科技論文英語寫作
English Scientific and Technical Writing

方克濤　著

全華圖書股份有限公司

目錄

作者序

　　二十多年前，受國立交通大學推廣教育中心之託，筆者應邀為交大教授與研究生修改英文科技研究報告，幫助他們以英語發表自己的研究成果。當初，我每週只收到兩三篇論文，但不久後，收到的篇數開始不斷增加。再到後來，我每週幾乎都要修改十到二十篇論文。這時，我才發覺臺灣的理工科學者對英文編輯服務的需求非常大，而這些學者要在臺灣找到專業的外國編輯幫助他們修改論文，卻是相當困難的。因此，我開始投入英文編輯技巧的研究，細心複習以前曾經學習的英文修辭原則，以增進自己修改論文的專業能力，並研究如何更有效地幫助論文作者有效表達自己的研究結果。同時，我經常發現在修改論文中所看到的錯誤英文，有不少都是不同作者一再重複的幾種基本問題。於是，我開始收集許多在修改論文過程中所注意到的常犯錯誤。當時我認為，假若能編寫一本中文參考書，為需要撰寫英文研究報告的人群詳細說明如何避免這些常犯的錯誤，那麼對臺灣的理工學者一定會有很大的幫助。

　　從事修改論文的工作幾個月之後，我也開始教授英文科技論文寫作的課程。當初很幸運地在很短的時間內便找到了幾本不錯的英文教材，但是之後，由於學生在課堂上所提出的種種疑問，以及自己在修改論文時所觀察到的一些問題，我發現雖然這些專業書籍的說法既正確又清楚，但往往不夠完整，而且並不特別適合中國人的需求。

　　鑒於臺灣的學術界很顯然需要這方面的中文書籍，我開始著手列出本書的大綱，並開始準備相關資料。我本來並沒有想到本書的篇幅會這麼長，但是在寫作的過程中，愈寫愈發現還有問題需要討論，因此就不斷增加了新的內容。經過兩三年的努力，本書的初稿終於在1995年暑假完成了。我出版此書，誠摯地希望能幫助臺灣的理工科學者提升自己英文寫作的品質，並在國際學術界較為順利地發表其重要的研究成果。

　　《英文科技寫作》初版廣受台灣理工界的學者與研究人員好評。能為這些研究人員提供參考，我感到十分欣慰，在此我也對本書的讀者及選用本書為教科書的大專教師，一併致謝。九五年的初版雖然暢銷，但成書倉卒，缺乏時間校對，書中難免出現不少錯別字，而部分的習題與例句亦未盡清晰。由於初版是由英文稿翻成中文，所以初版最嚴重的問題是有太多硬翻的「英式中文」。而亦因英中翻譯之故，使不少段落出現模糊和累贅的字句。要在初版中找出違背書中的修辭原則的詞句，俯拾皆是，這點是要向廣大讀者道歉的。

在完成初版後，我便開始投入別的研究工作，一直無暇全篇修改，以補初版之缺失。初版自出版以來，訂購數目不斷增加。我雖然不再從事英文寫作教學，惟眼見研究人員對本書的需求愈來愈殷切，決定推出修訂版，自覺責無旁貸。

在眾多朋友同仁的幫助之下，《英文科技寫作》（1995）的修訂版《科技論文英語寫作上冊》（2003）終於面世了。修訂版的主要目的是修正初版的一些錯誤、覆核部分例子和習題，及校正初版的英式中文。同時，2003版亦簡化突出了書中某些標題，像第一篇已由「文法與標點符號」改為「文法規則」，第二篇則由「寫作風格與可讀性」改為「修辭原則」，目的是讓標題更鮮明醒目。此外，修訂版的另一變更是初版的第六章「撰寫論文的過程」以及附錄一「撰寫使用手冊的準則」皆已省略，而該部分則納入《科技論文英語寫作下冊》中出版。

同時，《科技論文英語寫作下冊》為初版自序中所提及的姐妹篇《英文科技論文與會議簡報》，後來也於1996年順利發行。該書詳細討論了科技研究報告的結構與常用句式，且提供許多具體例子給讀者參考。

由於我近十幾年都生活工作在香港，過往出版發行的書籍慢慢在台灣市場上絕版，我也一直無暇顧及這兩本書的異地再版工作。儘管如此，每一年我都會收到熱忱的讀者從台灣發來的郵件詢問什麼時候在哪裡可以買到再版的書籍，因此我終於下決心將此書的再版發行工作移交給台灣專業的出版社負責，希望這兩本書能夠有專人負責出版發行工作，並在台灣市場上保有可持續的長足發展。

新版書將上冊和下冊合併在一起，分為「文法規則」、「修辭原則」、以及「科技期刊論文寫作和會議簡報」三篇。同時，鑒於學術界研究、台式電腦技術以及互聯網的飛速發展，本書過往的一些章節也難免顯得老套陳舊，因此不合時宜的段落和附錄也被刪除，希望可以更有效、更便捷、更貼時代前沿地幫助讀者全面迅速提升英文寫作能力。

本書的完成得力於許多人的支持與貢獻，我深深感激他們給予的大力幫助。

首先，我要謝謝曾經上過本人在交通大學和清華大學所開過課的學生和教師，以及曾經請我修改研究論文的作者。他們給了我撰寫此書的動機，而他們的問題和意見更對本書的內容有多方面重要的貢獻。在此我把這本書獻給所有的這些研究者。

孔德文先生 (C. A. Carelli) 和石家祺先生 (Daniel Strychalski) 仔細閱讀了本書的部分英文初稿，並提供了很多寶貴的建議，這些建議大幅增進了書中說明的清晰度，也幫助我糾正了初稿中的許多小錯誤。此外，我在寫書的過程當中，多次和這兩位先生討論英文文法和用法的問題。我非常感謝他們所提供的忠告與鼓勵。

另外，我要感謝國立交通大學推廣教育中心的蘇正芬小姐與劉素梅小姐、資訊工程研究所所長黃書淵教授、控制工程研究所所長鄧清政教授、國立清華大學工學院院長陳文華教授、工業工程系主任王小璠教授、工業工程研究所桑慧敏教授、國立交通大學電機資訊學院院長魏哲和教授、電信工程系主任彭松村教授，在我撰寫此書的這段時間，他們都給予我熱忱的支持。還有，我也很感激李錫堅教授、楊丁元博士和張慶輝教授，他們提供了列在本書封底的評語。

我非常感激李錫堅教授和魏哲和教授曾經為本書撰寫的序言，也特別感謝他們給出有關修改本書中文初稿的建設性意見。李教授閱讀了整本書的中文初稿，並針對書的內容、組織以及一些重要專業術語的中文翻譯，提供了極多寶貴的建議。他的幫助大幅提升了本書內容的清晰度和完整性。

本書中引用了許多研究者的專業著作，在寫作的過程中我也曾參閱不少專家寫的英文參考書，在此我要感謝所有這些學者。書中所有引文的原作者，在註釋中都有指明，在此我也謝謝這些允許我引用這些著作的期刊和作者。此外，我很感激 G. Gopen, J. Swan, T. Huckin 以及 L. Olsen 這幾位學者，雖然本書沒有直接引用他們的著作，但是他們的著作提供了本書第九章其背後的許多基本概念，此外，本書第二章部分的說明以及第六章關於關係子句的討論，都根基於 Huckin 及 Olsen 的著作。

在撰寫本書的中文稿時，鄭光明先生提供了大力協助，使我受益良多。他翻譯了幾個章節的初稿，也細心修改了中文初稿的一些部分。他的幫助深度優化了本書的可讀性和寫作品質，在此我非常感謝他的支持及耐心。他總是欣然回答我對中文語法以及相關雜事的極多煩瑣的問題，在此我深深感佩。李素瑛教授、吳龍庸教授、楊士偉先生以及郭曉潔小姐都參與了中文初稿的修改工作，他們幫助我進一步改善本書的中文，使得本書更清楚易懂，在此非常謝謝他們的協助。此外，我也很感謝其他幫助我翻譯中文初稿的人，尤其是盧德瑢小姐和周秀娟小姐。

感謝梁韻兒小姐、林康琪小姐對修訂版的細心校譯，對本書內容提出修改意見，並作增刪。

在我撰寫本書的過程當中，不少人曾提供重要的支持和鼓勵。我感謝歐柔婉小姐的支持與耐心，也謝謝林正弘教授在我開始規劃寫作此書時，提出了一些很實用的寶貴意見，猶如撥雲見日，即使到現在，仍然非常受用。此外，我也很感謝何志青教授的友誼與支持，他對不少英文概念的中文翻譯，使我深受啟發。

最後，我要特別感謝我的太太遲穎小姐孜孜不倦地反覆潤色、校正、編輯全書，及對本書的所有內容和出版做出的系統性的編纂和統籌工作。

我謹望新版書能繼續幫助學界的更多學者和讀者。

方克濤

二零一五年
香港大學

導論

　　隨著台灣科技研究事業的蓬勃發展, 越來越多的研究生與專業學者需要用英文撰寫研究報告, 並在國際學術界上發表自己的重要研究成果, 以提升學術界的研究水準、促進國際學術交流。當代理工學者的學術成就, 也常取決於其研究報告有否經常刊登於國際專業期刊; 大學教師必須出版一定數量的研究報告, 才有機會升等; 理工科系的研究生需於國際期刊上發表研究成果, 才能獲得博士學位。而要在國際專業刊物發表研究報告就得使用英文, 所以理工學者必須具備撰寫專業英文研究報告的能力, 或者說現今理工學者皆需面對使用英文撰寫學術研究報告的挑戰。

　　遺憾的是, 雖然科技研究人員迫切需要英文寫作的訓練, 然而到目前為止, 大多數國內大學與專科學校的理工課程只強調專業的科技知識, 而沒有提供完善的語言訓練。同時, 坊間也很難找到一本優秀的專門教人撰寫英文學術研究報告的中文書籍。較好的專書通常為英文本, 但大多數的學生都不知這類書籍的存在, 選哪本好, 而就算知道, 閱讀英文專書, 學生亦會感到既吃力又耗時。還有, 英文專書大多是針對以英文為母語的學生的需要而設計, 並不特別適合中國學生。因此, 一本詳盡討論英文科技論文寫作的中文專書, 讓中國學生在撰寫論文時避免許多常犯錯誤, 顯然非常重要。

　　本書便是針對這個需求而設計的, 力求以精簡的方式來介紹國內科技研究人員在撰寫英文研究報告時所需要的基本知識。書中的內容皆為筆者從過去豐富的教學與編輯經驗所累積的心得, 許多例子更為筆者在編輯論文時所收集整理得來的; 筆者過去在大學教授英文科技論文寫作的課程, 也曾於多間著名高科技公司擔任編輯。工作期間, 筆者修訂了數以千計的英文科技研究報告, 累積了多年修改英語論文的經驗。本書討論了不少學生常感頭痛的英文文法, 也詳細介紹了標準的英文修辭技巧。讀者只要仔細研讀本書所介紹的寫作原則與常用句型，便能儘快掌握撰寫英文科技報告的基本技巧。此外，本書提供豐富多樣的習題，不僅可做自學寶典，而且也是英文老師的首選教科書。

本書以準備撰寫英文論文或對英文論文有少許經驗的自然科學、社會科學、工程學的專業研究人員與研究生為主要對象。不論是撰寫研究報告、技術或專案報告、研究計劃、碩士博士論文，還是投稿於專業期刊之研究論文，本書所介紹的寫作原則都會有效地助你提升寫作能力。

此外，本書也有一個章節專門討論英文會議簡報的技巧。對於需要在國際研討會上發表研究報告的研究人員而言，該章所提供的資料俱有很高的參考價值。

「只要內容有價值，無庸關心寫作素質？」

也許有些理工學生認為論文的內容有價值便可，寫作素質並不是很重要。他們可能都忽略了一個重要的事實：如果一篇論文不知所云，根本不會有人注意到論文內容的價值。科技論文必須清楚易懂，讀者才能瞭解論文內容，從而注意到它的價值。千萬別相信只要論文內容本身有價值，不管寫得好或壞，讀者都會熱切去解讀。

事實上，一篇論文的價值，本來就端賴於寫作的素質。一方面，撰寫科技研究論文的主要目的，是與其他學者分享研究成果，一篇清晰簡要的論文可較有效地達到這個目的。另一方面，科技論文的價值不僅在於其所提供的數據，更重要的是作者對自己研究成果的分析與解釋。例如，作者必須指出研究的重要性，分析研究結果，並與其他學者的研究作比較。只有把論文寫得清楚聯貫，作者才可以為自己的研究成果提出一個完整、合理和具說服力的分析與解釋。

即使一篇論文的文法稍有瑕疵，只要研究題材新穎有趣，亦有可能被專業期刊接受。然而，作者仍應盡量用字清楚，組織嚴謹，以便讀者容易閱讀，從而明瞭其研究思路與結果。如果論文中夾雜錯誤英文，或內容艱澀難懂，讀者根本難以瞭解論文，更會有些讀者認為英文如此糟透，就視如敝屣，不屑一顧。儘管這並不公允，但文筆拙劣的論文，讀者都會直覺地否定其內容的價值，故論文給讀者的第一印象尤其重要。

當研究者藉論文把自己的研究成果與他人分享時，作者和讀者都各有責任。讀者必須先具備某種背景知識，並細心閱讀，作者則應盡量表達得清楚而合符邏輯，好讓讀者能易於瞭解文意。科技論文的讀者一般為專業研究者，具備科技背景知識，通常都能迅速掌握新的研究報告的重點。一篇表達清楚、結構嚴謹的論文，對這班專業讀者而言，不可能構成問題。所以如果有讀者覺得論文難懂的話，這大概是因為作者沒有盡責。撰寫科技論文時，作者應不厭其煩地不斷修改，直到確定論點清楚而合符邏輯為止。一篇論文可修改兩、三次，甚至更多次。因為即使是天才或諾貝爾獎得主，也不可能一下子就能完成一篇完美無缺的論文。所有專業作家在論文出版前都會一再修改，以臻完善。

理工研究生還需要瞭解，筆記本上的一大堆原始資料、數據，並不等於實驗或研究計畫的最後成果。如想成為專業科學家或工程師，還要對這些資料、數據做解釋與分析，然後提出一篇清楚簡潔而結構嚴謹的論文，否則研究計畫還不算完成。因此，撰寫研究論文本來就是研究活動中非常重要的部分，而非計畫完成後一項額外的工作。

用外語撰寫學術論文，的確非常艱巨，要寫得駕輕就熟，更不能一蹴即至。但幸好英文科技論文寫作實有標準格式可循，只要認識慣用的結構與詞句，並學會一些基本寫作技巧，就能寫出一篇符合基本要求的英文研究報告。如果讀者對撰寫論文的正確規則勤加練習，並模仿英語國家專業人士的寫作方式，定能寫出正確通順的英文。

在這裡我還想指出一點，想要加強自己英文科技論文寫作能力的學生或研究人員其實很幸運，因為科技研究報告中所使用的英文相當標準化。在各種不同研究領域裡所發表的研究論文中，常會出現相同的標準句型與論證模式。對於非以英文為母語的研究人員而言，這確實是好消息，只要掌握這些標準句型與論證模式，就能很快地提升自己的科技寫作能力，並開始寫出符合基本標準的英文研究論文。本書列有不少由不同研究領域的專業期刊摘錄下來之科技英文的實例，以便讀者有機會瞭解以英文為母語的專業研究人員如何應用本書所介紹的寫作原則寫作。此外，本書也提供許多習題，以幫助讀者練習標準的句型及段落結構。

此外，立志成為專業的科學家或工程師，其實光靠專業知識與技巧還是不足夠的，積累靈活豐富的溝通能力和專業知識同等重要。要清楚表達自己的論點，就必須學習清楚簡要的寫作技巧。一個人文章寫得清楚，表示這人頭腦也清楚。換句話說，增進寫作素質，等於同時訓練嚴謹準確的思考習慣。總而言之，增進寫作能力與溝通技巧，是培養自己成為專業科學家或工程師極為重要的一步。

本書組織

本書係專為理工學者撰寫論文時作參考之用，也可作為科技論文寫作課程的教材。本書分為三篇：「文法規則」、「修辭原則」與「論文寫作及會議簡報」。

前五章屬於第一篇，旨在讓讀者重溫英文文法的基本概念，包括說明冠詞、動詞以及標點符號等正確的使用方式。但這裡不會徹底講解所有的文法規則，而只會針對一般科技論文作者最感疑惑的部分來討論。當中的第四章介紹中國學生在撰寫英文科技論文時常犯錯誤。對希望能以正確英文來撰寫論文的讀者而言，此章非常重要。

接下來的五個章節為第二篇「修辭原則」。修辭原則和第一篇的文法規則有別，它們並非作者必須嚴格遵循的絕對規則，而是一般性的原則。若不遵循第二篇所介紹的英文修辭原則，未必表示寫法不正確；但貫徹這些原則，能使文章更清楚簡潔，讀者更易瞭解文意。第六章將介紹一些指導準則，有助於寫出較簡明的英文，第七章和第八章則解釋如何撰寫通順自然的句子以及合理聯貫的段落。對於希望掌握英文寫作的基本技巧的讀者而言，第六章至第八章極為重要。第九章陳述的一些準則，簡易而實用，遵從這些準則將能使論文內容的鋪排更符合讀者的期望，令論文更清晰易讀。末章會列出許多學生經常誤用的字詞與句子，並說明如何避免這些常見錯誤，讓讀者不會重蹈他人之覆轍。

第三篇為《英文科技寫作》（1995）一書之姊妹篇，現合併為一本書出版。這一篇則主要討論科技論文、研究報告的結構以及常用句型，並針對研究報告不同章節裡的標準段落組織、動詞時態等等提供許多具體的應用原則。就許多方面而言，第三篇和前面兩篇密切的關係。就某些專題而言，前面已有詳細的討論，作者也在這一篇適當的地方建議讀者參閱前面的相關內容。

本書是以作為科技寫作的參考書及教科書而設計，自學的讀者可依據自身需要而選讀某些章節。例如，想掌握英文基本文法的，可順本書次序閱讀。已有寫作研究論文經驗的，則可直接從第四章開始，且看自己有否曾犯該章所列出的錯誤。對於想瞭解英文寫作的基本原則，並要應用在自己文章中的讀者而言，第六章到第八章甚為關鍵。對有寫作經驗的讀者來說，認識第九章所介紹的可讀性準則，對寫作技巧將很有幫助。第十章則列出許多特定英文字詞與句子的正確使用法，讀者可順序一次看完，也可分數次閱讀。如果只想瞭解科技論文的寫作方法和原則，也可以直接跳到後面的十個章節研讀。

本書所附的習題是為讀者自我練習之用，並非以測驗學生為目的。當中有些習題非常困難，所以不要期望在讀過一兩遍內容後就能熟練回答所有習題。本書的附錄中，附有所有習題的完整答案。從這些答案中，應可瞭解英語國家的人如何把本書講授的原則應用在實際寫作上。

除了詳讀本書之外，為了更快、更有效地增進自己的英文論文寫作能力，讀者還應該注意下列兩點：

一、應多研讀以英文為母語的專家所寫的文章

開始閱讀本書之前，應先到圖書館影印五六篇自己研究領域裡以英文為母語的專家所出版的研究報告（如果你還是學生，那麼可以請教授推薦幾位資深專家的著作）。在閱讀本書每個章節之後，讀者也應參考自己所收集的文章，以比較這些文章的組織、寫作風格、常用句型以及時態的用法和本書所介紹的典範之間的同異之處。如此一來，就能多方面加強自己的英文能力，例如：

- 參考了更多專業研究人員所寫的科技英文之後，讀者便能更瞭解專業研究人員應用本書所介紹的句型及論證模式的方式，並能進一步熟悉、應用這些句型及論證模式。
- 一般而言，本書所介紹的寫作原則對各種研究領域都有效。儘管如此，不同專業領域的學者有時還會有個別領域中約定俗成之獨特的寫作方式。假如一邊研讀本書的寫作原則，一邊比較自己研究領域中不同專家所寫的文章，如此一來，就能很快發現自己的領域中是否有任何和本書所介紹之原則不同的特殊寫作習慣。
- 一般而言，文章讀得越多，寫作能力就會越好。不論是學生或專業研究人員，大家都應該養成時時閱讀自己研究領域中資深學者所寫的英文報告的習慣。

只要常常閱讀好的文章，自然而然就會慢慢開始倣效那些文章中正確、流暢的英文。

二、練習，練習，再練習！

在閱讀本書時以及讀完本書之後，應該常常撥出時間來練習撰寫英文研究報告或報告中的不同章節。本書提供不少習題以幫助讀者研習，但除了做這些習題之外，還要練習寫自己的題目才是。例如，應嘗試針對自己曾經進行的研究或實驗或曾經參閱的研究資料寫一篇簡單的導論（只要寫一兩頁即可），或針對自己熟悉的題目寫一篇簡短的「研究回顧」（請記住：我們目的只是要練習，因此篇幅不必很長）。然後，可以請一位教授或英文教師修改你的文章。也可以嘗試為一些對自己研究領域完全不熟悉的朋友、同事或老師寫一篇研究摘要。這是一種很有價值的訓練方法，因為要訓練自己寫出清楚、結構嚴謹的文章，最有效的方法之一就是嘗試撰寫一些連外行人都易於瞭解的文章（也可以使用這種方法來訓練自己撰寫更清楚、結構更嚴謹的中文文章）。

請記住：要掌握任何一種技能，一定要多練習才行。如果我們要在半年或一年後參加一場一萬公尺的賽跑，那麼我們一定會在好幾個月之前就開始練習，對不對？同樣地，如果我們以後打算寫正式、專業的英文研究報告，那麼便應先好好地練習本書所介紹的基本寫作技巧才是。

第一篇
文法規則

第一章
基本文法

本章將扼要陳述英文基本文法概念以及主要詞類，讓讀者可馬上重溫一些曾經學習過的英文文法。倘若讀者在本書的其餘章節遇到一些專門文法術語而不知所指的話，本章也可作為一索引。

1.1 句子

無論我們說話還是寫文章時，我們都是以不同的方式來組合字詞。例如，*The round table* 是一組字詞，我們會用以指稱某個物體，即一張圓桌子。*Early in the morning* 則是另外一組字詞，我們會用以指稱某段時間。不過，這兩組字詞都沒有陳述出一個完整意思：前一組字詞提到某個物體，卻沒有進一步提供關於該物體的資料；至於後一組字詞，則只提及某段時間，卻沒有道出該段時間內所發生的事情。

如果一組字詞表達一個完整意思，這組字詞稱為「句子」(sentence)。例如：*The method is efficient, Our aim is to solve this problem* 。這兩組字詞都表達一個完整意思：前一組字詞交代某個方法的特性，後一組字詞則陳述某位作者的目的。但這兩組字詞之所以為句子，並非由於它們比較長，而是它們都表達了一個完整意思。例如 *after we have described the design of the system* 比上面兩組字詞還要長，卻絕非句子。因為它只提到某段時間，並沒有陳述出一個完整意思。如果這組字詞要成為一個句子的話，那它得要和另外一組字詞結合而構成一個完整意思。例如：*After we have described the design of the system, we will analyze its effectiveness*.

同時，句子分為兩個主要部分——主詞 (subject) 和述詞或賓詞 (predicate)。主詞包含一個名詞片語，表示句子所敘述的人、地、物。述詞包含一個動詞，有時也會包含其他的字詞，用來陳述或詢問和主詞有關的事實。例如，在 *The method is efficient* 這句中，*the method* 是主詞，點出所要談論的對象；*is efficient* 則是述詞，以陳述和主詞有關的事實。一組字詞必須包含主詞和述詞，才稱得上是一個完整的句子。（祈使句是例外：它表面上不包含主詞，卻還是道道地地的句子。它只是省略主詞「你」而已。詳見本章1.10節。）

下面將討論字詞的種類，以及能構成英文句子的字詞組合。

1.2　名詞

指稱人、地、物、行動、狀態和概念的字詞，稱為「名詞」(noun)，如 *Tom, computer, university, tennis, intelligence* 等。至於專有名詞 (proper noun)，則用以指稱某特定的人、地或物，而字首通常為大寫，如 *Aristotle, George Washington, New York* 及 *Oxford University* 等。普通名詞 (common noun) 則是指稱某人、地或物之總類底下的一個或一些個例，如 *woman, desk, island, laboratory* 等。

名詞可作句子主詞，或作動詞及介系詞的受詞（稍後會介紹動詞及介系詞）。名詞可以分為可數名詞 (countable or count noun)、不可數名詞 (uncountable or mass noun) 和集合名詞 (collective noun)。可數名詞可以在字尾加 *s* 或 *es* 而變成複數名詞 *(computer, computers)*，但有些可數名詞的複數形式是不規則的 *(man, men; maximum, maxima)*。不可數名詞通常為無法計算的物體，如水 *(water)* 及地心引力 *(gravity)* 等，它們沒有任何複數形式。集合名詞雖是指稱一群人或事物所組成的單位，卻也有單數形式，如 *class, set* 及 *team* 等。（可數和不可數名詞的討論，詳見第二章。）

1.3　代名詞

顧名思義，代名詞 (pronouns) 就是代替名詞的字詞。與名詞一樣，代名詞既可作主詞，也可作動詞或介系詞的受詞。英語的代名詞共有八種：人稱代名詞、關係代名詞、疑問代名詞、指示代名詞、不定代名詞、相互代名詞、加強代名詞以及反身代名詞。

種類	代名詞	例句
人稱	*I, you, he, she, it, we, they* *me, you, him, her, it, us, them* *my, your, his, hers, its, our, their* *mine, yours, his, hers, its, ours, theirs*	
關係	*which, that, who, whom*	This is the book *that* I want. That is the teacher *whom* I admire.
疑問	*what, who, which*	*What* is that?

種類	代名詞	例句
		Which building are we going to?
指示	*this, that, these, those*	
不定	*all, one, any, each, everyone, someone*	
相互	*each other, one another*	
加強語氣	*myself, yourself, himself, herself, ourselves, yourselves, themselves*	He *himself* will do the job. *himself* 強調了 *he*。 The student wrote the paper *herself*. *herself* 強調了 *the student*。
反身	*myself, yourself, himself, herself, ourselves, yourselves, themselves*	He hurt *himself* while working in the lab. *himself* 和 *he* 實指同一個人。 To ensure she would not forget the appointment, she wrote *herself* a note. *herself* 和 *she* 實指同一個人。

　　一個代名詞所「代替」的那個名詞，稱為該代名詞的「前述詞」(antecedent)。使用代名詞可令作者在行文時非常方便，好處很多。但在使用時，作者必須要讓讀者清楚看出各代名詞的前述詞是甚麼，而不用猜測代名詞所指的人或事物──不定代名詞是例外，因為它根本不需前述詞。（第四章4.13節會再深入討論代名詞和前述詞。）

1.4 動詞

　　動詞 (verb) 是表示行為、事件、時態、擁有或狀態的字詞（例如 *run, sit, have, are, become, seem* 等）。英文中，每個句子必須至少有一個動詞，否則不能算是一個完整句子。辭典裏所列出的動詞形式，稱為原形動詞或「不定詞」(infinitive)。（句中的不定詞之前通常需加上 *to*；這個 *to* 稱為「不定詞標記」(infinitive marker)。）除了原形之外，動詞也有其他形式，像用來表示過去的行為或事件的「過去式」(past tense)。

　　表示某種動作的動詞稱為「動態動詞」(active verb)，這種動詞很多。下面例句中以斜體字標示的皆為動態動詞：

　　Cindy *wrote* quickly.

　　Karen didn't *eat* much.

　　The students are *working* on the project.

　　表示某種狀態的動詞稱為「靜態動詞」(stative verb)。下面例句中以斜體字標示的都是靜態動詞:

　　The doctor *believes* Sam is not badly injured.

　　She could *feel* that the weather was hot.

　　This graph *represents* the first group of data.

　　此外，還有一種動詞稱為「聯繫動詞」(linking verb)，它處於句子的主詞與述詞名詞 (predicate noun) 之間，或在主詞與述詞形容詞 (predicate adjective) 之間，充當聯繫作用。常見的聯繫動詞有 *be, become, seem, appear*。表達感官知覺的聯繫動詞，則有 *look, smell, taste, feel, sound* 等。下面例句中，以斜體字標示的都是聯繫動詞。

　　He *is* the professor.

　　Sally *became* a neurosurgeon.

　　You *look* beautiful.

　　The soup *tastes* good.

　　區分雖然有三種，但事實上這三種動詞間並不互相排斥。有時一個動詞在某句中是動態動詞，但在另一句中卻會變成靜態動詞或聯繫動詞。下面的第一句中，*look* 是聯繫動詞; 在第二句中，*look* 卻為動態動詞:

　　Jerry *looks* tired.　聯繫動詞

　　Jerry *looked* around the room to see if his friends were there.　動態動詞

　　動詞亦可與某些助動詞（如 *be, can, do, may, will* 及 *must* 等）連用，以表示特殊的意思。動詞不同的形式也可與某些助動詞連用，以表示不同的時間或語態關係（如: *have been working, will be going, might have gone*）。

　　此外，動詞也有主動、被動兩種語態。主詞是動詞的「施事者」(actor)，乃主動語態。如 *The car hit the bus* 這句中，主詞 *the car* 是施事者; 但若「受事者」(receiver) 做主詞，則乃被動語態。例如，在句子 *The bus was hit by the car* 中，主詞 *the bus* 是動詞 *hit* 的受事者。

1.5　修飾詞

　　修飾詞 (modifier) 可以是單字，也可以是一組字詞，用以描述或修飾另一個或一組字詞。形容詞 (adjective) 與副詞 (adverb) 是單字的修飾詞，片語 (phrase) 則為充當形容詞或副詞的一組字詞。（有關片語，詳見1.8節。）

形容詞

形容詞係作修飾名詞及代名詞之用，也可用來表示某東西是何種事物。它們不是在其所修飾的詞之前，就是緊接在其所修飾的詞之後。這裏以斜體字標示的皆為形容詞：*good* work, *effective* method, *large* animal, *difficult* problem, *Chinese* culture.

副詞

副詞既可修飾動詞、形容詞及其他副詞，有時也可修飾整個句子。副詞在修飾形容詞或其他副詞時，常緊接在其所修飾的詞後面。副詞在修飾動詞時，也常緊接在其所修飾的動詞之後（但副詞有時也會在動詞前面，或在句首或在句尾）。副詞可用來表示時間、地點、原因、方式、順序或頻率。這裏以斜體字標示的皆是副詞：talking *quietly*; playing *happily*; *deeply* unhappy; *Strangely,* he didn't notice the big dog running around the room。

1.6 具有連接功能的詞

具有連接功能的詞，既可連接字和字，也可連接一組組字詞。具有連接功能的詞可用來清楚界定不同概念間的關係。具有連接功能的詞包括介系詞 (preposition)、連接詞 (conjunction) 和連接副詞 (conjunctive adverb)。

介系詞

介系詞的語法功能，是表示名詞或代名詞和另一個詞之間的關係，而這名詞或代名詞稱為介系詞的受詞。介系詞和其受詞結合而成的介系詞片語，係用來修飾和介系詞受詞有關聯的詞。例如，句子 *Tom ran down the hall* 中，介系詞 *down* 將名詞 *hall* 和動詞 *ran* 關聯起來，而 *down the hall* 這介系詞片語即修飾動詞 *ran*，並指出 Tom 跑到哪裏去。此外，有些單字的介系詞（如 *in, to, of* 等），也可以和其他詞結合而成為片語形式的介系詞 (phrasal preposition)，如 *by means of, in addition to, such as* 等。

連接詞

連接詞的功能是將詞、片語或子句關聯起來，藉此指出它們之間的關係。連接詞有三種：對等連接詞 (coordinating conjunction)、相關連接詞 (correlative conjunction) 和附屬連接詞 (subordinating conjunction)。

對等連接詞

對等連接詞包括 *and, but, or, nor, for, so* 和 *yet*。此種連接詞可把對等的詞、片語或子句連接。

We played cards *and* chess. 連接詞 *and* 把 *cards* 和 *chess* 兩個詞連接。

She wants to go to the movies *or* to a restaurant. 連接詞 *or* 把 *to the movies* 和 *to a restaurant* 兩個片語連接。

He planned to graduate in December, *but* he didn't finish his thesis on time. 連接詞 *but* 把 *He planned…* 和 *he didn't finish…* 兩個子句連接。

相關連接詞

相關連接詞準會一對成雙出現，這種連接詞包括 *both…and…, either…or…* 和 *neither…nor…*。它們可把對等的詞、片語、子句或完整的句子連接。

Neither John *nor* Susan is coming to the dinner party. 連接兩個對等的詞。

Both the basketball team *and* the football team won last weekend. 連接兩個對等的名詞片語。

Either you do the job *or* I will do it. 連接兩個對等的獨立子句。

附屬連接詞

對等連接詞和相關連接詞，皆可連接對等的詞、片語或子句。附屬連接詞則只能把子句和子句連接，且連接的都只能是不對等子句。

以附屬連接詞開首的子句，稱為「附屬子句」（或「從屬子句」）(subordinate or dependent clause)。附屬子句不是一個完整句子；它必須與獨立子句（或主要子句）(independent or main clause) 連接，才能構成一完整句。換句話說，附屬子句是依附於相關主要子句的。下面兩個句子中的第一個子句，都是以附屬連接詞開首的附屬子句：

Because the traditional method is time-consuming, a new approach is needed.

If we set up the experiment in this way, we obtain some surprising results.

在上面兩個例句中，主要子句表達了句子的主要意思 (*a new approach is needed; we obtain some surprising results*)，而附屬子句則支持、補充或說明了主要子句。故附屬子句的意思可說是附屬於主要子句的意思。

下面是英文科技論文中常用的附屬連接詞：

常用的附屬連接詞			
after	even though	so that	whenever
although	if	than	where
as	in order that	that	whenever
as if	instead of	though	whether
because	owing to	unless	while
before	rather than	until	
even if	since	when	

特別需要注意，*after, as, before, since, until* 這些字詞，也可作介系詞使用。試比較下列句子中的 *since*：

Since he's not here yet, let's have a cup of coffee. 附屬連接詞。

Sally has been studying for her doctorate *since* 1990. 介系詞。

連接副詞

顧名思義，連接副詞是具連接功能的副詞。下面是一些常用的連接副詞：

常用的連接副詞			
accordingly	furthermore	in most cases	on the other hand
also	further on	in other words	otherwise
as a result	generally	in particular	rather
as mentioned in	hence	in practice	second
as shown in	however	in principle	still
by contrast	i.e.	instead	that is
consequently	in addition	in summary	then
e.g.	in comparison	in theory	therefore
finally	in conclusion	later	thus
first	in contrast	moreover	to be sure
for example	indeed	namely	too
for instance	in fact	nevertheless	
for this reason	in general	on the contrary	

連接副詞與附屬連接詞在功能上差別很大。附屬連接詞表示同一個句子中的兩個子句（即主要子句與附屬子句）之間的關係；連接副詞則表示兩個獨立而完整的子句、甚至兩個段落之間的關係。連接副詞是很重要的轉接詞，高明的作者常能巧用它來闡明不同句子或子句間的邏輯關係，或是把段落中不同的概念關聯起來。下面以斜體字表示的都是連接副詞：

The conventional method is slow, complex, and inaccurate. *Consequently,* we believe a different method should be used.

The argon process has a higher start-up cost than the oxygen process; *on the other hand,* the argon process is cleaner and more efficient.

In theory, this system can be represented by a simple model. *Nevertheless,* in practice the behavior of the system is difficult to predict.

連接副詞通常放在句首或子句的前面，但有時也可放在句子的中間或最後。同時，必須以逗點來區分連接副詞和句子的其他部分。如果連接副詞的位置在句子中間，則必須用兩個逗點把句子前後部分隔開。

The new system has many advantages. *However,* it also has several important disadvantages.

The new system has many advantages. It also, *however,* has several important disadvantages.

The new system has many advantages. It also has several important disadvantages, *however.*

如果要以連接副詞把兩個獨立子句連接而成一複合句，則必須在連接副詞前面
加上分號，而在其後加上逗點：

The new system has many advantages; *however,* it also has several important disadvantages.

1.7　動狀詞

動狀詞 (verbal) 是動詞的變形，可作名詞或修飾詞使用。英文的動狀詞計有三
種：不定詞 (infinitive)、分詞 (participle) 和動名詞 (gerund)。

不定詞

不定詞（即原形動詞）的典型特徵，是動詞前面有一個 *to*（如 *to be, to live*），
但有時會給省略。不定詞可作名詞、形容詞或副詞使用。

To win an Olympic gold medal is a difficult task. 作名詞。

We are looking for a place *to live.* 作修飾 *place* 的形容詞。

The secretary is ready *to type the letter.* 作修飾 *ready* 的副詞。

分詞

分詞有兩種形式：現在分詞 (*jumping, working, studying*) 與過去分詞 (*worked,
eaten, tried*)。而分詞通常都會作形容詞使用。

Looking toward the future, we are confident that we will achieve our goal.
現在分詞 *looking* 修飾主詞 *we*。

Exhausted, she fell onto the sofa. 過去分詞 *exhausted* 修飾主詞 *she*。

動名詞

動名詞和現在分詞外表雖相同（兩者都有 *-ing* 字尾），功能卻有別。當動狀詞
以 *-ing* 結尾，作形容詞使用（如上面第一個例句中的 *looking*），稱為「現在分
詞」；當動狀詞以 *-ing* 字尾，則作名詞使用，稱為「動名詞」。

Jennifer loves *dancing. Dancing* 為 *loves* 的受詞。

Studying all day long is boring. *Studying* 為 *is* 的主詞。

動狀詞不能作句子的述詞使用，卻可以有受詞，並可受副詞修飾：

Sam wants *to marry* Sandy. *Sandy* 為不定詞 *to marry* 的受詞。

Working quickly, Susan finished the test in less than an hour. 副詞 *quickly* 修飾分詞 *working*。

以上已介紹了英文科技寫作中常見的詞類。接著會介紹兩種重要的字詞組，即片語及子句。

1.8 片語

片語 (phrase) 是一組字詞，作單詞（如名詞或副詞）使用，但不能表達完整意思。英文的片語共可分成七大類：獨立片語、動名詞片語、不定詞片語、名詞片語、分詞片語、介系詞片語和動詞片語。

獨立片語

獨立片語 (absolute phrase) 包含一個當主詞的名詞（或代名詞）以及一個分詞。獨立片語和其他的片語不同，除了動狀詞之外，這種片語同時包含一個主詞。獨立片語並非修飾句子中的單字，而是整個句子，但這種片語在英文科技論文中並不常見。

The experiment having been completed, we cleaned up the lab and went home.

Demand for its products growing steadily, the firm appeared likely to become a success.

動名詞片語

動名詞片語 (gerund phrase) 包括一個動名詞和動名詞的修飾詞，有時還會包括動名詞的受詞。動名詞片語是作名詞使用的。

Talking to students sometimes helps teachers to clarify their own ideas. 動名詞片語為句子主詞。

John prefers *working alone.* 動名詞片語為 *prefers* 的受詞。

不定詞片語

不定詞片語 (infinitive phrase) 包含不定詞和不定詞的修飾詞，有時還可能包含不定詞的受詞。不定詞片語可作名詞、形容詞或副詞使用。

I prefer *to work alone.* 作名詞使用，即 *prefer* 的受詞。

Do you have a book *to read on the plane?* 修飾 *book* 的形容詞。

They were all ready *to begin the test.* 修飾 *ready* 的副詞。

名詞片語

名詞片語 (noun phrase) 包含名詞及名詞的修飾詞，可作主詞或受詞使用。

A beautiful new car was parked in *the driveway.* 第一個名詞片語是句子主詞；第二個則為介系詞 *in* 的受詞。

分詞片語

分詞片語 (participial phrase) 包含現在或過去分詞和分詞的修飾詞，有時還可會包含分詞的受詞（如果有的話）。分詞片語可作形容詞。分詞片語在外表上和動名詞片語完全一樣，在功能上卻有所不同：動名詞片語只能當名詞，而分詞片語則只能當形容詞。

Our professor is the man *talking to those students.* 修飾 *the man*。

Staring at the blackboard, Julie suddenly thought of the answer. 修飾 *Julie*。

介系詞片語

介系詞片語 (prepositional phrase) 包含介系詞、介系詞的受詞以及介系詞受詞的任何修飾語。介系詞片語通常作形容詞或副詞使用，偶爾也可作名詞使用（但在科技論文中很少見）。

We bought a gift *for him.* 修飾 *gift* 的形容詞。

The lecture began *at 10 o'clock.* 修飾 *began* 的副詞。

After class is a good time to meet. 作名詞使用，即句子的主詞。

動詞片語

動詞片語 (verb phrase) 包含動詞和修飾動詞的修飾詞或動詞的補語。

We *will be leaving early tomorrow morning,* if you want to come along.

1.9 子句

子句 (clause) 是包含一個主詞與述詞的字詞組。英文的子句可分成兩大類：獨立（或主要）子句 (independent or main clause) 和附屬子句 (subordinate or dependent clause)。

獨立子句

獨立子句包含主詞和動詞，可作為一個完整獨立的句子。獨立子句不能作名詞或修飾詞，也不能以附屬連接詞開首。下面句子皆為獨立子句：

Education is important.

Mark bought a new computer.

附屬子句

附屬子句以附屬連接詞（參閱上面1.6節）或關係代名詞（即 *who, which* 或 *that*）開首。附屬子句並非完整句子，它必須與獨立子句結合，才能成為完整句。附屬子句表達的意思都是依附於主要子句上的。下面以斜體字標示的子句，都是附屬子句。

Education is important if you wish to enjoy a rewarding career.

After his old one broke down, Mark bought a new computer.

附屬子句可以分成三種：形容詞子句 (adjective clause)、副詞子句 (adverbial clauses) 和名詞子句 (noun clause)。

形容詞子句

形容詞子句是修飾名詞或代名詞的附屬子句，通常以關係代名詞（作子句的主詞或受詞）開首。（以關係代名詞開首的子句，稱為「關係子句」(relative clause)。）

We have developed a system *that can perform this task.* 附屬子句是修飾名詞 *system* 的形容詞子句；關係代名詞 *that* 是附屬子句的主詞。

This is the system *that we developed.* 附屬子句是修飾名詞 *system* 的形容詞子句；關係代名詞 *that* 是附屬子句的受詞。

副詞子句

副詞子句可修飾動詞、形容詞、副詞或整個主要子句，一般用以說明事件發生的時間、地點、原因、方式、始末或結果。

The machine stopped functioning *when I spilled my coffee on it.* 附屬子句是修飾動詞 *stopped* 的副詞子句。

We'll try this plan first, *unless you have a better idea.* 附屬子句修飾整個主要子句。

This program solves the problem more slowly *than that one does.* 附屬子句修飾副詞 *slowly*。

名詞子句

名詞子句是作名詞使用的子句，並可作句子的主詞、述詞名詞或受詞。

What I have been working on is secret. 作句子主詞。

This is *what I have been working on lately.* 作述詞名詞。

Tell me *what you have been working on.* 作動詞 *tell* 的受詞。

The experimental evidence suggests *that this hypothesis is incorrect.* 作動詞 *suggests* 的受詞。

以上已介紹了大部分構成英文句子的詞類以及字詞組，接著將講解英文句子的基本句式。

1.10 基本句式

所有英文句子都是由幾個基本句式構成的。無論句子有多長、有多複雜，都可還原成一些基本句式。本節將會介紹一些常用句式。

句式一： 主詞 + 動詞

這是所有英文句子最簡單和最基本的句式。（本章1.1節經已說明，一組字詞必須至少包含一個主詞和動詞，才能為一個完整句。）

主詞	動詞
The class	began.
A dog	barked.
Morning	came.

句式二： 主詞 + 及物動詞 + 直接受詞

此句式包含直接受詞 (direct object)（所謂直接受詞，即動詞行為對象的名詞、代名詞或作名詞的片語或子句）。能加上直接受詞的動詞稱為「及物動詞」(transitive verb)。

主詞	及物動詞	直接受詞
The children	enjoyed	the ice cream.
The girl	hit	the ball.
The teacher	taught	the class.

句式三： 主詞 + 及物動詞 + 直接受詞 + 受詞補語

某些動詞的直接受詞後面，可接修飾詞或另一個名詞，以賦予受詞另一個名稱或性質。這修飾詞或名詞稱為「受詞補語」(object complement)。

主詞	及物動詞	直接受詞	受詞補語
They	called	the child	Jill.
The student	elected	him	president.
Your remark	made	him	very happy.

句式四： 主詞 + 及物動詞 + 間接受詞 + 直接受詞

這類句式包含間接受詞 (indirect object)。間接受詞位於直接受詞之前，指「接受」直接受詞的人或事物。

主詞	及物動詞	直接受詞	受詞補語
I	bought	you	a gift.
Sharon	has found	herself	a good job.
The family	gave	the boy	some money.

句式五： 主詞 + 聯繫動詞 + 述詞名詞或述詞形容詞

這種句式包含一個特殊的動詞——聯繫動詞。聯繫動詞的功能在於連結句子的主詞和述詞名詞或述詞形容詞（即聯繫動詞後面的名詞或形容詞）。常用的聯繫動詞包括 *to be, to become, to seem, to appear*。而如 *to feel, to taste, to smell, to look, to sound, to act* 及 *to grow* 等動詞，也可作聯繫動詞。緊接聯繫動詞後面的是主詞補語 (subject complement)，即形容主詞或主詞的另一個名稱。這種句式中，形容句子主詞的形容詞，稱為「述詞形容詞」；至於主詞另一個名稱的名詞，則稱為「述詞名詞」。

主詞	聯繫動詞	述詞名詞或述詞形容詞
Her brother	is	a pilot.
The apartment	was	bright.
The pie	tasted	sweet.

句式六： 疑問句

英文的疑問句都是上面基本句式之變形。只要對調句中的主詞與動詞，就能造出疑問句：

直述句： *You are* my cousin.

疑問句： *Are you* my cousin?

此外，我們也可以把助動詞加在「主詞 + 動詞」的基本句式前面：

直述句： *You live* near your office.

疑問句： *Do you live* near your office?

句式七： 祈使句

祈使句是把直述句中的主詞省略而成的句子。

直述句： *You* go home.

祈使句： Go home.

直述句： *You* do your homework.

祈使句： Do your homework.

在祈使句中，省略的主詞通常是 *You*。

句式八： 被動語態的句子

在被動語態的句子中，主詞不是動詞的「施事者」，而是動詞的「受事者」。要表示被動語態，可以在句子的主要動詞前加上一個助動詞。至於動詞的施事者，則可加上以 *by* 開首的片語來表示，或甚至可以省略。

主動句： Lightning *struck* the house.

被動句：　　The house *was struck* by lightning.

主動句：　　The police *arrested* the thief yesterday.

被動句：　　The thief *was arrested by* the police yesterday.

被動句：　　The thief *was arrested* yesterday.

當施事者身分不明或無關宏旨時，就可使用被動句。

句式九：虛主詞結構

在虛主詞結構 (expletive construction) 中，虛字 *there* 或 *it* 會擺在句首，而主詞則擺在動詞後面。

There was a package lying on the table.

There are two lines in the graph.

It is clear that the reaction rate increases with temperature.

要強調主詞，便可使用虛主詞結構，即把主詞擺在動詞後面。但在虛主詞結構中，虛字 (如 *there*) 通常不是句子的主詞，接在動詞後面的名詞片語或名詞子句才是句子的主詞。

根據子句結構作句子分類

英文句子可用句中所包含的子句結構作分類：

* 簡單句 (simple sentence)：只有一個主要子句的句子。

  Education is important.

* 複合句 (compound sentence)：含有兩個或以上主要子句的句子。

  Education is important, but experience is also necessary.

* 複句 (complex sentence)：含有一個主要子句以及一個或以上的附屬子句的句子。

  If you want to find a good job, education is important.

* 複合複句 (compound-complex sentence)：含有兩個或以上的主要子句以及一個或以上的附屬子句的句子。

  If you want to find a good job, education is important, but experience is also necessary.

第二章

冠詞

　　要寫出漂亮的英文，必須瞭解定冠詞與不定冠詞 (*a, an, the*) 的正確用法，因為這些字能幫助釐清英文名詞及名詞片語的意思。本章將說明這些重要字詞的使用準則。

　　普通名詞 (common noun) 是用來指稱一般事物或概念的。（一個普通名詞若單獨出現，而不加其他修飾詞，則非某一特定人或物之名稱。專指某一特定人或物之名詞稱為「專有名詞」(proper noun)。）一個普通名詞，可用來指稱某個事物或概念的總類中任何一個或某一個個例。例如，在 *A computer is a powerful tool* 這句中，*computer* 是一個普通名詞，所指為某個總類（所有的電腦）中的任何一個個例。在 *A 586 computer is faster than a 486 model* 這句中，*computer* 這字詞也是指某個總類中的任何一個個例，但這時總類是指所有型號為 586 的電腦。雖然這個句子中所指的總類比第一個句子中 *computer* 所指的要小（586 電腦相對於所有的電腦而言），但當中 *computer* 仍是指某個總類中的任何一個個例。

　　再來參考 *I really like the computer I bought last week* 這個句子。在這句中，*computer* 並非泛指一般電腦，而是特指某一臺電腦，是指我上星期買的那臺。正確的使用英文冠詞，先要能夠區分一個名詞何時是指某個總類中的任何一個或一些個例（如例子 *a computer* 所示），何時特指某個或某些事物（如例子 *the computer* 所示）。

2.1 不定冠詞

不定冠詞 (*a* 或 *an*) 是用來表示某個單數名詞，所指稱的事物是某個總類中的任何一個個例。英文不定冠詞的使用規則如下：

一、如果一個普通名詞是用來指稱某類事物中的單數且可數的個例，則這名詞前面應加上不定冠詞 (*a* 或 *an*)。

二、如果一個名詞是複數、不可數，或是特指某事物或概念，則前面不加不定冠詞。（這有兩種可能：加定冠詞或不加任何冠詞。）

在應用上述的規則前，需瞭解三個關鍵概念：一個名詞是單數或複數，是可數或不可數，是指某總類中的任何一個個例或是特指某事物。

單數與複數名詞

第一個概念很簡單：一個名詞單指某事物是單數，而如果它指一個以上的事物，則是複數。在英文中，複數名詞常會寫成特別的複數形式（在名詞後加上 *s* 或 *es*，或是整個字改頭換面，如 *child* 的複數形式是 *children*），很易辨認。由上述規則可得知，如果一個名詞是複數，則不加不定冠詞。

可數與不可數名詞

第二個概念稍微複雜些。有一些事物或概念沒有明確形狀，並通常不能被分解成最小的個別單位。在英文中，指稱這一類事物或概念的名詞就是不可數名詞，例如 *water, salt, information, chemistry, anger* 等。不可數名詞一定不會有複數形式，且不會以 *a* 或 *an* 來修飾。例如，不會有人說 "three waters" 或 "one anger"。這點不難瞭解，但要記住哪些名詞是不可數卻不容易。

常用的不可數名詞包括以下幾種：

- 指涉沒有固定形狀的物質，如液體、汽體及粉狀的東西。例如 *water, oil, rice, sand, flour, air, oxygen*。

- 指涉抽象概念。如 *anger, happiness, information, force, strength, power*。

- 指涉處理方法或過程。例如 *integration, photolithography, fabrication, pollution, etching, purification*。

- 指涉不同學術領域。例如 *physics, chemistry, economics, mathematics, engineering*。

下面的名詞都是科技論文常會出現的不可數名詞，請緊記使用時不能把它們寫成複數形式。

research   Much *research* has been published in this field.

information Not much *information* is available on this phenomenon.

  equipment　The new *equipment* has already been installed.

  software　We are developing advanced *software* to complement our new line of workstations.

  hardware　A company cannot rely only on advanced *hardware*.

此外，下列名詞在一般的文章中偶爾會作可數名詞使用，且可作為複數。不過，它們在科技論文中通常都是不可數的。

  literature　In the *literature*, little attention has been devoted to this problem.

   這裏的 *literature* 是不可數名詞，指某一特定學術領域中所有已發表的文獻。當 *literature* 用來特指某一文學傳統時，則可變成複數，如 *Chinese literature and English literature are two of the world's great literatures* 。

  work　Recent *work* has overcome these drawbacks.

   這裏的 *work* 指的是工作或著作的整體，而非某一篇特定的報告或一項特定的研究工作，因此這裏的 *work* 是不可數的。

  notation　The *notation* used in this paper is summarized below.

   這裏的 *notation* 是指由一些不同符號組成的一組符號。因為作者指的只是一組符號，而非一些個別的符號，所以 *notation* 是單數，且是不可數的。

  terminology　In this paper, we employ standard *terminology*.

   這裏的 *terminology* 是指由一些不同術語組成的一組術語。因為作者指的只是一組術語，所以 *terminology* 是單數，且是不可數的。

  可數名詞則指稱可分解成個別單位的事物。可數名詞有複數形式且可用數字和數量詞來修飾，例如：*two computers, one office, a dozen flowers, three children, several techniques, many approaches* 等。有某些抽象名詞也是可數的，例如 *concept* 和 *idea*。（注意：一個可數名詞如果前面有數字或是像 *several* 或 *many* 這樣的數量詞，則當然不可加不定冠詞。）

  在英語中，複數形式的可數名詞可直接用數字和數量詞來修飾。至於不可數名詞，則與漢語的名詞的情況相同，需要加上相應的量詞 (counters) 才可以用數字和數量詞來修飾。英語的不可數名詞通常是借一些度量衡單位或器物名稱作量詞使用。例如，*water* 這個名詞可使用的量詞包括 *cup, glass* 和 *liter* (a *cup* of water, a *glass* of water, a *liter* of water)。*Equipment* 所使用的量詞是 *piece* (a *piece* of equipment)。而量詞就像其他可數名詞一樣，可加上不定冠詞或用數字和數量詞來修飾。

一般指稱與特定指稱

  最後一個要弄清的概念是：所指稱的事物究竟是某個總類中的任何一個個例，還是某個特定事物。可數名詞常用來指某個總類中的個例。例如，*A computer is a powerful tool*，*computer* 指的是一般的電腦，而整句意思是「任何一臺電腦都是功能很強的工具」。這不僅指我書桌上的那臺、實驗室裏的或是圖書館裏的電腦，而是指任何一臺電腦。相反，*The computer on my desk is new*，*computer* 則指特定的一臺電腦：我書桌上的那臺。因為在 *A computer is a powerful tool* 這句中，*computer* 是單數且可數的，指一般電腦中的其中一臺，所以它前面會加不定冠詞 *a*。但在 *The computer on my desk is new* 這句中，*computer* 指的是特定的一臺電腦，所以它前面會加定冠詞。

　　很多人都會有相同的疑問：某個名詞事實上只指涉一件事物，但它不是特指一個事物，那麼應否加上不定冠詞？例如，*There is a book on my desk* 這個存在句已清楚指出我桌上只有一本書。然而，句子沒有特指是哪一本書。假如我在書桌上放了一本字典，*There is a book on my desk* 這個句子便為真。就算我將書桌上的字典拿走，然後換上一本英文課本，這個句子仍然為真。只要我的書桌上有一本書，無論它是哪一本書，皆足以使這個句子為真。此句中的單數可數名詞 *book* 並未指一本特定的書，所以應該用不定冠詞。

　　在大部分的情況下，如果在一個中文的名詞前，可以加上「一種」、「任何一個」或「某一個」，則所指大概就是某個總類中的任何一個個例，而在對應的英文名詞前大概都要加上不定冠詞。

A 和 *An*

　　英文有兩個不定冠詞，即 *a* 和 *an*，現在來重溫兩者不同的用法。某個名詞前應使用不定冠詞 *a* 還是 *an*，要視乎名詞第一個音節的發音而定。如果名詞第一個音節的發音是以子音開頭，則必須使用冠詞 *a*，即使這個字是以母音開始也不例外。

a machine	a blackboard	a universal joint
a union	a one-step method	a unique solution

上述例子中，有些字的拼法是以母音開頭，但它們第一個音節的發音是子音，所以都必使用冠詞 *a*。

　　相反，在以母音發音開頭的名詞前，應使用冠詞 *an*，即使它的第一個字母是子音，也不例外。

an algorithm	an iteration	an SRAM chip
an X-ray machine	an RNA molecule	

上述例子中，有些字詞的第一個字母是子音字母，但這些子音字母發的是母音，亦應使用冠詞 *an*。

　　如果一個加上不定冠詞的名詞前面有形容詞，應否使用 *a* 或 *an* 則視該形容詞的第一個音節發音而定。

a simple algorithm	a new element
an unusual machine	an interesting subject

兩用名詞

有些特別的英文名詞，在不同的文脈下，有時會作可數名詞，有時則會作不可數名詞。這一類名詞在科技寫作中十分常見，稱為「兩用名詞」(two-way noun)。大多數兩用名詞無論是在可數或不可數的時候，基本概念都相同。在多數情況下，兩用名詞都是不可數的，只有當要用來指該基本概念特定的個例時，才是可數的。

Language 就是兩用名詞的一個好例子。它可作不可數名詞，例如：

Language is what sets humans apart from animals.

但是，*language* 也可作可數名詞：

Professor Smith is fluent in four *languages*.

第一個例句的 *language* 是不可數名詞，所指為一般的語言溝通。而在第二個例句中，*four languages* 可解釋為 *four types of language*。（後者的 *language* 是取其不可數意義。）

有很多兩用名詞就像 *language* 這名詞一樣，可作可數名詞用來表示 *a type of x*，而這裏的 *x* 則是取其兩用名詞的不可數意義。這類兩用名詞包括：*metal, material, acid, noise, motion, force, friction*。

The door is made of *metal*. 不可數意義

Gold, silver, and bronze are three different *metals*. 可數意義，指三種不同金屬

兩用名詞當作可數時也常用來指 *an amount of x* 或 *a degree of x*。例如，*pressure* 這字詞通常是作不可數名詞，例如：

Pressure varies proportionately with temperature. 不可數意義

它也可作可數名詞用來指 *an amount of pressure*，例如：

In the second experiment, the reaction was carried out at *a greater pressure* than in the first. 可數意義

在這例子中，*a greater pressure* 的意思是 "a greater amount of pressure"。此外，其他可作可數名詞來指 *an amount of x* 的兩用名詞還有 *mass, force, velocity, acceleration*。

以上只是兩用名詞最常見的兩種解釋。英文中還有許多兩用名詞，且尚有其他不同解釋。但應注意：並非所有的不可數名詞皆可兩用。因此，在將一個不可數名詞視作兩用名詞使用前，最好先參考在同一學術領域內，以英文為母語的作者有否如此使用。

練習 2-1 可數與不可數名詞

請判斷下列名詞是可數還是不可數。

device	file
hydrogen	hydrochloric acid
substrate	deposition
telecommunications	system
equipment	liter of hydrochloric acid
research	concept
software	term
evidence	terminology
project	gold
information	rain
biology	kilogram
mass	efficiency

練習 2-2 兩用名詞

請指出下列畫線部分的名詞屬於可數還是不可數。

1. According to this law, <u>force</u> is the product of <u>mass</u> and <u>acceleration</u>. An object with a <u>mass</u> of 10 kilograms and an <u>acceleration</u> of one meter per second, per second, will have a <u>force</u> of 10 newtons.

2. Much research <u>effort</u> has been devoted to this problem.

3. We wish to thank Professor Chen for his <u>efforts</u> over the years on behalf of our <u>association</u>.

4. A <u>company</u> must not overburden itself with <u>debt</u>. In the last 18 months before its collapse, Technocorp had taken on several unwise <u>debts</u>.

5. <u>Voltage</u> is the electrical <u>pressure</u> that exists between two points and produces a flow of <u>current</u> when a closed <u>circuit</u> is connected between the points. The <u>unit</u> of <u>measurement</u> of <u>voltage</u> is the volt. One <u>volt</u> is the difference in electric <u>potential</u> required to make a <u>current</u> of 1 ampere flow through a <u>resistance</u> of 1 ohm.

6. The <u>feasibility</u> of this production <u>method</u> requires further <u>study</u>.

7. The <u>movement</u> of the snake is produced by four <u>mechanisms</u>. Each of the animal's <u>movements</u> can be analyzed as the <u>result</u> of one or more of these mechanisms.

8. The <u>solubility</u> of these salts in water varies with their chemical structure. The first two samples, for instance, have different <u>solubilities</u>.

2.2 定冠詞

定冠詞 *the* 是用來指一特定的人、概念或事物。與不定冠詞有別，定冠詞可與單數或複數名詞合用，也可與可數或不可數名詞合用。它既可用以表示獨一無二及特定的概念或事物之名詞，也可用來表示特定的一組概念或事物的名詞。

「如果一個名詞指的是一個或一組特定的事物，則應加上定冠詞」。這項規則是每個曾經學過英文的人都知道的，但實際上它幫助不大。因為對母語非為英語的人來說，最大的問題在於如何分辨一個名詞在甚麼情況下是指某一特定的事物，而非某個總類中的任何一個個例。要判斷名詞或名詞片語 *N* 應否使用定冠詞，有一個粗略的方法：當閱讀名詞或名詞片語 *N* 時，就問自己：「作者所說的是哪個 *N*？」如果之前的句子或該句子本身已經提供明確的信息，以指定所說的是哪個 *N*，則這名詞 *N* 可加定冠詞。我們來參考：

I am working on a new research project.

我們可以問自己：「作者所說的是哪項研究計畫？」如果作者在此以前並未提到這項研究計畫（且我們也不知道這項計畫），則這個句子就無法提供一個明確的答案。倘若如此，這裏用不定冠詞 *a* 是正確的。相反：

The new research project that I am working on is very challenging.

當我們問：「作者所說的是哪項研究計畫？」，大家已明確地知悉，所說的就是他正在進行的那個研究計畫。倘若如此，這裏用定冠詞是正確的。

以下將提出一些說明在甚麼情況下會使用定冠詞的指導準則。但這裏必須講明：除了第一條準則之外，這些準則並非絕對的。撰寫科技論文的作者不能完全依賴這些準則，還是要自己考慮清楚，一個由某特定名詞所指涉的事物究竟是某個（或某組）特定的事物，還是某個總類中的任何一個（或一些）個例。

提及過之名詞

如果一個名詞或名詞片語所指涉的，與同篇文章中已提過的名詞或名詞片語所指涉的事物或概念相同，則通常應加上定冠詞 *the*。請看下面例子：

A bus master either oversees the transfer of data between devices or, more often, exchanges information with one or more slaves. *The bus master* selects slaves by placing address information on the bus; each slave compares this information with its own address. If the addresses match, *the master* and slave establish a connection and the slave becomes a responder.

這段文字中，作者首次提及 *bus master* 這名詞時，*bus master* 並沒有特定的指稱，這時 *bus master* 可以是指任何一個 bus master，因此作者在這名詞前面使用不定冠詞 *a*。然而，第二和第三句中的 *bus master* 及 *master*，和第一句中的 *a bus master* 所指相同，故它們的前面應加上定冠詞 *the*。

當要確認一個名詞是否已在文章較前部分提及過，不能只檢視有否出現過相同字眼，更要判斷有否出現過所指的事物或概念。試看下面例子：

A solar water heater can be constructed as shown in Figure 2. At the top left of *the water heater* is a cold-water inlet, where water flows into *the apparatus*. The main portion of *the heater* consists of many coils of plastic pipe connected together in an accordion fashion....

在第二和第三句中的名詞片語都和作者第一句所使用的名詞片語不同。其中兩個名詞片語 (*the water heater* 和 *the heater*) 是第一句中的名詞片語 (*A solar water heater*) 的變形，而另一個名詞片語 (*the apparatus*) 的首語 (*apparatus*) 和第一句中的片語的首語完全不同。但實際上，第二和第三句中的三個名詞片語所指的，皆為第一句中提到的熱水器。因此，這三個名詞片語都應加上定冠詞 *the*。

接著限定子句或片語之名詞

　　如果一個名詞的後面接著一個子句或片語，用以說明或限定這個名詞所指為何，則這個名詞前面通常要加上定冠詞。這項準則最常見的例子，就是當一個名詞後面接著限定的關係子句：

This is *the network design that our firm is currently using*.

The method proposed by Johnson and Smith is the most efficient way to factor the logic terms.

　　第一個例句中，*that our firm is currently using* 這子句說明了句中所指的網路為何。從這個子句以及作者使用定冠詞來看，讀者可推斷作者的公司目前只使用一種網路設計。同樣，第二個例句中 *(that was) proposed by Johnson and Smith* 這子句說明了句中所指的方法為何。從這個子句和作者使用定冠詞來看，讀者亦可推斷約翰生和斯密夫只提出了一個方法。

　　如名詞後面接有以 *of* 開首的介係詞片語，經常應在該名詞前面加上定冠詞。下面的句子中，介係詞片語就說明了作者所指的發明、理論以及速率為何：

Future historians will surely regard *the invention of the integrated circuit* as one of the most important technological developments of the twentieth century.

Some scholars have argued that Einstein's wife helped him to develop *the theory of relativity*.

The rate of precipitation was extremely rapid.

　　然而，「接著限定子句或片語之名詞」與「提及過之名詞」的準則不同，它無法自動判斷作者該用定冠詞還是不定冠詞。作者仍須自行判斷他用的名詞究竟是指某一個（或一組）特定事物，還是某個總類中的一個（或一些）個例。試比較下列兩句的意思：

This is *the network design* that our group recently developed.

This is *a network design* that our group recently developed.

這兩句都是正確英文，而應選用哪個句子則需視乎上下文關係而定。使用定冠詞的句子，暗示作者的研究小組最近只研發出一種新的網路設計。如果作者認為讀者知道此設計的發展，則他會用第一句。反過來說，假使作者認為讀者對他的研究小組及工作內容完全不熟悉，或者這研究小組最近完成了幾種不同的設計，而句中所指的只是其中一個，則他會選用第二句。

再來看另一個例子：

Smith presented *a detailed analysis of the process.*

The analysis of the process that Smith presented was very clear.

第一個句子中，作者之所以選用不定冠詞 *a* 是因為斯密夫對這過程所提出的只是其中一個分析，而別人或斯密夫自己仍然可能有別的分析。但若作者把 *a* 改為 *the*，意思就迥然不同了。這表示可行的分析只有一個，且就是斯密夫的那一個。而在第二個句子中，作者選用定冠詞 *the*，暗示斯密夫只提出了一個特定的分析。

上面網路設計的例子顯示出，即使一個名詞後面接有一個限定或說明的子句或片語，要選擇用定冠詞或不定冠詞，有時還是要取決於讀者對主題瞭解的程度。

共有和專業的知識

當作者認為讀者都瞭解某個名詞具有特定的指稱時，通常會在這個名詞前加上定冠詞。在這種情況下，即使這個名詞在文章較前部分未曾提及過，也可用定冠詞。試看下面例子：

The Chernobyl accident drew attention to the dangers presented by poorly designed, inadequately maintained nuclear reactors.

這個例子中，作者在 *The Chernobyl accident* 這名詞片語中用定冠詞 *the*，因為他假設讀者都知道1986年在車諾比爾核電廠發生的重大意外事件。然而，這個假設是否恰當要視作者預設的讀者群而定。在1986年任何一位看得懂報紙或電視新聞節目的人都知道這宗意外。因此如果作者預設的讀者群是三十歲以上的成人，則他的假設完全成立，而用定冠詞是恰當的。相反，如果作者的文章是針對那些在1986年只是幼童的人而寫的，則假設便不成立。他或許應該使用 *an accident* 來改寫：

An accident that occurred at Chernobyl in 1986 drew attention to the dangers presented by poorly designed, inadequately maintained nuclear reactors.

由此可見，在決定是否在一個特定的名詞前加上定冠詞時，作者不但要考慮這個名詞有否特定的指稱，還要考慮到讀者群是否同樣已知道有此特定指稱。同一個名詞，在對象是專業讀者的論文中會使用定冠詞；但在另一篇以普羅大眾為對象的論文中，很可能需要用不定冠詞。例如，在一篇對象為專業研究人員的論文中，作者會這樣寫：

To study the roots of linguistic meaning, we can consider *the process called radical interpretation.*

這裏作者在 *process* 前加定冠詞，因為他確信看這篇文章的讀者都知道「徹底詮釋」的意思，且肯定在他們的學術領域中只有一種分析法叫做 "radical interpretation"。

這種情況就是作者與他的讀者都共同擁有一種「專業知識」。相反，如果作者的寫作對象是一般普羅大眾，他們都不瞭解何謂徹底詮釋，則作者就該用不定冠詞：

> To study the roots of linguistic meaning, we can consider *a process called radical interpretation*.

再舉另一個例子，請參考下面句子中定冠詞的用法：

> Sandy jumped into a taxi and said, "Take me to *the train station*."

句子中選用定冠詞的理由，就是作者與讀者對城市與火車站都有一些共同的想法。一般人皆知道，大多數的城市裏都只會有一個火車站，所以在 *the train station* 這名詞片語前面用定冠詞，讀者會認為是很自然的。相反，假如 Sandy 要求司機載她到 "a train station" 去的話，句子就會顯得十分奇怪——司機甚至可能會把她載到另一個城市的火車站！

如要採用一些用以指涉所有人都知道之特定事物的名詞，使用定冠詞是正確的。這一類的名詞包括 *the world, the sun, the moon, the sky, the earth, the ground, the north pole* 等等。（但有兩個特別的情況：名詞 *space* 的前面不會用定冠詞；還有，在口語中，以英文為母語者習慣說 "on earth"。）而專有名詞像 *the United States* （或 *the U.S.A.*）、*the United Kingdom* （或 *the U.K.*）、*the Republic of China* （或 *the R.O.C.*）以及 *the People's Republic of China* （或 *the P.R.C.*），此類名詞都要加上定冠詞（地址除外）。此外，指稱一段時間的名詞，一定要加上 *the*，如：*the past, the present, the future, the 1990s, the twentieth century* 等。

有些專有名詞的前面必須加定冠詞，特別是它的首語 (head noun) 本身是個普通名詞（在英文中，首語通常是名詞片語中最右邊的名詞）。這類專有名詞包括國家名稱，例如 *the United States*，和某些廣大的地理環境名稱，例如 *the Nile River, the Pacific Ocean, the Atlantic Ocean, the Alps* 和 *the Himalaya Mountains*。

然而，很多首語為普通名詞的專有名詞，並不會加上定冠詞。例如個別的山的名稱前通常不加定冠詞 (*Taiping Mountain*)，湖泊名稱前亦通常不加定冠詞 (*Sun Moon Lake*)。只有當某一地理環境真的非常廣大時，才會特別為它的名稱加定冠詞。

特定的歷史事件名稱前通常要加定冠詞，例如 *the chemical revolution* 和 *the industrial revolution*。還有，特定的科學理論或定律的名稱，如 *the phlogiston theory* 和 *the uncertainty principle*，也要用定冠詞。如果一個名詞指的是某個研究領域的總稱，而非某一特定理論，則不需加冠詞：*set theory, game theory, psychoanalytic theory*。

特殊的形容詞

有些用來修飾名詞的形容詞，能使名詞清清楚楚地特指某個事物。例如，最高級形容詞將所修飾的名詞，限定其僅指涉一件事物。像 *largest, oldest, fastest, leftmost, most expensive* 這樣的形容詞，只看形式便可知它們指涉的事物是獨一無二的。所以這些形容詞修飾的名詞都一定要加定冠詞：

> His family owns *the oldest house* in the city.

　　序數形容詞 (*first, second, nth, last*) 亦是一種將名詞限定為只有一個指涉對象的形容詞。任何一組事物，從第一個到最後一個組成分子，每個皆是獨立的個殊。因此，用序數形容詞修飾的名詞幾乎都要加定冠詞：

> *The first batter* hit *the third pitch* out of the park.

　　然而，有些特殊情況，序數形容詞前面也會加不定冠詞。例如：*A second approach to the problem is to use a Markov model*。在這裏，"second" 的意思不是「第二個」，而是「另一個」。

　　此外，有一些形容詞也會使它所修飾的名詞有唯一的指稱，例如 *only*。在 *This is the only road to Kalamazoo* 這句中，形容詞 *only* 將 *road* 這名詞的指稱限定為一條特定的路。這類形容詞還包括 *sole, exact, ideal, present, same, following*：

> *The sole way* to find *the exact solution* for *the ideal case* is by using *the following method*, which is *the same method* as that used in our earlier paper.

　　當然，即使有這些標記，作者在加上定冠詞 *the* 之前，仍需確定這個名詞所指的是否為一特定的事物。再看下面的例子：

> This is *an exact method* for finding *the exact solution*.

這裏 *an exact method* 指的是一個精密的方法（可能還有好幾個精密的方法），而 *the exact solution* 指的是某個獨一無二、正確可行的解救方法。

總稱

　　定冠詞有時可用來賦予某個單數且可數的名詞一個「總稱」意義，用來代表該名詞所指為某個總類的事物，而非某個特定的事物。這類總稱的名詞片語最常用於指稱某種特別的設備、機器或動物。以下是幾個例子：

> *The integrated circuit* is one of the most important inventions of the twentieth century.

> Because of rampant poaching, today *the tiger* is in danger of becoming extinct.

> *The computer* has changed the way business is conducted in many industries.

　　複數名詞當然也可用來指某個總類中的一些個例，因此上述句子中斜體字部分的單數名詞，和不加定冠詞的複數名詞的意思十分相近。例如，上述第二句和 *Because of rampant poaching, today tigers are in danger of becoming extinct* 的意思並沒甚不同。同樣，上述第三句和 *Computers have changed the way business is conducted in many industries* 的意思也沒多大差別。

隱含的獨特性

　　有時作者為了暗示某個名詞只有一個指涉對象，即使讀者可能不瞭解某個名詞有唯一的指涉，作者還是會在這個名詞前加上定冠詞。這個做法是希望讀者能由此推斷出這個名詞事實上只有唯一的指涉。這種情形最常出現在作者描述某種設備或機器時。試看以下例子：

> ...The jumper is on the bottom of the modem, near the back panel. To set up the modem as the answering side, remove *the plastic jumper cap* from the jumper.

這段是從一本教人安裝數據機的技術手冊中節錄下來的。在這段落之前，作者已提過數據機、jumper 及 answering side，而他並沒提過 plastic jumper cap。但作者在這裏仍加上定冠詞，顯然是暗示它是唯一的。因此，即使讀者不怎麼瞭解甚麼是數據機、jumper 或 jumper cap，仍然可立刻從這段落推斷出，作者所指的 jumper 只有一個 plastic jumper cap。

再參考另一個例子。下面的文字是從一本教人安裝雷射印表機碳粉匣的說明書中節錄下來的：

> ...Remove the new toner cartridge from its bag.... Grasp the tab of *the sealing tape* and firmly pull the tape out of the cartridge. Insert the cartridge into the printer, taking care not to touch *the photoconductive drum*.

在這段文章之前，作者已先提到碳粉匣，但並沒提到密封帶或感光鼓。但只要讀者一看到作者在這兩個名詞片語前面用定冠詞，自然就能推斷出這裏只有一條密封帶和一個感光鼓。

常犯錯誤

以下是中國作者在科技論文中，使用定冠詞時常犯的兩個錯誤，希望各位留意。

1. 經常會用一個普通名詞和數字組成的專有名詞，來指稱報告中的某一章節，或報告中提出的方程式或定理。試看幾個例子：

equation (9)　　　　section 4　　chapter 3　　theorem 2.1

這些專有名詞是不能加定冠詞的。下列句子都是錯誤的寫法：

> 誤：　The solution will be presented in *the* section 4.

> 誤：　We can derive the solution from *the* equation (9).

正確寫法如下：

> 正：　The solution will be presented in section 4.

> 正：　We can derive the solution from equation (9).

2. 在科學、工程學或數學中，有很多廣為人知的定理、方程式及公式，都是以發現者的名字來命名的。有些定理或方程式的名稱必須加上定冠詞，有些則只要在發現者的名字後面加上屬格（或稱「所有格」，即加上 *'s*）便可。試看這兩個例子：

Shannon's theorem　　　　　　the Ricatti equation

要學習這些定理或方程式之名稱的正確寫法，最好參考在同一學術領域內以英文為母語的專家的寫法。此外，要緊記一項準則——如果發現者的名字加了屬格，則不可用定冠詞 *the*；反過來說，如果已經加了定冠詞，就不可在人名後面再加屬格。

　　誤：　the Newton's laws
　　正：　Newton's laws

　　誤：　the Barcan's formula
　　正：　the Barcan formula

練習 2-3　定冠詞與不定冠詞

在下列的空格內填上 *a, an* 或 *the*，有些可能不需填寫。並請說明理由。

1. Laser Printers

In _the_ late 1970s, ＿＿ laser printer had just arrived on ＿＿ market. It used ＿＿ complex and expensive optical system to scan ＿＿ diode laser beam in straight lines across ＿＿ photoconductive drum. This optical system consisted of ＿＿ rotary polygonal-mirror scanner and ＿＿ special focusing lenses. ＿＿ laser beam is simultaneously modulated and deflected by ＿＿ rotating mirror so that it repeatedly scans straight lines, forming ＿＿ electrically charged image on ＿＿ photoconductive drum. This image is then transformed into ＿＿ visible image on paper by ＿＿ electrophotoconductive process of ＿＿ kind used by photocopiers.

　Vital to ＿＿ optical system of ＿＿ early laser printer was ＿＿ high-precision, mirror-scanner motor, needed to minimize fluctuations in ＿＿ placement and straightness of ＿＿ scanning lines. In laser printers, about 10 scanning lines are generated per rotation. Each line must scan exactly ＿＿ same position on ＿＿ photoconductive drum. If ＿＿ shaft of ＿＿ motor rotating ＿＿ scanner wobbles, ＿＿ scanning line also will deflect. ＿＿ permissible runout angle for motor shafts of ＿＿ mirror scanners is about 5 arc seconds, depending on ＿＿ system. In ＿＿ typical scanner, ＿＿ placement error should be less than 25 micrometers, which usually corresponds to ＿＿ deflection angle change of less than 10 arc seconds. ＿＿ line produced by ＿＿ laser printers may curve no more than ±0.1 millimeter over ＿＿ entire scanning range of about 260 mm. To correct placement errors due to mirror wobble, cylindrical lenses often are used.[1]

2. Using Fusion for Power

Thermonuclear fusion is ____ process through which light nuclei—such as hydrogen and its isotopes, deuterium and tritium—fuse at ____ extremely high temperatures to produce heavier elements. It is ____ fundamental source of energy in ____ universe, providing ____ power for ____ sun and all other stars. Ultimately, all forms of energy used on Earth—including ____ fossil fuels, ____ hydroelectric power, and ____ solar power—derive from ____ fusion energy. Even ____ energy stored in uranium was originally ____ product of fusion reactions in ____ nearby supernova.

Since ____ nuclei are all positively charged, very high temperatures—over 100 million Kelvin—are required to give them sufficient energy to overcome coulomb electrical repulsion and to react. ____ basic problem of controlled fusion reactions is, therefore, to produce these high temperatures and simultaneously to confine ____ resulting plasma long enough and at sufficient density for ____ release of ____ economically significant energy.

There are two main approaches to ____ use of ____ fusion for ____ power generation: inertial confinement and magnetic confinement. Of these two, ____ magnetic confinement has yielded ____ best results so far. Magnetic confinement makes use of ____ fact that ____ charged ions and electrons that make up ____ thermonuclear plasma tend to spiral around magnetic lines of force rather than move across them. With good design, therefore, magnetic "bottles" can be devised to contain ____ plasma even at ____ very high temperatures, while ____ combination of ____ magnetic field compression and other methods can be used for heating.[2]

3. Progress in Computer Technology

Early computers required ____ special environment, with raised floors to carry ____ interconnecting cables and large air-conditioning units to remove ____ dissipated heat; ____ maintenance man had to be summoned frequently. At ____ cost of over ____ dollar for either ____ discrete transistor or ____ bit of memory, ____ price of early computer systems generally came to ____ few million dollars. ____ high cost forced compromises on computer designers, such as ____ use of ____ single accumulator register as ____ source of one argument in every operation of computer logic or arithmetic. This simplified ____ control structure but generally necessitated time-consuming transfers of data that were extraneous to ____ intended calculation.

Since that time, ____ speed, cost, reliability, and size of computer circuitry have changed beyond recognition. ____ cost of ____ single transistor or bit of memory is less than ____ hundredth of ____ cent, ____ circuits operate for thousands of hours without failing, and ____ computing unit that far exceeds ____ capabilities of ____ ENIAC measures about ____ centimeter on ____ side, consumes ____ fraction of ____ watt, and can be bought for only ____ few dollars. This has been brought about, on ____ supply side, by ____ remarkably diverse body of new technology and, on ____ demand side, by ____ emergence of new, massive, and diverse applications of ____ computational resources, which for ____ most part bear little resemblance to those for which ____ general-purpose computer was originally intended.[3]

4. Radio Astronomy

Radio astronomy—the measurement of radio frequencies emitted by interstellar molecules—is ____ chief method for observing how stars form from ____ interstellar clouds of gas and dust, or die and release such clouds. We live about 30,000 light years from ____ center of our galaxy, but interstellar dust blocks most of ____ distance from view by optical telescopes. However, radio waves travel through ____ dust and can be recorded by special receivers, since ____ wavelengths are much longer than ____ size of ____ dust grains.

Radio telescopes are somewhat similar to optical telescopes. Radio waves from interstellar space are reflected off ____ antenna—a bowl-shaped mirror—onto ____ secondary mirror. ____ waves are reflected down to ____ center of ____ bowl, where they enter ____ radio receiver, or radiometer. ____ signal is then amplified, filtered, and processed by ____ detector with ____ short integration time—about 0.1 ms, or ____ response time suitable for ____ loudspeaker.

In making ____ observation, ____ astronomer typically steers ____ antenna toward ____ radio source, such as ____ nebula. ____ signals from various species of molecules—at least 40 have been identified so far—are measured by tuning ____ receiver to ____ wavelength characteristic of each species. ____ observed peak output power of many regions of ____ interstellar cloud can be plotted as ____ map with isophotes.[4]

5. Computers and Speech Recognition

____ computers would seem much friendlier if it were possible to verbally ask them for ____ information or command them to carry out ____ task, and if they could respond by talking in ____ natural, conversational English. However, ____ prospects for automatic recognition of fluent, continuous speech in ____ near future are not encouraging, in part because of ____ complexity of ____ task and in part because of inadequate research support.

____ fundamental question in automatic speech recognition by computers is how much information is contained in ____ acoustic wave patterns that make up ____ words and sentences used in communicating by voice. In other words, can ____ machine decipher ____ voice command and act on it simply by decoding ____ wave pattern, or does it need to "know" certain additional information? In all cases, ____ answer seems to be that ____ extra knowledge must be programmed into ____ computer.

____ speech recognition by ____ computer comprises two operations. ____ first is ____ decomposition of acoustic wave patterns into ____ basic sounds or elements of speech, called phonemes. ____ existing speech recognition machines do this job with no more than 65 percent accuracy, in part because ____ wave patterns corresponding to neighboring phonemes tend to overlap. ____ second operation is to arrange ____ phonemes into words and ____ words into sentences, taking into account that ____ substantial fraction of ____ phonemes may be misidentified, and it is here that ____ need for linguistic and contextual knowledge arises.[5]

6. Chemical Reactions in Combustion

The molecules of most fuels have far too many atoms for combustion to proceed as ____ concerted event. Imagine ____ tangle that would arise if ____ eight carbon atoms and ____ 18 hydrogen atoms of ____ octane molecule (C_8H_{18}) were to disengage from one another and combine all at once with ____ surrounding molecules of diatomic oxygen (O_2), forming ____ new chemical bonds of carbon dioxide (CO_2) and water (H_2O). No fuel burns that way. Instead ____ breakdown of fuel molecules and ____ formation of ____ combustion products proceed in long sequences of steps; each step involves only ____ small rearrangement of chemical bonds.

____ step of this type is termed ____ elementary reaction; ____ various molecules created along ____ way are called reactive intermediates, and ____ set of all elementary reactions that together account for ____ net chemical transformation is ____ reaction mechanism. ____ equation describing ____ overall chemical reaction that takes place in ____ flame gives no hint of what ____ individual molecular changes are; ____ equations describing elementary reactions, however, do represent real chemical events at ____ molecular level. Only when all ____ important elementary reactions are known can ____ path from fuel to combustion products be accurately described in terms of ____ rearrangements of atoms in molecules.[6]

7. A Special Kind of Atom

As far as chemists and biologists are concerned, ____ basic building blocks of matter are ____ atoms and molecules, combinations of atoms that are bound together electrically. ____ atom consists of ____ nucleus, which has ____ positive electric charge, surrounded by one or more electrons that are negatively charged. ____ electrons are over ____ thousand times less massive than ____ nucleus, but they usually occupy ____ volume with ____ diameter more than ten thousand times that of ____ nucleus. Thus, to all intents and purposes, ____ size of ____ atom is determined by its electrons.

Since oppositely charged particles attract one another, electrons in ____ atom tend to stay as close to ____ nucleus as possible. If one of ____ electrons is given additional energy, however, ____ force binding that electron to ____ nucleus is partially or totally overcome. When ____ compensation is partial, we speak of ____ process of excitation; when total, of ionization.

The more ____ attractive force within ____ atom is counterbalanced, ____ greater ____ separation of ____ excited electron and ____ nucleus. If one electron in ____ atom is at ____ much greater distance from ____ nucleus than all ____ others, ____ atom is called ____ Rydberg atom, ____ highly excited electron ____ Rydberg electron, and ____ rest of ____ atom (____ nucleus plus ____ less distant electrons) ____ core of ____ Rydberg atom.[7]

8. Successful Integrated Circuits

More complex circuits are generally more specialized in their functions and thus are less in demand. ____ efforts of integrated circuit designers have focused on developing ____ commercially viable products using integrated circuits in ____ face of this and other constraints.

Undoubtedly ____ most successful such product has been ____ memory circuit, which makes ____ large data bases practical; ____ second most successful class of devices has been ____ microprocessor and its successor ____ microcomputer, which is, literally, ____ computer on ____ chip. ____ programming of microcomputers often involves ____ program written permanently into ____ special read-only memory (ROM) on ____ chip during ____ manufacturing process, which makes it possible to use this class of circuits in ____ wide variety of ways.[8]

9. The Expansion of the Universe

The expansion of ____ universe was discovered when it was found that ____ cosmic objects move away from us with speeds that are higher ____ farther away ____ object is located. ____ speed at which objects move away from us increases by about 15 km/sec for every 106 light years distance from us. ____ expansion must be imagined not as ____ penetration of ____ limited amount of ____ matter into empty space surrounding it, but as ____ increasing dilution of matter everywhere in ____ universe. Each point can be considered ____ center of this dilution. Indeed, regardless of his location in ____ universe, ____ observer would see exactly ____ same thing with respect to ____ objects around him; that is, objects would recede from him at ____ rate of 15 km/sec/106 light years. ____ expansion of ____ universe does not distinguish any point and is ____ same all over space.

This expansion leads to ____ remarkable conclusion when we try to extrapolate it toward ____ past: one can easily calculate that about 18 billion years ago ____ density of matter must have been infinite. Thus we can indeed calculate approximately ____ date of ____ Primal Bang.

It is important to keep in mind that ____ Primal Bang is not ____ local phenomenon. ____ descriptions of it in ____ popular literature are often grossly misleading; it is wrong to imagine that ____ Primal Bang occurred at ____ given point in ____ space, matter being expelled in all directions. Actually, ____ Primal Bang was ____ beginning of ____ decompression of ____ infinite universe. This means that ____ whole universe, ____ infinite space, was filled with ____ infinite density of matter at time zero. Immediately afterward ____ density became finite though still very high. With ____ passage of time ____ density decreased further until it reached ____ present value.[9]

10. How a Bus Works

The function of _____ bus is to transfer information in _____ form of electric signals between _____ different parts of _____ electronic system. _____ generic term for system components connected by _____ bus is devices. _____ group of devices is connected to _____ bus segment.

Only one device, _____ bus master, is allowed to control _____ bus and initiate data transfers at any one time. Several masters may be present on _____ bus, so contention between them must be resolved using _____ arbitration rules.

_____ bus master either oversees _____ transfer of _____ data between _____ devices or, more often, exchanges information with one or more slaves. _____ bus master selects slaves by placing _____ address information on _____ bus; each slave compares this information with its own address. If the addresses match, _____ master and slave establish _____ connection and _____ slave becomes _____ responder. Addresses that identify more than one slave are called _____ broadcast addresses. _____ particular device may act as both master and slave, but not at _____ same time.

Once _____ slaves are connected, _____ bus master exchanges data with them over _____ bus. _____ master breaks _____ connection with its responders after all _____ data have been transferred. This sequence of actions—making _____ connection, transferring data, breaking _____ connection—is called _____ transaction. The master may either relinquish bus mastership after _____ transaction or continue with other transactions.[10]

第三章

動詞

本章將討論動詞的三個用法：一、時態要統一；二、主詞與動詞必須一致；三、動詞的語氣。

3.1 時態

英文研究報告中動詞時態 (tense) 的用法，有很清楚的使用準則，但這些準則卻相當複雜。這裏只打算介紹最基本的動詞時態的使用原則。英文科技寫作最常用的時態，計有簡單現在式、簡單過去式、現在完成式、現在進行式以及未來式（即語態助動詞 *will* 加上原形動詞）五種。本節將分述前四種時態的用法。

簡單現在式

簡單現在式 (simple present tense) 是用來陳述不受時間影響的普遍事實。當研究報告作者要指出某個科學的事實時，就可用現在式來陳述，例如：

Water *boils* at 100 degrees centigrade.

A junction diode *permits* current to flow through in only one direction.

Whales *are* aquatic mammals.

上面句子所指為普遍的科學事實，無論任何時候，這些事實皆恆常為真。

簡單現在式也可用來指出現時為真、將來亦會一直為真的事實。雖然將來情況可能有變而使句子不再為真，但就目前而言，它們都陳述大可能會持續不變的事實。像下面的例子：

The factors that control this process *are* poorly *understood*.

Modeling this type of fluid flow *is* extremely difficult.

Few tigers *can be found* in China today.

AIDS *is* a lethal illness.

簡單現在式也可用來陳述作者或他人的信念、解釋及想法。這些信念、解釋及想法皆為他們目前的心理狀態，而且將來可能會一直為真：

Doctors *believe* that if this condition is detected early, major surgery can be avoided. 這信念將來大概不會改變。

We *propose* an alternative mechanism to explain this reaction. 論文的作者將來很可能一直認為這說明是合理的。

We *recommend* that the batch-means technique be used for these cases. 作者將來很可能一直認為這建議是恰當的。

This paper *presents* a new method for finding the optimal solution. 這篇論文提出一個新方法，這事實將來會一直為真。

簡單現在式也可用來表示數學上的演算、分析或定義：

To obtain the solution, we *can* now *integrate* expression (12) over the interval from 0 to 1.

The relationship between these parameters *is defined* by equation (5).

由於科技寫作中常需要指出普遍事實或表示學者的想法，所以簡單現在式是其中一個最常用的時態。

簡單過去式

簡單過去式 (simple past tense) 是用來指出過去曾發生或存在，但現在已不再發生或存在的事物。例如，當研究報告的作者想在研究報告的方法章節裏，描述曾經做過的實驗，就可以用過去式：

To test the model, we *ran* a series of simulations.

The samples *were* then *placed* in the test chamber and the temperature *was increased*.

作者要敘述實驗的結果，可用過去式來表達：

When water *was added* to the solution, the deposition rate *increased*.

Our method *found* the solution faster than Wheaton's method in nine of ten trials.

作者想敘述其他研究人員的發現（如在研究報告的文獻回顧部分），也可用過去式來表達：

Johnson (1987) *found* that raising the temperature of the substrate increased the deposition rate.

Stewart (1974) *was* the first to study this phenomenon. He *reported* that it occurred throughout the population.

如果句子中提到過去某個特定的時間，則必須用過去式來表達：

Professor Chen *returned* to Taiwan from the United States in 1989.

Our company *began* manufacturing the new memory chip last month.

在科技研究報告中，有時作者也會用過去進行式，例如：

As the solution *was being stirred*, silica powder was gradually added to it.

但一般而言，如果可以用簡單過去式，就不要用過去進行式：

As the solution *was stirred*, silica powder was gradually added to it.

現在完成式

現在完成式 (present perfect tense) 是用來描述過去已開始存在，而且現在仍然一直存在的行動或狀態。撰寫研究報告的人在文獻回顧中，常會使用現在完成式來描述過去一直持續到現在的某種趨勢，例如：

Neural networks *have attracted* much attention in recent years.

Several researchers *have studied* the relationship between sunspots and weather.

第一句表示神經網路在過去已受到廣泛的注意，而且情況將會持續。第二句則表示從以前到現在，不少科學家曾經研究太陽黑子和氣候之間的關係，還可預見科學家會一直研究下去。

此外，千萬不要把現在完成式和過去式混淆，因為這兩種時態各代表不同的意義。過去式是用來指稱過去已完成的狀態或行為，現在完成式卻是用來指稱過去已開始存在，而且現在仍然一直存在的狀態或行為。舉個例說，當科技論文作者引用某個研究者或研究小組已出版的研究報告時，通常會用過去式，因為研究計畫早已完成：

Williams (1998) *applied* fuzzy logic to control the movement of a robot limb.

相反，如果作者要概論一個研究趨勢，就得用現在完成式。當作者用現在完成式時，可指出所描述的不是過去孤立的研究個案，而是從過去持續到現時，並由眾多學者造成的研究趨勢。

Williams (1998), Gregg (1999), Kirk (2001), and others *have developed* a wide range of new applications of neural networks.

現在完成式的另一種功能是可表達過去曾發生，而現在仍然有效的行為。例如：

We *have invited* Dr. Holmes to lecture here next Friday afternoon.

雖然邀請荷姆斯博士這行為在過去已經完成，但現在這項邀請仍然有效（下星期五還未到，荷姆斯博士一直是在受邀請中），所以應使用現在完成式。

科技論文作者當要描述自己過去的某項研究時，有時會用現在完成式而不用過去式，因為他們想表達自己過去的行為仍然「有效」。例如：

The proposed algorithm *has been implemented* on a workstation in C.

在這例中，作者要指出自己根據演算法所開發的電腦程式仍然有用，而將來還打算再使用這套程式，所以用現在完成式。然而，作者的研究已在過去完成，改成過去式亦屬正確。事實上，像這類型的句子，對母語不是英文的人來說，還是用過去式較好，因為這可使自己習慣以過去式去表達過去已完成的行為：

The proposed algorithm *was implemented* on a workstation in C.

請切記在這種情況中，絕對不可以用現在式來表達：

誤：The proposed algorithm *is implemented* on a workstation in C.

要強調某行為是最近才完成的，也可用現在完成式：

We *have* just *developed* a new memory circuit.

Morton *has* recently *published* a survey of work in this area.

在文法上，這些句子都沒有錯誤，但在科技論文中，尤其在文獻回顧中，不論事件是否最近發生，還是應一律用過去式來表達過去發生的事件。

Morton recently *published* a survey of work in this area.

此外，請注意現在完成式是 *have* 的現在式（即 *have* 或 *has*）加上過去分詞，不要混淆現在完成式和過去完成式，因為它們各自代表不同的意思。請看下面例句：

現在完成式：Chiptech *has developed* a new memory chip.

過去完成式：Chiptech *had developed* a new memory chip.

現在完成式是用來表示最近才剛完成的行為或狀態，或用來表示過去已經開始，而現在仍然持續發生的行為或狀態。相反，過去完成式卻是用來表示在一個過去的特定時間前已完成的行為，這種時態很少出現在科技寫作中。

Chiptech *has* recently *developed* a new memory chip, which the company will begin offering for sale next month. 現在完成式

By the mid-1980s, when personal computer sales began to grow, Chiptech *had already developed* its first memory chip. 過去完成式

現在進行式

現在進行式 (present progressive tense) 是用來描述目前正在發生的行為，在科技論文中較少用到。因為科技論文的內容不是和普遍的事實，就是和過去的行為有關。儘管如此，科技論文的作者有時也可用現在進行式，表達當下正在進行的行為或研究趨勢：

We *are* currently *developing* an advanced RISC processor.

Digital signal processing *is becoming* more and more widely used.

讀者應留意在現在進行式和現在完成式的差別。如果作者想強調數碼訊號處理的進展是當下發生的，會用現在進行式表達：

Digital signal processing *is becoming* more and more widely used.

但如果要強調數碼訊號處理已發展了一段時間，則作者就應該用現在完成式表達：

Digital signal processing *has become* more and more widely used over the past five years.

實際上，這兩句的意思非常接近。唯一的分別是第一個句子特別強調行為是當下發生的，而第二句則強調事態於近五年來一直發生。

大多數的英文動詞都表示某個動作，這類動詞稱為「動態動詞」，例如 *study, read, walk, investigate, speak* 等。有些動詞並非表示某個動作，而是表示事物的狀態，這類動詞稱為「靜態動詞」，例如 *appear, be, correspond, know, represent, seem* 等。靜態動詞沒有進行式，因為這些動詞皆為指稱事物的狀態，而並不像動作般有開始、經過以至結尾的過程。現在進行式是表示動作在進行中，故此一個現在進行式的動詞，只能是動態動詞，而不能是靜態動詞。

動詞 *develop* 是動態動詞，所以下面句子是正確的：

New semiconductor manufacturing processes *are being developed* at a rapid rate.

相反，下列句子的動詞是靜態動詞，所以這些句子都是錯誤的：

誤： This network structure *is corresponding* to the first graph in Figure 1.

誤： In equation (3), the letter F *is representing* force.

這兩個例句中的動詞，必須改成簡單現在式：

正： This network structure *corresponds* to the first graph in Figure 1.

正： In equation (3), the letter F *represents* force.

下面是科技論文中常用的靜態動詞，使用時不可用進行式：

常用的靜態動詞			
appear	constitute	involve	represent
be	contain	know	satisfy
believe	correspond	mean	seem
concern	differ	need	understand
consist of	exist	possess	yield

練習 3-1 動詞時態

請選出最適合的動詞時態。（第四章練習 4-5 中有更多習題。）

1. Antarctic Fishes

   In February of 1899 the British ship Southern Cross ____put____ (put / has put / had put) 10 men ashore at Cape Adare in Antarctica, thus beginning the first expedition to endure a year on the world's southernmost continent. Today many zoologists _____ (credit / credited / have credited) the expedition, which ushered in the "heroic" era of Antarctic exploration, with a discovery that _____ (intrigue / intrigued / has intrigued) them for almost a century: the coldest marine habitat in the world _____ (is / was / has been) actually alive with fishes. The team's zoologist, Nicholai Hanson, _____ (does / did / has) not _____ (survive / survived) the year on the icy land, but before his death he _____ (collect / collected / has collected) examples of previously unknown fish species.

   Almost a century later investigators _____ (are / were / have been) still trying to understand the adaptations that _____ (enable / enabled / have enabled) fish to survive in a region once thought to be virtually uninhabitable. Of particular interest _____ (are / were / have been) the evolutionary adaptations of the suborder Notothenioidei, a group of teleosts, or advanced bony fishes, that _____ (are / were / have been) related to the perchlike fishes common in virtually all marine habitats. This suborder of between 90 and 100 species _____ (is / was / has been) primarily confined to the Antarctic region; there it _____ (dominates / dominated / has dominated), accounting for an estimated two thirds of the fish species and 90 percent of the individual fish in the area.[1]

2. From the results section of an experimental report:

   Figure 2 _____ (shows / showed / has shown) the current-voltage (I-V) characteristics of aluminum contacts on boron-doped polycrystalline diamond films deposited from gas mixtures with different concentrations of boron. The I-V characteristics _____ (are / were / have been) determined by applying a voltage to the Al contact on the diamond film surface while grounding the rear of the Si substrate. Poor rectifying characteristics _____ (are / were / have been) obtained as a result of excess reverse leakage current. When the boron concentration _____ (increases / increased / has increased), the forward current _____ (decreases / decreased / has decreased). This decrease in the forward current _____ (may be / was / has been) attributed to impurity scattering on the diamond film. For a given temperature, the mobility _____ (decreases / decreased / has decreased) with increasing impurity concentration because of enhanced impurity scattering. The smaller forward current _____ (is / was / has been) due mainly to the smaller hole and electron mobility.

Figure 3 _____ (shows / showed / has shown) the I-V characteristics of diamond films deposited with various boron concentrations and annealed at a constant temperature in helium ambient at 900° C for 30 min. After the annealing treatment, there _____ (is / was / has been) no deterioration in the I-V characteristics of the undoped films. In the boron-doped films, the leakage current for the 10V forward voltage _____ (doubles / doubled / has doubled) and deterioration in the rectifying characteristics _____ (is / was / has been) observed.[2]

3. From the introduction to a scientific report:

The amplification of ultrashort pulses in erbium-doped fiber amplifiers (EDFAs) _____ (is / was / has been) intensively studied both theoretically and experimentally. Several theoretical models _____ (are / were / have been) proposed that _____ (use / used / have used) different gain descriptions for the pumped erbium ions [2–6]. Numerical studies _____ (are showing / have shown / had shown) that an accurate analysis _____ (requires / required / has required) the use of the Maxwell-Bloch equations with all the higher-order dispersive and nonlinear terms [7]. However, previous studies all _____ (are / were / have been) concerned with the amplification in an EDFA of a single ultrashort pulse with negligible gain saturation. For this case, our previous work _____ (is showing / has shown / had shown) that solving the Bloch equations for the pumped erbium ions _____ (is / was / has been) equivalent to using a complex Lorentzian gain profile [9]. Here we _____ (extend / extended / have extended) our previous results to include the important phenomenon of gain saturation, which _____ (occurs / occurred / has occurred) in the amplification of the pulse train in the amplifier.

This paper _____ (presents / presented / has presented) a model that fully _____ (characterizes / characterized / has characterized) the amplification of an ultrashort soliton pulse train in an EDFA. This model _____ (employs / employed / has employed) the general formalism of a two-level system to treat the coupled set of Maxwell-Bloch equations. The model _____ (provides / provided / has provided) a general expression for the propagation of the pulse train in the amplifier. The population relaxation time in the Bloch equation _____ (is / was / has been) modified to include the pumping rate, and the pump absorption _____ (is / was / has been) taken into account by solving the pump intensity evolution equation. This approach _____ (allows / allowed / has allowed) us to estimate the range of pulse widths in cases in which the simpler rate-equation approximation [8] _____ (is / was / has been) valid. The paper also _____ (discusses / discussed / has discussed) the problem of the nonlinear nonreciprocity of soliton transmission in EDFAs with different pumping configurations.[3]

4. Observing Jupiter's Moons

For three and a half centuries after their discovery, the Galilean satellites of Jupiter _____ (are / were / have been) studied through telescopes. Then, on 20 August 1977, the first of two Voyager spacecraft _____ (has been / was / had been) launched from Kennedy Space Center. A year and a half later, the two spacecraft _____ (pass / passed / have passed) through the Jupiter system, and in a few days the Galilean satellites _____ (are / were / have been) transformed from small points of light into four separate worlds that could be mapped and studied in great detail. Hundreds of high quality images of the two largest moons, Ganymede and Callisto, _____ (are / were / have been) obtained. These objects _____ (are / were / have been) of great interest not only because of their great size—Ganymede _____ (is / was / has been) larger than the planet Mercury, Callisto only slightly smaller—but also because of their composition. All the planets and moons studied in detail prior to Voyager _____ (are / were / have been) composed of rock and, in some cases, metal. Ganymede and Callisto, however, _____ (have / had / have had) densities so low—1.9 and 1.9 g/cm^3—that roughly half their mass must _____ (be / had been / have been) ice. There _____ (are / were / have been) many other icy bodies in the solar system, including the planet Pluto and most of the moons of Saturn, Uranus, and Neptune. Ganymede and Callisto _____ (provide / provided / have provided) the first look at this previously unexplored class of planetary objects.[4]

5. From the introduction to a research paper:

For many years now, kinship _____ (is / was / has been) recognized as an important factor in human social behavior, and recent studies _____ (are demonstrating / have demonstrated / had demonstrated) that kinship _____ (influences / influenced / has influenced) the social behavior of many other species as well. The widespread occurrence of nepotism, or favoritism shown to genetic relatives, and the rarity of close inbreeding among free-living animals _____ (imply / implied / have implied) that most animals _____ (possess / possessed / have possessed) mechanisms for distinguishing relatives from nonrelatives and close from distant kin.

However, until the last few years little attention _____ (is / was) paid to mechanisms of kin identification. In this paper, we _____ (consider / considered / have considered) some of the theoretical and empirical issues relevant to animal kin recognition, _____ (describe / described / have described) recent work on this topic, and _____ (outline / outlined / have outlined) several mechanisms by which kin might be identified. Finally, we _____ (summarize / summarized / have summarized) the results of our four-year laboratory and field investigation of kin recognition using ground squirrels.[5]

6.　The Origin of Stars

The origin of stars _____ (represents / represented / has represented) one of the most fundamental unsolved problems of contemporary astrophysics. Stars _____ (are / were / have been) the basic objects of the universe. Indeed, the discovery of the nature of most stars as hydrogen-burning thermonuclear reactors and the subsequent development of the theory of stellar evolution _____ (rank / ranked / had ranked) among the greatest triumphs of twentieth-century science. Deciphering stellar genesis, on the other hand, _____ (proves / proved / has proven) to be a formidable challenge for astronomers. Until a quarter of a century ago, only a rudimentary understanding of the subject _____ (exists / existed / has existed). This state of comparative ignorance _____ (prevails / prevailed / had prevailed) because no substantive body of empirical data _____ (exists / existed / had existed) that could be used to critically test even the most basic hypotheses concerning stellar origins.

In our galaxy, stars _____ (form / formed / have formed) within the dust-enshrouded dense cores of molecular clouds. The obscuration provided by the solid grains that permeate the clouds _____ (renders / rendered / has rendered) newly forming stars (protostars) completely invisible at optical and shorter wavelengths. Moreover, the molecular gas that gives birth to young stars _____ (is / was / has been) itself extremely cold (10 to 20 K) and, with a few exceptions, _____ (can be / could be / has been able to be) observed in emission only in the submillimeter and millimeter regime, a spectral window opened by radio astronomers only in the 1970s.

During the last two decades, impressive advances in technology _____ (provide / provided / have provided) astronomers with the ability to observe star-forming regions in considerable detail at infrared, millimeter, and submillimeter wavelengths. With this new instrumental capability, a direct assault on the star-formation problem _____ (becomes / became / had become) possible. Indeed, over the last few years, observations with filled-aperture telescopes and interferometric arrays _____ (produce / produced / have produced) a series of remarkable, exciting, and unexpected discoveries that _____ (begin / began / have begun) to remove the veil of mystery that surrounds the star-formation process in our galaxy. As a result of these discoveries, now we _____ (are / were / have been) beginning to understand the processes of star formation and early stellar evolution and _____ (are / were / have been) developing the foundation for a coherent theory of star formation.[6]

7. From the method section of a scientific report:

The experimental apparatus used _____ (is / was / has been) shown in Fig. 3. The reactant gas pressure _____ (is / was / had been) set at 3.3 kPa (25 Torr). An optical pyrometer _____ (is / was / has been) used to monitor the substrate temperature, which _____ (is / was / had been) maintained at about 820° C by keeping the microwave power at 450 W. CH_4-CO_2 gas mixtures without additional H_2 gas _____ (are / were / have been) used. The flow rate of CO_2 _____ (is / was / has been) fixed at 30 sccm and the flow rate of CH_4 _____ (is / was / has been) varied from 19.2 to 20 sccm. Then the silicon substrates _____ (are / were / have been) prepared for diamond deposition by carrying out the following steps.[7]

8. Africanized Bees

As Figure 1 _____ (shows / showed / has shown), Africanized honeybees _____ (are / were / have been) nearly indistinguishable in appearance from the bees familiar in North America and Europe, and sting for sting they _____ (are / were / have been) no worse than our own honeybees. What _____ (earns / earned / has earned) the Africanized bees the undeserved notoriety as killer bees _____ (is / was / has been) their extreme aggressiveness. Numerous studies _____ (document / documented / have documented) the fierce defensive behavior of this bee (Michener 1972; Collins et al. 1982; Rinderer 1986; Boreham and Roubik 1987). Many _____ (report / reported / have reported) that a particularly dangerous attribute of the bees _____ (is / was / has been) their aggressiveness after slight jarring or vibration of the hive. Africanized bees _____ (can react / could react / have reacted) to an intruder three times faster than do European bees, _____ (can inflict / could inflict / have inflicted) ten times as many stings, and _____ (pursue / have pursued / will pursue) their aggressors over much longer distances, up to a kilometer. However, some evidence _____ (suggests / suggested / has suggested) that climate _____ (has / had / has had) more influence on aggressiveness than racial differences and that Africanized bees _____ (are / were / have been) more aggressive under warmer conditions (Brandenburgo et al. 1977).[8]

9. Mutation and DNA

In recent years an extraordinary increase _____ (occur / occurred / has occurred) in the attention, both popular and scientific, that _____ (is / was / has been) paid to mutation and its consequences. The sources of this interest _____ (are / were / had been) the recognition that components of our environment _____ (pose / posed / have posed) a largely unevaluated threat to the conservation of genetic material and the realization that mutations frequently _____ (have / had / have had) serious consequences for human health that encompass, at the least, birth defects and cancer. The resulting research effort _____ (improves / improved / has improved) our understanding of the fundamental genetic substance, DNA, and of the intricacies of its metabolism and organization into genes.

Contemporary investigations into the mutation process _____ (involve / involved / have involved) the structure of DNA and all the processes that _____ (affect / affected / have affected) it. Inherent in the now-classical description of DNA structure by Watson and Crick in 1953, and immediately recognized by them, _____ (is / was / has been) the notion that variations in the electronic structures of the DNA bases _____ (can / could / has been able to) cause incorrect base pairings, and hence mutations. In the early models, however, DNA _____ (is / was / has been) viewed as structurally static when not undergoing replication. More recently, the identification of numerous families of alternative structures _____ (leads / led / has led) to an expanded view of DNA as far more variable in form. Some of these structures _____ (provide / provided / had provided) explanations for mutational events that _____ (are / were / have been) previously mysterious, and others _____ (offer / offered / had offered) intriguing hints for future exploration.[9]

10. Maps and Computers

Maps _____ (are / were / have been) one of the oldest forms of written communication. Land boundary maps on clay tablets _____ (are being / were being / had been being) used in Babylonia as early as 2200 B.C. Through the centuries various materials _____ (are / were / have been) used for maps. The ancient Egyptians _____ (use / used / had used) sheets of papyrus, the Chinese _____ (use / used / had used) pieces of silk, Eskimos _____ (make / made / had made) maps on seal skins, and Polynesians _____ (use / used / had used) a network of bamboo canes, with each crossing point indicating an island. Today printed maps _____ (pervade / pervaded / have pervaded) our lives, ranging from sketch or location maps in newspapers and advertisements, to parcel maps showing property boundaries, to small-scale maps in atlases.

The techniques used to produce maps _____ (change / changed / have changed) dramatically over the past fifty years, in a transition from field workers and mule trains to jet aircraft, satellites, and computers. Before World War II, the predominant method for creating maps _____ (is / was / has been) field surveying. After World War II, map-making methods _____ (begin / began / have begun) to include manual photogrammetry (measurement from photographs). Although manual photogrammetry _____ (is / was / has been) still used today, it _____ (is being / was being / had been) supplanted by digital cartography, and computers _____ (are / were / had been) becoming the hub of the mapping process.

Soon after their introduction in the 1950s, digital computers _____ (are / were / have been) used for various phases of the mapping process, especially for trigonometric calculations of survey data and for orientation of aerial photographs on map manuscripts. In addition, computer-controlled plotters _____ (are / were / have been) used to draw simple outline maps. The process of collecting data for the plotters _____ (is / was / has been) slow and expensive, and the drawings _____ (are / were / had been) not as precise as those produced by the best manual cartography. Only in the last ten to fifteen years _____ (does / did / has) it become technologically feasible and cost-effective to assemble and use the data required to automate the mapping process.[10]

3.2　主詞與動詞一致

　　本節將強調一個重要的文法規則——主詞和動詞必須一致地使用同一個數的形式 (subject-verb agreement) 。這即是說，如果主詞是單數，則動詞也必須是單數；如果主詞是複數，則動詞也必須是複數。漢語沒有像英語般複雜的語法形態變化，所以不少中國作者在書寫英文時，偶爾會不自覺地忽略句子中主語和動詞都有單、複數的變化，結果未必每次都能使兩者配合。

　　複數主詞和以 *and* 連接而成的複合主詞（即由兩個以上名詞組成的主詞）必須用複數動詞。尤其要注意的是倒裝句，倒裝句的主詞都放在後面，所以遇到倒裝句時，就要確定主詞是否複數主詞。

　　The R&D director and sales manager *are* both at the meeting.

　　On the agenda *were* incoming orders, production planning, and delivery schedule.

　　動詞的數應配合的，不是句中述詞名詞或其他名詞的數，而是主詞的數。下面首個例句中，動詞之後雖然緊接著兩個名詞，但單數主詞 *field* 才是整句的主詞，故動詞仍應為單數。第二個例句中，動詞之後雖然緊接著一個單數名詞，但複數主詞 *systems* 才是整句的主詞，故動詞仍應為複數。

　　His field of research *is* molecular biology and neurology.

　　Computer-aided design systems *are* an important type of tool used in the product development process.

　　在虛主詞結構 *there is* 或 *there are* 中，動詞的數應與緊接其後的主詞的數一致。（第一章1.10節已說明過虛主詞結構。）

　　There *is* a unique solution to this equation. 主詞是 *solution*。

　　There *are* several ways to approach this problem. 主詞是 *ways*。

　　兩個單數主詞之間出現 *or* 或 *nor* 時，必須用單數動詞；兩個複數主詞之間出現 *or* 或 *nor* 時，必須用複數動詞。而如果句子中出現由單數主詞和複數主詞以 *or* 或 *nor* 連接而成的複合主詞，則動詞的數應與之最接近的主詞的數配合。

　　Raising the temperature or increasing the flow of hydrogen *causes* the reaction rate to increase.

　　Neither the experimental results nor the theoretical results *are* valid.

　　Either the experimental results or the theoretical analysis *is* invalid.

第三個例句用了單數動詞。有些作者認為這雖合符文法，卻不太自然，他們寧可對調組成複合主詞的兩個名詞片語，再使用複數的動詞：

Either the theoretical analysis or the experimental results *are* invalid.

凡加上 *every, each* 或 *no* 的單數主詞，必須配合單數動詞，即使句中的主詞是由兩個或以上的單數主詞組成。

No student *graduates* without having submitted an acceptable thesis.

Every paper, thesis, and letter *is stored* in this computer.

以 *-one, -body, -thing* 結尾的不定代名詞（如 *everyone, something*），必須用單數動詞。此外，*another, each, either, neither, one* 這些不定代名詞也必須用單數動詞。

Another simplified design *is* that proposed by Thomson (1987).

代名詞 *all, any, most, more, some*，單、複數動詞皆可連接，這要看代名詞所指稱的，究竟是單數名詞（通常是不可數的）還是複數名詞而定。

Most of the salt *dissolved* when the solution was stirred. *Most* 指稱 *salt* 這單數（不可數）名詞。"Most of the salt" 表示「大部分的鹽」。這句回答了「How much 鹽溶解了？」。

Most of the trials *were* successful. *Most* 指稱 *trials* 這個複數名詞。"Most of the trials" 表示「大多數的試驗」。這句回答了「How many 試驗成功了？」。

不定代名詞 *none* 與 *all, most, some* 一樣，通常也可用單數或複數動詞，這完全視乎它所指稱的名詞而定。然而，當 *none* 表示 "not one" 的意思時，儘管它表面上似是指稱複數的前述詞，但仍然必須用單數動詞。

None of the students *have arrived*. *None* 指稱複數的 *students*。這句是表示："No students have arrived."

None of the methods *is* efficient enough to be used for real-time processing. *None* 表示 "not one" 方法，所以用單數動詞。這句是表示："Not one of the methods is efficient enough."

當關係代名詞 *who, which, that* 作關係子句的主詞時，子句動詞的數必須與關係代名詞的前述詞的數一致。

The project that *has drawn* the most funding has yet to produce any concrete results. 關係子句是 *that has drawn the most funding*。這裏必須使用單數動詞，因為動詞的數必須和關係代名詞 *that* 的前述詞（即 *project*）的數一致。

The projects that *have been* the most successful have all been relatively inexpensive. 關係子句是 *that have been the most successful*。這裏必須使用複數動詞，因為動詞的數必須和關係代名詞 *that* 的前述詞（即 *projects*）的數一致。

Those of you who *study* diligently are likely to do well on the test. 關係子句是 *who study diligently*。這裏必須使用複數動詞，因為動詞的數必須和關係代名詞 *who* 的前述詞（即 *those*）的數一致。

緊接著以 *one of* 開首的片語的關係子句，當中動詞的數必須和關係代名詞的前述詞的數一致。

Joanie is the only one of the students who *has* not turned in her paper. *Who* 指稱 *one*，而非 *students*。這裏可省略 *of the students* 而無改句意。

She is one of those people who never *finish* their work on time. *Who* 指稱 *people*，這句的意思是：有些人經常不如期完成工作，而她是其中一個。這裏 *of those people* 不能省略，否則會改變句意。

就第二個例句而言，如果不確定句中的動詞 (*finish*) 應否用複數，則只要先把它暫時改寫成下列形式，就可以看出動詞正確的數：

Those people never *finish* their work on time. She is one of them.

單數主詞的後面，即使緊接著以 *as well as, together with, along with, in addition to* 等類似字詞開首的片語，動詞仍然是單數。

The growth in the economy together with the stable political situation *has* led to a significant increase in GDP. 句子主詞 *growth* 是單數名詞。

The computer hardware as well as the software programs *is* outdated. 句子主詞 *computer hardware* 是單數名詞。

單數主詞和其動詞之間，儘管出現複數的字詞或片語，動詞亦不會變成複數。

One of the advantages of the new computers *is* that they are easy to use. 句子主詞是 *one*，而非 *advantages* 或 *computers*，故動詞是單數。

在集合名詞中，如果集合的成員行動一致，則用單數動詞；如果成員行動不一致，則用複數動詞。（集合名詞是單數名詞，因為它們即使是指一群人或事物，但仍然同屬一個較大的整體，如 *band, class, committee, crowd, family, faculty, majority, team, variety* 等。）

The team *is* playing well today. 球隊成員行動一致。

The team *are* already on their way home. 各自回家，行動不一致。

A variety of factors *have contributed* to this growing problem. 不同的原因都各自對問題構成影響。

The committee *was surprised* by the news. 委員會成員反應一致。

A total of 25 samples *were collected*. 分別收集了二十五個樣本。

For men, the total number of correct answers was 43. For women, the total *was* 56. *The total* 指稱一個數字。

A series of six experiments *were conducted*. 分別進行了六個實驗。

有一點值得大家留意：英語國家的人常對這些規則的應用方式有不同看法，亦有很多人根本不遵循這些規則。英國人經常不管集合名詞中成員行動是否一致，亦一律使用複數動詞。因此，有些英國人可能會說 *The team are playing well*。有些美國人又總是把集合名詞配以單數動詞，會說 *A variety of factors has led to this problem*。

為避免使用上的混淆，最好還是不要把集合名詞（如 *variety, total, series* 等）當成句子的主詞。如果句中的主詞是集合名詞，其實非常容易以別的字詞代替，因為集合名詞常是累贅的。例如：

原句：　　*A variety of* factors have contributed to this growing problem.
修正：　　*Many factors* have contributed to this growing problem.

原句：　　*A total of 25 samples* were collected.
修正：　　*Twenty-five samples* were collected.

原句：　　*A series of six experiments* were conducted.
修正：　　*Six experiments* were conducted.

指稱特定範疇的學科或知識的名詞（如 *physics, economics, mathematics* 等），表面上是複數形式，但動詞卻必須為單數。另外，如 *politics, statistics, athletics* 這些名詞，則可用單數或複數動詞，這要看它們究竟是指單數還是複數的概念。在正式寫作中，*data* 會當作複數名詞。

Economics *is* often referred to as "the dismal science."

Statistics *is* taught in the Sociology Department at our university. *Statistics* 是單數名詞，因為它是指一門學科。

Statistics *show* that special educational programs and psychological therapy are more effective than incarceration in preventing recidivism among juveniles. *Statistics* 是複數名詞，因為它指的是不同研究中的不同統計數據。

The experimental data *agree* with the predictions derived from the theoretical model.

表示固定數量（如金錢、時間、數量等）的名詞片語，可以是單數名詞，也可以是複數名詞，這取決於它們指的是一個整體（單數名詞），還是整體的個別部分（複數名詞）：

Thirty thousand dollars *is* a good price for that car.　一個整體

Forty percent of the budget *has been spent* already.　一個整體

The majority in the parliament *is* Liberal.　一個整體

The majority of these algorithms *are* unsuitable for VLSI implementation. 個別的演算法

Only sixty percent of the students *were* in class today.　個別的學生

有少數特殊的複合主詞或複數主詞，所指實際上是單一的整體，因此必須用單數動詞：

Spaghetti and meatballs *is* his favorite dish.

Roberts & Sons *is* a dependable paper supplier.

Research and development *has* always been one of Chiptech's strong points.

R&D *is* an important aspect of the company's operations.

表示數學演算關係的複合主詞，既可以是單數名詞，又可以是複數名詞。不過較多人把它視為單數名詞：

Two plus two *equals* four. 較常用

Two plus two *equal* four.

The number of 用單數動詞，但 *a number of* 卻必須用複數動詞。

The number of new accounts opened *has* increased each year since 1987. *The number of* 指一個數字。

A number of researchers *have* investigated this problem. *A number of* 的意思是「許多」。

練習 3-2 主詞與動詞一致

請填入正確的動詞形式。（第四章練習 4-4 中提供更多的習題。）

1. Physics _____ (is / are) a subject that has fascinated him since high school.

2. Smith's approach as well as Turner's _____ (has / have) several serious short-comings, which _____ (render / renders) it unsuitable for practical applications.

3. The RAM and two I/O ports _____ (is / are) an important part of the chip.

4. Each of the samples _____ (was / were) annealed for 20 minutes.

5. The number of passengers using the airport _____ (has / have) increased each year since 1984.

6. After the members of the examination committee and the department chairman _____ (approves / approve) the plan, it should be submitted to the Dean's Office.

7. After the members of the examination committee or the department chairman _____ (approves / approve) the plan, it should be submitted to the Dean's Office.

8. The increase in the number of free hydrogen atoms along with the higher temperature _____ (cause / causes) the reaction rate to increase.

9. Be careful how your research team _____ (interpret / interprets) those figures. Statistics _____ (is / are) sometimes highly misleading.

10. An attribute name or a class name _____ (is / are) entered in this dialog box.

11. Also of interest _____ (is / are) why samples immersed in solution A exhibited a higher growth rate.

12. The automatic power-saving function _____ (is / are) just one of the many features that _____ (makes / make) the Droog 2000 the most cost-effective system on the market today.

13. All of the authors _____ (has / have) sent in their papers and every paper _____ (has / have) been received.

14. A number of samples _____ (was / were) collected from a different geographical region to see whether the phenomenon occurred there as well.

15. Included in the search _____ (is / are) all child nodes on the right-hand side of the node of interest.

16. A major problem with this type of system _____ (is / are) the many errors that occur in the acceleration stage.

3.3 語氣

　　英文有三種語氣 (mood)：直述語氣 (indicative)、祈使語氣 (imperative) 以及假設語氣 (subjunctive)。直述語氣係用來陳述及詢問問題；祈使語氣作指使或懇求他人之用；假設語氣則會用在條件句中，表示反事實 (counterfactual) 的狀態，又或是用於緊接著某些動詞後面的子句中。

　　　　直述語氣：　The weather *is* warm.
　　　　　　　　　　Is the weather warm?

　　　　祈使語氣：　*Let* F_r represent the force in the radial direction.
　　　　　　　　　　Note that we neglect the effects of friction.

　　　　假設語氣：　Users require that there *be* sufficient bandwidth to handle all of the requests.
　　　　　　　　　　If I *were* healthy, I would not need to see a doctor.

　　英文的祈使句前面是不需要加上 *please* 的。例如，一般的使用手冊裏，祈使語氣句都不會加上 *please*，*Connect the device to the communication port*，不會寫成 *Please connect the device to the communication port*。

　　假設語氣句中，大部分動詞形式都是最簡單的動詞原形，即省略 *to* (不加上 *s*)。*To be* 的假設語氣是例外，這種句式的動詞皆為 *were* 或 *be*，而非 *am, is, are* 或 *was*。在假設語氣的條件句中，表示條件的子句使用假設語氣，表示結果的子句則使用語態助動詞 *would* 加上動詞原形（如：*would have, would go, would be* 等等）。

　　If I *were* the leader of the United Nations, I *would stop* the war.

　　If she *were* rich, she *would* still *be* unhappy.

在科技寫作中，使用假設語氣有兩種可能情況：

1. 假設語氣可用來表示反事實的狀態、表示可能性、也可用以提出假設或推測。

> If the children *were* already grown up, we wouldn't have these financial problems. 反事實

> If I *were* you, I would accept the job offer. 反事實

> If the fuel *were* cleaner, it would burn more efficiently. 假設

> If the system *were* to incorporate more processors, this performance bottle-neck would vanish. 假設

上面的句子都表示反事實的狀態。事實上，小孩還沒長大、我不可能是你、燃料並不乾淨、系統也沒有更多的處理器。

然而，以 *if* 開首的子句，並非所有都表示反事實的狀態。相反，有些這類子句還可用以表示指稱的狀態有可能在未來達成。

> If this new product *is* a success, the company will earn a lot of money this year.

在這句中，以 *if* 開首的子句並非表示反事實的狀態，而是陳述一個條件，如果條件得到滿足，則會達成主要子句所陳述的結果。

2. 在某些表示請求、要求、建議、命令或期望的動詞後面，都會加上以 *that* 開首的名詞子句，這種子句必須使用假設語氣。這些動詞包括 *ask, command, order, recommend, request, require, stipulate, suggest, wish* 等。

> 誤：　We suggest that the user *to try* to run the program again.
>
> 誤：　We suggest that the user *tries* to run the program again.
>
> 正：　We suggest that the user *try* to run the program again.

> 誤：　The manufacturer recommends that the unit *to be* placed at least three meters away from a radio or television.
>
> 誤：　The manufacturer recommends that the unit *is* placed at least three meters away from a radio or television.
>
> 正：　The manufacturer recommends that the unit *be* placed at least three meters away from a radio or television.

假如作者不想使用假設語氣，則可使用意思近似的直述句代替：

> 假設語氣：　*The manufacturer recommends that the unit be placed* at least three meters away from a radio or television.
>
> 直述語氣：　*The unit should be placed* at least three meters away from a radio or television.

> 假設語氣：　The president asked *that she attend* the meeting.
>
> 直述語氣：　The president asked *her to attend* the meeting.

> 假設語氣：　She wishes that she *were* a movie star.
>
> 直述語氣：　She wishes that she *could be* a movie star.

假設語氣： The judge ordered *that the policeman remove* the unruly man from the courtroom.

直述語氣： The judge ordered *the policeman to remove* the unruly man from the courtroom.

諸如 *suggest, recommend, stipulate* 或 *require* 之類的動詞，後面加上以 *that* 開首的名詞子句，動詞必須使用假設語氣。請留意這類句式於科技論文中相當常見：

假設語氣： This constraint stipulates that the distance between the poles *exceed* the size of the air gap.

假設語氣： We require that T *be* perpendicular to the gradient of the function in Equation (3).

作者如果不想使用假設語氣，或是不確定應否使用，則可以考慮使用下面較簡單的句子：

直述語氣： This constraint states that the distance between the poles *must exceed* the size of the air gap.

直述語氣： T must *be* perpendicular to the gradient of the function in Equation (3).

第四章
科技論文中常見錯誤

科技論文中的英文必須通順正確，讀者才能瞭解以至接受論文的觀點。論文若不遵循標準的文法規則，讀者可能要反覆參看上下文，才可推斷出文意。這樣的文章會讓讀者感到非常吃力，儘管吃力，有時可能還是不知其所云。最嚴重的情況是，若論文中出現太多文法錯誤，論文內容乃至作者的專業能力都會受到質疑。

本章將討論中國人撰寫英文科技研究報告時常犯的文法及造句錯誤。讀者如果多注意以下的英文文法準則，則可避免許多錯誤。

4.1 不完整句

別以為一個句子只是一連串由大寫開首、以句點結尾的字詞。正式的英文文章裏，每個句子必須表達一個完整的意思，及必須至少包括一個含有主詞、動詞的獨立子句。如果不能滿足這兩個要求，造出來的就是不完整句。許多作者時常將一組尚未包含至少一個獨立子句的字詞當為一個句子。這些不完整句必須和其他字詞合併，構成至少一個獨立子句，並表達一個完整意思，方可成為一個完整句子。

常見的一種不完整句是一個孤離的附屬子句。（附屬子句係由附屬連接詞開首，例如：*after, although, because, before, if, since, when* 或 *while*。詳見第一章。）這種不完整句通常可與前後的獨立子句結合。

不完整: *Although a preprocessing stage is required and the proposed method is slower.* Our method is much more accurate than the traditional approach.

修正句：　*Although the proposed method requires a preprocessing stage and is slower than the traditional approach,* it is much more accurate.

不完整：　The technology was adopted quickly and successfully. *Because the technology was highly mature and trained technicians were available.*

修正句：　The technology was adopted quickly and successfully, *because it was highly mature and trained technicians were available.*

某些情況中，亦可省略附屬連接詞，把附屬子句修改成完整句。

不完整：　*Whereas* many nodes in the network contain incompletely specified functions of the primary inputs.

修正句：　Many nodes in the network contain incompletely specified functions of the primary inputs.

另一種不完整句是作者把複合述詞中的第二個述詞分割出來。在這種情況下，分割出來的述詞應併入之前的句子。

不完整：　Section 4 presents the results of simulations conducted to test the effectiveness of the proposed approach. *And compares its performance with that of previous methods.*

完整：　Section 4 presents the results of simulations conducted to test the effectiveness of the proposed approach *and compares its performance with that of previous methods.*

經常造成不完整句的原因，就是孤立使用介系詞片語、動狀詞片語、名詞片語或同位語。這類不完整句通常可以併入前後的完整句中。

不完整：　*For this reason.* Logic optimization techniques have been introduced.

修正句：　*For this reason,* logic optimization techniques have been introduced.

不完整：　Designers apply logic optimization techniques. *Reducing the chip area.*

修正句：　Designers apply logic optimization techniques *to reduce the chip area.*

請注意：祈使句雖然在形式上缺少主語，但並非為不完整句。如下所示的祈使句都是完整的英文句子，句子的主詞讀者早已理解，就是 "you"。

Turn on the computer. *You* turn on the computer.

Let x=3 and y=5. *You* let x=3 and y=5.

Assume that the system is at equilibrium. *You* assume that the system is at equilibrium.

4.2 散亂句

在英文中，一個句子不僅必須表達完整的意思，長度還必須適切。撰寫論文時，作者應該使用各種不同長度的句子：以短的作強調之用；以較長的來表達較複雜的意思（關於句子種類的詳細說明，請參閱第八章8.1節）。寫作論文時，其實不應企圖同時表達太多的意思而令句子過於冗長，使讀者難以瞭解。過於冗長或複雜的句子，我們稱之為「散亂句」(rambling sentence)。散亂句可以分成兩大類：一類是由多個雜亂附屬子句和主要子句所構成的複雜句子。另一類是用 *and* 或 *but* 連接一長串簡單子句的散亂句子。

下面的例子就是第一種散亂句。這個句子是以兩個附屬子句開首，再接一個獨立子句和另一個附屬子句，最後還有三個獨立子句，而且其中一個是複合述詞。這個句子相當冗長而複雜，必定無法表達一個清楚的意思，實在令人難以閱讀。

> 散亂句：　*Because* there is still a great deal of material in this field that I have yet to study, and *because* my desire to obtain a doctoral degree is strong, *moreover*, my institute also has agreed to provide expenses for me to travel abroad to study, *therefore, if* your graduate institute accepts my application, I hope to begin my studies there in the fall of next year, *and* plan to complete my degree objectives in four years, *and* then I will return to my country and work for the research institute here again.

要修正這個散亂句，必須把它分成幾個短句，讓每個句子都分別表達一個清楚特定的意思。以下是一種修正方法：

> 修正：　There is still a great deal of material in this field that I wish to study, and I am highly motivated to pursue a doctoral degree. Moreover, the research institute where I work has agreed to provide funds for me to study abroad. If admitted to your graduate institute, I plan to begin my studies there next fall. I hope to complete my degree in four years; after graduating, I will return to my country to continue my work at the research institute here.

修正後的段落把原句分成四個獨立句子，每一句陳述一、兩個清楚的意思。修正後句子的意思較清楚，中心更突出，易讀得多。

下面的句子則是第二種散亂句。相對上例，這個句子的結構比較簡單：句子大部分都是由一連串用 *and* 連接的子句組成。

> 散亂句：　None of the proposed object-oriented or object-based specification languages is completely satisfactory, *because* the language of PROTOB incorporates standard programming languages to specify object behavior, *and* the language of OBSERV does not provide any mechanism for specifying inheritance relationships and system functions, *and* the language proposed by Lee cannot specify classes or relationships between objects, *and* the language of ENVISAGER does not provide any mechanism for

specifying system functions or a large-scale model partitioning structure.

這個散亂句中的第一個子句陳述了一個清楚的中心意思，而其餘的子句則提供支持這個中心意思的例子。因此，要修正這個例子，可以把原句分成三個或以上不同的句子，並以首句陳述整段文字的重點：

修正：　None of the proposed object-oriented or object-based specifi-cation languages is completely satisfactory. For example, the language used in PROTOB relies on standard programming lan-guages to specify object behavior, and the language proposed by Lee cannot specify classes and relationships between objects. On the other hand, the language of OBSERV fails to provide a mechanism for specifying inheritance relationships and system functions, and that of ENVISAGER provides neither a mechanism for specifying system functions nor a large-scale model partitioning structure.

修正過後，首句是一個把主要意思陳述清楚的短句，接著的兩句則分別作支持主要意思的例子。這樣便能讓讀者易於閱讀與瞭解。

4.3 缺乏連接詞

只用逗點來連接兩個獨立子句，而缺乏任何連接詞的，是錯誤的句子。例如：

缺乏連接詞：　A significant learning cost is involved in transferring a technology from the R&D stage to the production stage, part of this cost should be defrayed by the government re-search institute that developed the technology.

缺乏連接詞和不完整句一樣，都會令讀者混淆，但原因正好相反。這兩類句子表面上都表達一個完整的意思，但實際上不完整句沒有表達一個完整的意思，而缺乏連接詞的句子，卻不只表達一個意思。

先看以下例句：

缺乏連接詞：　The samples were dipped into the etching solution, they were then washed with a chemical cleanser.

缺乏連接詞的句子，有四種不同的修正方法：

- 把逗點改成句號（切記把逗點後的第一個字母改回大寫）：

The samples were dipped in the etching solution. They were then washed with a chemical cleanser.

- 把逗點改成分號：

The samples were dipped in the etching solution; they were then washed with a chemical cleanser.

- 在逗點後面加上對等連接詞 *(and, but, for, or, nor, so, yet)*：

The samples were dipped in the etching solution, and then they were washed with a chemical cleanser.

- 把其中一個獨立子句改成附屬子句:

After the samples were dipped in the etching solution, they were washed with a chemical cleanser.

在這個例子中，第四種修正方式大概最恰當，因為最能清楚表達兩個子句之間的關係。但在修改原本缺乏連接詞的句子時要特別注意，不能只把 *then* 移到 *they* 前面，例如:

誤:　The samples were dipped into the etching solution, then they were washed with a chemical cleanser.

Then 不是對等連接詞，而是連接副詞，所以這句仍然缺乏連接詞。

連接副詞 (*also, consequently, furthermore, however, moreover, otherwise, then, therefore, thus*) 的前面，和連接兩個獨立子句的轉接片語 (*for example, in contrast, in fact, on the other hand*) 的前面，都必須加上句號或分號。這類字詞的後面通常都會緊接著一個逗點，但當後面的子句非常短時，*hence, otherwise, then, therefore, thus* 這些字則可以不接逗點。

誤:　Assume the system can be modeled by equation (10), then we obtain the following expression for the equilibrium state.

正:　Assume the system can be modeled by equation (10). Then we obtain the following expression for the equilibrium state.

正:　Assume the system can be modeled by equation (10); then we obtain the following expression for the equilibrium state.

正:　If we assume the system can be modeled by equation (10), then we obtain the following expression for the equilibrium state.

誤:　The value of this variable must be greater than zero, otherwise we obtain a contradiction.

正:　The value of this variable must be greater than zero. Otherwise, we obtain a contradiction.

正:　The value of this variable must be greater than zero; otherwise, we obtain a contradiction.

當然，如果兩個子句之間沒有任何標點符號，也是錯誤的。所以必須加上適當的標點符號，清楚表示第一個子句的結尾以及第二個子句的開始。

誤:　The samples were dipped in the etching solution then they were washed with a chemical cleanser.

正:　The samples were dipped in the etching solution, and then they were washed with a chemical cleanser.

練習 4-1 不完整句

　　請找出不完整句，並與前後的句子合併。（提示：修改某些句子時，必須改寫句子的標點符號，並要注意更改大小寫。）

1. Given an input rate r. We can obtain the solution using equation (3). If r is unknown but T is known. We can apply equation (5).

2. The amount of fluorine incorporated into the film on the substrate surface can be controlled. By reducing the amount of water added to the immersing solution. When there is less water, more fluorine atoms are released. As shown in the reaction equation above. Because of the increase in free fluorine atoms in the solution. A greater amount of fluorine is incorporated into the film.

3. While there are at least a dozen major different designs for devices that use magnetic fields to control thermonuclear fusion. The best results to date have been achieved with the tokamak. Which was developed in the 1960s by Soviet scientists seeking to overcome the inherent instability of earlier magnetic confinement schemes. After the announcement in 1969 of results showing much longer confinement of the plasma under fusion conditions. The United States redirected its fusion program to emphasize tokamak research, and today major tokamak projects are being conducted by the U.S., the European Economic community, Japan. And China.[1]

4. Although physics has made monumental strides in the last hundred years. Theoretical descriptions of complex phenomena such as turbulent flow in fluids have remained outstanding unsolved problems. The difficulty lies in the nonlinear character of the mathematical equations which model the physical systems. The Navier-Stokes equations for fluid flows and Newton's equations for three or more interacting particles. Since these equations do not generally admit closed-form analytical solutions. It has proved extremely difficult to construct useful theories that would predict, for example, the drag on the wing of an airplane. Or the range of validity of statistical mechanics. However, in

the last ten years, considerable progress has been made. Using a unique synthesis of numerical simulation and analytical approximation.

The key to recent progress has been the use of high-speed digital computers. In particular, high-resolution computer graphics. These tools have enabled the "experimental" mathematician to identify and explore ordered patterns which would otherwise be buried in reams of computer output. In many cases the persistence of order in irregular behavior was totally unexpected; the discovery of these regularities has led to the development of new analytical methods and approximations. Which have improved our understanding of complex nonlinear phenomena.[2]

練習 4-2 散亂句

下面都是由一些冗贅的散亂句所構成的段落。試將這些段落分成幾個長度適切的句子，換上正確的標點符號，並把贅詞刪除。（提示：正確的修正方式並非只有一種。）

1. A communication network can be modeled as a graph, and a network under attack or with other sources of failure can be modeled as a random graph, regarding which, for the purpose of clarification, a graph, in the sense used here, consists of vertices (or points) and edges, of which each vertex corresponds to a command center or other node in a communication network and each edge represents a two-way communication link between two command centers—in a random graph, an edge may fail, leaving intact the vertices connected by the edge, or a vertex may fail, destroying all the edges connected to the vertex.[3]

2. Slime molds reproduce by means of spores, each of which is an independent, one-celled organism, however, the cells originating from spores divide repeat-edly, and eventually the offspring swarm together in a heap to form a common amoeboid mass, and then the original cell boundaries sometimes disappear,

and the once-independent cells take on specialized functions, somewhat like organs in a larger animal, and the creeping mass of protoplasm, in some cases as large as 30 cm in diameter, is difficult to classify as plant or animal or, indeed, as either a collection of individuals or a larger, single organism, but at any rate, it is one of the most curious examples of self-organization in all biology.[4]

練習 4-3 缺乏連接詞

下面的句子都缺乏連接詞。請修改句子的標點符號，或在必要時加上連接詞。

1. Let X be the Cartesian product of these sets, A is their union.

2. Consider the circuit shown in Figure 2, we can draw its Norton-equivalent circuit as shown in Figure 3.

3. Assume the input power of port 1 is P1 and the output power of port 2 is P2, then we have the following equation.

4. Suppose C can be factored into a product of D and a cube q, then we replace C in the above expression by q.

5. The samples were fabricated by a standard chemical vapor deposition process, N-type Si (100) substrates were scratched using diamond powder to enhance the nucleation density of the deposits.

6. Rearrange the above equation, we obtain the solution.

4.4 主詞與動詞一致

在英文中，動詞的單複數必須和相對應的主詞的單複數一致。在句意上，主詞與動詞一致極為重要。因為如果動詞的數和主詞的數不一致，則讀者就不能確定作者所談論的是一個，還是很多事物：

誤： Methods has been introduced to solve this problem.

作者的意思究竟是「有些學者曾提出幾種不同的方法」，還是「有一個學者曾提出一個方法」？讀者必須猜測句意，且可能會猜錯。

這個錯誤顯然是作者疏忽所致。但許多主詞和動詞不一致的情形，並非疏忽所致，而是作者無法確定句中的動詞應該是單數還是複數。第三章裏已討論過主詞和動詞的一致，所以這裏將只討論幾種容易犯錯的字詞。

由 *every, each* 或 *no* 所引介的單數主詞必須配合單數動詞，即使主詞不只一個，也要配合單數動詞。此外，不定代名詞 *another, each, either, neither, one* 也是應該配合單數動詞的。

> Every paper, report, and letter *is* stored in this computer.

> Neither of these methods *is* truly effective.

即使單數主詞後面緊接著以 *as well as, together with, along with, in addition to* 開首的片語，而當中還包含其他名詞，單數主詞仍是單數：

> The growth in the economy together with the stable political situation *has* led to a significant increase in GDP. 主詞是 *growth*。

> One of the advantages of this approach *is* that it is extremely simple. 主詞是 *one*。

動詞的數必須配合主詞的數，然而與補語的數無關。像下面的句子，補語是複數，但主詞 *sensitivity* 仍是單數。

> 誤： The nominal sensitivity *were* 200 and 270 mV/mil for 4140 steel and stainless steel, respectively.

> 正： The nominal sensitivity *was* 200 mV/mil for 4140 steel and 270 mV/mil for stainless steel.

4.5 時態

英文動詞的時態有十二種，而只有五種是科技寫作中常用的：

科技寫作常用時態

- 現在式：表達不受時間影響的普遍科學事實，以及論文作者的意見和建議。
- 過去式：記錄過去已完成的行為，如實驗中的步驟或電腦模擬。
- 現在完成式：
  - (一) 用來描述行動或狀態在過去已開始存在，而現在仍然一直持續。
  - (二) 用來表達行為在過去曾發生，而現在仍然有效。
  - (三) 用來表達行為「最近」才完成。
- 現在進行式：用來描述行為當下正在發生而尚未完成。
- 未來式：用來描述將來會發生的行為。

當要考慮句子應使用哪種動詞時態時，可參考下列重點：

不要用現在完成式來描述過去的事件。 雖然它亦可用來描述事件在過去已開始存在，但已在過去完成了的事件是應該使用過去式來表達的。所以，下面句子都有文法錯誤：

> 誤： Greenspan *has presented* an ingenious graph reduction technique *in 1982.*

> 誤： *At the conference,* we *have introduced* our new memory chip.

這兩個句子都提到過去一個特定的時間（"in 1982," "at the conference"），事件大概已完成了，所以必須使用過去式。

> 正： Greenspan *presented* an ingenious graph reduction technique *in 1982.*

> 正： *At the conference,* we *introduced* our new memory chip.

千萬不要把現在完成式和過去完成式混淆。 現在完成式是助動詞 *has* 或 *have* 加上主要動詞的過去分詞；過去完成式則是過去式的助動詞 *had* 加上主要動詞的過去分詞。過去完成式是用來表示一個行為已在過去一特定事件之前完成：

> By the time his mother came home, he *had cleaned* all of the windows.

這句提及了兩個過去的事件：「男孩的母親回到家裏」和「男孩洗窗戶」。動詞之所以使用過去完成式，是由於第二個過去的事件在第一個事件之前發生。

在科技寫作中，需要使用過去完成式的機會微乎其微，所以這裏不詳加討論。但現在完成式與過去完成式都是表示發生的事件已經過去了，故不要把兩者混淆，尤其在使用現在完成式時，應避免把 *has* 或 *have* 誤寫成 *had* 。

靜態動詞是沒有進行式的。 現在進行式表示當下進行的動作，靜態動詞是描述主詞狀態而非動作的動詞，因而不會有進行式。靜態動詞包括：*appear, be, believe, concern, consist of, constitute, contain, correspond, exist, know, mean, need, possess, represent, result in, satisfy, seem, understand, yield* 等等。下面句子都有文法錯誤：

> 誤： Solubility *is appearing* to increase with temperature.

> 誤： This case *is corresponding* to equation (6).

這些句子都應該修正為簡單現在式：

> 正： Solubility *appears* to increase with temperature.

> 正： This case *corresponds* to equation (6).

若要查閱動詞時態用法的詳細說明，可參考第三章。

4.6 錯誤的動詞補語

除了動詞的修飾詞之外，動詞補語 (verb complement) 亦是能對動詞作補充說明的字詞，而常以動詞的直接受詞或間接受詞形式出現。在科技論文中的動詞，其後大多數會加上 *to* 或 *that* 開首的補語，看下面的例子：

We intend *to propose a new method.* 動詞後面緊接著以 *to* 開首的補語，這個補語是動詞的直接受詞。

The experimental results show *that the new method is feasible.* 動詞後面緊接著以 *that* 開首的補語，這個補語是動詞的直接受詞。

然而，有些動詞（例如 *try*）是使用 *-ing* 形的補語 （*try* 也可用 *to* 開首的補語）：

Smith tried *using multivariate analysis.*

Smith tried *to use multivariate analysis.*

有些動詞（特別是 *make* 和 *let*）的補語則為動詞原形。

Raising the temperature makes the water *boil* off more rapidly. 補語沒有以 *to boil* 開首，而只以 *boil* 一個字詞開首。

Let F *represent* force and E *represent* energy. 補語沒有以 *to represent* 開首，而只以 *represent* 一個字詞開首。

Let there *be* six individuals in the domain. 不寫 *to be*，而只寫 *be* 。

Let *it be.* 不寫 "Let it to be"，而只寫 "Let it be"。

研究報告的作者尤其應注意下列動詞，其補語必須為動詞原形或 *-ing* 形。

make, let:	動詞原形
suggest, recommend:	*-ing* 形或 *that* 開首的補語
discuss, consider, *depend on, result in:*	*-ing* 形

簡而言之，動詞應配合正確的補語。請參考下列的例句：

誤： The author should consider *to give* a more detailed proof.
正： The author should consider *giving* a more detailed proof.

誤： I suggest *to include* a more detailed proof.
正： I suggest *including* a more detailed proof.

練習 4-4 主詞與動詞一致

請找出主詞與動詞不一致的地方，並加以改正（第三章中練習 3-2 提供更多練習）。

A centralized compression service are economical, but it hampers creativity when developers want to experiment with applications and data. Accordingly, digital video interactive (DVI) technology offer another kind of compression: edit-level video, done on the developer's DVI system in real time. Edit-level video are lower in quality than the presentation-level video made by centralized compression but are adequate for software development.

The user employ edit-level video to develop and test new software. When the user have made his choices and polished the program, he send the final analog video through the centralized compression service. When the presentation-level compressed video come back, the user substitute it for the edit-level files. The newly developed software run just as it did in testing, but now with higher-quality video.

The heart of the DVI video display processor is two chips: one for processing images stored in memory, the other for displaying the processed images. Each chip are a CMOS chip containing about 132,500 transistors. The set can connect to almost any computer, as long as it have the requisite computing speed and data transfer and width—usually this mean a 16-bit or 32-bit processor that operate at a clock speed of 6 megahertz or higher.[5]

練習 4-5 時態

請找出錯誤的動詞時態，並加以改正。（提示：有些動詞是正確的。）

1. When researchers a few years ago had uncovered a strong link between the sunspot cycle and weather patterns on Earth, many atmospheric scientists have been intrigued. Indeed, the correlation was seeming so convincing that a few meteorologists even began to plug solar activity into official long-range

forecasts. But the whole notion takes a battering recently, and it may have a tough time recovering.

Many skeptics, in fact, are always saying that the postulated correlation was not as firm as it seemed. For starters, they had pointed out that it could be traced back only about 40 years, which struck them as too short a record to be convincing. On top of that, solar activity was seeming to affect weather patterns one way when winds in the stratosphere above the equator were blowing in a westerly direction and another way when they were easterly; statistically speaking, that effectively cut in half an already short record. And most disturbing was the absence of any physical mechanism to explain such behavior. But the skeptics nevertheless are having a hard time disproving the link, which had withstood every statistical test—until the winter of 1989.[6]

2. Chain-propagating steps alone are being insufficient to account for flames. It is recognized in the 1930s that chain-initiating, chain-terminating, and chain-branching steps are being also necessary. The 1956 Nobel prize in chemistry had been awarded jointly to Cyril N. Hinshelwood of the University of Oxford and Nikolai N. Semenov of the Institute of Chemical Physics in Moscow for their leading roles in showing how the main features of oxidation reactions could explain in terms of branched-chain reaction mechanisms. (At the time of their research chemists have had only provisional ideas about what the actual elementary reactions might be and almost no information at all about the values of the rate coefficients.)[7]

3. While scientists and engineers are agree that fusion can be working, there is no general agreement on what will be the most economical and desirable type of fusion reactor. To date, the best results had been achieved with the tokamak, a doughnut-shaped machine with powerful magnetic coils, and the optimism that a viable reactor can be built is being primarily based on the tokamak's performance. Although it now is appearing probable that tokamak reactors

will one day produce energy at a cost around that of petroleum and below the cost of solar energy, many scientists are thinking that alternative magnetic fusion devices could produce energy even more cheaply.[8]

4. The sun produced the heating and confinement needed for atomic fusion through its immense gravitational fields. On earth, large-scale fusion reactions are being achieved for 30 years in thermonuclear weapons, where the temperature has been provided by a plutonium bomb explosion and the confinement is simply by inertia—that is, the reaction is going so fast that the fusion fuel, lithium deutride, does not have time to disperse. Inertial confinement is being one of the two principal approaches to the use of fusion for power generation. Inertial fusion reactors would use lasers, electron beams, or ion beams to compress and heat pellets of fuel, allowing them to explode in chambers and thereby drive energy generation equipment.[9]

練習 4-6 動詞補語

請修正下面句子中錯誤的補語。

1. The aim of this paper is propose a new simulation method that dramatically reduces the time needed carry out the simulations.

2. Increasing the annealing temperature beyond 900° C causes the samples become brittle.

3. Adding more oxygen makes the deposition rate to increase significantly.

4. Let N represents the number of customers and t represents the time.

5. Assume that half of the customers to exit the system at the same time.

6. Let there are 10 processors in the network.

7. The author should consider to prove theorems I and II instead of only to state the theorems.

8. We suggest to solve the problem by using a Fourier transform.

9. The referee recommends to accept the paper for publication.

10. The success of this method depends on to solve equation (5) quickly.

11. Let X is the desired recognition accuracy and S is the desired recognition speed.

12. We discussed to treat practical applications of the new technique in the paper, but we decided doing so would make the paper too long.

4.7 誤用被動語態

被動語態常出現在科技論文中，尤其當作者需要描述某種方法、過程或因果關係，而不知道行為的施事者是何人何物，或是該人或事物是無關重要的。例如，在研究報告的方法章節中，作者往往以 *The samples were placed in the reaction chamber* 這樣的被動句子取代主動句子 *We placed the samples in the reaction chamber*。這裏所討論的焦點是樣本，而不是研究者，並且從上文下理讀者已可知行為之施事者就是研究者。因此，這句使用被動語態是很恰當的。

有時在科技論文中使用被動語態是適當的，可是有些作者往往都過度或錯誤使用被動語態。所以使用時，應記住以下事項：

假若使用被動語態來指涉自己的行為，便要清楚表示自己就是該行為的施事者。當研究報告的作者使用被動語態來描述自己的行為、陳述自己的研究目的或提出建議、主張，務必讓讀者清楚知道作者本身就是該行為的施事者。例如，在研究報告中的方法章節裏，就大可放心使用被動語態。因為從文章的脈絡，讀者已經可以清楚知道行為的施事者就是作者。相反，如果科技研究報告的文獻回顧中出現這樣的句子：

不清楚：　*It is suggested* that the stability of the film deteriorates at high temperatures.

這句未能清楚表明那個建議到底是作者的，還是別人的。英文中，*it has been suggested/proposed/found that* X 這種句式的意思是「曾經有人建議／提出／發現 X」。當作者想強調緊接著動詞後面建議或發現的內容，而不用理會是誰建議或發現，便可使用這種句式。因此，讀者看到上面的句子時，自然會猜測建議是別的學者曾提出的，但作者卻又誤用了現在式（現在完成式才正確）。要修正上面的句子，作者就應清楚表示建議是自己的。其中一種修正方式是以代名詞 *we* 做句子的主詞：

清楚：　*We suggest* that the stability of the film deteriorates at high temperatures.

另一種修正方式就是省略動詞 *suggest*，然後再使用語態助動詞或試探性動詞，以表示作者正在提出建議：

> 清楚：　　The stability of the film *may deteriorate* at high temperatures.

> 清楚：　　The stability of the film *appears to deteriorate* at high temperatures.

模糊而不自然的被動句子結構中，經常會出現這些動詞：*argue, assume, believe, desire, present, propose, recommend, suggest, suppose*。例如：

> 不清楚：　Previous techniques for solving this problem all have serious drawbacks. Hence a new method *is proposed*.

外國讀者看到這句的被動動詞 *is proposed* 時，會立刻追問句中的方法是誰人在何時提出的。首句指出了其他研究者所提出的技術。第二句則是作者想藉被動語態句來表達自己打算提出一個新方法。但對讀者而言，這並非明顯易見的。所以，作者應重寫第二句，好讓讀者清楚看出新方法是誰提出的。下面有三種修改方式，各修正句中都加上一個字詞或片語，以清楚表達作者的意思：

> 清楚：　　Hence *in this paper* a new method *is proposed*.

> 清楚：　　Hence in this paper *we propose* a new method.

> 清楚：　　Hence *this paper presents* a new method.

下面是另一個意思含糊及語氣不自然的被動語態句：

> 不自然：　Therefore, *it is desired* to define event types using independent variables.

在這句中，*it is desired* 是非常生硬的寫法。擬使用獨立變數來定義事件種類的人是誰？難道是所有人嗎？大多數人根本不會瞭解作者的討論，也不在乎作者如何定義事件的種類。下列有四種修改方法：

> 自然：　　Therefore, *we need* to define event types using independent variables.

> 自然：　　Therefore, *event types should be defined* using independent variables.

> 自然：　　Therefore, *it would be desirable* to define event types using independent variables.

> 自然：　　Therefore, *it would be best* to define event types using independent variables. 或可使用更精確的形容詞，如 *it would be more effective* 或 *it would be simpler*。

修改過的句子，意義都稍有不同。前兩句都暗示使用獨立變數來定義事件種類是可能的。第一句表示需要用這種方式做定義；第二句則表示應該用這種方式做定義。相較之下，第三和第四句則暗示作者還不太確定是否真的有辦法用獨立變數來定義事件種類。（這可能是個有價值的目標，但未必能達成。）有些資深的作者會認為第三句過於冗長，會避免使用。第四句的意思和第三句大致相同，但寫作風格較口語化。

當作者根據自己研究結果提出假設或結論時，切忌使用加上像 *believe* 這種動詞的被動語態。

含糊：   Hence *it is believed* that annealing improves the electrical characteristics of the films.

在這句中，使用被動語態是不適當的。因為使用 *it is believed* 來表示「我們認為」的意思，既生硬又模糊。這句應修改成主動語態，或換上如 *appear* 之類的試探性動詞：

清楚：   Hence *we believe* that annealing improves the electrical characteristics of the films.

清楚：   Hence annealing *appears* to improve the electrical characteristics of the films.

清楚：   Hence *it appears* that annealing improves the electrical characteristics of the films.

一般來說，如果以英文為母語的作者把如 *believe* 之類的動詞寫成被動語態，又不明確表示該信念是誰抱持的，則意思並非「我們認為」，而是表示該信念是普遍（或幾乎普遍）的信念。例如：

Legionnaires' disease *is believed* to be caused by bacteria.

Sunspot activity *is believed* to vary according to a cyclic pattern.

這類句子中，被動動詞 *is believed* 並非表示「我們這樣認為」或「我個人這樣認為」，而是意味著「絕大多數專家都這樣認為」。因此，當英語國家的人閱讀上面第一個例句時，他們會理解為「絕大多數的醫生、醫學研究人員以及其他的專家都認為，外籍兵團症是細菌感染所致」。而當讀到第二個例句時，他們則會理解為，「大多數的天文學專家都認為，太陽黑子活動是以周期的模式變化」。同樣，當以英文為母語的人看到 *Only high-speed SRAMs are recommended for use with this computer system* 時，他們會想作者的意思是「對這個電腦系統瞭如指掌的人（尤其是電腦系統的製造廠商）都會一致建議，這系統只應配以高速靜態隨機存取記憶體」。

另一個例子：

含糊：   Two examples *are employed* to illustrate the fringe effect.

科技論文中使用這句來介紹所指的兩個例子，既含糊又不自然。下面三個句子都比上面的好得多。

清楚：   Two examples *will be employed below* to illustrate the fringe effect.

清楚：   Two examples *will be employed here* to illustrate the fringe effect.

清楚：   *The following examples* illustrate the fringe effect.

前面兩個修正句都仍然使用被動語態，但它們均指明了動作發生的地點（"below," "here"），因此讀者可清楚看出作者便是動作的施事者。這裏可推而廣之成為一普遍的準則：假如句子本身已指明了動作的發生地點，則可以使用被動語態，因為讀者已能清楚瞭解施事者是誰。例如：

> *In section 4*, two examples *are employed* to illustrate the fringe effect.
>
> *In this paper*, two examples *are employed* to illustrate the fringe effect.
>
> *In Russell's paper*, two examples *were employed* to illustrate the fringe effect.

這些都是自然的英文句子，它們都清楚指出句中的施事者：在前兩句中，施事者是該篇論文的作者，而第三句的施事者是羅素這個人。下面是另一篇科技研究報告的摘要節錄：

> This paper presents a new method for modeling the fringe effect at the edges of an air gap in a magnetic bearing. The accuracy of the proposed model *is demonstrated* by means of two examples.

在這例中，只看第二句並不會獲知誰是施事者，但首句有清楚表示論文作者將會提出新的模型。因此，第二句使用被動語態是恰當的。

　　總而言之，當要使用被動語態來指涉自己的動作時，必須確定讀者能夠清楚看出，作者自己正是該行動的施事者。如果不能的話，就需修改句子。

　　被動語態所陳述的事件必須符合事實。 以英文為母語的作者也會使用被動語態的現在式動詞來陳述普遍的事實。經驗豐富的作者亦常會使用被動語態的現在式動詞去描述某種標準的做法或程序。因為無論是誰在任何特定情形下實行這種做法或程序，這種作法或程序的正確描述都是真實的。請看下面的例子：

> Deuterium *is obtained* from sea water.
>
> In indirect scanning, a small beam of light *is moved* across the subject and then reflected to a battery of phototubes.
>
> The solution to this problem *is* usually *obtained* by applying a Fourier transform.

上面首例使用被動語態是正確的，因為這句所陳述的是一個普遍事實——氘（重氫）都自海水中獲得。在第二和第三例中，使用被動語態也是正確的，因為它們都正確地描述某種標準的做法或程序。這些句子所指涉的行為都是標準程序，故句中的描述皆不受作者寫作時的特定情形影響。

　　使用被動語態的現在式動詞來指出某件事情，或做某種觀察時，都應注意被動語態的句子必須表達一個普遍事實。下面卻是一反例：

> 不自然：　It *is seen* from the figure that the two systems perform equally well.

這個句子非常不自然，它其實是 "it is seen (by everyone) that…"，意即「每個人都能看出兩個系統皆運作良好」，但事實並非如此。很多人根本沒有看到句中所指出

的圖表，所以並非每個人都知道兩個系統運作良好。如果要把這句修改成合符事實，
有這樣一個方法：

> 自然：   It *can be seen* from the figure that the two systems perform
> equally well.

在被動動詞前面加上語態助動詞 *can*，句子所陳述的內容就變得具有普遍的真實性，
這才是正確的英文。事實上，任何受過專業訓練的人，一旦看過這圖表，就可看出
這兩個系統皆運作良好。另一個更直接的修改方式，是將句子改寫成主動語態，以
the figure 作主詞：

> 修正句：   *The figure shows* that the two systems perform equally well.

試看另一個類似的例子：

> 不自然：   It *is observed* that steps 2 and 3 of the algorithm are repeated
> several times.

> 修正句：   It *can be observed* that steps 2 and 3 of the algorithm are repeated
> several times.

> 修正句：   *Observe* [或 *Note*] that steps 2 and 3 of the algorithm are re-
> peated several times.

本節曾引用過這個例子：

> The solution to this problem *is* usually *obtained* by applying a Fourier
> transform.

這裏使用被動語態來描述某種標準程序是正確的。因為這裏要陳述的是一個普遍的
事實——事實上，作者討論的方案都是利用傅立葉轉換而得。相反，下面是一個有
問題的句子：

> From equation (12), x = q/2 and y = r.   Equation (9) *is* now *rewritten* as
> follows.

如果在作者的研究領域中，用作者所指的方式來改寫方程式 (9) 是標準的做法，則
此句使用被動語態或許是正確的（但其實作者亦應把 *now* 這個字改成 *then*）。然
而，這句似乎並非真的描述了某種通用的做法，反而是指作者自己的建議。這句也
許要表達「現在我已經得到了 x = q/2 和 y = r，所以我能將方程式 (9) 改寫成下
列的形式」。如果作者本來是要指涉自己的建議，則應改寫成：

> 修正句：   From equation (12), x = q/2 and y = r.   Equation (9) *can* now *be*
> *rewritten* as follows.

修正句的陳述明顯合符事實，意思比原句清晰得多。任何人只要由已得出的 x = q/2
與 y = r，便能如作者所說，重新改寫方程式 (9)。另一個修改方法是使用主動語態：

> 修正句：   From equation (12), x = q/2 and y = r.   *We can now rewrite*
> equation (9) as follows.

上面兩個修正句都比原句更清楚暢達。

　　要決定不定詞應使用主動抑或被動語態，先要確定它暗示的主詞為何。 如果主詞是不定詞所指行為的施事者，則應使用主動語態；相反，如果主詞是行為的「受事者」，則應該使用被動語態。下面是典型的錯誤：

　　誤：　The parameters are difficult *to be measured* directly.

在原本文章的脈絡中，這句決非表示「參數正在被計算」，而是表示「直接計算參數是一件很困難的工作」。這個意思可使用不定詞表達：

　　正：　It is difficult *to measure* the parameters directly.

原句中的 *to measure* 所暗示的主詞並非「參數」，而是如「研究者」、「我們」或「任何人」之類的主詞。為了方便澄清這點，應將暗示的主詞「研究者」插入句中：

　　正：　It is difficult [for researchers] to measure the parameters directly.

然後將這句改寫成和原本例句相同的句式：

　　正：　The parameters are difficult [for researchers] to measure directly.

由於不定詞 *to measure* 所暗示的主詞是產生不定詞所指行為的「研究者」，因此不定詞應該使用主動語態。現在將不定詞所暗示的主詞「研究者」刪除，以得出最後的修正句。

　　誤：　The parameters are difficult *to be measured* directly.

　　正：　The parameters are difficult *to measure* directly.

下列的例句則正好相反，不定詞所暗示的主詞是句子的主詞：

　　正：　Sally felt happy *to be measured* for her wedding dress.

　　正：　The circuit design is expected *to be completed* by July.

首句意思是莎莉為結婚禮服度身，她為此而感到高興。由於莎莉是不定詞「度身」所暗示的主詞，且也是不定詞所指行為的受事者（施事者為裁縫師），所以使用被動不定詞 *to be measured* 是正確的。第二句的意思則是某些人期望線路設計在七月前完成。由於線路設計是不定詞「完成」所暗示的主詞，也是不定詞所指行為的受事者（施事者則為一組工程師），所以使用被動不定詞 *to be completed* 是正確的。

　　在以下兩個簡單的例句中，不定詞都應用主動語態：

　　誤：　This kind of sensor is easy *to be installed*.

　　正：　This kind of sensor is easy *to install*.

　　誤：　This problem is difficult *to be solved*.

　　正：　This problem is difficult *to solve*.

　　確定動作的施事者是誰，以免混淆主動與被動語態。 很多人在描述實驗方法或陳述實驗結果時，都會把被動語態和主動語態的意思混淆。要表達某些方法或結果時請注意：被動語態是表示某個行為由研究者所產生；主動語態則表示某個行為或事件是自己產生，或是另一個行為或事件的結果，而非由研究者的某個直接行為所致。比較下列句子：

> After the samples were placed in the reaction chamber, the temperature *was increased* gradually from 100° C to 250° C.

> As the chemical reaction proceeded, the temperature *increased* gradually from 100° C to 250° C.

首個例句中，被動動詞 *was increased* 表示所描述的行為是由研究者所產生的。研究者將樣本置於反應槽中，然後增加槽內溫度。第二個例句中，主動動詞 *increased* 表示溫度增加純粹是化學反應的結果而並非研究者做出任何動作去導致溫度增加。

不及物動詞不可使用被動語態。 許多英文動詞本來就沒有被動形式。例如不及物動詞的後面從不接直接受詞，所以根本不可能有被動形式。像動詞 *proceed* 就無法使用被動語態。

誤：　The experiment *was proceeded* by the researchers.

正：　The experiment was performed by the researchers.

正：　The experiment was carried out by the researchers.

下列動詞在科技論文中很常見，它們皆沒有被動形式：

沒有被動形式的動詞			
appear	correspond	occur	tend
arise	depend on	proceed	work
be	exist	remain	yield
become	happen	result in	
come	have	rise	
consist of	let	seem	

避免過度使用被動語態。 在科技寫作中，不應該濫用被動語態。因為這會使論文變得笨拙而生硬，還常會產生不自然或難以理解的句子。此外，濫用被動語態也會導致孤立修飾詞（詳見4.9節），這亦是英文科技寫作中最常犯的錯誤。當然，在研究報告中被動語態的句子還是可以使用，尤其在論述實驗方法時。但若被動語態佔了全篇論句子的25%以上，則可能是過度使用了。

練習 4-7 被動語態

　　下面的句子都是不自然或錯誤的被動語態結構。請使用主動語態或較自然的被動語態結構來修改。

1. From these figures it is seen that the classification accuracy increases as the size of i and j increases.

2. It is believed that the annealing treatment improved the electrical characteristics of the films.

3. The difference between the two curves is attributed to the different values of b used in the two cases.

4. Now that the method has been modified, it is used to analyze the oscillator.

5. The following example is considered.

6. It is desired that the country's economy improve quickly.

7. From these data it is seen that the phase modulation and the frequency shift are enhanced by forward pumping.

8. Coding of coefficients is difficult to be accomplished in real time.

9. The appearance of C-H bonds is attributed to the large number of non-equilibrium hydrogen atoms in the plasma.

10. Now these values are substituted into the equations of motion and the solution is obtained.

11. The arrival rate is assumed in this example to be able to be modeled as a Poisson process.

12. The theoretical model is indicated from Figure 6 to predict the experimental values accurately.

4.8 隨意更換主詞或語態

在英文科技論文中，句中的主詞以及主動與被動語態應避免不必要的更換。這樣會使得句子的焦點不明確，就像是作者本人亦不能確認自己想表達的主題，更別說要讓讀者瞭解句子的重點。請看以下例子：

When we carried out the second trial, the following results were obtained.

這句的文法是正確的，但因為第一個子句與第二個子句的主詞、語態都不同，使得整句很不自然，且焦點欠清晰。第一個子句採用主動語態，主詞是 *we*；第二個子句則採用被動語態，主詞是 *the results*。假如統一兩個子句的主詞和語態，句子就會變得較自然暢達：

When *we carried out* the second trial, *we obtained* the following results.

修改過的句子好多了，可是要求較高的作者不會就此滿意。這個主動句強調了研究者的行為，但作者真正的意思似乎是要提出一組實驗結果，所以把兩個子句都改成被動語態是較為達意的：

When the second trial *was carried out,* the following results *were obtained.*

這句似乎比第一個修改句子恰當。試驗及結果是句子的主要意思，故即使主詞由第一個子句的 *trial* 轉為第二個子句的 *results* 仍是正確的。再者，把這兩個名詞各自成為兩個子句的主詞，更可統一地使用被動語態。在某些文章脈絡中，這句甚至可進一步修改，用一個較簡短的介系詞片語來取代前面的引導附屬子句。

In the second trial, the following results were obtained.

The results *of the second trial* were the following.

有時候更換動詞語態是恰當的，但必須要根據上下文的結構或句意，方可更換。以下便是一個正確的例子：

As soon as *the samples were exposed* to the gas, *they began* to deteriorate.

在這句中，動詞語態從第一個子句的被動語態，更換為第二個子句的主動語態。這是因為作者希望將焦點集中在「那些樣本」上，而它們剛好是兩個子句的主詞。

概括而言，科技論文作者應該格外小心，句中的主詞或主被動語態有可能在不知不覺間轉換。這些轉換亦常會令句子出現孤立的修飾詞（請參閱下一節）。

4.9 孤立的修飾詞

孤立的修飾詞（dangling modifier，也可譯為「邊垂的修飾詞」）是指句子中沒有任何合理修飾對象的修飾詞。以下例句的 *after reading this book* 就是一個孤立的修飾詞：

After reading this book, some common errors can be avoided.

在英文中，如果像 *after reading this book* 這修飾詞在句首出現，則通常是用以修飾句中的主詞。然而，這裏 *after reading this book* 卻不能合理修飾句子的主詞 *some common errors*。這句的意思為「常犯錯誤」能看懂這本書。但「常犯錯誤」怎能看書？因此，這句根本語意不通。

以上例句產生孤立修飾詞的原因，是作者在句中將主動語態更換成被動語態。這個句子若以主動語態開始，則主詞應是某個正在閱讀的人。然而，當了解到這個主詞和動詞時，卻發現作者突然轉用被動語態，把 *some common errors* 當作主詞。如要把它修改成合理的句子，必須提供一個主詞，能受 *after reading this book* 這片語合理修飾，並一貫使用主動語態。以下是一種修改方式：

> After reading this book, *students* may be able to avoid some common errors.

正如此例，孤立的修飾詞經常是由於作者在句子中將主動語態更換為被動語態所致。因此，當句中有被動的主要動詞時，科技論文作者應特別小心，不要造成孤立的修飾詞。

孤立修飾詞種類很多，最常見的包括有孤立的分詞片語、動名詞片語、省略子句以及不定詞片語，這些都常出現在中國人撰寫的科技論文中。以下是各種孤立的修飾詞的例子，例句將會顯示出，孤立的修飾詞常出現在句首。根據文法原則，它們應修飾句子的主詞，但它們卻無法合理地修飾主詞，使句子變得毫無意義。

孤立的分詞片語

分詞片語包含一個分詞（即 *-ed* 或 *-ing* 形的動詞）、分詞的受詞、修飾分詞及修飾分詞的受詞。出現在句首的分詞片語應修飾句子主詞，若不能修飾句子主詞，便要修改句子，刪除孤立的片語。

> 誤：　*Examining this problem,* the following fact can be observed.
>
> 正：　Examining this problem, we observe the following fact.
>
> 正：　Concerning this problem, the following fact should be observed.

> 誤：　*Turning now to the second case,* it can be seen that it is much simpler than the first.
>
> 正：　Turning now to the second case, we see that it is much simpler than the first.
>
> 正：　The second case, on the other hand, is much simpler than the first.

> 誤：　*Running the second trial,* an unusual problem occurred.
>
> 正：　When the second trial was run, an unusual problem occurred.
>
> 正：　In the second trial, an unusual problem occurred.

在以上錯誤的例句中，分詞片語在表面上修飾句子的主詞，但主詞卻無法合理產生分詞片語所指稱的動作。第一和第二個例子的首個修正句，均提供了另一個能讓分詞片語合理修飾的主詞 (“we”)。在修改第三個錯誤例句時，則用一個附屬子句或一個介系詞片語，取代孤立的分詞片語。

在英文中，有少數介系詞（如 *concerning, considering* 和 *regarding*）及附屬連接詞 *(providing)*，本身即為 *-ing* 形。以這類字詞開首的片語或子句並不算是孤立的修飾詞。

包含動名詞的孤立片語

動名詞是動詞的 *-ing* 形，作名詞使用。在一個帶有動名詞的孤立片語中，動名詞通常作介系詞的受詞使用。

誤：　*After substituting this term for y in Equation (3),* the equation can be rewritten as follows.

嚴格來說，介系詞片語 *After substituting...* 應修飾句子的主詞。然而，主詞是 *the equation*，一個方程式不可能做出「以某詞項取代 *y*」這個行為。

這例子中出現孤立的修飾詞的原因，與本節曾提及的原因相同：作者以 *After substituting...* 開首，似乎有意撰寫一個主動語態的句子，但後來卻寫出一個被動的動詞。原句至少可用三種方式修改，這些修改方式的共同點是取消由主動語態轉為被動語態。

第一個修改的辦法是插入一個主詞，能受 *after substituting...* 合理修飾，並讓句子貫徹使用主動語態：

正：　After substituting this term for y in Equation (3), *we can rewrite* the equation as follows.

另一個修改方法是把孤立的片語改成附屬子句，並以被動語態改寫：

正：　*If this term is substituted for y in Equation (3),* the equation can be rewritten as follows.

第三個修改方法是省略 *after* 這字詞，直接用 *substituting* 這動名詞來作句子主詞，並使用主動語態。

正：　*Substituting* this term for y in Equation (3) *yields* the following equation.

正：　*Substituting* this term for y in Equation (3) *gives* the following equation.

此外，有時句首會出現包含動名詞的介系詞片語，而該介系詞片語表面上是可以合理修飾句子的動詞。以下是一範例：

原句：　*By focusing the scene to be imaged on the photocathode of the tube,* the image is intensified.

有些作者可能會認為介系詞片語 *By focusing...* 不是一個孤立的片語，因為它可合理修飾句子的動詞（它說明了增強影像的明暗度的方法）。然而，這個片語顯然是錯置的。假如把這個片語移到句尾，句子就通順得多，讀者也會清楚這個片語係用來修飾動詞：

修正句：　The image is intensified *by focusing the scene to be imaged on the photocathode of the tube.*

其實原句的結構較接近中文句子結構，但就英文而言，修正句是較為自然的。

孤立的省略子句

所謂省略子句是指一個省略主詞的附屬子句。作者省略一個主詞，是因為該主詞與主要子句的主詞相同。然而，若不小心把與主要子句的主詞不相同的主詞省略，省略子句就會頓成孤立的修飾詞。要修改孤立的省略子句，可在省略子句中加入適當的主詞，或重新改寫這個省略子句，使該子句能合理修飾句子主詞。

誤：　*When attempting to integrate this term*, the following problem is encountered.

正：　When attempting to integrate this term, we encounter the following problem.

正：　When this term is integrated, the following problem arises.

誤：　*While constructing the menu hierarchy*, subfunctions and services invoked by the system functions are not used.

正：　While constructing the menu hierarchy, programmers do not need to use subfunctions and services invoked by the system functions.

正：　When the menu hierarchy is constructed, subfunctions and services invoked by the system functions are not used.

誤：　*When simple,* we can solve this type of problem quickly using the direct method.

正：　When simple, this type of problem can be solved quickly using the direct method.

第一和第二個錯誤例句中的孤立修飾詞，都是因作者混用了主動語態和被動語態而造成的。故修正句都一律使用主動語態或被動語態來貫穿整句。

孤立的不定詞片語

不定詞片語包含不定詞、不定詞的受詞以及任何修飾不定詞或其受詞的字詞。一般來說，位於句首的不定詞片語應修飾句子主詞；如果它沒有修飾句子主詞，亦很可能是孤立的修飾詞。

誤：　*To design an effective system,* information about users' needs should be collected first.

正：　*To design an effective system,* programmers must first collect information about users' needs.

誤：　*To write a good paper*, much research is necessary.

正： To write a good paper, a student must do much research.

在錯誤的例句中，句首的不定詞片語都不能合理修飾句子主詞（「資料」不能設計系統，「研究」也不能寫文章）。因此，修正句都插入適當的主詞，能讓不定詞片語修飾。

在科技論文中，如果句首的不定詞片語不能修飾句子主詞，但只要句子不會因此變得毫無意義，或閱讀起來不會不自然，有時也能為專業的作者和編輯接受。作者有時會認為這種以不定詞片語開首開首的句子，表達得最為簡潔，且會認為有時即使不定詞片語不能合理修飾主詞，但它可修飾句子的主要動詞。但像以上兩例使用的不定詞片語，專業的作者都會反對。因為 *to design* 和 *to write* 無論是用來修飾句子主詞或主要動詞，都很怪誕。相比之下，以下句子中的不定詞片語就比較自然，這是因為不定詞片語可合理修飾句子的動詞：

> *To resolve this performance bottleneck*, a small, fast memory buffer was placed between the central processor and main memory.

許多以英文為母語的作者會認為這句把不定詞片語 *To resolve...* 擺在句首，是無可厚非的。然而，有些資深的作者卻會認為以下的修正句更達意：

> This performance bottleneck was resolved by placing a small, fast memory buffer between the central processor and main memory.

此外，有些作者會認為以下句中不定詞片語的位置並無不妥，因為該不定詞片語可合理修飾句子的動詞：

> *To determine how the parameters vary over time*, the experimental data were analyzed using a computer model.

然而，有些專業編輯會認為以下的句子比原句來得通順：

> To determine how the parameters vary over time, we analyzed the experimental data using a computer model.

面對這類例子，科技論文作者必須自行決定，讀者能否接受句子以不定詞片語開首。

練習 4-8 隨意更換主詞或語態

請修改下列句子，刪除不必要的主詞或動詞語態更換。

1. When we tested the system, excellent performance was obtained.

2. If users plan to carry out complex calculations, purchase of a high-performance workstation is recommended.

3. This type of network is insensitive to differences in scale, translation, and rotation, but an unusually large number of processing elements and connections are required.

4. If we attempt to solve the equation in this form, several difficulties are encountered.

5. This algorithm provides accurate results, but a great deal of processing time is required for the algorithm.

6. The sensors detect errors quickly, and information about the errors is fed from the sensors to the controller.

練習 4-9 孤立的修飾詞

請修改下列句子，刪去孤立或誤置的修飾詞。

1. After determining the mapping of A_i from L_1 to L_p, the next array dimension can be processed in the same way.

2. When applying Smith's method in our simulations, the modeled objects had an unrealistic shape.

3. By choosing an appropriate reference plant model and robustness filter, the IMC structure will produce a controller of the desired order.

4. By further decreasing the input pulse width, pulse splitting due to SFS is observed.

5. After performing the simulations, the following results were obtained.

6. To write effective software programs for banks, training in both computer science and finance is necessary.

7. By verifying the prototype at this stage, specification errors can be detected and corrected earlier.

8. Using an NPN bipolar junction transistor as an example, there are three parts: the collector, base, and emitter.

9. Comparing Chen's method with ours, the difference between them is that we don't use external forces to join the panels in the model together.

10. By applying the finite difference method, the elastic force for an M × N grid of points in vector form is the following.

11. Each cluster contains a different number of spectral vectors after performing the iterative procedure for producing the codebook.

12. To develop a high-performance bicycle, it is important to use lightweight materials.

13. Before discussing the design of the damper, the main design factors must be identified.

14. By applying the proposed load compensation technique, the results indicate that system performance improves significantly.

15. To directly apply this analysis to the present case, two difficulties arise.

4.10 修飾詞誤置

　　英文句子裏，字詞或字詞組的位置，可顯現出其與句子中其他字詞間的相互關係。如果具有修飾功能的字詞位置不當，文章就會變得令人費解。

程度副詞

　　程度副詞（如 *only, nearly, almost, even* 以及其它類似的字詞）應直接擺在其修飾的字詞前面。撰寫英文文章時，應注意這些副詞在句中的正確位置，通常與中文句子的位置不同。

誤置句： The system *only needs* three iterations to find the solution.
修正句： The system needs *only three* iterations to find the solution.

誤置句： The computation took two seconds *approximately*.
修正句： The computation took *approximately two* seconds.

在第一個例子中，*only* 不是用來修飾 *needs*，而是 *three*。在第二個例子中，*approximately* 應放在 *two* 前面。

　　注意以下兩個句子的差別：

The calculations are *nearly all* completed.

The calculations are all *nearly completed*.

在首句中，*nearly* 這字詞用來修飾 *all*，這句指出「大部分計算都已完成，但有些還沒有」。在第二句中，*nearly* 修飾的是 *completed*，所以意思是「沒有一個計算是完成的，但所有的計算都會快將完成」。

以下展示了一個很有意思的情形，同一個句子，整句意思會隨 *only* 位置的改變而改變。（底線是標明 *only* 所修飾的字詞。）

Only <u>Arnold</u> said that he ate his apple. 其他人都沒這麼說。

Arnold only <u>said</u> that he ate his apple. 他只是說這件事，沒做甚麼。

Arnold said only <u>that he ate his apple</u>. 他除了說出這件事，沒有說別的了。

Arnold said that only <u>he</u> ate his apple. 吃了這蘋果的只有他。

Arnold said that he only <u>ate his apple</u>. 他只吃了蘋果，沒做過別的事。

Arnold said that he ate only <u>his apple</u>. 他只吃了自己的蘋果，沒有吃其他屬於自己或別人的東西。

Arnold said that he ate his only <u>apple</u>. 他吃掉自己僅有的蘋果。

Arnold said that he ate <u>his apple</u> only. 他只吃了自己的蘋果，沒有吃其他屬於自己或別人的東西。

其他副詞

請注意副詞 *easily* 的位置：

The solution can be *easily* found by using the following method.

這句在文法上是正確的，但以英文為母語的作者都會認為，若將副詞 *easily* 置於助動詞 *can* 和 *be* 之間，整句會較自然。

The solution can *easily* be found by using the following method.

副詞在修飾一個動詞時，通常是放在該動詞的前後。但在某些情況下，假如將副詞放在句尾，則會使句子更通順。尤其是當作者有意強調某個副詞，或當副詞片語很長時，則可把副詞放在句尾。試比較下列句子：

The new algorithm *quickly and accurately* finds the solution.

The new algorithm finds the solution *quickly and accurately*.

兩句同是文法正確的英文，但第二句就要比第一句來得通順自然。在第二句中，動詞直接放在主詞後面，會使句子比較易讀，同時，把副詞放在句尾，亦較能強調副詞的意義。

避免不明確的修飾詞

作者在寫作時應要明確表示修飾詞所修飾的特定字詞。有時候，修飾詞的位置不當，會使讀者不瞭解哪個是受修飾的字詞。請注意以下句中 *often* 這字詞的位置。

不清楚： The professor encouraged the class *often* to do extra homework.

讀者實在難以看出這裏 *often* 修飾的是 *encouraged* ，還是 *to do*？作者應表明 *often* 修飾的究竟是哪個動詞，再在下列修正句中任擇其一。

> 修正句：　The professor *often encouraged* the class to do extra homework.

> 修正句：　The professor encouraged the class *to do* extra homework *often*.

片語

修飾名詞的片語應直接放在它修飾的名詞後面，否則句子會令人非常費解。試看下面例句：

> 誤置句：　Stuart bought a new computer system from a discount store *with a scanner and a printer.*

> 修正句：　Stuart bought a new computer system *with a scanner and a printer* from a discount store.

片語 *with a scanner and a printer* 似乎是修飾名詞 *store*，但事實上它卻應修飾 *system* 。

副詞片語可直接放在其所修飾的字詞後面，也可放在句首或句尾。當選擇副詞片語的位置時，句意必須要很清楚。試參考下面的例子：

> 誤置句：　Then a new design is proposed for the system *in the second section.*

> 修正句：　Then, *in the second section,* a new design is proposed for the system.

> 修正句：　Then a new design for the system is proposed *in the second section.*

在原句中，*in the second section* 這片語是用來修飾名詞 *system*。然而，作者原本是想說：新設計將在論文某個章節中提出。同樣，以下例子裏，*on paper* 這片語似乎是修飾 *system*；但事實上它卻修飾了 *reproduces*。

> 誤置句：　The facsimile recorder reproduces the image transmitted by the facsimile system *on paper.*

> 修正句：　The facsimile recorder reproduces *on paper* the image transmitted by the facsimile system.

關係子句

關係子句通常應緊接著它所修飾的字詞。下面的「誤置句」，是句中關係子句位置出了錯，令人不知其所云。在第一個誤置句中，關係子句應修飾 *drive*，而非 *device*；在第二個誤置句中，關係子句應修飾 *information*，而非 *memory*。

> 誤置句：　A laser disk drive is used in the CD-ROM device *that is the same size as a traditional 5.25-inch drive.*

> 修正句：　A laser disk drive *that is the same size as a traditional 5.25-inch drive* is used in the CD-ROM device.

修正句：　The CD-ROM device has a laser disk drive *that is the same size as a traditional 5.25-inch drive.*

誤置句：　Information can be loaded into memory *that is stored on a CD-ROM* and then displayed or printed.

修正句：　Information *that is stored on a CD-ROM* can be loaded into memory and then displayed or printed.

　　上述準則有個例外：假如關係子句太長，而直接放在它所修飾的名詞後面，就會令句子變得笨拙。所以應把關係子句移到較恰當的位置（譬如，把子句放在句尾）。在下列句子中，假如關係子句放在動詞後面，便會較通順。（請參閱第九章9.4和9.5節。）

不通順：　A design *that prevents slow master modules from being handicapped in their attempts to gain control of the bus while permitting faster modules to transfer data at high speed via the same bus* has been developed.

修正句：　A design has been developed *that prevents slow master modules from being handicapped in their attempts to gain control of the bus while permitting faster modules to transfer data at high speed via the same bus.*

以 *based on* 開首的片語不應擺在句首。

不通順：　*Based on the simulation results,* the second algorithm is faster and requires less memory.

這例中的分詞片語 *based on the simulation results* 並沒任何合理修飾對象，因此是孤立的修飾詞。作者真正的想法是：

The second algorithm is faster and requires less memory. This conclusion is *based on the simulation results.*

但這修正法卻太冗長間接。以下任何一個修正句都比原句達意，尤其第三個修正句特別簡潔直接：

修正句：　*On the basis of the simulation results, we can conclude that* the second algorithm is faster and requires less memory.

修正句：　*From the simulation results, we can conclude that* the second algorithm is faster and requires less memory.

修正句：　*The simulation results show* that the second algorithm is faster and requires less memory.

　　在正式的文章中，假如關係代名詞是介系詞的受詞，則介系詞通常應是關係子句中的首個字詞。

不自然：　The speed *which the reaction occurred at* surprised us.

修正句：　The speed *at which the reaction occurred* surprised us.

但這也有例外。為使句子較自然，資深的作者有時會把介系詞放在子句的結尾。下面的例子很著名（據說是前任英國總理邱吉爾提出的）：

不自然： This is something up with which we will not put.

修正句： This is something we will not put up with. 這是一件我們無法忍耐的事。

當關係代名詞之後緊接著動詞 *to be* 時，關係代名詞以及動詞有時是可省略的。請參考下面的例子：

The results *that were* obtained are shown in Figure 1.

這個句子可簡化成這樣：

The results obtained are shown in Figure 1.

這裏 *obtained* 表示一個縮短的關係子句，所以應把 *obtained* 放在它所修飾的名詞後面。中國人寫英文文章時，有時會顛倒名詞和修飾詞的次序：

The *obtained results* are shown in Figure 1.

雖然以上句子並非不正確，但聽起來就有點不對勁，因為 the results obtained 始終要比 the obtained results 自然得多。

副詞子句

以 *although, because, since, until, after* 等字詞開首的副詞子句，可放在其所修飾的字後面，或放在句首或句尾。在選擇副詞子句的位置時，作者應確定句意清楚明確。例如：

誤置句： The samples were used in the experiments *after they were doped with boron.*

修正句： *After they were doped with boron*, the samples were used in the experiments.

副詞子句的意思是「實驗本身灌入了硼」。但作者原意是「樣本被灌入了硼」。因此，我們應該把副詞片語移到句首。如此一來，子句中的 *they* 很清楚是指稱樣本，而非實驗本身。

中國的作者應留意代名詞 *they* 在以上修正句中的位置。在中文裏，比較自然的寫法是先提及名詞，才使用代名詞。所以，中國作者可能會認為，應該先提及名詞 *samples*，才使用代名詞 *they*：*After the samples were doped with boron, they were used in the experiments*。但在英文中，先用代名詞、然後才用名詞的 *After they were doped with boron, the samples were used in the experiments*，亦同樣正確。

練習 4-10 修飾詞誤置

指出下列句子中誤置的修飾詞，並加以修正。

1. In this case, it would only be necessary to search for the largest subset template.

2. The samples were placed in an oven wrapped in foil.

3. Based on the two parameter studies, the appropriate parameters for the recognition system are $N = 12$, $M = 4$, and $T = 18$.

4. We can assume that the applied force is always in the +y direction without loss of generality.

5. Based on the mathematical model presented above, a computer program was developed to generate the complete tooth profile.

6. The technique only partitions a data set into two subsets.

7. Generally, an observer-based scheme for generating residuals is depicted in Figure 2.

8. The system can be divided into two parts basically.

9. This is a problem in classical physics of great complexity.

10. The parameters were used to test the model measured in the experiment.

4.11 誤用冠詞

冠詞是英文中最難以掌握的詞類之一，許多非以英文為母語的人都難以決定甚麼名詞該用甚麼冠詞。如第二章討論過的，為正確使用冠詞，作者必須知道如何分辨某個名詞是指稱一個總類中的任何一個個例，或是指稱一個特定事物。

中國作者使用英文冠詞常犯的錯誤，就是當要以單數且可數的名詞來指稱一個總類的任何一個個例時，卻省略了不定冠詞 *a*。

　　誤： In this paper, we propose mechanism to explain this phenomenon.

顯然，作者是想提出 *a mechanism* 來說明這現象。在這裏不定冠詞是必要的，因為 *mechanism* 是一個單數且可數的名詞，且是指稱一個總類中的某一個個例。這裏不定冠詞之所以必要，是由於作者打算從多種可能的說明中提出一個。即使作者提出的是唯一正確的說明，但這仍不是唯一可能的說明。（若在同一個段落或章節中再需要提到時，就會寫成 *the mechanism* 而非 *a mechanism*。）

　　另一個常犯錯誤是當有必要使用定冠詞 *the* 時，卻將它省略。如以下例句所示，當缺少了定冠詞時，句子就變得難以理解。

　　誤：　Range of low frequencies passed by low-pass filter within a specified limit is called pass band of filter. Point considered to be upper end of pass band is at critical frequency, f_C, which is frequency at which filter's output voltage is 70.7% of maximum.

加上適當的定冠詞後，句子遂變得比較清楚。

　　正：　*The* range of low frequencies passed by *a* low-pass filter within *a* specified limit is called *the* pass band of *the* filter. *The* point considered to be *the* upper end of *the* pass band is at *the* critical frequency, f_C, which is *the* frequency at which *the* filter's output voltage is 70.7% of *the* maximum.

　　然而，有些作者卻犯了相反的錯誤，即使應使用不定冠詞或沒有必要使用任何冠詞時，也一律在每個名詞前面加上 *the*。

　　誤：　*The* ordered binary decision diagram is *the* directed acyclic graph with *the* fixed variable ordering that represents *the* Boolean functions. *The* graph includes two kinds of *the* nodes, *the* non-terminal and *the* terminal, as stipulated by *the* Shannon's theorem.

　　正：　*An* ordered binary decision diagram is *a* directed acyclic graph with *a* fixed variable ordering that represents Boolean functions. The graph includes two kinds of nodes, non-terminal and terminal, as stipulated by Shannon's theorem.

　　在 "Shannon's theorem" 之前不必加上 *the*，因為接著「屬格」（又稱「所有格」）的名詞不需要加上任何冠詞。方程式的名稱（如 "equation (9)"）以及論文中的章節或小節（"chapter 6," "section II"），也不需要冠詞。

　　要重溫冠詞更詳細用法，請參閱第二章。

4.12 錯誤的複數名詞

　　有時造成主詞和動詞不一致，並非作者不懂文法規則，而是忘記把複數主詞寫成複數形式之故。當要修改英文研究報告初稿時，一定要留心複數形式的用法。如果名詞是複數的話，就不要忽略名詞的複數形式。此外，千萬不要把單數名詞寫成複數形式，尤其不可把不可數名詞寫成複數形式。中國人撰寫英文科技論文時，就經常把下列不可數名詞誤以複數形式表示：

literature	research	work
notation	terminology	information
equipment	software	hardware

其他不能寫成複數形式的名詞還包括任何加上 *every, each, no, another, either, neither, one* 等字的名詞。例如，下面兩句的主詞都應是單數：

Every *product* undergoes two phases of quality testing.

No *student* may leave the room during the test.

若一個單位之前有一數字，除非數字剛好為 1，否則應是複數形式。

This event lasts only 1 second.

The launch was aborted just 1.8 seconds before lift off.

Valid data must be present for a minimum of 0.5 microseconds before and after the strobe pulse.

Integrated circuits are now manufactured with line widths of less than 0.001 millimeters.

4.13 含糊的代名詞

每個代名詞必須有一個清晰的前述詞（前述詞是代名詞所指稱代替的名詞）。假如一個代名詞的前述詞會讓讀者覺得不夠明確（尤其是較不熟悉文章內容的讀者），代名詞就應改成名詞或名詞片語。例如：

含糊：　There are several differences between static memory and dynamic memory. First, because *it* does not lose its contents as long as power is applied, *it* eliminates the need for periodic refresh cycles.

第二句的代名詞 *it* 是指哪種記憶體？有電子知識背景的讀者也許能猜中，但這本來並非他們的責任。作者應讓讀者能清楚看出代名詞的前述詞，他可用名詞取代這代名詞：

修正：　There are several differences between static memory and dynamic memory. First, because *static memory* does not lose its contents as long as power is applied, *it* eliminates the need for periodic refresh cycles.

撰寫英文文章時，應避免在同一句中使用代名詞 *it* 來表達兩個或三個不同的意思。例如，如果使用 *it* 作虛主詞，則不應在同一句中再使用它來指稱一特定的前述詞。請參考以下例句：

模糊：　If a diode fails the quality test, *it* is necessary to replace *it*.

清楚：　If a diode fails the quality test, *it* must be replaced.

清楚：　Any diode that fails the quality test must be replaced.

模糊：　When *it* is important for a system to handle complex data, *it* is difficult to design *it* so that *it* also finds solutions quickly.

清楚：　*It* is difficult to design a system that both handles complex data and finds solutions quickly.

如果要使用一個代名詞來指稱前一句的意思，則不可使用代名詞 *it*。在這種情形中，使用代名詞 *this* 較為適合。

誤：　Fax machines allow documents to be transmitted to remote locations quickly and conveniently. *It* is one reason they are so popular.

正：　Fax machines allow documents to be transmitted to remote locations quickly and conveniently. *This* is one reason they are so popular. 第二句沒有文法錯誤，但句意模糊。

誤：　A conventional MVC application is composed of several fixed subwindows that share the same model, and each subwindow works through a view and a controller. *It* is sufficient when a window application is simple.

正：　A conventional MVC application is composed of several fixed subwindows that share the same model, and each subwindow has a view and a controller. *This* is sufficient when a window application is simple. 第二個句子沒有文法錯誤，但句意模糊。

但一般而言，除非代名詞所指意思已非常清楚，否則作者應盡量避免使用 *this*, *that* 或 *which* 來指稱整個句子或子句的意思。若是以代名詞來指稱的意思不夠清晰，不如乾脆刪除代名詞，並將句子重新改寫，或加入能夠澄清句意的名詞。例如：

模糊：　Fax machines allow documents to be transmitted to remote locations quickly and conveniently. *This* is one reason they are so popular.

清楚：　Fax machines allow documents to be transmitted to remote locations quickly and conveniently. *This capability* is one reason they are so popular.

清楚：　One reason fax machines are so popular is that they allow documents to be transmitted to remote locations quickly and conveniently.

模糊：　The maximum number of generalizations is related only to the number of attributes, *which* is consistent with the points in section 2.

清楚：　The maximum number of generalizations is related only to the number of attributes. *This relationship* [或 *this property*] is consistent with the points in section 2.

模糊：　A conventional MVC application is composed of several fixed subwindows that share the same model, and each subwindow has a view and a controller. *This* is sufficient when a window application is simple.

清楚：　A conventional MVC application is composed of several fixed subwindows that share the same model, and each subwindow has a view and a controller. *This design* is sufficient when a window application is simple.

同時也應避免使用不必要的代名詞。

誤： For a program with n iterations, there are n iterations in *its* corresponding DFG.

正： For a program with n iterations, there are n iterations in the corresponding DFG.

正： A program with n iterations has n iterations in its DFG.

誤： We can now extend the uniform case to a general distribution, which we view *it* as the prior distribution of U in Bayesian statistics.

正： We can now extend the uniform case to a general distribution, which we view as the prior distribution of U in Bayesian statistics.

在第二個錯誤的例子中，關係子句中出現了不必要的代名詞。因為這個代名詞與關係代名詞 *which* 是指同一個對象，即 "a general distribution"，故可以說，這代名詞是累贅的。假如 *We view it as the prior distribution of U in Bayesian statistics* 這個子句是一個獨立子句的話，則把代名詞 *it* 放在動詞後面是正確的。然而，當這個子句以關係子句出現時，關係代名詞 *which* 就取代了代名詞 *it*，因此應該省略後者。

4.14 代名詞與前述詞一致

除了前述詞必須交代清楚之外，代名詞的數必須符合其前述詞的數。請注意下列各項：

- 指稱不定前述詞 *any, each, either, neither, person* 和 *-one, -body, -thing* (*everyone, anybody, something*) 結尾的字詞時，必須使用單數代名詞。
- 如果前述詞是由兩個以上單數的名詞組成，並以 *and* 連接的話，就應使用複數代名詞。
- 如果前述詞是由兩個以上單數的名詞組成，並以 *or* 或 *nor* 連接的話，則應使用單數代名詞。
- 假如前述詞是由一個複數名詞與一個單數名詞組成，並以 *or* 或 *nor* 連接的話，那代名詞則應與它所在位置最接近之前述詞名詞的數一致。

傳統上，陽性單數代名詞 *he, him, his* 皆可指涉男性或女性的單數前述詞，如 *someone, everyone, person, student, user, reader* 這些字詞。然而，現今許多讀者卻反對以陽性代名詞兼稱兩性。這裏倒有些折衷的辦法。請看下面的例子：

Any author who wishes to present a paper at the conference should submit *his* paper before April 30.

如果像這句中的代名詞只出現一次，則作者就可用 *he or she* 來代替 *he*，並以 *his or her* 來代替 *his*：

Any author who wishes to present a paper at the conference should submit *his or her* paper before April 30.

然而，如果代名詞在句子中多次出現，即一直重複使用 *he or she*，句子將會變得冗長笨拙。另一個不錯的解決辦法，就是將句中的單數代名詞與相應的前述詞都改寫成複數。

> *Authors* who wish to present a paper at the conference should submit *their* papers before April 30.

第三個方法則是刪除句中所有代名詞：

> Any author who wishes to present a paper at the conference should submit the paper before April 30.

十九世紀以來，一般英文文法參考書都表示，在正式文章中，用複數代名詞 *they, them, their* 指稱單數前述詞是錯誤的。但近年有學者指出，英文文學史上許多著名的作者（如莎士比亞）都慣用第三人稱複數代名詞指稱單數不定前述詞，因此這應亦為正確。

> *Anyone* who wishes to present a paper at the conference should submit *their* paper before April 30.

然而，很多期刊的編輯仍不容許此用法，所以本書建議使用以上介紹的方法，避免這種單複數形之混合使用。

在正式文章中，不應將代名詞合併使用，如 *his/her* 與 *s/he*。

> 劣：   Any *author* who wishes to present a paper at the conference should submit *his/her* paper before April 30.

指示形容詞 (*this, that, these, those*) 的數必須符合其所修飾名詞的數。尤其是指示形容詞後面接著 *kind of* 或 *type of* 這類字詞時，應與 *kind of* 或 *type of* 後面所接的名詞的數一致。

> 正：   This type of method [*this, type, method* 皆為單數。]

> 正：   These types of processors [*these, types, processors* 皆為複數。]

> 正：   This kind of book

> 正：   These kinds of instruments

> 誤：   This type of computers [*This type* 是單數，*computers* 卻是複數。]

> 誤：   These types of design [*These types* 是複數，*design* 卻是單數。]

使用關係代名詞時：*who* 指稱人，*which* 指稱事物，*that* 則指稱事物或人。而當 *which* 與介系詞連用時，會使句子顯得不自然，則屬格 *whose* 亦可用來指稱事物。

> 不自然：   The least squares method is used to simplify a piecewise multivariate polynomial regression model *the regression function of which* must satisfy certain continuity conditions.

修正句：　The least squares method is used to simplify a piecewise multivariate polynomial regression model *whose regression function must satisfy* certain continuity conditions.

在這裏，關係子句 *whose regression function must satisfy...* 要比 *the regression function of which must satisfy...* 來得自然。

關係代名詞 *that* 只可用在限定關係子句中。限定關係子句是指對句意不可或缺的子句，而且不能用逗點將它與句子其他部分隔開。相反，非限定子句是指對句意可有可無的子句，而且可以逗點把它與句子其他部分隔開。（參考第五章5.2節的詳細說明。）*Which* 可用在限定子句或非限定子句。為了清楚起見，許多英文寫作參考書會建議作者在限定子句中使用 *that*，而 *which* 只用在非限定子句中。但這準則也有個例外的情形，如在同一句中，過度使用 *that* 的話，則不妨可交替使用 *which*。

練習 4-11 代名詞與前述詞

找出不清楚的代名詞，或與前述詞的數不一致的代名詞。試修改這些句子，使得每個代名詞都有一個清楚的前述詞，且兩者的數都相符合。

1. When a formal financing system does not exist, a pre-selling system is established to make the market more effective. It can be found in a number of Asian countries.

2. A centralized compression service is economical, but they hamper creativity when developers want to experiment with applications and data. Accordingly, digital video interactive (DVI) technology offers another kind of compression: edit-level video, done on the developer's DVI system in real time. Edit-level video is lower in quality than that made by centralized compression but is adequate for software development. Users employ it to develop and test new software. When they have made their choices and polished the program, they send the final analog video through it. When the presentation-level compressed video comes back to them, they substitute it for the edit-level files. Their newly developed software runs just as they did in testing, but now with higher-quality video.[10]

3. The solar water heater used in the experiment is shown in Figure 2. At its top left is a cold-water inlet, where water flows into it. Its main portion consists of

many coils of plastic pipe connected together in an accordion fashion and covered with a sheet of heat-absorbing plastic. The water flows through them, absorbing heat from the sun, and then exits the heating apparatus through the outlet at the lower right of the heater. From the outlet it flows into an insulated storage tank in the basement of the house, from which hot water is drawn when needed.

4. While scientists and engineers agree that fusion can work, there is no general agreement on what will be the most economical and desirable type of fusion reactor. To date, the best results have been achieved with the tokamak, a doughnut-shaped machine with powerful magnetic coils, and the optimism that a viable one can be built is primarily based on its performance. Although it now appears probable that they will one day produce energy at a cost around that of petroleum and below the cost of solar energy, many of them think that alternative magnetic fusion devices could produce it even more cheaply.[11]

4.15 冗長或錯誤的複合名詞

複合名詞 (noun compound) 是指由兩個以上名詞組成的名詞片語，例如：*a research paper, the electronics laboratory, mathematics textbooks*。英文複合名詞中，最右邊的名詞叫「首語」 (head noun)，首語前面的名詞則是作修飾詞之用。例如，在 *mathematics textbooks* 這個複合名詞中，*textbooks* 是首語，*mathematics* 則是用來修飾 *textbooks*，以告訴讀者教本種類。

複合名詞非常重要，它可以幫助作者簡潔地表達一些複雜的意思。然而，中國人撰寫英文科技論文時，千萬別造出不自然或錯誤的複合名詞。想確保所寫的複合名詞是清楚正確的英文，應記住以下的重點。

使用複合名詞時，最重要的原則是複合名詞要簡短。一個複合名詞的組合若是超過三個名詞，個別名詞之間的關係必定是模糊的，會令讀者費解。當讀者遇到如 *computer simulation test program analysis method* 的複合名詞時，根本不可能清楚了解作者的意思。這裏所指至少有三個可能：

一、 用以分析電腦模擬測試的程式的方法 (a method for analyzing programs used in computer simulation tests)。

二、用以分析電腦模擬程式的試驗性方法 (a test method for analyzing programs used in computer simulations)。

三、使用電腦模擬來分析測試程式的方法 (a method that uses computer simulations to analyze the effectiveness of test programs)。

故此，假如發覺自己使用了超過三個字詞組成的複合名詞，趕緊用介系詞或關係子句把這個複合名詞分成兩個或兩個以上的部分。例如，冗長的複合名詞 *a new power plant control system design approach*，可修改成 *a new approach to designing control systems for power plants*，這樣便清楚得多。尤其當一個名詞片語在文章中首次出現時，應如後者般清楚交代該名詞片語所指的意思。在介紹這名詞片語過後，才可把它縮短為一個複合名詞。

在撰寫複合名詞時，必須正確使用複數形式。一般而言，只有首語（複合名詞中最右邊的名詞）才可以為複數形式。修飾首語的名詞皆須為單數形式，即使這名詞可能表達複數意思。舉個例說，*circuit designer* 這複合名詞，即使某位線路設計者可能會設計出很多不同線路，但 *circuit* 仍是單數。又例如在複合名詞 *computer science* 中，即使電腦科學家研究多種不同的電腦，*computer* 仍是單數。假如將這些複合名詞寫成 *circuits designer* 與 *computers science*，對以英文為母語的人來說，都是光怪陸離的寫法。

但這些規則還是有例外，對非以英文為母語者的確造成很多麻煩。例如在複合名詞 *systems technology, communications satellite* 及 *teachers college* 中，修飾首語的名詞都要寫成複數。對這些例外的複合名詞，只有死背一途了。

在中文的名詞片語中，我們常用「的」字來類比為英文介系詞 *of*。中文的「的」字也可用來表示名詞的屬格，而英文的屬格則用 *'s* 來表示。因此有些人便誤以為可用 *'s* 來翻譯所有中文的「的」字，結果常將複合名詞誤當成屬格來使用。例如，他們會將 *a laser printer controller, a home entertainment center, an IBM personal computer* 誤寫成 *a laser printer's controller, a home's entertainment center, an IBM's personal computer*。但複合名詞的首語之前的名詞是修飾詞，而決非屬格。當要表達一家名為 Technocorp 的公司的商業合約時，應寫成 "the Technocorp contract"，而非 "the Technocorp's contract"。（相反，如果要提到某些屬於 Technocorp 的事物，則應使用屬格，如 "Technocorp's organizational structure"。）

同樣，「不使用名詞的屬格」這項規則也有例外，其中一個就是寫科技論文的人可能會遇到的 *user's guide*。縱然與規則有所抵觸，但這已經是一種約定俗成的標準說法。這種例外的情形，作者除了牢記，亦別無他法。

複合名詞就是由一個或以上的名詞修飾另外一個名詞。在英文中，如果可以用一個恰當的形容詞來修飾一個名詞，便不應用名詞來修飾。例如，作者應使用 *computational complexity* 來代替複合名詞 *computation complexity*，用 *industrial technology* 來代替 *industry technology*，或用 *Fast, precise operation is required* 這句來代替不自然的 *Fast and precision operation is required*。

練習 4-12 複合名詞

請修改下列含糊或錯誤的複合名詞。

1. In this paper we introduce a new actuator location selection method.

2. To achieve realistic modeling, we need to develop an object penetration avoidance method.

3. We will now discuss architecture implementation issues.

4. Next, we will find the service time for cycle k using the random numbers stream R_i.

5. Section 3 presents our feedback gain matrix computation method.

6. Existing network bandwidth assignment methods are not suitable for this case.

7. Mitchell [4] described an efficient distributed operating system file transfer technique.

8. The government has enacted new technology investment stimulation legislation.

9. The company has developed a new integrated circuit production machinery operator training program.

10. This document is a government research institute technology development guidance model proposal.

4.16 模糊的比較

　　當比較兩個項目時，一定要合理而完整，而項與項之間定要是可比較的。還有，必須把比較的項目陳述清楚，避免模稜兩可。下列「不合理」的例句，就是把兩個不同種類的項目做比較：

不合理：　The flexibility of joint 1 is greater than joint 2. 把關節的彈性與關節本身做比較。

合理：　　The flexibility of joint 1 is greater than *that of* joint 2.

合理：　　Joint 1 is more flexible than joint 2.

不合理：　The performance of our algorithm is better than the conventional algorithm. 把一個演算法的性能與另一個演算法做比較。

合理：　　The performance of our algorithm is better than *that of* the conventional algorithm.

合理：　　Our algorithm outperforms the conventional algorithm.

不完整的比較常出現於有字詞 *similar* 的句子中。以下的例句中，作者並沒有指出與論證做比較的是甚麼。

錯誤句：　To prove this, we can use *a similar argument as* in [5].

這句既不合理，又不正確，因為 *similar* 所接的介系詞應該是 *to*，而非 *as*。作者應這樣修改句子：

修正句：　To prove this, we can use *an argument similar to that* in [5].

在 *Sarah reads faster than her sister does* 這句中，*does* 是可省略的。因為 *Sarah reads faster than her sister*，既不影響句意，也不會造成歧義。但在某些例子中，省略助動詞、介系詞或其他字詞，句中的比較對象就會變得模糊。

模糊：　　Jeffrey likes Mary more than her husband. 這句的意思是：　Jeffrey 喜歡 Mary 多於他喜歡 Mary 的丈夫？ 還是 Jeffrey 喜歡 Mary 多於 Mary 的丈夫喜歡 Mary？

清楚：　　Jeffrey likes Mary more than *he likes* her husband.

清楚：　　Jeffrey likes Mary more than her husband *does*.

模糊：　　The optimum absorber damping is less sensitive to the damping level of the system than the optimum tuning frequency.

清楚：　　The optimum absorber damping is less sensitive to the damping level of the system than the optimum tuning frequency *is*.

模糊：　　The overall performance depends more on the bus speed than the memory access time.

清楚：　　The overall performance depends more on the bus speed than *it does on* the memory access time.

清楚：　　The overall performance depends more on the bus speed than *on* the memory access time.

練習 4-13 模糊的比較

請修正以下句中錯誤或模糊的比較對象。

1. The alignment problem is simpler in imperative languages than the functional language Alpha.

2. The cost function and alignment algorithm are also similar to [11].

3. The cost of the filter is about half of the approach in (Wason, 1990).

4. Compare the voltage drop between node 1 and node 2 and node 3 and node 2.

5. Lane developed an alternative approach with performance similar to (Long, 1992).

6. The accuracy of the new robot arm is greater than the conventional one.

7. Machine recognition of handwritten Chinese characters is more difficult than handwritten English letters.

8. This strategy yields a greater variance reduction than [3].

9. These results are consistent with Rogers et al. (1985).

10. Low-frequency noise is filtered out more effectively by the AGC than the limiter.

4.17 「主題與評論」句

　　在中文裏，作者為求強調句子的主題，經常會在句首的片語中開門見山地點出主題，而通常又會在這片語後，接著一個對該主題做評論或描述的子句。這種把主題放在句首的方式，稱為「主題化」 (topicalization)，有人稱這種句式為「主題與評論」句 (topic-comment pattern)。在「主題與評論」句中，句首所提到的主題時常會在其後「評論」子句中再次出現，且有時會以代名詞來指涉：

　　　　在自動化技術方面，近幾年已開發出多種新的技術。

　　　　至於第二種方法，最大的優點是這方法成本比較低。

雖然在英文裏，這樣的句子結構或可接受，但還是不夠自然簡潔。以下是把上面兩個中文句子，未經修飾而直接翻譯成英文：

　　不自然：　In regard to automation technology, in recent years many new technologies have been developed.

　　不自然：　As to the second method, the most important advantage is that the cost of this method is lower.

這些句子都沒有文法錯誤，可是卻嫌不夠通順。如果省略這兩句的引導片語，直接陳述重點，句子就醒目得多了。引導片語的意思通常可輕易地併入句子的主詞片語中，或改為動詞的受詞。例如：

　　修正句：　In recent years *many new types of automation technology* have been developed. [或： In recent years we have developed many new types of automation technology.]

修正句：　*The most important advantage of the second method* is that it has a much lower cost. [或："…it costs much less."]

　　以下的「不自然」句都是「主題與評論」句，而它們的結構明顯是直接從中文翻過來的英文，所以都應予以修改。但這兩句的結構實在太過不自然，根本不能清楚表達作者的真正意思。因此，這裏只好盡量猜測作者的意思而嘗試修改：

不自然：　*Regarding the overload condition of the destination gateway*, it is assumed to have a traffic intensity of greater than one.

修正句：　We assume that the destination gateway is overloaded whenever it has a traffic intensity of greater than one.

修正句：　The destination gateway is overloaded whenever it has a traffic intensity of greater than one.

修正句：　Overload of the destination gateway occurs whenever the traffic intensity of the gateway is greater than one.

不自然：　*Concerning rotor flux detection*, the indirect control method has been used because it offers the advantage of no flux sensor installation and ease of operation at low speeds compared with the direct vector control scheme.

修正句：　One effective method for detecting rotor flux is the indirect control method, which eliminates the need for flux sensors and is easier to use at low speeds than the direct vector control scheme.

　　撰寫英文科技研究報告時，中國的作者應格外留意以 *as for, as to, concerning, considering, for, in respect to, in the area of, regarding* 等這類字詞開首的句子，可能就是不通順的「主題與評論」句。刪除這種句子的引導片語，直接陳述重點，這樣的句子才鮮明易讀。

練習 4-14 「主題與評論」句

請修改以下的句子，刪除不必要的引導片語或字詞。

1. As for Smith [15], he gave a parametric solution for the eigenvalue assignment.

2. For SPS, it is an extensible operating system for creating system services.

3. Regarding Lee's algorithm, it can be divided into two parts for discussion.

4. In application aspects, many applications of fuzzy neural networks have been reported.

5. Concerning this problem, the following approach was adopted to solve it.

6. For each character image, it is identified as belonging to a set of m candidate characters.

7. Comparing the differences between Lee's approach and our approach, the main difference between them is that our method is much simpler to use.

8. As to the history of the institute, it has been in operation for twenty years.

9. For some I/O devices, software written for them can program the devices so that interrupts can be shared with other devices.

10. Regarding the effect of the Rayleigh number on the wall temperature of the inner cylinder, it is illustrated in Figure 4(a).

第五章
標點符號

　　標點符號是用來表示句子結構與意思的重要工具。中文的標點符號使用原則頗寬鬆，不像英文有很明確的使用規則。在英文中，儘管不同作家偶爾會對同一句有不同標點方式，但一般來說，凡受過訓練的英文作者對標點符號的正確用法，看法都相當一致。

　　本章將討論英文標點符號和數字的基本使用規則，並指出中國研究人員在撰寫英文科技論文時的常犯錯誤。讀者若想對英文標點符號的用法有更深入的認識，可參考一些其他的英文工具書，例如 *The Chicago Manual of Style* (University of Chicago Press) 及 *Webster's Standard American Style Manual* (Merriam-Webster)。此外，完備的英文字典也會有一個章節，特別討論標點符號的用法。

5.1 句尾標點符號

　　句尾標點符號表示英文句子的完結，包括句點、問號和感嘆號。在這三種標點符號中，常在科技論文出現的只有句點。

句點 (Period)

1. 用在直述句、祈使句或間接問句的句尾。

   The higher temperature resulted in a higher reaction rate.

   Increase the temperature.

   We investigated whether a higher temperature would increase the rate of the reaction.

2. 用於名字的縮寫字母或縮寫字的小寫字母後面。

    L.Y. Li   J. C. Smith   Dr.   Ms.   etc.   et al.

3. 大寫字母的縮寫字或政府機關名稱的縮寫，常會省略句點。

    PC   UN   GDP   CPU   CIA   GATT

    用於學位的縮寫。（注意：字母之間沒有空格。）

    Ph.D. M.S.   B.A.   M.D.

    亦可用於國家名稱的縮寫，但這些縮寫字的後面通常不須標點。

    USA 或 U.S.A.   UK 或 U.K.

4. 縮寫的測量單位後面通常沒有句點，但英語國家的傳統單位如英里、分、秒等字的縮寫後面卻會使用。

    20 cm   25 km   10 m   10 mi.   20 min.   12 sec.

5. 如果句尾是帶有句點的縮寫字，則不可以再標上句點。

    誤：   The name on the door was Sandra Jones, M.D..

    正：   The name on the door was Sandra Jones, M.D.

6. 用於大綱或垂直式一覽表的字母、羅馬數字或阿拉伯數字後面。

    Advantages:

     1. Low cost

     2. High speed

     3. Simple design

但不可以在這種目錄式標點中同時使用句點與括號。以下幾種標示方式都是錯誤的：

    Advantages: Advantages:

    (1.) Low cost   (1). Low cost

    (2.) High speed   (2). High speed

    (3.) Simple design   (3). Simple design

7. 句點總是置於引號內，即使它不是用以標示引號內的資料。這是標準的美式用法。而英式的用法是，只有當句點是用以標示引號內的資料時，句點才置於引號內。

    Chicago is called "the Windy City" and New York "the Big Apple." 美式

    Chicago is called 'the Windy City' and New York 'the Big Apple'. 英式

    His paper is entitled "Recent Developments in Parallel Processor Architecture." 美式

    His paper is entitled 'Recent Developments in Parallel Processor Architecture'. 英式

8. 一個置身括號內的獨立句子，其句點應標於括號裏。但若括號內的句子、子句或片語是屬於其前後句子的一部份，則必須省略括號內的句點。

The Siberian tiger still has a good chance of survival. (In contrast, the South China tiger may already be doomed.) Several strategies for saving this tiger have been adopted. 括號內是獨立句子。

The first of Hunt's articles was published in 1974 (the others were published soon afterward). Yamamoto's work, on the other hand, was not published until five years later. 括號內是首句的一部分。

9. 傳統的打字稿中，每句的句點後面都會留兩個空格（如果句點後面有一閉引號或閉括號的話，則會留兩個空格於此引號或括號後面），印刷資料中的句點後則只須留一個空格。現今多數作者在使用先進的文字處理設備或桌上型印刷設備時，句點後面都只留一個空格。

在縮寫字中，字與字間的句點之前後，不須留空格。

| i.e. | e.g. | a.m. | p.m. | Ph.D. |

傳統上，名字字首的句點後面須留一個空格。然而，許多作者在使用具有自動邊界線的文字處理軟體時，為了使名字的首兩個字皆能位於文章的同一行，因而省略了兩個字之間的空格（但名字和姓氏之間必須要有空格）。

正：　Mr. C. Y. Chang　　　　　J. P. Morgan

正：　Mr. C.Y. Chang　　　　　J.P. Morgan

劣：　Among those at the meeting was Mr. W.
　　　H. Wang, who is the company's sales manager.

佳：　Among those at the meeting was Mr. W. H. Wang,
　　　who is the company's sales manager.

10. 英文文章中，句尾的句點前面絕對不可以加空格。

問號 (Question Mark)

1. 用於直接疑問句的後面。

What is the purpose of this project?

When will the new product be released?

Are you the project leader?

直接問句常以疑問代名詞如 *what, when, who* 等字詞開首，並且常是動詞（或助動詞）在主詞前面的倒裝句。間接問句並不直接詢問問題，而是一種隱含或指涉問題的陳述。英文的間接問句並不會使用問號。

The purpose of the experiment was to determine whether the deposition rate could be increased by adding water to the solution.

Another important problem is how to improve the educational system.

正式的科技寫作中很少出現直接問句，反而常會使用間接問句。

直接問句：　The purpose of this research is to answer the following question: Does this equation have a unique solution? 不常見

間接問句：　The purpose of this research is to determine whether this equation has a unique solution. 常見

2. 當問號標示的只是引號內的資料而非整個句子時，問號應置於閉引號內。當所標示的是整個句子時，問號應置於閉引號之外。

The teacher asked, "Have you all done the homework?" 標示的是老師的問題。

Can you explain to me why New York is called "the Big Apple"? 標示的是整個句子。

3. 傳統的打字稿中，每句的問號後面都會留兩個空格（如果問號後面有閉引號，則兩個空格須加於此引號後面），印刷資料上的問號後面則只須留一個空格。與句號相同，現今多數作者在使用先進的文字處理設備或桌上型印刷設備時，句中的問號後面都只留一個空格。

感嘆號　(Exclamation Point)

1. 在感歎語詞或表示驚嘆的句子後面，會使用感嘆號。

Help!　　　Fire!　　　Follow me!　　　You can't be serious!

2. 感嘆號的使用規則和問號大致相同。在正式英文文章中，感嘆或驚嘆語氣詞句後面不能使用兩個或以上的感嘆號，即不要在句尾後面使用一連串的感嘆號。

誤：　He broke the record!!!

正：　He broke the record!

3. 正式的英文科技寫作中幾乎不會使用感嘆號。

5.2　句內標點符號

句內標點符號係用來表示句中各組成部分之間的關係，共有五種：逗點、分號、冒號、破折號和括號。

逗點　(Comma)

英文的逗點有特定的使用規則。標示逗點並非只為讀者在閱讀時提供一個停頓處而已，故不可任意在英文句子中標示逗點。

1. 可隔開對等連接詞 *and, but, or, nor, for, so* 或 *yet* 所連接的主要子句。

The samples were soaked for thirty minutes, and then they were washed with a chemical cleanser.

This is a challenging problem, but recent engineering breakthroughs have enabled us to solve it.

在包含三個或以上子句的句子中，可用逗點或分號來隔開子句。如果子句很短或子句內沒任何標點符號，則通常使用逗點來隔開幾個不同的子句；如果子句很長或子句內有標點符號，則通常使用分號來把句中的子句隔開。

> The economy is shrinking, the unemployment rate is up, and a major political shake-up seems likely.

> The economy is shrinking, with no prospects for growth in sight; unemployment is up, as foreign manufacturers close their doors and the largest domestic employers continue to lay off workers; and a major political shake-up seems likely, if only to placate the armed forces.

逗點通常不會用來隔開只有兩個述詞的複合述詞。（所謂複合述詞，是指一個句子中有兩個或以上的動詞，且它們都是對應同一個主詞。）例如，下列句子並不需要任何逗點：

> The samples were soaked for thirty minutes and then washed with a chemical cleanser. *The samples* 是 *were soaked* 和 *washed* 的主詞。

> We examined the device but failed to discover the source of the problem. *We* 是 *examined* 和 *failed* 的主詞。

如果複合述詞內的各部分都很長，某些作者會用逗點來隔開當中的述詞（即在連接詞 *and, but, or* 等前面加上逗點）。此外，有些作者如要強調兩個述詞間的轉折關係，亦會在連接詞 *but* 前面加逗點。

> We hoped to collect some interesting results, but did not expect to refute the theory.

2. 主要子句前面的附屬子句或片語後面，通常都會標示逗點。

> Before we present the new algorithm, let us first review recent developments in this field.

> To further understand the mechanism, we repeated the experiment using different initial conditions.

> In the second experiment, we used a different solvent.

當引介性的子句或片語很短，且在不影響句意的情況下，可省略逗點。

> In 1987 our second factory opened.

> After school he went home to face his father.

3. 逗點必須將句中的非限定修飾詞隔開，但千萬不要在限定修飾詞前後使用。限定修飾詞 (restrictive modifier) 是用來定義或限定它所修飾的詞句的意義，而它可以是子句、片語或字詞。限定修飾詞一經省略，句子的基本意思即會隨之而改變，因此不可省略。相反，非限定修飾詞 (nonrestrictive modifier) 的內容都只是補充作用的，因此就算省略亦無改句子基本意義。參閱下列句子：

> 限定的：　　No student *who has failed more than three courses* will be permitted to graduate.

非限定的：　　Dana, *who is a diligent student,* will graduate near the top of the class.

在第一個例句中，如果省略關係子句 *who has failed more than three courses*，即 *No student will be permitted to graduate*，則整個句意已全然不同。因此原句中的子句 *who has failed more than three courses* 是限定修飾詞（在此例中是限定的關係子句），故不使用逗點。在第二個例句中，如果省略子句 *who is a diligent student*，即 *Dana will graduate near the top of the class*，則句子的主要意思仍然不變。因此子句 *who is a diligent student* 是非限定關係子句，故需要以逗點隔開。除非非限定子句是位於句首或句尾，否則都需要兩個逗點一前一後的分隔開來。

　　同樣的規則亦適用於同位語 (appositive)：非限定同位語應以逗點把句子的其餘部分隔開，限定同位語則不需加逗點。（同位語是一名詞片語，它給予在它前面的名詞片語一個不同的名稱，例如句子 *John, my brother, is tall* 中的字詞 *my brother* 就是同位語。）非限定同位語是指省略而無改句意的同位語。

　　下面例句中的名詞片語 *the famous physicist* 是非限定同位語，因此以逗點將它與句子的其餘部分隔開。（省略 *the famous physicist* 並無改整句的基本意思。）

非限定的：　　Albert Einstein, the famous physicist, was never fully satisfied with the theory of quantum mechanics.

　　相反，下面例句中的名詞片語 *classical logic* 是限定同位語，因此不能以逗點隔開。（如省略 *classical logic*，整句會變得毫無意義。）

限定的：　　In this text the term *classical logic* refers to a logic in which there are only two truth values.

　　4. 如果在主要子句後面的附屬子句或片語的內容，是非限定而具補充作用的，則應使用逗點隔開；如果它的內容是限定的，則不用逗點。

We will accept this paper for publication if you make the following minor revisions. 限定的：省略 *if* 開首的子句會改變句意。

He is not in his office because he has a class at 1:30. 限定的

This is an excellent paper, although I don't completely agree with the conclusion. 非限定的：省略 *although* 開首的子句而句意不變。

He is not in his office, because his answering machine is on. 非限定的

第一和第二個例句中的附屬子句的內容是限定的。第一個例句的附屬子句是指出論文接受出版的必要條件，第二個例句的附屬子句則陳述了某人不在辦公室這事實的特定原因。第三和第四個例句中的附屬子句的內容是附加而非限定的。第三個例句的附屬子句是作者補充自己對主要子句的看法，第四個例句的附屬子句則提供支持主要子句為真的證據。簡而言之，限定的附屬子句是指它與主要子句關係密不可分，非限定的則不然。

　　片語 *as follows* 是一範例，它常以限定或非限定意義在科技論文中出現（片語 *as shown below* 亦同樣）。

By substituting this expression into equation (3), we obtain a concise formulation of the equations of motion, as follows. 非限定的

The initial conditions are as follows. 限定的

The solution can then be derived as follows. 限定的

第一個例句中，片語 *as follows* 是非限定的，它並非構成句子主要意思的必要部分，原則上可以省略。因此可加上逗點將 *as follows* 和句子的其餘部分隔開。相反，第二個例句中的 *as follows* 有限定意義，是句子主要意思的一部分，因此句中的 *as follows* 不能加上逗點。同樣，第三個例句中的 *as follows* 也有限定意義，因為它所引介的內容（即字詞 *as follows* 後面的方程式）正是獲得解答的方法。這裏作者的意思並非只是 "the solution can be derived"，而是 "the solution can be derived in the following way"。因此句中的 *as follows* 不能加上逗點。

5. 獨立片語和主要子句總是以逗點隔開。（有關獨立片語的說明，請參閱第一章1.8節。）

The lecture over, the students left the room.

The conviction having been overturned, the defendant was free to go.

6. 逗點可把插入語和句子的其餘部分隔開。插入語包括：轉接字詞或片語，例如 *moreover, in contrast, indeed, finally* 等；引導例句的字詞或片語，例如 *for example, e.g., that is, i.e., namely* 等；還有 *respectively*。

The second approach, on the other hand, is faster but far more costly.

This function has a constant value, namely, 1.

The recognition rates for the first and second algorithms were 92% and 97%, respectively.

Failure to control such a plant effectively could be disastrous; indeed, it could result in catastrophic loss of human life.

如插入語位於句子中間，必須用兩個逗點一前一後地分隔開來。

誤： In the high temperature trials, however there was a discrepancy between the predictions and the experimental results.

正： In the high temperature trials, however, there was a discrepancy between the predictions and the experimental results.

連接副詞 *hence, otherwise, then, therefore, thus* 的後面有時並不加逗點，尤其是副詞後面接著很短的子句時。

Failure to control such a plant effectively could be disastrous. Hence an accurate and reliable control algorithm is needed.

另外，像 *indeed* 或 *finally* 之類的字詞在用法上並非總是轉接詞，當這些字詞非作轉接之用時，則不須加逗點。

Our work was finally finished.

We predicted that conductivity could be improved by boron doping, and the experimental results show that this is indeed true.

7. 逗點可用來做分項，把包括三個或以上的對等字詞、片語或子句分成數項，而分項的形式有如 *a, b, and c* 或 *a, b, or c*。

Our method is faster, cheaper, and more accurate than the conventional method.

The new building will include a manufacturing plant, warehouse, and laboratory.

在 *a, b, and c* 或 *a, b, or c* 這種形式中，當中 *and* 之前的逗點稱為「系列逗點」(serial comma)。某些作者會省略系列逗點 (這是報紙或新聞雜誌的標準慣例)。但許多時，系列逗點都能幫助澄清句子意思，所以許多英文寫作指南，都會建議作者一致使用系列逗點。例如：

The new building will include a manufacturing plant, a laboratory with complete testing equipment and offices.

這句中沒系列逗點，閱讀時著實較困難。事實上，有些讀者首次閱讀這句子時，總難以看出辦公室究竟是實驗室的一部分，還是整個建築物的另一部分。但在使用系列逗點後，句子就清楚得多：

The new building will include a manufacturing plant, a laboratory with complete testing equipment, and offices.

為使行文清晰一致，這裏亦建議作者養成使用系列逗點的習慣。

8. 逗點可用來區分三個或以上的對等形容詞。對等形容詞是指對同一個名詞作個別修飾的幾個形容詞。

We have developed a *fast, inexpensive, accurate* method.

相反，累積形容詞則各自修飾隨後的字詞。例如，在下面句子中，*first* 修飾 *direct numerical method*，*direct* 則修飾 *numerical method*，而 *numerical* 修飾 *method*。

Ours is the *first direct numerical* method to be introduced.

在要決定形容詞是對等形容詞或累積形容詞時，可看是否能將 *and* 插入這些形容詞之間。例如，在首個例句中，如果用 *and* 取代逗點，則所得句子仍然合理，所以是對等形容詞；在第二個例句中，如果將 *and* 插入形容詞之間，則句子會變得沒有意義，所以是累積形容詞。

9. 逗點可用來隔開直接引言和指示說話者的片語或子句。

"You will find this course challenging," said Professor Zane.

Professor Zane said, "You will find this course challenging."

但當句中的引言是句意的一部分時，引言的前後不須加任何逗點：

"Novel and thorough" was the reviewer's response to Jack's paper.

當所引述的片語或句子有限定意義時，不須以逗點作分隔。如前所述，限定片語一經省略，句意會隨即改變，故是不可省略的。下面第一個例句中的引述字詞具有限定片語功能；第二個例句中的引述字詞則為非限定片語。

> Enclosed is a paper entitled "Regeneration of Forelimbs in Amphibians."

> Did you read the paper I published last spring, "Genetic Algorithms and Machine Learning"?

間接敘述句不須使用逗點。

> He told me that the class had just started.

10. 逗點可用來引介直接問句。即使問句前後沒有加上引號，或問句的第一個字非大寫，也需要使用逗點。

> The question is, How do we improve the system?

11. 逗點可用來劃分句子中的對比語辭。

> They invited Professor Wang, not Professor Lin.

> This interesting, though unpersuasive, argument ought to be developed further.

> We expect the yield to increase, but only by about 10%.

但當以 *but* 或 *or* 連接兩個形容詞而它們都共同修飾一個名詞時，*but* 或 *or* 前面不需要加逗點。

> These interesting but incomplete results should be supplemented by further research.

12. 當對稱子句之間存在對照或比較關係，兩個子句間必須以逗點隔開（除非子句非常短）。

> The greater the amount of water added to the solution, the slower the reaction rate becomes.

13. 當一前一後的兩個字詞可以有兩種解讀時，逗點可用以避免誤解。

> To Jane, Frederick was the brother she had never had. 如果省略逗點，讀者可能會將 "Jane Frederick" 誤解為一個人的名字。

在只有兩個項目的一覽表中，首個項後面通常不用逗點。

> There are two types of three-terminal semiconductor devices: bipolar junction transistors and field-effect transistors.

在必須防止誤解的情況下，可加逗點。例如，下述句子如果省略字詞 *clauses* 後面的逗點，則可能會使句意不清。

> Rambling sentences may be divided into two types: excessively complex sentences with many subordinate clauses and independent clauses, and sentences formed of a long string of simple independent clauses joined together by coordinating conjunctions.

14. 如果日期是以月、日、年的順序書寫，則須在日與年之間加逗點。如果句子中使用這種記載形式的日期，則通常在年的後面也會加逗點。

> January 3, 1990

> They were married on October 12, 1983, and left for their honeymoon the next day.

如果只標示月、年，則月與年之間及年的後面都不用逗點。

> He was hired in August 1987 and was promoted less than a year later.

如果日期書寫形式是日、月、年，則不用逗點。

> 4 July 1776

15. 可用逗點來隔開名字與頭銜。

> The guest lecturer will be Robert Jones, Ph.D.

> Robert Jones, Ph.D., will join the faculty in September.

16. 可用逗點來隔開地址的內容或地理名詞。

> Their address is 125 Elm Street, Waltham, Massachusetts.

> He visited his sister in Osaka, Japan, for three weeks.

但書寫信封格式的地址，每行的結尾處皆不用逗點。

> Professor J. C. Chang
> Department of Physics
> City University
> 555 Main Street
> Metropolis, NY
> U.S.A.

17. 在大數目中使用逗點以顯示千位數。

> 125,000　　42,500　　　1,375　　　　1,235,983

然而，在表示年份的數字中不應該用逗點來顯示。

> Cynthia joined the department in 1993.

18. 逗點後面都要留一個空格（表示千位數的逗點例外）。此外，在逗點前面千萬不要留空格。

分號 (Semicolon)

1. 分號用於隔開關係密切但沒有對等連接詞（*and, but, or, nor, for, so, yet* 等）相連的主要子句。利用分號暗示兩個獨立子句之間的緊密關係，可令句子較為簡潔。如以下的句子中，句子的前後部分都有一種因果或對比的關係。（但如果這些子句中前後沒有密切的關係，則應使用句點而非分號。）

> Today is Tuesday; I don't think we can complete the project by Thursday.

Some of these methods scan the rows from top to bottom; others scan from right to left.

作者也可偶爾不用逗點而使用分號，以隔開以對等連接詞連接的長獨立子句。

He criticizes many aspects of civilization and scorns the scheming and striving of the members of the elite class; yet his ideal of leading mankind back to a more primitive state of existence is itself the conscious scheme of a member of the elite.

2. 分號可用來隔開由連接副詞連接的主要子句。連接副詞包括 *consequently, for example, furthermore, however, in contrast, indeed, moreover, nevertheless, on the other hand, otherwise* 等字詞。（第一章有更詳細的連接副詞表。）連接副詞通常必須以逗點和句子的其餘部分隔開。

Plastic film capacitors are generally more reliable and smaller than paper capacitors; however, they are also more expensive.

要隔開連接副詞和對等連接詞、附屬連接詞等相關字詞相當容易。連接副詞的不同，在於它可放在子句中不同的位置，而不會改變子句的意義。以下三個例句都是正確的英文（雖然許多作者會認為第二個例句不太自然）：

Plastic film capacitors are generally smaller and more reliable than paper capacitors; however, they are also more expensive.

Plastic film capacitors are generally smaller and more reliable than paper capacitors; they are also, however, more expensive.

Plastic film capacitors are generally smaller and more reliable than paper capacitors; they are also more expensive, however.

3. 一連串的項目中，個別項目本身有內在標點符號時，應用分號來隔開這些項目。

At the meeting were John Smith, the general manager; Michael Thompson, from the Sales Division; Peter Watson, a production engineer; and Robert Black, the project leader.

分號使讀者能較易認清序列項目中的個別項目。如果以逗點取代上述例句中的分號，則讀者閱讀時會出現困難，甚至可能根本不知道作者所提到的是四個人還是六個人。

4. 分號的後面必須留一個空格，前面則不應該留。

冒號 (Colon)

1. 當一些子句、片語、字詞組或單字詞都是說明、闡述、強調或重述主要子句的意思時，可用冒號來隔開它們與主要子句。

In this lecture we shall discuss the most complex parallel processor in existence: the human brain.

The personal computer is a truly versatile device: it can be used to design an automobile, to write a great novel, to compose a symphony, to send messages around the world, and to play solitaire when one can't think of anything else to do.

2. 可以在 *as follows* 或 *the following* 後面加上冒號，以引介連串的數個項目。

Commonly used capacitors include the following: paper capacitors, plastic film capacitors, mica capacitors, ceramic capacitors, and electrolytic capacitors.

冒號前面應為完整句子，故這些例句都不應使用冒號。

誤：In this chapter, we will describe several common types of capaci-tors, such as: paper capacitors, plastic film capacitors, mica capacitors, ceramic capacitors, and electrolytic capacitors.

誤：In this chapter, we will describe several common types of capaci-tors, including: paper capacitors, plastic film capacitors, mica capacitors, ceramic capacitors, and electrolytic capacitors.

修改上述兩句有三種方法：第一，省略冒號；第二，省略 *such as, including*；第三，於 *such as, including* 後面加上字詞 *the following*。

正：In this chapter, we will describe several common types of capaci-tors, such as paper capacitors, plastic film capacitors, mica capacitors, ceramic capacitors, and electrolytic capacitors.

正：In this chapter, we will describe several common types of capaci-tors: paper capacitors, plastic film capacitors, mica capacitors, ceramic capacitors, and electrolytic capacitors.

正：In this chapter, we will describe several common types of capaci-tors, including the following: paper capacitors, plastic film capacitors, mica capacitors, ceramic capacitors, and electrolytic capacitors.

3. 冒號可用來把方程式或例子隔開，但冒號前面必須是完整句子。

We now obtain the following equation:

$$x = y + z.$$

4. 要指稱書名時，就算該書封面上的書名沒有冒號，引述時亦可加上冒號來隔開書名的主標題與次標題。

Her newest book is *What Machines Can't Understand: A Critique of Artificial Intelligence.*

5. 商務信件的提稱語後面應使用冒號。

Professor Gregory: Dear Ms. Wilson:

6. 傳統打字稿中，冒號後面要留兩個空格，排板稿件則留一個。如同句號和問號的用法一樣，許多作者在使用先進的文字處理設備或桌上型印刷設備時，只會在冒號後面留一個空格。此外，冒號的前面和在數學比例中所使用的冒號後面（例如：3:5），也絕對不可以留空格。

破折號 (Dash)

英文的破折號有兩種：長破折號與短破折號。長破折號的作用是把插入的字詞、說明、例子或其他字句，從句子的主要意思中劃分出來。（長破折號在英語中稱為 "em dash"，因為它的長度和小寫字母 "m" 相同。）括號亦有這樣的功能，但破折號則更強調劃分出來的插入字句。此外，逗點也可用以劃分諸如非限定子句的插入字句，但卻只用於劃分和句子主旨非常密切的插入字句。

如插入字句是在句子的中間，則必須使用兩個破折號，一前一後地把字句隔開來；如插入的字句在句末，則只需在字句前面加上一個破折號。

短破折號通常只會被置於兩個數字之間，用以表示「至」的意思。（短破折號在英語中稱為 "en dash"，因為它的長度和小寫字母 "n" 相同。）

破折號與連字號 (hyphen) 是不同的。長破折號是較長的橫線 ("—")，短破折號是較短的橫線 ("–")，而連字號是最短的 ("-")。破折號是無法在標準英文鍵盤上找到的特殊記號。一般文字處理設備都有特殊的長短破折號符號，作者可參看附於軟體的說明，學習輸入這些符號。例如，使用者可以設定微軟公司的 Word™ 軟件，自動將連字號格式化，造出短破折號及長破折號。如果所使用的文字處理軟體沒有破折號，則可用兩個中間及兩邊皆沒有空格的連字號 ("--") 代替長破折號，以連字號 ("-") 代替短破折號。

1. 長破折號用於表示句子結構的突然轉變或中斷。

   Our new microprocessor—as well as several other exciting products—is scheduled to be introduced in March.

2. 長破折號可用來劃分非限定同位語或需要強調的插入字句。

   Tantalum capacitors—a commonly used type of electrolytic capacitor—are known for their large capacitance value.

3. 短破折號是用來表示「至」的意思。

   The data are presented on pp. 22–26 of the paper.

   Few people know that Isaac Newton (1642–1727) wrote more about alchemy and astrology than he did about physics.

括號 (Parentheses)

1. 括號可括著句子中非必要的資料、說明或評論。

   Theorem 1 leads directly to the equation shown below (the details of the derivation are given in the Appendix).

2. 括號可括著標示項目的數字或字母，使數字或字母更見清晰。

   Installing the modem involves three simple steps: (1) selecting a communication port setting; (2) installing the modem in an expansion slot on the host computer; and (3) connecting the telephone line to the line jack on the back of the modem.

左右括號應同時使用，而不能單使用右括號。

3. 括號與被括著的資料或其後的標點符號之間不能有空格。如果括號在句子中間，開括號（即左括號）前面必須留一個空格；如果閉括號（即右括號）後面沒有標點符號，則其後也須留一個空格。下面例句中，開括號前面沒留一個空格，是錯誤的用法：

> 誤： Do not use parentheses like this(there should be a space before the left parenthesis).

開括號後面不能有空格；閉括號前面亦不能有空格。例如：

> 誤： This is an example of incorrect usage (do not leave a space between parentheses and the words inside them).

> 正： This example (of how to use parentheses) is correct.

4. 在某些編輯格式中，括號可用來援引參考作品或參考頁碼：

> Russell (1985, p. 32) described the structure of several types of neural networks.

> Several authors (Russell 1985, Henson 1987, Hardwick 1988) have studied the application of neural networks to traffic control.

不同的專業期刊使用不同的引文格式，但所有的期刊都會定期印發論文格式的詳細指導規章，以供作者投稿之用。因此，想知道該使用何種格式的參考引文，可參閱期刊規章。

引號 (Quotation Marks)

在美式文章中，雙引號 ("…") 用於標示引言。（英式文章則通常使用單引號 ('…') ）。

1. 如要在一個句子中加上引言，除了必須使用引號作引述之外，通常亦要在開引號之前加一個逗點。但如果引言很短或引言之前的文字和引言的內容密切相關的話，則常會省略此逗點。

> The professor said, "She is one of the finest students I have had in fifteen years of teaching."

> I shouted "Stop, thief!" and began to run after the man.

> Jane's professor said that she was "one of the finest students ever to graduate from this university."

2. 引號可用於引述文章標題或較長著作內各文章的標題（即它們並非獨立的書或著作）。同時，在演講稿、詩詞、短篇故事、書中章節、歌曲、收音機和電視節目中，亦可用引號以括著當中的標題。

> His paper was entitled "An Analysis of Chordal Graphs."

> Richard's recently published article, "Water: The Twenty-First Century's Most Important Liquid," has received much attention in the media.

3. 要劃分開啟式引言與句子的其他部分，可加上逗點；但如果引言是以問號或感嘆號結束，則會省略逗點。

> "That's all for today," the doctor said.

> "Is that all?" asked the patient.

4. 在美式文章中，逗點和句點應在引號以內，分號和冒號則應在引號之外。除非問號和感歎號是引言的一部分，才置於引號內，否則會置於引號外。(英式的逗點和句點，除非是引言的一部分，才會放在引號內，否則應放在引號外。)

> The doctor said, "That's all for today."

> The patient asked, "Is that all?"

> What is "fool's gold"?

但上述規則有一例外：當一個字詞在句中的功能，非用以表達一個意思，而只作為一個字詞來討論。這種情形主要在語言學、邏輯學和哲學中出現。在這種情況中，應該使用單引號，而且句點或逗點應置於閉引號後。例如：

> There are five letters in the name 'Tully'.

> I know how to spell 'potato'.

以上兩例中的引用字詞皆非字義上的使用，而是純當作字詞來使用。第一個例句中，引號內的字詞並非指叫 Tully 的那個人，而是指 *Tully* 這個字詞（叫 Tully 的那個人並非由五個字母構成，但字詞 *Tully* 本身就是）。同樣，第二個例句中，引號內的字詞 *potato* 並非指一個馬鈴薯，而是指 *potato* 這個字詞。在這句中，說話者說他知道如何拼出 *potato* 這個字詞，而不是如何拼出馬鈴薯這個植物。

上述例句中的引號亦可省略，而把字體改以斜體字表示：

> There are five letters in the name *Tully*.

> I know how to spell *potato*.

應用斜體字是一種較簡單的方式，及可避免句點應置於引號內還是引號外的疑問。（參閱本章5.3節「斜體字」的規則 2。）但使用斜體字時，應注意不可同時使用引號：

> 誤：There are five letters in the name "*Tully*."

5. 引言內的引言應該用單引號來引述。

> John said, "I know why New York is called 'the Big Apple.'"

方括號　(Brackets)

1. 方括號 "[...]" 可用來括著評論、校正或其他附加資料，尤其是插入引言的補充資料。

> The Senator said, "I fully supported his [President Obama's] health care plan."

這段文字中，上下文可能都沒有清楚表明代名詞 "his" 是誰，而作者插入字詞 "President Obama's" 就可避免可能的誤解。

> In his statement to the press, the Senator claimed that his own "many years of effort" had "establish[ed] a blueprint for this program. "

在這例句中，作者利用方括號去標明自己更改了引言中動詞的時態。原來引言的動詞 *establish* 可能是 *establishing*，或是 *establishes*，它們都跟文章句子的時態不配合。作者遂加上 "[ed]" 把引言的時態改成過去式，從而使引言能跟正在撰寫的句子文法一致。

作者要自行改變引言的一些字詞的時態或大小寫，以配合行文的文法。只要沒有破壞引言的原意，這種做法是沒有問題的，但必須加以註明。這時便應使用方括號來表示。

2. 在數學方程式或化學公式中，方括號和括號合用，可顯示出複雜的內含關係：

$32y+5x[(3x+2y)(2y+3x)]$

3. 在某些編輯格式中，方括號用於引用參考資料。下列句子中，方括號內的數字，是指於論文結尾的參考資料中，第四和第五項論文或書籍。

> For examples of this type of neural network, see [4] and [5].

不同專業期刊使用不同的引文格式，想知道該使用何種格式，可參閱各期刊的規章。

省略號 (Ellipsis Points)

1. 省略號是由三個句點 (...) 組成的，用來表示省略的資料。在學術著作中，如果要引用某段文字，並省略原文的部分文字，則必須插入省略號以表示省略部分。如果要省略的部分在句尾，應使用四個句點，一個表示句子結束，另外三個則表示省略部分。如果句尾的省略號接著加上括號的頁碼，則應在頁碼前置入省略號，並且將句子的句點置於閉括號後面。

> Wind power is nonpolluting...and in principle it is fairly easy to turn wind into electricity. The problem, however, lies in producing electricity from wind at a price competitive with that of electricity produced by burning fossil fuels.... This is a problem the wind power industry has yet to fully overcome... (p. 120).

省略號必定是由三個句點組成，其他所有的標示方法都是錯誤的。

2. 省略號可用於方程式或數學式中，代表沒有列出的項目。

T_i, where $i = 1, 2, 3, ..., n$

$A_V = V_{on} / V_{i1} = A_{v1} * A_{v2} * A_{v3} * \cdots * A_{vn}$

$var(x_1) = var(x_2) = \cdots = var(x_n)$

如以上首例所示，省略號通常是在本文字行行底，即與句點或逗點同等的位置。然而，當省略號的前後接有像加號（"+"）或等號（"="）等數學符號時，如以上第二和第三個例子所示，則常會將省略號提高至和前後符號同等的位置。

同時，省略號的前後，必須是對等的標點或數學符號：

正：　$x_3, \ldots, x_n$

誤：　$x_3, \ldots \quad x_n$

誤：　$x_3 \ldots, x_n$

即使是用以省略一系列項目，省略號亦必須為三個句點，切勿使用少於或多於三個句點。

誤：　$T_i,$ where $i = 1, 2, 3,.., n$

誤：　$T_i,$ where $i = 1, 2, 3,\ldots\ldots\ldots, n$

5.3 大寫字母、斜體字及字詞的標點符號

在英文中，大寫字母、斜體字、粗體字、屬格符號和連字號，都用於顯示句中字詞的特殊用法或功能。本節將介紹大寫字母、斜體字、粗體字及字詞標點符號的標準用法和規則。

大寫字母 (Capitalization)

字詞大寫，即一字詞的首個字母是大寫字母 (capital or uppercase letter)，而其他字母則仍用小寫字母 (small or lowercase letters)。

1. 舉凡句子、直接引言（甚至它在句法上不是另一個句子）或括號或方括號內的完整句子，首個字詞都必須大寫：

> We shall argue that the received view is mistaken.

> To each of the reporters' questions, the police spokesman replied, "We have no comment on that at this time."

> The reaction rate increased when the temperature was increased, but it decreased when water was added to the solution. (See Figure 2.)

句子中的直接問句，首個字詞都應大寫。

> The question we now need to consider is, How can this process be made more efficient?

2. 如果接於冒號後的獨立子句，不僅強調或闡明冒號前面的子句，還陳述新信息的話，則有些作者會將此獨立子句的首字大寫。

> Our first reason for rejecting instrumentalism is simple: The arguments its proponents advance in support of their position are invalid.

但若冒號後面的獨立子句只是重述或說明前面的子句，則不必大寫。

Competitors' products have become popular because of their low price and high quality: they offer quality comparable to that of our product at only half its price.

3. 專有名詞必須大寫，如人名、族名、國家名、語言名稱和地名。以下是某些專有名詞的通用寫法：

專有名詞的通用寫法		
Nelson Mandela	Michael Jordan	John Lennon
Chinese	African	Turkish
Israeli	Thai	French
Cantonese	Beijing	Hong Kong
Okinawa	Kuala Lumpur	Shanghai

以顏色來命名的名稱通常不用大寫，例如用以指稱黑人的 "blacks" 或白種人的 "whites"。

The survey found that the majority of both blacks and whites support the policy.

組織、歷史事件、時代及歷史條約的名稱皆必須大寫。

the Treasury Department	the United Nations
the Civil War	World War I
the Magna Charta	the Treaty of Versailles

周日、月份及假日必須大寫。

Monday	July	Thanksgiving	Mother's Day

書本、戲劇、影片、電視節目、雜誌、報紙、文章標題，以及所有的版權、商標名稱或產品，全部必須大寫。同時，出現於刊物標題冒號後面的首個字詞也要大寫。這些標題及名稱中，除了冠詞、連接詞、不定詞 *to* 和少於五個字母的介系詞以外，其餘字詞及首個字詞都必須大寫。

The Lord of the Rings	*Heart of Darkness*	*Newsweek*
Death of a Salesman	*The New York Times*	*Kleenex*

人名前面的職銜、人名後面的學位縮寫和專業名銜也應為大寫。

President Clinton	Dr. John Fitzpatrick	Professor Chen
W. H. Wang, Ph.D.	Vice President Chang	Ronald Blake, M.D.

接在人名後面的公司、學院或政府的職銜，則不可以大寫。

C. F. Chen, professor of physics	F.L. Lin, director of finance
R. J. Smith, general manager	Edward Kennedy, senator from Massachusetts

如 *road, street, avenue, park, island, river, lake, ocean, sea* 等此類字詞，本來是普通名詞，但如果把它們加於專有名詞後面而變成專有名詞時，必須大寫。

the Amazon River	Franklin Street	Harvard University
the Indian Ocean	the Pearl River	Oak Island
Elm Lake	Central Park	Marston Road

然而，當普通名詞為複數時，便不應大寫：

He has sailed solo across the Atlantic and Pacific oceans.

The patrolmen were assigned to cruise up and down Maple and Elm streets.

4. 科學定律與原理的專有名詞和地質學時期的術語，必須大寫，但接於其後的普通名詞則不用。此外，化學元素與化合物的名稱不須大寫。

Ohm's law	Newton's laws	the Ricatti equation
the Jurassic era	carbon dioxide	sodium phosphate

5. 撰寫書或論文時，如果要指出書中或文章中的通用標題（例如序言 (preface)、導論 (introduction) 或附錄 (appendix)），必須大寫。

A proof of the theorem is given in the Appendix.

This problem was mentioned in the Introduction. *Introduction* 是指該論文的導論，故為大寫

Baker states the central aim of his research in the introduction of his book. *introduction* 非指該論文的導論而是指另一本書中的導論，故為小寫。

6. 字詞 *chapter, section* 是用來指稱書或論文中的章節，這些字詞應否用大寫並沒一致的通則。許多作者會將它們視為專有名詞，自然使用大寫；但亦有某些著名的格式指導手冊則建議不應大寫。

The experimental procedure is described in Section 3.

Relevant work in the literature is discussed in section 2.

7. 圖形、表格及方程式的名稱通常為大寫，但某些作者喜用小寫來表示。要瞭解是否須要大寫，可參閱各特定期刊的格式規章。

The results of the experiments are shown in Figure 3 and Table 1.

The relationship between the two parameters is plotted in figure 6.

The solution can be derived from Equation (9).

This term is defined in equation (3).

8. 各羅盤方位（即東西南北）或季節的名稱不用大寫。

east	west	summer	winter

但當羅盤方位所指為地理區域時，則必須大寫。

She has lived in the South all her life.

Is this your first visit to the Far East?

He believes in using a Western management style.

9. 當普通名詞用以替代專有名詞時，不可大寫。

正：　　Michael is a student in the Mathematics Department at Princeton University.

誤：　　Michael is studying Mathematics in University.

正：　　Michael is studying mathematics in university.

誤：　　Our Company is one of the fastest-growing firms in the Asian Semiconductor Industry.

正：　　Our company is one of the fastest-growing firms in the Asian semiconductor industry.

10. 撰寫英文文章時，切勿任意使用大寫字母。將一個字詞或片語的所有字母大寫，是表示吶喊的意思。除了書寫頭字語、字首語、縮寫及某些特定語辭（如某些電腦程式語言的名稱）外，千萬不要把一個字詞的所有字母以大寫書寫。頭字語和字首語是由數個單字字首組成的縮寫字。頭字語 (acronym) 是數個字詞的縮寫，且能在拼音上組成單字，例如 *random access memory* 的縮寫是 *RAM*，可發單字 "ram" 的音。字首語 (initialism) 雖也是數個單字的縮寫，但發音是逐個縮寫字母地發，例如 *Graduate Record Examination* 的縮寫 *GRE*，應發三個字母 "G"、"R"、"E" 的音。

PC　　DOS　　CPU　　IBM　　BMW　　NATO　　ISDN

頭字語和字首語皆由數個字詞的縮寫組成，每個縮寫字母都各代表一個字詞，故全部應以大寫字母書寫。然而，請注意下列的書寫形式：

FAX　　MODEM　　SUN workstation

這些縮寫和名稱的大寫字母並沒代表任何字詞，所以都是錯誤的。正確的書寫形式應該是：

fax　　modem　　Sun workstation

在英文文件中，公司名稱應為大寫，但公司名稱的所有字母不應以大寫書寫：

誤：　Our firm, CHIPTECH, INC., has developed a new memory module.

正：　Our firm, Chiptech, Inc., has developed a new memory module.

11. 研究論文中，圖表字詞大寫的用法有各種不同的習慣。圖表標題的首個字詞和表格各記錄開端的首個字詞，都必須大寫。亦有某些刊物將圖表標題及表格中的每個字詞全都以大寫（介系詞、連接詞及冠詞除外）。圖表字詞的大寫用法，應參閱投稿期刊的規定。

斜體字 (Italics)

1. 書本、雜誌、學術期刊及其他刊物的標題，均必須為斜體字；但期刊或論文集的文章和書中章節的標題，則不應以斜體表示。

> *The Atlantic Monthly*　　　　　*The Wall Street Journal*
>
> *Romeo and Juliet*　　　　　　　*The Old Man and the Sea*
>
> *Proceedings of the Sixth*　　　　*The Journal of Mechanical*
> *　Conference on Neural Networks*　*　Engineering*

2. 指稱字詞、字母或數字時可使用斜體。

> The sixth letter in *government* is *n*.
>
> Some people think my *6s* look like *4s*.

3. 斜體字用於標示首次引介或界定的特殊語辭。已引介或界定過的語辭，則不需以斜體書寫。

> The *farad* is the basic unit used to measure capacitance. A farad is the amount of capacitance in a capacitor in which a charge of 1 coulomb produces a change of 1 volt in the potential difference between the capacitor's terminals.

4. 斜體字亦可用於表示非英語的外來字詞，如下例中的 *chun jie*（春節）和 *hong bao*（紅包）。

> During *chun jie*, Chinese children receive *hong bao* from their parents and relatives.

如果一個外來語（例如 *ad hoc*）已列於標準英文字典中，而且在字典中亦非以斜體表示，則不須使用斜體。

> The committee held an ad hoc meeting on Wednesday, September 5.

5. 拉丁文縮寫，例如 *cf., e.g., et al., etc., ibid., i.e.* 和 *op. cit.*，傳統上為斜體字。然而，現今多數作者和刊物在使用時，已不再以斜體字表示。

6. 斜體字有時用於強調一些字詞或片語。

> Applications must be received *on or before April 1*. No application received after that date will be considered.
>
> Julie said she *couldn't* come to the beach; she didn't say she didn't *want* to come.

切勿過度使用斜體字來強調字詞。事實上，某些編輯也許會認為上述例句亦可不需使用。在科技寫作中，真正需要使用斜體字的機會微乎其微。

7. 在專業科技期刊和書籍中，數學符號（向量除外）與數學公式經常會以斜體字表示。

粗體字 (Bold Print)

粗體字只適宜用於標題或小標題，而不適宜用於強調論文中的字詞。當真的需要強調某特殊的意思時，則可使用斜體字表示。

粗體字亦用於表示向量、矩陣等形式的數學符號。

屬格符號 (Apostrophe)

1. 單數名詞、專名、不定代名詞及字尾非 *s* 的複數名詞，它們的屬格都應使用屬格符號加上字母 *s* 來表示（最後一個字母為 *s* 的單數名詞也不例外）。

Alice's mirror	the men's club	everyone's opinion
Charles's paper	the dog's ball	Chris's bicycle

2. 複數且字尾為 *s* 的名詞，只需在 *s* 後加上屬格符號便為屬格。

the teachers' parking lot   the employees' welfare

3. 當句中提及的一個物件有兩個或以上的擁有者時，只有最後一個指涉擁有者的名詞才需為屬格。如句中出現的物件，都各有不同的擁有者，指涉擁有者的名詞都必須為屬格。

I read Bill and John's paper this morning. 文章是 Bill 和 John 共同寫的。

I read Bill's and John's papers this morning. 我讀了兩篇文章，分別是Bill 和 John 寫的。

4. 屬格符號可用來表示省略了的字母或數字。

does not	→	doesn't	1992 →	'92
it is	→	it's	I am →	I'm

年份的縮寫（如 "2003"）為 '03，而非 03'。此外，正確的日期縮寫（如 "December 30, 2003"）為 "12/30/03"（美式）或 "30/12/03"（英式），"12/30/'03" 是錯誤的。

5. 小寫字母要構成複數，可加上屬格符號。（這類字母亦常為斜體。）

x's and *y*'s   *p*'s and *q*'s   three *q*'s

大寫字母的複數形式亦可加上屬格符號，但有時會省略。

two A's   four Bs

加有標點的片語或複合名詞縮寫，可加上屬格符號以表示複數形式。

M.S.   →   M.S.'s   Ph.D.   →   Ph.D.'s.

沒加標點的片語、複合名詞或數字縮寫，通常不用屬格符號來表示複數形式。

two SRAMs	four ICs	two BIOSs	100 DRAMs
the 1980s	two XJ-100s		

不同的英文格式指導書在複數的屬格符號用法上有不同的規則。如果要將論文投遞到學術或專業期刊，還是應查閱該期刊的格式規章。

6. 如果科學定律、理論或數學方程式的名稱中包含人名，則只有在不使用定冠詞 *the* 時，才會使用 *'s* 的屬格形式。換言之，如果使用了定冠詞 *the*，則不使用屬格符號和 *s*。

誤：　the Ohm's law
正：　Ohm's law

誤：　the Ricatti's equation
正：　the Ricatti equation

誤：　the Einstein's theory of relativity
正：　Einstein's theory of relativity

斜線號 (Virgule)

1. 斜線號（有人稱為 *slash*，但 *virgule* 較正確）在測量單位中表示 *per* 或 *to* 的意思，有時也用來表示 *at*, *for* 或 *with* 等字詞的意思。

25 gm/100 cc　　a 30/70 split　　　　a price/performance tradeoff
U.C./Berkeley　fax/modem　　　　　Executive Assistant/Planning

2. 當有兩種選擇並列時，斜線號有時也可用來代表字詞 *and* 或 *or*。

boys/girls camp　　　　parent/guardian　　　　input/output

3. 斜線號有時用於表示 *and*。

The class of 1944/45　　the April/May order　　a camping/fishing trip

但許多時，以斜線號表示 *and* 或 *or* 常會導致文意曖昧不明。例如：

The functional departments/divisions will provide the resources needed to complete the project.

在這句中，斜線號使句意變得不明確。句子的意思是 "departments and divisions" 嗎？ 如果是的話，則作者應使用 *and* 而非斜線號。再者，這裏根本沒必要同時提及 departments 和 divisions。（"Division" 比 "department" 大，如果用 "division"，則讀者會瞭解一個 "division" 可能包括數個 "departments"。） 如果作者刪除其中一個，又或者用 *and* 或 *or* 取代斜線號，則句意會明晰得多。作者在撰文時，千萬不要任意使用斜線號作縮寫，因追求簡潔而犧牲了文意的清晰。

4. 某些縮寫是以斜線號作標點。

c/o　(care of)　　　　w/　(with)　　　　　w/o　(without)

5. 斜線號可用於標點日期和分數。

6/11/02　　　4/20/84　　　　1/2　　　3/4

（美式日期縮寫的順序是月、日、年，例如，"12/30/03"；但英國和歐陸國家的順序則是日、月、年，例如，"30/12/03"。）

連字號 (Hyphen)

連字號用於構成複合字詞，還可用來連接一個剛好介乎於兩行之間的字詞。連字號是條短橫線，是英文鍵盤上 '0' 字右方的鍵。連字號直接接在字母後面，不須留空格。連字號不同於底線符號：連字號位於字行的中間，底線符號則位於字行行底。同時，連字號亦與破折號不同（參閱上面5.2節），連字號 ("-") 都較長破折號 ("—") 和短破折號 ("–") 短。

1. 連字號可用來連結兩個或以上的形容詞，而變成複合形容詞去修飾名詞。但如果一個複合形容詞是接於動詞之後，而作述詞使用（即非直接置於所修飾名詞的前面），則通常不應使用連字號。

> One well-known method for solving this problem was proposed by Thompson [9].
>
> Thompson's method [9] is very well known.
>
> A 16-bit or 32-bit bus may be used.
>
> The bus width may be 16 bits or 32 bits.
>
> Our firm will introduce a new, high-technology model early next year.
>
> The New York-based firm plans to go public next year.
>
> We propose a neural-network-based system for controlling robot motions.

字尾是 *ly* 的副詞和其他字詞之間不應使用連字號。

> 誤：　a rapidly-growing market segment
>
> 正：　a rapidly growing market segment

2. 連字號會用來連結一些尚未成為單一字詞的複合字詞。（要知道複合字詞是否需要加上連字號，應翻查字典。）

> built-in　　　　　custom-designed　　　　　time-sharing　　　all-in-one

3. 使用連字號可避免產生含混不明的字母組合。例如，*recover* 的意思為重新獲得原有的力量（即「康復」），但 *re-cover* 則為再次覆蓋的意思。當懷疑一字詞是否需要用連字號時，應翻查字典。

4. 書寫英文數字二十一到九十九時，都需用到連字號。當使用分數去修飾名詞時，分數中的分母和分子亦應使用連字號連結；當分數不是用以修飾名詞時，分母和分子之間則不應加上連字號。

> twenty-three　　　　　　sixty-seven
>
> two thirds　　　　　　　one half
>
> one-half cup of milk　　　a two-thirds majority in the legislature
>
> two thirds of the water　　a six-inch silicon wafer

5. 連字號常和某些字首或字尾合用，例如 *self-, ex-* 和 *pre-*。

> This is a self-correcting system that learns from its mistakes.

連字號與分節法

當一個字詞書寫到一半卻已到了行尾時，另一半便需要於下一行繼續，該字詞會被分割成兩半。在英文中，字詞只能以音節來割斷，並必須在割斷的地方插入連字號。在這種情形下，連字號必須緊接在字詞前部分的後面，而不可置於下一行的開始。

現今多數文書處理軟體都有自動分音節和插入連字號的斷字功能。但如果真的要自行斷字，可參閱字典。英文字典裏，每個字詞中都會出現一些點子，這就是區分音節的標記（像 syl•la•ble, text•book, ob•ser•va•tion）。

斷字的方法，有兩個重要規則：

1. 不可分割只有一個音節的字詞。

   誤：　tir-ed, pho-ne, tra-in

   正：　tired, phone, train

2. 如一個字詞在斷字後，會令其中一行剩下一個字母，則切勿斷字。

   誤：　a-round, o-ver, cream-y

   正：　around, over, creamy

5.4 方程式的標點符號

撰寫科技論文的人常都關心一個問題：句中的數學方程式或公式後面，應否加入標點符號（如逗點或句點）？參考下例：

If V_{CC} and R_L are known, the load line equation may be written as

$$V_{CC} = I_C * R_L + V_{CE} \,.$$

句尾是方程式，因此在 "V_{CE}" 後加上句點似乎很合理。再看下例：

Under these assumptions, the load line equation may be written as

$$V_{CC} = I_C * R_L + V_{CE} \,,$$

where V_{CC} and R_L are known.

字詞 *where V_{CC} and R_L are known* 是一個非限定關係子句，用以修飾方程式，所以在文法上 "V_{CE}" 後應有一逗點。

在上述情況中，應否使用標點符號並沒明確規則。有些作者認為在方程式與公式後面使用標點符號，可有助釐清句子的文法結構，令文章更清晰易讀。在某些情況中，標點符號更可避免讀者誤解。不過，亦有作者則會省略方程式或公式後的標點符號。他們或許認為釐清句意並不需要標點符號，又或許他們認為在載有大量數學公式的文章中，使用標點符號會讓頁面過於擁擠，文章反而變得不夠清晰易讀。然而，使用標點符號似乎還是較合理的，因為方程式與公式確實是句子的一部分。不過，在決定使用前，亦應先查閱投稿期刊的格式指導規章。

　　如果數學方程式或公式與句子其餘部分沒有隔開，且在句子結構上有需要的情況下，則應使用標點符號。

5.5 數字

　　英文數字 (numbers) 和阿拉伯數字 (numerals) 的使用規則會隨著文字脈絡的不同而有所改變。如報紙的規則和出版社的便有所不同，而它們的規則亦跟科技期刊的不一樣。然而，除非投遞論文的期刊有特別的規定，否則科技論文作者都應遵循下述的使用規則。

　　1. 論文文章中，十以下的整數應寫成 one, two, three 般的文字。

　　誤：　We conducted 2 experiments, each with 5 trials.

　　正：　We conducted two experiments, each with five trials.

　　正：　The conference committee accepted 25 papers.

但在量度單位前面，應使用阿拉伯數字。如果量度單位是縮寫或符號形式，更必須使用阿拉伯數字。

　　誤：　The two samples were both eight cm long and each weighed about one kg.

　　正：　The two samples were both 8 cm long and each weighed about 1 kg.

如果在同一個句子或段落中出現兩個或以上可比較的數字，則數字的格式應當一致，而通常是以最大的數字的格式為準。

　　正：　In the first set of experiments, six of the eight trials were successful.

　　誤：　In the second set of experiments, eight of the 12 trials were successful.

　　正：　In the second set of experiments, 8 of the 12 trials were successful.

　　2. 以阿拉伯數字開首的句子是錯誤的。如果句子無可避免要以數字來開首，則數字必須以英文拼出，否則便應改寫句子。

　　誤：　32 engineers attended the meeting.

　　正：　Thirty-two engineers attended the meeting.

　　正：　There were 32 engineers at the meeting.

　　3. 阿拉伯數字可用於表示時間、錢數、測量值、小數和百分比。

| 10:30 a.m. | 3:15 | 75% 或 75 percent |
| $10.56 | 4 mm | 4.56　　3.1415 |

然而，"o'clock"，必須是 "ten o'clock"，不可以寫成 "10 o'clock"。

　　4. 十以下的序數切勿縮寫，十以上的序數則可以。

　　誤：　1st, 2nd, 3rd

　　正：　first, second, third

　　正：　15th, 21st, 52nd

5. 小於一的分數必須以字詞表示。

one-half kilogram of rice　　　　　　　　　one third of the passengers

6. 一百萬以上的數字應以阿拉伯數字與字詞合用：

The company sold 4 million cars last year.

Sales this year are expected to reach 6 million units.

7. 書中的章節與頁碼通常為阿拉伯數字。

See chapter 4.

This analysis is presented on page 9 in section 3.

8. 阿拉伯數字的後面可接著符號或縮寫。同時，阿拉伯數字和符號或縮寫之間必須留一個空格。

a 1 MB cache memory

6 MHz

Absolute zero is 0 K.

（例子 "0 K" 是 "zero kelvin" （開式溫度）的縮寫，開式溫度不會加上度 （""）的符號。）

9. 在小於一的分數中，小數點之前應加上一個 "0"。

0.5　（非 ".5"）　　　　　0.1　（非 ".1"）

10. 複合數字形容詞的首個數字應以字詞表示，第二個應為阿拉伯數字。

　　誤：　12 256K SRAMs

　　正：　twelve 256K SRAMs

11. 如已以英文拼出了數字，切勿再重複書寫阿拉伯數字，並加上括號。

　　誤：　We ran four (4) trials.

　　正：　We ran four trials.

　　例外：　On May 16, we sent you an order for six (6) buzzword eliminators.
　　　　　只有在某些法律或商業的文件中才會這樣。

12. 用阿拉伯數字來書寫日期時，切勿以縮寫的序數來表達。（雖然日期必然會唸成序數，但書寫上必須是基數形式。）

　　誤：　I suggest we meet on May 1st and begin operations on June 15th.

　　正：　I suggest we meet on May 1 and begin operations on June 15.

5.6 複數

　　大多數英文名詞的複數 (plurals)，都是由單數名詞加上 *s* 而成的。如果一個單數名詞的字尾為 *s, x, z, ch* 或 *sh*，要把它改為複數的話，則應加上 *es*，因為這些名詞需要一個額外的音節才能發音。如果一個名詞的字尾是 *y*，而 *y* 字的前面為子音，要把它改成複數，就要將 *y* 改為 *i* 再加上 *es* 。

　　不過，事實上也有不少英文名詞的複數，並不符合這些通則。所以當要撰寫一些特殊名詞時，要知道它們正確的複數形式，最好是翻查字典。假如一個名詞的複數是不規則的，字典定會列出；如果字典沒有列出，則此名詞的複數極可能是根據上述通則來構成。

　　以下列出許多於科技論文中常見的特殊複數形式。

　　1. 單一字詞的縮寫，常會加上句點。句點前面可以加上 *s*。（以下分別是 *figures, tables* 和 *sections* 的縮寫。）

fig.　→　figs.　　　　tab.　→　tabs.　　　　sec.　→　secs.

　　2. 帶標點的片語或複合語詞縮寫，可在最後一個句點後加上 ’*s*。片語或複合語詞縮寫而沒有標點的，則可直接在縮寫後加上 *s*。

M.S.　→　M.S.’s　　　　Ph.D.　→　Ph.D.’s

BIOS　→　BIOSs　　　　DRAM →　DRAMs

　　3. 只有一個小寫字母的縮寫而又非測量單位，可重複字母而構成複數。

pp.　(*pages*)　　　　　　cc.　(*copies*)

　　4. 一般測量單位的縮寫，其單複數形式相同。

100 cc　　　30 min.　　　75 m　　　10 cm　　　50 sec.

　　5. 外來語的複數形式，通常是與其外語中的複數形式一樣。但有時亦可寫成英文中的規則複數（即加上 *s* 或 *es*）。

phenomenon	→	phenomena
schema	→	schemata 或 schemas
formula	→	formulae 或 formulas
thesis	→	theses
datum	→	data
series	→	series
index	→	indices 或 indexes
appendix	→	appendices 或 appendixes

　　6. 英文字母的複數通常是加上 ’*s* 而成的。

a series of *x*’s and *y*’s　　　　　　　ten A’s and B’s in the matrix

　　7. 斜體字、片語及字母的複數形式，通常是在單數的字尾後，加上屬格符號和非斜體的 *s* 而成。

two *yes*'s and three *no*'s　　　　　　　a series of *x*'s and *y*'s

8. 雖然某些編輯會選用 's 來表示數字的複數形式，但亦可在單數形式的後面只加上 *s*。此外，英文數字字詞的複數形式，通常只會在字尾加上 *s*，而不加上屬格符號。

the 1990s　　　　　　　　　an order for ten XJ-100s
two 2s and three 3s　　　　　he threw two sevens in a row

9. 當只指涉一個字詞，而非使用該字詞以表示一個意思時，該字詞的複數形式，通常會於字尾接著非斜體的屬格符號和 *s*。

a string of clauses connected by *and*'s or *but*'s

replace all of these *&*'s with *and*'s

change the *you*'s to *we*'s

10. 一個名詞，受包含複數受詞的 *of* 片語修飾，可以是單數，也可以是複數。這要視乎句子想強調的意思而定。

The *price* of these components *has* been increasing.

The *prices* of these components *have* been increasing.

這兩句都是正確的，但第二句強調了那些零組件各有不同的價格。

以下兩個句子都是正確的：

Next, record the *value* of V_s, f, R, C, and V_o.

Next, record the *values* of V_s, f, R, C, and V_o.

第一句中，動詞的受詞可解釋為 "the value of V_s, that of f, that of R, etc."。第二句中，動詞的受詞則可闡釋為 "the values of all of these parameters: V_s, f, R, etc."。兩者的意思都很合理，亦皆為正確的句子。

以上兩例中，字詞 *value* 指一種參數值。如果取 *value* 較抽象之意，則使用單數形式會較自然。例如：

The *value* of houses in our city has been increasing.

11. 如果一個符號在用法上是作某個名詞的限定同位語，則不可同時以複數表示此名詞與符號。以下是一個怪句：

誤：　From this equation, we obtain the error signals δ's for the different
　　　cases.

作者應以下列其中一個句子取代：

正：　From this equation, we obtain the error signal δ for the different
　　　cases.

正：　From this equation, we obtain the value of the error signal δ for the
　　　different cases. 假如要強調有許多不同的案例，而這些案例各有不同
　　　數值，則 "value" 亦可改為複數 "values"。

正： From this equation, we obtain the value of δ for the different cases.

12. 當某個數字後面接有量度單位時，除非前面的數字剛好是一，否則此量度單位通常應以複數形式表示。

0.3 inches (非 0.3 inch)　　　　　　0.5 microns (非 0.5 micron)

0 wait states (非 0 wait state)　　　　0.8 degrees (非 0.8 degree)

量度單位只有在單獨使用時，才以複數形式表示。假如量度單位後面接有名詞，則不寫複數，並必須以連字號和前面的阿拉伯數字連結。

0.5 microns　　　　　a 0.5-micron manufacturing process

8 inches　　　　　　an 8-inch silicon wafer

13. 當 *the number of* 是用來表示 "how many" 的意思時，不可寫成複數。

誤： We wish to determine *the numbers of* airports needed to serve a large metropolitan area.

正： We wish to determine *the number of* airports needed to serve a large metropolitan area.

當 *the number of* 用來表示一個特定的數字時，則可寫成複數形式。

What are *the numbers of* those two basketball players? 那兩個籃球選手的運動衫上各有不同的號碼。

5.7 專業術語的縮寫

若要使用專業術語的縮寫形式，應在專業術語首次出現於論文時，寫出術語的全寫，並在後面加上縮寫和括號。在論文接下來的段落中，該科技術語即可用縮寫表示。

On the front panel of the terminal adapter is a three-inch liquid crystal display (LCD). The LCD is used to display menus, through which the user may adjust the configuration of the adapter. The LCD also displays messages concerning the status of the adapter during data communication.

Genetic algorithms (GAs) have attracted a great deal of interest in recent years. GAs are useful in a wide variety of applications. . . .

上述兩個段落的首句都分別對 "LCD" 和 "GA" 等縮寫定義清楚，讀者應已瞭解這些縮寫的意思，作者遂可放心在接下來的段落使用縮寫。

5.8 縮進排印

每個英文段落的首行，都應從左邊縮進排印，除了下列的例外：

一、方程式或引言，應整句或整段從左邊縮排。如果引言中只有一個段落的話，就算是段落的開始，仍不需再縮排。而如果引言中連續有兩個或以上的段落，則首段的首行不需要再縮排，而從第二個段落起，每段的首行皆需再縮排。

二、論文與章節的首段首行，某些作者和刊物會不縮排，副標題下的首段首行亦是如此。

5.9 使用標點符號之常犯錯誤

本節將敘述中國作者撰寫的英文科技論文中，使用標點符號時常犯的幾個錯誤。中英文的標點符號，用法上有許多差異。研讀本節，可能你會發現，某些習以為常的用法原來是錯誤的。

空格

在打字時，要注意字詞及標點符號空格是否正確。（正確的空格規則，已在各種標點符號的次小節中講述。）下列幾個要點尤其重要：

打字稿中，各英文字詞間只能有一個空格。逗點和句點之前絕對不可加上空格。逗點、分號、冒號和句點後面必須留一個空格。

右括號前面和左括號後面都不能有空格。

誤： (This, for example, is wrong.)

正： (This is correct.)

當然，左括號前面和右括號後面都應留一個空格，但若右括號後面接有逗點或句點，則括號與逗點或句點間不可留空格。

誤： Do not omit the space before a left parenthesis(like this) or the space after a right (like this)parenthesis.

在中文中，當作者要把資訊列於一覽表或表格時，都會習慣把各行的冒號對齊，排成一條垂直的線。

```
Name        :    Technocorp
Established  :    1987
Employees   :    400
Location     :    Taipei
```

但如把這做法搬到英文去，便會顯得非常奇怪。英文正確的排列方式，是直接把冒號加於第一欄的字詞後面。

```
Name:        Technocorp
Established:  1987
Employees:   400
Location:    Taipei
```

百分比符號前面不須加上空格。百分之五十二是 "52%"，而不是 "52 %"。

　　溫度符號前面不應留空格。攝氏四百度是 "400° C"，而非 "400 °C"。但溫度符號與字母 "C" 之間必須留一個空格。此外，絕對溫度的縮寫沒有溫度符號，絕對零度是 "0 K"，而非 "0° K"。

　　字詞和阿拉伯數字之間應留一個空格，正確的寫法是 "pin 1 and pin 2"，而非 "pin1 and pin2"。

　　在研究論文中，方程式號碼常與方程式列於同一行，且會寫於靠近右邊界的括號內。方程式和方程式號碼之間的空格應為空白，切勿在方程式和號碼之間置入虛線或一連串的連字號。

　　要投出去接受評審的論文，每行間應有兩行行距，同時四個邊界也不應太狹窄。

逗點

　　逗點可用來區分非限定子句或片語與句子的其餘部分。切勿在限定子句或片語的前後插入逗點（詳見5.2節中討論逗點的第三項）。限定子句或片語的作用在於限定名詞的意義，因此是無法省略的，否則會影響整句的語意。然而非限定子句即使是省略而仍不改句子主要子句的意思。

非限定的：　　The personal computer, *which became popular in the 1980s*, has revolutionized many types of work.

限定的：　　The personal computer *that I bought on Saturday* is much faster than my old one.

　　方程式後面常緊接著附屬子句（"where" 為開端的附屬子句最常見），以說明方程式中符號的意義。此種子句為單一子句，如果子句內只有兩個主詞和兩個動詞，則不應在第一個主、動詞和第二個主、動詞之間加入逗點。

誤：

The force can be calculated as follows:
$$F = ma,$$
where *m* represents mass, and *a* represents acceleration.

正：

The force can be calculated as follows:
$$F = ma,$$
where *m* represents mass and *a* represents acceleration.

只有在包含三個或以上的主詞及動詞的子句中，才使用逗點：

正：

This law can be expressed as follows:
$$F = ma,$$
where *F* represents force, *m* represents mass, and *a* represents acceleration.

（亦可縮短成："where *F* represents force, *m* mass, and *a* acceleration"。）

字詞 *respectively* 和拉丁文縮寫 *i.e.* 及 *e.g.*，必須用逗點將它們和句子的其餘部分分開。假如這類字詞出現在句子的中間，則必須在字詞的前後加上逗點。

The growth rate of samples A and B increased by 25% and 30%, respectively, when oxygen was added to the reaction mixture.

書寫英文時，切勿在主詞和動詞之間加逗點，除非是使用一對逗點以隔開插入的非限定片語。下列的錯誤句中，逗點正正把主詞 *hypotheses* 和動詞 *may be* 分開了：

誤： Hypotheses derived from other training instances or taken from other sources, may also be valid.

正： Hypotheses derived from other training instances or taken from other sources may also be valid.

當句首出現類似 *thus* 或 *therefore* 的字詞時，通常不須在這類字詞後面加逗點，尤其是短句。

We originally planned to go, but that morning it rained heavily. *Therefore* we decided to stay home.

Transistors are rated according to their ability to dissipate power. *Thus* a transistor used as a low-level audio amplifier may have a power rating that is quite low.

在諸如 *show that* 之類的表達形式中，千萬別在字詞 *that* 後加逗點：

誤： Michelson's work shows that, the theory is valid for this range of values.

正： Michelson's work shows that the theory is valid for this range of values.

當只提到兩個項目時，逗點不能用來表示 "and" 的意思。

誤： For cases 1, 2 we apply equation (12).

正： For cases 1 and 2 we apply equation (12).

誤： Substituting these values for x, y, we obtain the following solution.

正： Substituting these values for x and y, we obtain the following solution.

參考引文數字是例外，這類引文數字往往會置於方括號內，如 [2, 3]。

英文中沒有頓號（、）（在英文中，頓號稱做 *semicomma*）。當列出數個項目時，切勿以頓號取代逗點。

誤： The results for algorithms A、B and C are shown in Table 3.

正： The results for algorithms A, B, and C are shown in Table 3.

大寫字母的用法

　　請勿因覺得一些字詞重要，就任意將字詞大寫。專有名詞（或名稱）當然要大寫，但專有名詞相對於所有的名詞來說，是非常少的，故文章中不應有太多大寫字詞。

　　誤：　The new Local Bus design allows the Processor to access Memory faster.

　　正：　The new local bus design allows the processor to access memory faster.

　　只有頭字語和字首語才會將一個字詞的所有字母大寫，因為它們都是縮寫的形式，即每個字母都代表一個字詞。例如，"CPU" 是正確的，因為 "C" 代表 "central"，"P" 代表 "processing"，而 "U" 代表 "unit"。 "ROM" 也是正確的，因為 "R" 代表 "read"，"O" 代表 "only"，而 "M" 代表 "memory"。相反，雖然 *fax* 是 *facsimile* 的縮寫，但 "FAX" 是錯誤的，因為字母 "F, " "A" 和 "X" 各自不代表任何事物。同樣，"MODEM" 亦是錯誤的（"MODEM" 中的 "O" 代表甚麼？），故應寫成 "modem"。

　　除非公司或組織的名稱是縮寫，否則不要將名稱的所有字母大寫。Sun workstation 是一種高性能的電腦，不能寫成 SUN workstation。Ford 是一個有名的汽車製造廠商，也不能寫成 FORD。還有，"IBM" 和 "GM" 是正確的：第一個縮寫是代表 International Business Machines，第二個則是 General Motors。

　　在英文中，將字詞的所有字母大寫就像代表著吶喊，在論文中不能以此作強調之用。（信封上的國家名稱常全部大寫，是為了便於傳遞郵件。）

　　論文或書本標題中的冠詞、連接詞、用於不定動詞的 *to* 或者長度少於五個字母的介系詞，都不可以大寫。當上述字詞是標題中的第一個字或冒號後面的第一個字時，則應大寫。此外，標題中長度五個字母以上的介系詞也要大寫（例如，*About, Before, Between*）。

冒號

　　冒號前面應為完整句子。下例的用法很不自然：

　　誤：　The frequency can be expressed as:

句子應修正成：

　　正：　The frequency can be expressed as follows:

　　正：　The frequency can be expressed as　直接寫出方程式

下列句子都是正確的：

　　The dB attenuation is as follows: 使用冒號最恰當的用法

　　The dB attenuation is　直接接著數學方程式而不加冒號

The dB attenuation is: 根據某些編輯格式指南，如果接著的方程式和句子其他部分是分開的，或接著列出的項目很多，則在 *to be* 或 *to include* 等動詞後面加冒號，也算正確。

介紹方程式時，要使用完整句子。在下例中，字詞 *then* 並非完整句子：

When designing an attenuator, we already know R_1, R_2, and P_1/P_2. Then: [方程式]

如果改寫為以下的句子，則文章會更順暢好讀：

When designing an attenuator, we already know R_1, R_2, and P_1/P_2. Thus we have the following equation: [方程式]

When designing an attenuator, we already know R_1, R_2, and P_1/P_2. Thus we have: [方程式]

其他錯誤

一個句子只能標一個句點。就算句末的最後一個字詞是縮寫（例如 *etc.* 或 *et al.*），亦不應在縮寫後面多加一個句點。

誤：　He is going to school in the U.S..

正：　He is going to school in the U.S.

在正式的英文中，請勿以記號 "&" 取代字詞 *and*。在某些期刊的參考格式中有時會允許使用 "&"，但最好還是查閱投稿期刊的格式規章。

請勿使用 "～" 這符號來代表 *to* （「至」）這字，這絕非標準英文標點符號。需要代替 *to* 時，應使用短破折號（"–"）。短破折號比長破折號（"—"）稍短，但比連字號 ("-") 長。如果文書處理系統沒提供短破折號這符號，可嘗試使用減號或連字號，或直接把 *to* 拼寫出來。

誤：　the 1995～1996 school year

正：　the 1995–1996 school year

文章的標題（或任何非獨立刊物的標題）要放在引號內，書名或期刊的名稱（即獨立的刊物）則使用斜體字或底線。

Smith, John. 1989. "Recent Advances in Widget Design." *Widget News*, Vol. 5, No. 2, April 1989, pp. 21–36.

Smith, John. 1988. *Widget Design and Implementation*. New York: Widget Technology Research Institute.

不要把連字號放在副詞和其所修飾的字詞中間。

誤：　One *commonly-used* method is chemical vapor deposition.

正：　One *commonly used* method is chemical vapor deposition.

括號內的字詞結尾處，不能加上句點。除非括號內的字詞，是獨立於括號外的完整句子時，才可使用句點。

誤： We can use an ohmmeter (a digital meter used for diode testing.) to check these values.

正： We can use an ohmmeter (a digital meter used for diode testing) to check these values.

誤： To check these values we can use an ohmmeter (a digital meter used for diode testing.)

正： To check these values we can use an ohmmeter (a digital meter used for diode testing).

正： We can use an ohmmeter to check these values. (An ohmmeter is a digital meter used for diode testing.)

年份的縮寫，例如 1992，是 '92，而非 92'。

括了括號的補充字詞，應置於冒號前面，而不應放於冒號之後。

誤： The contents of this register are shown below: (for RGB mode and 24-bit YCbCr mode)

正： The contents of this register are shown below (for RGB mode and 24-bit YCbCr mode):

練習 5-1 標點符號

修正下列句中錯誤的標點符號。有些句子有多於一個錯誤，有些則完全沒有錯誤。如果句子的標點符號沒有錯誤，請說明理由。

1. Consider the circuit shown in Figure 10-1 where R_1 is in port 1 and R_2 is in port 2.

2. As just mentioned the input and output impedance of the attenuator should match those of the original circuit's.

3. The personal computer which became popular in the 1980s has had a far-reaching impact on the way research in this field is conducted.

4. Researchers who do not enjoy teaching should not become university professors.

5. Professor Thompson sitting in the second row raised his hand to ask a question.

6. The difference between their method and ours is, as follows.

7. Next, connect the current source as shown in Figure 8.

8. The market radius decreases as population density increases as shown in Figure 5.

9. The students sitting in the back could not hear the lecturer.

10. Sales revenue in the local computer industry has grown rapidly over the last three years as shown in Figure 4.

11. Consider the case in which t > 0.

12. Let a represent x, and b represent y.

13. An objects radar cross section (RCS)may depend more on it's shape than on it's physical size.. A small truck with its sharp edges, abrupt flat surfaces can reflect electromagnetic waves, better than a smooth edged Jumbo Jet. The RCS of a pickup truck (measured head-on at Microwave frequencies.) is about 200 square meters while that of a Jumbo Jet Airliner is only about 100.[1]

14. The last twenty years have seen major developments in clinical transplantation , particularly of such vital organs as the Heart、 liver & kidneys . However despite these apparent breakthroughs the success of tissue transplants remains dependent on first overwhelming and then chronically suppressing the patient's Immune System with a variety of drugs. The drug therapy currently in use , has many undesirable side effects(particularly in children), because it is based on nonselective cyclotoxic drugs, which indiscriminately kill all rapidly dividing cells.An encouraging development of the 1980s was the introduction of CYCLOSPORIN A, an immunosuppressant with more specific effects on the Immune System , that leave the patient with some resistance against infection. Nevertheless even this immunosuppressive drug , is not free from side effects, including damage to the Kidneys.[2]

第二篇
修辭原則

第六章
簡明的英文

本章及第七章皆旨在介紹英文基本的修辭原則。修辭原則與文法規則不同，原則是大體的，而非絕對的規條。不遵循這些原則，未必表示文章的英文不正確。但如要學好英文寫作，除了按照文法規則寫出正確的英文之外，還必須遵循一些修辭原則，表達才會自然暢達。

英文寫作一個很重要的原則是表達要簡明。這是說，文章應該精確具體，避免不必要的字詞。本章將介紹十個英文修辭原則，好讓寫論文的作者了解，怎樣表達才會更簡潔清晰。

中英文寫作有許多不同之處。許多作者書寫中文時，為求使句子結構較均稱、聲韻較和諧，字詞都寫一雙成對的，甚至有時寧犧牲文章的簡潔；資深的英文作家寫作時，一般則較直接簡潔。在中文文章中，作者時會假定讀者知道句子的主詞所指為何，因此會省略主詞；然而在英文文章中，每個句子定要有一個主詞。在中文裏，於文章的開首，或在支持重要的論點時，作者都喜用成語、俗語；相反，絕大多數好的英文文章中，都鮮有成語或俗語。本書不打算深入討論中英寫作原則異同，只希望中國的研究人員，特別注意這兩章所介紹的英文修辭原則，能避免用中文寫作或修辭方式去撰寫英文論文。

6.1 句意要精確具體

文章要寫得好，就必須學會把句子寫得精確具體，遣詞精準而簡煉。資深的作者都用字精煉，描述事物絕不模稜兩可。

撰寫科技論文必須表達得精確具體，但有些作者往往未能做到。例如，許多撰寫工程研究報告的人，就常濫用 *good* 和 *better* 這兩個形容詞。以下是兩個典型的例子：

Our method is *better* than Smith's method.

The proposed algorithm performs *better* than Chen's algorithm.

這兩句並沒有文法錯誤，但卻不夠精確具體。在第一個例句中，作者的方法如何比斯密夫的方法「更好」？到底是更快、更準確、更精密、更容易程式化、抑或是其他？此句傳達給讀者的具體內容實際上非常少。在第二個例句中，也有相同的問題：作者的演算法究竟如何比陳氏的演算法好？作者應具體直接地告訴讀者。

這兩句應怎樣修改呢？在這兩句中，作者必須指明評價方法或性能優劣的標準。例如：

Our method is *more accurate* than Smith's method and *nearly twice as fast*.

The proposed algorithm is *more efficient* than Chen's algorithm.

這兩句很明白地指出了作者的方法與演算法，為何比別的方法與演算法要來得好。

再看另一個例子。以下亦是一段很模糊的文章：

Kemp and Tate [4] proposed a method for transferring files between nodes of the network, but there are several points that their method does not consider. Therefore, in this paper we propose a new file transfer technique.

坎普和泰特忽略的 "several points" 是甚麼？他們的方法有何不足？作者應明確指出，自己要補足別人的方法的哪些缺點。

再看以下這個不精確的英文句子：

The present method is limited to treating binary patterns, but it can be extended to treat analog input vectors by applying the idea used in [8].

在這句中，參考文獻 [8] 運用的方法是甚麼？讀者沒有責任要記得參考文獻 [8] 的內容。而且，作者真正所指的是哪項方法，讀者也未必能確定。所以，作者應直接明確地告訴讀者：

The present method is limited to treating binary patterns, but it can be extended to treat analog input vectors by incorporating fuzzy logic techniques in a manner similar to that described in [8].

讀者現在便可清楚知道作者所討論的是哪種方法。如果讀者想回頭參閱參考文獻 [8]，還可很快找到該方法。

以下同是不夠精確的例子：

The choice of which calcium compound to use in wastewater processing is important. The amount of sludge produced may vary by a factor of 15 depending on whether calcium hydroxide or calcium chloride is used.

這段文章的作者到底認為在廢水處理中，應使用 calcium hydroxide 還是 calcium chloride？除非讀者非常熟悉這課題，否則根本無從猜測作者的意思。作者應說明清楚，這兩種混合物中哪個較有效減少污泥數量：

> The choice of which calcium compound to use in wastewater processing is important. If calcium chloride is used instead of calcium hydroxide, the amount of sludge produced can be reduced by a factor of 15.

簡言之，科技論文作者不應寫出模稜兩可的句子，不可要讀者猜測句子所指為何。作者應當提供精確具體的信息，好讓讀者清楚瞭解論文的意思。

6.2　省略贅詞

撰寫科技論文時，除了表達要精確具體之外，還必須懂得辨識並省略贅詞。但這並不表示句子要寫得很短，亦非是說論文不可以有詳細說明。省略贅詞是指當找到對句子毫無意義的字詞，就應該省略。句中每個字詞，都應是句子整體意義不可或缺的一部分。

中國人撰寫的英文句子，常有一些贅詞。例如 *phenomenon* 這字：

累贅：　We must also consider the phenomenon of the fringe effect.

這裏字詞 *the phenomenon of* 對整個句子毫無意義，說 "the fringe effect" 和說 "the phenomenon of the fringe effect" 沒任何差別。因此，省略 *the phenomenon of*，可使句子較為簡潔直接：

簡潔：　We must also consider the fringe effect.

另一個常見的贅詞是 *basically*。例如：

累贅：　Basically, the process can be divided into two parts.

在這句中，*basically* 有甚麼作用呢？「把過程分成兩個部分」和「基本上，把過程分成兩個部分」，沒任何差別。因此，這句應省略 *basically*。

簡潔：　The process can be divided into two parts.

假如作者要強調那兩個是「基本」的部分，則亦不應把副詞 *basically* 放在句首，而應以形容詞（如 *basic* 或 *main*）來修飾 *parts*，例如：

The process can be divided into two main parts.

The process can be divided into two basic parts.

像 *very, somewhat, rather, quite* 這類修飾詞，通常是多餘的：

累贅：　The proposed algorithm is *very* simple in design and is *quite* fast and *somewhat* easier to program than previous methods.

簡潔：　The proposed algorithm is simple, fast, and easier to program than previous methods.

以下是典型的冗長英文句子：

冗長：　It is the aim of the research in this paper to propose and justify recommended modifications to the conventional method so as to enhance and strengthen the performance and effectiveness of on-line control systems.

這段文章中，既然用了 *research*，又何必再用 *paper*？有必要同時用 *propose* 和 *justify* 嗎？為何要加上 *recommended*？（假如作者不推薦那些修正，根本不會撰寫報告。）*Enhance* 和 *strengthen* 的意思不是大同小異嗎？*Performance* 和 *effectiveness* 不是指同一件事情嗎？

　　或許這段文章的作者，認為這樣可更清楚而「完整」地表達自己的意思。又或許他覺得論文的論點非常重要，必須用較多的字詞來強調。但贅詞只會阻礙閱讀，無法令讀者馬上掌握句意。作者大可省略這些贅詞，表達會更見簡潔：

簡潔：　The aim of this paper is to modify the conventional method so as to enhance the effectiveness of on-line control systems.

修改過後，省略的字詞近一半，但句子內容無改。而且，讀者可更快更易看到文句的重點。

　　中國作者亦應特別注意避免累贅動詞。例如，以下兩個例句，每個例句中到底有多少個動作呢？

The final estimates *are summarized and listed* in Table 8.

The generating function for node x *is given and derived* as follows.

事實上，這兩句各自都只描述一個動作而已，作者何必每句都用兩個動詞呢？在這兩個例句中，各應省略一個動詞：

The final estimates *are listed* in Table 8.

The generating function for node x *can be derived* as follows.

　　論文作者不要以為唯有不斷重複，讀者才能理解文意。作者表達一個論點時，必須清楚扼要，一氣呵成。

　　贅字固然要省略，「贅句」同樣也應省略，且原則雷同。當發現一個句子並非段落中必要的，或只是重複一個已相當清楚的意思，便應刪除。在一個段落中，每個句子應清楚地表達一個獨立的意思，而不應只換上不同的字眼去述說同一個論點。請仔細看下面描述地震儀的段落，當中有否對段落整體沒大意義的句子？

[1]The intensity and frequency of earthquakes can be measured by means of seismometers. [2]A seismometer consists of a mass suspended by a spring or other elastic mechanism inside a metal frame that is anchored to the ground. [3]A magnet is attached to the mass and an electric coil to the frame. [4]Any vibration of the ground shakes the seismometer's frame, but inertia tends to hold the mass in its place. [5]In other words, the frame moves, while the mass stays in its original position. [6]Thus the coil on the frame moves in relation to the magnet on the mass, and this movement generates an electrical signal that represents the intensity and frequency of the movement.[1]

像第四句已清楚說明，當地震儀周圍的地層震動時，地震儀的外架會搖動，但儀內的質量仍在原位。而第五句只是第四句的重複，它既沒為前句作澄清或補充，又沒帶來新內容。故省略此句，可使段落更簡潔直接。

關係代名詞

關係代名詞（即關係子句前面的代名詞）有時是不必要的，可以省略。如果限定關係子句以關係代名詞以及 *to be* 助動詞開首，而後面又緊接著動詞片語，則可省略關係代名詞和助動詞。（限定和非限定的關係子句之間的差別，詳見第五章5.2節中逗點的規則三。）下列的例句中，都可省略關係代名詞以及助動詞，而句意無改。

> We expect the new processor *that was* developed by our firm to be popular.
> We expect the new processor developed by our firm to be popular.

> The flame *that is* produced by this fuel is extremely unusual.
> The flame produced by this fuel is extremely unusual.

> The professor *who is* teaching the course this year is very knowledgeable.
> The professor teaching the course this year is very knowledgeable.

如果決定省略關係代名詞和助動詞 *be*（即 *is, are, was* 和 *were*），則兩個都必須同時省略，而不能只省略助動詞。例如，下面句子的文法是錯誤的：

> 誤： The nodes *that produced* by isolated strokes must be deleted.

在這句中，作者要不省略 *that*，要不就用 *that are* 這兩個字詞。

> 正： The nodes *produced* by isolated strokes must be deleted.

> 正： The nodes *that are produced* by isolated strokes must be deleted.

應否省略句子中的關係代名詞和助動詞，是有準則可循的：如果緊接在關係代名詞和助動詞後面的字詞是需強調的，則不要省略。如果緊接在關係代名詞和助動詞後面的字詞並非句中的重要概念，則可省略。

> The professor *who is* teaching the course this year is knowledgeable.

> The professor teaching the course this year is knowledgeable.

這句的主要意思是：教授是個學問淵博的人。字詞 *teaching* 並非句子的重要概念，故省略 *who is*，表達會較簡潔暢達。但如果：

> The professor *who designed this course* is knowledgeable, but the professor *who is teaching the course* this year is not an expert in the field.

在這句中，作者大概想強調 *teaching* 這字詞，因而強調設計課程的教授和講授課程的教授之間的分別。這種情形下，作者可保留 *who is*，就可引導讀者自然而然地注意到 *teaching* 這個字。（英語口語自然的節奏是當讀者唸到句子的第二個子句時，會傾向於先強調 *professor*，而會較輕聲唸 *who is*，再強調字詞 *teaching*。）

如果關係子句以關係代名詞開首而接著名詞片語或另一個代名詞，只要句意依然清楚，則可省略該關係代名詞。

> The statistical treatment *that we propose* is highly efficient.
> The statistical treatment *we propose* is highly efficient.

> The phenomena *that any acceptable theory must explain* are the following.
> The phenomena *any acceptable theory must explain* are the following.

如果關係子句以關係代名詞開首而接著一主要動詞，則可省略關係代名詞，並把該主要動詞改為 *-ing* 形（即現在分詞）。

> Planes *that travel* in these areas may experience radio disturbance.
> Planes *traveling* in these areas may experience radio disturbance.

> Algorithms *that involve* complex calculations are difficult to apply in real-time control systems.
> Algorithms *involving* complex calculations are difficult to apply in real-time control systems.

然而，如果緊接在關係代名詞後面的是語態助動詞，如 *can, may, will* 或 *should*，或以助動詞 *to be* 或 *to have* 形式的動詞，則不能使用這規則。

> 正：　There are many problems *that must be solved* before the system will be ready for practical application.

> 誤：　There are many problems *must being solved* before the system will be ready for practical application.

> 正：　All of the samples *that were produced* in the second run met the specifications.

> 正：　All of the samples *produced* in the second run met the specifications.

> 誤：　The samples *being produced* in the second run met the specifications.

許多時，作者可能決定不省略關係代名詞並把動詞改成 *-ing* 形。如果要強調關係子句，或關係子句表達的是句子的核心意思，則應用完整的關係子句，同時不把動詞改成 *-ing* 形。如果關係子句的內容非句子的重點，則把動詞改成 *-ing* 形可能較適當。請看下面的例句：

> A bandpass filter is a filter *that passes* only frequencies within a specific range.

在這句中，關係子句表達的是句子的核心意思，所以把關係代名詞和動詞 *that passes* 改成 *-ing* 形 *passing* 顯然不合適（事實上，如果動詞是 *-ing* 形 *passing*，則這句很不自然）。此句陳述通帶濾波器的定義，而關係子句是陳述此類濾波器的特徵。如果使用完整的關係子句，則可引導讀者更注意該子句，並強調 *passes* 這字詞，進而強調這意思：一個濾波器究竟是否通帶濾波器，正決定於它過濾頻率的方式。

比較下面的例句：

The factors *that affect* the reproduction of these organisms have been thoroughly investigated, but the factors *that affect* their development are poorly understood.

The factors *affecting* the reproduction of these organisms have been thoroughly investigated, but the factors *affecting* their development are poorly understood.

這兩句都是正確的英文，但有些人會認為第二個例句（即動詞是 *-ing* 形的）比第一個來得通順。兩個例句都在比較影響有機體繁殖和有機體發展的因素，述詞 *thoroughly investigated* 及 *poorly understood* 來表示比較的重點。在這兩個句子中，關係子句和 *affect* 這字詞皆非句子重點，假若用 *affecting*，會使讀者的視線從前後兩主詞 *the factors* 迅速轉移到 *reproduction* 和 *development* 上，再會注意到比較的重點。相反，如果用完整的關係子句 *that affect...*，則會使得讀者較為注意到關係子句，這耽擱了讀者看出兩個主要子句的核心意思（即 *thoroughly investigated* 及 *poorly understood* 的對比）。因此，在這句中，動詞是 *-ing* 形真的比 *that affect* 來得恰當。

6.3 直接表達

要寫出簡明的英文，作者應直接乾脆敘述句子的重點，避免不必要的修飾詞或迂迴的敘述。請看下列例句：

迂迴： In this paper, *we concentrate our efforts* on these issues.

作者撰寫這論文目的究竟是甚麼？"concentrate our efforts on these issues" 是何解？何不更直接來敘述這句的重點？

直接： In this paper, we investigate these issues.

直接： In this paper, we propose a method for solving these problems.

下面同樣是需要修改的例句：

迂迴： In this paper, we will try to propose a new method to solve this problem.

迂迴： In this section, we will focus on investigating the relationship between these parameters.

第一個例句中，*try to* 是贅詞。作者不應如此間接寫 *we will try to propose*，而應直接寫 *we will propose*。第二個例句中，*we will focus on investigating* 一點也不直接。動詞 *investigate* 已能表達出句子的重點，故把主詞、動詞直接改成 *we will investigate*，句子會更直接、簡潔：

直接： In this paper, we will propose a new method to solve this problem.

直接： In this section, we will investigate the relationship between these parameters.

　　上一節已討論過贅詞，即可省略而不改句意的字詞。作者如果不細心修改自己的文章，不刪除贅詞，就常會寫出冗長的句子。不過，有些冗長的句子，並非句中包含太多贅詞之故，而是由於作者行文迂迴。例如：

> Based on the well-known characteristic that the peak value of the passband code detector output has a close relationship with the peak value of the channel pulse response, we can use the detector output to tune the AGC gain.

這個句子中，第一個子句非常冗長，可是卻非贅詞太多的緣故。因為除了 *well-known* 之外，這子句已沒有可省略的字詞。就算隨便去掉幾個單字，亦不足以使句子變得簡潔直接，可能還會改變句意。所以唯一可行的方法是徹底改寫：首先，刪除字詞 *well-known characteristic*，因為提醒讀者句子所指的關係是廣為人知的，實在沒有必要。第二，描述偵測器的輸出和瞬間波動反應之間的關係，可用更精準的字詞，如 *is proportional to, is determined by* 或 *can be controlled by*（熟悉電子學的讀者或許會想到更恰當的字詞）。最後，應把 *because* 放在句首來更直接表達兩個子句間的因果關係。因為句子意謂第二子句所述的事情是基於第一子句的內容。

> *Because the peak value of the passband code detector output is proportional to the peak value of the channel pulse response,* we can use the detector output to tune the AGC gain.

改寫過的第一個子句，字數從29個減到21個，而重點無一遺留。從這個例子可看出，簡單直接的表達方式不僅可減少冗詞，同時可使讀者更易瞭解文章內容。

6.4 避免堆砌名詞以及弱動詞

　　中國人常會寫出「堆砌名詞」的英文句子。這些句子常包含太多名詞，使名詞與其他詞類（尤其是動詞和形容詞）不成比例。例如：

> This method has the advantage of accuracy but the disadvantage of slowness.

這句共有字詞十二個，其中五個是名詞，只有一個動詞，沒任何形容詞。塞滿名詞的句子，既生硬，又難讀。為了使得句子通順易讀，必須刪除部分的名詞，或可以以其他詞類來取代。

　　仔細看句中的名詞，其中兩個 *advantage* 和 *disadvantage* 是贅詞。有必要告訴讀者「準確」是優點，而「速度慢」是缺點嗎？這些是連外行人都知道的事情。因此，這裏可先省略這兩個名詞：

> 劣：　This method has accuracy but slowness.

這樣便可清楚地看出句子的結構是多麼的不自然。不論中文或英文，把 "This method is accurate"，（「此方法很準確」）寫成 "This method has accuracy"，（「此方法具準確性」），既間接又不自然。因此，名詞 *accuracy* 和 *slowness* 應改成形容詞 *accurate* 和 *slow*，並用動詞 *is* 取代 *has*。試比較修改前後的句子：

劣： This method has the advantage of accuracy but the disadvantage of slowness.

佳： This method is accurate but slow.

刪除不必要的名詞，並把部分名詞改成形容詞，句子就會簡明得多。

假如可使用動詞，則應避免使用名詞；假如可用子句，則應避免使用名詞片語或一連串介系詞片語。下面是個不自然而冗長的例句：

This problem is caused by the lack of consideration of the effect of the bandwidth gain that results from the termination request.

這句的主要動詞後面緊接著很長的介系詞片語，這介系詞片語是由三個介系詞片語組成，而最後一個介系詞片語還包含一個關係子句。此外，句子中間還出現了五個名詞：*lack, consideration, effect, bandwidth* 以及 *gain*。這樣的句子，堆滿了名詞，難於閱讀——讀者可能要讀上兩三次才能理解句意。如要句子變得直接易讀，應改寫整句，把至少一個名詞改成動詞，並省略介系詞片語。

修改的第一步是先去掉一個名詞，*consideration* 用不定詞 *to consider* 取代，以 *failure* 取代 *lack*，並以動狀詞 *resulting* 取代 *that results*。

This problem is caused by *the failure to consider* the effect of the bandwidth gain *resulting* from the termination request.

這句比原句簡潔，不過還是堆滿名詞，仍有點笨拙。因此，可進一步把名詞 *failure* 變成動詞 *fail*，同時把動詞後面冗長的介系詞片語改成一個附屬子句。另外，最好亦把被動式改成主動動詞，並加上一個主詞，做這個主動動詞的施事者。下面是兩種修改方式：

This problem occurs because we failed to consider the effect of the bandwidth gain resulting from the termination request.

This problem occurs because the proposed model fails to consider the effect of the bandwidth gain resulting from the termination request.

最後，考慮到名詞 *effect* 非為整句意思不可或缺的字詞，所以是累贅的，應該省略：

修正句： This problem occurs because we failed to consider the bandwidth gain resulting from the termination request.

修正句： This problem occurs because the proposed model fails to consider the bandwidth gain resulting from the termination request.

此外，*fail to consider* 其實還可用 *neglect* 這動詞來取代：

修正句： This problem occurs because we *neglected* the bandwidth gain resulting from the termination request.

修正句： This problem occurs because the proposed model *neglects* the bandwidth gain resulting from the termination request.

用動詞取代名詞，並以附屬子句（"because..."）來取代冗長的介系詞片語，就可寫出比原句簡短直接而容易瞭解的句子。

下面是另一個堆砌名詞的句子：

> This approach solves the problem at the cost of various amounts of band-width wastage.

這句的主要動詞和直接受詞後面，有三個介系詞片語，而這些片語中又包含了四個名詞。如前所示，以動詞取代句中的名詞，可使句子較易讀。同時，這裏應該考慮至少刪除一兩個介系詞片語。所以，可先從名詞 *wastage* 著手，用動狀詞 *wasting* 來取代：

> This approach solves the problem at the cost of wasting various amounts of bandwidth.

這句比原句通順，但卻沒有比原句簡潔。要做到簡潔，就可用一簡短的子句取代介系詞片語 *at the cost of wasting...*。並且，字詞 *various amounts of* 對整體句意是多餘的，可以省略：

> This approach solves the problem but wastes bandwidth.

修改後的句子簡潔直接。還有，直接使用動詞來表達而不用一連串介系詞片語，使之比原句更強而有力。

名物化名詞和弱動詞

撰寫科技論文的人應避免另一種冗長而間接的句子結構——名物化名詞和「弱動詞」連用句。所謂的「名物化名詞」(nominal) 是一個由動詞加上名物化字尾所變成的，這些名物化字尾有如 *-tion, -ance, -ness, -ment* 等。例如，*performance* 是由動詞 *perform* 變成的名物化名詞，*calculation* 是由 *calculate* 變成的，*achievement* 是由 *achieve* 變成的。

名物化名詞本是英文中很重要的一種詞，有時作者要表達某個特定的意思時，也許就只有這種名詞正能表達出那特定意思。然而，當句子中出現此種名詞時，常要配合「弱動詞」("weak" verb) 作主要動詞，如 *do, give, have, make, take, achieve, effect, conduct, perform* 等。這些動詞的意思既微弱，又模糊，故稱之為「弱動詞」。這種句子中，弱動詞代替了名物化名詞背後較「強」而具體的動詞，使句子較冗長，表達的動作較間接。

如要修改名物化名詞和弱動詞連用結構，而想寫出較簡潔直接的英文，那必須把名詞背後較「強」而具體的動詞抽出，作句子的主要動詞。試看這個名物化名詞和弱動詞連用結構的句子：

> 弱動詞：　*The calculation* of this parameter *can be performed* using Lee's algorithm.

句子主要動詞 *perform* 是一個弱動詞，句中 *calculation* 是名物化名詞。修改這句其實很容易，只要用較強而具體的動詞 *calculate* 取代 *the calculation...can be performed*，並把 *calculate* 轉成被動語態，這樣句子便會變得簡潔直接：

> 簡潔：　This parameter *can be calculated* using Lee's algorithm.

修改後的句子不單較原句簡明，且更強而有力。此外，原句本來就不夠精確，作者原意大概不會是利用李氏演算法算出「參數」，而是算出「參數值」。所以，句子還應進一步修改：

精確：　　The *value of* this parameter can be calculated using Lee's algorithm.

現在來看另一個例句：

弱動詞：　They *reached the conclusion* that a disruptive approach is more effective.

這句中，*reach* 是弱動詞，而名詞 *conclusion* 可改為動詞。為求把句子修改得簡潔直接，最好是用動詞 *concluded* 取代 *reached the conclusion*：

簡潔：　　They *concluded* that a disruptive approach is more effective.

練習 6-1　簡明的句子

請把下列句子修改得較簡明。其中有些句子可能要大幅修改。

1. In this paper, we try to propose an algorithm to handle noisy and uncertain data. The new proposed algorithm easily handles false negative training instances.

2. The values obtained in the first two trials are plotted and compared in Figure 3.

3. In application aspects, many applications of fuzzy neural networks have been reported.

4. The procedure is outlined and described below.

5. The second method uses a relatively more complex formulation.

6. For the purpose of comparison, consider and compare the performance of Chen's method.

7. Section 6 shows the summary of the results. For the sake of simplicity, the results have been divided into two sets.

8. The reasons for this poor performance can be characterized as the following.

9. This paper concentrates on an attempt to study the effects of three types of mutation on the performance of genetic algorithms.

10. Table 4 shows the comparison of the speed of our algorithm with that of the other algorithms.

11. In this paper, we focus on the analysis of the stability of clamping with passive friction forces.

12. The data have been simplified for the reason that we can treat this problem well and more easily in the finite element analysis.

13. In order to respond to this requirement, development of an optimization technique for implicit-form problems becomes necessary.

14. This allocation technique may lead to longer delays and blocked connections in time-insensitive and time-sensitive applications, respectively.

15. The shortcomings of the application of the general cell mapping method can be eliminated by combining application of this method with application of interpolated cell mapping.

16. For the purpose of examining the variation in tensile strain along the free edge, we have calculated and plotted the relationship between tensile strain and element number in Fig. 5.

17. A larger scale of operations is needed not only because of manufacturing cost reduction considerations, but also for R&D investment justification.

18. If we compare Chang's method with ours, we find that the major and most significant difference between them is that our technique does not rely on external forces to ensure smooth, natural animated motion.

19. The proposed algorithm is better than Matsumoto's method, which is slower and takes up much more memory.

20. With the consideration of the algorithm level and architecture level in our design approach, the resulting filter design has the features of programmability, low cost, and an accumulation-free tap structure.

練習 6-2 名物化名詞和弱動詞

請刪除下列的弱動詞，並把名物化名詞改為動詞。

1. The proposed method offers great improvement in the accuracy of the analysis.

2. In section 4 performance comparisons between the proposed method and several existing methods are discussed.

3. In section 2, a brief survey is made of existing blending techniques.

4. This policy may result in a considerable amount of bandwidth wastage.

5. The conclusion is made in section 6.

6. The activation of the triggers was done sequentially.

7. The modal controllability has a more compact expression as follows.

8. The level sufficient for successful identification is dependent on several factors.

9. Under the condition of the use of high-temperature processing, the phenomenon of reduction of yield occurs.

10. The stability analysis of these solutions will be studied below.

11. Chen [5] states the definition of the problem in a similar way.

12. To make a comparison of the performance of the two processors, we ran another series of tests.

13. This technique can be used to achieve an improvement in the performance of CAD systems.

14. The compiler is responsible for the insertion of communication instructions. Insertion of instructions will occur wherever the compiler judges they should be.

15. With this new method, a substantial reduction in the severity of the staircase effect can be achieved.

16. The effect of speed adjustment can be accomplished by means of the technique described in section 2.

6.5 多用主動語態

通順的科技論文中，句子大多使用主動語態。與被動語態相比，主動語態令句子更直接，且更強而有力。同時，用較多主動語態的文章會較簡潔而直截了當。請看下面兩例句：

The mice *were shown* by the experimental results to prefer sweet foods.

The experimental results *showed* that the mice preferred sweet foods.

這樣就可看出主動和被動語態的分別。第二個句子是主動語態，故較清楚直接，通順有力。這句的主要子句和動詞後的名詞子句，結構都非常簡單直接：主詞後緊接著主動動詞，然後再接著直接受詞。

試看更多的例子：

被動：   *It can be observed* that steps 2 and 3 of the algorithm are repeated several times.

主動：   *Observe* [或 *Note*] that steps 2 and 3 of the algorithm are repeated several times.

或：   Steps 2 and 3 of the algorithm are repeated several times. 此句雖然也使用被動語態，但比原句簡潔直接得多。

被動：   *From these data it can be seen* that the phase modulation *is enhanced by* forward pumping.

主動：   *These data indicate* that forward pumping *enhances* the phase modulation.

然而，這並非說文章應一律避免使用被動語態。資深的作者亦會使用被動語態：事實上，他們的文章中平均有 25% 的句子是被動語態，但他們都是有好理由時才使用：在某些句子中，使用被動語態會比主動語態更簡潔。或者有時要強調某個字詞，而把它作句子的主詞，亦會使用被動語態。還有當要描述某個標準的過程，而無需提及過程的執行者時，用被動語態就最好不過了。此外，以被動語態來描述實驗的程序也是約定俗成的。但如果只因慣性或暫時未想到更好的寫法而濫用被動語態，都是不妥當的。（詳見第四章4.7節濫用被動語態問題。）唯有在比較使用被動和主動語態的優劣後，並認為被動語態確實較為恰當，才可使用。

想進一步瞭解如何適當使用被動語態，還可參考第九章9.3節。

6.6 正面表達

科技論文貴能一語道破研究重點，正面的言說方式可使文句清楚直接。如非必要，作者不應使用反面的說法（必要的情況非常少）。一般來說，作者不應說「某人某物沒做甚麼」，而應說「某人某物做甚麼」。

> This technique *does not produce good results.*

這句子用了一個否定動詞，使句意既間接，又模糊。讀者詮釋這句時，不僅要消化句子的表面意思，還要進一步思考「這技術不產生理想效用」的意思。句中 "not good" 意思並不清楚：到底是指「很差」，還是「雖不理想，但可接受」？如果省略否定動詞並以 *good* 的相反詞代替，則句子就較清楚直接了：

> This technique produces poor results.

> This technique produces unsatisfactory results.

這例可看出：盡量用正面而肯定的動詞來表達，句子會較直接簡潔。

類似的原則可應用在修飾詞上：別告訴讀者「事情非如此」，而應該說「事情到底是怎麼樣」。請看下列例句：

> The construction of a TLT is not difficult, but the construction of a PAT is not easy.

句中的否定詞會阻礙讀者掌握句意。如要句子變得較易瞭解，應省略否定詞，並更改形容詞，換上它的反義詞：

> The construction of a TLT is easy, but the construction of a PAT is difficult.
> 亦可用 *straightforward, simple* 等同義字取代 *easy*

此外，如果把 the construction of 改為動名詞，句子會更簡潔：

> Constructing a TLT is easy, but constructing a PAT is difficult.

科技論文非文學作品，不應只說事情非這非那，留下疑團讓讀者「細味」。正面直接告訴讀者你的意思，這往往更適當。

練習 6-3 主動語態及正面表達

請用主動語態及正面方式改寫下列句子，使它們變得更簡潔清楚。（提示：一句可能不只一種正確修正方式。）

1. The reaction did not occur quickly.

2. It has been observed by several researchers that in solving this type of problem genetic algorithms tend to be attracted by local minima.

3. A valid schedule cannot have an iteration period that does not exceed this bound.

4. We cannot provide only one plot.

5. The conventional method is shown by the experimental results to be outperformed by the proposed algorithm.

6. The effects of computer-assisted instruction and traditional instruction techniques have been compared in this study.

7. The analysis is not valid.

8. For the hardware cost to be reduced, a more efficient filter design must be developed.

9. Designing an on-line control system for this application is not a simple task.

10. The electrical properties of the films were found to be improved after the films were doped with boron.

11. The iterations do not stop if the convergence test is not satisfied.

12. As shown by the simulation results, with the proposed control algorithm the cutting system can be adjusted quickly and effectively in response to different cutting conditions.

6.7 少用虛主詞

　　句首為 *it is, there is* 或 *there are*（或這些表達形式的其他時態），稱為「虛主詞結構」(expletive construction)。當要強調句子動詞後面的觀念時，可使用虛主詞結構句。比較下列兩個例句：

Two tall trees were in front of the house.

There were two tall trees in front of the house.

這兩句提供同樣的信息，但強調的重點卻不同。第一個句子較強調樹木的位置，讀者閱讀這句時，會自然而然強調 *in front*；第二個句子則較強調「兩棵樹」，由於閱讀時會自然而然強調 *two tall trees*。

　　同時，虛主詞結構會讓讀者的注意力集中在某個事實或某個行為所產生的結果，而不會去注意實踐行為的人或物。比較下列例句：

Scientists have little evidence to support this theory.

There is little evidence to support this theory.

相比之下，第二個句子較強調「理論欠缺證據」，證據是誰掌握並不重要，使用虛主詞就可不用指明是誰掌握了證據。

　　另外還有兩個例句：

We can approach this problem *in three ways.*

There are three ways of approaching this problem.

第一個句子強調「我們」處理問題，並且有三種處理方式；第二個句子則沒有指明是誰處理問題，而會較強調「有三種處理問題方法」這個事實。誰都可用這些方法，所以誰在考慮使用並不重要。

　　當要強調句子裏某些特定的意思時，使用虛主詞結構有時是非常適合的。然而，虛主詞卻常為文章中的贅詞。如果省略虛主詞會使句子更簡明，則應避免使用。如在下列例句中，*there is* 和 *there are* 顯然都是累贅而應省略的：

There are fourteen cases presented here.

There is no desired velocity specified in the equilibrium control.

在這兩例中，主詞（"fourteen cases" 和 "desired velocity"）後面緊接著關係子句（兩個子句 "presented here" 和 "specified in the equilibrium control" 都省略了關係代名詞和助動詞）。如果刪除兩句中的虛主詞，而把關係子句的動詞作句子主要動詞，則這兩個句子就會變得較簡潔：

Fourteen cases are presented here.

No desired velocity is specified in the equilibrium control.

　　這樣可推出一個普遍的原則：如果一個虛主詞結構句中包含一個關係子句或名詞子句，則應省略虛主詞，並把子句中的動詞作句子主要動詞。這通常會使句子變得較為簡潔。現再舉幾個例子：

劣：   There are several methods that have been proposed for selecting the fittest individuals.

佳：   Several methods have been proposed for selecting the fittest individuals.

劣：   There are seven companies that participated in the program.

佳：   Seven companies participated in the program.

劣：   It is clear from the data that raising the temperature led to an increase in the deposition rate.

佳：   Raising the temperature clearly led to an increase in the deposition rate.

佳：   The data clearly show that raising the temperature led to an increase in the deposition rate.

有些中國人會濫用虛主詞結構，使句子沒有任何具體內容，例如：

劣：   There are some important characteristics of the common-base amplifier. The first is that…

以英文為母語的作者一定不會這樣使用 *there are*。正確的寫法應該是：

佳：   The common-base amplifier has a number of important characteristics. The first is that…

佳：   Important characteristics of the common-base amplifier include…
        直接列出重要特性

句首出現諸如 *it should be noted that* 或 *it can be observed that* 之類的詞語，句子的重點必定是於 *that* 後面的子句中。刪除不必要的虛主詞結構，突顯句子的重點，好讓讀者能更快看到句子的重點。

冗長：   *It should be noted that* program enrollment is inversely proportional to economic growth.

簡潔：   Program enrollment is inversely proportional to economic growth.

冗長：   *It can be observed that* the rate increases as a function of temperature.

簡潔：   The rate increases as a function of temperature.

若 *it should be noted* 或 *it can be observed* 是句意必要的部分，不能刪除，常可用祈使語氣來改寫，而變得較簡潔。

冗長：   *It should also be noted* that…
簡潔：   *Note* that…

冗長：   *It can be observed* that…
簡潔：   *Observe* that…

練習 6-4　虛主詞結構

刪除下列句中不必要或錯誤的虛主詞結構，並省略贅詞。（提示：第五題是文法錯誤的句子。）

1. It should be noted here that the analysis presented above is not applicable to nonlinear systems.

2. There have been many filter designs proposed in the literature.

3. It would be time-consuming to solve equation (5) directly.

4. There are many new applications of neural networks that have been proposed in the last ten years.

5. *There needs an on-chip buffer for raster-scan ordering of the pixels.

6. It can be concluded from these results that hypothesis H_1 is false.

7. There are three types of events defined in the program.

8. There is another advantage to this method in that we need only a shifter and an adder to complete the circuit.

9. It is the purpose of mission planning to maximize instrument operating time subject to various constraints.

10. From these figures it can clearly be seen that the classification accuracy increases as i and j increase.

6.8　第一人稱句

科技研究報告中，有些作者會以為要讓文章看來「科學」、「客觀」，最好避免使用第一人稱複數代名詞 *we*。但這理由是站不住腳的。研究廣告或政治宣傳的人都知道：避免使用第一人稱，不會讓文章更「客觀」；即使使用第一人稱，也絕不會讓文章過於「主觀」。報告內容的客觀程度，是不受有否使用第一人稱影響的。

只要整篇文章的語氣連貫，且沒累贅之虞，在正式的科技論文中還是可使用第一人稱。在很多文脈中，例如在科學及數學教科書中，*we* 根本不是指作者自己，而是泛指作者和讀者。不過有時候，*we* 也確是指作者自己，以表示論文研究目的、發現或結論是作者本人之見。如此使用第一人稱，既無迫使讀者接受作者觀點之嫌，反能讓讀者看出作者所扮演的角色——資訊的提供者，好讓讀者進一步評斷作者的觀點。

可惜有些撰寫科技論文的人，誤以為凡使用第一人稱都會讓論文「不夠科學」或過於「主觀」。他們會千方百計地避免代名詞 we，就算要被迫寫出不自然而迂迴的句子。下面是一個正確的英文句子：

佳： We need to show that the proposed method is more accurate than the conventional one.

曾經有位作者就是為了避免使用 *we*，把這句「修正」如下：

劣： The proposed method requires to be shown to be more accurate than the conventional one.

原句是自然正確的英文，然而那位作者就把句子「修正」得既不自然，又使句意模糊。有些編輯甚至還會認為這樣的句子有語法錯誤。

如果那位作者實在不想用第一人稱，其實他亦大可保留句子的主動語態，而另找一個新主詞。他也可用下面這些句子來取代原句：

The following analysis will show that the proposed method is more accurate than the conventional one.

The purpose of this section is to show that the proposed method is more accurate than the conventional one.

是否使用第一人稱，主要是依作者個人寫作風格而定；但有些學術領域的論文使用第一人稱的情況可能沒那麼普遍；而有些作者覺得這可讓文章較通順自然且口語化，就像自己在演講般。使用第一人稱既可避免濫用被動語態，有時還可有助避免不自然的句子（尤其是在包括很多數學方程式的論文）。在某些情形下，使用以 *we* 為主詞的句子來陳述某個論點，可能是最簡單直接的寫法。作者在衡量一個句子的主詞要不要用第一人稱時，不要擔心論文內容會因而變得不夠「客觀」，而應考慮：可否寫出較通順的句子；是否與論文整體的風格一致；在特定的句子中，*we* 是否累贅而應省略。

試比較下面兩個意思大致相同的例句：

The solution can be obtained by substituting this value into expression (22).

To obtain the solution, we can substitute this value into expression (22).

兩個句子的英文皆正確。有些作者可能比較喜歡第一句，或許是它看來較正式。但有些作者會較喜歡第二句，因為它是主動語態，比較口語化，沒那麼生硬。兩句都適用於科技研究報告中，而皆有各自適合的文章脈絡。

我們再列出兩對例句，讀者可作比較：

This paper presents a new algorithm that performs character thinning quickly and reliably.

We present a new algorithm that performs character thinning quickly and reliably.

Here the following method will be employed.

We will employ the following method.

同樣，上面四句都是正確的英文，且也適用於科技寫作。應選用哪個句子，則要看文章脈絡及作者個人的寫作風格而定。這裏要強調：沒有一條普遍規則是「非第一人稱句定比第一人稱句好」。

某些句子中，*we* 可能是不必要的，因此作者可考慮省略：

From the graph, we observe that the value of x increases sharply after time *t*.

The graph shows that the value of x increases sharply after time *t*.

某些文章脈絡中，像第一個句子中的 *we observe that*，可能是累贅的。整個句子的重點是描述圖形，所以第二個句子就比第一個合適。相反，在下列例句中，*we believe that* 是句子的重點：

We believe that the actual mechanism has yet to be discovered.

在這句中，作者用 *we believe that* 來陳述出自己的看法，所以不能省略，否則會影響句意。如果作者想避免用 *we* 來陳述出自己的想法，還可以用臆測動詞（如 *appears*）來改寫：

It appears that the actual mechanism has yet to be discovered.

（"Has yet to be discovered" 和 "has not yet been discovered 意思一樣。）

然而，雖然在科技論文中可使用第一人稱，但切勿過多使用。下面就是濫用代名詞 *we* 的例子：

We can judge whether a diode we test is good if the forward-biased resistance we read is much less than the reversed-biased resistance we read.

這句的作者實在沒必要重複 *we* 四次。以下有兩種修改方式：第一種是只保留一個 *we*，第二種則省略所有的 *we*。

We can judge whether a diode is good by checking whether the forward-biased resistance is much less than the reversed-biased resistance.

A diode is good if the forward-biased resistance is much less than the reversed-biased resistance.

請注意這兩句的語氣有何不同。第一句使用代名詞 *we*，較口語化，而且突出了作者的行為（也許亦指讀者）。這句的意思是：「我們的目的是要檢查兩極真空管是否良好，而達致這個目的所採取的方法是……」；第二句則突出了兩極真空管及其特性，卻完全省略作者的行為。這句幾乎是一個定義，句中既沒有提到是誰想應用那定義，也沒交待定義目的。如果作者認為研究者的動作在句中很重要（例如專供實驗課程使用的教科書），則第一個修正句會較恰當。相反，如果作者是想說明甚麼是兩極真空管，以及描述它的特性，則第二個修正句會較恰當。

雖然在科技研究報告中可使用第一人稱 *we*，像論文是由多位作者共同撰寫的，但絕不可以使用第一人稱單數代名詞 *I*。即使只有一位作者，在報告中還是可使用

we。（也有少數作者會使用 *the author*。）此外，偶爾也可以在科技論文中使用不定代名詞 *one*，但如濫用的話，文章的語氣便會變得生硬。

6.9　避免偽術語

　　無論任何學術領域，專家都需要一些專業術語以方便溝通。使用專業術語是用較簡潔的方式，來表示一些較複雜的概念。很多專業術語所表達的意思，都是不能在日常語言中找到對應的詞彙來表達，各學術領域的專家才會構造出這些術語。在研究報告中，當要提到某研究領域的專家已通曉的概念時，使用他們已有共識的專業術語來指稱，就不需再作長篇解釋。

　　然而，論文作者卻應避免用偽術語 (jargon)。與前段所描述的情形不同，偽術語是不必要的專業術語，它所表達的概念根本就是可用日常語言的字詞來表達的，而它通常卻又比日常語言模糊或冗長。在撰寫論文時，如果想使用的專業術語，沒有比日常語言更清楚精確，則應使用日常語言，以避免濫用專業術語。

　　例如：當 *first step* 已可表達得當，就不應寫 *initial phase*；當你可以寫 *The system will be reviewed immediately*，就別寫成 *The system review operation has been prioritized*；可以寫 *to refer* 或 *to retrieve* 時，就不要寫 *to reference*；明明可寫 *to affect*，就別寫成 *to impact*；本來可以寫 *to connect*，寫 *to interface* 就是作態；*function* 已很恰當，為何要寫 *functionality*？有 *important, central, main, primary* 或 *crucial* 等如此多字詞可選擇使用，為何只用 *key* 來形容所有重要的事物？電子產品推銷員別再把每個新產品（或產品線）稱為 *total solution*，應改用更精確的字詞來告訴客戶產品有甚麼特別功能；描述所有硬體或軟體設備之間的關係時，別再用 *support*，而應該用 *provide, include, can be used with, is compatible with* 等較精確的字詞；*costdown* 根本就不是正確的英文字詞，作者應該用 *reduce costs*（動詞）或 *cost reduction*（名詞）。總而言之，在一個句子中，如果有兩個字詞都是正確的選擇，就應使用較精簡的一個，別以為非用「專業」字詞不可。

　　撰寫科技論文時，當首次提到某個專業術語時，必須同時定義清楚這術語並以斜體字標示之。此外，論文中首次提及一個「頭字語」(acronym)（即由數個字詞的首個字母組成的字詞）或縮寫字時，也應完整地列出這些字母所代表的字詞，並用括號括著頭字語或縮寫。這樣，作者便可假定讀者已瞭解頭字語或縮寫的意思，而可放心在論文中使用。如果必須用到特別多的縮寫或術語，可以考慮加上 "nomenclature"或"notation" 的小節來結集所有術語的定義。（英文的 *nomenclature, notation* 及 *terminology* 意思是一組術語或符號，都是不可數名詞，故沒複數形式。）作者應盡量避免用過多專業術語，如果是萬不得已的話，應確定讀者都已知道這些術語的意思。

6.10 避免直接疑問句

在英文科技論文中，當作者需要帶出一個問題或新的課題時，通常會使用直述句或間接疑問句，而不會使用直接疑問句。試看以下例子：

> An important question is, "Why do we need normalization?" This question will be addressed in the next section.

這句文法雖正確，但作者卻用了太多字詞來表達實際上很簡單的意思。作者應使用間接疑問句或直述句來取代，這在說明為何需要 normalization 時，會較簡潔直接。

> The question of why normalization is needed will be addressed in the next section. 這句仍稍嫌冗長

> The next section will explain why normalization is needed. 比較簡潔

在某些文章脈絡中，還是可把直接疑問句當作有效的主題句：

> Why is normalization needed? Normalization allows us to compensate for the variation in the data that results from collecting samples from many different speakers.

不過，有些資深的作者會認為這個直接疑問句也是多餘的，應該省略。他們會建議把這段文章修改為：

> Normalization is needed to compensate for the variation in the data that results from collecting samples from many different speakers.

這樣就能用較簡潔的方式來表達相同的論點。

中國作者應特別注意避免寫出不自然或文法有誤的直接疑問句。在中文裏，直接和間接疑問句之間並沒有很清楚的區別，但英文中，它們在句法上有很大的分別。例如，下例兩個「劣」句似乎是由中文直接翻成的英文。這些英文句子非常不自然，應該修改成間接疑問句：

> 劣： We must now discuss, Does the proposed modification increase the computational complexity of the method?

> 佳： We must now discuss *whether* the proposed modification *increases* the computational complexity of the method.

> 劣： The next step is to consider, How can the speed of the system be increased?

> 佳： The next step is to consider *how* the speed of the system *can* be increased.

> 佳： The next step is to consider *how to increase* the speed of the system.

要把第一個「劣」句修改成間接疑問句，必須加上 *whether* 這字詞，並省略直接疑問句裏的助動詞。當我們把第二個「劣」句修改為間接疑問句時，必須改動助動詞的位置。

練習 6-5 直接疑問句

請把下列直接疑問句修改成間接疑問句或直述句。（提示：下面六個習題中，只有第一個是文法正確的句子。）

1. An interesting question is, Is the relationship between these chromosomes an original form or is it itself a result of evolution?

2. Let us now consider, How does the circuit work?

3. We must now explain, Why did the samples immersed in the HF solution show increased selectivity during the second deposition phase?

4. Section 3 discusses the proposed algorithm outperforms the conventional method in what types of applications?

5. In section 4 we evaluate How does the performance of the proposed method compare with that of the conventional method?

6. In the second experiment, we investigated, Does the amount of fluorine incorporated into the film depend on the amount of water in the immersing solution?

第七章
通順的句子

若要寫出流暢得體的英文，則必須學習造出自然通順的句子。這一章將介紹五個基本修辭原則，在撰寫或修改英文句子時，這些原則皆有助作者寫出自然通順的英文。

7.1 善用不同的句子結構

高明的作者往往懂得利用不同的句子結構來反映不同的句子內容。一個既簡單且重要的意思，應使用簡短有力的句子來表達。相反，一個複雜詳盡的說明，則需要用較長而複雜的句子來陳述。帶出新的話題、提出重要論點，或是陳述段落或章節的結論，可用短句；詳細說明並支持段落的主要論點，可用長句。簡言之，作者應學會運用句子結構來強調文章內容，從而使句子意思更清晰。

要把握以結構強調內容的技巧，應多觀察以英語為母語的專家如何使用不同的句子結構。在他們的文章中，常看到一種組織模式：先是一個有力的短句，用以介紹新論點；接著有一個或一些長句，用以展開、推陳或說明該論點；然後再來一個短句，用以敘述結論或提出另一個新論點。在撰寫英文論文時，如果發現初稿中有太多的長句，則應予以修改。先找出主要論點，並使用短句直接有力地表達出來，然後再以一些長句來討論這些論點。

注意下列段落如何有效地利用不同句子結構：

> [1]Today color constancy, if it is mentioned at all, is treated by a skeptical footnote in textbooks on vision. [2]The skepticism is not hard to understand. [3]Since many of us virtually live our lives under artificial lighting, we have

become inured to the experience that faces and cosmetics, for example, change color between incandescent and fluorescent lighting. [4]Yet the skepticism is wrong. [5]Investigators of a century ago knew that color constancy poses a serious problem for efforts to understand perception. [6]The constancy is so reliable that one routinely compares by memory the face color and lip color of someone who now stands under one form of daylight with the colors seen an hour ago, a day ago, a week ago, and under another form of daylight, and thus detects changes due to blushing or paling or signifying disease such as jaundice (which turns the skin yellow) or anoxia (which turns it blue). [7]Such changes are much smaller than the possible changes in daylight color. [8]It is as if, in the words of the 19th-century physiologist Hermann von Helmholtz, we "discount the illuminant" when we perceive color.[1]

段落的開首是中等長度的句子（句子 1），指出當代流行的「色彩不變說」的懷疑論態度（贊成「色彩不變說」的學者認為，無論日光照明有何變化，人類知覺到事物的顏色是大致不變的）。接著是一個有力的短句（句子 2），敘述一個簡要的論點：有些人抱持這種懷疑論態度並不難瞭解。然後是一個長句（句子 3），提供資料去支持前面短句的論點。跟著，作者使用另一個短句（句子 4）以表達一個極鮮明的論點：懷疑論是錯誤的。緊接在後是幾個長句，其中一個（句子 6）特別長，作者用它來強調，即使隨著時間不同，日光照明有所變化，人類知覺到事物的顏色，大致上還是不變的。

　　總而言之，一個好的英文段落中，句子會有不同的結構。撰寫論文時，作者應根據句子內容來選用合適的句子結構。

7.2 避免散亂句

　　英文的句子結構不應過於冗長或複雜。一般而言，一個句子只應表達一兩個主要意思，且必須清楚易懂，能讓人一讀就能瞭解句意。冗長或過於複雜的句子，或一個包含太多意思的句子，稱之為「散亂句」。

　　以下是一散亂句。在這句中，先出現兩個附屬子句，其中一個子句本身又包含兩個附屬子句，接著是一個很長的介系詞片語，主要子句最後才出現，且也是相當長的。這句結構極冗長複雜，未能表達出清楚易明的論點，使讀者難以閱讀與瞭解。

散亂句：　When a technology is to be transferred from the R&D stage to the production stage, if the learning cost of the technology is so high as to create a situation where, when private companies are deciding whether or not to adopt the technology, research institutes are unable to provide investment support, then from the perspective of converting new technology to commercial applications, the possibility of the industrial sector transferring the results of government-funded R&D to commercial applications is not high.

像這樣的句子，讀者通常很少能一讀便能瞭解句意。就傳達信息的效率而言，可說是非常差。當閱讀一個句子時，我們通常不會逐字來消化句子內容，散亂句提供過多信息，使讀者無法同時記得整句的內容，因而擾亂正常的閱讀過程。

　　想修改以上的散亂句，必先找出句中的幾個主要意思，然後把它們以獨立的句子來表達。即是說，把原句分割成兩個以上的句子，而分割後的句子都只表達一或兩個意思。在修改這類極繁雜迂迴的句子時，還必須細心考慮原句的重點，可否更直接去表達，並看原句陳述的意思中，有否多餘而可省略的部分。

　　下面是一種修正方法。為使整段文章變得較清楚直接，我們把原來的散亂句分成兩個句子，同時刪除了一些不必要的子句：

> 修正：　The learning cost involved in transferring a technology from the R&D stage to the production stage may be very high. If part of this cost is not defrayed through investment by the government research institute that developed the technology, then private companies may be unwilling or unable to apply the new technology commercially.

修正後表達都較直接簡潔。由於原來的散亂句極迂迴，故還可以有很多修正方法，在此僅列一種，以供參考。

　　散亂句未必都像以上的例子般那樣長。下列句子也是一例：

> In this situation, the sizes of the pitch radii and addenda will be altered and are known as operating sizes which were first discussed by Johnson [9] and are expressed as follows.

這句不特別長（僅31字），但它同樣雜亂無章。此句共有四個動詞，兩個是在一個長的關係子句中，即 "which were first discussed... and are expressed..."（這個關係子句為非限定子句，故子句前應加上逗點）。作者似乎要把幾個不同的意思都塞進一個句子裏去，故句中沒清楚的焦點，且句中不同意思間的邏輯關係並不明瞭，實在令人費解。讀者根本不可能會瞭解句中哪個動詞要和哪個主詞搭配，哪些動詞受片語 in this situation 修飾，或動詞之間的關係。要修改此句，必須把它分成至少兩句，每句表達一個清楚的論點。以下有三種可能的修改方法：

> In this situation, the size of the pitch radii and addenda will be altered; the altered sizes are known as operating sizes, which were first discussed by Johnson [9]. The operating sizes can be expressed as follows.

> In this situation, the size of the pitch radii and addenda will be altered. The altered sizes, which were called operating sizes by Johnson [9], can be expressed as follows.

> In this situation, the size of the pitch radii and addenda will be altered. The altered sizes, which are known as operating sizes (see Johnson [9]), can be expressed as follows.

第一個修正句把原句分割成兩個獨立句子，在保留了原句的所有資料之餘，補充了幾個字詞以闡明句意。第二與第三個修正句則省略了原句部分資料，以造出較簡潔的句子。三個修正句都是清楚自然的英文，尤以第二與第三句為通順，而第一個修正句還是缺乏精確的焦點。

在修改論文初稿時，應注意文稿中有否散亂句。如果有的話，則可應用上述的方法來修改：先找出句子的主要意思，並考慮有否可省略的地方。然後把原句分成兩個或以上較短的句子，每句表達原句中一兩個意思。（關於散亂句子的詳細討論，請參閱第四章4.2節。）

7.3 避免片斷句成篇

在7.1節曾說明，撰寫英文文章時應善用不同的句子結構：短句用以陳述簡單直接的重點，長句則用以陳述較詳細複雜的說明。一篇論文不可能只有一個個孤零的重點，卻沒有詳細的說明，因此文章中應避免出現一連串短句。如果短句太多，則表示作者無法聯繫不同句子內容之間的關係。同時，這樣的文章會非常沉悶，如同小學國文讀本一樣。當文章中連續出現許多片斷句時，應使用適當的對等結構及附屬結構來把這些片斷句合併，並闡明句子之間的關係（有關對等結構和附屬結構的進一步討論，請參閱下面7.5節）。

以下段落是由一連串片斷式的句子所組成的：

> The substrates were mounted on brackets. The brackets were placed in the reaction chamber. The chamber was sealed. The microwave power was turned on. The temperature was set to 600° C. The gas mixture was introduced into the reaction chamber. The reaction was allowed to continue for four hours. Then the samples were removed from the chamber. Next, the samples were submerged in distilled water. The samples were placed in the water for 30 minutes.

這段英文非常呆板。作者把許多零星的意思，都用一個個短句來表達，短句間互相獨立，中間看似沒甚關係。事實上，段落中各句子所表達的意思之間都密切相關，這段英文卻沒有表達出這些關係。

要把這段落修改得通順流暢，必須把關係密切的意思合併成一句，再以主要子句來表達主要意思，以附屬子句來敘述次要意思。此外，段落中的句子應有不同的結構。以下是一種修改方法：

> The substrates were mounted on brackets and placed in the reaction chamber, which was then sealed. The microwave power was turned on, and the temperature was set to 600° C. The gas mixture was then introduced into the reaction chamber. The reaction was allowed to continue for four hours, after which the samples were removed from the chamber and submerged in distilled water for 30 minutes.

原來的段落共有十個短句，修正段落則只有四句，句子也有長短的變化。修正段落通順流暢，每句之間的關係亦清楚得多。

練習 7-1 散亂句

下面的文章都是一些散亂句。請改寫這些句子，使文章變得更簡短，焦點更清晰。在某些句子中，需省略一些累贅的轉接詞，才能造出合理的句子。（第四章中練習 4-2 有更多習題。）

1. Another type of network used in neural-network-based object recognition is the neocognitron, which is a hierarchical multilayered network based on the model of the human visual system, in which the initial stage is an input layer, and each succeeding stage has a layer of S-cells followed by a layer of C-cells, and thus layers of S-cells and C-cells are arranged alternately throughout the whole network, a detailed analysis of the training process used with this type of network can be found in Matsumoto [8].

   The neocognitron has two disadvantages, of which the first is that the training process is very slow, because the number of cells in the model increases almost linearly with the number of objects it is required to learn to distinguish, and second, the network must be completely retrained for each new set of patterns.

2. Housing is an extremely heterogeneous product, reflecting the uniqueness of each building site, the long life of the structure, and particularly the decentralized means of production, which shows up sharply in a comparison with the automobile, which for most people is second only to housing in size and cost, but only a few manufacturers produce automobiles, whereas in housing, however, the 100 largest developers produce only about 15 percent of the annual new construction, and the remainder is mostly built by companies of small or medium size or by individuals—all with their own idea of what constitutes a house. Moreover, the builder, unlike the automobile manufacturer, makes no systematic effort to control the quality of maintenance once the product has been sold, but instead the owner must deal with an even more decentralized system of local repair and remodeling services—all with their own views of what should be done, and local building codes are one of

the few sources of standardized construction and maintenance procedures, yet they are notorious for differing from one another and for being circumvented by owners in any event.[2]

練習 7-2 片斷式句子

以下的文章都包含過多片斷式的句子。請把這些句子與其前後的句子合併，以造出較順暢連貫的文章。在某些句子中，可能需省略一些贅詞，或可能需修改或補充一些字詞。

1. To the observer, a change in state is a sudden and dramatic event. It renders a material essentially unrecognizable after it occurs. Certainly, at first glance, an ice cube seems to have more in common with a quartz crystal or a diamond. It seems to have less in common with the steam pouring from a kettle of boiling water. On a microscopic scale, however, all three forms of water contain the same two atoms of hydrogen to one of oxygen. All are held together by the same electromagnetic force. Moreover, despite the apparent abruptness of a change in state, the sequence of events that precedes it is anything but sudden and dramatic. Typically, it is a smooth and unremarkable continuum. Lower the temperature of a glass of water degree by degree. At some point the change from water to ice will take place. Experience tells us at what temperature the change will occur. But no simple theoretical formula predicts it.[3]

2. In the 1920s, researchers realized that the brain was in ceaseless electrical activity. So the idea became popular that memories could take the form of recurrent electrical signals between cells. But memories can withstand all sorts of shocks to the head or brain. These shocks range from concussion to electroconvulsive therapy. These shocks totally disrupt this electrical activity. So memories cannot be stored in purely electrical form. On the other hand, such damage does tend to result in loss of very recent memory. Recent memory is memory for events minutes to hours before the shock. This is why

people who have been in crashes often cannot remember the events that led up to the accident.

Hence researchers came to believe that memory exists in at least two forms. One is memory for very recent events. This is called short-term memory. It is relatively labile and easily disruptable. The other is long-term memory. It is much more stable. Not everything that gets into short-term memory becomes fixed in the long-term store. A filtering mechanism selects things that might be important. It discards the rest. If this were not the case, we would remember everything that impinged upon us. If we remembered everything that impinged upon us, we would soon become hopelessly overloaded.[4]

7.4 對稱法

當英文論文中提到兩個或以上的對等概念時，這些對等概念應皆以對稱的文法結構去表達，這原則稱為「對稱法」(parallelism)。對等的概念是指兩個或多個概念在某一個文脈中，是同等重要的，例如用以描述同一個事物的連串形容詞，或一個程序中的幾個必要的步驟。表達對等概念的字詞可以是單字、片語或整個子句。對稱法有助作者以語文結構來反映內容，只要以對稱結構來寫對等的字詞、片語或子句，讀者便能較快較易地掌握文章內容。

下列例句都包含對稱結構：

A research report should be *clear* and *concise*. 兩個對等的形容詞

The baseball sailed *over the tree, through the open window,* and *into Mrs. Smith's soup.* 三個對等的介系詞片語

The technician *holds* the module at a 45 degree angle from the system board, *inserts* it into the socket, and gently *presses* it forward until it snaps into place. 三個對等的動詞

Before annealing, the samples were soft and flexible; after annealing, they were hard and brittle. 兩個對等的獨立子句

序列的項目亦應使用對稱結構。參考以下的序列：

The process may be divided into four phases:

Harvesting
The drying procedure
Roasting
Product is packaged

把以上各項目改成對稱形式，會令序列更清晰。第一和第三個項目都是動名詞（即動詞的 *-ing* 形）；第二個項目包含一個動名詞與一個名詞；第四個項目則包含一個動詞 ("packaged")，而這動詞可輕易改成動名詞。所以最簡單的修改方式就是把全部項目都改為動名詞：

> The process may be divided into four phases:
>> Harvesting
>>
>> Drying
>>
>> Roasting
>>
>> Packaging

修改後，序列項目的文法結構都對稱一致，會更順暢易讀。

有時候，作者必須正確使用對稱結構，句意才不會含糊。譬如，根據文法結構，下面句子的意思似乎是：動畫系統能創造出兩種事物的表象，即「實際的景觀」和「模型上的交互作用」。

> The animation system is designed to create lifelike representations of real scenes and modeling interactions between objects in a scene.

然而，作者的原意是這個系統有兩種功能，它能創造出實際景觀的表象，並做出景觀中事物間交互作用的模型。因為指稱這兩個功能的動詞沒有寫成對稱的形式，因此很易誤導讀者：

> The animation system is designed *to create* lifelike representations of real scenes and *modeling* interactions between objects in a scene.

如果把兩個動詞改寫成對稱形式，句意會清楚得多：

> The animation system is designed *to create* lifelike representations of real scenes and *to model* interactions between objects in a scene.

英文文法規定，相關連接詞 (*not only...but...*, *both...and...*, *either...or...*) 後面的內容必須為對稱結構。

誤：The algorithm *not only must avoid* local maxima *but also converge* as quickly as possible.

正：The algorithm *not only must avoid* local maxima *but must converge* as quickly as possible.

正：The algorithm must *not only avoid* local maxima *but converge* as quickly as possible.

誤：Light can *either be treated as* waves *or as* particles.

正：Light can *either be treated as* waves *or be treated as* particles.

正：Light can be treated *either as* waves *or as* particles.

當對稱結構中的字詞或片語要加上冠詞或介系詞時，可以只加在首個字詞或片語前面，否則必須加在每個對等字詞或片語的前面。

正： We will analyze *the* structure, computational complexity, and performance of the algorithm.

正： We will analyze *the* structure, *the* computational complexity, and *the* performance of the algorithm.

誤： We will analyze *the* structure, computational complexity, and *the* performance of the algorithm.

如果對稱結構中的字詞各須加上不同的介系詞，則必須在每個對等字詞前或後面加上適當的介系詞。

誤： This interface is used for *reading* and *writing to* memory.

正： This interface is used for *reading from* and *writing to* memory.

在某些句子中，必須在對稱結構中的對等項前面都加上一個介系詞或其他字（例如 *that* 或 *to*），才能突出對稱結構，使句意更明確。看以下的例句：

Our aim is to *identify the difficulties* faced by customers who *purchase these devices* and *develop more user-friendly products*.

這句子的意思模稜兩可：要開發新產品的是作者還是其客戶？作者原本想強調的對等結構是 *identify the difficulties* 和 *develop more user-friendly products* 兩個不定詞片語。這兩個片語的形式確實對稱，但剛好後者的形式和 *purchase these devices* 也對稱，故對稱的片語究竟是哪兩個？要澄清句意，作者必須在第二個對稱的不定詞片語前面也加上 *to*：

Our aim is *to identify* the difficulties faced by customers who purchase these devices and *to develop* more user-friendly products.

以下是另一個例子：

The experimental data confirm that the proposed method is *accurate* and *fast* algorithms based on this method can be implemented in practical applications.

這句相當容易誤導讀者。乍看之下，還以為作者的意思是自己的方法既準又快。作者應多加一個 *that*，使能突出句中的對稱結構：

The experimental data confirm *that* the proposed method is accurate and *that* fast algorithms based on this method can be implemented in practical applications.

對稱法不但可應用在句子中對等的概念，還可應用到段落中有對等關係的句子上。對稱法應用到句與句之間，可讓段落中在內容和功能上相似的句子，以相似的文法結構標示出來。這樣的段落會更鮮明易讀。試參考這例：

On the front panel of the modem are seven control buttons and a row of LED indicators. An RS-232 connector, a line jack, a phone jack, and a power connector can be found on the rear panel.

這段的寫法有點笨拙，且很容易會把讀者搞糊塗。讀者會期待描述數據機背面板的第二句，與描述正面板的第一句在結構上對稱。所以，應把第二句改寫成與第一句對稱，這才明瞭通順。

> *On the front panel of the modem are* seven control buttons and a row of LED indicators. *On the rear panel are* an RS-232 connector, a line jack, a phone jack, and a power connector.

下面是另一個例子：

> The algorithm we have proposed is superior to the conventional algorithm in two ways. Our algorithm is much faster than the conventional algorithm, especially in applications with only a small number of parameters. And, particularly in applications involving large sets of data, the conventional method is more difficult to program than our method.

這段文章中，第三句的結構和第二句的不對稱，使段落不通順，尤以第三句更見笨拙難懂。作者在首句指出自己的新演算法有兩方面比傳統的優勝，遂於第二句把新演算法和傳統的作對照，並舉例說明新的速度明顯較快。在看過第二句後，讀者會期待接著的第三句是兩演算法之間的另一個對照，還會期待它的結構會和第二句的對稱。為了滿足這些期望，作者應把 *our method* 當作第三句的主詞，並把這主詞放到句首：

> The algorithm we have proposed is superior to the conventional algorithm in two ways. *Our algorithm is much faster* than the conventional algorithm, especially in applications with only a small number of parameters. *Our method is also easier to program* than the conventional method, particularly in applications involving large sets of data.

修改後的段落，意思更明瞭合理，結構更見工整。

練習 7-3 對稱結構

請將下列對等的字詞、片語或子句改寫成對稱形式，並刪除贅詞。

1. We are developing a new memory product with large capacity, requires low power, and it has fast access speed.

2. My report discusses how to increase sales, how to improve quality, and developing new products.

3. The terms will either be a sequence of 1's or 0's.

4. In our latest work, we have prepared fiber with liquid crystal cladding, a measurement system has been set up, and theoretical formulas have been derived.

5. The selection criteria for government-funded R&D projects are the following:

- A major technology essential to economic growth is developed

- Requires substantial funding

- The project fills a gap in private firms' development plans

6. The new method is simpler and faster than the conventional method, and it has higher accuracy compared with the conventional method.

7. The indirect control method has two advantages: no need to install flux sensors and easy to use at low speeds.

8. When the principal point lies on the right side of the graph, the angular velocity is negative and the direction of the friction force is counterclockwise. The direction of the friction force is clockwise and the angular velocity is positive when the principal point lies on the left side of the graph.

7.5 善用對等與附屬結構

　　一個句子中所包含的概念，不一定都同等重要。除了主要意思的部分外，句中可能也有一些次要或補充的部分。在英文中，用來標示句中不同意思之間關係的文法結構有兩種：對等結構和附屬結構。對等結構 (coordinate construction) 用來表達相關而對等的意思；附屬結構 (subordinate construction) 則用來表達補充而次要的意思，即非句中的主要意思。句子的主要重點可用主要子句來表達，而次要且附屬的意思則可用附屬結構表達。

　　對等結構以對等連接詞、相關連接詞或連接副詞作連接而構成。對等連接詞 (and, but, or, nor, so, yet, for)及相關連接詞 (not only...but..., either...or..., both...and...) 是連接句子內對等的字詞、片語或子句的。至於連接副詞（however, therefore, nevertheless, consequently 等等）則用來表示兩個句子之間的對等關係。

　　以下是兩個對等結構的範例。在首句中，有三個以 and 連接的對等述詞。第二句中則有兩個以 but 連接的對等獨立子句。

　　The precipitate was *filtered* out of the solution, *dried*, and *weighed*.

　　The substance was not soluble in water at room temperature, but *it was soluble in water heated to 75° C.*

以上兩個例句中，以斜體字表示的都是對等的概念：首句所提到的三個步驟都同等重要，第二句敘述的那兩個事實也一樣重要。因此，這兩句都應寫成對等結構。

　　附屬結構是包括附屬子句、關係子句、同位語、分詞片語以及獨立片語。這種結構常用來表示因果關係（以 *because, since* 等字詞引介的附屬結構）、條件關係（*if, unless*）、讓步關係（*although*）、目的關係（*in order to, so that*）、時間關係（*after, before, when, while*）或地點　（*where*）。附屬結構能清楚地表示出句中不同概念之間的關係，是造出簡明英文句子的重要工具。如能善用附屬結構，可有助突出句子的重點，並顯示出句中其餘的概念和重點的關係。

　　要瞭解附屬結構的重要，可參考下面這個段落。在這段落中，所有內容都以對等結構表達，沒有任何附屬結構。

> The Vu Quang ox is a rare mammal, and it resembles cattle, goats, and antelope in different respects. The Vu Quang ox lives in an isolated, inaccessible region of Vietnam, and the existence of this species was unknown to scientists until 1992. A hunter captured a young female Vu Quang ox, and scientists recently obtained the first living specimen of this unusual animal.

這段文章的內容全都以對等形式表達，所以文中的句子皆缺乏清晰的焦點。此文章提供了許多信息，但信息之間的關係卻不清楚。第二句中，兩個子句之間的關係為何？第三句中，獵人所捕捉的動物和科學家獲得的動物是否為同一隻？若改用適當的附屬結構，文中概念之間的關係得以闡明，將有助讀者更易瞭解文意。

> The Vu Quang ox is a rare mammal *that in different respects resembles cattle, goats, and antelope. Because the Vu Quang ox lives in an isolated, inaccessible region of Vietnam*, the existence of this species was unknown to scientists until 1992. Scientists recently obtained the first living specimen of this unusual animal *from a hunter who captured a young female Vu Quang ox.*

修改過後，文章通順得多，模糊之處都已澄清：第二句中，清晰顯示出兩個子句之間的因果關係，第一個子句是因，第二個子句是果。第三句則表明了，獵人捕捉了一隻動物，然後交給了科學家。

　　要寫出流暢自然的英文科技論文，必須學習適當使用對等結構與附屬結構。中國作者寫的英文文章中有一常犯錯誤：必須用附屬結構時，卻不使用。以下句子是兩個以連接詞 *and* 連接的對等子句：

> The number of directions in each frequency contour is at most two, *and* we divide the contours into two sections.

兩個子句的關係不夠明瞭：句子的主要意思是甚麼？好像是 *we divide the contours into two sections*，而它與第一個子句之間的關係又似乎是因果關係：因為方向最多只有兩個，所以作者決定把每條線分成兩節。假設這個詮釋正確，作者應在句首加上附屬連接詞（如 *because* 或 *since*），使第一個子句附屬於第二個子句：

> *Since* the number of directions in each frequency contour is at most two, we divide the contours into two sections.

下面的句子也沒有適當使用附屬結構：

> The dynamic Coulomb friction between two sliding surfaces always opposes the direction of motion and is given by the following expression.

這句非常不自然。讀者可看出句中兩個動詞 (*opposes* 和 *is given*) 的意思並不對等：第一個動詞指科學的事實，第二個則指作者使用的某特定數學公式。再者，句中兩個對等動詞在文法結構上都受副詞 *always* 修飾，這有點荒謬。摩擦力怎樣「總是」以接著的方程式表示？（如果沒有物理學家，根本不會有任何方程式表示這摩擦力）。為了把這句改得合理通順，應該將其中一個動詞併入一附屬結構。假設重點是可使用作者所介紹的方程式來表示摩擦力，此句應修改如下：

> The dynamic Coulomb friction between two sliding surfaces, *which always opposes the direction of motion*, can be expressed by the following equation.

但如果重點是摩擦力的方向和動作的方向總是相反，則此句應改寫成：

> The dynamic Coulomb friction between two sliding surfaces, *which can be expressed by the equation below*, always opposes the direction of motion.

> The dynamic Coulomb friction between two sliding surfaces always opposes the direction of motion, *as shown in the equation below*.

在這個例子中，第一個修正句大概較能表達出作者原意。其實無論選擇哪個修正句，最重要是選出其中一個動詞來作句子的重點，並把另一個動詞併入關係子句中，使它附屬於這個重點。

練習 7-4 對等與附屬結構

　　請改寫下列句子和段落，以適切的附屬子句或片語來表達次要的意思。（提示：修改時可能需更改句子結構和標點符號，或修改、刪除、補充一些字詞。第 7、8 題中，斜體字是應改成附屬結構的部分。）

1. When designing practical controllers, one often encounters systems with uncertain parameters and these can be represented mathematically as follows.

2. This type of job dispatching balances the workload of the processors and is called dynamic load balancing.

3. The upper row displays eight icons, and users can assemble these into query graphs.

4. The results of the first trial were surprising, and we repeated the experiment using a new set of data.

5. Live-line workers approach their jobs with the care accorded lion training and skydiving. *A significant electrostatic field surrounds a live power line for several tens of meters and increases in strength the nearer to the line*, and a lineman's body is

energized well before he touches the conductor. Within a meter or so, the field may be 20-30 kV less than the conductor's voltage. Despite that difference, a human body has a relatively small mass. *The lineman contacts the line with his wand,* and a current of no more than a few microamperes is induced in his body. *That difference in voltage exists,* however, and an arc will leap between conductor and wand as the lineman approaches the conductor. (*Such sparks are not strong enough to be fatal.* They can cause a brief loss of sensation in the hand.)

6. The lineman's wand and steel-mesh suit prevent the spark from touching his body: the arc jumps from line to wand rather than to a gloved hand or finger, and the suit equalizes the charge across its surface. *The suit works on the principle of a Faraday cage. The lineman is bonded,* and then contact is maintained through a short tie from suit to conductor, and *the tie is called a bonding lead. The suit is required at voltages above 150 kV,* and it also protects the lineman against the corona effect, the ionization of the air around a person's body. *The ionization results in a distinct buzzing sound and a prickly sensation on protruding body parts such as the ears.*[5]

第八章
統一連貫的段落

　　第六章和第七章已介紹有關英文論文由字詞使用到句子結構的修辭原則，本章則進一步討論段落結構。

　　一個段落 (paragraph) 是由一些共同針對某一特定主題的句子所組成的。段落是文章的基本單位，因此想寫一篇好論文，便要從統一連貫、組織嚴謹的段落開始。如果一篇論文的段落組織緊湊，會讓研究人員易於閱讀，較易瞭解論文內容。

　　一個緊湊的段落通常有三個主要特性：

- 統一 (unity)：一個段落應集中討論一個主題或重點，並應先在主題句中清楚點出，然後再詳細敘述或舉例說明。

- 連貫 (coherence)：一個段落應有清楚的組織，段中的每個句子，都應支持段落的主題或主要論點。

- 發展 (development)：一個段落必須包括一些例子、數據和解釋，來具體地闡述主題或主要論點，從而使讀者相信論點合情合理。

本章將討論兩個段落寫作之基本要點：主題句及段落組織。

8.1 主題句

　　主題句 (topic sentence) 通常是在段落的首句或首幾句。一個清晰具體的主題句大致有三個作用：

一、　直接告訴讀者段落的重點或主題。

二、　讓讀者能看出段落的內容與讀者的背景知識有何關聯。

三、 可作為一背景脈絡，使段落中其他的句子，都能針對著一個重點展開討論或予以支持。

當讀到一個段落時，每個人都自然想儘快知道該段將會講甚麼，或是該內容與自己的背景知識有何關聯，故一個好的主題句應能滿足這些要求。同時，主題句也應能讓讀者在瀏覽文章時立即瞭解各段重點，以便決定哪些段落要仔細閱讀或略過。

科技論文的每個段落中都應該有主題句。主題句通常是在段首，但有時也會出現在別的位置。一般來說，主題句的位置可以有三種：

- 段落首句。科技論文的導論或「討論」(Discussion) 章節中的段落，常以主題句開首。

- 段落的首幾句。有時段首會以一個句子或子句來承接上文，而第二個子句或第二、三句才會是主題句。

- 段落末句。在科技研究報告的「結果」(Results) 章節中，作者經常會先陳述一些資料，然後再以歸納形式作結，因此會順理成章把歸納得來的結論放於段末。這個結論就是段落的主題句。

雖然並非每個段首都是主題句，但段落首句都應明白地指出：（一）段落的內容和作者的背景知識有何關聯。（二）整段到底要表達甚麼。例如，下列是一篇論文的結果章節中某段落的首句：

The electrical characteristics of the six samples are shown in Table 2.

雖然這句並非該段落的主題句（在原文中，由表二的資料所歸納得來的結論，即主題句，其實是在段落的末句），但它告訴讀者這個段落將會討論甚麼，同時也指出該段內容和前段的關聯。（在原文中，導論和「方法」(Method) 章節已交代過，論文目的在於探討不同環境下製造的樣本，其電子特性的差異。）

主題句不單要點明段落將會討論甚麼，還要提供具體的內容。舉個例說，假設某段落的首句是這樣的一個句子：

The structure of the system will be described now.

這是一個不妥當的主題句，因為內容太少。這句表示該段落將要描述一個系統的結構，但卻未真正提供有關這系統結構的任何信息。一個較妥當的主題句應是這樣的：

The system consists of two main parts.

這句不單指出將會描述一個系統，同時也確切地陳述有關這系統結構的一些信息。

儘管主題句非常重要，但有時仍然會給不少作者忘記。試看下列這個討論電腦程式語言缺點的段落：

Among the proposed object-oriented or object-based specification languages, the language of PROTOB incorporates standard programming languages to specify object behavior, and the language of OBSERV does not provide any mechanism for specifying inheritance relationships and system functions. The language proposed by Lee cannot specify classes and relationships between objects, and the language of ENVISAGER does not provide any mechanism for specifying system functions or a large-scale model partitioning structure.

這段沒有主題句，使段落的要義不明。作者清楚地述說了一些內容，但卻沒指出述說的目的，或這些內容所用作支持的論點。想修改這段落，必須找出它的主要論點，然後寫成一個主題句。在原文中，作者曾在這段落之前提出過良好的程式語言所應符合的條件。據此，我們可推斷這段落的主要論點是：作者所批評的語言中，沒有一個能滿足所有這些條件。故此，以這論點作為主題句的基礎非常恰當。下面以斜體字標示的便是主題句：

None of the proposed object-oriented or object-based specification languages satisfies all of the criteria we have set forth. The language used in PROTOB relies on standard programming languages to specify object behavior; the language proposed by Lee cannot specify classes and relationships between objects. The language of OBSERV fails to provide a mechanism for specifying inheritance relationships and system functions, and the language used in ENVISAGER provides neither a mechanism for specifying system functions nor a large-scale model partitioning structure.

科技論文作者時會在同一個段落中陳述很多事實，有時這些事實彼此間表面上會出現矛盾，令人困惑。這時明確的主題句就特別重要。試看以下這個比較風力與化石燃料的段落：

Wind power is more expensive than energy generated from traditional sources such as fossil fuels. In general, energy produced by wind turbines costs more than twice as much as energy produced from natural gas, and it is also more expensive than energy produced from oil or coal. The technology for producing energy from wind is improving steadily, and the cost of wind-generated energy may soon be competitive with that of energy generated from fossil fuels, especially if the prices of fossil fuels rise. The earth's reserves of fossil fuels are limited and will one day be depleted, but wind is an infinitely renewable resource. Wind turbines are nonpolluting, and they can coexist with agriculture. In addition, energy sources such as oil and coal have hidden social costs, because they pollute the environment and, particularly in the case of coal, cause a variety of occupational illnesses. Wind power has no such hidden costs.

這段落的主要論點似乎是：雖然現今以風力產生能源，較其他自然資源昂貴，但仍有許多理由能證明風力是甚具潛力的資源。然而，作者並沒直接表示這論點，讀者只能從段落內容中推斷出來。更嚴重的，是段首兩句很易誤導讀者。乍看之下，這兩句像是與上述推斷出來的論點相牴觸。讀完首兩句，讀者可能會假設段落重點是指出風力的缺點，卻非肯定它的價值。由於這段落陳述了幾個表面上互相矛盾的事實，作者實在有必要在段落的開首加上明確的主題句，以便讀者掌握段意。以下是一個修改方法，以斜體標示的是主題句：

Although wind power is currently more expensive than energy generated from traditional sources such as fossil fuels, it is a promising source of energy for the future. In general, energy produced by wind turbines costs more than twice as much as energy produced from natural gas, and it is also more expensive than energy produced from oil or coal. Yet the technology for producing energy from wind is improving steadily, and the cost of wind-generated energy may soon be competitive with that of energy generated from fossil fuels, especially if the prices of fossil fuels rise. Energy sources such as oil and coal have hidden social costs, because they pollute the environment and, particularly in the case of coal, cause a variety of occupational illnesses. Moreover, the earth's reserves of fossil fuels are limited and will one day be depleted. In contrast, wind power has no such hidden costs. Wind turbines are nonpolluting and can coexist with agriculture, and wind is an infinitely renewable resource.

加上明確的主題句之餘，段落也應重組，以闡明風力與傳統能源來源的對比。同時，作者也應該採用一些「信號」字眼 (*yet, although, in contrast*) 來闡明或強調某些概念之間的關係（有關「信號」字眼，詳見第九章9.7節）。在首句中，加上 *although* 這字眼尤其重要，它有助澄清一個轉折關係：雖然首個子句對風力的報告像是負面的，但段落對風力的整體評價仍屬正面。

練習 8-1 主題句

為下列段落選出最適當的主題句。（假設所選句子是該段的首句。）

1. The longer and deeper they stay below, the more of the gas dissolves in their blood. Eventually too much of it is driven into solution by the sea's greater-than-atmospheric pressure. Subsequently, if a diver returns to the surface without letting his body adjust to the lower pressure, the gas starts bubbling out of the blood and blocking circulation. This causes the bends, the effects of which can be permanently crippling or lethal. In essence, the deeper the dive from the surface, the shorter the stay on the bottom should be.[1]

   主題句：

   (a) Divers must pay careful attention to the effects of nitrogen gas.

   (b) What ultimately limits divers' time under water is nitrogen gas.

   (c) One danger of deep-sea diving is the bends, a phenomenon caused by nitrogen gas dissolved in divers' blood.

2. Jupiter's latitudinal bands, the zonal jet streams, and the long-lived oval spots were known before Voyager. The intense eddy activity at scales below the resolution of Earth-based telescopes was an important Voyager discovery that served to deepen the mystery surrounding the long-lived ovals and latitudinal bands. The 1800-km/hour winds of Saturn, three times faster than those of Jupiter, were another important discovery. The existence of latitudinal bands on Uranus, despite that planet's peculiar orientation, showed that planetary rotations, not energy sources, control the patterns of atmospheric circulation. Neptune was a surprise because its wind speeds were greater than any seen elsewhere in the solar system, despite its low solar energy input. The power

per unit area that drives Neptune's Great Dark Spot, for example, is 5% of that which drives the Great Red Spot of Jupiter.[2]

主題句：

(a) A major discovery due to the Voyager spacecraft was that the winds on Saturn are much faster than those on Jupiter.

(b) The two Voyager spacecraft have allowed us to compare characteristics of the outer planets in new ways.

(c) The two Voyager spacecraft revealed much about the dynamics of the atmospheres of the outer planets.

3. They must be longer, relative to the body, than the legs of most slower animals, yet they must oscillate very fast. They must also be relatively light, yet strong enough to deliver enormous thrust and to sustain tremendous loads. All of this must be done with sufficient economy of effort to provide endurance. It is evident that nature places greater demands on the mechanical design of horse legs than on the legs of most other animals, even including those of the faster but smaller cheetah.[3]

主題句：

(a) The legs of a horse have a unique structure, unmatched in the animal world.

(b) The horse's great running ability coupled with its large size places unusual demands on its legs.

(c) In comparison with the legs of a cheetah, a horse's legs are longer, lighter, and stronger.

4. The tubular body of the leech is built of 32 similar segments and offers the possibility of understanding the entire animal by studying just one of its segments. Of the 32 segments the frontmost four make up the specialized structures of the head, including a pair of eyes on the dorsal, or upper surface and a front sucker on the ventral, or lower surface. The rearmost seven segments make up the specialized structures of the tail, including the anus and a large rear sucker. The anatomy of the intervening 21 mid-body segments is highly stereotyped. Each segment has a complete set of visceral organs, including circulatory vessels, kidneys, and gut. The skin of each segment is subdivided into a fixed number of annuli, or rings; the middle annulus bears an array of sensory organs distributed around the circumference of the body tube. The body wall of each segment is girded by circular muscles that can constrict the body tube. Deeper in the wall lie longitudinal muscles; their contraction shortens the body tube.[4]

主題句:

    (a) The leech's simple body plan makes it an attractive animal to the experimental biologist.

    (b) The structure of the leech's body has been the subject of extensive study by biologists.

    (c) The body of the leech is similar in structure to that of the earthworm, its close relative.

5. In a topping system (Fig. 1), electricity is delivered first, and the thermal power exhausted is captured for further use. In a bottoming system (Fig. 2), thermal energy is extracted from the heat source after it has been used in a process, and it is used to drive a turbine to generate electricity. Both types of systems vary in size and hardware, depending on the electrical and thermal needs of the user.[5]

主題句:

    (a) A bottoming system is usually more efficient than a topping system.

    (b) Both topping and bottoming systems have been used in many applications.

    (c) There are two basic types of cogeneration systems.

6. Algorithmic computing is ideal for accounting, aerodynamic and hydrodynamic modeling, and the like. Neural networks are ideal for pattern recognition, fuzzy knowledge processing, and adaptive control. Neurocomputers should not be used to balance checkbooks. Algorithmic computers should not be used to recognize speech. The two types of computing can be used together and can be integrated easily in hardware.[6]

主題句:

    (a) Both algorithmic computing and neurocomputing have many important applications.

    (b) Neural computing is unlikely to replace algorithmic computing.

    (c) Algorithmic computing and neurocomputing complement each other well.

8.2 段落組織

    本章8.1節曾指出,一個緊湊的段落有三個基本特性: 統一、聯貫和發展。要寫出統一聯貫的段落,首先要確定段落中有明確適當的主題句。接著是給予段落恰當的組織形式,這除了有助段落統一聯貫外,更可保證段落中包含足夠的內容,從而發展並支持主題句中所提出的論點。

修改段落時，要找出段落的組織形式，並評估該段主題是否明確且能獲得有力的支持。接著再看是否需要進一步修改，例如調動、合併、增加或刪除一些句子。

以下是科技寫作中最常用的一些段落組織形式。這些組織形式並不互相排斥，有時還可兩三個形式合用。例如，作者可列出一連串過程並同時比較其優劣點，或是依時間順序來描述一連串事件，並解釋事件之間的因果關係。

依時間順序

依照事件發生的先後次序來描述一連串事件，是依時間順序的組織形式。這種組織形式通常用於科技研究報告的方法章節，也常用於研究報告中文獻回顧的段落中。（以時間順序表達的段落，如實驗報告方法章節中的段落，有時只描述實驗步驟而不寫主題句。）

在依時間順序的段落中，一定要用轉接詞和表示時間的用語，讀者才能清楚瞭解所描述事件之間的關係。可能使用到的時間用語包括 *afterwards*, *as soon as*, *at the same time*, *before*, *finally*, *first*, *immediately*, *later*, *next*, *second*, *soon*, *third*, *until*, *when* 以及 *while* 等。

以下是一個以時間順序來組織的例子。注意段落如何以表示時間用語和轉接詞（以斜體字標示）來闡明事件發生的先後次序：

> Donor and control nests were located in two areas of north-central Florida where there are large numbers of nesting bald eagles. Aerial surveys *during the breeding seasons from 1985 to 1987* were initiated *prior to egg-laying (in October and November)* and repeated *approximately every week until nearly all the eggs hatched (mid-March). From mid-March until the eaglets fledged,* surveys were conducted *approximately every two weeks* to monitor chronology and productivity at all nests. A total of 42 suitable donor nests were *eventually* located, and 87 eggs were removed *over three breeding seasons.* One egg-collecting trip was made *in 1985* and two *in 1986 and 1987.* Eggs were removed by climbers and *then* quickly dispatched to the research center.[7]

空間順序

依物件或景觀的空間結構來描述，是段落中空間順序的組織形式。它通常是按照一般人親身觀察時的順序描述，例如：從上到下、從前到後，或從左到右地描述物件的各部分。論文的方法章節或材料與方法 (Methods and Materials) 章節常會使用這種組織形式。描述物件之間關係的常用字有 *above, below, on the right, at the top, at the bottom, in the middle, in the center, at the top right (bottom right, top left, bottom left)* 等介系詞。

下面描述水底研究站的例子，就是用空間順序的組織形式。請注意段落中的描述手法：先描述水底研究站的大致情形，再以合理的順序，描述研究站的每個部分——依照人們身臨其境時自然觀察的次序。以斜體標示的字詞皆有助闡明描述物件之間的關係。

In its final form, the underwater habitat weighs 73,500 kilograms and has three chambers (see Figure 3). Divers enter and leave the habitat *through a hole in the floor of a wet porch.* An entrance lock 2.4 meters long and 2.75 meters in diameter *connects the porch to the main lock, where* scientists eat, sleep, relax, and do their desk work. A tube 6.5 meters long with a 2.75-meter diameter, *it contains* six bunks, a dining and work table, and a small kitchen. Air, fresh water, and electricity flow *down into* the habitat *through* umbilical pipes and cables *from* equipment *on* a 13-meter life support buoy anchored permanently *overhead.*[8]

因果分析

　　要解釋某事發生的原因、過程或運作方式，進而預測即將發生的事，都可運用因果分析的段落組織形式。在解釋因果關係時，最好先說明原因再敘述結果，因為這樣會較簡潔自然。除非結果是句中的「舊」內容，才可能先說結果再說原因（有關這裏所指的先後次序，詳見第九章9.1節「先舊後新」）。

　　作因果分析時，必須用轉接詞和附屬子句來標示所描述的因果關係。這類的字詞包括 *accordingly, as a result, because, consequently, hence, if, since, so, then, therefore* 以及 *thus* 等。

　　以下段落便是因果分析之組織形式的例子。注意以斜體字表示的動詞和轉接詞，如何幫助闡明此段落中的因果關係。

The atomic structure of ceramics *gives* them a chemical stability that is manifested as imperviousness to environmental degradation, such as dissolution in solvents. Also, *because* many ceramics are composed of metal oxides, further oxidation (whether by combustion or by other chemical reaction) is often impossible. (In essence, a metal-oxide ceramic has already been "burned" or "corroded," *so* the final ceramic object cannot be further subjected to either of these degradations.) The strength of the bonds in ceramics *endows* them with a high melting point, hardness, and stiffness. Unfortunately, this strength also *prevents* planes of atoms from sliding easily over one another; the material cannot deform to relieve the stresses imposed by a load. *As a result,* ceramics maintain their shape admirably under stress until a certain threshold is exceeded; *then* the bonds suddenly give way and the material fails catastrophically. A further *consequence* of this brittleness is that ceramics can withstand compressive loads far better than they can withstand tensile or shear loads. Under compressive loads incipient cracks tend to be squeezed shut, whereas under tensile loads the crack surfaces tend to be pulled apart, further widening the cracks.[9]

邏輯論證

　　這種組織形式是因果分析的個例，它通常用以支持或反駁某種觀點、理論或解釋。在邏輯論證方式的段落中，常出現的轉接詞包括：*although, as a result, because, but, consequently, even though, for, hence, however, if, otherwise, since, so, then, therefore* 以及 *thus* 等。

　　以下段落是邏輯論證的例子。請注意以斜體字表示的轉接詞，如何幫助闡明段落中論證的結構。

> Fission hypotheses, which assert that the material for the moon came from the earth's mantle, encounter two basic difficulties. The angular momentum of the earth-moon system, *although* large, is insufficient by a factor of about four to support rotational fission. There is no acceptable mechanism for removing the excess angular momentum following lunar formation. A second objection is even more telling. Fission models have become the most readily testable of all following the collection of lunar samples, *since* they predict that the chemistry of the moon should bear some recognizable signature of the terrestrial mantle. *However,* the moon contains 50% more iron than the earth's mantle and has distinctly different signatures of trace siderophile elements. The best estimates for the abundances of the refractory elements in the moon exceed those in the terrestrial mantle by 50%. *Even though* mechanisms for depleting the volatile elements can be incorporated into fission models, the enhancement of iron and the refractory elements cannot be accomplished by such means. The hypothesis *thus* fails the test of finding an identifiable chemical signature of the terrestrial mantle.[10]

比較與對照

　　科技論文的作者經常需要比較與對照不同的對象或現象。尤其是工程學論文的作者，更常需要比較和對照不同過程或方法的特性，進而決定選用哪種方法，或要顯示出自己提出的新方法是怎樣優越。

　　在寫比較和對照的段落時，有兩點必須注意。首先，要用「信號」字眼來闡明比較和對照的目的或要義，例如：

> The recognition rate of our program is 98.5%, and that of Smith's program is 92%.

上述兩種程式的的辨識率皆已達百分之九十以上，讀者一般都會相信這兩種程式均相當有效。但現在假設另一種情況：在同類的程式中，只要辨識率是低於百分之九十五的，就已是毫無用處的。如果是這種情況的話，則那兩種程式之間就有很大的差別。上述句子並未能指出這要點，所以應修改為：

> The recognition rate of our program is 98.5%, *whereas* that of Smith's program is *only* 92%.

在修改句中，附屬連接詞 *whereas* 和字詞 *only* 強調了作者的程式遠比斯密的程式有效，且這個性能的差別才是重點所在。

　　此外，如果要比較的兩件事物，有幾項特性（如製作過程的成本、效率、準確度、開發時間或簡易性等），則要避免每句交替且重複地說第一個事物是怎麼樣，第二個又是怎麼樣，這樣會十分生硬。要從某幾項特性去比較兩個事物，應先仔細將那些特性分組，然後一組一組來討論；或者可先舉出一項的所有優點，再談另外一項的優點，最後談兩者的缺點。

在比較和對照的段落中，用來顯示概念之間關係的轉接詞或其他用語有：
although, at the same time, but, by contrast, conversely, despite, however, in contrast, likewise, more, nevertheless, less, on the other hand, similarly, still, than, unlike, whereas, while, yet 等。

以下段落就是用比較和對照的組織形式。請注意以斜體字標示的字詞，如何幫助闡明段落的對照。

Because of its large size, the running horse places more deflecting forces on its legs (in turning, or in stepping on angled surfaces) *than* do many smaller, slower animals. *Yet* its musculature, being adapted to function largely in one plane, is, if anything, *less* suited to stabilize the joints. This animal *instead* employs mechanisms that are better suited for speed and endurance, because they are lighter than muscles and are passive—hence, free of energetic cost. For example, *whereas* the human wrist joint, being ellipsoid, allows motions in two planes of space, that of the horse is a hinge that turns only front and back. The joints between our palm bones (metacarpals) and finger bones likewise work in two planes (making a fist and spreading the fingers), *in contrast to* the corresponding joint of the horse, which again is a hinge. These hinges, and those at the elbow and heel—the horse's hock (Fig. 2)—are strengthened against dislocation by having a flange on one member of the hinge that turns in a groove in the other (Fig. 3). Rotation of the forearm is prevented by fusion of the two bones there (radius and ulna). The head of the human thigh bone (femur) forms a large part of a nearly perfect sphere, and the hip joint is thus a ball and socket, allowing freedom of motion in all planes but requiring muscles to prevent unwanted sideways motions. *By contrast,* the head of a horse's femur is a lesser part of a sphere, and is somewhat cylindrical on top (with axis transverse to the body), thus passively restraining motions that are not front and back.[11]

列舉法

列舉法也是科技寫作中常用的段落組織形式。這種方式通常出現在研究報告的導論，用來回顧相關的研究著作。列舉法有時也會用在報告的材料 (Materials) 章節，以描述某項實驗所用到的材料類型。在使用列舉法的段落中，所列出的每個項目都應該用對稱結構來表達（如果所列項目很多，則可分組，而每組中的各項目仍須以對稱結構來表達）。此外，用列舉法的段落必須以明確的主題句開首，也就是在列舉之前，先說明列出項目的原因。

在使用列舉法的段落中經常出現的轉接詞包括：*also, and, and then, equally important, finally, first, further, furthermore, in addition, last, likewise, moreover, next, second, similarly, third, too* 等。

請注意以下段落如何以斜體標示的字詞來強調各列舉項目。

A variety of interrelated reasons have contributed to problems with the accuracy of radar speed readings. *First,* the police radar industry is highly competitive and has been growing rapidly. Because of this competition and the fact that most operators are technically unknowledgeable, a number of "convenience" features of dubious merit have been introduced to help sell equipment. *Second,* operator training has been left, by default, in the hands of equipment manufacturers, and no standards for operator training have been established. The equipment manufacturers, by and large, have instructed operators, or instructors of operators, in the nominal setup and use of the radar, but have fallen short on explaining equipment shortcomings. *Third,* there are no standards for equipment performance except for the Federal Communication Commission's frequency and power output requirements and licensing procedures. But this simple license has itself led to serious misconceptions among some equipment users, since the FCC is concerned only with a small portion of the equipment and not with the accuracy and performance of the complete device. *Finally,* there are no standards for the calibration or maintenance of the equipment.[12]

由概括到個別描述

如果作者在一段首已提出一個概括的論點，然後再列出一些具體事項來支持，這種組織手法便是由概括到個別描述。在這類段落中，句子的描述範圍會隨著段落的發展而漸漸縮小，在科技論文中十分常見。

例如，以下段落的首句表示了一個概括的論點：「地球－月球」系統在太陽系中是相當獨特的，接著再指出一些該系統具有的特質來支持首句的論點。

The earth-moon system is unmatched among the inner, or terrestrial, planets. Neither Venus, close in size to the earth, nor Mercury has a moon, while Phobos and Deimos, the two moons of Mars, are probably tiny captured asteroids, with primitive compositions. The satellites of the outer planets are mostly ice-rock mixtures. The orbit of the moon about the earth is neither in the equatorial plane of the earth nor in the plan of the ecliptic, but is inclined at 5.1° to the latter, and the angular momentum of the earth-moon system is anomalously high compared to that of the other planets.[13]

在某些段落中，由概括到個別描述還可能會與歸納法（歸納法即由個別到概括描述）合用。即是說，會先作概括論述，遂提出具體事項來支持，最後再以另一概述結尾，扼要說明全段重點或結論。

歸納法

在科技論文中結果章節和討論章節中，有時會使用歸納法。使用這種形式時，作者應先提出一些資料，然後討論這些資料的涵意，最後再推出一個或多個結論。在這種類型的段落中，句子的描述範圍會隨著段落的發展漸漸擴大。還有，段中末句可能會以這些字詞開始： *in conclusion, in short, in summary, on the whole, to conclude, to summarize, to sum up* 等。

下列段落節錄自一篇論文的結果章節，而這段就採用了歸納法。段落的前六句指出了實驗工作的結果，最後兩句便扼要說明這些結果，並從中推出結論。請注意這段使用了 *to summarize* 這轉接詞來帶出歸納的結果。

For the first set of 10 odorants, including the brand names, the number of correct responses ranged from 1 to 9, with a mean of 4.4, or 44%, and a standard deviation of 1.9. The mean number of correct responses for the five brand names was 2.4, with a standard deviation of 1.3. The mean for the five other odorants was 2.1, with a standard deviation of 1.2. For the scratch-and-sniff experiment with 13 odorants, the number of correct responses ranged from 1 to 8, with a mean of 4.2, or 32%. In both experiments, women were significantly more successful than men in identifying the odors, with a mean number of correct responses of 4.9 versus 4.1 for men in the first experiment and 4.9 versus 3.8 for men in the second. Regarding differences between odors, the percentage of correct identification ranged from 27% for rose to 75% for bubble gum in the first experiment and from 0% for musk to 83% for licorice in the second experiment. *To summarize,* although there are individual differences, people are not good at naming even very familiar odors. The main point is that, on the average, fewer than half of the odors were correctly named, even with a liberal scoring system.[14]

分類法

分類法是用來描述可分為不同種類的物件，或可把某些類別的事物細分為一些次類別。這種方式常用於論文的文獻回顧或討論章節。如果需要討論的資料相當多，可先將討論對象分組，然後再逐組討論，並比較每組裏的項與項或是組與組本身的特性。

下列的段落所用的是分類法。作者先說明高能雷射可分為兩類及分類的基準，然後再描述這兩大類別下的次類別。

It is becoming common to speak of two classes of high-power lasers, light and heavy. The classification depends mainly on the power. Light lasers operate in the range from a few tens of watts to a few hundred. Many of these lasers are fairly small solid-state devices: ruby lasers (with a wavelength of 0.69 micrometers), neodymium-doped glass lasers, and neodymium-doped yttrium aluminum garnet lasers (both with a wavelength of 1.06 micrometers in the infrared). Ruby and neodymium-doped glass lasers are usually operated in the pulsed mode; neodymium-doped yttrium aluminum garnet lasers can be operated either in the continuous-wave mode or in the pulsed mode. The light class of lasers also includes certain gas lasers (argon and carbon dioxide), which are operated mostly in the continuous-wave mode. The heavy lasers range in power from a few kilowatts to a few tens of kilowatts. At present, however, only experimental or laboratory devices exceed 20 kilowatts. Most of the heavy lasers are carbon dioxide lasers operating in the continuous mode.[15]

定義

當作者需要為一個複雜精密的概念或過程下定義時，通常會作一種延伸且仔細的定義。在這種段落中，作者可能會先下一個概略的定義，再說明定義中所提到的概念，或是進一步補充要定義的概念的一些相關細節。作者也可能先概述要定義的概念，接著用列舉法、比較與對照或其他的技巧來描述此概念的其他面向。

　　以下的段落為陶瓷作了詳細的定義。段落先提出一個概略的定義，然後再補充說明有關陶瓷的一些資料，並列出陶瓷的類型及其應用。這些細節對不熟悉化學的人很重要，因為他們大概不會瞭解首句中那概略的定義。

> Materials scientists generally define ceramics as including all solid materials that are neither metals nor polymers (although they may contain metallic and polymeric elements as constituents or additives). Ceramics can be fabricated from a wide variety of raw materials other than clay (some of which are not found in nature), and they come in a wide variety of forms: glasses, crystallized glasses, monolithic crystals, conglomerations of small crystals and combinations of these. They serve as abrasives and cutting tools, as heat shields and electrical insulators, and as lasing crystals, nuclear fuels, and artificial bone implants. The diverse applications of ceramics make them not only common materials but also indispensable ones in modern society.[16]

　　想寫出統一聯貫、結構嚴謹的段落，論文作者必須細心檢查草稿，找出與段落不聯貫或不通順的句子，然後不斷修改、調動或省略一些句子，以及修改或重組段落。

練習 8-2 段落組織

　　請指出下列段落所用的組織形式。

1. Perceptions of odors and colors operate according to different principles. Colors involve a lexical system which is organized in memory in a relatively abstract and rigidly controlled way. By contrast, odor perception is characterized by flexibility and adaptability, and a relatively concrete but open-ended nonverbal coding system. This manner of organization in turn affects odor memory. What is stored about odors is not likely to involve semantic categories which can be used to retrieve odors. Rather, odor memory involves perceptually unitary episodes described in an idiosyncratic lexicon (Engen 1982). Because the odor is an integral part of the episode, what is stored in memory is not interfered with or even forgotten through frequent experience with similar names or closely related sensory information. Another important difference between odor and color lies in the direction of association between a name and a stimulus. Once one has presented a color chip and had a subject name it, the subject can conjure up a mental image of the color of the chip when the name is subsequently presented (Dorcus 1932). But in odor perception there is no such reciprocity: while perception of an odor may elicit an associated name, such a name cannot be used later to bring back the

original odor perception. The strength of the association is weak from odor to name and nearly zero from name to odor.[17]

2. The result of this analysis is shown in Fig. 7. The left-hand curve is $d\bar{u}/dy$, and the center and right-hand curves are $r(u',v')$ from Voyager 1 and Voyager 2, respectively. Here $r(u',v')$ is the correlation coefficient, $\overline{u'v'}$ divided by standard deviations of u' and v' for the latitude. For the planet as a whole the standard deviations of u' and v' are 10 and 6, respectively. Figure 7 shows that the correlation coefficients are of order 0.3 and that the sign of $r(u',v')$ tends to be the same as that of $d\bar{u}/dy$. The implied rate of energy transfer is enough to double the kinetic energy of the zonal jets in 75 days. If such transfers are occurring over a layer 2.5 bars deep, the transfer rate is 2.3 W/m^2, or 15% of the total thermal energy flux at Jupiter. For Earth, the same term in the mechanical energy cycle is only 0.1% of the total thermal flux. Either Jupiter is much more efficient than Earth in converting thermal energy to mechanical energy, or else the measurements are misleading.[18]

3. The solar water heater used in the experiment is shown in Figure 2. At the top left of the water heater is a cold-water inlet, where water flows into the apparatus. The main portion of the heater consists of many coils of plastic pipe connected together in an accordion fashion and covered with a sheet of heat-absorbing plastic. The water flows through the pipes, absorbing heat from the sun, and then exits the heating apparatus through the outlet at the lower right of the heater. From the outlet the water flows into an insulated storage tank in the basement of the house, from which hot water is drawn when needed.

4. What is a transform? Think of a function $f(x)$, for example, $\exp(-|x|)$, on which some explicit operation $\mathbf{T}$ is carried out, leading to another function $\mathbf{T}\{f(x)\}$. Call this other function $F()$. We say that $F()$ is the such-and-such transform of the function $f()$ that we first thought of. The symbols for the independent variables are deliberately omitted in order to focus attention on the idea that the function shape $F()$ derives from the original shape $f()$, not from either the value of the independent variable or its identity. With the Fourier transform, the operation $\mathbf{T}$ is as follows. "Multiply the function $f(x)$ by $\exp(-i2\pi sx)$, where s is the transform variable, and integrate with respect to x from $-\infty$ to ∞." Applying this operation to $f(x) = \exp(-|x|)$, we find that $\mathbf{T}\{f(x)\} = F(s) = 2/[1 + (2\pi s)^2]$, which is the Fourier transform of $\exp(-|x|)$.[19]

5. The intensity and frequency of earthquakes can be measured by means of seismometers. A seismometer consists of a mass suspended by a spring or other elastic mechanism inside a metal frame that is anchored to the ground. A magnet is attached to the mass and an electric coil to the frame. Any vibration of the ground shakes the seismometer's frame, but inertia tends to hold the mass in its place. Thus the coil on the frame moves in relation to the magnet on the

mass, and this movement generates an electrical signal that represents the intensity and frequency of the movement.[20]

6. The silicon substrates were prepared for diamond deposition as follows. First, p-type or n-type silicon wafers were chemically cleaned and the nucleation sites were patterned with SiO_2. Next, ultrasonic agitation was performed for various lengths of time in water containing diamond powder with a grain size of 1 to 2 mm. Acetone and HF were then used to remove the SiO_2 pattern. Finally, the substrates were dipped into a solution of $HF:HNO_3:H_2O$ (1:1.1:10) for various lengths of time to increase the selectivity during the second stage of diamond growth.[21]

7. The search for extraterrestrial intelligence has already been productive in several respects. It has contributed to the development of new technologies, such as the 8.4 million channel spectrometer developed for the META program at Harvard. It has prompted members of the scientific community to think deeply about basic questions regarding the probability of the emergence of planetary systems, life, intelligence, and technological civilizations. It has also posed fundamental questions about the further development of our own civilization. What are the relative likelihoods of our alternative futures: annihilation, planet-bound stagnation, or continued growth and expansion into the galaxy?[22]

8. The amount of H_2O added to the immersing solution used in liquid phase deposition affects the concentration of fluorine in the resulting silicon oxide. Specifically, a decrease in the quantity of H_2O per 100 ml of immersing solution results in a linear increase in the fluorine concentration. It appears that as the quantity of H_2O in the immersing solution decreases, the concentration of HF increases. This increased HF concentration causes the Si-OH on the substrate to be subject to HF attack, with the result that more fluorine is incorporated into the LPD oxide.[23]

9. The popular stereotype of jackals as skulking scavengers with base and reprehensible behavior is belied, as is so often the case, by long-term observations. Jackals are one of the few species of mammals in which males and females form long-term pair-bonds, often lasting a lifetime. They hunt together, share food, groom each other, jointly defend their territory, and provision and defend their pups together (Fig. 1). Some of the pups stay with their parents and at the age of one year help raise the next litter, their full brothers and sisters.[24]

10. Speculation inspired by Hart's paper led to the formation of the N=1 school, researchers arguing for the uniqueness of our own technological civilization. Several scientists asserted that the creation of life is highly unlikely because of the exceedingly small probabilities for the random assembly of polypeptide sequences (e.g., Monod 1971 and Shklovskii 1978). More recent research on

problems of chemical evolution relating to the origin of life, however, tends to argue in the opposite direction. For example, it has been demonstrated that the coupling of autocatalytic cycles ("hypercycles") could well produce self-replicating macromolecules in relatively short times, rather than the billions of years that would be required by random assembly (Field 1985). Similarly, the phenomenon of RNA catalyzing its own synthesis (see Lewin 1986) supports the idea that the appearance of life may not be particularly unlikely. Shapiro (1986) has explored this complex debate in greater detail. In any case, fossil evidence (stromatolites) indicates that life appeared fairly quickly on earth within one billion years of its formation, perhaps as soon as meteoric bombardment of the primordial crust had subsided.[25]

11. 在練習 8-1 中，請指出每個段落所用的組織形式。

第九章
易讀的論文

　　本章將提出一些基本寫作準則，有助科技論文作者寫出較易閱讀的英語論文。第六章和第七章所介紹的，是標準英文作文遣詞造句的基本規則；本章則集中討論如何鋪排英文句子與段落的內容，令文章更易讀。

　　本章所介紹的是一般的「準則」，而非必須固守的嚴格「規則」。在某些特殊情形下，違反這些準則或許更能寫出簡潔的句子。此外，這些準則偶爾可能會互相衝突，此時作者必須自行取捨。但一般而言，撰寫論文的作者只要遵循這些準則，便可寫出較連貫流暢的文章。

結構與內容

　　本章介紹的準則，皆出於一個基本的假定：文章的表達結構，經常影響讀者對文章內容的理解。換言之，句子與段落的結構，會增進或阻礙讀者對論文內容的理解。因此，作者在鋪排句子與段落內容時，應以讀者較易理解的先後次序為依歸。本章將提出幾個準則，望能指導科技論文的作者達到這目的。這些準則共同的基礎是信息的表達應符合「讀者的期望」(reader expectations)。只要句子與段落遵循這些準則，便能滿足讀者的期望，從而令文章更易讀。

　　舉個簡單的例子，便可說明信息的「結構」如何影響讀者對信息的領悟，以及「結構」與「讀者的期望」的關係。假設我們打算前往異國旅行，希望旅行時能享受到明媚的風光和怡人的天氣，所以要避開雨季。我們遂瀏覽該國旅遊局的網站，查看當地各月的平均雨量。網站提供很多旅遊資料，其中包括下列圖表：

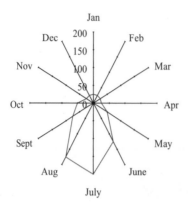

Average Monthly Rainfall
in Country X, 1980-1990

這個圖表已提供我們所需的資料，但是讀這圖表卻非常吃力。它表達資料的方式既不自然，又不清楚。因此，我們把圖表上的資料抄寫在筆記本上：十二月和十一月的雨量大約各為 25 公釐；十月的為 50 公釐；九月為 75 公釐；八月為 175 公釐；七月為 200 公釐；六月為 125 公釐；五月為 50 公釐；至於四月到一月大約各為 25 公釐。接著我們重畫了另一個圖表。因為我們想知道每月雨量變化的情形，所以把月份畫在 x 座標上，雨量畫在 y 座標上，結果如下：

Average Monthly Rainfall in Country X,
1980-1990

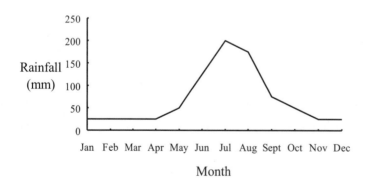

修改後的圖表一目瞭然，當地雨季顯然是從五、六月開始，七月達高峰，而於九、十月結束。

兩個圖表包含的資料相同，但為何第二個圖表較易閱讀？這就是因為它顯示資料的結構較符合讀者的期望。讀者會希望圖表的自變數畫在 x 座標上，而修改後的圖表正是如此：我們把自變數（即時間）畫在 x 座標上，並把因變數（即雨量）畫在 y 座標上。此外，讀者也會希望圖表中的資料是從左往右排列，因為易於閱讀與瞭解。修改後的圖表也滿足了這期望：只要從左往右讀，立刻就可看出 X 國每年雨季及乾季的周期。相反，原來圖表的結構，卻與一般讀者的期望相反，因此難以理解。

　　由上面的例子可以看出：使用符合讀者期望的表達方式，可以使讀者更易瞭解所要表達的內容。反之，使用間接而違反直覺的表達方式，即使是很簡單的內容，也會變得難以瞭解。因此，撰寫科技研究報告時，作者應使用可滿足讀者期望的結構來表達，以便讀者更容易瞭解文章內容。簡單來說，應把讀者希望看到的內容放在讀者希望看到的地方。下面幾個準則就是以這概念作為主要的理論基礎。

9.1 先舊後新

　　讀者閱讀科技論文時，自然想儘快掌握一個新的句子和讀過的句子之間的關聯。為了滿足這需求，作者可採用下列技巧：首先重複一些「舊」內容（即已提過的內容），然後才提出「新」內容。這樣不僅可清楚交待句子和前文內容的關係，還可交待句中的新內容在整個段落脈絡中的角色。此外，在英文中，讀者傾向於強調處於句尾的字詞。作者應明白這閱讀習慣，把希望讀者注意的新內容放在句尾。

　　舉個例說，下面這個段落摘錄自一篇科技管理研究報告。請從頭到尾閱讀一遍，但不要重讀，然後再自問：要瞭解這段需付出多少心力。

> There is often a significant learning cost involved in transferring a new technology from the R&D stage to the production stage. Frequently, investment by the research institute that developed the technology will defray part of this cost. Private industry will probably show little interest in finding commercial applications for a new technology if such investment is unavailable.

大多數讀者都會覺得要把這個段落讀懂，需要付出相當大的心力，也覺得它「不夠流暢」。由於第二、三句與第一句的關係不夠清楚，所以閱讀每一句時，必先記下一大堆資料才能瞭解句意。

　　只要檢查這個段落內容的排列順序，馬上就能瞭解它難讀的原因。試把每句裏的名詞片語都當是一個資料「項目」。我們便會發現，段落首句已提到兩個主要的資料「項目」：「學習成本」和「從研發階段到生產階段的技術移轉」。在看完首句後，我們自然希望進一步認識這兩個資料「項目」，但第二句卻讓我們的期望落空。作者先提到一個新的資料「項目」（即研究機構的投資），並強迫我們一直讀到第二句句尾，才終於提到 "this cost"。接著當讀到第三句時，期望又再次落空。因為在讀完第二句後，我們希望馬上可以對學習成本或研究機構的投資認識更多。然而，第三句的首個名詞片語卻又是另一個新的資料「項目」"private industry"，我們還是必須多讀十六個字詞，才能讀到期待已久的 "such investment"，這正是第三句應進一步解釋的資料「項目」之一。

　　當開始讀一個句子的時候，我們總希望知道該句和前面提過的資料「項目」（即「舊」內容）有何關係。以上面段落為例，斜體字表示了第二和第三句中的「舊」內容：

> There is often a significant learning cost involved in transferring a new technology from the R&D stage to the production stage. Frequently, investment by the research institute that developed the technology will defray part of *this cost*. Private industry will probably show little interest in finding commercial applications for a new technology if *such investment* is unavailable.

這個段落難讀的原因，在於第二和第三句中的「舊」內容都在句尾，並且是在「新」內容之後。要這個段落較易讀，必須重寫這兩句，並將「舊」內容（即第二句中的 *this cost* 和第三句中的 *such investment*）置於「新」內容的前面。以下是一種修改方式（「舊」內容以斜體字標示）：

> There is often a significant learning cost involved in transferring a new technology from the R&D stage to the production stage. Frequently, part of *this cost* will be defrayed through investment by the research institute that developed the technology. If *such investment* is unavailable, private industry will probably show little interest in finding commercial applications for a new technology.

　　修改後的段落通順易讀，只要看它的內容排列方式，就會瞭解原因所在。與閱讀原文一樣，看完首句後，我們希望馬上可進一步認識「學習成本」或「從研發階段到生產階段的技術移轉」。修改後便能滿足讀者這個期望，因為第二句句首便提到「學習成本」。在開始閱讀第三句時，我們希望能多瞭解「學習成本」或「研究機構的投資」，而修改後句首又馬上提供相關內容：「研究機構的投資」。

　　再以修正後的段落中的三個句子為例。斜體字表示句中的舊和新內容，也是三個句子相關的關鍵。請注意這些以斜體字標示的名詞片語如何像吊鉤一樣，把三個句子連在一起。

There is often *a significant*
　　　learning cost involved in transferring a new technology....

Frequently, part of *this cost* will be defrayed through
　　　investment by the research institute that developed the technology.

　　　　　If *such investment* is unavailable, private industry will probably show
　　　　　little interest in finding commercial applications for a new technology.

　　提到「舊」內容可以有許多不同方式。其中一種是直接重複前文的名詞片語，但這常會造出冗贅的句子。因此，大多數作者在提到舊內容時，不是用代名詞（如 "it" 或 "this"）來指稱曾經提過的名詞片語，就是把原來的名詞片語稍作變形或縮短。例如，在以上段落的首句中，名詞片語 *a significant learning cost* 在第二句中縮

短為 *this cost*。至於第二句中的名詞片語 *investment by the research institute that developed the technology*，在第三句中則縮短為 *such investment*。

這個「先舊後新」的原則，並非表示句首定要為舊內容的字詞（在很多句子中，要做到這點是不可能的）。這準則是要強調，科技論文作者應該養成習慣，在介紹讀者未知的新資料之前，應先提到一些曾經討論的相關舊資料。（但請注意「先舊後新」的原則有時並不適用於新段落中的首句，因為首句可能只會包含新內容。）

先重複曾經提過的內容，建立一個能讓讀者輕鬆進入的脈絡，是有效溝通的基本原則。然而，為何有這麼多作者（如本節開首的段落）違反「先舊後新」這個準則呢？這大概由於這準則和作者於寫作時的心態恰好背道而馳。在撰寫論文初稿時，作者會急於表達新的內容，或想儘快把它記下來。因為新內容特別顯眼，亦可能是因作者怕會忘記或遺漏任何重點。故此，在撰寫初稿時難以遵守「先舊後新」，是很自然的。但在初稿完成後，作者必須特別檢查文章中的句子有否遵循這準則，看應否作出修改。

9.2 主題作主詞

把舊內容放在新內容之前，是鋪排句中內容時的首要準則。然而，如果句中包含二個或以上的舊資料項目，則作者必須決定以哪個項目作句子的主詞。作者在決定時，仍是應以考慮讀者的期望為依歸。讀者總希望作者會針對某個特定的主題作聯貫的討論，而句子的主詞就是討論的主題。在這種情況下，作者應挑出實際討論的焦點，並把這焦點作主詞。

試參考這個段落：

> The algorithm we have proposed is superior to the conventional algorithm in two ways. Our algorithm is much faster than the conventional algorithm, especially in applications with only a small number of parameters. And, particularly in applications involving large sets of data, the conventional method is more difficult to program than our method.

讀者自然會假定句子的主題就是句中的主詞。因此，這段首句的主題是 "the algorithm we have proposed"。這個句子指出，新演算法有兩方面比傳統演算法優勝。第二句的主題也是新演算法，此句則闡明了新演算法較優勝的一個向面。然而，第三句卻有一個問題，這句不僅出現了兩個舊資料項目："the conventional method" 及 "our method"。而且由於前者是句子主詞，表面看來它是討論的主題。但事實上，段落討論的焦點並非為「傳統演算法」，而是比它優勝的新演算法。因此，作者應在第三句中，把真正的討論焦點「新演算法」當作句子主詞，同時把新演算法（即舊的內容）置於演算法的應用（即新內容）之前：

> The algorithm we have proposed is superior to the conventional algorithm in two ways. *Our algorithm* is much faster than the conventional algorithm, especially in applications with only a small number of parameters. *Our*

method is also easier to program than the conventional method, particularly in applications involving large sets of data.

讀者讀到第三句時，會期望以「新演算法」為討論的主題，並希望能進一步瞭解「新演算法」。因此，只要把 "our method" 當作第三句的主詞，就可以滿足讀者的期望。此外，在修改後的段落中，第二和第三句亦改寫成一對稱結構，加強了段落的整體結構。

9.3 被動語態

在第六章6.5節中曾經奉勸科技論文作者不要濫用被動語態，但同時亦指出一項事實：資深作者大約會使用25%的被動語態句子，被動語態顯然是英文寫作中的重要部分。

甚麼時候使用被動語態呢？在此可以提供兩個判準，它們便是9.1節和9.2節中的寫作準則：如果唯有使用被動語態才能遵循「先舊後新」或「主題應作主詞」這兩個準則，則科技論文作者就有很好的理由使用被動語態。試回想在9.1節中一段修改過的段落：

There is often a significant learning cost involved in transferring a new technology from the R&D stage to the production stage. Frequently, part of this cost *will be defrayed* through investment by the research institute that developed the technology. If such investment is unavailable, private industry will probably show little interest in finding commercial applications for a new technology.

段中第二句是被動語態，而被動動詞為 *will be defrayed*。此句使用被動語態是恰當的，因為這能使句子符合「先舊後新」的準則。這句的舊內容是 *this cost*，新內容則是 *investment by the research institute*。如果把句子改成主動語態，則句子就會變成「先新後舊」：

Frequently, *investment by the research institute* that developed the technology *will defray* part of *this cost*.

因此這句使用被動語態，比主動語態要來得好。

濫用被動語態，會使文章生硬冗長。但如果作者使用被動語態，是為了遵循9.1節和9.2節的寫作準則，則這反而會使文章更易讀。

9.4 先短後長

英文科技寫作中常出現這類不通順的句子：主詞是很長的名詞片語，再接著很短的動詞片語。閱讀這種結構的句子，會讓人非常傷神。如果論文中出現很多這種句子，定會使讀者吃不消：

In this paper, the molecular director configuration of a closed cylinder of liquid crystal (CCLC) with negative dielectric anisotropy in an external field is studied.

閱讀這句時，需要消耗許多短暫記憶力，令人難以消化句意。人類的短期記憶力只能在一段時間內保有一小部分的新資訊（僅約五到九項）。如果一個字詞是一項資訊，則可以說：能在句子或子句約前九個字詞中，就可看到主要部分（至少主詞和動詞），最易會讓人掌握到句意。瞭解「九個字詞」這限制後，再看以上的例句。例句強迫我們在從頭到尾看完整整共24個字詞後，才可看到句子的主詞和主要動詞，知道主角是誰和在發生甚麼事情。在還未弄清句子是描述甚麼行為之前，我們就已經被迫接收一大堆資訊。

科技論文中，句子超過九個字詞是很正常的。但作者亦絕不可忽略讀者的需要：儘快看到句子的主角及其行為。因此，作者應把主要的文法單元（至少主詞和動詞）放在句子的開首。要達到這目的，可用以下方法：把「短」片語放在「長」片語前面，如果句子包含一個以上的子句，則在子句中亦是先放「短」片語。讀者通常會逐一消化句中的所有子句，所以只要每個子句都是「先短後長」，即使到第二或第三個子句才出現主詞和主要動詞，整句仍會順暢易讀。

參考下面的段落，便可瞭解「先短後長」的重要：

Based on the Cholesky decomposition of the Gram matrix formed by successively received data vectors, a new fast recursive least-squares algorithm in transversal filter form is derived. Related issues such as sensitivity to the finite precision effect, numerical stabilization methods, and initialization considerations are also addressed.

段落中的兩個句子都是「先長後短」結構。首句是一個很長的分詞片語，再接著一個很長的名詞片語（"a new fast recursive least-squares algorithm in transversal filter form"）和一個很短的動詞片語（"is derived"）。同樣，第二句也有一個很長的名詞片語（"related issues such as sensitivity to the finite precision effect, numerical stabilization methods, and initialization considerations"），其後接著一個很短的動詞片語（"are also addressed"）。

要用「先短後長」的準則來修改這類句子，便應把每句中的動詞放在長的名詞片語前面。同時，也可以把句子從被動語態變成主動語態。以下有兩個修改方法。多數讀者都會覺得這些修正句較易解讀（在修正句中，每個子句的主詞和動詞皆以斜體字標示）。

This paper presents a new, fast recursive least-squares algorithm in transversal filter form; *the algorithm is based* on the Cholesky decomposition of the Gram matrix formed by successively received data vectors. *The paper also addresses* related issues such as sensitivity to the finite precision effect, numerical stabilization methods, and initialization considerations.

We employ the Cholesky decomposition of the Gram matrix formed by successively received data vectors to derive a new, fast recursive least-squares algorithm in transversal filter form. *We* also *address* related issues such as sensitivity to the finite precision effect, numerical stabilization methods, and initialization considerations.

即使要保留被動語態，仍可用「先短後長」的準則來修改。首先，把原文中放在首句句首的長片語調到句尾。接著可把第二句句首的名詞片語分成兩部分，並把這片語中較長的部分調到句尾（每個子句的主詞和動詞皆以斜體字標示）：

A new, fast recursive least-squares algorithm in transversal filter form is derived by applying the Cholesky decomposition of the Gram matrix formed by successively received data vectors. *Related issues are also addressed*, including sensitivity to the finite precision effect, numerical stabilization methods, and initialization considerations.

修改後，段落的首句並沒違反「先短後長」這準則，因為句中放在動詞前面的名詞片語，遠比動詞後面的片語短。

以上三個修改過的段落都比原來的好，至於採用哪一個修改方法，則視乎個人寫作風格。

另一種違反「先短後長」準則的句子，通常是一個很長的主詞後面接著聯繫動詞，動詞後面又接著一個很短的述詞名詞或述詞形容詞。以下就是這種結構的句子（動詞以斜體字標示）：

That increasing the concentration of fluorine atoms around the silicide/silicon interface improves the high temperature stability of thin cobalt silicide film *is* clear.

其中一種修改方法是把原本的主詞移到句尾，並以虛主詞 "it" 替代：

It is clear that increasing the concentration of fluorine atoms around the silicide/silicon interface improves the high temperature stability of thin cobalt silicide film.

另一種修改方式是取出名詞子句中的動詞（"improves"），作句子的主要動詞。接著把述詞形容詞 "clear" 改成副詞，用來修飾主要動詞：

Increasing the concentration of fluorine atoms around the silicide/silicon interface *clearly improves* the high temperature stability of thin cobalt silicide film.

雖然句子的主詞還是有點長，但動詞前後部分的長度大致相同，句子整體尚算平衡。只要主詞不是太長，也算符合「先短後長」準則。

除此之外，「先短後長」準則也適用於介系詞片語。試看以下句子中接在動詞後面的兩個介系詞片語：

The signals are relayed *by means of a beam of highly directional high-frequency waves* from one station to another.

以斜體字標示的片語遠比接在其後的片語長。因此，我們可應用「先短後長」準則，把這兩個片語前後對調：

The signals are relayed from one station to another *by means of a beam of highly directional high-frequency waves.*

把長片語 *by means of a beam of highly directional high-frequency waves* 調到較短片語 *from one station to another* 後面，句子便較易於閱讀與瞭解。

練習 9-1 句子內容的順序

請依據9.1節到9.4節所介紹的準則來修改下列段落。

1. In this paper, we propose a new service for digital mobile communication systems. Two or more users can hold a secure electronic conference using this service.

2. A block of four DIP switches is located on the bottom of the UT620. The unit can be configured for different types of systems by adjusting these DIP switches. Table 2 below shows the correct DIP switch settings.

3. Much recent research on machine pattern recognition has focused on the use of neural networks. Extracting the features of the patterns to be recognized is an important step in most existing neural-network-based methods. The recognition rate achieved is determined largely by the quality of feature extraction.

4. A distinctive feature of the MOS resistor is that its resistance value can be adjusted by varying the gate voltage. Thus the gain of the wideband amplifier can be tuned by the MOS resistor. However, the frequency response is degraded slightly by the parasitic capacitance of the MOS device.

5. If the CPU address does not match the tag, a cache miss occurs. The controller will check whether the alter bit of the cache line involved is clean or dirty when a cache read miss occurs. The main memory will be updated by the controller with the data currently stored in the cache if the alter bit is dirty.

6. The solar water heater used in the experiment is shown in Figure 2. A cold-water inlet, where water flows into the apparatus, is at the top left of the water heater. Many lengths of plastic pipe connected together in an accordion

fashion and covered with a sheet of heat-absorbing plastic make up the main portion of the heater.

7. The atomic structure of ceramics gives them a chemical stability that makes them impervious to environmental degradation, such as dissolution in solvents. Characteristics such as a high melting point, hardness, and stiffness are the result of the strength of the bonds in ceramics. Also, because metal oxides are components of many ceramics, further oxidation is often impossible.[1]

8. In this paper, the financial investment and technological requirements involved in putting nitrogen-based techniques for fabricating widgets to use in commercial manufacturing are investigated. The per-unit cost of traditional methods of manufacturing widgets is higher than the per-unit cost of nitrogen-based techniques, so these techniques are an attractive investment. However, a number of technical problems must be overcome before nitrogen-based techniques can be adopted.

9. A bus master either oversees the transfer of data between devices or, more often, exchanges information with one or more slaves. Slaves are selected by the bus master by placing address information on the bus; each slave compares this information with its own address. A connection is established by the master and slave and the slave becomes a responder if the addresses match. Broadcast addresses are what addresses that identify more than one slave are called. A particular device may act as both master and slave, but not at the same time.[2]

10. Perceptions of odors and colors operate according to different principles. A lexical system which is organized in memory in a relatively abstract and rigidly controlled way is involved in color perception. By contrast, flexibility and adaptability, and a relatively concrete but open-ended nonverbal coding system, are the characteristics of odor perception. Odor memory is in turn

affected by this manner of organization. What is stored about odors is not likely to involve semantic categories which can be used to retrieve odors. Rather, perceptually unitary episodes described in idiosyncratic terminology are involved in odor memory.[3]

練習 9-2　長短片語的順序

請根據9.4節介紹的「先短後長」準則，修改下列句子。

1. The problem of the nonlinear nonreciprocity of soliton transmission in an EDFA with different pumping configurations is also discussed in this article.

2. In this paper, through the use of an internal model control method a fully digital servo control for an AC induction motor is developed.

3. In this paper, the molecular director configuration of a closed cylinder of liquid crystal with negative dielectric anisotropy in an external field is investigated.

4. A global calibration scheme to resolve the coordinate equivalence problem encountered when CAD systems are integrated with robot manipulators is proposed.

5. In section 7, experiments in which the proposed method is applied to control a standard industrial robot manipulator are described.

6. In this report, an efficient algorithm that employs the concept of static equilibrium to determine the stability of clamping is developed.

9.5　縮短主動詞距離

　　讀者開始閱讀一個句子時，會希望能儘早知道句中的人物和行為的施事者。當讀者讀到主詞後，會想儘快看到搭配主詞的動詞。為滿足讀者期望，科技研究報告的作者一般都應盡量在主詞之後及早接上動詞。如果修飾的片語或子句可放在其他地方（如擺在主詞前面），則應避免把這些片語或子句插在主詞和動詞之間，尤其當修飾的片語或子句特別長。雖然資深的作者有時亦會把修飾的片語或子句放在主詞和動詞之間，但在科技論文中把片語或子句放在其他位置，通常會令論文句子較易閱讀。

比較下列兩對原句和修正句：

原句：　The port enable input, *when high*, disables ports A and B by placing them in high-Z condition.

修正：　*When high*, the port enable input disables ports A and B by placing them in high-Z condition.

原句：　The architecture, *as shown in Figure 3*, incorporates two modules linked together by a map field.

修正：　*As shown in Figure 3*, the architecture incorporates two modules linked together by a map field.

兩個原句中，主動詞之間的字詞似乎破壞了句子的流暢，並暫時干擾讀者把主動詞聯結。修正後的兩句，不僅較通順，且更易讀。

現在請看這段特別長的段落：

A two-phase extraction procedure (see Figure 3), with one phase that identifies the similarities between nodes on the same level in the graph and one that uses these features to extract the common parts of the nodes, is used to identify complementary pairs and common factors among the nodes in the graph. The extraction procedure, which begins from the lowest level of the graph, where all nodes contain only terminal child node zero and terminal child node one, and moves upward level by level, eventually yields the output logic functions in a minimized factored form.

這個段落非常難讀，因為每句的主動詞間夾著的字詞都非常多。下面是同一個段落，只是主詞和動詞都已以斜體字標示。現在就可清楚看出每句的主動詞間到底插入了多少字詞：

A two-phase extraction procedure (see Figure 3), with one phase that identifies the similarities between nodes on the same level in the graph and one that uses these features to extract the common parts of the nodes, *is used* to identify complementary pairs and common factors among the nodes in the graph. *The extraction procedure*, which begins from the lowest level of the graph, where all nodes contain only terminal child node zero and terminal child node one, and moves upward level by level, eventually *yields* the output logic functions in a minimized factored form.

要讓文章變得易讀，必須把句子的主動詞放在一起，再加以改寫。首先，必須把原來兩句各分成兩個以上句子；我們可以把主動詞間的長片語或子句全部刪除，並將它們改寫為獨立的句子。下面是一種修改方式，其中每句的主詞和動詞都以斜體字來標示：

A two-phase extraction procedure is used to identify complementary pairs and common factors among the nodes in the graph (see Figure 3). *The first phase identifies* the similarities between nodes on the same level in the graph. *The second phase uses* these features to extract the common parts of the nodes. *The extraction procedure begins* from the lowest level of the graph, where all nodes contain only terminal child node zero and terminal child node one.

It then *moves* upward level by level, eventually yielding the output logic functions in a minimized factored form.

段落已分成五句，而修正後的每句中，主動詞都連在一起。這比原文來得易讀。

練習 9-3 主動詞相連

請把下列句中的主詞皆與其動詞連在一起。（提示：有些句子需要在中間斷句。）

1. The solar cell may, in strong light conditions, deliver a supply voltage that is so high that the LCD display segments cannot be switched off.

2. The techniques used to produce maps, progressing from field workers and manual surveying to satellites and computers, have changed dramatically over the past fifty years. The predominant method for creating maps, before World War II, was field surveying. After World War II, map-making methods began to include manual photogrammetry. Manual photogrammetry, although still used today, is being supplanted by digital cartography, and computers are becoming the hub of the mapping process.[4]

3. In recent years an extraordinary increase in the attention, both popular and scientific, that has been paid to mutation and its consequences has occurred. The sources of this interest, which has led to research that has improved our understanding of DNA and of its metabolism and organization into genes, are the recognition that components of our environment pose a largely unevaluated threat to the conservation of genetic material and the realization that mutations frequently have serious consequences for human health.[5]

4. These insects, as Figure 1 shows, are physically dissimilar from species common in North America, and they have a voracious appetite. Numerous studies—see, for example, James (1982), Halton (1987), Mayumi (1989), and Brandom (1992)—have documented the unusually large amount of vegetation an individual of the species can consume in a single day.

5. Impressive advances in technology during the last two decades, which have led to the development of sophisticated new instruments such as filled-aperture telescopes and interferometric arrays, have provided astronomers with the ability to observe star-forming regions in considerable detail at infrared, millimeter, and submillimeter wavelengths. Over the last few years, observations with these and other instruments have produced a series of remarkable, exciting, and unexpected discoveries concerning the star-formation process in our galaxy. Astronomers, as a result of these discoveries, are beginning to understand the processes of star formation and early stellar evolution.[6]

6. The test apparatus, which is based partly on the design described by Susky and Hopfeld [4]—although it is easier to move and assemble than their device, requiring only two people for transportation and setup—samples and records the rate of evaporation over a 4 × 5 meter area.

9.6 動作以動詞表達

　　大多數句子都會描述某種動作，而讀者總希望動作可由動詞來表達。如果句中動作表達得不明顯，或是句子的動作都不用動詞表達，反是隱藏於名詞之中，則讀者就難以明白句子的動作是甚麼。請看下面這個段落，當中的動詞皆以斜體字標示：

> After etching, a decrease *was observed* in the intensity of the Si(2s), Si(2p), and C(1s) peaks, but an increase *was observed* in the intensity of the O(2p) and O(1s) peaks at 103.4 and 531.6 eV. This *may be* because of removal of undesired crystallites and oxidation of the silicon due to a mixture of nitric acid (HNO_3) and hydrofluoric acid (HF), which *resulted* in the formation of silicon oxide. At low HF and high HNO_3 concentrations, the etching rate *is* HF-dependent, evidently because HF *causes* the removal of SiO_2 during SiO_2 formation.

這個段落表達得很不夠清楚直接，讀者必須費許多心力去理解作者的意思。主要理由是：整個段落從頭到尾既沒有清楚交待句子的動作，也沒有交待動作的施事者。像第一句的動作就隱藏在名詞 *a decrease* 和 *an increase* 中，沒以動詞表達出來。至於第二句的動作更藏得無影無蹤：第二句的動詞只是聯繫動詞加上語態助動詞 (*may be*)。末句作者更捨動態動詞不用，反而使用聯繫動詞 *is*。整個段落中的動詞幾乎都是弱動詞（參考第六章6.4節），根本沒有表達任何具體的動作（全段動詞包括 *was observed, may be, resulted, is* 及 *causes*）。

要這個段落更清楚易讀，必須把每句（或子句）中的動作用動詞來表達。如果可以的話，作者也應指出動作的施事者，並以之作句子的主詞。以下是一種修改方式，以斜體字標示的都是動詞：

> After etching, the intensity of the Si(2s), Si(2p), and C(1s) peaks *decreased*, but the intensity of the O(2p) and O(1s) peaks at 103.4 and 531.6 eV *increased*. This *may be* because a mixture of nitric acid (HNO₃) and hydrofluoric acid (HF) *removed* undesired crystallites and *caused* the silicon to oxidize, *forming* silicon oxide. At low HF and high HNO₃ concentrations, the amount of HF available *determines* the etching rate, evidently because HF *removes* SiO₂ as it *forms*.

現在的段落有力易讀多了。只要把首句改成主動語態，並用主動動詞 *decreased* 和 *increased* 來取代冗長被動的結構 *a decrease is observed* 和 *an increase is observed*。第二句用了動詞 *remove* 及 *caused . . . to oxidize* 來取代名詞 *removal* 和 *oxidation*，並以動狀詞 *forming* 來取代冗長的 *resulted in the formation of*。末句則用了較精確的說法 *the amount of HF available determines the etching rate* 來取代模糊的 *the etching rate is HF-dependent*。此外，我們也把名詞 *removal* 和 *formation* 改成動詞 *removes* 和 *forms*。如此一來，段落中的動作都一律以動詞來表達。

要確定句中的動作以動詞表達，必先找出句子的動作。有些句子的動詞很模糊，沒有把句子的動作具體表達出來。例如：

> Excess HNO₃ *may lead* to a thin oxide film on the substrate surface and thus inhibition of nucleation in non-target regions and an improved degree of selectivity.

這個句子沒有表達任何具體的動作。動詞 *may lead* 的意思很模糊，而它的三個直接受詞（*film, inhibition* 和 *degree*）與主詞 HNO₃，甚至三個受詞之間的因果關係，都不夠精確。此外，句中的兩個名物化名詞（*inhibition* 和 *nucleation*），指涉的皆為具體動作，為何不以動詞表達？以下是一種修改方法，動詞都以斜體字標示：

> Excess HNO₃ *may cause* a thin oxide film *to form* on the substrate surface that *inhibits* nucleation in non-target regions, thus *increasing* the degree of selectivity.

先刪除模糊的動詞 *lead to*，換上 *cause...to form*。還有，阻礙成核的似乎是氧化薄膜，而非 HNO₃。因此，應把名詞 *inhibition* 改成動詞 *inhibits*，並放在關係子句中，而以關係子句的主詞作指稱氧化薄膜的代名詞。最後，「選擇度的增加」似乎是由於在非目標區阻礙成核。為了闡明這種關係，應省略 *improved* 這形容詞而插入動狀詞 *increasing*。修改過的句子易讀得多，因為所有的動作都能精確具體地表達出來。

儘管如此，修改句還是有一值得商榷之處。有些讀者可能仍會認為修改句中，關係代名詞 *that* 所指的前述詞不夠清楚。從句子的意思，我們可以推斷 *that* 是指名詞片語 *a thin oxide film*；但根據句子的結構，*that* 也可以是指另一名詞片語 *the substrate surface*。對專業讀者而言，修改句相當清楚。因為根據上下文，他們可立刻推斷出動詞 *inhibits* 的主詞必定是 *a thin oxide film*。但假如文章的對象是不諳化學的大眾，則應考慮進一步修改，以保證讀者不會誤解句意：

> Excess HNO$_3$ may cause a thin oxide film to form on the substrate surface, thus *inhibiting* nucleation in non-target regions and *increasing* the degree of selectivity.

「動作以動詞表達」原則可補充第六章中的論點。6.4節建議讀者要避免弱動詞和名物化名詞，並盡量用清楚具體的動詞來表達句子的動作。6.7節則建議避免虛主詞結構，從而造出簡明的句子。從以下例子可看出，第六章的規則和本節陳述的原則是互補的。當中的弱動詞、名物化名詞和虛主詞結構，都以斜體字標示：

> Increasing the acidity of the nutrient solution *has* two effects on the growth of strain B. First, *there is* a general *inhibition* of growth, and second, *destabilization* of existing healthy cultures *is observed*.

首句包含一個與名詞 *effects* 連用的弱動詞 *has*，第二句則包含一個 *there is* 結構及兩個名物化名詞：*inhibition* 和 *destabilization*。要修改首句，必須用較具體的動詞 *affects* 來取代弱動詞 *has* 及名詞 *effects*。同時，第二句必須捨虛主詞結構 *there is an inhibition of growth*，改用動詞來表達句子的動作，即 *it inhibited growth*（"it" 指稱「增加溶液的酸度」）。最後，作者應刪去名物化名詞及弱動詞 *destabilization… is observed*，改為 *it destabilizes*（"it" 再次指稱「增加溶液的酸度」）。下面是修改好的句子，以斜體字標示的是動詞：

> Increasing the acidity of the nutrient solution *affects* the growth of strain B in two ways. First, it *inhibits* growth generally, and second, it *destabilizes* existing healthy cultures.

應用以上這種修改方式，既可用動詞來表達句子的動作，也可避免弱動詞、名物化名詞以及不必要的 *there is* 結構。無論修改的理由是以何種原則去說明，修改後的句子顯然較流暢易讀。

練習 9-4 動作以動詞表達

請修改下列段落，使每句或子句中的動作都能以動詞表達。

1. Measurement of the intensity and frequency of earthquakes can be performed using seismometers. A seismometer consists of a mass suspended by a spring or other elastic mechanism inside a metal frame that is anchored to the ground. A magnet is attached to the mass and an electric coil to the frame. Any vibration of the ground causes shaking of the seismometer's frame, but inertia tends to hold the mass in its place. Thus movement of the coil on the frame in

relation to the magnet on the mass is observed, and this movement results in generation of an electrical signal that is a representation of the intensity and frequency of the movement.[7]

2. Control of the amount of fluorine incorporated into the silicon film can be achieved by reduction of the amount of water added to the immersing solution. Addition of less water results in the release of more fluorine atoms, as shown in the reaction equation. The increase in the number of free fluorine atoms in the solution leads to incorporation of a greater amount of fluorine in the film.

3. Since each sensor receives information from only a limited range, combining information from many sensors is necessary.

4. As closing of landfills takes place, many communities are passing recycling laws and undertaking construction of waste-to-energy plants. Although waste-to-energy plants face many of the same technical, regulatory, and political obstacles as conventional power plants, some issues are peculiar to them. Unlike most power plants, municipal waste incinerators perform burning of many different types of materials, resulting in creation of different types of toxic byproducts. Whereas fossil fuel plants may lead to air pollution, waste incinerators may result in pollution of the earth. Since most ash is buried along with garbage in municipal landfills, environmentalists fear that seeping of contaminants into groundwater may occur.[8]

9.7 邏輯關係要清楚

　　讀者期望科技研究報告中的討論是合理、合符邏輯及井然有序的。為滿足這期望，科技論文作者應清楚明確地顯示段落中各句子間的邏輯關係，避免突然從一個主題跳到另一個。此外，也該用適當的字眼作為「信號」（如 *however, since, because, so, thus, although, in contrast, only* 等等），為讀者闡明不同子句或句子間的邏輯關係。

　　撰寫論文時，別以為句子間的邏輯關係不用表明，讀者亦可領會。例如：

Requirements analysis is the most error-prone step in the software development process. A widely accepted technique for solving this problem is rapid prototyping.

"Rapid prototyping" 所要解決的「問題」是甚麼？這個句子連一個問題都沒提過。作者指出的「需求的分析」是個容易出錯的「步驟」，卻不是「問題」。顯然，作者希望讀者能自行推斷出：需求的分析過程中常出現的錯誤本身便是「問題」。儘管這種省略看來微不足道，卻可能會把讀者弄糊塗。就算讀者真的能推斷成功，但他並沒這種責任。我們應改寫原句，以避免出現邏輯的「跳躍」：

Requirements analysis is the most error-prone step in the software development process. Errors in requirements analysis can often be prevented by applying a widely accepted technique known as rapid prototyping.

Most errors in the software development process occur during requirements analysis. These errors can often be prevented by applying a widely accepted technique known as rapid prototyping.

由於對自己的研究非常熟悉，作者時會錯誤假定內容之間的邏輯關係是不言而喻的，因此很容易會發生邏輯的「跳躍」。例如：

Process A generally requires test information that is not directly available from the specifications. As an alternative to the expensive test evaluation, we will adopt Process B, which is widely recognized as an effective design technique. To reduce the complexity of Process B, we propose to modify it in the following way.

這個段落至少有兩個閱讀障礙：首句與第二句、第二句與末句之間，都遺漏了重要的信息，使讀者難以看出句子間的關係。在第二句中，作者提出以另一種處理方式去取代方式 A，因為方式 A 需要昂貴的試驗。但作者既沒事先明白的指出處理方式 A 需要昂貴的試驗，也沒有交待該昂貴的試驗是指花費昂貴、曠日費時，還是其他？在末句中，作者介紹了一個計畫，可減少處理方式 B 的複雜度，但卻沒有事先指出處理方式 B 太複雜，也沒指出過是哪方面複雜。作者從頭到尾都假定讀者已經知道自己的想法。然而，這個假定是站不住腳的。讀者未必會知道段落中的內容之間有何關聯，作者有義務將意思逐步合理地表達出來。

如果這個段落的作者想把自己的意思有效傳達給讀者，則必須填補句子間的三個邏輯「跳躍」。以下是一初步的修改方式：

Process A generally requires test information that is not directly available from the specifications, *and the testing needed to obtain this information is costly*. This expensive testing can be avoided by adopting Process B, which is widely recognized as an effective design technique. *In its present form, however, Process B has a major drawback: it requires extremely complex calculations*. To reduce the complexity of Process B, we propose to modify it in the following way.

在修改過的段落中，已經清楚解釋了處理方式 A 需要昂貴的試驗，而處理方式 B 所需的計算太複雜。所以句子間的邏輯關係已得以闡明。（如果我們知道「昂貴」

和「複雜」實指為何，則還能進一步修改。）只要不用讓讀者自行去推斷句子間的邏輯關係，能簡化讀者的詮釋工作，我們的文章就會更易於閱讀及瞭解。

科技論文作者應明白句子之間必須有清晰的邏輯關係，且也應擅於在文章中找出且避免邏輯「跳躍」。千萬別假定讀者和自己一樣熟悉文章的主題；即使是博學多聞的讀者，也可能不常接觸自己討論的主題，同樣需要文章提供背景知識及詳細的說明。如果邏輯「跳躍」是無關緊要，則只會阻礙讀者閱讀；但如果邏輯「跳躍」是嚴重的話，則會使讀者覺得文章莫名其妙。

反過來說，不存在邏輯關係的地方，就不應該暗示存在著邏輯關係。請看下面的例子：

> We have now obtained all of the solutions, so they are summarized in Table 3.

這個句子看來極不自然。連接詞 *so* 暗示了前後兩子句間蘊含邏輯或因果關係，但在句意上，它們之間卻沒有這種關係。「作者在表3列出解答」，並非「獲得所有解答」的邏輯或因果上的結果。我們可一方面獲得解答，另一方面不把這些解答列於表3中，兩者沒必然或因果關係。因此，連接詞 *so* 必須用其他字詞替代。由於第一個子句表達了句子的主要意思，所以可把第二個子句改成關係子句，並把它納入附屬結構：

> We have now obtained all of the solutions, which are summarized in Table 3.

這個句子比原句合理自然得多。

為了向讀者強調重要的概念，並闡明文章的概念之間的邏輯關係，以及不同子句或句子之間的轉接，科技論文作者應常使用適當的「信號」字眼。常用的「信號」字眼有：*although, because, but, however, since, so, thus, in comparison, in contrast, few, despite, only, little* 等等。「信號」字眼可能是連接詞、連接副詞，也可能是一般形容詞和副詞。

「信號」字眼在溝通中尤其重要，現以一淺顯例子作說明：

> Experimental trials show that the proposed algorithm has an average recognition rate of 98% and the conventional algorithm has an average rate of 91%.

這句的重點是甚麼？它陳述了兩個明顯的事實。然而，只要不知道上下文，就無法瞭解作者撰寫這個句子的目的。我們只知道兩個演算法都有很高的平均辨識率，作者並沒指出辨識率差異的重要。

這句則加上了「信號」字眼，試觀察當中的差別：

> Experimental trials show that the proposed algorithm has an average recognition rate of 98%; *in contrast*, the conventional algorithm has an average rate of *only* 91%.

現在即使不知原句的脈絡，仍可大略猜測作者的撰寫目的。*In contrast* 這字詞把句子中的兩個子句關聯起來，並指出了句子主要目的在於提出一個新演算法，以跟現有的演算法作對照。至於 *only* 則暗示作者肯定演算法辨識率差異的重要。要強調這差異，大概是由於作者認為新演算法較傳統演算法優勝，並可取代它。原句和修正句都表達了相同的事實，但修正句中的「信號」字眼，卻可讓讀者瞭解到作者的態度，以及句子在原來脈絡中的目的。

練習 9-5 邏輯關係不清

指出下列不清楚或錯誤的邏輯關係，並一併改正。

1. Roski [3] studied the characteristics of the built-up edge (BUE) and developed a chamfered main edge cutting tool. This method involves tool geometries that produce a BUE that flows away continuously in the form of a separated secondary chip. Therefore, we conducted cutting experiments on carbon steel and pure aluminum to examine the mechanism underlying secondary chip formation.

2. Based on a trade-off between the operating cost and the travel cost, this paper has formulated a nonlinear programming problem to determine the optimal market size.

3. In this paper, we analyze the stability of clamping with passive friction forces. Based on the concept of the instant center of rotation, the stability analysis is transformed into a search for a static equilibrium state. Other properties are also studied and then applied to increase the efficiency of the search algorithm.

4. A distinctive feature of the data model is how names are used. Users can specify multiple names for classes, attributes, methods, and reference relationships. Multiple names must have the same semantics. For example, *person, people,* and *human* are good names for a class which contains information about persons. When users want to retrieve information about persons, they can use one of these names in their query.

5. The reaction between n-butyl bromide and phenoxide ions exhibits a slow reaction rate because the two substances consist of different phases. Many investigators have devoted a great deal of effort to solving this problem by using various catalysts.

6. Vendor selection is one of the most important parts of the purchasing process. Recently, the concept of dimensional analysis was used to propose a supplier performance measure and to obtain an index called INY. The performance criteria used in INY include quantitative and qualitative criteria. For qualitative criteria, a two-directional evaluation is employed instead of the one-directional approach used in INY. Then all scores for quantitative and qualitative criteria are combined into a sum of weighted averages called INZ. The use of INZ is compared with that of INY by means of several examples.

第十章
字詞誤用

本章旨在討論中國人撰寫的英文科技論文中經常誤用的字詞及片語。誤用的情況中，有些是文法錯誤；有些則為文法正確，然而文章欠清晰通順。

A, an. 名詞前應使用不定冠詞 *a* 還是 *an*，是取決於名詞第一個音節的發音而定，而非取決於名詞的首個字母是否為母音字母。如果名詞首個音節的發音是以子音開頭，則必須使用 *a*。如果名詞首個音節的發音是以母音開頭，則必須使用 *an*。

> The doctor sent him to have *an* X-ray taken.

> I am working on *a* unified approach to these problems.

A lot of. *A lot of* 是口語，因此在正式論文中應避免使用，而應以 *many, much* 或 *a great deal of* 去表達。

Above. 可用以指稱曾經提過的資料。以 *above* 指稱的資料應是在前幾句或前段中出現過的，而不應用以指稱前幾個段落甚至前幾頁中曾提過的資料，因為讀者可能並不知道其所指為何。

> We can now apply *the above technique*… 如果是剛提及該技術，則此乃正確的寫法，否則應該改用以下的寫法。

> We can now apply *the technique introduced in section 2*…

> We can now apply *the technique introduced earlier*…

Adopt, adapt. 不要把這兩個字詞混淆。*Adopt* 的意思是「採用」或「選擇並遵循」。然而 *adapt* 卻是「為使之更適合而作修改」或「適應」之意。

> We shall *adopt* Watson's technique, but we must *adapt* it slightly so that the reaction will take place at a lower temperature.

Affect. 不要把 *affect* 和 *effect* 混淆。*Affect* 是動詞，意思是「影響」。然而 *effect* 既可作動詞，也可作名詞: 作動詞時的意思是「實現」或「達成」，作名詞時的意思則是「結果」或「影響」。（*Effect* 在科技論文中通常作名詞使用，而少會作動詞使用。）

Increasing the annealing temperature *affected* the junctions in two ways.

Increasing the annealing temperature had two *effects* on the junctions.

Aforementioned. 撰寫科技研究報告時，應避免使用如 *aforementioned* 或 *hereinafter* 之類的生硬古語。在當代英文中，這種古語只在某些正式的法律文件中使用。即使是法律上的使用，英文修辭學專家之間也有爭議。

生硬:　We shall now use *the aforementioned method* to solve this problem.

自然:　We shall now use *the method described above* to solve this problem.

自然:　We shall now use *the proposed method* to solve this problem.

生硬:　This set will *hereinafter* be referred to as set S.

自然:　This set will be referred to *below* as set S.

自然:　We will refer to this set as set S.

Alternate, alternative. *Alternate* 是指每隔一個的意思，亦可表示「交替者」; *alternately* 則表示兩者交替輪流。*Alternative* 是兩個選擇中的其中一個; *alternatively* 則是非此即彼之意，可視作「要不然」。在提出另一個可能的選擇時，應使用 *alternative* 或 *alternatively*，而不要使用 *alternate*。

The traditional algorithm processes the data from the bottom up. An *alternative* approach is to begin from the top and work downward.

Alternatively, we can use the following method.

Although...but. 將兩個子句連接時，不能同時使用 *although* 和 *but* 這兩個連接詞，必須在兩者中選擇一個來使用。

誤:　*Although* the algorithm is precise, *but* it is slow.

正:　*Although* the algorithm is precise, it is slow.

正:　The algorithm is precise, *but* it is slow.

Among. 一般而言，如想表示「從幾個可能的選擇中選出一個項目」，不應只用 *among*，而應使用 *from among*。

劣:　This algorithm selects the optimal solution *among* all possible dynamic alignment patterns.

佳:　This algorithm selects the optimal solution *from among* all possible dynamic alignment patterns.

Among, between. *Among* 這介系詞，是表示把東西分給三個或以上的人或物，或表示某事物和其他事物間的關係。至於 *between* 則指某種相對或一對一的關係，

而不論相關者的數目。所以千萬別以為只要指稱三個或以上的人或物，就必須用 *among*。在科技寫作中，*between* 比較常用。

劣： Messages are passed *among* objects in two ways.

佳： Messages are passed *between* objects in two ways.

劣： Let us examine the relationships *among* the three variables.

佳： Let us examine the relationships *between* the three variables.

正： The additional profits were divided *among* the stockholders.

正： Professor Chen is *among* the leaders in her field.

Amount, number. *Amount* 用以指稱不可數名詞，*number* 則用來指稱可數名詞。

劣： The system must handle a large *amount* of objects.

佳： The system must handle a large *number* of objects.

正： In the second trial, the *amount* of oxygen added to the system was increased.

And. 一般而言，英文句子不應以 *and* 開首。不過，資深的作者有時也會為造出某種特殊效果而違反這規則。儘管如此，在科技寫作中的句子，不太可能有好理由以 *and* 開首。

劣： *And* our theory explains why the anomalous Hall effect does not occur in conventional superconductors.

佳： *Moreover,* our theory explains why the anomalous Hall effect does not occur in conventional superconductors.

And/or. *And/or* 意思十分模糊。我們應兩者擇一，否則乾脆用 *or both*。

模糊： This modification may improve the efficiency *and/or* accuracy of the algorithm.

清楚： This modification may improve the efficiency *and* accuracy of the algorithm.

清楚： This modification may improve the efficiency *or* accuracy of the algorithm *or both*.

很多以斜線把兩個字詞相連的句子，意思都是模稜兩可的。讀者在碰到這種字詞時，都會不解作者為何不另選較精確的字詞表達。在大部分的情形下，作者以 *and* 或 *or* 來取代斜線，或乾脆在兩個字詞中選擇其一，通常會使句意更清楚。

Anymore. 在正式英文文章中，如果句子有 *anymore* 及否定動詞，都應改寫成 *no longer* 及肯定動詞。

劣： After this cycle, the memory *does not contain* invalid data *anymore*.

佳： After this cycle, the memory *no longer contains* invalid data.

Apparently. 這字詞有「顯然」之意，不過也常有「似乎（但未必）為真」或「似乎（但不確定）」之意。為免混淆起見，在科技寫作中，不應用 *apparently* 來表示 *obviously* 或 *clearly*。

不清楚：　*Apparently,* the number of defects decreased as the temperature increased. 這句意思似乎是 "The number of defects *seems* to have decreased as the temperature increased."

清楚：　*Clearly,* the number of defects decreased as the temperature increased.

清楚：　The number of defects *clearly* decreased as the temperature increased.

Appendix. 如果研究報告只有一個附錄，則文章中應以 *the Appendix* 來指示這附錄（*Appendix* 前面加定冠詞）。如果研究報告有兩個或以上的附錄，則應以 *Appendix A, Appendix B* 等（或 *Appendix I, Appendix II* 等）來指明這些附錄，而不應加上定冠詞（這裏 *Appendix A, Appendix B* 等是作專有名詞使用）。

誤：　The proof of Theorem I is stated in detail *in Appendix.*

正：　The proof of Theorem I is stated in detail *in the Appendix.*

正：　The proof of Theorem I is stated in detail *in Appendix A.*

Approach. *Approach* 作動詞使用時，後面不應接著介系詞 *to*。

誤：　As *x* increases, the value of the function *approaches to* zero.

正：　As *x* increases, the value of the function *approaches* zero.

Approach 作名詞使用時，後面常會緊接著介系詞 *to* 及另外一個名詞。如果 *approach to* 後面緊接著一個用來修飾 *approach* 的動狀詞，（即表示是怎樣的 *approach*），則該動狀詞必須以 *-ing* 結尾（即動名詞）。*Approach* 後面不能接不定詞，因為緊接其後的 *to* 是介系詞，而非不定詞前面的 *to*。

劣：　This paper proposes a new *approach to solve* this problem. 如果 *to solve this problem* 這片語是用以修飾動詞 *propose*，則這句是正確的。但作者似乎是想用這片語來修飾名詞 *approach*，所以這裏 *to solve* 是錯誤的。

正：　This paper proposes a new *approach to solving* this problem.

正：　This paper proposes a new *approach to* this problem.

A priori. 小心把這個片語與 *prior* 混淆。*A priori* 是拉丁文，意思為「先驗」、「先於經驗」或者為「不倚仗經驗」之意。*Prior* 則表示「在前」或「優先」。

As. *As* 配合過去式或進行式的動詞使用時，可表示「正在」或「當中」之意。但如果 *as* 跟現在式動詞配搭，要表示 "when"（「當」或「屆時」）之意，則句子會看來不太自然。此外，在科技寫作中應避免以 *as* 來表示「因為」或「由於」，以免使句意模稜兩可。

自然： *As* the solution *was stirred*, more water was added.

自然： *As* we *were preparing* for the experiment, we heard a loud explosion in the lab next door.

劣： *As* node CS *receives* a message, type analysis begins.

佳： *When* node CS *receives* a message, type analysis begins.

劣： *As* the force is large enough, the asperities are completely deformed and the body begins to slip.

佳： *When* the force is large enough, the asperities are completely deformed and the body begins to slip.

佳： *Because* the force is very large, the asperities are completely deformed and the body begins to slip.

As follows. *As follows* 和 *the following* 都是正確的用法（*as shown below* 也是正確的）。

正： This relationship can be expressed *as follows*:

正： Commonly used methods include *the following*:

正： The equations of motion can be written *in the following way*:

誤： as the followings

誤： as followings

列： as below

As follows 作非限定修飾詞使用時，前面必須加逗點（詳見第五章 5.2節中逗點的第四條規則）。*As follows* 及 *the following* 後面，通常必須接著冒號，但有些情況也可接句號。一般而言，如果 *as follows* 或 *the following* 所介紹的項目很短（如只有幾個數學方程式），則後面就應接著冒號。但如果 *as follows* 或 *the following* 所介紹的項目很長（如很長的例子或演算法），則應接著句點。

一般而言，在論文中不應使用 *as follows* 來介紹新的小節。例如，在結束一個小節而開始另一個之時，不應以 "We will discuss this problem as follows" 結尾，而應寫 "We will discuss this problem below" 或 "We will discuss this problem in the next section" 般的句子。

As mentioned above. As mentioned previously. 兩者的用法稍有不同。*As mentioned previously*（或 *as mentioned earlier*）通常是用來指涉幾個段落或幾頁前提過的內容。至於 *as mentioned above*，雖然也可這樣使用，但通常是指讀者印象猶新的內容，如前一兩段剛提過的。此外，作者想指稱前幾句提過的內容時，則可使用 *as just mentioned*。

作者應盡可能用較精確的字詞來取代 *as mentioned above* 或 *as mentioned earlier* 這些片語。例如，如果作者要指稱上一節的內容，大可用 *as mentioned in the preceding section* 來代替 *as mentioned above*。

As you know. As we know. 在科技論文中，千萬別使用這些片語。不管句子內容是甚麼，它們必定是贅詞。

As well as. 這個片語的意思和 *and* 不盡相同。*As well as* 相等於 *in addition to*，是用來強調前面的名詞。例如，*John as well as Mary is coming* 這句所強調的是專有名詞 *John*：讀者本已知 *Mary* 要來，但不知道 *John* 也一同前來。同樣，*This material can be used in cars, motorcycles, and bicycles as well as airplanes*，這句中，讀者早已知悉所指的材料可用來製造飛機，但句子要強調的，亦是讀者不知道的，是這種材料也可用來製造汽車、機車以及腳踏車。

Aspect. 在英文句子中，*aspect* 及 *area* 之類的字詞經常是累贅的。

累贅：　Regarding the application *aspect* of fuzzy neural networks, many approaches have been proposed.

累贅：　In the *area of* application of fuzzy neural networks, many approaches have been proposed.

簡潔：　Many approaches to the application of fuzzy neural networks have been proposed.

簡潔：　Many applications of fuzzy neural networks have been proposed.

Assume. 這個動詞後面不應緊接 *as*。正確寫法是 *assume to be*。

誤：　The parameters of the price indices can be *assumed as* constants.

正：　The parameters of the price indices can be *assumed to be* constants.

正：　*We can assume that* the parameters of the price indices are constants.

Assure. 請參見 *ensure*。

At. At Table 2, at Figure 3, at row x in the matrix 這些片語中使用 *at* 是錯誤的，應改用 *in*：*in Table 2, in Figure 3, in row x in the matrix*。

At first. 不要把 *at first* 和 *first* 混淆。*At first*（即「當初」）表示所述情形已隨時間而改變。至於 *first* 則是指一系列項目、事件或步驟中首個行為或事物。

At first she wanted to use the *first* method, but later she decided to use the second one.

At last. 同理，亦別將 *at last* 和 *last* 混淆。*At last* 是指「終於」，但 *last* 卻是指一系列項目、事件或步驟中最後一個行為或事物。

At last we reached the *last* house on the street.

Based on. 以 *based on* 開首的句子通常都是不精確的，甚至有時還會有文法錯誤。*Base* 是動詞，而非介系詞。因此，如果句首是以 *based on* 開首的片語，則這就是分詞片語。根據英文文法，這個分詞片語應修飾句子的主詞（參見第四章 4.9 節）。然而，絕大多數以 *based on* 開首的句子中，這分詞片語卻都不能合理地修飾句子的主詞。因此，應盡量以 *on the basis of, by, from, according to* 或其他字詞來取代 *based on*，否則應重寫句子，清楚指出甚麼是甚麼的「基礎」。

劣：　*Based on* the conventional method using Lagrange multipliers, the closed form solution can be written as follows.

佳：　*According to* the conventional method using Lagrange multipliers, the closed form solution can be written as follows.

佳：　The conventional method using Lagrange multipliers yields the closed form solution:… 直接列出解答

佳：　*Applying* the conventional method using Lagrange multipliers, we can write the closed form solution as follows.

佳：　*If we apply* the conventional method using Lagrange multipliers, we can write the closed form solution as follows.

誤：　*Based on* Eq. (8), it is obtained that…

正：　*From* Eq. (8), we obtain…

正：　Equation (8) entails that…

劣：　*Based on* our experimental results, we conclude that…

佳：　*On the basis of* our experimental results, we conclude that…

佳：　*From* our experimental results, we conclude that…

佳：　Our experimental results show that…

劣：　*Based on* decomposition of the matrix formed by successively received data vectors, we develop a fast, recursive least-squares algorithm in transversal filter form.

佳：　*Through* decomposition of the matrix formed by successively received data vectors, we develop a fast, recursive least-squares algorithm in transversal filter form. [或 *By decomposing* the matrix…]

佳：　We present a fast, recursive least-squares algorithm in transversal filter form. *The algorithm is based on* decomposition of the matrix formed by successively received data vectors.

　　假如以 *based on* 開首的片語真的可以修飾句子的主詞，則應把這片語放在句首（但這種情形很少見）。例如，下列例句中，以 *based on* 開首的片語便可以用來修飾句子的主詞。這個句子的涵意是：XPG 系統的架構是以 "advanced digital technology" 為基礎。

　　Based on advanced digital technology, *the XPG system* provides reliable operation with minimal maintenance.

　　-based. 以連字號加上如 *-based* 之類的字尾，有時很有用，尤其是它可把很長的名詞片語縮短（例如，可把 *a computer system that is based on a Pentium microprocessor* 縮短成 *a Pentium-based computer system*）。然而，在首次使用一個名詞片語時，應寫出整個片語。還有，應盡量使用更文雅且精確的字詞，避免使用這種字尾的寫法。

模糊：　　We propose *a neural-network-based control system.* 如果同一篇論文中曾經提到以神經網路為基礎的控制系統，則可使用這種寫法，否則應用以下的寫法。

清楚：　　We propose *a control system based on a neural network.*

更清楚：　We propose *a control system that uses a neural network* to maintain the operating parameters within the proper range.

Basically. 人們常濫用這個字詞。在大多數的英文句子中，這是個模糊並應省略的修飾詞。有時使用「基本上」可造出通順的中文，但在相同情況下卻不能造出通順的英文。

累贅：　　There are *basically* two types of reactors.

簡潔：　　There are two types of reactors.

簡潔：　　There are two *basic* types of reactors.

Because of the fact that. 這是個冗贅的片語。*Of the fact that* 應省略，寫 *because* 便成。

冗贅：　　*Because of the fact that* the system is intended for real-time processing, a faster algorithm is needed.

簡潔：　　*Because* the system is intended for real-time processing, a faster algorithm is needed.

Because…so. 這兩個連接詞不能在同一句中並存。

誤：　　*Because* the method is fast, *so* it can be used for real-time processing.

正：　　*Because* the method is fast, it can be used for real-time processing.

正：　　The method is fast, *so* it can be used for real-time processing.

Because that. *Because* 後面緊接著 *that*，是不合文法的。

誤：　　*Because that* the system is intended for real-time processing, a faster algorithm is needed.

正：　　*Because* the system is intended for real-time processing, a faster algorithm is needed.

誤：　　This is *because that* the system makes full use of the link capacity.

正：　　This is *because* the system makes full use of the link capacity.

Become. 在英文中，*become* 的用法和中文的「成為」不盡相同。除非要描述某種變化，否則不應使用 *to become* 這動詞。下面的句子只陳述普遍的事實，並沒描述某種變化，所以句中的動詞應使用 *to be*，而不能使用 *to become*。

劣：　　Because official records do not include information on this type of sale, transaction records from realtors *become* the only source of detailed information.

佳： Because official records do not include information on this type of sale, transaction records from realtors *are* the only source of detailed information.

劣： For these cases, Monte Carlo simulation *becomes* a powerful technique for estimating the probability *p*.

佳： For these cases, Monte Carlo simulation *is* a powerful technique for estimating the probability *p*.

如果想以 *become* 來描述某種從過去到現在的改變，正確的動詞時態應為現在完成式，而非簡單現在式。

誤： Computers *become* more widely used in education in recent years.

正： Computers *have become* more widely used in education in recent years.

Behavior. 在英文的用法中，*behavior* 通常是不可數名詞，因此為單數。在某些特殊的文脈裏（如心理學的文章），作者為強調所指涉的是幾種不同類型的行為，會把 *behavior* 當作可數的複數名詞來使用。

Belong. 英文的 *belong* 與中文的「屬於」不能互譯來使用。在英文中，*belong* 通常表示「適合」或「屬於某人」之意。

正： This land belongs to the university.

正： This house belongs to Mr. Davis.

正： Robert is an excellent student, one who belongs at the finest university in the country.

誤： The frictional characteristics of this type of damper *belong to* dry friction.

劣： The frictional characteristics of this type of damper *fall under the category of* dry friction. 稍見冗長

正： The friction that occurs in this type of damper *is a form of* dry friction.

正： The friction in this type of damper is dry friction.

正： This type of damper is subject to dry friction.

誤： This problem *belongs to* a linear programming problem.

正： This problem *can be classified as a* linear programming problem.

正： This problem *is a type of* linear programming problem.

Besides. 正式英文文章中，要表示「此外」不應以 *besides* 作連接副詞來表達，而應使用 *in addition, moreover* 或 *furthermore* 表達。

劣： *Besides*, the following problem arises when we consider the effects of friction.

佳： *In addition*, the following problem arises when we consider the effects of friction.

佳：　*Moreover*, the following problem arises when we consider the effects of friction.

Better. *Good* 是英文最常見的褒詞，故意思相當含糊。當比較兩件事物時，用詞應力求精準，不要只說某方「較好」（即 "better"）。

模糊：　Our algorithm is *better* than the conventional one.

精確：　Our algorithm is *more accurate* than the conventional one.

精確：　Our algorithm is *faster* than the conventional one.

Build. 在大多數科技論文中，使用 *construct* 比 *build* 更恰當。

劣：　We shall *build* an efficient natural language parser.

佳：　We shall *construct* an efficient natural language parser.

劣：　The switched current approach to *building* the low-pass filter has several advantages.

佳：　The switched current approach to *constructing* the low-pass filter has several advantages

But. 一般而言，英文的句首不應使用 *but*。但與 *and* 相同，資深的作者偶爾也會為造出特殊的修辭效果而違反這規則。儘管如此，在科技寫作中，違反規則通常都是沒有好理由的。如果要在句首表示「然而」或「但是」之意，則應使用 *however*。（對等連接詞後面本來就不加逗點，故萬一在句首使用 *but*，亦千萬別加逗點。）

不恰當：　*But* Smith's theory does not explain why the anomalous Hall effect does not occur in conventional superconductors.

恰當：　*However*, Smith's theory does not explain why the anomalous Hall effect does not occur in conventional superconductors.

By this way. 這個片語正確的寫法是 *in this way*。

誤：　*By this way*, we can obtain the solution to equation (7).

正：　*In this way*, we can obtain the solution to equation (7).

Call. 千萬別在 *call* 後面加上 *as*；但 *refer to* 後面必須跟著 *as*。

誤：　We shall *call* this algorithm *as* the new GA.

正：　We shall *call* this algorithm the new GA.

正：　We shall *refer to* this algorithm *as* the new GA.

Called. 科技論文作者常用 *called* 來介紹新術語或某事物的別名。然而，*called* 有時是可省略的。

原句：　In the first phase, *called* graph analysis, the similarities between nodes on the same level are identified.

修正句：　In the first phase, graph analysis, the similarities between nodes on the same level are identified.

Can. 在英文中，*can* 常為贅詞。在一個中文句子中使用「可以」是很恰當時，但在意思相同的英文句子中卻可能沒必要加上 *can*。

累贅： Our method *can find* the optimal solution quickly.

簡潔： Our method *finds* the optimal solution quickly.

讀者應分清 *can* 和 *may* 的分別。*Can* 是指能力，但 *may* 則為可能或允許之意。

This technique *can* prevent the radiation from interacting with the natural convection.

There are many situations in which radiation *may* interact with natural convection.

首個例句表示：採用這個技術「可以」或「能夠」避免某種交互作用。第二個例句則表示：在很多情形下都有「可能」發生某種交互作用。

I *can* go for a walk today.

I *may* go for a walk today.

"You *may* go out and play," said the children's mother.

首個例句的意思是：我今天可以出去散步。（我有空，沒給事情絆住。）第二個例句的意思是：我今天可能出去散步。（我可能會去，但不一定。）第三個例句的意思則為：母親允許小孩子出去玩。

Cannot. 英文寫作中，*cannot* 通常應寫成一個字，尤其當它表示「不能」或「不可能」的意思時，更不應拆開。

劣： A car *can not* go as fast as an airplane.

佳： A car *cannot* go as fast as an airplane.

假如要表示「可以不必這樣做」或「能夠不必這樣做」之意，或者需要強調 *not* 這字，則 *can* 與 *not* 可以分開。

We have already received several interesting papers for the conference, so we *can not accept* late submissions, if we prefer. 我們可以不接受遲交的論文——我們沒必要接受

然而，正面的表達方式通常會更清楚：

We have already received several interesting papers for the conference, so we *can reject* late submissions, if we prefer.

Case. 名詞 *case* 後面的關係代名詞，必須使用 *in which* 或 *when*，而不能用 *that*。（有些資深的作者也會用 *where*，但這用法備受爭議。）

誤： Let us now discuss *the case that* q is greater than 0.

正： Let us now discuss *the case in which* q is greater than 0.

有時候，*case* 是贅詞。把它省略的話，句子會較簡潔。

累贅：　*In many cases*, these systems are slow and inaccurate.

簡潔：　Many of these systems are slow and inaccurate.

Change. 如果用 *change* 來描述因時而遷的變化，則其後的介系詞應是 *in*，而非 *of*。

劣：　The changes *of* the rotor temperature were measured at 30 second intervals.

佳：　The changes *in* the rotor temperature were measured at 30 second intervals.

Choose as. 下面這樣使用 *chose as* 是錯誤的：

誤：　We *choose* the frequency of the carrier *as* 300 kHz.

使用 *choose as*（或 *select as*）的正確方式如下：

正：　We *choose* 300 kHz *as* the frequency of the carrier.

此外，這些例句也是正確的英文：

We specify the frequency of the carrier as 300 kHz.

The frequency of the carrier is specified as 300 kHz.

The frequency of the carrier is set as 300 kHz.

The frequency of the carrier is set to be 300 kHz.

Classical, traditional, conventional. 雖然這三個形容詞的用法有時大致相同，但涵義卻有少許分別。*Classical* 強調某理論或方法是「經典」的，即是在過去廣為學者承認，但現已被新理論或方法取代。*Traditional* 通常表示某理論或方法已行之日久，或許現在仍有人使用，但很可能已經有更新的理論或方法提出。至於 *conventional* 則可形容某理論、方法或技術是時下最流行的或約定俗成的，但與 *traditional* 不同，它沒有表示歷時多久。當作者使用 *conventional* 這字詞時，大概是在暗示自己將會提出或已經出現更先進的做法或技術。

原句：　In *traditional* physics, force is considered to be the product of mass and acceleration.

修正：　In *classical* physics, force is considered to be the product of mass and acceleration.

原句：　The proposed architecture is more efficient than the *traditional* design, which was originally developed by researchers at IBM in 1993. 設計是近年發明的，用 *traditional* 不太妥當。

修正：　The proposed architecture is more efficient than the *conventional* design, which was originally developed by researchers at IBM in 1993.

Compare. *Compare to* 用以比較兩個有基本差異的事物的相同之處；*compare with* 則用以比較兩個大致相同事物的相異之處。因此，在科技寫作中，*compare with* 應比 *compare to* 常用。當比較不同的數據或結果時，尤應使用 *compare with*。

The human brain has been *compared to* a computer.

Let us *compare* these results *with* those obtained in the first experiment.

Compensate. *Compensate* 有「補充」或「抵消」之意。其後通常必須加上介系詞 *for*，而不加直接受詞。唯一例外的情況是當直接受詞正是得到補償的人或事物。

誤： This mechanism *compensates* the slower speed of the genetic algorithm.

正： This mechanism *compensates for* the slower speed of the genetic algorithm.

正： The boss *compensated* the staff *for* their hard work by paying them a bonus at the end of the month.

Complete. *Complete* 為及物動詞，必須接著直接受詞，除非句子是被動語態。若要表示某事情完成了，則應用述詞形容詞 *is completed.*

正： We *completed* the experiment on Tuesday.

正： The memory access *is completed* in one cycle.

誤： When the operation *completes,* the system enters standby mode.

正： When the operation *is completed,* the system enters standby mode.

Comprise. *Comprise* 意思為「包含」；避免使用 *is comprised of*。

誤： The system *is comprised of* four functional blocks.

正： The system *comprises* four functional blocks.

正： The system *consists of* four functional blocks.

正： The system *is composed of* four functional blocks.

正： Four functional blocks *constitute* the system.

Conclusion. *State* 及 *present* 這兩個動詞可跟 *conclusion* 搭配；但千萬別寫 *make conclusions* 或 *give conclusions*。想避免寫出不自然的句子，可以只寫 *conclude*，非常簡單。

劣： Finally, we *make a conclusion* in section 6.
佳： Finally, we *state* our *conclusions* in section 6.

劣： The final section of the paper *gives the conclusions.*
佳： The final section *states the conclusions of the paper.*
佳： Section 5 *concludes* the paper.

Consider. 如果 *consider* 是表示「相信」或「視為」之意，則其後不應有 *as*。（有些作者為求表達清楚，會用 *consider to be*。嚴格說來，*to be* 通常是可以省略的。）但 *regard as* 及 *view as* 都是正確的。

誤： For practical purposes, this may be *considered as* an adiabatic reaction.

正：　For practical purposes, this may be *considered* an adiabatic reaction.

正：　For practical purposes, this may be *regarded as* an adiabatic reaction.

當 *consider* 意指「評價」、「討論」或「考慮」，其後可加上 *as*：

正：　We *considered* him *as* a candidate for the job, but in the end we decid-ed to hire another applicant.

Contrary. 參見 *on the contrary*。

Currently. 參見 *recently*。

Criteria. *Criteria* 是複數，單數形式是 *criterion*。"Criterions" 是錯誤的。

There are three major design *criteria*. The first *criterion* is that the system must be shock resistant.

Data. 在正式文章中，*data* 應作複數名詞。

劣：　The data that *is* received *is* stored in the FIFO buffer.

佳：　The data that *are* received *are* stored in the FIFO buffer.

Decide. *Decide* 應為「做決定」或「判斷」之意。如果要表示「確定」、「辨認」或「定義」之意，則用 *determine* 會較自然。

We *decided* to use this approach for several reasons.

Determining which hypothesis is true is a difficult task.

The overall speed of the system *is determined* mainly by the speed of this algorithm.

Defect. 這個字詞不但指「缺點」，也指「瑕疵」或「毛病」。在某些文脈中，以 *defect* 來指某方法或系統的缺點是不自然的。因為即使該方法不是最理想的，但未必有很明顯的毛病。這種情況中，可用 *shortcoming, disadvantage* 或 *drawback* 來表示「缺點」的意思。

原句：　Smith's method has four major *defects*.

修正：　Smith's method has four major *shortcomings*.

修正：　Smith's method has four major *drawbacks*.

Defined. 當 *define* 在被動句中，跟它配合的介系詞應為 *in* 或 *by*，而非 *as*。

誤：　The variable z is defined *as* equation (12).

正：　The variable z is defined *in* equation (12).

正：　The variable z is defined *by* equation (12).

如果想指稱曾經定義過的變數或名詞，則可使用下面的句式：

The solution is 5z, where z is *as defined in* equation (12).

The solution is 5z, where z is *defined as in* equation (12).

此外，跟 *definition* 配合的介系詞應該是 *of*：

The definition *of* this term was stated in section 3.

The definition *of* this term was given in section 3.

This term was defined in section 3.

Demonstrate. 不要把 *demonstrates* 和 *illustrates, depicts* 或 *presents* 混淆。*Demonstrate* 指「清楚示範」，即向他人示範如何做某事情。此外，*demonstrate* 也可表示「證明」之意。

劣： Figure 3.6 *demonstrates* the effect of the Rayleigh number on the wall temperature of the inner cylinder.

佳： Figure 3.6 *illustrates* the effect of the Rayleigh number on the wall temperature of the inner cylinder.

劣： Figure 3.6 *demonstrates* the variation of the data over time.

佳： Figure 3.6 *depicts* the variation of the data over time.

劣： This paper *demonstrates* a new method for bandwidth allocation.

佳： This paper *presents* a new method for bandwidth allocation.

正： In section 3, we *demonstrate* how to estimate the bit error rate using the proposed method.

Denote. 當 *Denote* 在被動句中出現時，其後必須加上 *by*，而非 *as*。（但 *referred to* 後面卻是加上 *as*。）此外，*represent* 也可作 *denote* 的同義字使用。

誤： In this equation, the force in the radial direction *is denoted as* r.

正： In this equation, the force in the radial direction *is denoted by* r.

正： In this equation, the force in the radial direction *is represented by* r.

正： In this equation, r *denotes* the force in the radial direction.

正： In this equation, the letter r *represents* the force in the radial direction.

誤： Denote *r* to be the force in the radial direction.

正： Let *r* denote the force in the radial direction.

誤： Johnson and Kirk's method *is denoted* below *as* "the JK method."

正： Johnson and Kirk's method *is referred to* below *as* "the JK method."

正： Johnson and Kirk's method *is abbreviated* below *as* "the JK method."

正： A static random access memory is often *referred to as* an SRAM.

正： We will *refer to* these memories as SRAMs.

Depict. *Depict* 的基本意思是「用圖畫表示」。在科技寫作中，不應用 *depict* 來表示「描述」之意。

劣： The contents of each mission segment are *depicted* in section 3.

佳： The contents of each mission segment are *described* in section 3.

Desire. 要表達「需求」的意思，千萬別以 *desire* 與被動語態並用來表示；而應使用 *need* 或 *must*，並使用主動語態句。

誤：　Hence the reliability of the system *is desired to be* improved.

正：　Hence the reliability of the system *needs to be* improved.

正：　Hence the reliability of the system *must be* improved.

正：　Hence the system must be made more reliable.

Despite the fact that. 此冗長的詞語應以 *although* 或 *though* 來代替。

劣：　*Despite the fact that* this method is reliable, it is too slow for medical applications.

佳：　*Although* this method is reliable, it is too slow for medical applications.

佳：　This method is reliable but too slow for medical applications.

Detail. *Describe in detail* 是「詳細地描述」，*a detailed description* 則是「一個詳細的描述」。千萬別寫 "detailly" 或 "detailedly"，這些都是錯誤英文。此外，*detail* 不能作動詞，要表達「描述」或「說明」的意思，應該用 *describe*。例如：

劣：　The functions of the system *will be detailed* in section 2.

佳：　The functions of the system *will be described* in section 2.

Details. 中國人撰寫科技論文時，常會在介紹一項技術或程序後，接著寫 *The details will be described in the next section*（作者大概認為這句的意思是「下一節將詳細描述這些技術」）。但其實這是個意思不明的句子，因為它根本沒清楚指出要詳細描述的事物是甚麼。以下三句都是正確的英文：

The method will be described in detail in the next section.

The details of this method will be described in the next section.

A detailed description of this method will be given in the next section.

Difference. 當 *difference* 用來比較兩個事物時，應與介系詞 *between*（有時也可用 *in*）連用，例如："the difference between x and y"。

誤：　This risk is reflected in the difference *of* the prices *between* real estate in the pre-sales market and that in the finished housing market.

正：　This risk is reflected in the difference *between the price of* real estate in the pre-sales market *and the price of* real estate in the finished housing market.

正：　This risk is reflected in the difference *between the price of* real estate in the pre-sales market *and that* in the finished housing market.

正：　This risk is reflected in the difference *in* the price of real estate in the pre-sales market and that in the finished housing market.

Different. 正確與 *different* 配合的介系詞是 *from*。千萬別寫成 *different than*, *different to* 或 *different between*。

> 誤： The characteristics of the second sample were *different than* those of the first.

> 正： The characteristics of the second sample were *different from* those of the first.

> 誤： The operation is slightly *different between* x and y.

> 正： The operation of x is slightly *different from* that of y.

不過，如果使用名詞 *difference*，則應以 *between* 配合：

> 正： There is a slight *difference between* the operation of x and that of y.

此外，句子不應以 *different from* 開首。（可參見 *unlike*。）

Display. *Display* 及 *exhibit* 可指「呈現」，如 *The data display a decreasing trend*。然而，*display* 及 *exhibit* 卻不應用來表示「提出」：

> 劣： The analysis *is displayed* in section 3.

> 劣： The analysis *is exhibited* in section 3.

> 佳： The analysis *is presented* in section 3.

此外，*display* 也可表示「以圖表表示」（一般而言，作者多會使用 *show*）。但用 *exhibit* 來表示「以圖表表示」，則會顯得不自然：

> 正： The test results *are shown* in Figure 4.

> 正： The test results *are displayed* in Figure 4.

> 劣： The test results *are exhibited* in Figure 4.

Dramatic, drastic. *Dramatic* 通常指「興奮」或「轟動」。至於 *drastic* 則指「強烈」或「激烈」。*Dramatic* 的意思可以是正面或負面的；*drastic* 則通常是負面的。要表示「大幅增加」，通常應該用 *a dramatic increase* 來表示；至於 *drastic* 則常這樣使用：*The economy will improve only if drastic changes in the finance laws are made*。

Due to. 標準英文中，*due to* 只能修飾名詞，旨在指出事件起因。如果 *due to* 不修飾名詞，則應用 *because of* 代替。還有，別用 *due to* 作介系詞來表示「由於」之意。

> 正： The breakdowns were *due to* poor design.

> 正： We observed changes *due to* the presence of excess fluorine in the system.

> 劣： *Due to* this problem, a conventional controller cannot be used in this case.

佳： *Because of* this problem, a conventional controller cannot be used in this case.

Due to the fact that. 這冗長的詞語應以 *because* 代替。

冗長： This unexpected result occurred *due to the fact that* the raw materials were impure.

簡潔： This unexpected result occurred *because* the raw materials were impure.

Effect. 參見 *affect*。

E.g. 此乃拉丁文片語 *exempli gratia* 的縮寫，意思是「例如」。由於它是非限定片語，所以一定要用逗點把它與句子其他部分隔開。注意這縮寫的正確寫法是 "e.g."，兩個字母後都必須有句號。

Ensure. *Ensure* 和 *insure* 都是「確保」之意，但用 *ensure* 較好。至於 *insure* 則特指「防止財務損失」（例如保險 (insurance)）。此外，許多人常把 *assure* 和 *ensure* 混淆：*assure* 是「承諾」或「保證」，而不是「確保」。*Assure* 及 *insure* 都很少在科技寫作中出現。

Overflow protection *ensures* that recorded messages will not be lost when the memory is full.

She *assured* the professor that her report would be completed by the end of the week.

Equal. *Equal* 作動詞時，其後不應接介系詞。作形容詞時，其後才必須加上介系詞 *to*。

誤： A kilogram *equals to* 1000 grams.

正： A kilogram *is equal to* 1000 grams.

正： The value of this variable *equals* half the value of *z*.

Especially. 把 *especially*（或 *particularly*）放在句首或子句開首來表示「尤其」或「特別」是錯誤的，這時應使用 *in particular*。

劣： All of our algorithms performed well; *especially*, algorithm 3 was nearly twice as fast as the conventional method.

佳： All of our algorithms performed well; *in particular*, algorithm 3 was nearly twice as fast as the conventional method.

用 *especially* 來修飾形容詞是正確的：

正： All of the algorithms are fast, but Algorithm 3 is *especially* fast.

Et al. 這是拉丁文片語 *et alii* 的縮寫，意思是「以及其他人」。在援引書籍或論文時，如該書籍或論文的作者超過三位，就可只列出首位作者的名字，並把 *et al.* 放在這名字後面，來代表所有的作者（例如，"Smith et al."）。請注意這縮寫正確的寫法是 "et al."，"al." 之後應有一個句點（"et.al." 或 "et al" 都是錯誤的）。此

外，在論文的引文中，在首位作者和 *et al.* 之間，通常不加逗點。但在參考書目中，必須在首位作者和 *et al.* 之間加上逗點。

　　Etc. 此為拉丁文片語 *et cetera* 的縮寫，意指「以及其他事物」。但英文的 *etc.* 和中文的「等」，用法不盡相同。中文的「等」係用來表示一系列事物的結束，即使已沒有可提及的事物。英文的 *etc.* 意思和中文的「等等」較為相近。然而，在正式英文文章中，卻不應常用 *etc.*，尤其是中國人在文章中所用的 *etc.*，大多應省略。

　　Etc. 尤其不應出現在以 *such as, including, for example* 或 *e.g.* 引介的一系列項目的結尾。如果作者事實上已再沒有可以提及的事物，則不應使用 *etc.*。如果讀者並不明瞭作者所指的「其他事物」是甚麼，也不應使用 *etc.*。在很多句子中，即使有理由使用 *etc.*，然而片語 *and so on* 或 *and so forth* 仍是較佳的選擇。

- 劣： Computers can be used for a wide variety of applications, including word processing, graphics processing, and entertainment, *etc.*

- 佳： Computers can be used for a wide variety of applications, including word processing, graphics processing, and entertainment.

- 正： The items in the series will be denoted by i_1, i_2, i_3, etc. [讀者都明瞭作者所指的其他事物為何，即：i_4, i_5, i_6 等等。]

　　Evidence. 這是不可數名詞。「證據很多」是 *much evidence*，而非 *many evidences*。

　　Exhibit. 參見 *display*。

　　Exist. 以 *exist* 來表示「有」或「在內」或「包含」，是不自然的寫法。這樣的寫法應修改，以其他字詞來代替 *exist*。

- 劣： Many inconsistent training instances *exist* in the training set.
- 佳： Many inconsistent training instances *are present* in the training set.
- 佳： Many inconsistent training instances *can be found* in the training set.
- 佳： *There are* many inconsistent training instances in the training set.
- 佳： The training set *includes* many inconsistent training instances.

- 誤： We shall develop a method for guiding the motion of the robot *with the existence of* obstacles.

- 正： We shall develop a method for guiding the motion of the robot *in the presence of* obstacles.

- 誤： Many factors *exist* in designing a good learning system.

- 正： Many factors *must be considered* in order to design a good learning system.

- 正： Many factors *must be considered* in the design of a good learning system.

- 正： Many factors *are involved* in the design of a good learning system.

Fact. 如果句子中出現了 *the fact that*，則應把它省略，並改寫句子。改寫後的句子通常會較為簡潔。

冗贅：　*The fact that* the temperature rose caused the reaction rate to increase.

簡潔：　The rise in temperature caused the reaction rate to increase.

簡潔：　Because the temperature rose, the reaction rate increased.

Famous. 在科技論文中，*well-known* 常比 *famous* 恰當。

不自然：　A *famous* approach to solving this problem is the method introduced by Zucker [4].

自然：　　One *well-known* approach to solving this problem is the method introduced by Zucker [4].

Farther, further. *Farther*（「更遠」）是指距離，而 *further*（「更多」、「更進一步」）則指時間或數量。

Singapore is *farther* from here than Hong Kong.

We will now modify the algorithm *further* to improve its efficiency.

Feedback. *Feedback* 只能作名詞使用。如果想作動詞使用，則必須寫成兩個字：*feed back*（被動語態和過去式是 *fed back*）。

誤：　Each output neuron *is feedbacked* to the corresponding node in the input layer.

正：　Each output neuron *is fed back* to the corresponding node in the input layer.

正：　Each output neuron *is connected* to the corresponding node in the input layer.

Few, a few. *Few* 意指「很少」，而 *a few* 則指「一些」或「幾個」。

Few people know this. 很少人知道。

A few people have written papers about this problem. 已有幾個人對這問題發表文章了。

Fewer, less. 修飾可數名詞時，應使用 *fewer*；修飾不可數名詞時，則應使用 *less*。

The new method requires *fewer* cycles to complete the calculation.

In the second experiment, *less* nitrogen was used.

Finalize. 參見 *-ize*。

Firstly, secondly. *First, second* 等字詞比 *firstly, secondly* 等字詞文雅簡潔。*First, second* 加上了字尾 *-ly* 是強迫讀者多閱讀一個累贅的音節。

劣：　*Secondly*, the annealing temperature was higher for this group of samples.

佳：　*Second*, the annealing temperature was higher for this group of samples.

在下面的「誤」句中，*firstly* 的使用方式是錯誤的：

誤：　How to form a crossing region is *firstly* explained.

正：　We *first* explain how to form a crossing region.

正：　*First*, we will explain how to form a crossing region.

The following. 參見 *as follows*。

For example. *For example* 是正確的英文用法，*for examples* 則是錯誤的。注意 *for example* 是連接副詞，因此只能用來表示兩個子句、句子或段落間的關係。*For example* 之後不應有一連串例子：

誤：　The employees were asked to indicate the level of importance of 12 aspects of their jobs, *for example,* salary, benefits, safety, and opportunities for advancement.

正：　The employees were asked to indicate the level of importance of 12 aspects of their jobs, *such as* salary, benefits, safety, and opportunities for advancement.

正：　The employees were asked to indicate the level of importance of 12 aspects of their jobs, *including* salary, benefits, safety, and opportunities for advancement.

正：　The employees were asked to indicate the level of importance of 12 aspects of their jobs. *For example,* they were asked to compare the relative importance of salary, benefits, safety, and opportunities for advancement.

For +動名詞 (gerund)。參見 *To do x*。

Form, formulate. *To form* 指「形成」、「組成」或「產生」。*To formulate* 則指「寫成公式」或「規劃」。

When water boils, steam *forms*.

The girls *formed* a basketball team to play against the boys.

We can *formulate* the problem in the following way.

The soldiers *formulated* a detailed plan for the attack.

Functionality. 如果 *function* 可表達句意，則別寫 *functionality*。

劣：　The system has many convenient *functionalities*.
佳：　The system has many convenient *functions*.

模糊：　The *functionality* of the device has been expanded.
清楚：　The device has several new *functions*.

Get. 這字詞不夠正式。科技論文中應使用 *obtain, have, derive* 或其他字詞才是。

劣：　By inserting these values into equation (10), we *get* the following solution.

佳：　By inserting these values into equation (10), we *obtain* the following solution.

Give. 中國人撰寫英文科技論文時，常會濫用 *give*。*Give* 本身是個意思不精確的字詞，故在大多數情況中，使用如 *state, present* 或 *propose* 這些較精確的字詞，遠比使用 *give* 來得好。

模糊：　Smith *gave* a theorem that shows…
精確：　Smith *stated* a theorem that shows…
精確：　Smith *presented* a theorem that shows…
精確：　Smith *proved* a theorem that shows…

模糊：　First we will *give* the following definitions.
精確：　First we will *state* the following definitions.
精確：　First we will *define* the following terms.

在很多中國學生撰寫的研究報告導論中，常可看到這個句子：

劣：　The final section *gives* the conclusions.

這句是非常不自然的英文，應改寫如下：

佳：　The final section *states* the conclusions of the paper.

佳：　The final section *presents* the conclusions of the paper.

佳：　Section 5 concludes the paper.

佳：　The conclusions of the paper are stated in section 5.

Given. *Given* 不是限定動詞。因此，像 *given a set of data* 這樣的片語，並非完整句子，因此其後必須緊接一個主要子句。

誤：　Given that x=y. We can prove the theorem as shown below.

正：　Given that x=y, we can prove the theorem as shown below.

正：　Assume that x=y; the theorem can then be proven as shown below.

正：　If x=y, then the theorem can be proven as shown below.

Given as. 以 *given as* 指「從某處得到」或「表達」的句子，是非常不自然的：

劣：　The solution *is given as*…
佳：　The solution *is given by* the following equation.

劣：　The centripetal force *is given as* the following:
佳：　The centripetal force *can be expressed* as follows:

Good. 參見 *better*。

Happen. 在科技論文中，使用 *occur* 通常比使用 *happen* 好。

原句：　We then observed what *happened* as the experiment proceeded.

恰當：　We then observed what *occurred* as the experiment proceeded.

Her. 要指稱公司或機關學校，別用 *she* 或 *her*，而應用 *it* 或 *its*。

誤：　Technocorp agrees to fulfill *her* obligations promptly.

正：　Technocorp agrees to fulfill *its* obligations promptly.

Herein. 避免使用 *herein* 這種古英文字詞。

劣：　We *herein* select the ART I model.

佳：　*Here* we select the ART I model.

佳：　*In this study*, we will use the ART I model.

However. 如果要以 *however* 表示「可是」或「然而」的意思，則必須用逗點把 *however* 與句子其餘部分隔開。如果句子以 *however* 開首而缺少逗點，則 *however* 就是「無論」的意思。

However, little research has been done on the effects of excessive rainfall on this type of habitat.

However you attempt to stop me, I will still go.

The idea of. *The idea of* 和中文的「這個概念」或「這個主意」意思相似。在 *She found the idea of going to Canada for school very exciting* 及 *Everyone thought the idea of having a party was a good one* 這兩句中，*the idea of* 都是正確的用法。然而，想解釋自己的方法或理論背後的基本概念時，千萬別用 *the idea of*，而應用 *the idea behind* 或 *the idea underlying*。

劣：　*The main idea of* the proposed method is to use a region-growing technique to cluster the data.

佳：　*The main idea behind* the proposed method is to use a region-growing technique to cluster the data.

佳：　*The main idea underlying* the proposed method is to use a region-growing technique to cluster the data.

I.e. *I.e.* 係拉丁文片語 *id est* 的縮寫，指「即是」（"that is (to say)"）。*I.e.* 是非限定片語，因此必須用逗點把它與句子其他部分隔開。注意這縮寫正確寫法是 "i.e."，每個字母後面都必須有句號。

Illustrate. *Illustrate* 是「舉例說明」之意。因此，我們不能 "illustrate" 一個例子，對象應是一個論點或方法才是。

誤：　Two examples of the proposed method are *illustrated* in section III.

正：　Two examples are *presented* in section III to illustrate the proposed method.

正：　In section III the proposed method is illustrated by means of two examples.

Illustration. 不要混淆 *illustration* 和 *example*。

誤： A numerical *illustration* will show how the coordinates of these points can be found.

正： A numerical *example* will show how the coordinates of these points can be found.

Impact. 不要把 *impact* 作動詞來表示「影響」。

誤： Boron doping *impacts* the characteristics of the substrates in two ways.

正： Boron doping *affects* the characteristics of the substrates in two ways.

In such case. 這是錯誤英文，*in this case* 才是對的。

In this way. 參見 *by this way*。

In other words. *In other words*（「換句話說」）是正確的寫法，但 *in another word* 或 *in a word* 都是錯誤的。*In a word* 是正確的英文，而與 *in other words* 意思不同。*In a word* 意思類似於中文的「簡單地說」，但很少在科技論文中出現。

In order to. 很多有 *in order to X*... 的句子，都可省略 *in order*。

原句： *In order to overcome* this problem, we propose using a new mixture of gases in the reaction chamber.

簡潔： *To overcome* this problem, we propose using a new mixture of gases in the reaction chamber.

Insure. 參見 *ensure*。

It should be noted that. 如此冗贅的表達，可省略成 *note that*。（大部分的情形中，*it is noted that* 也是錯誤英文，因此應以 *note that* 取代。）

冗贅： *It should be noted that* these findings are subject to several restrictions.

簡潔： *Note that* these findings are subject to several restrictions.

Interesting, interested. *Interesting* 係表示某人對某主題或事物感興趣；*interested* 則用以形容某人對某事感興趣。千萬別以 *interested* 來修飾某主題或事物。

Many people find circuit design *interesting*, but I am more *interested* in software development.

Introduce. 可以用 *explain, describe* 或 *state* 時，就別用 *introduce*：

劣： We will *introduce* the geometric significance of the theorem in section 3.

佳： We will *explain* the geometric significance of the theorem in section 3.

Its, it's. *Its* 是屬格代名詞，指「它的」；*It's* 則表示 "it is"。

誤： We will design a fuzzy neural network and then test *it's* performance.

正： We will design a fuzzy neural network and then test *its* performance.

-ize. 別以這個字尾來造出新單字。避免使用如 *finalize* 及 *prioritize* 這種意思模糊的偽術語。

模糊： We have not yet *finalized* the design.

清楚： We have not yet *put* the design *into final form.*

清楚： We have not yet *finished* the design.

清楚： We have not yet *decided on the final design.*

Know. 英文的 *know* 是靜態動詞，不能用來表達從「不知道」變成「知道」的轉變。英文的 *know* 通常不用於表示「學習」、「看出」、「發現」或「得知」，只能用以表示「知道某事」的心理狀態。

劣： From the figure we can *know* that *x* increases with time.

佳： From the figure we can *see* that *x* increases with time.

正： From the figure we *know* that *x* increases with time. 此句之意非「從圖中資料，我們可以發現這點」，而是「根據圖中的資料，我們知道這點」。

誤： According to these test results, we can *know* that the genetic algorithm is more effective.

正： From these test results, we can *see* that the genetic algorithm is more effective.

正： *These test results show* that the genetic algorithm is more effective.

Latter, former. *Latter* 是指兩個曾經提及的項目中的次項，*former* 則指兩個項目中的首項。它們與 *first, last* 的意思不同。*First* 是指連續多個項目中的首項，就算只有兩項；*last* 則指連續三個以上項目中的最後一項。注意 *latter* 與 *later* 是不同的，*later* 是指「在一段時間後」。

Less. 請參見 *fewer*。

Less than. 嚴格說來，像 *with size less than 1* 及 *has value less than x* 的寫法都是錯誤的（但有些人把這些詞句當作正確的縮寫形式）。正確寫法應該是 *with a size of less than 1* 及 *has a value of less than x*。

誤： We then obtain a result *with error less than* the size of the cell.

正： We then obtain a result *with an error of less than* the size of the cell.

Let. *Let* 是動詞，並非附屬連接詞。因此以 *let* 開首的子句應接著句號或分號，而非逗點。否則便會造出缺乏連接詞的複句（請參考第四章 4.3節）。此外，正式科技論文中，最好別以 *let's* 來代替 *let us*。

誤： Let x=y, the following equation can then be obtained.

正： Let x=y; the following equation can then be obtained.

正： Let x=y. The following equation can then be obtained.

List. 惟真正列出幾個不同的項目時，才可用動詞 *list*，否則應用 *state, describe* 或其他字詞。

劣： The solution can be found by using the procedure *listed* in this section.

佳： The solution can be found by using the procedure *stated* in this section.

佳： The solution can be found by using the procedure *described* in this section.

劣： The proof is *listed* in the Appendix.

佳： The proof is *stated* in the Appendix.

佳： The proof is *given* in the Appendix.

正： The error rates for each of the trials are *listed* in Table 3.

Make. *Make* 為弱動詞，意思非常模糊。因此，應盡量使用較特定具體的動詞來取代 *make*。

模糊： From the results of the experiments, the following conclusions can be *made.*

清楚： From the results of the experiments, the following conclusions can be *drawn.*

清楚： The experimental results *support* the following conclusions.

清楚： From the experimental results, we can *conclude* that…[直接敘述結論]

模糊： A new, more detailed analysis of the problem is *made* in section 3.

清楚： A new, more detailed analysis of the problem is *presented* in section 3.

在上面「模糊」的例句中，*make* 使用得非常不自然。以英文為母語的作者絕不會寫出像 "make a conclusion" 或 "make an analysis" 的詞句。

Match. 比較不同資料時，用 *agree* 或其他字都常比 *match* 恰當。

原句： The test data *match* the theoretical predictions.

恰當： The test data *agree with* the theoretical predictions.

恰當： The test data *are in good agreement with* the theoretical predictions.

恰當： The test data *are consistent with* the theoretical predictions.

恰當： The test data *confirm the accuracy of* the theoretical predictions.

May. 與 *can* 的意思並不相同。*Can* 表示能力，*may* 則表示可能或許可。請參見 *can*。

Meanwhile. 中文的「同時」可以指「此外」、「也」或「而且」之意。但英文的 *meanwhile* 只能指「在同一段時間」。如果以 *meanwhile* 來表示中文的「同時」，則會非常不自然。

劣： This technique increases the rate of convergence; *meanwhile*, it prevents the algorithm from becoming trapped in local optima.

佳： This technique increases the rate of convergence; *moreover*, it prevents the algorithm from becoming trapped in local optima.

佳： This technique increases the rate of convergence; *in addition*, it prevents the algorithm from becoming trapped in local optima.

Method for. *Method* 後面常緊接介系詞 *for* 或 *of* 及一個動名詞，這樣通常比使用不定詞自然。

劣： We shall discuss two *methods to solve* this problem.

佳： We shall discuss two *methods for solving* this problem.

佳： We shall discuss two *methods of solving* this problem.

Modern. 許多時，*modern* 並不能清楚表示所指時代為何。*Modern* 可以是指從近幾十年到一百年或以上，但科技論文中提到的 "modern technology"，當然絕非指六十、八十年前的技術。相對地，使用 *contemporary* 或 *recent* 的話，意思會較清楚。

模糊： The cache memory has become a standard feature of *modern* computer designs.

清楚： The cache memory has become a standard feature of *contemporary* computer designs.

More than one. 使用這詞句作主詞時，必須用單數動詞。

More than one researcher *has* attempted to solve this problem.

Most, most of. *Most* 和 *most of* 表示不同的普遍程度。*Most* 指一個總類中的大部分個例，緊接其後的複數名詞不加任何冠詞。*Most of* 則指某一組事物中的大部分個例，其後必須接著定冠詞 *the*。當使用 *most of the* 時，如所指事物不是前文已提過或讀者早已知道的，句中就應清楚界定所指對象為何。許多時，*most* 都可代替一個句子中的 *most of the* 而使句意不變。相反，除非讀者已知所指的是哪些特定事物，否則以 *most of the* 代替 *most*，可能會使句意不清。

正： *Most* graduate students are hard-working.

誤： *Most of* graduate students are hard-working.

模糊： *Most of the* graduate students are hard-working.
不明所指為哪些研究生

清楚： *Most of the* graduate students *in our department* are hard-working.

清楚： *Most* graduate students *in our department* are hard-working.

Some 的使用規則，與 *most* 大致相同。

正： *Some* graduate students are lazy.

誤： *Some of* graduate students are lazy.

模糊： *Some of the* graduate students are lazy. 不明所指為哪些研究生

清楚： *Some of the* graduate students *in our department* are lazy.

Namely. 在很多句子中是不必要的，可以省略。

累贅： Two important components in the AGC loop, *namely*, the variable gain amplifier and the bandpass filter, must now be designed.

簡潔： Two important components in the AGC loop, the variable gain amplifier and the bandpass filter, must now be designed.

簡潔： Two important components in the AGC loop must now be designed: the variable gain amplifier and the bandpass filter.

Notation. 當 *notation* 是指一整組符號時，應作不可數名詞使用；但當所指為一個特定的符號時，則有時可作可數名詞使用，並寫成複數。然而，使用 *types of notation* 或 *symbols* 總比 *notations* 恰當。

正： The *notation* used in this paper is summarized in Table 1.

劣： The authors used two different *notations* to represent the same force.

佳： The authors used two different *types of notation* to represent the same force.

佳： The authors used two different *symbols* to represent the same force.

Obvious, obviously. *Obvious* 這形容詞的意思是「清楚而容易看出的」，且常是 *clear* 的同義詞。*Obviously* 這副詞的主要意思是「容易看出或瞭解的」（即「顯然」，卻非「明顯」），但有時不適合用作 *clearly* 的同義字。例如，下面句子使用 *obviously* 的方式不太自然，而應以 *clearly* 或 *significantly* 來代替。

劣： The intensity of the C-H bond absorption peaks decreased *obviously* as the annealing temperature increased.

佳： The intensity of the C-H bond absorption peaks *clearly* decreased as the annealing temperature increased.

佳： The intensity of the C-H bond absorption peaks decreased *significantly* as the annealing temperature increased.

正： *Obviously*, the annealing temperature affects the intensity of the C-H bond absorption peaks in some way.

Occur. 在正式文章中，使用 *occur* 比用 *happen* 或 *there is* 恰當。

原句： *There was a problem* during the preparation stage.

恰當： *A problem occurred* during the preparation stage.

Of. 中國人寫英文文章時，常會誤把介系詞 *of* 代替所有介系詞，例如往往把 *of* 和 *in* 混淆：

誤： We aim to prevent errors *of* the digitalization process.

正： We aim to prevent errors *in* the digitalization process.

誤： The samples were examined for changes *of* thickness.

正： The samples were examined for changes *in* thickness.

撰寫英文報告時需特別注意，不能把中文的「的」字直譯成英文的 *of* 來使用。下面以斜體字標示的介系詞都表示「關於」或「針對」之意，因此不能使用 *of*，而必須用 *about, on, concerning* 或 *regarding*：

誤： The test reports *of* our new product are finished.

正： The test reports *on* our new product are finished.

誤： Professor Chen has done some interesting research *of* neural networks.

正： Professor Chen has done some interesting research *on* neural networks

誤： This is a book *of* the design of mixed-signal circuits.

正： This is a book *about* the design of mixed-signal circuits.

誤： The information *of* the input pattern is stored here.

正： The information *on / concerning / about* the input pattern is stored here.

此外，千萬別混淆 *of* 和 *for*：

誤： All of the arrangements *of* the conference are finished.

正： All of the arrangements *for* the conference are finished.

誤： This is our strategy *of* expanding sales in Europe.

正： This is our strategy *for* expanding sales in Europe.

On the contrary, on the other hand, in contrast, in comparison. 這四個詞語意思都有所不同。*On the contrary* 用以否定前一個句子或子句的論點。

He argues that this strategy has increased sales. *On the contrary*, sales revenue has dropped 20% since the strategy was adopted.

千萬別混淆 *on the contrary* 與 *in contrast*（或 *by contrast*），後者是用來介紹一個與前句概念作強烈對照的新概念：

Approach A provides high speed at the cost of increased memory requirements. *In contrast*, approach B is slower but requires much less memory.

On the other hand 和 *in comparison*（或 *by comparison*）是用來提出新內容，並與前一個句子或子句的內容作比較或對照。

The serial design is still the most common design. *On the other hand*, the parallel design is becoming increasingly popular.

The parallel design is quite complex. *In comparison*, the serial design is much simpler.

On the other hand, in comparison 和 *in contrast* 的語法功能類似，且意思也相近。不過，與 *on the other hand* 或 *in comparison* 相比，*in contrast* 更強調句子內容和前文的對照。這三者與 *on the contrary* 的意思截然不同。*On the other hand, in comparison* 和 *in contrast* 的功能在於引導新概念，令讀者較注意下文內容；而 *on the contrary* 的功能則在於強調否定前文內容，會令讀者暫時較注意前文論點。

On the other hand 這片語只有在其引介句子的主題為前文提過時，或引介句子與前幾句主題有明顯的對照關係時，方可使用。下面句子中，*on the other hand* 用得很適當，因句中的兩種活動有明顯的對照：

I enjoy playing sports with my friends and going dancing on Saturday nights. *On the other hand*, I also enjoy many quiet, solitary activities.

相反，下面的 *on the other hand* 就用得很不自然。因為討論的兩個項目（"fuzzy set theory" 和 "neural networks"）既沒明顯的對照，前文也不曾提過。

Fuzzy set theory has been the focus of much research in the last decade, because it can be used to model ambiguous data or uncertain information. *On the other hand*, neural networks have also attracted a great deal of attention in the last ten years.

第二句最好是直接省略 *on the other hand*。下面是一種修改方式：

Fuzzy set theory has been the focus of much research in the last decade, because it can be used to model ambiguous data or uncertain information. Neural networks are another area of research that has attracted a great deal of attention in the last ten years.

-oriented. 凡為這字尾的字，意思通常是空洞模糊的。作者應以較精確的字詞去取代這種表達方式。

模糊：   Our firm emphasizes *market-oriented* products.
清楚：   Our firm develops products that meet the demands of the market.

模糊：   We provide *customer-oriented* operations.
清楚：   We provide excellent customer service.
清楚：   Our goal is to meet the customer's needs quickly and efficiently.
清楚：   Our strategy is to analyze the customer's needs and to design systems that meet those needs.

Otherwise. 要指稱某個狀態或情況，除非所指已非常清楚，否則不要使用 *otherwise*。下面是一個句意模稜兩可的例子，因為根本看不出 *otherwise* 所指的情況是 bit 2 不設為 0、數據不送到 pin R0，還是其他。因此，應使用更精確的陳述方式取代 *otherwise*。

不精確： If bit 2 is 0, the data will be transmitted to pin R0. *Otherwise*, the data will be transmitted to pin R1.

精確： If bit 2 is 0, the data will be transmitted to pin R0. If bit 2 is set to 1, the data will be transmitted to pin R1.

還有，*otherwise* 不可作連接詞使用。

誤： He must submit his thesis by September, *otherwise* he will not graduate.

正： He must submit his thesis by September, *or* he will not graduate.

正： He must submit his thesis by September; *otherwise,* he will not graduate.

Owing to the fact that. 這種表達方式太冗贅，應以 *because* 或 *since* 取代。

冗贅： *Owing to the fact that* X increases over time…

簡潔： *Because* X increases over time…

Particularly. 請參見 *especially*。

Performance. 在評估和比較不同的方法或系統時，理工學者常提到某個方法或電腦系統的 "performance"。在這種文脈中，*performance* 文法雖正確，卻略嫌模糊。故應換上較精確的字詞，如 *speed, throughput, accuracy* 或 *efficiency*，否則應定義好 "performance" 的意思。

模糊： When this technique is used, system *performance* is enhanced significantly.

清楚： When this technique is used, the speed of the system increases significantly.

清楚： This technique increases the accuracy of the system by 20%.

誤： Parallel computing is a popular technique for improving *the performance of scientific calculations.*

正： Parallel computing is a popular technique for improving *the speed of scientific calculations.*

Phenomena. *Phenomena* 是複數名詞，單數形式是 *phenomenon*。*Phenomenon* 即「現象」，在中文裏很常用，但在英文中會較少用到。所以英文句子中最好省略這字詞，而改用較具體的字詞。中國人應格外留意，若自己的句子中出現 *phenomenon*，很可能就是贅詞。

累贅： We must also consider *the phenomenon of* the fringe effect.

簡潔： We must also consider the fringe effect.

累贅： The *quenching and aging phenomena* in plastics have been studied extensively.

簡潔： *Quenching and aging* in plastics have been studied extensively.

Precise, accurate. *Precise* 是「精確」，指重複某動作或測量而可以絲毫無差。*Accurate* 指「準確」或「正確」，意思是某個動作或測量符合公認標準。具有高精確度 (highly precise) 的儀器若沒有經過正確的校正，仍然可能會不準確 (inaccurate)。

Present, propose. 這兩個動詞的意思稍有不同。"To present" /prɪˈzɛnt/ 是提出某意見供他人參考。"To propose" 亦有此意，卻也有指「建議」或「推薦」之意。一個學者可 "present" 某個自己不認同的理論。但 "propose" 一個理論，等於建議別人接受這理論。在理工論文中，要指出論文推薦的方法或技術，應以 *the proposed method* 或 *the proposed technique* 等名詞片語表達；如果用 "presented" 的話，則是錯誤的。

> 誤： *Our presented scheme* successfully extracts the objects in the image.

> 正： *The proposed scheme* successfully extracts the objects in the image.

Present /ˈprɛznt/（即「目前」）可用來形容論文作者提出的理論或方法。"The present method" 便是代表 "the method proposed in this paper" 或 "the method we are now proposing" 的意思。

> The *present* theory successfully explains how the increased concentration of boron affects the electrical characteristics of the films.

> The *present* method is simpler and more elegant than Miller's method.

Principal, principle. *Principal* 的意思是「主要」或「最重要」，*principle* 的意思則是「原則」或「原理」。

> The *principal* technique used is a modified Kalman filter.

> A number of *principles* may be used to explain this result, but we believe the most likely explanation is that suggested by Daniels (1991).

Propose. 只有指涉一個真正的提議時，才可用 *propose*。例如，在下面「誤」句中，*propose* 的使用方式是錯誤的：

> 誤： Smith *has proposed* theoretical aspects of the problem.

> 正： Smith *has studied* theoretical aspects of the problem.

> 正： Smith *has discussed* theoretical aspects of the problem.

Prove. 除非是指數學的證明，否則 *prove* 這個字的意思可能會太過強烈。所以應考慮以 *confirm, verify* 或其他字詞取代。

> These examples *prove* the effectiveness of our method.

> These examples *confirm* the effectiveness of our method.

Purpose. 在許多文脈中，*purpose* 都是贅詞。

> 累贅： The address counter is used for record and playback positioning *purposes.*

累贅：　The address counter is used for *the purpose of* record and playback positioning.

簡潔：　The address counter is used for record and playback positioning.

Reason is because. Reason why. 在 *the reason is because* 和 *the reason why* 中，*because* 和 *why* 都是贅詞。

冗贅：　*The reason* we were late *is because* our car broke down.

冗贅：　*The reason why* we were late is that our car broke down.

簡潔：　*The reason* we were late is that our car broke down.

簡潔：　We were late *because* our car broke down.

Reason is that. 需要說明某個事件或現象時，使用 *the reason is that* 是不夠精確的。*The reason for this is that* 較為清楚，但略嫌冗贅。最簡短直接的表達方式是 *this is because*。

冗贅：　It is clear from the figure that the two plots differ. *The reason for this difference is that* the temperature was higher in the second trial.

簡潔：　It is clear from the figure that the two plots differ. *This is because* the temperature was higher in the second trial.

簡潔：　The figure clearly shows that the two plots differ. *This difference occurred because* the temperature was higher in the second trial.

Recently. 在中文中，很多句子會以表示時間副詞片語開首，如「近幾年」、「近年來」或「目前」等等。中國人寫英文文章時，有時會把這種中文句式直譯成英文，把如 *recently* 或 *currently* 這類副詞擺在句首。在英文中，把表示時間的單一副詞擺在句首，雖沒有文法錯誤，但卻會不夠自然。

Recently, many researchers have investigated this phenomenon.

Currently, this problem is attracting a great deal of attention.

若將副詞擺在動詞前後或移到句尾，則句子會較自然通順：

Many researchers have investigated this phenomenon *recently*.

This problem is *currently* attracting a great deal of attention.

如果想強調某事件發生的時間，則可把句首的時間副詞改成副詞片語，如 *in recent years* 或 *at present*。同時，這樣會使句子較自然。

In recent years, many researchers have investigated this phenomenon.

At present, this problem is attracting a great deal of attention.

此外，*recently* 這字詞的意思極為模糊。對讀者來說，「最近」指的是哪一段時間，這並不清楚。「六年以前」算是最近嗎？對於一個發展一日千里的研究領域而言，六年前的研究結果已經是史料了。因此，表示時間應使用較具體的語詞，例如 *in the past decade* 或 *in the last four years*。

Refer. 當要引述參考資料時，不要把 *refer* 作被動動詞使用。這時 *refer* 應為主動動詞，並把句子寫成祈使語氣。

> 誤：　Detailed descriptions of the evaluation method *are referred to* Smith (1993).

> 誤：　Detailed descriptions of the evaluation method *can be referred to* in Smith (1993).

> 正：　For a detailed description of the evaluation method, *refer to* Smith (1993).

> 正：　For a detailed description of the evaluation method, *see* Smith (1993).

> 正：　A detailed description of the evaluation method *can be found in* Smith (1993).

> 正：　For a detailed description of the evaluation method, *readers are referred to* Smith (1993). 文法雖正確，但略嫌冗長

當 *refer* 表示「稱為」的意思，正確寫法是 "refer to...as..."（主動）或 "...is referred to as..."（被動）。

> Let us refer to this method as *the shortcut method.*

> This process is referred to as "etching."

Reference. 不要把名詞 *reference* 和動詞 *refer* 混淆。在電腦術語中，*reference* 有時可作動詞使用。但一般而言，應避免把 *reference* 作動詞使用，而應以 *refer* 或 *retrieve, read, recall, use* 等字詞取代。

> 誤：　For the details of the proof, *reference* the Appendix.
> 正：　For the details of the proof, *refer to* the Appendix.
> 正：　For the details of the proof, *see* the Appendix.

> 劣：　The CPU then *references* the data *in* memory.
> 佳：　The CPU then *reads* the data *from* memory.
> 佳：　The CPU then *retrieves* the data *from* memory.

Represent. 不要把 *represent*（即「代表」）和 *indicate*（即「表示」或「指出」）混淆。

> 劣：　This result *represents* that the coefficient is significant at the 95% level.

> 佳：　This result *indicates* that the coefficient is significant at the 95% level.

> 佳：　This result *shows* that the coefficient is significant at the 95% level.

Request, require. *Request* 指要求，但被要求者不受約束，可以不答應。*Require* 也指要求，但被要求者必須滿足要求。

Research. 與它配合的介系詞應為 *on*，而非 *of*。當代英文中，*research* 是不可數名詞，因此它是單數形式，不可寫成 *researches*。

誤：　Much research *of* this problem has been published.

正：　Much research *on* this problem has been published.

誤：　*Many researches* have been published in this area.

正：　*Much research* has been published in this area.

Respectively. 它是在科技論文中常被濫用的贅詞：

累贅：　We then measured the nominal sensitivity of the 4140 steel and the stainless steel, *respectively*.

正：　　We then measured the nominal sensitivity of the 4140 steel and the stainless steel.

在某些情況下，使用 *respectively* 雖沒文法錯誤，但如果省略它並改寫句子的話，則會使句子更直接易讀。

不清楚：　The nominal sensitivity was 200 and 270 mV/mil for 4140 and stainless steel, *respectively*.

清楚：　The nominal sensitivity was 200 mV/mil for 4140 steel and 270 mV/mil for stainless steel.

清楚：　The nominal sensitivity of 4140 steel was 200 mV/mil and that of stainless steel was 270 mV/mil.

讀者在閱讀首句時，在心裏會被迫停下來，把兩數字和兩種鋼鐵對應。第二和第三句將各種鋼鐵的名稱與數字一併列出，因此能讓讀者一目瞭然。若要提到多種項目，用上 *respectively* 的句子，格外令人費解。例如：

不清楚：　The initial values of b, h, k, q, x, a, b, and the coefficients in the x and y directions were 3, r/2, 183, 50, 60, 33/22, r/2, 0.45, and 0.38, respectively.

假如真的需要表達這麼多項目，則應用表格列出。這比以文章表達更清晰易明。

此外，*respectively* 與句子其他部分，必須以逗點隔開。

Restated. 不要將 *restated* 作轉接詞來引介某種解釋或結論。如使用 *in other words, that is, thus, in summary* 或其他字詞，句子會較清楚自然。

劣：　*Restated*, the value of x increases when y is increased.

佳：　*In other words,* the value of x increases when y is increased.

佳：　*In summary*, the value of x increases when y is increased.

Reveal. 這字詞只能表示「揭露原先被遮掩的事物」。如果可使用 *show* 或 *indicate*，則不要使用 *reveal*。

劣：　The test results are *revealed* in Table 6.

佳：　The test results are *shown* in Table 6.

正：　Experiments *revealed* that the theory was false.

不要把 *reveal* 與 *exhibit* 或 *display* 混淆。

劣：　The magnesium dopant also *revealed* less activation energy than the zinc dopant.

佳：　The magnesium dopant also *exhibited* less activation energy than the zinc dopant.

Right-hand. 諸如 *Right-hand* 和 *left-hand* 等形容詞，必須用連字號將兩個字連結，才是正確的拼法。

Look at *the right-hand side* of the equation.

Same. *A is the same as B* 是正確的，而 *A is the same with B* 卻是錯誤的。

Search. 當 *search* 後面加上介系詞 *for* 時，*search* 的意思會隨之改變。例如，*She searched her bag* 的意思是她在袋子裏找某東西；*She searched for her bag* 的意思則是她要找回遺失了的袋子。所以，不應該寫 *We searched the solution*，而應寫 *We searched for the solution*。還有，*We searched the set of possible solutions to find the optimal solution* 也是正確的。

Secondly, thirdly. 這些字在當代英文中聽來很生硬。應該使用 *second, third* 等等。（請參見 *firstly*。）

Show. 不要使用 *show* 來表示「提出」。

誤：　The paper *shows* simulation results that demonstrate the effectiveness of the method.

正：　The paper *presents* simulation results that demonstrate the effectiveness of the method.

誤：　Experimental results *are shown* in section 4 of the paper.

正：　Experimental results *are presented* in section 4 of the paper.

不要以 *show* 來表示「討論」、「探討」或「考察」。

誤：　We will *show* some properties of these types of graphs below.

正：　We will *examine* some properties of these types of graphs below.

在引介數學方程式時，別以 *show* 來表示「表示」或「寫出」。

誤：　The closed-loop gain can then be *shown* as follows.

正：　The closed-loop gain can then be *expressed* as follows.

正：　The closed-loop gain can then be *written* as follows.

如果可找到較清楚簡潔的動詞，就不要使用 *show*。

誤：　Table 4 *shows the comparison of* the accuracy of our learning algorithm with that of the other algorithms.

正：　Table 4 *compares* the accuracy of our learning algorithm with that of the other algorithms.

誤：　Section 6 *shows the summary of* the results.

正：　Section 6 *summarizes* the results.

Show 有時也有「證明」的意思，因此語意會變為較強烈。撰寫研究報告時，有些情況使用語意較弱的字來取代，可能會較恰當。

最強： Smith (1984) *showed* that the burn rate increases greatly under these conditions.

較弱： Smith (1984) *found* that the burn rate increases greatly under these conditions.

最弱： Smith (1984) *suggested* that the burn rate increases greatly under these conditions.

Significant. *Significant*（即「重要」、「有意義」）、*obvious*（「明顯」、「顯然」）、*apparent*（「顯然」、「表面上」）以及這些字的 *-ly* 副詞形式，意義都各有不同。例如，*an apparent change* 是指很容易憑外表觀察出來的變化，但 *apparent* 亦暗示那變化未必為真。*An obvious change* 則指清楚容易觀察出來的變化。*A significant change* 是指在特定情形中性質或數量方面的重要變化。通常 "obvious" 的變化也會同樣是 "significant"。但對沒有具備專業知識的人而言，"significant" 的變化卻未必 "obvious"。此外，一個 "apparent" 的變化卻可能並不 "significant"。

下面句中的 *obvious* 或 *significant* 都可修飾 *decrease*。若受 *obvious* 修飾，則句意是「這減少是可清楚觀察到的」，若受 *significant* 修飾，則是指「這減少在這特定文脈中相當重要」。在這例子中，除非要暗示「減少僅是表面的，並沒真正發生」，否則不應使用 *apparent*。

When the annealing temperature was increased, an *obvious* decrease in the C-H bond absorption peaks was observed.

When the annealing temperature was increased, a *significant* decrease in the C-H bond absorption peaks was observed.

Similar. 與它配合的介系詞應為 *to*，而非 *as*。此外，不要把名詞置於 *similar* 和 *to* 之間，參考下面的例句：

劣： The second element has a *similar structure to* the first.

正： The second element has a *structure similar to* the first.

嚴格說來，上面句子的比較項目是第一個和第二個元素的結構，因此可考慮進一步修改：

正： The second element has a structure similar to *that of* the first.

Similarly. 這字詞是用來指出兩個概念或事物之間相似的地方。當所指涉的並非相似關係，而是對照或相對關係時，則不應使用 *similarly*，應以 *in contrast, by contrast* 或 *conversely* 來表達。

劣： A sufficiently large scale of operations is needed to justify R&D investment. *Similarly*, a fruitful R&D program is necessary to support the growth of the company's operations.

佳：　A sufficiently large scale of operations is needed to justify R&D investment. *Conversely*, a fruitful R&D program is necessary to support the growth of the company's operations.

Simply. 這字詞有時可有效地強調一個複雜的和一個簡單的動作之間的對照。但許多時，*simply* 都是多餘的。

正：　Instead of carrying out this complex measurement procedure, we *simply* derive the value from Equation (3).

累贅：　Whenever a model changes its status, it *simply* broadcasts a change message to all its dependents.

簡潔：　Whenever a model changes its status, it broadcasts a change message to all its dependents.

Since. 當把 *since* 作附屬連接詞來表示「因為」時，*since* 後面不應接著 *that*。在以 *since* 開首的句子中，不應把 *then* 放在主要子句前面。

誤：　*Since that* the result was unsatisfactory, we repeated the experiment.

誤：　*Since* the result was unsatisfactory, *then* we repeated the experiment.

正：　*Since* the result was unsatisfactory, we repeated the experiment.

So. 在正式的英文中，這字不應用來表示 *very* 的意思。

劣：　These exercises are *so* difficult.

佳：　These exercises are *very* difficult.

由於 *so* 為對等連接詞，英文句子一般不應以 *so* 開首。但資深的作者偶爾也會為求得某種特殊效果而違反這準則。儘管如此，科技寫作中，如果想在句首表示「所以」或「因此」之意，則應使用 *thus* 或 *hence*。此外，對等連接詞後面本來就不加逗點，所以如果真的要在句首使用 *so*，千萬別在後面加上逗點。

劣：　Any vibration of the ground shakes the seismometer's frame, but inertia tends to hold the mass in its place. *So,* the coil on the frame moves in relation to the magnet on the mass.

佳：　Any vibration of the ground shakes the seismometer's frame, but inertia tends to hold the mass in its place. *Thus* the coil on the frame moves in relation to the magnet on the mass.

So-called. 構成這複合形容詞的兩個字，必須以連字號連接：

誤：　so called

正：　so-called

So far. 在研究報告的文獻回顧部分，最好別以 *so far* 或 *until now* 來表達「到目前為止」的意思，它們都太口語，所以使用 *to date* 會較適合。如果使用現在完成式，則沒必要用 *to date* 去指涉事發的時間，因為現在完成式本身就已清楚交代了「從過去持續到目前」的意思。

劣： *So far*, little research has been done on this problem.

佳： *To date*, little research has been done on this problem.

佳： Little research has been done on this problem.

So that. 在表示目的或理由的子句前，用 *so that* 比 *so* 來得適合。

模糊： First the cache memory is cleared *so* the result will not be affected by stale data.

精確： First the cache memory is cleared *so that* the result will not be affected by stale data.

So that, such that. *So that* 引介的子句，是敘述主要子句中的動作的目的或理由。*Such that* 則用來陳述某種條件，通常用以修飾其前面的名詞。

誤： I went to the library *such that* I could study.

正： I went to the library *so that* I could study.

正： There exist two objects x and y *such that* x does not equal y and x and y are members of the set S.

表達因果或邏輯關係時，應使用 *so* 而不應使用 *such that* 或 *so that*。在以下例句中，第二個子句非但沒表示出第一個子句中動作的目的，反而卻是第一個子句的結果。

誤： Here Cb and Cr share the same field *such that* both are forced to be identical.

正： Here Cb and Cr share the same field, *so* they must be identical.

Solution. 當談到某個問題或方程式的解答時，*solution* 後應加上介系詞 *to*，如 *the solution to the problem (or equation)*。當談到某方程式 E 中的某一個變數 y 的值時，*solution* 後應加上介系詞 *for*，如 *the solution for y in equation E*。（參見 *solve*。）

只有在真正遇上問題或困難而必須解決時，才可使用 *solution* 這字詞。科技寫作中，應避免以術語 *solution* 來代替 *system, package, kit, design* 等這些較精確的字詞。

模糊： This is a complete office automation solution.
精確： This is a complete office automation system.

冗贅： We have a new design solution.
簡潔： We have a new design.

模糊： Our firm will soon release an exciting new LAN solution.
精確： Our firm will soon release a new LAN chip set.
精確： Our firm will soon release a new LAN card.

Solve. 在表示要解決某個問題或方程式時，應寫 *solve the problem* 或 *solve the equation*。在指稱由某方程式得出的變數 x 值時，應使用 *solve for x*。

> *Solving* the above equation, we obtain the following value for the angular momentum.

> *Solving for x* in Equation (3), we obtain the following expression for the angular momentum.

只有當確實有問題要解決時，才可用 *solve* 這動詞，否則應使用 *treat, handle* 或更精確的動詞。

> 劣：　The case in which the sample rate is uniform can be *solved* by using direct duplication of serial registers.

> 佳：　The case in which the sample rate is uniform can be *treated* by using direct duplication of serial registers.

Some. 英文文章中，使用 *some, very, rather* 及 *quite* 之類的修飾詞常會使句意模糊而微弱，故可免則免。若必須使用 *some* 的話，則應考慮使用 *several, a number of* 或 *many* 代替。例如，如果要以 *some* 表示「某一組」之意，則應以 *specific* 或 *certain* 代替。

> 模糊：　In recent years, *some researchers* have proposed *quite a few* methods for solving this *rather challenging* problem.

> 清楚：　In recent years, *researchers* have proposed *many* methods for solving this *challenging* problem.

Such. *Such a* 有時可表示「這種」(this type of) 的意思，但千萬別以 *such* 來表示「這個」(this) 的意思。不少中國人撰寫 *In such a case, the strategy is invalid* 時，其實應寫成 *In this case, the strategy is invalid*。

> 誤：　*Such* selection operator guarantees that the best M strings will always survive.

> 正：　*This* selection operator guarantees that the best M strings will always survive.

Suffer. 若使用 *suffer* 這動詞來指出某方法或做法的缺點，則其後必須接著介系詞 *from*，否則不但是語法有錯，而且句意可能會與作者的原意背道而馳，因為 *suffer* 也有「忍耐」之意。

> 誤：　This method *suffers* several problems.

> 正：　This method *suffers from* several problems.

> 正：　There are several problems with this method.

> 正：　This method has several problems.

> 正：　This method is subject to several problems.

Suggest. 一般用法的意思為「建議」。此外，這字詞還有「表示」之意，可用來表達由某些證據推出結論。*Suggest* 的意思沒有 *indicate* 或 *show* 般強。

正：　These data *suggest* that deposition rate depends on the amount of nitrogen available.

正：　The survey results *suggest* that men tend to prefer sour flavors.

Support. 從事資訊電子業的工程師往往濫用這字詞，他們會用它來指涉任何兩種項目（包括人類、電子零件、電腦與其他硬體設備、軟體等等）之間所有的關係。故應特別注意要避免濫用 *support*，而應另找較精確的字詞取代。（請參見第六章 6.9節。）

模糊：　The computer *supports* many popular software applications.
清楚：　The computer *can run* many popular software applications.

模糊：　We *support* customers with a variety of services.
清楚：　We *provide* customers a variety of services.

模糊：　The system *supports* two operating modes.
清楚：　The system *has* two operating modes.

模糊：　The program *supports* both Windows™ and DOS.
清楚：　The program *is compatible with* either Windows or DOS.
清楚：　The program *can be used with* either Windows or DOS.

Suppose. 別把 *suppose* 和 *if* 混淆。*Suppose* 是動詞，所以 *suppose that x is true* 是獨立子句，可當為一完整句子。*If* 則為附屬連接詞，以 *if* 開首的就是附屬子句，不能當完整句使用。以 *suppose* 開首的子句應接著句號或分號，但接逗點是錯誤的。唯一可接逗點的情況是，逗點後接有以連接詞（*and, but* 等等）開首的獨立子句。

誤：　Suppose that all the parameters are set to 1, then the system will achieve maximal efficiency.

正：　Suppose that all the parameters are set to 1. Then the system will achieve maximal efficiency.

正：　Suppose that all the parameters are set to 1; then the system will achieve maximal efficiency.

正：　If all the parameters are set to 1, then the system will achieve maximal efficiency.

正：　Suppose all the parameters are set to 1, and the system runs for one hour.

Terminology. 在絕大多數情形下，*terminology* 是不可數名詞，因此不應該寫成複數形式（詳見第二章 2.1節）。

That. 在限定關係子句中，應以 *that* 作關係代名詞，而不用 *which*。（參閱第四章 4.15節「代名詞和前述詞一致」。限定子句和非限定子句的區分，詳見第五章 5.2節中逗點的討論）。

原句： This is the computer *which* I bought last week.

恰當： This is the computer *that* I bought last week.

但如果限定關係子句以介系詞開首，則關係代名詞必須用 *which*。

誤： The node numbers determine the order *in that* each producer writes its message into the buffer.

正： The node numbers determine the order *in which* each producer writes its message into the buffer.

使用 *that* 這字來引介名詞子句時，*that* 後面不加逗點。

誤： The results show *that,* the theorem is true.

正： The results show *that* the theorem is true.

當 *that* 出現在名詞子句或關係子句的開頭時，如果 *that* 後面緊接著名詞片語或代名詞，只要句意依然清楚，則可省略 *that*。

正： Suppose *that* the system includes ten processors.

正： Suppose the system includes ten processors.

下面兩個例子中，假若省略 *that*，則句子會變得不自然而易令人誤解，因此 *that* 不應省略。在名詞子句或關係子句前面使用 *that*，可使句子更清晰，通常亦不會使句子不通順。所以在科技研究報告中，一般而言還是保留 *that* 較恰當。

清楚： The phenomena *that* the theory must explain are very complex.

模糊： The phenomena the theory must explain are very complex.

清楚： It has been suggested *that* the stability of the film deteriorates at high temperatures.

模糊： It has been suggested the stability of the film deteriorates at high temperatures.

Then. 因為 *then* 非對等連接詞，而是連接副詞，所以 "A, then B" 是錯誤英文。在 *then* 前面必須加上對等連接詞，如 *and* 或 *but*，或是把 *then* 前面的逗點改成句號或分號（參閱第四章 4.3節）。

誤： The samples were dipped into the solution, *then* they were washed with water.

正： The samples were dipped into the solution, *and then* they were washed with water.

正： The samples were dipped into the solution. *Then* they were washed with water.

There exists. 不要任意以 *there exists* 代替 *there is* 來表示「有」或「存在著」。在討論邏輯或數學時，可用 *there exists* 以表示存在量詞（"∃"）。但在一般情形下，寫 *there is* 或 *there are* 通常較恰當。

　　劣： *There exist* two techniques for controlling this type of system.

　　佳： *There are* two techniques for controlling this type of system.

They. 第三人稱複數代名詞 *they* 不應用來指稱單數前述詞，如 *each person* 或 *everyone* 等等。如果使用第三人稱單數代名詞 *he* 或 *she* 不太恰當的話，則應修改句子，把前後的名詞及代名詞都一致改為複數。否則，應省略代名詞，並改寫句子。（詳見第四章 4.14節。）

　　誤： When *each person* arrives, *they* must check in.

　　正： When *each person* arrives, *he* must check in.

　　正： When *the guests* arrive, *they* must check in.

　　正： Upon arriving, *each guest* must check in.

　　正： Upon arrival, *each guest* must check in.

This. 如果以 *this* 來指涉一整個子句或句子的意思，則所指意思必須清楚明瞭。否則，最好在 *this* 後面加上一個名詞，以指出 *this* 所指為何。（詳見第四章 4.13節。）

　　劣： The subjects identified fewer than half of the odors correctly. *This* was surprising.

　　佳： The subjects identified fewer than half of the odors correctly. *This result* was surprising.

　　佳： The subjects identified fewer than half of the odors correctly. *This low success rate* was surprising.

Those. 在許多情形下，名詞前面使用指示詞 *those* 會使句子不自然。這時應以 *the* 取代，或乾脆把 *those* 刪除。

　　劣： We must also factor in the service time of *those* customers that arrive before the labeled customer.

　　佳： We must also factor in the service time of *the* customers that arrive before the labeled customer.

　　佳： We must also factor in the service time of customers that arrive before the labeled customer.

Thus. 只有當第二個句子或子句的意思，確實為第一個句子或子句的意思所蘊涵的結果時，方可用 *thus*（或 *therefore*）來連接。例如，下面例子中，第二句並非第一句在邏輯或因果上的結果，所以使用 *thus* 會令人費解。這例子中的 *thus* 應省略，或可以 *for example* 來取代。

劣：   R&D projects undertaken by the institute aim to develop major industrial technologies essential to the development of the nation's
economy. *Thus* project A, project B, and other projects related to automation technology were carried out to increase productivity in
several important industries.

To do x, for doing x. 要解釋某事物的功能或某行為的目標時，如果受修飾的對
象為名詞，則通常使用介系詞（通常是 *for*）加上動名詞來修飾。但如果受修飾的對
象為動詞，則常以不定詞來修飾。（這並非絕對的規則，但往往是對的。）下列例
句中，不定詞片語修飾了句子的動詞，以說明進行掃瞄的原因，所以使用得非常自
然。

Scanning was performed *to confirm* the accuracy of the results.

但如果以 *for confirming* 取代 *to confirm* 這不定詞，則句子會變得很不自然：

劣：   Scanning was performed *for confirming* the accuracy of the results.

下面例句中，片語 *for designing mixed mode ICs* 修飾名詞 *system*，這片語說明所購
買的是何種系統。因為被修飾的是名詞，所以使用介系詞加動名詞而成的介系詞片
語，會比較自然。

We recently purchased a new CAD system *for designing* mixed mode ICs.

雖然在文法上動名詞和不定詞都可作句子主詞使用，然而使用動名詞比不定詞
常會較自然。

劣：   *To prove* the uniqueness of problem (i) is equivalent to proving that *X*
is negative at R.

佳：   *Proving* the uniqueness of problem (i) is equivalent to proving that *X*
is negative at R.

上面句子中，緊接 *is equivalent to* 後面的字詞該是動名詞而非不定詞，因為此
時 *to* 是介系詞，而非不定詞開首的 *to*。

誤：   Proving the uniqueness of problem (i) is equivalent *to prove* that *X* is
negative at R.

Totally. 意思是「完全」，並不能表示「總共」或「一共」之意。如果要表示
「總共」之意，則應用 *a total of* 或 *altogether*。

誤：   There are three solutions *totally*.

誤：   There are *totally* three solutions.

正：   There are *a total of* three solutions.

正：   There are three solutions *altogether*.

Type of. *Type of, form of* 及 *kind of* 這些詞語的數和接在其後的名詞的數必須一
致。在正式文章中，寫 *type of* 比寫 *kind of* 恰當。

正：   We are designing a new *type of computer*.

正： There are four *types of methods* that can be used to solve this problem.

誤： This is Sarah's favorite *kind of shoes*.

正： This is Sarah's favorite *kind of shoe*.

Unlike. 英文的 *unlike* 可放在句首，來表示中文「與 x 不同，……」或「不同於 x，……」的意思。若把 *different from* 或 *differing from* 放在句首，則句子會顯得很不自然。

劣： *Differing from* previous authors, we use the mean age and mean excess to obtain the formula for the mean waiting time.

劣： *Different from* previous authors, we use the mean age and mean excess to obtain the formula for the mean waiting time.

佳： *Unlike* previous authors, we use the mean age and mean excess to obtain the formula for the mean waiting time.

Until now. 在研究報告的文獻回顧中，應該以 *to date* 表示「到目前為止」。在大部分正式文章中，使用 *until now* 及 *so far* 都是不恰當的。

劣： *Until now*, however, the effect of boron on the reaction rate has not been examined.

佳： *To date*, however, the effect of boron on the reaction rate has not been examined.

因為英文的現在完成式本身就表示「到目前為止」之意，所以在大部分使用 *until now, so far* 或 *to date* 的句子中，這些詞語都可以省略。

佳： However, the effect of boron on the reaction rate has not been examined.

佳： However, the effect of boron on the reaction rate has yet to be examined.

Utilize. 撰寫科技論文時，應避免使用 *utilize*，而以 *use* 取代。如此一來，語法會較簡單直接。*Employ* 也比 *utilize* 恰當。

原句： We will *utilize* an LP parser for the parsing procedure.

更恰當： We will *use* an LP parser for the parsing procedure.

Versus. 這個字詞正確的縮寫是 *vs.*，"v.s." 是錯誤的寫法。

Very. 這個字詞是用來加強形容詞形容程度的副詞，但它的意思卻微弱。大部分情形下，*very* 並非句子必要的部分，通常應省略。

累贅： *Very many* researchers have studied this problem.

簡潔： *Many* researchers have studied this problem.

Whether or not. 在大多數使用 *whether or not* 的文脈中，*or not* 可以省略，以使得句子更簡潔。只有當要特別強調有兩種可能情形時，才有必要寫 *whether or not*。如果意思是「無論如何」，則寫 *whether or not* 也是正確的。

累贅：　After the first iteration, we check to see *whether or not* the weight exceeds the threshold q.

簡潔：　After the first iteration, we check to see *whether* the weight exceeds the threshold q.

正確：　*Whether or not* excess oxygen is available, the fuel will still burn. 意思是「無論如何」

Which. 限定關係子句中（限定關係子句的說明，詳見第五章 5.2節），以 *that* 作關係代名詞比以 *which* 恰當。然而，如果關係子句以介系詞開首，則必須以 *which* 作關係代名詞。

原句：　This is the system *which* we shall use.

恰當：　This is the system *that* we shall use.

誤：　The water flows into a storage tank, from *that* hot water can be drawn when needed.

正：　The water flows into a storage tank, from *which* hot water can be drawn when needed.

While, when. *When* 可指一個頃刻或一段時間，*while* 則只能指一段時間。在 *while* 開首的子句中，常使用進行式的動詞（有時也可用簡單現在式或過去式）。

正：　*When* the magnesium *was added* to the solution, a precipitate immediately formed.

正：　*While* the engine *was running*, three different types of faults were simulated.

劣：　*While* the solution *begins* to boil, the temperature levels off.
　　　"Begins to boil" 是指一個頃刻，故用 *while* 不自然。

佳：　*When* the solution *begins* to boil, the temperature levels off.

Without loss of generality. 這片語正確的寫法是 *without loss of generality*，下面前三個例句的寫法都是錯誤的。

誤：　*Without the loss of the generality*, we can assume that…

誤：　*Without losing the generality*, we can assume that…

誤：　*Without lost generality*, we can assume that…

正：　*Without loss of generality*, we can assume that…

第三篇
科技論文與會議簡報

第十一章
一般原則

11.1 基本原則

簡明直接（看完本節之後，請再看兩次。）

　　有時候，買了新書，我們只會偶爾拿起來翻一翻，或僅僅參考一下，並沒有仔細閱讀整本書的內容。如果你是剛買或是正在書店翻閱本書，請仔細閱讀本節。因為本書的其它部分你都可以暫時不予理睬，但千萬不要略過本節。

　　一、撰寫英文文章時，應努力把每個句子的意思寫得清楚明了，而且要非常清楚，以保證讀者不會誤解你的意思。如果你希望通過文章向讀者傳達準確的信息，那麼你必須完整地、直接地如實相告，而不要一廂情願地對你的讀者報以期望，期望他們能根據文章的上下文自行做任何假設推斷。在英語寫作中，對於「清晰度」的要求往往比中文寫作要高得多。因此在撰寫英文文章時，作者對「清晰度」也就越執著越好。

　　二、英文寫作應盡量直接表達。每當文章中有冗長而迂迴的句子時，應刪掉，並採用更為簡短、直接的句子來代替（若原句很長，則應把句子分為兩三個較簡短的句子來寫）。此外，盡量選用容易而常見的詞彙，並多使用主動語態。例如：

> 劣： The confutation of this contention will be undertaken, so that the inadequacies of Smith's explanatory strategy are revealed.

> 優： We will show that this claim is unjustified, and so Smith's explanation fails.

　　三、如果句子里存在任何非必要的字詞，都應刪掉。

宜用短句

很多華人不善於寫出清晰而簡潔的英文句子。如果你也遇到同樣的難題，請不要灰心！反之，你應僅記以下兩點：

第一，大多數以英文為母語者也一樣面對相同的難題，認為要寫出清楚、簡潔的英文句子並非易事。

第二，只要你下定決心並努力把文章寫得更清晰、更簡潔，同時以此當作你的人生目標，你便獲得成功的一半了。

下面講述一些實用的寫作方法，可助你獲得成功的另一半：在撰寫初稿時，盡量用簡短的句子來表達所有內容。然後在修改初稿時，注意是否出現連續片斷的短句。一旦出現，你就應添加對等連接詞（如 *and, but* 或 *so*）或附屬連接詞（如 *after, because* 或 *if*）把一些句子合併成完整的一句。

一個好的英文段落是由多種結構及長度的句子組成的（請參閱本書第七章）。從這點出發，把清晰而簡潔的句子合併起來，組成具有多種結構、多種長度的句子，是不是比修改冗長迂迴而語焉不詳的段落要容易多了？

行文應如交談般自然

撰寫科技研究報告的作者應把寫文章當成和讀者說話一樣，使用自然而順暢的表達方式來描述自己的研究工作和成果。（但同時也要避免使用俚語或過於通俗的言辭。例如，應使用 *find, discover* 或 *obtain* 來取代如 *get* 等稍嫌不正式的言辭。）

為了避免出現生硬的句子並使文章更通順易讀，在修改文章時，應反覆自問：「在說英語時，有沒有人會使用這樣的句子？」請看下面的例子：

> From Figure 3 it is observed that under the condition of use of high-temperature deposition, the phenomenon of formation of large grains occurs.

在英文會話中，是沒有人會說出如此生硬的句子啊！（即便有，此人恐怕也很難找到聊天或討論的夥伴！）因此，要表達和上面例句相同的意思時，以英文為母語者通常會說：

> Figure 3 shows that high-temperature deposition causes large grains to form.

> Figure 3 shows that when high-temperature deposition is used, large grains form.

> Figure 3 shows that high-temperature deposition produces large grains.

上述三個句子均適合在英文的演講或會話中使用，而且這三句都比原句要清楚、流暢得多。

（請參閱本書第四、六章。）

摸清讀者的閱讀習慣

說到專業研究者的閱讀習慣，有一些研究結果指出：他們在閱讀專業學術期刊上的研究報告時，其實一般是直奔主要結論，根本不會把整篇文章從頭到尾讀完。為了迎合這種閱讀習慣，建議作者在撰寫研究報告時，採用以下方式來突顯自己的主要研究結果：

在文章的標題中，直接點題或暗示主要的研究結果。例如，與其說 "Effects of Adding Oxygen on Film Samples"，不如說 "Increasing the Hardness of Film Samples by Adding Oxygen"。如此一來，這個標題既能簡明扼要地傳達自己的研究目的，又能讓讀者大致推斷出其主要結果。

在摘要中，必須明確闡述主要的研究結果及結論。

在導論中，一定要清楚敘述研究目的，以便讀者根據該目的推斷主要的研究結果。請看下列例句：

> The purpose of this research was to investigate the effects of adding oxygen on film samples.

雖然此句意思清晰，但是讀者還是不太容易能推斷出研究結果，下面幾句則更為適當：

> In this research, we attempted to increase the hardness of film samples by adding oxygen.

> The purpose of this research was to determine whether the hardness of film samples could be increased by adding oxygen.

> This experiment attempted to increase the hardness of film samples by adding oxygen.

看完這三句後，讀者就能了解到其研究目的不只是要找出氧氣的一般影響，而是要看看多加氧氣是否會增加樣本的硬度。讀者大概可以推斷主要的研究結果不是「會增加」，就是「不會增加」。

在結果章節及討論章節中，應盡量保證每個段落都有一個提綱挈領的的主題句。主題句不是出現在段首發揮引導作用，就是在段尾做總結。（請參閱本書第八章。）

在結果章節與討論章節中，應有清楚、能提供具體信息的副標題（關於副標題，本章稍後將作進一步討論）。

在結論中（如果報告沒有獨立的結論章節，那麼即為討論章節結尾處），應使用清晰而精簡的方式敘述主要的結論。如果條件允許，應考慮把結論分為幾個單獨的要點，以列表形式呈現，並給每項標上序號。

先陳目的，後述結果

在撰寫研究報告時，一般應先具體說明研究的目的或動機，然後再描述研究方法，最後給出結果。在知道研究的詳細過程或結果之前，讀者會期望首先瞭解為什麼要作該項研究。

現舉一個簡單例子，以說明這個原則：

To examine the effect of language immersion on progress in learning a second language, students with similar scores on a placement test were divided into an immersion class and a non-immersion class. After six months, students in the immersion class scored an average of 25% higher on a second placement test than students in the non-immersion class.

該段落先解釋目的，接著描述研究方法，最後給出結果，所以整個段落既通順又易懂。相反，下列段落所提供的信息和上面段落完全一樣，但是作者卻先描述結果及方法，最後才解釋目的：

After six months of study, students in an immersion class scored an average of 25% higher on a placement test than students in a non-immersion class. The two classes consisted of students with similar scores on an earlier placement test, who had been divided into an immersion class and a non-immersion class in order to examine the effect of language immersion on progress in learning a second language.

由於這段話提供信息的順序較為不自然，因此讀者在閱讀時會感到有些吃力。

當然，你也可以用一句話來兼述幾個行動的目的，例如：

X was mixed with Y at high pressure in an attempt to develop a more heat-resistant Z.

The aim of this experiment was to develop a more heat-resistant Z by mixing X with Y at high pressure.

要特別注意的是，最好不要先忙著具體描述某個行動，給出大量細節，廣征博引、縱橫捭闔，再告訴讀者行動的目的。這樣會讓讀者讀得雲裡霧裡的，還不知你為什麼要這麼做。

如果要介紹某種新方法或新技術，應先言簡意賅地說明該方法的主要目的或應用，然後再詳細描述方法本身。在描述了方法之後，亦應附上一些具體的例子來充實該方法的應用。

同樣道理，在論述自己如何解決某個問題以前，還應先把問題陳述清楚。曾經看過一篇研究報告，整個文章的內容只有分析並描述一些方法，從頭到尾都沒有提到過究竟什麼才是研究的問題。看完文章後，讀者甚至還搞不清作者到底為什麼要進行該項研究。

按步討論

如果作者需要針對幾個單獨的小題目給出結果，或者必須描述由幾個複雜步驟所組成的方法或分析，那麼一定要按步就班、井井有條地處理每一個課題。在處理過程中，應先確定當下的課題都已討論完畢，再開始討論下個課題。此外，在每個小題目或步驟討論完畢後，應該給出明確的小結或結論。若有必要，還應說明本課題和下個課題之間的關係。（如果方便，也可在一開頭就先解釋所有小題目或步驟之間的關係。）如此一來，文章讀起來會更流暢聯貫，讀者對文章也會覺得更容易理解。

曾經看過一篇華人撰寫的英語研究報告，作者常在三四個不同的小題目之間跳來跳去，但從未深入解釋這些小題目之間的關聯，在討論每個小題目過後也沒給出任何結論。結果是看完整篇文章後，才能猜出幾個課題之間的關係。這就好比讀中國的武俠小說一樣，作者為了製造懸念吸引讀者，把最關鍵的內容放在故事最後的大結局。有人說這種寫法引人入勝，讀後意猶未盡。但閱讀研究報告不同於武俠小說，為了真正瞭解整篇文章的內容，我還需要再看一次！

專業術語必須前後統一

在研究報告中，專業術語的使用應前後一致。首次使用某個專業術語時，應先提供精確的定義。如果打算使用縮寫的術語，則應在首次提到這術語時就使用括號來介紹它的縮寫。不要在報告的前幾頁先用某名稱來指稱某事物，接著在後文突然換上另一個。若同時使用兩個不同的術語來指稱同一事物，就應同時介紹這兩個術語，並說明兩個術語所指為同一事物。

仿效英美行文寫法

英文和中文的文法以及表達方式大不同，究其原因還在于說英文的人和說中文的人有著完全不同的思維方式和文化傳統。華人用英語寫作時，常會寫得語法不正確或不自然；或許這並非因為他們對英文文法不熟悉，而是因為所採用的表達方式不符合英語系國家的寫作規範及習慣。

要避免這種問題並提高英文寫作能力，就要僅記：學習任何一種語言都是從模仿開始的。兒童在牙牙學語時會模仿父母，學生會模仿老師或教科書，而外國人要想學好一門語言就不得不向母語者討教。因此，要想提高自己的英文寫作能力，最基本且最關鍵的第一步，就是要模仿在相同專業領域、且以英語為母語的諸位專家的寫作風格。也就是說，要經常閱讀以英語為母語的專家所寫的著作，仔細研讀其寫作風格，觀察他們所採用的字詞、所寫的句子結構以及段落的組織，並留意他們遣詞造句的方式方法，以便日後借用到你自己的報告中可能會討論到的一些概念。你更可進一步花些心思比較不同作者的寫作習慣，並整理出在你所關注的學術領域內一些標準的寫作風格與語法。最後，當你在撰寫自己的文章時，就可以試著去效仿你所學習到的標準寫作風格與語法。

相信各位同學、同事在小學、中學的語文課程裡都認真研習過寫作的技巧。在中文寫作中，優秀的範文通常能巧妙地運用比喻修辭，博古通今，以華麗的辭藻渲染氣氛，恰當之處再引用幾個古代詩詞典故點睛就更好了。讀者讀後雖然感覺語焉不詳，好似觀摩一幅水墨畫，輪廓遠近都很模糊。不過「內行人」都知道，欣賞大師的作品必須充分發揮想象力，而這個想象力的空間又是與個人修行的深淺密不可分的，看不懂是緣於你的修行不夠。所以中國文化中大多數世代流傳的經典作品都是在意境上有所保留的，要的就是那種「欲迎還拒，欲語還休」的感覺，能不能領會文章主旨全靠讀者的悟性。同時，由於受封建禮教和等級觀念的影響，好多話不能直接說，好多文字不能明白寫，因此寓言故事、委婉暗示、比喻雙關、歇後語、諺語成語典故等修辭手法也就貫穿了整個華夏文明。

有人說這才是中國文化的博大精深之處！然。但你若把這種博大精深的習作手法應用於英文寫作就顯得完全不合時宜。西方人認為論文是以辯證和邏輯為基礎的，而對辯證和邏輯的表述就必須直接、清晰、簡潔、全面，不能指望借用讀者的想象力、悟性來填補作品中的空白。在本書中，你會發現我一再重復強調直接、清晰、簡潔、全面的重要性。英文寫作水平不僅僅是靠強大的詞彙量來提升的，這其實是一個思維方式的轉變。

誠然，並不是每一位以英語為母語者的文筆都那麼清楚有條理，值得做為英文寫作效仿的榜樣。有些著名研究人員的著作，行文複雜含糊，讀上去含混晦澀又令人費解。就算是以英語為母語的讀者，都會覺得閱讀他們的文章好比經受精神折磨那樣令人沮喪。這些研究人員之所以著名，是因為他們研究結果的學術價值很高，或許可以抵消其拙劣的文筆。然而，他們的文章實在無法令人滿意。要模仿的不是這種作者，而是用詞簡潔明瞭、言簡意賅、行文流暢易懂的人。

用外語撰寫研究報告是一門很難掌握的技巧。不過，如果想在國際學術領域內有長足發展或是成為一位專業的研究人員，這種技巧卻不可或缺。其實，你的英文寫作能力不一定要達到日臻完美的水平，因為專業學術期刊通常可以接受英語非母語的作者在文章中存在一些小瑕疵。但話說回來，追求卓越的你也應該為自己明確樹立學術領域的專業標準，並且盡力去達到這個標準。

作者的責任：滿足讀者

身為作者，你的責任就是將自己的想法用最清楚的方式表達出來，讓讀者輕易地瞭解你的想法，繼而輕鬆愜意地閱讀。別以為讀者能自行推斷你的想法，或是可以自動填補你論證或解釋過程中的缺失。好的作者應提供足夠的信息，以便讀者讀懂你的文章，並且用清楚、合乎邏輯的方式將這些信息組織起來。如果讀者對你的文章產生任何誤解，你應該把它歸咎為自己的責任，而非讀者的錯。

閱讀時，讀者自然會對文章抱持某些期望：他們期望文章內容易於理解，結構合乎邏輯。在你撰寫報告時，應儘量滿足讀者的這些基本期望及需求，並圍繞這些期望和需求來組織及表達報告內容。

要說服讀者，文章的內容必須清楚、精簡及聯貫，文章的論證必須公平合理、詳細全面。只有這樣，讀者才能較為容易地去瞭解及評價報告中的主張，也會比較尊重作者及其觀點。相反，如果文中充滿過於片面空洞、錯漏百出、不合邏輯的論證及不合理的批評，或者文章結構散亂而不知所云，那麼當然不能說服讀者。

作者應把報告當做是「為讀者」而寫，而非「為自己」而寫。因此在寫作過程中，要常常自問：讀者能夠容易地理解這個段落嗎？這個說法有沒有說服力？我該如何去讓一個半信半疑的讀者，義無反顧地接受我的主張？讀者對我的說法會持有什麼可能的反證呢？我該如何表達以避免或駁回這些反證？多問些這樣的問題可引導我們寫出更易讀、更具說服力的文章。

11.2 寫作過程

完成一篇好的科技論文、研究報告或專業文件需要花很多功夫，除了進行實驗性或理論性的研究和分析外，作者還必須規劃如何陳述結果，初擬草稿，之後再仔細檢查、多次修改並認真校對。本節將大致介紹撰寫報告的整個過程，並說明撰寫研究報告時需要特別注意的事項。

撰寫一篇科技研究報告的過程和撰寫任何文件是一樣的，大致可分為四個基本階段：準備、計畫、撰寫初稿以及修改。

一、準備 (preparation)

準備階段包括所有與界定研究課題有關及與進行研究相關的工作。在此階段，通常要首先回顧相關的研究文獻，參考其他學者的研究成果，進而質問：他們的方法、分析及解釋是否合理，有沒有說服力？他們的結論可曾忽略了其它合理的解釋？他們的結果與討論能不能衍生出什麼新的研究課題？接下來，界定具體的研究課題，並對此課題陳述初步的假設 (hypothesis)。然後，指定自己的研究方法以及採用這些方法的理由。最後，開展研究工作、收集分析資料，推出結論。

在進行研究的過程中，需要常常提醒自己，撰寫報告時需要解釋研究工作中的每一個步驟、每一個結果及其重要性。因此，在工作的過程中，應該養成記筆記的好習慣，而且記得越詳細越好。

獲得研究資料之後，需要分析、評價及解釋這些資料，並審查這些資料是否支持自己的假設。首先，分析研究資料並給出初步的解釋，然後考慮這些解釋是否能覆蓋說明所有的資料、是否符合初步的假設？再者，需要考慮是否存在其它解釋可能代替自己現有的解釋？你的解釋與其它解釋的區別是什麼，有什麼優點和缺點？能否修改自己的解釋以增加其說服力或使之更完備？在評價自己的結果與解釋時，也可以考慮與同事討論你的研究結果，他們的意見可能會幫你找到不同或更完美的結論。

二、計畫 (planning)

計畫一篇科技研究報告，通常比其它領域的論文簡單，因為科技研究報告的結構一般都遵循標準的行文格式。然而，計畫的階段對報告作者來說卻有著統籌全局的重要性，因此作者必須謹慎規劃如何清楚陳述報告的主旨，並構思導論及討論章節的論證。此外，整理後的研究資料必須於報告的結果章節中發表，並清楚解釋你的研究結果對相關學術領域有哪些貢獻和意義。因此，精心的計畫對撰寫科技研究報告的整個過程而言，有著舉足輕重的地位。

計畫工作的第一步就是確定自己需要將哪些內容納入報告中。為了方便計劃報告的主要重點，你可以嘗試以下方法：

（一）先在一張白紙或電腦文檔上寫下你的研究題旨或假設。接著，概括描述你所採用的方法、主要的研究結果、以及你對研究結果的解釋。最後，分析解釋的優劣，並列出這些研究結果其它可能的解釋。此外，別忘了說明這些其它解釋的長短之處，以及為什麼你的解釋更有說服力。

　　（二）在審查回顧剛剛寫下的所有重點之後，為報告定下清楚、具體而恰當的題目。

　　（三）考慮如何編排報告的內容：你需要構思如何解釋概念、資料和論題，怎樣有條不紊地編排章節次序。

　　（四）最後，為你的報告起草大綱。採用分層的方式（可參考下列範本）：把報告各部分切割開來（如導論、方法、結果等等）分成章 (I, II, III, ...)，把章下的每一個 主要部分再次分為節 (A, B, C, ...)，然後再細分用條 (1, 2, 3, ...) 與款 (a, b, c, ...) 以表示特定的要點。為每個小節定下標題，並為每個段落歸納一個主題句以清楚顯示該段落的重點。最後，在大綱中填入報告所有重點的細節。　明確地註明各段落的主要內容，不要只寫一些含糊的筆記。大綱起草得越具體細緻，撰寫報告時也就越容易。

三、擬寫初稿 (writing)

　　在擬寫初稿的階段，作者應以大綱為基礎來拓展完成初稿。擬寫初稿的主要目的是確保大綱中所有重點，都是以完整的句子與段落的形式表達，報告內容對所有重要的概念、議題、方法、推論、結果、結論等等都提供了適當的解釋。撰寫初稿的過程中，要常常自問：報告的鋪陳是否清楚，讀者能不能理解？每個段落都有明確的主題句嗎？如果你有一大段話要告訴讀者，應先做概述，為下文的細節描述或解釋整體結構做鋪墊，然後再給出具體詳盡的描述或解釋，這樣讀者會更容易瞭解其中每一句的關係。

　　初稿中也許有些句子或段落在文法、結構或選詞上不夠完美，還存在些小瑕疵。在此階段無需太過在意，在接下來的修改階段還有機會修正。

四、反覆修改 (revising)

　　完成報告初稿後，還必須仔細地閱讀全文，檢查是否在文法、內容或格式上存在錯誤，並審查初稿是否符合原先的計劃及主旨。當發現錯誤或論述不清之處時，應修改，做到使報告清晰、簡潔且正確。反覆修改，是將研究報告寫得清晰、有條理的秘訣。

報告大綱範本

你的題目

I. 導論
  A. 背景
    1. 概括議題
    2. 具體議題
    3. 報告主題
  B. 文獻回顧
    1. 第一套研究結果
    2. 第二套研究結果
    3. 其他研究結果
    4. …
  C. 研究問題
    1. 上述研究所衍生的新問題
  D. 本研究的目的
    1. 主要目的
    2. 次要目的
  E. 本研究的價值或意義
    1. 要點一
    2. 要點二
    3. …

II. 方法
  A. 基本概述
    1. 研究方法
    2. 採用此方法的理由
    3. 其他要點
  B. 材料
    1. …
    2. …
  C. 詳細程序
    1. 步驟一
    2. 步驟二
    3. …

III. 結果
  A. 結果一
    1. 小節一
    2. 小節二
  B. 結果二
    1. 小節一
    2. 小節二
  C. …
    1. …
    2. …

IV. 討論
  A. 結果一的解釋
    1. 要點一
    2. 要點二
  B. 結果一的涵義含義
    1. 要點一
    2. 要點二
  C. …
    1. …
    2. …

V. 結論
  A. 結論一
    1. …
    2. …
  B. 結論二
    1. …
    2. …

  …

　　許多研究生因趕著投稿而忽略反覆修改文章的重要性。這些研究生需要提醒自己：沒人能於首次陳述一個概念或提交一份草擬階段的文章，便將自己的意思表達得完全清楚、正確、無懈可擊。即使是有數十年寫作經驗的研究人員，也很難不經修改就寫得出完美的報告。專業作者在發表文章之前常常修改十次以上。所以，在撰寫報告初稿之後，一定要給自己足夠的時間仔細改寫、反覆潤色。

　　至於修改的方法，可以這樣做：完成初稿後，先將它閒置在旁一兩天。然後，用批判的眼光去審查初稿。（最好把初稿列印出來，因為有些問題在列印稿上會比較容易注意到。）首先審視報告的結構：報告的題目是否適切？研究目的是否清晰明確地交代出來？有沒有直接準確地給出主要的研究結果？這些內容易理解嗎？每段都有一個主題句嗎？各段的要點都清晰嗎？各課題的鋪陳次序都合乎邏輯、聯貫和容易理解嗎？報告得出的結論站得住腳嗎？論述的各段落是不是都合理支持結論？這種關係是否顯而易見？

　　此外，在閱讀時需要常常自問：在拼字、語法或標點各方面有沒有錯誤？（要記得用檢查拼字的軟體工具檢查報告中是否存在錯字。）每個句子都有主詞和動詞嗎？所陳述的內容都合理嗎？論證是否清楚、有說服力？用詞是否準確？會產生歧義嗎？句子是否精確地表達你的意思，還是句子本身另有所指？句子之間的關繫緊湊嗎？有沒有句子只是簡單地重複前文？每句都是論述的必要組成部分嗎？能不能在不影響論述的情況下刪除？

　　經過這樣的檢查，你就會發現初稿中存在不少錯誤、含糊、不夠精確、累贅及組織不當之處。因此，你需要修改資料內容（添加或刪除一些內容）、概念用語、句子結構以及文章組織（例如，句子在段落中的前後次序或是段落在章節中的層次）。

　　首輪修改工作完成後，建議你把報告放在一旁，待兩天後拿出來再次修改（假如第一次是在電腦上檢查，這次一定要在列印稿上檢查。）在提交報告前，應至少修改三次。

　　修改文章時必須非常專心，絕對不能趕時間。就一般研究報告而言，最好不要嘗試在一天下午就把它全部改完，而應該安排連續兩三天，每天修改一部分。

　　總之，在發表報告前，千萬要記得仔細修改，反覆修改。唯有反覆修改，才能真正令文章變得清楚、簡練而具說服力。

初稿應儘早動手

　　撰寫研究報告和進行報告中所描述的研究工作同等重要，因此應給予同等的時間並儘早動手撰寫初稿。

　　在撰寫報告時，你可能會發現自己的研究還有一些不完善或過失之處。如果早點動手寫初稿（甚至在研究工作還沒有完成時就開始），則還會有充裕時間補充資料或調整改善。

批判思考

在修改研究報告時，要盡可能地以批判性的眼光來審視，把自己當作一個從未讀過此文的讀者，尋查論述中有沒有不清楚、不聯貫或不易理解的地方，辨識論證環節是否存在薄弱或無效之處。身為作者，應該盡一切可能避免讀者對作品產生誤解。

修改報告時，要特別注意有沒有由於粗心所造成的明顯的錯誤，包括文法、拼字、打字或格式。許多很明顯的錯誤，相信不是因為作者不熟悉英文而造成，而是因為並未專心仔細檢查自己的文章。下例就是出自一位國立大學的研究生之手：

> 誤： Because method A excessive memory space requirement and inefficiency, so we develop method B.

例句中第一個子句沒有動詞，只有一長串的名詞和形容詞，不能表達清楚的意思。此句可修正如下：

> 正： Because method A is inefficient and requires excessive memory, we will develop method B.

如此明顯的文法錯誤，大多數讀過高中英文者都能輕易指出並改正。修改了一兩次後的文章，如果還出現這樣粗心的錯誤，一定是因為作者尚未採用批判眼光、從讀者的立場去審查自己的作品。

在修改一兩次後，還要儘可能請他人閱讀並評價你的報告，指出欠清晰、不通順或說服力不足的地方。請他們特別注意有沒有哪些句子需要看兩三遍才明白，或存在累贅的字詞或句子（請他們標記）。

特別注意

千萬不要將別人對自己文章的批評當作人身攻擊。在中國文化中，有許多人都不太樂意接納別人對自己文章的批評，而且也極少會去批評別人的文章。因此，讀者即便看不懂，通常也只是自行猜測文章的內容和揣摩作者的意思。回避正面批評的這種做法，從人際關係或談判氛圍的角度來看是促進團結友誼的一種很有效的手段，但這種習慣卻無法促進學術研究的發展或幫助研究人員提高他們的寫作能力。身為研究人員，應悉心聽取別人對自己文章提出批評與建議，並判斷其是否有理，有理的話，則應虛心接納並改進，而不要抵觸逃避。

11.3 善用各個章節

選擇標題 (Title)

學術界很多讀者一般只看報告的標題及摘要而略過其它內容，因此一定要確保標題與摘要寫得既清楚又具體。如果你儘早開始計劃標題，在撰寫報告時就可以有較多時間慢慢修改。

在選擇標題時，可以先將幾個關鍵詞記下來，然後再考慮如何把這些關鍵詞連接組合起來。你的標題的內容寫得越具體越好，而且標題必須準確地反映出文章的內容（別做虛假廣告哦！）。可能的話，儘量用報告的標題提綱寫領地顯示主要的研究結果。舉例來說，"Reducing Hyperactivity Through Placebo Use" 就很清晰，而 "Hyperactivity and Placebo Use" 就有點讓人不知所云。

有專家建議：盡量以關鍵詞作為標題中的首個字詞。另外，也有些專家認為，不應該把 *the* 當作標題中的首個字詞（雖然有很多作者這樣做）。有一位著名的專家曾建議：研究報告的標題不應該出現如 *study* 或 *investigation* 之類的字詞。比如說，假設原來的標題為 "An Investigation of Microarthropod Communities in Wetlands"，則應該修改為較簡短的標題 "Microarthropod Communities in Wetlands"。

多使用副標題 (Subtitle)

在研究報告的結果章節及討論章節中（尤其是在討論章節中），可以把文章分為多個小節並在每個小節前面加一個副標題。這既可以令文章結構更清晰、更易讀，又能吸引讀者的注意。此外，當報告中有很多副標題時，忙碌的專業讀者便能輕易找到想閱讀或詳細研讀的部分。

在撰寫副標題時，應注意以下兩點：（一）研究報告中的任何標題都應該包含至少一個名詞，而不應僅僅把單一的形容詞當作標題。（二）報告中的標題或副標題應該提供具體的信息。應避免使用如 "Part I" 此種千篇一律的副標題，而應採用具體貼切的詞句如 "Reaction Rate" 或 "Dependence of Reaction Rate on Temperature" 或 "Increase in Reaction Rate with Temperature"。

導論 (Introduction)

研究報告的導論具有兩個主要功能：第一，說明研究的動機；第二，敘述研究的目的。在寫報告時，應保証導論能清楚而精確地實現這兩個重要功能。

導論文獻回顧是用來指出一個值得研究的課題或論點——即說明作者企圖解決的問題。文獻回顧的目的並不在於證明什麼，只需引述一些能幫助讀者瞭解與自己的研究動機相關的參考文獻即可。

在導論中應避免照搬摘要中的內容，更不要直接複製粘貼摘要裡頭的句子。導論和摘要各有不同的作用與長度，因此這兩部分的內容及表達方式應各有差別。況且，一模一樣的句子或段落，有哪位讀者想看兩遍呢？

如果研究報告為傳統常見的實驗報告，大概無需多費筆墨描述文章的行文結構。想想看，如果有誰在導論結尾再安排一個段落來交代「第二節描述實驗方法，第三節列出研究結果，第四節敘述結論」，這麼一來就顯得既無聊又多餘，因為讀者只要看報告下文中的副標題就一目瞭然了。只有在讀者對報告的結構不太熟悉時，才有必要加以說明（當報告篇幅很長或組織架構比較特別時）。如果你決定在導論中加上一段來描述文章的結構，那麼該段落必須能提供具體的信息，而且句子結構也盡量不要重複。

有些人建議在導論的結尾處應簡略地敘述報告的主要結論，但我個人並不贊成：概述結論的章節應是摘要而不是導論。假如讀者想對結論有更深入的瞭解，他們可以先跳到結論章節，然後再回頭閱讀方法章節或結果章節。

（對於導論的標準寫法，請參考本書第十二、十三章。）

方法章節 (Method)

研究報告方法章節是要讓其他學者能夠重複作者的實驗以驗證作者得到的結果，因此方法章節中的描述必須既清楚又准確。作者應按照前後順序逐一描述曾操作過的所有試驗步驟；同時在描述材料時，因為有些讀者可能對作者所採用的品牌不熟悉，因此應該用一般名稱或化學名稱，而不是僅僅提及個別品牌的名稱。

為了確保方法章節寫得清楚、完整，作者可以考慮請他人按照方法章節中的描述，在作者不在場時重複一次實驗。如此一來，大家就會很容易發現在實驗方法的描述中是否存在錯誤，或遺漏了任何重要的信息。

方法章節的英文名稱應該是 "Method"、"Materials and Method" 或 "Procedure"。不要使用單一的形容詞當作方法章節的標題，例如 "Experimental"。"Experimental Procedure" 或 "Experimental Method" 其實都是適切的標題，但在這裡 "experimental" 就顯得完全多餘。

（對於方法章節的寫法，本書第十五章將有進一步的討論。）

結果章節 (Results)

在結果章節部分，只要陳述最主要的結果即可，至於細節，則應使用圖表來列出。圖表的內容應盡量一目瞭然、通俗易懂，讓讀者不需先看完文字說明，就能容易領會圖表中的信息。因此圖表的標題及說明必須清楚完整。

（對於結果章節的標準結構與常用句型，請參考第十六章。）

討論章節 (Discussion)

在討論章節中，作者必須針對自己的研究結果提出合理的解釋，說明這些結果的重要性，並指出自己的研究對當代知識界將做出哪些貢獻。作者應指出研究結果是否符合自己原先的假設，並嘗試說明造成這些結果的原因。如果是獨具創見的研究結果，則應特別強調。假如作者在導論中曾把研究目的敘述成間接的疑問（如 "The purpose of this study was to determine whether X affects Y"），那麼在討論章節中就應該正面回答此疑問，並指出研究結果如何支持自己的答案。

在構思及撰寫討論章節的內容時，應反覆自問：「我的假設或理論會不會很容易就被反駁？」以及「針對這些結果，可不可能還有其它的解釋？」應細心考慮研究結果是否真能支持自己的假設，抑或根本不能支持這個假設，還是甚至可以用來反駁自己的假設？佛南·布斯 (Vernon Booth) 指出：曾經有兩位學者在研究報告中展示了一些圖表來支持自己的理論，後來沒想到有另一位學者正好就採用了同一張圖表來否證他們的理論！

討論章節的內容對整篇研究報告的價值而言有至關重要的影響。在此章節中，作者不僅需對自己的結果給出解釋，而且還需說明結果的涵義。有位專業編輯曾告誡說：就算報告所提出的研究結果再有意思，只要討論章節不夠嚴謹、完整或存在瑕疵，就可能會被退稿。所以，作者在撰寫與修改此章節時要特別留意自己的分析和解釋是否深入、完備、正確。

（對於討論章節的內容，請參考第十七章。）

結論 (Conclusion)

有些讀者在看完了研究報告後，可能只記得結論中一兩個關鍵的句子，或甚至只記得幾個關鍵的字詞而已。因此，報告的結論一定要敘述得盡量清楚、精確。

要記住，結論章節主要用來陳述作者的結論，而不應重複一大堆前文已經講過的內容。如果你的報告已經有適切的討論章節（請參考第十七章），作者不需要在結論中再次解釋研究的背景、目的或實驗方法。

報告的主要結論應在摘要和結論中（或討論章節中）各自提到。在這兩處，敘述結論的方式應該稍有不同，而且在結論中應該陳述得更為詳細。在這兩個章節採用不同的表達方式，或許有助於讀者更瞭解結論的重點。

千萬不要在摘要、導論以及結論中重複同一個句子。摘要、導論及結論的功能各有不同，能符合其中一個功能的句子大概就不適合在另外兩個地方再次使用，而且也不要虐待讀者，強迫他們重複閱讀一模一樣的句子。在這三個地方可能有必要提到一些相同的要點，但是每次都應該採用不同的方式和句子結構來表達。

如果需要敘述好幾個主要結論，則應該考慮採用排列要點的格式，並在每個結論前打個序號。在結論上面亦可以寫一個介紹句，如 "The results of this research support the following conclusions" 或 "The following conclusions can be drawn from the results presented in this report"。

（對於結論章節的寫法，請參考第十八章。）

摘要 (Abstract)

摘要是整個研究報告中最最重要的部分。作者在寫摘要時，應暫時假定讀者無法或無暇閱讀報告的任何其它部分，所以摘要基本上就是你這篇報告的廣告招牌，顧客進不進門惠顧就靠它了。作者還應提醒自己：摘要的內容必須能讓讀者清楚領會作者究竟進行了怎樣的研究工作、為何要做這些研究，最後得到了甚麼樣的結果。

在摘要中千萬不要引用一大堆數據，因為這些數據對讀者而言可能完全沒有意義。應該用文字的方式來說明自己的研究，最多只引述幾個關鍵的數據以供讀者參考。摘要還要言簡意賅地敘述主要的結論。但如果你實在無法提出一個具體精簡的結論，則可以寫 "The effect of X on Y is discussed" 或 "The implications of these data are discussed"。

研究報告的摘要不能過長，否則讀者恐怕無意全部看完。

（對於摘要的結構與寫法，請參考第十九章。）

11.4 投稿

查閱格式指導說明

在準備把研究報告投稿到學術期刊時，一定要先查閱該期刊編輯對於文章的結構及格式的說明，還應翻閱期刊以往出版的幾篇文章，瞭解一般的格式，如註解格式、參考書目格式、圖表格式，以及關於文章篇幅及圖表數量的規定等。

應投什麼期刊？

準備投稿時，一個重要的問題就是應該把自己的文章投遞到什麼期刊比較適合呢？作者應儘量把稿子投到自己研究領域裡比較知名或地位比較高的期刊，但在選擇時還要注意，比期刊的名氣更重要的是：你的文章主題是否符合該期刊所關注的主要焦點。根據1985年對於85名專業期刊編輯之問卷調查的結果，專業期刊被退稿的最普遍理由在於文章的主題不適合或超出期刊的所關注的範圍！所以，投稿前一定要先確定自己文章是否切合所投期刊的旨趣。

被退稿怎麼辦？

剛開始投稿到學術期刊時，每個研究人員一定會遭遇被退稿的苦惱，這很正常。如果你的文章被退稿，不要過於沮喪，而應該把這段經歷視為有價值的學習過程（別忘了，你至少可以免費獲得兩三位審稿人及編輯對報告提出的寶貴意見！）。作者應該根據審稿人的意見細心修改自己的文章，然後再投稿到其它期刊。只要報告的研究具有價值、內容清楚而有條理，終究會如願以償地找到樂意刊登你的文章的期刊。

編輯意見

在上述1985年問卷調查中，受訪的編輯表示：退稿的次要理由是文章內容的重要性令人置疑。另外一些其它的退稿理由，還包括結果的正確性無法令人信服、討論及分析不夠深入、文章篇幅太長、文章結構混亂，以及表達方式欠妥等。

問卷中還有一部分，請編輯指出投稿的研究人員最常犯的錯誤。受訪者特別強調了文章結構或表達方式不當的問題。他們指出：作者行文時應保持清晰的焦點，還應清楚解釋研究問題以及研究結果的重要性。此外，也有不少編輯強調：投稿前，作者一定要多次修改文章的內容，請同事先過目並提供意見。

第十二章
背景資料

本章及下一章將討論如何撰寫研究論文的導論。導論用於介紹論文的主題，並讓讀者對閱讀下文的詳細資料做好心理準備。導論常常是論文最難寫的部分之一，因為作者必須言簡意賅、準確適切地總結論文的全篇內容，同時還必須嚴格控制篇幅。因此，每次撰寫研究論文時，應確保自己有足夠的時間慢慢擬定導論的草稿並細心修改，這樣才可能寫出提綱挈領的好論文。

12.1 基本內容及組織

一篇好的導論應清楚交代下列四個項目：

- 主要的研究活動：進行研究的人究竟做了些什麼事情？
- 研究活動的目的：做這些事情的目標是什麼？
- 進行研究的理由或背景：進行這研究的動機為何？
- 研究在相關領域中的地位：此項研究與其它相關研究有什麼關係？

作者在提供這些訊息時，通常會採用倒序的方式，也就是說，先描述某個研究領域的近況，從而進一步指出研究的理由，然後再介紹此項研究及其目的。一般而言，為了清楚傳達這些訊息，報告的導論通常會至少包括四個基本的「步驟」：

步驟一：背景資料。導論伊始首先介紹作者的研究領域，並提供相關的背景資料，為報告下文將要探討的問題或現象做好鋪墊。

步驟二：文獻回顧。接下來，討論其他學者對此問題或現象發表過的研究。

步驟三：指出問題。然後，作者便指出仍然有某個問題或現象值得進一步研究。

步驟四：研究內容與目的。最後，作者描述自己的研究內容，並明確指出此項研究的具體目的。

上述四個步驟在每一篇科技研究報告的導論中幾乎都會出現。此外，導論有時候還會包括一兩個其它的步驟，用來說明本研究潛在的價值以及介紹研究報告的組織架構。不過這兩個步驟可有可無，它們在某些研究領域的報告中常常出現，但其它領域的報告中，則較為罕見。

步驟五：研究價值（本步驟可有可無）。作者解釋該項研究對相關領域的貢獻，例如理論的應用或實用價值。

步驟六：組織架構（本步驟可有可無）。作者簡略地介紹報告的組織結構，以方便讀者熟悉全文和瞭解研究結果。

一般而言，碩士、博士論文的導論中都會涉及步驟五。如果作者接受某機構團體所贊助的研究經費來進行研究時，研究報告中也常常會包含這項步驟。儘管如此，還是有不少投稿專業期刊的報告將此步驟省略。當報告篇幅很長時，就應該包括步驟六；在某些專業領域（如某些工學領域），因為不同報告有不同的結構，因此這項步驟便顯得尤為必要。反之，當專業領域中的報告都採取統一的標準結構（如導論、方法、結果、討論）時，則可以省略此步驟。

以下範本摘錄自一篇科技研究報告的導論，這篇典型的導論包括了步驟一到五（步驟六的範本將在第十三章提供）。

The Effect of Indentation on Program Comprehension

步驟一：
背景資料

Managers of data-processing centers and other organizations often find it practical to establish standards regarding the format of computer programs. The use of programming standards may make programs easier to comprehend and thus may enhance programmer productivity. In recent years, a variety of standards have been proposed in the literature. Yet often these proposals are offered with no more foundation than the experiences of a small number of professionals. To be effective, programming standards must be based on empirical data concerning program comprehension and the factors that affect it.

步驟二：
文獻回顧

A number of researchers have begun to collect empirical evidence regarding the effects of various factors on program comprehension. Woodfield et al. (1981) investigated modularization and comments and found that subjects given programs containing comments were able to answer more questions correctly about the program than those who did not have comments and that subjects given an abstract data type version of the program could answer more questions correctly than those given any of three other types of modularization. Sheppard et al. (1979) studied the effect of structured coding and mnemonic variable names on program comprehension. They found that unstructured programs were the most difficult to reconstruct and that there were no differences in program comprehension among the levels of variable mnemonicity.

Shneiderman (1976) compared the logical and arithmetic IF statements of Fortran and found modest support for the hypothesis that beginning programmers tend to find the logical IF easier than the arithmetic IF, whereas experienced programmers find them equally difficult. Green (1977) investigated nested and jumping-styled forms of the conditional statement in the context of two typical programming tasks: tracing and reporting the truth-conditions needed to reach a point in the program. He found that both tasks took longer when the program conditionals were written in the jump form.

步驟三：
指出問題

Although these studies have provided much valuable information on the relationship between various factors and program comprehension, there are still many factors that have not yet been explored. This paper describes an empirical study that investigated the effect of indentation on program comprehension. We tested three different indentation styles for the same program control structures: no indentation, moderate indentation, and excessive indentation. The results of this study may be of interest to managers and educators attempting to develop programming standards and to researchers interested in the psychological aspects of computer programming.

步驟四：
研究目的

步驟五：
研究價值

練習 12-1 導論中的五個步驟

請指出下列導論中步驟一到五各步驟所包含的句子。

The Influence of Oxygen on SiO_2 Sputtering

[1]Silicon dioxide (SiO_2) is by far the most common insulator used in microelectronics. [2]Thus the properties of SiO_2 have been the subject of numerous investigations in the past few decades. [3]With the rapidly increasing use of ion beams in the manufacturing of microelectronics, an interest in the properties of ion-bombarded SiO_2 has emerged.

[4]The surface structure of ion-bombarded SiO_2 has been thoroughly evaluated using x-ray photoelectron spectrometry and Auger electron spectrometry for low ion energies and ultrahigh vacuum conditions (Thomas and Hofmann, 1985; Lang, 1989). [5]It appears that ion bombardment causes the outermost atomic layers of SiO_2 to become depleted in oxygen.

[6]Sputtering yields have been determined, mostly for ion energies between 1 and 30 keV, but insufficient control of vacuum conditions and hence oxygen partial pressure has resulted in widely scattered data.

[7]Argon ion sputtering yields obtained by previous researchers range from 0.78 atoms/ion at 1 keV ion energy (Cantagrel and Marchal, 1973) and 1.0-1.3 atoms/ion at 10 keV to 1.0-1.8 atoms/ion at around 20 keV ion energy (Edwin, 1973; Bach, Kitzmann, and Schroeder, 1974). [8]The latter ion energy is close to the maximum nuclear stopping power of argon ions in SiO_2 (Biersack, 1987). [9]Although Cantagrel and Marchal (1973) found that the sputtering yield of 1-keV Ar bombarded SiO_2 was affected by oxygen, no systematic investigation of the effects of an oxygen ambient during ion bombardment of SiO_2 has been carried out.

[10]In this research, high-energy argon-ion sputtering of thin SiO_2 films was performed and the relationship between sputtering yield and oxygen partial pressure was studied. [11]The data reported here may be of importance in understanding ion-beam-induced oxidation of silicon.

接下來，我們將討論報告導論的前半部分（即步驟一、二）的內容及常用句型，至於步驟三至六，則留待下一章作進一步討論。

12.2 步驟一：背景資料

在撰寫報告導論的第一個步驟時，作者必須說明報告的主題在其所屬的研究領域中有著什麼樣的學術地位、關係；同時必須提供足夠的背景資料，以便讀者瞭解報告內容的重要性。我們一般采用這種約定俗成的方法：先介紹報告內容所屬研究領域的大氣候，接著再把視野聚焦到其中一個次領域，並針對該領域交代一些較為有針對性的概況。最後，深度聚焦到與報告所探討的問題直接對應、更為具體的課題，並針對這個課題再次補充說明現狀。所以，撰寫背景資料的時候，是先有一兩個比較宏觀籠統的句子，然後逐漸轉為微觀具體的句子，最後一兩句應儘量點題切題，定焦於報告的重點。

讓我們舉一個具體的例子來展開說明這一點。下面一段文字摘錄自一篇研究報告導論的背景資料部分。作者的第一句介紹了一個較為廣泛的題目，即 "programming behavior"，接著第二、三句就介紹與之相關但比較具體的課題，即 "comprehension"。然後，在第四、五句中作者把焦點推進到與 "comprehension" 相關這樣更具體的題目，即 "psychological complexity"。這個題目就與研究報告的課題直接相關。

[1]As research into human factors in software development continues, it has become important to develop a detailed cognitive model of programming behavior. [2]One of the major components of programming behavior is comprehension. [3]Comprehension is involved in nearly all aspects of programming work, including writing, debugging, and modifying software. [4]Thus factors that relate to program comprehension must be explored. [5]One of these factors is psychological complexity,

which one expert has defined as "characteristics that make it difficult for humans to understand software."

在這裏，背景資料的內容大都是一般學者公認的事實，因此通常不需引述參考文獻。然而，有的作者偶爾還是會引述一些參考資料，以提供這些內容之來源。

背景資料的範圍

撰寫導論的背景資料時，作者必須根據報告的不同讀者群來準備不同的內容。如果讀者主要是某個專業領域裡的專家，那麼背景資料就可以寫得相當簡短（甚至只需兩三個句子足以），同時在這個步驟之前的那些敘述大背景的句子也可以描述得相對具體些。相反，假如閱讀期刊的讀者來自其它領域，那麼此期刊所刊載的文章大都需要提供較完整的背景資料（或許有兩個段落以上），而背景資料開篇所涉及的層面也可能會較為宏觀。

「先舊後新」

在充實背景資料時，作者應細心運用「先舊後新」的原則，務求文章易讀易懂。也就是說，在敘述宏觀的研究領域和自己具體的研究主題之間的關係時，作者每寫一句，應以「舊」的訊息開頭，即前文提過的名詞片語，然後再給出「新」的訊息，即尚未出現過的名詞片語。這種寫法能令讀者緊跟作者思路，清楚瞭解每項新的訊息和整個研究背景的關係。作者在呈現「舊」的訊息時，可以直接重複前文曾提及的名詞片語；若不想重復，也可以採用代名詞或涵義相同的字詞代替（例如，可以採用 *the machine* 或 *the system* 來取代前面曾提及的舊訊息 *the computer*）。

請注意下面一段文字如何運用「先舊後新」的原則。每句都先重複上句提過的「舊」訊息，然後才介紹新概念。這樣一來，每句的「舊」訊息便能發揮引導作用，讓讀者比較容易瞭解每句的內容以及整個段落的重點（各句中的「舊」訊息都用下劃線標出）。

> As research into human factors in software development continues, it has become important to develop a detailed cognitive model of programming behavior. One of the major components of programming behavior is comprehension. Comprehension is involved in nearly all aspects of programming work, including writing, debugging, and modifying software. Thus factors that relate to program comprehension must be explored. One of these factors is psychological complexity, which one expert has defined as "characteristics that make it difficult for humans to understand software."

關於「先舊後新」原則的進一步討論，請參考本書第九章。

練習 12-2 背景資料

下列句子摘錄自一篇研究報告的導論，但卻沒有依照原文的順序列出。請注意每個句子所涉及的範圍及名詞片語的位置，然後根據「先舊後新」的原則來判斷各句子的原文順序。

Brewery Effluent in China

____ With an estimated annual production of 6 million cubic meters of beer, China has become the fifth-largest beer-consuming nation in the world, after the United States, Germany, the United Kingdom, and Russia.

____ As a result of this heavy output of effluent, the brewery industry has become one of the major polluters in China.

____ As the standard of living has improved in the last ten years, beer, a Western beverage, has become very popular in China.

____ For each cubic meter of beer produced, these breweries in general generate 20-30 cubic meters of effluent, much more than that reported to be produced by modern plants in Western nations.

____ Of the thousands of beer factories, or breweries, in China, most are located in rural areas, use outdated technology, and, until recently, have been little concerned with pollution.

時態

在論述背景資料的時候，作者通常會描述某些現象或某研究領域的一般事實。在英文中，當句子所描述的事實不受時間限制時，主要動詞應使用簡單的現在式。請參考下面的例句：

Managers of data-processing centers often *find* it practical to establish programming standards.

Comprehension *is involved* in nearly all aspects of programming work, including writing, debugging, and modifying software.

For each cubic meter of beer produced, these plants in general *generate* 20-30 cubic meters of effluent.

The use of programming standards *may make* programs easier to comprehend.

此外，撰寫背景資料時，作者有時候還需交代一些專業領域的最新趨勢。在描述既有並一直持續到現在的趨勢或事件時，應採用現在完成式。另外，現在完成式也可以用以表示最近才發生的某個事件。

As the standard of living has improved in the last ten years, beer, a Western beverage, *has become* very popular in China.

In recent years, a variety of standards *have been proposed* in the literature.

關於英文動詞時態的使用原則之進一步討論，請參考本書第三章。

練習 12-3 時態

請為下面文章選擇適當的動詞時態填空。

Knowledge of the wind-induced local pressures expected to act on the building envelope during its lifetime _____ (is / was / has been) needed for the rational design of glass and cladding on buildings. This requirement _____ (becomes / became / has become) more important in recent years because of the popularity of tall buildings with large areas of glass and lightweight cladding. Fluctuations in pressure on wall surfaces _____ (are / were / have been) caused by the turbulence in the wind flow approaching the building and by flow disturbances generated by the building and its surface elements, such as mullions or vertical ribs. Mullions and ribs _____ (are / were / have been) common because of cladding requirements or simply for decorative purposes.

Wind standards and building codes _____ (state / stated / have stated) guidelines for the design of building cladding. However, the applicability of these guidelines to buildings with mullions or ribs _____ (is / was / has been) doubtful. In addition, wind tunnel modeling commonly _____ (assumes / assumed / has assumed) that the surfaces of the buildings being simulated are smooth. It _____ (is / was / has been) unclear whether wind pressures measured on smooth building surfaces _____ (can / could) also represent those acting on a model with mullions or ribs.

練習 12-4 背景資料

請採用下面的字詞組，正確補上動詞、介系詞、冠詞以及其它字詞造句，並完成此背景資料段落。

Passive Ranging Using a Moving Camera

one / most challenging problems / the field of computer vision / analysis of visual motion from image sequences

besides / relevance to the understanding of biological vision systems / motion analysis / practical applications / robotics, vehicle navigation, traffic safety, intelligent vehicle and highway systems, aviation, and space exploration

one / major areas of interest in motion analysis / passive ranging

in passive ranging / 3-D environment of moving camera / reconstructed / analyzing / a sequence of images obtained by the camera

12.3 步驟二：文獻回顧

導論中的第二個步驟為文獻回顧。在這一步驟中，作者通常會繼續講述研究工作的背景及目的。一方面，作者會指出自己對其他學者發表過的相關研究很熟悉，另一方面還會說明自己的研究跟這些學者過去的研究有何關係和區別。

> **特別注意**
>
> 1985年發佈的一篇專業期刊編輯問卷調查表示，科技研究報告投稿者最常犯的錯誤之一，就是報告中沒有引述足夠的相關研究，以清楚表示作者的研究目的及其重要性。一篇論文必須能夠推動相關研究領域的發展，才會被學術期刊接受。而要讓審稿人及讀者感受到這一點，作者就得先將相關研究領域的近況論述清楚。

文獻回顧的長度

文獻回顧的長度應視文章類別與研究領域而定。在專業學術期刊發表過的報告中，文獻回顧有時候只由幾個句子組成，不過通常情況下會有一兩個段落。相比之下，博士論文的文獻回顧則常常是一整個獨立的章節。假如你所研究的問題是眾多學者近年來探討過的技術問題，那麼就可能要討論很多參考資料。相反，如果要處理的是一個新近提出而且非常專業的數學問題，則只需討論一兩篇參考文獻就足夠了。

在准備將報告投稿到專業期刊時，作者應避免引述一大堆不相干的參考文獻，以此來炫耀自己學識淵博。恰當地整理、引述參考資料，找出一個有意思的研究課題才是作者應挖空心思鑽研的方向。要知道，引述各種參考資料不是為了證明作者文章讀得多、見識廣，而是為了進一步闡明研究動機與目的，並藉此表明本項研究能夠在此基礎上提供哪些新的發現或解決哪些新的問題。

文獻回顧的組織形式

撰寫文獻回顧的時候，我們一般會依照參考文獻與報告主題的密切程度來作編排。也就是說，作者先把跟研究報告關係不大密切的資料排到前面，然後再把關係最為密切的參考資料擺在後面。以下的文獻回顧範本就採用了這種結構。這篇報告是一項實地研究，探討小麥秸稈如何在土壤表面消失的現象。在文獻回顧中，作者首先描述其他學者以往在實驗室進行過的相關研究，接著討論將樣本埋入泥土中的實地研究，最後才提到將樣本留在土壤表面上的實地研究。

Wheat Residue Loss from Soil Surface
under No-till Management

Several laboratory studies have been conducted to determine actual decomposition rates of wheat and other small grain straws using ^{14}C-labeled plant material. Martin et al. (1980), using optimal conditions of -33 kPa water potential and 23° C, determined that 74% of the carbon in wheat straw evolved into the atmosphere as CO_2 after 2 years. A companion study showed that after 1 year the ^{14}C from wheat straw that had not evolved as CO_2 could be accounted for in the soil microbial biomass (Stott et al., 1983).

Most field studies have used straw-filled cloth or fiberglass bags buried in soil, and decomposition has been measured as weight loss. Smith and Douglas (1968) noted an average 44% weight loss in 12 weeks from buried wheat straw. In another study, weight loss from straw of 23 varieties of small grains ranged from 54% to 75% after 1 year (Smith and Peckenpaugh, 1986).

Few studies have been done on surface-residue loss. Brown and Dickey (1970) used fiberglass bags to compare decomposition rates of buried straw and straw left on the soil surface. Over 1.5 years, surface straw disappeared at one-third the rate of buried straw. A study by Douglas et al. (1980) showed similar results after 2 years.

另一種編排文獻的方法是依時序來排列：先討論早期的文獻，然後才提到近期的資料。下面的文獻回顧就是用這種方法編排的。

Wind Pressures on Buildings with Mullions

The effect of mullions on wind pressures on buildings has not been extensively examined. Hoerner (1957) discussed the effects of vertical ribs on a circular cylindrical storage tank and reported that the suction peaks are eliminated by ribs on the outside structure of the storage tank. The drag, however, is higher on a cylinder with ribs than on a tank with a smooth surface. Leutheusser (1970) performed a series of wind tunnel studies on building models with various architectural details, including mullions. Other than very local effects of wind-induced pressures between mullions, the overall trend for most regions showed no difference between the cases with and without mullions.

Roshko (1970) also carried out tests on circular and prismatic cylinders in an aeronautical wind tunnel and discussed the effect of surface roughness modeled by mullion-like grooves. He reported that the pressure distribution depended on the Reynolds number.

The effect of the Reynolds number was also discussed by Standen et al. (1971), who attempted pressure measurements on a full-scale building with mullions, as well as on a wind tunnel model of the building. They deduced that the scale of the mullions should be proportional to the local boundary-layer thickness. Templin and Cermak (1976) carried out full-scale and wind tunnel studies concerning the effect of mullions on wind-induced loads on buildings and found that the mullions reduced the magnitude of the mean and RMS pressures on the sides of the building on which the main flow reattached after separating from the upwind corner. Finally, Leadon and Kownacki (1979) discussed fluctuating pressures generated by I-shaped external mullions on a curtain wall in a two-dimensional flow.

第三種常見的組織形式是把要討論的參考資料分為不同類別，比如說根據研究方法來分類。當作者要討論很多參考文獻時，這種方法就顯得特別有用。在分類後，可以依關係的密切程度或依時序來組織各類文獻，以便討論。下面的文獻回顧就是採用了分類法。作者把所要討論的參考資料分成兩大類：流行病學研究以及實驗研究，然後針對這兩大類中的資料分別依時序編排並加以討論。

Back Pain and Exposure to Whole Body Vibration in Helicopter Pilots

In several epidemiological studies on back pain in helicopter pilots, a distinction has been made between transient back pain and chronic back pain (Shanahan et al., 1986; Froom et al., 1986). According to Bowden (1987), chronic back pain can be compared to idiopathic low back pain in the general population. Back pain prevalences in helicopter pilots reported by several authors vary from 21 to 95% (Schulte-Wintrop and Knoche 1978; Fischer et al. 1980; Delahay et al., 1982). The prevalence of back pain during or shortly after flight ranges from 34 to 64%. Back pain not primarily associated with flight is reported in 11 to 27% of the respondents (Shanahan et al., 1986; Froom et al, 1986)....

A number of experimental studies have also been conducted. In a mock-up of a UH-1H helicopter seat and control configurations, 11 subjects were asked to adopt the posture they assumed in normal flight and were tested for two separate periods of 120 min, one with simulated helicopter vibration and one without (Shanahan and Reading, 1984). No significant difference was found between the vibration and non-vibration conditions for either time of onset or intensity of pain. Pope et al. (1986) tested the change in muscle response due to sustained posture and vibration in a simulated UH-1H cockpit. Marginally significant fatigue occurred only as a result of the sustained static posture. In contrast, all tests both with and without vibration produced discomfort in the lower back.

Froom et al. (1987) compared the onset and intensity of back pain between aviators occupying the pilot's seat and the gunner's seat of a helicopter. Most pilots experienced pain or discomfort in both positions. However, the intensity was greater and the onset of the pain quicker in the pilot's seat....

12.4 文獻回顧常用句型

一般而言，用於文獻回顧的句子可以分成四大類，每一類都有特定的句型，而動詞也需要使用特定的時態。

- 資料導向引述
- 研究領域的一般描述
- 多位作者導向引述
- 作者導向引述

作者在起筆撰寫文獻回顧時，大都會先採用前三種方式引述。如此引述一兩項研究資料後，作者通常會轉用第四種方法來引述。如果文獻回顧有兩段或兩節以上，則便會採用前三者作為新段落的起首句或主題句。

下面我們將進一步討論這四種引述的句子結構。

資料導向引述

文獻回顧中的首句常常用來敘述跟研究報告內容有關的一般事實，這種句子稱作「資料導向引述」。在這種引述中，句子用於交代訊息，而被引述文獻的作者姓氏及出版年代則放在句尾的括號中。（至於文獻名稱以及其它詳細資料，則在報告結尾的參考書目中列出。）在資料導向引述中，作者通常會把自己正在討論的主題當作句子的主詞。

資料	參考引述
Correct sensor and actuator placement is crucial in determining the performance of a control system	(James, 1985).
Knowledge of the differences between advertising styles used in different countries is essential for corporations that advertise in a variety of national markets	(1, 2, 4).

如上面例句所示，資料導向引述有兩種標準格式，其中一種格式是將參考文獻作者的姓氏以及出版年代放在句尾的括號裡，另一種則是把參考文獻的序號放在括號裡，而這個序號就是指參考文獻在該篇報告結尾參考資料目錄中作者所編的序號。在決定該使用何種格式時，應事先瞭解、查閱你意向投稿期刊所印行的格式說明。

此外，文獻回顧的首句有時候還可以在形式上和資料導向引述完全一樣，不過僅僅陳述一些資料而已，而省略參考引述。這樣做是因為作者考慮到所陳述的資料為公認的事實，沒有必要引述參考文獻來支持。

在資料導向引述中常常會用到兩種時態。最常用的時態為簡單現在式，只要所引述的資料為普遍事實（例如科學上的普遍事實），不會受時間限制，則應使用此時態。

主題	現在式動詞	補語或修飾詞	參考引述
The success of no-till management systems	depends	on knowledge of how rapidly crop residues decompose	(Stott, 1990).
Acid rain	is	a serious prob-lem in many areas of Asia	(1).

當所引述的資料是某種趨勢或變化時，則應使用現在完成式。

主題	現在完成式動詞	補語或修飾詞	參考引述
The computer	has become	an important educational tool in the past decade	(Johnson, 1993).
Outbreaks of dengue fever	have decreased	in recent years	(4).

另外，作者有時候會採用資料導向引述方法來陳述過去的事件或事實，這時由於句子所指的是過去的事情，那麼當然應該用過去式。

主題	過去式動詞	補語或修飾詞	參考引述
The original treatment guidelines	were published	in 1989	(2).

採用資料導向引述方法將一些關於研究主題的一般事實陳述完畢，作者接下來通常會把討論的焦點轉到其他學者進行過的研究。

研究概況的描述

另一種常見的句型是對研究領域的一般描述。這種句型有時會在文獻回顧的起首幾句出現；但亦可能是新段落的開首。這種句子主要是交代有關研究的發展現狀，藉以說明學術界對該問題的研究有多深入。由於這些句子論及的通常是公認的事實，所以一般而言不需要引述任何參考文獻。同時，考慮到這些句子描述的是從過去持續到現在的研究趨勢，所以我們便應使用現在完成式。此外，由於討論的焦點是研究主題，而不是從事研究工作的人，所以這種句子常常採用被動語態。標準的句型如下：

研究程度		現在完成式動詞 （被動語態）	主題
Much Little No	work research	has been done on has been devoted to has been conducted on has been published regarding	the differences between advertising styles used in different cultures.
Much Little	attention	has been devoted to has been directed toward has been focused on	the effects of boron doping.
Many A number of Several Few	studies experiments	have been conducted on have been done regarding have been performed on have been published on	the prevalence of back pain in helicopter pilots.

請注意：上面第一、二列的主詞是不可數，因此句子的動詞必須使用單數形。第三列的主詞則是可數而且是複數，因此動詞必須使用複數形。此外，如果要指出確實有些人曾研究過某個問題，則應該採用 "several" 或 "a number of"，如 "Several studies have been done on X"。相反，如要強調曾研究這問題的人極少，則應該採用 "few" 或 "little"，如 "Few studies have been done on Y" 或 "Little research has been done on Y"。

在上面的例句中，研究主題都是在動詞之後給出。其實在此種描述中，也可以把主題當作主詞。此外，類似這種句子常常會提到特定的一段時間。如果打算把主題當作主詞時，是否應該使用被動還是主動語態，則要視動詞的意思而定。請參考下面兩個表格中的例句，這些例句包括主動、被動語態以及單數、複數主詞。

主題	現在完成式動詞 （主動語態）	研究程度	時間 （可有可無）
The problem of back pain in helicopter pilots	has been	the subject of much research	in recent years. in the last decade. since 1990.
The effects of surface structures on wind flow	have been	the subject of few studies the focus of much research	
The problem of back pain in helicopter pilots	has drawn has attracted	much attention much interest little attention	in recent years. in the last decade. since 1990.
The effects of surface structures on wind flow	have drawn have attracted		

主題	現在完成式動詞（被動語態）以及研究程度	時間（可有可無）
The problem of back pain in helicopter pilots	has been extensively examined has been widely discussed has been thoroughly investigated has seldom been discussed	in recent years. in the last decade. since 1990.
The effects of surface structures on wind flow	have been extensively examined have been widely discussed have been thoroughly investigated have seldom been discussed	in recent years. in the last decade. since 1990.

　　另一種常見的句型是使用虛主詞結構來指出對某個問題的研究。在此種句子中，若表示研究數量的名詞為不可數，則必須搭配單數形動詞；若是可數，則必須搭配複數形動詞。

虛主詞及現在完成式動詞	研究程度	主題
There has been	much research little research	on the prevalence of back pain in helicopter pilots and other aviators.
There have been	many studies few reports	

　　在描述了相關領域中對某個問題的研究程度之後，作者通常會開始詳細討論個別學者曾進行過的研究。

多作者導向引述

　　在文獻回顧一開頭或在文獻回顧中新段落開頭時，作者也常常會使用一個句子來描述多個學者的研究。這種句子稱為「多作者導向引述」。正如對於研究程度的一般描述一樣，多作者導向引述描述諸多學者從過去到現在的研究，因此應該使用現在完成式。在這種引述中，可以把 "several researchers" 之類的名詞片語當作主詞，或採用主動語態，或採用被動語態。至於文獻的資料則放在句尾的括號中。

多作者	現在完成式動詞（主動語態）	主題	參考引述
Several researchers A number of authors Many investigators Few writers	have studied have investigated have examined have explored have reported on have discussed have considered	the role of computers in classroom instruction	(4, 6, 7, 9).

注意：當要強調罕有學者研究過此問題時，才可以使用 "few writers" 或 "few researchers" 當作主詞。如果要表達的意思是「有些學者研究過此問題」，則用 "several writers"、"several researchers" 或 "a few researchers" 才正確。

主題	現在完成式動詞 （被動語態）	多作者	參考引述
The role of computers in classroom instruction	has been studied has been investigated has been examined has been explored has been reported on has been discussed has been considered	by several researchers by a number of authors by many investigators by few writers	(Frickert, 1989; Smith, 1990; Roberts, 1992).

此外，多作者導向引述也會偶爾會使用以 *that* 開頭的名詞子句來描述某些學者的研究結果。至於子句中動詞的時態，下面將進一步討論。

多作者	現在完成式動詞 （主動語態）	That	研究結果	參考引述
Several researchers	have shown have found have reported have suggested	that	the use of computers may stimulate independent learning	(Chen, 1989; Smith, 1992; Rose, 1994).

作者導向引述

提出資料導向引述、對研究程度的一般描述或多作者導向引述之後，作者通常會在兩三句內把焦點轉移到跟本研究相關的個別參考資料，並詳細討論這些研究結果。用來引述這些個別參考文獻的句子，我們稱之為「作者導向引述」。在這種引述中，個別學者的姓氏通常會被用作句子的主詞；而且因為句子內容是指學者過去的行為和觀點，所以主要動詞通常使用過去式。研究成果則用以 *that* 開首的名詞子句交代，並緊接在主要動詞之後。

作者 及文獻引述	過去式動詞 （主動語態）	That	研究結果
Chen (1992) Rogers [2]	showed found reported noted suggested observed pointed out	that	the use of computers in a high school class-room enhanced creativity and independent thinking.

　　作者導向引述中有兩個動詞，第一個為句子的主要動詞，第二個為以 *that* 引入的名詞子句中的動詞。主要動詞通常使用過去式。至於名詞子句中動詞的時態，則要視子句所表達的資料而定。關於這點，下面將作進一步討論。

　　有時候，可以把作者導向引述分成兩個句子，第一句只描述某位學者的研究活動，第二句再敘述其研究結果。這時兩個句子的主要動詞都應使用過去式，第二句的結構和上面作者導向引述一樣，須包括以 *that* 開頭的名詞子句，但可以省略出版年代。

作者 及文獻引述	過去式動詞 （主動語態）	主題	第二句： 作者導向引述
Chen (1992)	studied examined investigated explored	the effect of X on Y.	He found that...

　　注意：在科技研究報告中，因為作者導向引述中的主要動詞，是指被引述的學者過去進行研究時之行為，所以幾乎總是使用過去式。然而，在人文學科的研究論文中，跟作者導向引述結構相同的句子則常常使用現在式，如下例所示：

　　Davidson (1978) *defines* weakness of the will as the agent's failure to take the action he judges to be best, all things considered.

　　不過在人文學科的研究論文中，我們一般都是使用現在式撰寫這類句子。這是因為句子本身不是在描述該學者本人過去的行為，而是文獻所表達的觀念（因為文獻表達此觀念係為不受時間影響之事實，所以得使用現在式）。因此，即使被引述的人是數千年前的人物，仍然可以使用現在式來表達其著作中的觀念。

　　Aristotle *uses* the term *akrasia* to refer to a person's failure to act according to his or her best judgment.

　　在經濟學、管理學、心理學、社會學以及其它社會科學中，研究報告的作者通常會遵循科技研究報告的習慣，在作者導向引述中使用過去式。然而，有時候也會如人文學科一樣使用現在式。因此在撰寫研究報告之前，應先借鑑自己專業領域的常規做法，並參考意向投遞報告的期刊曾刊登過的數篇文章，以便瞭解應該使用何種時態。

練習 12-5　參考引述中的時態

請在下列句子中填入適當的動詞形式，其中一些動詞應該為被動語態。

1. Many studies _____ (*examine*) the relationships between physical characteristics of the work environment, attitudes, and behavior.

2. Goodrich (1982) _____ (*find*) that the use of a VDT focuses workers' attention. He _____ (*suggest*) that use of a VDT would reduce workers' need for privacy.

3. Several different measures of these factors _____ (*employ*) to study a variety of samples and settings.

4. The effects of devices such as VDTs _____ (*investigate*) by several authors (Brown, 1982; Forman, 1986; McGee, 1988).

5. Roberts (1987) _____ (*show*) that interaction with a VDT tended to increase employees' levels of fatigue, muscular tension, and eyestrain.

6. Degree of openness _____ (*be*) an important characteristic of the physical work environment (Smith, 1990).

7. Several researchers _____ (*find*) that muscle aches and joint pain can be reduced by the use of adjustable workstation furniture (Kleeman, 1988; Roberts, 1990; Paul, 1993).

8. Many authors _____ (*suggest*) that office technology affects the ways in which employees work (Kruk 1987; Smith 1989; Black, 1990; Lane, 1992).

9. Stellman et al. (1987) _____ (*find*) that stress effects are greater for clerical employees than for managerial employees.

10. The negative effects of improper VDT use and poor work station design _____ (*be*) costly (Kruk, 1989).

11. A number of researchers _____ (*demonstrate*) that physical characteristics of the work environment have an impact on outcome variables such as

satisfaction, motivation, and performance (Becker, 1981; Sundstrom, 1982; Carlopio, 1991).

12. Kleeman (1988) _____ (*suggest*) that VDT users are more prone to stress symptoms than are non-VDT users.

12.5 名詞子句中的動詞時態

作者導向引述及一些多作者導向引述都包括兩個動詞。第一個為句子的主要動詞，用來描述被引述之學者的活動。第二個動詞則是以 *that* 開頭的名詞子句中的動詞，這個動詞描述該學者所提出的資料或研究結果。所以，作者除了要正確選擇主要動詞的時態外，還要恰當選擇名詞子句的動詞時態。至於名詞子句的動詞應該採用哪種時態，則要視子句內容的性質而定。下面我們會予以詳細解釋。

子句中的資料為普遍事實

在英文中，描寫普遍事實一般都會採用現在式。因此，作者若認為（以 *that* 開首的）名詞子句所引述的資料並不僅僅在研究環境下才有效，而且不受時間限制，那麼當中的動詞便會採用現在式。

作者 及文獻引述	過去式動詞	That	研究結果： 現在式動詞
Marks (1932)	showed found reported noted suggested observed pointed out	that	water *boils* at 100° C.
Gorden (2)			the gravity of the largest moon *affects* the orbits of the other moons.

作者有時還需要論及其他學者提出的技術或方法。雖然這些方法或技術可能是從前提出的，但由於已經成為標準並廣為採用，即可視為不變的事實，因此便用現在式。不過，若作者認為方法已經過時並已無人採用，那就可以使用過去式。

作者 及文獻引述	過去式動詞	受詞	關係子句： 現在式動詞
Rogers (1987)	developed described introduced	an algorithm a technique a method	that *solves* the problem quickly.
Chen [4]	designed presented proposed		that *produces* a clearer image.

子句的資料只在特定情形下才有效

　　有時候，報告作者會認為 *that* 子句中所提出的資料只在特定情形下有效，而並非恆久不變的普遍事實。例如，作者可能認為引述的研究確實獲得了某些結果，但尚未得到學術界普遍接受。那麼這時，作者應把 *that* 子句中的動詞寫成過去式。

作者 及文獻引述	過去式動詞	That	研究結果： 過去式動詞
Bolan (1987)	found reported suggested observed	that	young girls *scored* higher than boys on communication skills.
Reed (2)			reducing the amount of oxygen *caused* the deposition rate to drop sharply.

子句的資料僅僅為建議或假設

　　有時候，引文在原來的文獻中其實就是以假設的口吻提出的；或者這些資料不過是建議或假設而已，尚未經研究論證。這時作者便應把句子的主要動詞改為 *suggested* 或 *hypothesized* 之類的臆測動詞，而且在 *that* 開頭的子句中使用現在式，並在動詞前加上如 *may* 之類的語態助動詞。

作者 及文獻引述	過去式之臆測動詞	That	資料：現在式動詞加 上語態助動詞
Ross (1990)	suggested hypothesized proposed argued	that	reducing the duration of school vacations *may help* children to retain more of what they learn in class.

評論引述資料

　　有時候作者在描述某個學者的研究之後，還會加以評論。這時，描述研究工作的句子應使用過去式。至於作者評語的句子，如果評論的是過去的行為或事件，則句子的主要動詞應使用過去式；如果是指不受時間限制或目前仍然有效的事實，則應該使用現在式。

　　Rogers (1982) performed the first systematic study of this illness. His data *provided* the starting point for many later investigations.

　　Smith (1978) presented a method for solving problems of this form when $x \leq 1$. However, his method *is* not applicable to the general case.

Smith (1978) presented a method for solving problems of this form when $x \le 1$. However, his method *was* not applicable to the general case.

在例一中，因為評論的是過去的事件，所以採用過去式。在例二中，作者認為評論句為不受時間限制或目前仍然有效，因此使用現在式。在這個例子中，之所以要使用現在式，是因為論及的方法儘管有侷限，但仍然可以採用：換句話說，該方法尚未過時。例三跟例二幾乎完全一樣，只有評語句的時態不同。例三的作者使用了過去式，藉以暗示句子所論及的事情「已經過去了」，這可能是因為史密斯方法的侷限性早已廣為人知，並已無人採用。請注意：在上述例子中，描述學者研究工作的首句都應使用過去式。

練習 12-6 "That" 名詞子句中的時態

請根據下列句子裡以 *that* 開頭的名詞子句中動詞的時態來判斷作者認為子句說明的是普遍事實、特定情況或過去的事實，還是建議或假設。

1. Goodrich (1982) observed that the use of a VDT focuses workers' attention.

2. Brown and Dickey (1970) found that surface straw disappeared at one third the rate of buried straw.

3. Goodrich (1982) suggested that use of a VDT may reduce workers' need for privacy.

4. Roberts (1987) found that interaction with a VDT tended to increase employees' levels of fatigue, muscular tension, and eyestrain.

5. Martin et al. (1980) determined that 74% of the carbon in wheat straw evolved into the atmosphere as CO_2 after 2 years.

6. Stellman et al. (1987) showed that stress effects are greater for clerical employees than for managerial employees.

7. In a wind tunnel study, Lockhard (1974) found that under uniform flow conditions there were no significant differences between the cases with and without mullions.

8. Several authors have hypothesized that office technology may affect the ways in which employees work (Kruk 1987; Smith 1989; Black, 1990).

9. Hoerner (1957) reported that the drag is higher on a cylinder with ribs than on one with a smooth surface.

10. Froom et al. (1987) reported that the onset of pain was quicker for aviators sitting the pilot's seat.

練習 12-7 文獻回顧

下面是一篇研究報告的導論，其中步驟一、三以及四都已完成，但步驟二的文獻回顧卻只有大綱而已。請根據大綱內容完成步驟二，並在必要之處加入動詞、冠詞、介系詞及其它字詞。

注意：請把大綱的內容悉數寫出，同時必須使用完整的句子，即包括主詞、動詞；在撰寫時應回顧本章介紹過的常用句型，並留意句子的時態。

提示一：撰寫文獻回顧時，不要把過多的資料硬塞進一個句子內。如果某個句子太長，便應該分成兩句來寫。

提示二：一般而言，應該先描述被引述學者的研究活動，然後才概述他們的研究結果。 "Researcher A did X and found that Y"，這種形式的句子會比 "Researcher A found that Y by doing X" 順暢得多。請參考下面的例子：

劣：　　Smith found that students in language immersion classes progressed much faster than students in regular classes by examining language programs in a Canadian school system.

佳：　　Smith examined language programs in a Canadian school system and found that students in language immersion classes progressed much faster than students in regular classes.

The Relationship Between Privacy and Job Satisfaction

步驟一：
背景資料

Individuals may have a vocational need for privacy. Privacy may help employees to regulate and maintain an optimal level of social interaction and may provide a greater sense of control in the workplace. It seems likely that the level of architectural privacy employees experience in their office setting may have an effect on how they view their job and in particular on different components of job satisfaction.

步驟二：
文獻回顧

A. Several researchers: workers prefer architecturally private offices to open offices; lack of privacy affects the level of job satisfaction (Sundstrom, 1982; Oldham, 1988)

1. Oldham and Brass (1979): employees before and after they moved to an open-plan office

   Findings: job satisfaction declined considerably after move and remained low at time of follow-up survey

2. Hedge (1982), similar study of office workers: open office caused too many disturbances and distractions

3. Block and Stokes (1989), laboratory experiment: subjects more satisfied working in a private office than in office shared with three other individuals

B. Several studies: relationship between privacy and overall job satisfaction (Sundstrom, 1980; Burt et al., 1981); few researchers: relationship between privacy and individual aspects of job satisfaction

1. Altman (1975): privacy may function to reduce overload and distractions by providing worker the ability to regulate number of outgoing and incoming interactions

2. Steele (1973): privacy increased employee's sense of social status in company

3. Justa and Golan (1977): privacy may give worker greater sense of freedom

4. Sundstrom (1986): privacy generally serves to improve working conditions

步驟三：
指出問題

步驟四：
研究目的

Although these writers have provided many interesting preliminary results, to date no systematic studies have been carried out concerning the relationship between privacy and different components of job satisfaction. The study reported here attempted to correlate the levels of architectural privacy reported by employees with 10 different components of job satisfaction.

第十三章
介紹研究主題

　　當作者交代過背景資料，並討論了其他學者的相關研究之後，導論的後半部就應把焦點轉到要研究的問題上。這個部分通常至少包含兩個主要步驟，即步驟三「指出問題」與步驟四「研究目的」。在「步驟三」中，作者會指出過往的研究還有問題尚未處理，或衍生了其它問題，以便讀者瞭解報告的研究動機，亦可以為下文的討論做好鋪墊。在「步驟四」中作者便可以介紹自己的研究活動或目的了。

　　此外，導論有時候還會包括另外兩個步驟，即步驟五與步驟六。在步驟五中，作者會指出研究結果可能產生的理論或應用價值；而步驟六則說明報告的組織結構。這兩個步驟其實可有可無，有些研究報告會省略。

　　本章將詳細說明導論中步驟三到六的內容與常用句型。

13.1　步驟三：指出問題

　　請參閱下列摘錄自一篇研究論文的導論，並嘗試指出步驟二文獻回顧的結尾，即作者準備介紹研究主題的地方。

Wheat Residue Loss from Soil Surface
under No-till Management

[1]The benefits derived from directly drilling wheat into stubble in terms of timely seedings, reduced soil erosion by water and wind, and conservation of energy and water are widely recognized. [2]However, if large amounts of wheat residue remain on the soil surface at seeding, decreases in yield can occur. [3]Thus the successful adoption of no-till

management systems will partially depend on knowledge of how rapidly surface-managed wheat residues are broken down and lost from a field site.

[4]Several laboratory studies have been conducted to determine actual decomposition rates of wheat and other small grain straws using ^{14}C-labeled plant material. [5]Martin et al. (1980), using optimal conditions of -33 kPa water potential and 23° C, determined that 74% of the carbon in wheat straw evolved into the atmosphere as CO_2 after 2 years. [6]A companion study showed that after 1 year the ^{14}C from wheat straw that had not evolved as CO_2 could be accounted for in the soil microbial biomass (Stott et al., 1983).

[7]Most field studies have used straw-filled cloth or fiberglass bags buried in soil, and decomposition has been measured as weight loss. [8]Smith and Douglas (1968) noted an average 44% weight loss in 12 weeks from buried wheat straw. [9]In another study, weight loss from straw of 23 varieties of small grains ranged from 54% to 75% after 1 year (Smith and Peckenpaugh, 1986).

[10]Few studies have been done on surface-residue loss. [11]Brown and Dickey (1970) used fiberglass bags to compare decomposition rates of buried straw and straw left on the soil surface. [12]Over 1.5 years, surface straw disappeared at one-third the rate of buried straw. [13]A study by Douglas et al. (1980) showed similar results after 2 years. [14]To date, however, no studies have attempted to measure surface-residue loss without employing litter bags. [15]This is a notable shortcoming, because the use of litter bags in previous studies may have resulted in underestimation of residue loss.

[16]The objective of the present study was to determine rates of loss of wheat residues left directly on the soil surface in different wheat-growing regions. [17]In addition, we monitored changes over time in the percentage of the soil surface covered by residues.

在這個例子中，句四到十三是文獻回顧，句十四與十五則指出跟過去研究相關的問題，以結束文獻回顧。指出問題的句子屬於步驟三。在此步驟中，作者指出上文提到的研究尚有問題未處理，促使讀者將注意力轉移到作者的研究中去。讀者看到這裡便自然知道，作者正準備介紹研究主題，亦可猜想到此項研究必是意在提供相關的資料，或者是解決有關問題。

步驟三通常只要用一兩句交代即可，其主要內容通常包含下列四項：

- 以前的學者尚未研究，或處理得不夠完善的重要課題。
- 過去的研究所衍生的問題，尚有待進一步探討。
- 提出過兩個以上的理論或觀點，而且互不相容。唯有進一步研究，才有望解決這種衝突。
- 可以將過去的研究擴展到別的領域；或是可以改善已有的方法或技術，進而應用到別的地方。

閱讀前文導論時，我們又該如何認定文獻回顧結束、步驟三開始的地方呢？讀者大概都會覺得，要找出文獻回顧結束的地方並不是很難，因為步驟三一開始便有一個清楚的「信號」字眼——*however*。該詞便意味著下文將要指出過去研究不足之處。此外，步驟三的首句還會出現另一個信號字眼—修飾詞 *no*。這樣的句子為步驟三最常用的兩種句型之一，這句型的句首常常會出現 *however* 這個詞，接著便表示目前資料仍不充分。句子表示資料不足的部分常會用到如 *few, little* 或 *no* 等修飾詞。緊接在修飾詞後面的，則是指涉及研究主題之名詞片語。

信號字眼	使用如 *few, little, no* 之信號字眼 以指出過去研究之不足	研究主題
However,	few studies have been done on few studies have reported on few studies have been published on few researchers have studied no studies have investigated little research has been devoted to little attention has been paid to little information has been published concerning no work has been done on little literature is available on there is little literature available on little is known about insufficient data are available on	surface- residue loss.

　　此外，複句也是步驟三常用的句型。句子的首個子句旨在說明雖然不少學者已經研究過某課題，而下面的子句緊跟著指出相關課題研究仍然不足。這種句型通常以信號字眼 *although* 或 *while* 開頭。由於兩個子句的內容通常要強調對比，所以第一個子句會出現如 *some, many* 或 *much* 等修飾詞，第二個子句則會出現 *little, few* 或 *no* 等修飾詞。

信號字眼	主題一的研究程度	主題二的研究程度
Although While	much work has been done 　on X, much research has been 　devoted to X, many researchers have 　investigated X, many studies have been 　published concerning X, much literature is 　available on X,	little research has been done on Y. little attention has been paid to Y. little information is available on Y. little work has been published on Y. few researchers have studied Y. few studies have investigated Y.

　　作者會在 X 與 Y 的位置填上兩個對比鮮明的課題，例如：

Although much research has been done on *CO₂ levels in agricultural soils*, little work has been done on *CO₂ levels in forest soils*.

有時候句首雖然沒有 *although* 或 *while*，而第二個子句開首一定會出現連接詞 *but* 或 *yet*。

CO_2 levels in agricultural soils have been studied extensively, *but* little attention has been devoted to CO_2 levels in forest soils.

Much research has been done on CO_2 levels in agricultural soils, *yet* to date forest soils have been relatively neglected.

另外，有時候第一個子句之後也會插入參考引述，例如：

Although CO_2 levels in agricultural soils have been studied extensively (Smith, 1990), little information is available on CO_2 levels in forest soils.

當然，我們不見得一定要採用這兩個基本句型來撰寫步驟三。最重要的是要指出問題，讓讀者瞭解研究動機。

撰寫步驟三時，應注意下列兩點：

一、*Work, literature, research* 及 *attention* 等字詞皆為不可數，因此應寫成單數形並搭配單數動詞；此外，修飾詞應使用 *much, little* 或 *no*，不能用 *many* 或 *few*。*Studies, papers, investigations, researchers* 及 *investigators* 等字詞皆為可數，因此應寫成複數形並搭配複數動詞，而修飾詞應使用 *many, few* 或 *no*。

二、一般來說，句子的動詞時態不是現在式，就是現在完成式。若敘述的是不受時間限制的一般事實，則應使用現在式，例如 "little is known about X" 或 "little literature is available on X"。若要描述從過去持續到現在之事件，則應使用現在完成式，例如 "few studies have been done on X" 或 "little attention has been devoted to X"。

有時候，尤其是當文獻回顧很長時，步驟二、三可能會穿插進行。作者可以先討論研究主題某方面的研究，然後指出其不足之處；接著便討論另一個問題的研究，然後再指出其中尚有待解決的問題。

練習 13-1 步驟三中信號字眼與時態

請在下面兩篇文章中填上適當的信號字眼與動詞。填上動詞時，還要注意時態與語態。

Photochemistry of Solid Ozone

Depletion of atmospheric ozone is a major environmental problem, especially in the polar regions [1]. Several studies have examined the photodissociation of ozone and subsequent reaction of the fragments with O_3 [2-11], H_2O [12-23], and other small molecules [24-31]. _____, the importance of ozone photochemistry in stratospheric ice crystals _____ largely unknown [32, 33], and to our knowledge _____ experimental research on this reaction in the solid state _____ reported until now. The present paper describes cross sections for photodestruction of solid ozone at 308 nm. . . .

CO_2 Dynamics in Acid Forest Soils

...Studies performed on CO_2 levels within the soil profile have established that significant variations in soil CO_2 occur seasonally, between soils, and with depth (Richter and Jacobs, 1972; Miotke, 1974; Rightmire, 1978; Gunn and Trudgill, 1982; Buyanovsky and Wagner, 1983). Measurements of CO_2 concentrations for an entire annual cycle _____ rare, _____, and most of these _____ reported for just one depth. Moreover, _____ annual CO_2 cycles _____ studied extensively under agricultural conditions (Buyanovsky and Wagner, 1983), to our knowledge there _____ _____ intensive investigations into CO_2 dynamics and the possible effects on water quality in mountainous and forested regions....

13.2 步驟四: 研究目的

撰寫步驟四時, 作者一般還會用一兩個句子來敘述研究的性質及目的, 用來表示如何解決步驟三指出的問題。

我們不妨再參考上文列出的導論樣本。可以看到, 作者在步驟三指出問題後, 便立即敘述研究目的。

Wheat Residue Loss from Soil Surface under No-till Management

步驟三:
指出問題

…To date, however, no studies have attempted to measure surface-residue loss without employing litter bags. This is a notable shortcoming, because the use of litter bags in previous studies may have resulted in underestimation of residue loss.

步驟四:
研究目的

The objective of the present study was to determine rates of loss of wheat residues left directly on the soil surface in different wheat-growing regions. In addition, we monitored changes over time in the percentage of soil surface covered by residues.

撰寫研究報告時, 作者可以利用幾種不同的方式來介紹研究主題或目的。大多數作者會採用如 *purpose, aim* 或 *objective* 等字眼來直接指出研究目的, 例如:

The objective of this research was to determine the impact of the N-application rate during the early portion of the sugarcane growth cycle on the NO_3 distribution in the soil profile.

The purpose of this experiment was to examine whether listeners' gender affects their response to background music.

也有些作者只簡略地描述主要研究活動, 讀者可以跟據此描述聯繫上下文來推斷研究目的。

This study investigated visual strain in a laboratory task that required gaze shifts between a printed document and a visual display unit (VDU) screen.

The present paper describes cross sections for photodestruction of solid ozone at 308 nm.

另外, 也可以用主句敘述主要的研究活動, 用不定詞片語 (infinitive phrase) 來敘述研究目的。

An empirical study was carried out to investigate the effect of indentation on program comprehension.

To investigate the prevalence of back pain in helicopter pilots, a survey was conducted of all licensed helicopter pilots in three provinces of the country.

一般來講, 上文介紹過的三種句型, 採用第一種及第三種較為適合。這是因為這兩種句式直接了當地交代了研究目的, 因此不須讀者自行推斷。不過, 如果研究目的既不單一也不具體，作者便可能會採用第二種句型。總之，無論使用哪一種句型，作者都一定要清楚地說明究竟這項研究做了甚麼工作。

論文導向與研究導向

　　要介紹自己的研究，可以根據文章的焦點而選擇兩種導向：一是以研究論文本身為焦點，另外一是以研究活動為焦點。若敘述以論文為焦點，我們可稱之為「論文導向」。這樣一來便會使用如 *paper, report, thesis* 或 *dissertation* 等詞來指代研究論文本身。如果論文所提供資料不受時間限制，那麼我們便應使用現在式。

論文導向（現在式）	研究主題
The purpose of this paper is The aim of this report is The objective of the present 　　paper is	to analyze the effect of X on Y. to determine whether X can be used to 　　increase Y. to show that X is superior to Y.
The present paper reports This report presents This thesis describes This thesis discusses	the results of experiments in which X was 　　mixed with Y. data collected during a two-year survey of X.
This paper proposes This thesis describes This letter presents	a new method of synthesizing X. a new algorithm for sorting X. a proof that X can be reduced to Y.

有些作者也會以 *we* 作主詞：

　　In this report, we present data collected during a two-year survey of X.

　　In this paper, we propose a new algorithm for sorting X.

上述例子都是用主動語態的句子，不過也可以用被動語態，例如：

　　In this paper, experimental results are presented to show that X.

　　In this report, a new synthesis method is described that dramatically reduces X.

　　In this thesis, a detailed analysis of X is presented to show that Y.

另外，因為句子所指涉的內容將要在下文中交代，所以也可以使用未來式：

論文導向（未來式）	研究主題
This paper will propose This thesis will present This paper will evaluate This paper will discuss	a new method for analyzing X. several approaches to improving X. a theory that attempts to explain X. new equations for expressing X.
This paper will argue This report will present evidence 　　to show This letter will present a proof In this paper, we will argue In this report, we will attempt 　　to show	that the conventional technique 　　generates errors in special cases. that Smith's hypothesis is false. that X is equivalent to Y.

要注意一點：當提到如 *purpose, aim* 或 *objective* 等名詞時，通常不應採用未來式，而用現在式。

如果作者意在介紹新技術或方法、分析問題、或提出論證，那麼報告則應採用「論文導向」來撰寫。如果報告的焦點傾向于介紹研究活動，旨在提供調查或實驗結果，那麼報告則應採用「研究導向」。採用「研究導向」時，可以用 *study, research, investigation* 或 *experiment* 等字眼指代該研究。另外，由於研究活動發生在過去，所以要用過去式。「研究導向」的兩個常用句型如下：

研究導向（過去式）	研究主題
The purpose of the experiment 　　reported here was The aim of this study was The objective of this research 　　was	to investigate the effects of adding X 　　to Y at various temperatures. to determine whether increasing X 　　affected Y.

研究導向	研究活動（過去式）
In the experiments reported 　　here, In the research described here, In this research, In the present investigation, In this study,	this theory was tested by examining X. we investigated the effects of X. samples of X were tested by placing 　　them in Y. a survey of X was conducted.

值得注意的是，無論是「論文導向」還是「研究導向」，上述例句都至少有一個名詞片語（如 *this paper* 或 *the experiment reported here*），能夠清楚表示句子指涉的是作者本人，而不是其他學者的研究。這點非常重要，步驟四的句子一定要讓讀者清楚知道，作者已經不再討論文獻回顧中的參考資料了，而是在說明自己的研究之目的或內容。所以下面例句斜體字強調的部分就顯得很不恰當：

In summary, previous methods are all extremely inefficient. *Hence a new approach is developed to process the data more efficiently.*

這個例句讀起來就會讓人覺得很困惑，這是因為它未能清楚表示何人何時要開發新技術。為令讀者瞭解要開發新技術的人就是作者自己，我們可將上述例句修改如下：

In summary, previous methods are all extremely inefficient. *In this paper, a new approach will be developed to process the data more efficiently.*

In summary, previous methods are all extremely inefficient. *In this paper, we will present a new approach that processes the data more efficiently.*

In summary, previous methods are all extremely inefficient. *This paper will present a new approach that processes the data more efficiently.*

In summary, previous methods are all extremely inefficient. *This paper presents a new approach that processes the data more efficiently.*

練習 13-2 研究導向及論文導向

在習題一至六中，請判斷該句是「研究導向」還是「論文導向」。在習題七至十中，請根據所屬導向填上正確動詞形式。

1. This paper addresses the problem of designing an adaptive force controller that asymptotically attains the tracking force objective.

2. This report describes a new method for reducing variance in common cases.

3. The purpose of this research was to investigate the effect of elastic scattering on the angular and depth distributions for the five electron lines of gold.

4. In the present paper, the nature of seasonal shell structural changes that occur in a common salt-marsh bivalve will be described in detail.

5. The objective of this research was to determine the variability of soil CO_2 temporally, spatially, and with depth in two acid soils in a mountainous, forested catchment.

6. In this study, we examined vertical nutrient mixing in late summer in a test area 20 kilometers off the coast.

7. The present paper _____ the influence of tempo and loudness on two types of hedonic responses to music. （論文導向）

8. The aim of this research _____ to determine the preferred viewing distance for work at a visual display unit. （研究導向）

9. This study _____ the direct and interactive relationships among several elements of the physical work environment. （研究導向）

10. This report _____ detailed data on sputtering yields in an oxygen ambient. （論文導向）

13.3 步驟五: 研究價值

在步驟五中，作者應指出研究結果可能產生的貢獻或用途，從而指出研究價值。有些研究報告會省略此步驟。一般而言，應學位考試委員會的要求，碩士、博士論文中都會包含此步驟，因此想取得學位，作者就必須指出論文之創意或貢獻。另外，因為工程方面的研究通常有實際用途，所以相關的研究報告也常常會包含步驟五。相反，那些意欲投稿到學術期刊的實驗報告，卻常常會省略這步驟。

一般而言，步驟五敘述的若不是研究的實用價值，就是其理論價值。若是實用價值，那麼作者會指出研究結果對某些具體的應用問題或工作有哪些參考價值。若是理論價值，那麼作者會指出該研究結果可能幫助某個領域中的研究人員說明某個現象、解決某個問題或提出未來的研究方向。以下都是步驟五的典型句式，分別摘錄自多篇研究論文。

應用價值

This research may provide a useful reference for researchers and managers attempting to increase employee productivity through optimization of the work environment.

The results reported here could be beneficial to educators attempting to design more effective language programs.

The results of this study may be of interest to managers and educators attempting to develop programming standards and may help to increase programmer productivity.

Data from this research may help other factories to reduce the impact of acidic effluent on the local environment.

This information should aid in the design of management schemes that will optimize the benefits of crop residues remaining on the soil surface.

理論價值

The results of this study may help to explain how the amount of fluorine incorporated into the films is affected by the presence of water in the immersing solution.

Our results may help to clarify whether the fission hypothesis or external origin hypothesis is valid.

Further data of this kind are of importance for the understanding of ion-beam-induced oxidation of silicon.

The results of this survey may aid researchers in better understanding the adverse health effects of long-term exposure to whole-body vibration.

Knowledge of the seasonal dynamics of soil CO_2 is necessary for a quantitive assessment of watershed acidification.

　　有些作者偶爾會利用介系詞片語、不定詞片語或關係子句把步驟四及五合併成一句，例如（步驟五以斜體字表示）：

> The objective of this study was to collect data on the results of various teaching methods *for reference in designing more effective language teaching programs.*

> The objective of this study was to collect data on the results of various teaching methods *in order to design more effective language teaching programs.*

> This paper describes a new channel assignment algorithm *that may significantly increase quality of service and system utilization.*

> This report presents experimental data on ozone decomposition *that may be of importance in explaining the breakdown of atmospheric ozone.*

　　另外，學者在說明研究價值的時候，往往會運用假設的語氣以示謙虛謹慎。例如，作者很少宣稱自己的研究能完全解決某個問題；反之，就算作者對研究結果非常有信心，也只會表示這些結果可能「幫助」我們解決某個問題，或能提供一個「可能」的答案。因此，為了表現得謙遜，作者常常會將語態助動詞和現在式主要動詞一起使用。語態助動詞清楚表示這只不過是臆測或假設：最常用的助動詞為 *may*，其次還有 *should* 及 *could*。

研究結果	現在式動詞加上語態助動詞	價值
Our results	may help	to clarify whether the fission hypothesis or the external origin hypothesis is valid.
The technique presented here	may facilitate	the development of advanced robotic vision systems.
The proposed technique	could be	useful in maximizing the efficiency of systems with heavy traffic.
The analysis presented in this paper	should simplify	the task of finding a comprehensive solution.

　　此外，若用到間接問句來介紹研究目的，則要利用語態助詞 *could* 或 *would*。

> The aim of this research was to investigate *whether* pilot back pain *could be reduced* by modifying the cockpit design.

> The purpose of this study was to determine *how* the addition of water *would affect* the reaction rate.

> This survey examined *whether* students' test scores *could be improved* by intensive preparation.

　　下表列出了步驟四及五中常用的語態助動詞以及其確定程度。

助動詞	確定程度	例句
will	最確定：表示作者一點也不懷疑句子的內容	The results of this experiment *will provide* further data concerning the performance of the two systems.
would	在某些條件下很確定：只要滿足條件，就確定	If a second processor were added, the system *would run* 40% faster.
should	很可能，但不完全確定	This modification *should improve* the efficiency of the system, but it has not yet been tested in practice.
may	句子所表達的事情是可能的，但作者不確定是否會發生	These findings *may be* useful to researchers attempting to increase employee productivity.
might	同上，但比較不確定	These data *might help* to clarify whether the fission hypothesis is valid.
could	作者更不確定事情是否會發生	Our results *could be* beneficial to educators attempting to design more effective language programs.

13.4 步驟六：文章組織

　　有些導論的結尾還會出現一個段落，用來說明研究報告的組織架構。我們可以把它稱為「步驟六」。只有在讀者不清楚報告的結構時，才有必要添加此步驟。一般來講，傳統實驗報告的組織結構往往大同小異，所以此步驟通常可以省略。相反，如果工學研究報告的組織結構複雜多變，那麼有些編輯及作者則認為有必要添加這樣一個段落來說明文章的組織。是否應該包括步驟六，建議先翻閱意欲投稿的期刊，以確定以往刊載的文章是否也包含此步驟。

　　下面給出步驟六的兩個典型範例。值得注意的是，這兩個段落的作者都盡量避免重複使用相同的句子結構；在內容上，兩個段落都提供了不少具體的信息，以便讓讀者瞭解整篇報告的內容及組織結構。

> This paper is organized as follows. In Section 1, we lay out the basic backstop capacity model, using a social planning framework. The analytic solution to this model is then outlined. In Section 2, we develop the Stackelberg model, in which the backstop capacity model is used for the follower, and the leader is the depletable resource sector. Finally, in Section 3 we present the results of numerical implementations of these two models. These numerical examples allow us to compare the Stackelberg and social planning solutions and to study the sensitivity of the models to backstop capacity costs. In Section 4, we summarize our results.

> The paper is organized as follows. Section 2 presents the dynamic models and problem formulation. Section 3 introduces the controller

structure for the ideal case, in which the exact dynamics and environment parameters are known. Section 4 presents the proposed adaptive scheme and the main stability result. Section 5 presents stronger analytical results for the single-link case. In section 6, the robustness of the scheme is discussed. Section 7 discusses simulation results for the single revolute link case. Finally, section 8 offers brief concluding comments.

如果步驟六為獨立的段落，那麼段首常會出現這樣的主題句：

The organization of this report is as follows.

This paper is organized as follows.

The remainder of this paper is organized as follows. 如果導論篇幅很長，此句便十分適用。

通常來講，步驟六句子裡的動詞不是用現在式就是未來式。請看下列例句：

現在式

Section 2 *presents* the basic analysis and describes the proposed method for finding the solution.

In section 2, the basic analysis *is presented* and the method for finding the solution is described.

Section 3 *describes* simulations in which the proposed algorithm was tested using three data sets.

In section 4, we *describe* experimental results that confirm the effectiveness of the proposed method.

In section 4, experimental results *are presented* that confirm the effectiveness of the proposed method.

The conclusions of the paper *are stated* in section 5.

Section 5 *summarizes* the conclusions of the paper.

Section 5 *presents* concluding remarks.

未來式

Section 2 *will present* the basic analysis and describe the proposed method for finding the solution.

Section 3 *will describe* simulations in which the proposed algorithm was tested using three data sets.

In section 4, we *will present* experimental results that confirm the effectiveness of the proposed method.

In section 4, experimental results *will be summarized* that confirm the effectiveness of the proposed method.

如以上例句所示，句子的動詞使用主動或被動語態均可適用。跟被動語態的句子相比，主動語態的句子通常比較簡短、直接、有力。然而，被動語態卻可讓作者以章節作為主詞，藉以強調章節的內容。採用被動語態時，應避免在句首嵌入過長的主詞，而接下來的動詞卻過於簡短。這種大頭小尾不平衡的句子讀起來讓人十分費神。請看以下例句：

> In section 4, experimental results that confirm the speed, accuracy, and reliability of the proposed fuzzy logic controller in a variety of common applications are presented.

這種句子應這樣修改（請參考本書第九章9.4節）：

> In section 4, experimental results are presented that confirm the speed, accuracy, and reliability of the proposed fuzzy logic controller in a variety of common applications.

> Section 4 presents experimental results that confirm the speed, accuracy, and reliability of the proposed fuzzy logic controller in a variety of common applications.

練習 13-3 步驟三至步驟五

下面列出兩篇研究報告的導論。第一篇導論的步驟一、二都已完成，但步驟三、四卻只有大綱，尚未完成（該導論的原作者省略了步驟五）。請根據大綱內容完成步驟三、四，並在必要之處填上動詞、冠詞、介系詞以及其它字詞。而第二篇導論的步驟三到五還尚未完成，請根據大綱內容將之完成。

Carrier Lifetime in MBE-grown Si:Sb and Si:In Layers

步驟一： 背景資料	Measurements of the carrier lifetime τ in a semiconductor material can give valuable information on the crystal and interface quality of the material. τ is also an important device parameter. In low-doped Si, grown by molecular beam epitaxy (MBE), τ is usually determined from the reverse characteristic of p-n diodes or by the Zerbst method [1]. Generation and recombination mechanisms have also been studied by DLTS measurements [2].
步驟二： 文獻回顧	
步驟三： 指出問題	Problem: at high doping levels conventional methods usually give erroneous values of τ because of the resistivity and short lifetime in such materials
步驟四： 研究目的	Research reported here: • investigated carrier recombination in MBE-grown silicon films highly doped with Sb or In • unlike earlier work, used transient grating method under strong pumping conditions—attempt to obtain more accurate values of τ

Integrating Formal and Functional Approaches
to Language Teaching in French Immersion

步驟一：
背景資料

The immersion approach to language teaching has become increasingly common in Canadian and American schools. In this approach, the children's second language is used as the language of instruction and means of communication for all or most of the school day. This provides children with the opportunity to learn their second language much as they had their first language, that is, through using it in natural and meaningful situations.

步驟二：
文獻回顧

Extensive research has attested to the effectiveness of immersion programs in enabling children to attain high levels of communicative proficiency in the second language, while at the same time allowing them to acquire subject matter content and progress in the mother tongue at rates equivalent to their peers in regular English programs (Swain and Lapkin, 1982; Genesee, 1987; Day and Shapson, 1989). However, research has also shown that there are still major gaps in immersion children's acquisition and control of many aspects of grammar despite the fluent, functional proficiency they achieve in their second language (Adiv, 1980, 1984; Harley and Swain, 1984; Day and Shapson, 1987).

步驟三：
指出問題

Many immersion educators: called for curriculum-based research—how to improve immersion students' oral and written grammar skills?

步驟四：
研究目的

Purpose of this research:

- conduct an experimental study to determine whether middle-school immersion students' acquisition and use of a specific grammatical form could be improved

- develop curricular materials integrating formal and functional approaches in order to effect this improvement

步驟五：
研究價值

Results of this research: of interest to educators involved in designing language immersion programs and teaching materials

第十四章
數學分析

在數學、理論科學以及工學研究報告中，導論之後常常會出現一篇較長的「分析」章節。作者會利用這章節來分析問題、解釋技術的理論基礎，或是說明所開發的理論模型。本章將討論撰寫「分析」章節的基本原則。

14.1 「分析」章節的基本結構

在不同論文中，「分析」章節的內容可能迴異，所以其結構便不會像研究報告的其它章節（例如導論）那樣有章可循。不過總的來說，「分析」章節通常會包含以下內容。

數學分析

在介紹數學分析的章節中，常常會涉及以下資料項目：

- 介紹題目
- 說明相關假設、條件或定義
- 敘述主要問題或基本的方程式
- 進行分析並得出結果（此項目可能重複多次）
- 說明或討論上述結果，或根據結果推出某種結論（此項目可能重複多次，或跟前一項穿插進行）

我們可以參閱下面的例子。此段落一開頭先介紹一個題目 ("Consider...")，然後再說明一些假設及定義 ("let...")。接下來，列出一條方程式並進行分析及演算。最後，根據整個段落的內容得出結論。

Consider a unitary matrix B whose eigenvalues $\mu_1, \mu_2, ..., \mu_n$ all lie on the unit circle. Let $P_N(z)$ be a polynomial that has a peak at $z = 1$ and is constructed to be close to zero on the unit circle away from the vicinity of $z = 1$. Let the eigenvectors of B be $g_1, g_2, ..., g_n$ and the initial vector v_0 be expanded as $v_0 = \sum_{j=1}^{n} \alpha_j g_j$. We have

$$u(\lambda) = P_N(e^{-i\lambda}B)v_0 = \sum_{j=1}^{n} \alpha_j P_N(e^{-i\lambda}\mu_j)g_j.$$

Clearly, if λ is chosen such that μ_{j_0} is close to $e^{i\lambda}$ and other eigenvalues of B are not "close" to $e^{i\lambda}$, then the coefficients of g_j will be small except when $j = j_0$. Thus $u(\lambda)$ can be regarded as an approximation to the eigenvector of μ_{j_0}. If the polynomial $P_N(z)$ is written as

$$P_N(z) = \sum_{j=0}^{N-1} \beta_j z^j,$$

then we have that

$$u(\lambda) = \sum_{j=0}^{N-1} \beta_j B^j v_0 e^{-ij\lambda}$$

$$= \sum_{j=0}^{N-1} \beta_j v_j e^{-ij\lambda},$$

where $v_j = B^j v_0$. Therefore, if the vectors v_j are computed first, the fast Fourier transform can be used to compute $u(\lambda)$ at many different values of λ simultaneously.

介紹模型

在介紹理論或數學模型的章節中，常出現的內容包括：

- 模型的背景或理論基礎（有時候需要引述其他學者的著作）
- 方法或模型之基本假設或根據（當模型有多個部分時，應就每個部分逐一說明其假設或根據）
- 基本方程式與分析
- 模型的詳細描述（當模型有多個部分時，應逐一討論每個部分，然後再作總結）

- 說明或討論模型的重要特性
- 解釋如何應用此模型，進而討論一些應用例子
- 對例子中的結果加以評論

此外，介紹完模型之後，一般還要比較模型所得出的推測和實驗數據分析，用來論證該模型是否有效。

下面是兩篇介紹不同模型的文章。在第一篇文章中，作者清楚交代了模型的背景，並詳細說明了製作模型的不同假設或條件。最後，作者給出了模型。在此報告的其餘章節中，作者還解釋了如何將自己的模型運用在許多特定問題上，並討論了模型對這些問題的理論涵義。在此，我們省略了這些章節。

The model and analysis presented here were originally developed in Powell (1983). A closely related discrete time model was developed by Switzer and Salant (1980) and recently published in French (Switzer and Salant 1986)....

We assume that a social planner controls the rate of production of all energy resources. These resources are of two types: depletable energy, which is costless to produce but available in a limited amount, and backstop energy, which has a constant production cost and unlimited (physical) availability. The two resources are perfect substitutes; that is, consuming a unit of each provides the same gross utility to society....

The social planner's problem is to choose the optimal rates of production of depletable and backstop energy, as well as the rate of investment in backstop capacity. We assume the existence of a concave social utility function defined on total energy production. Furthermore, we assume the planner's objective is to maximize the present value of social utility net of production and investment costs. The operative constraints are, first, that total production of depletable energy may not exceed the fixed stock; second, that backstop capacity increases in each period by the rate of backstop investment; and third, that backstop production is limited in each period by the current level of backstop capacity. Formally, the planner's problem can be written as follows....

在第二個例子中，作者一開始就介紹一個基本的方程式，並說明這個方程式以及一些重要的假設。然後，作者利用此方程式及其它資料得出一個模型。在這篇報告的其餘部分（在此省略），作者則討論了自己模型的各種特性。

In the absence of friction and other disturbances, the joint-space dynamics of an n-link constrained rigid robot manipulator can be written as

$$H'(q)\ddot{q} + C'(q,\dot{q})\dot{q} + g'(q) + J^{\mathrm{T}}(q)f_{\mathrm{e}} = \tau \qquad (1)$$

where q is the next n × 1 vector of joint displacement, t is the n × 1 vector of applied joint torques (or forces), $H'(q)$ is the n × n symmetric positive definite manipulator inertia matrix, $C'(q,\dot{q})\dot{q}$ is the n × 1 vector of centripetal and Coriolis torques, $g'(q)$ is the n × 1 vector of gravitational torques, $J(q)$ is the n × n manipulator Jacobian matrix, which is assumed to be non-singular, and F is the n × 1 vector of forces/moments at the end-effector. We assume that the manipulator described by (1) is non-redundant. We also assume that the robot is equipped with joint position and velocity sensors and a force sensor at its end-effector.

Now let us derive the Cartesian-space arm dynamics. Following Slotine and Li (1987), we first fix a frame of reference R_0 on the robot base and then use a set of independent parameters x, composed of the Cartesian position and Euler angles of the end-effector, to represent the end-effector configuration. Since the manipulator is assumed to be non-redundant, the vector x is also an n × 1 vector, and in a singularity-free region, it represents a set of generalized coordinates that completely describes the manipulator's motion. The relationship between joint positions and the end-effector configuration is

$$x = f(q) \tag{2}$$

with the corresponding velocity relation

$$\dot{x} = J(q)\dot{q} \tag{3}$$

where $J(q) = \partial f(q)/\partial q$ is the Jacobian matrix.

The Cartesian dynamic model can be derived directly from the joint-space model (1). Differentiating the velocity relation (3) and solving for $\ddot{q}$ yields

$$\ddot{q} = J^{-1}(q)[\ddot{x} - \dot{J}(q)\dot{q}] \tag{4}$$

Substitution of the above into (1) leads to

$$H'J^{-1}[\ddot{x} - \dot{J}\dot{q}] + C'J^{-1}\dot{x} + g' + J^{\mathrm{T}}F_e = \tau$$

where we have suppressed the arguments for brevity. Multiplication of both sides by J^{-T} leads to the Cartesian-space dynamics

$$H(x)\ddot{x} + C(x,\dot{x})\dot{x} + g(x) + F_e = F \tag{5}$$

with the following relations between the Cartesian and joint-space formulations:

$$\left.\begin{array}{l} F = J^{-T}\tau \\[4pt] H(x) = J^{-T}H'J^{-1} \\[4pt] C(x,\dot{x}) = -J^{-T}H'J^{-1}\dot{J}J^{-1} + J^{-T}C'J^{-1} \\[4pt] g(x) = J^{-T}g' \end{array}\right\} \tag{6}$$

Important properties of the Cartesian dynamics include the following....

基本要點

撰寫「分析」章節時，應該注意以下基本要點：

- 運用假設或引述概念前，先將其定義解釋清楚。
- 解決任何問題前，先把問題陳述清楚。
- 若需要討論的項目有很多，應有條不紊地逐一解決，並將這些項目之間的邏輯關係交代清楚。討論完一個問題後，要記得先將主要論點總結一下，再討論下一問題。

方程式標點符號的運用

科技論文的作者大都遇到過這樣的問題：數學方程式或公式雖然屬於句子一部份，但卻自成一行；若所屬句子須加標點，那麼公式之後是否還應加上標點呢？例如：

If V_{CC} and R_L are known, the load line equation may be written as

$$V_{CC} = I_C * R_L + V_{CE} .$$

這個例子的方程式位於句尾，因此 "V_{CE}" 之後有句點似乎頗合理。再看第二個例子：

Under these assumptions, the load line equation may be written as

$$V_{CC} = I_C * R_L + V_{CE} ,$$

where V_{CC} and R_L are known.

這個例子中，字詞 *where V_{CC} and R_L are known* 是修飾方程式的非限定關係子句，所以在文法上 "V_{CE}" 後面應有一逗點。

　其實，遇到這些情況時，加標點與否可以說是因人而異，並沒有一定規則。有些作者及期刊編輯認為在方程式與公式後面應加標點，因為這樣會令句子的文法結構更鮮明，文章更易閱讀。此外，為了避免混淆，有些時候一些公式後也會加上標點。不過有些作者及學術期刊卻會省略方程式或公式後面的標點，他們的理由可能是含有方程式或公式的句子的意思已很清楚，毋須再加標點釐清；另一個理由是，在含有大量數學公式的文章中使用標點符號會使頁面過於擁擠，所以刪繁就簡。我們看到，上文引述的兩篇文章，一篇在方程式後都使用了標點符號，另一篇則完全沒有。

　筆者認為，使用標點是較為合理的，因為方程式與公式確實是句子的一部分，因此建議使用。然而，在決定應否使用標點前，作者應先查閱投稿期刊的格式指引。

　至於沒有跟句子其餘部分區隔開來的數學方程式與公式，若句子結構有需要，也應使用標點符號。

方程式的位置

當數學方程式跟文章其餘部分區隔開來時，方程式上下要至少空一行，而且應縮進排印。縮排的距離應至少跟新段落首行縮進的距離一樣，最好比新段落首行縮進的距離還多一點（如 0.5 – 1.0 英寸）。有些學術期刊習慣把區隔開來的方程式排在頁面正中間（置中）。因此，投稿之前應查閱期刊的格式指引。

不少作者及期刊習慣在數學方程式的右方標上序號。此序號應放在括號內，而且方程式和序號之間應該留空白，不要用虛線把方程式和序號連起來。

14.2 時態

「分析」章節的內容大部分都是論述數學或邏輯關係，因此屬不受時間限制的普遍事實。敘述這些事實自然要使用現在式。請參看下面的例子：

Consider a unitary matrix B whose eigenvalues all lie on the unit circle.

Then we *have* the following equation: …

If A *is chosen* such that $A_1 = B_1$, then the two expressions *are* equivalent.

We *assume* that a social planner controls the rate of production of all energy resources.

The solution *can be obtained* by solving Equation (1).

The social planner's problem *is* to choose the optimal rates of production of depletable and backstop energy.

偶爾，作者也會採用未來式來介紹新題目，或過渡到新段落或新章節。用條件句表示可能的結果時，我們也可以使用未來式。

We *will* now *discuss* the nonlinear case.

In the next subsection, we *will show* how to solve this equation.

If an appropriate value of λ is chosen, then the coefficients of g_j *will be* small.

有時候，敘述模型或數學分析時，作者需要提及已完成的實驗研究。這時，由於實驗研究是作者過去的行為，而不是不受時間限制的事實，因此必須用過去式。請參看下例：

[1]For three modes, Equation (5) *provides* 42 equations. [2]If the stiffness matrix *is assumed* to be symmetric, then there *are* 105 unknown terms in the matrix. [3]Consequently, the coupling between nodes *must be* arbitrarily reduced. [4]In the initial evaluation of the experimental data, the coupling *was reduced* so that only adjacent nodes *were coupled* in the stiffness matrix.

此段落的前三句中，作者討論的是數學分析，由於是不受時間限制的事實，因此這三句便使用了現在式。然而，第四句則指作者過去的實驗研究，因此得使用過去式。

練習 14-1 時態

請在下面兩篇文章中填上適當的動詞形式。填上動詞時，應注意時態與語態（部分的動詞是被動語態）。

An Adaptive Controller

We _____ (*consider*) now the case in which the dynamic link parameters and the environment stiffness _____ (*be*) unknown. A pure controller _____ (*propose*) here to solve the resulting adaptive tracking control problem. The adaptive controller _____ (*consist*) of a control law and a parameter update law. Note that the adaptive controller _____ (*be*) not a "certainty equivalent" implementation of the inverse dynamics controller (8). A non-trivial modification, similar in spirit to the one needed for the adaptive control of linear systems of relative degree two, must _____ (*introduce*) to ensure global convergence.

An Important Assumption

Here we _____ (*assume*) that beyond some critical rate of investment (per period), the marginal cost of backstop capacity _____ (*increase*). The rationale for this assumption _____ (*be*) simple. Recall that the backstop _____ (*represent*) an entire industry, which _____ (*expect*) to grow very fast over a short time according to the standard model. Such growth _____ (*place*) severe demands on the supply of skilled labor and on scarce materials. At some rate of growth, these demands _____ (*begin*) to drive up the prices of these key inputs. Eventually, an absolute scarcity of some input _____ (*impose*) a hard constraint on the feasible rate of expansion of the backstop sector.

14.3 修辭原則與常用句型

　　與撰寫任何英文文章一樣，撰寫「分析」章節時要把文章寫得准確、清楚及簡潔，儘量避免過於生硬、晦澀的寫作手法（關於自然、順暢的英文寫作風格之進一步討論，請參考本書第六章）。在「分析」章節中，應採用自然、易讀的寫作方式，就如經驗豐富的教授在課堂上講課一樣。寫作時，千萬不要為了讓文章看起來很專業、很高深，而故意把文章寫得晦澀難懂；事實上，只要文章寫得簡單直接，論述又仔細清楚，讀者自然看得出作者的專業水準。

　　本章所摘引的例子，都寫得自然通順及易讀，是英文寫作的典範。我們可以看到，這些文章讀起來就像跟讀者說話一樣，或者就像我們坐在教室裡聽作者講解他們的數學分析一樣。這些文章寫的都是「正式」的英文——也就是說，作者並沒有使用俚語或非正式的言辭。儘管如此，文章卻顯得自然流暢，絲毫沒有矯揉造作的痕跡。

　　「方法」章節大多會避免使用 *we* 而多採用被動語態，但「分析」章節則恰恰相反。撰寫「分析」章節時，作者應儘量避免以 *it is*、*there is* 或 *there are* 為句子的開頭。如果覺得採用第一人稱複數代名詞 *we* 會使句子讀起來較自然通順，則不妨多加採用，而不要擔心文章看起來會「不夠正式」。請參看下列例句：

生硬：　*It is assumed here* that the social planner controls the rate of production of all energy resources.

自然：　*We assume* that the social planner controls the rate of production of all energy resources.

自然：　*Let us assume* that the social planner controls the rate of production of all energy resources.

自然：　*Assume* that the social planner controls the rate of production of all energy resources.

　　撰寫「分析」章節時，還須避免使用孤立的修飾詞 (dangling modifier)。這類修飾詞沒有明確的修飾對象，或是由於誤置而無法發揮任何修飾作用。另外，若句子旨在說明自己的目的、動機或興趣，則必須令讀者知道作者正在描述自己，而不是別人。(有關這些問題，請參本書第四章 4.7 節及 4.9 節之進一步討論。) 我們可以參考下列例句：

劣：　*Before describing the adaptive controller in detail,* the ideal case in which the dynamic model is exactly known will be considered.

佳：　Before describing the adaptive controller in detail, we will consider the ideal case in which the dynamic model is exactly known.

佳：　Before describing the adaptive controller in detail, we consider the ideal case in which the dynamic model is exactly known.

佳：　Before describing the adaptive controller in detail, let us consider the ideal case in which the dynamic model is exactly known.

在這個例子中，句首的片語沒有修飾對象，要將之改寫成後三句才成。我們再看下面的例句：

劣： The relationship between these two variables is now considered.

劣： The relationship between these two variables will now be considered.

佳： Now let us consider the relationship between these two variables.

佳： Consider the relationship between these two variables.

佳： These two variables are related in the following way.

佳： The two variables are inversely proportional to each other. When x increases...

這個例子中，首句並不能告訴讀者誰在考慮兩個變數的關係，而且動詞時態亦不自然；第二句的時態雖然正確，但我們仍然不知道誰是施事者。第三、四句明確指出是作者自己考慮，所以句意清楚。後兩句則直接描述二者的關係，不另加施事者，句意亦清楚明白。特別是最後一句將引介詞省略掉，表達更加直接。

常用句型

下面是「分析」章節常用句型的例子。要進一步瞭解如何撰寫行文自然、組織嚴謹的「分析」章節，則要多參閱所屬研究領域的專家撰寫的研究報告。

Consider the case in which A is equal to B.

As an example, consider the case in which A = B.

Let us now consider the case in which A = B.

We assume that A = B.

Let A be equal to B.

If A = B, then we have the following equation: [列出方程式]

Given that A = B, we obtain... [列出方程式]

This problem can be written as... [列出方程式]

This problem can be expressed as... [列出方程式]

This problem can be written as follows: [列出方程式]

Substituting A into Equation 2, we obtain... [列出方程式]

We will now integrate Equation 3 in order to derive the solution.

A is inversely proportional to B, as shown below.

The relationship between A and B is as follows: [列出方程式]

The relationship between A and B can be expressed as... [列出方程式]

The solution is... [列出方程式]

We can now derive the solution to Equation (3).

We will now reduce Equation (3) to a simpler form.

Given these assumptions, the system can be modeled as follows: [列出方程式]

Under these conditions, the equation can be rewritten as shown below.

第十五章

方法章節

「方法與材料」("Method and Materials") 或「方法」("Method") 章節在研究報告中扮演了極為重要的角色，因為讀者可以通過這一章節來了解作者的研究方法是否正確可行，進而判斷其研究結果是否有效。本章將討論作者在撰寫「方法」章節時應注意的要點。

工學研究報告若旨在介紹新技術、新模型或演算法，那麼通常要有一個章節專門描述對這等新技術進行的測試過程。這類章節的寫作原則跟「方法」章節大同小異，讀者也可以參考本章的說明。

15.1 基本內容及組織

實驗報告的「方法」章節必須將作者的實驗程序說明得既清楚又詳細，以便讓其他學者能按照這一過程重複作者的實驗。因此，本章節應包括下列基本內容：

- 描述所採用的材料、儀器以及設備。
- 逐步解釋實驗程序。

此外，若有需要，還可能會包含下列內容：

- 概述整個實驗（只用一兩句交代即可）。
- 描述調查的抽樣 (sample) 或樣本總體 (population)。這部份的內容可能會包括下列項目：
  - 關於抽樣所屬樣本總體背景資料的描述。
  - 抽樣的方法或基準。

- 樣本的限制或特殊條件。
- 實驗環境的特殊情況，如極高或極低溫度、極高或極低電壓、輻射、特殊的光線等等。
- 選用特定材料、設備或方法的理由。
- 實驗設備或方法（包括問卷或測驗的內容）之詳細描述。
- 對所採用的統計分析方法的描述（一般作者把這些資料放在「方法」章節中，但也有一些作者習慣放在「結果」章節）。

　　至於應該如何安排「方法」章節的內容，則要視研究領域、學術期刊及作者的習慣而定，並沒有一定的準則。不過一般來說，作者應按照實驗進行的先後次序來敘述。也就是說，在「方法」章節之首，應先對整個實驗作概述，並描述此實驗的預備工作以及研究對象、樣本或材料。之後，應按順序描述實驗程序的步驟。（有時候，實驗步驟及材料的描述可以合併在一起。）最後，還要說明一下如何收集實驗結果及分析結果，或對所採用的儀器設備進行描述。

　　如果研究程序中包括測驗或問卷調查，那麼在描述完研究對象之後，應敘述測驗或問卷的內容（也有作者將這些內容放在統計分析方法前敘述)。

　　某些研究領域的作者常常把「方法」章節分成幾個小節，每小節專門介紹上述其中一項內容。以社會科學的研究報告為例，可能會有一個小節專門描述研究對象以及抽樣方法，另一個小節則專門描述測試或調查方式以及測驗或問卷的內容。而化學或物理實驗報告還可能會有一個小節專門描述實驗材料、儀器或設備。

　　下面的例子，就「方法」章節的標準寫法給出了示範，其內容均是「方法」章節常見的內容。文章有刪節，原文對樣本（研究對象）、研究程序、測驗方式與測驗內容的描述都要詳細得多。

An Experimental Approach to Language Teaching

Method

概述

To evaluate the effect of the proposed approach to language teaching, pretests, posttests, and follow-up tests of oral and written French were administered to experimental and control classes comprising 350 grade 7 French immersion students in a large metropolitan area. In all, 12 classes participated in the study.

抽樣方法及樣本的特性

Classes were selected that were similar in general socioeconomic background and ability level of the students and in the teaching experience of the instructors. The assignment of classes to the experimental or control group was stratified by district and made on a random basis; the pretest results and information provided by the school districts were used to match the two groups. There were six classes in each group, with between 25 and 30 students in each class....

實驗程序

The experimental group received instruction in a specially designed curriculum unit over a period of five to seven weeks, while the control group received normal classroom instruction....Written and oral measures of French were administered to both groups prior to the beginning of the experimental curriculum (pretest) and immediately after its completion (posttest). Tests were administered near the end of the school year to determine the long-term effects of the treatment (follow-up test).

測驗方式　　The test instruments developed for the study consisted of a cloze test, a written composition, and an oral interview. The cloze tests consisted of....

統計分析　　Statistical comparisons were made between the pretest results of the two groups to determine their relative standing at the start of the experiment. Repeated measures analysis of variance was used to statistically compare the progress of the two groups in French writing and speaking over the three testing times. Only students who participated in all three testing sessions were included.

練習 15-1 內容排列

下列句子摘錄自一篇研究報告的「方法」章節，但卻沒有依照原來的次序列出。請根據句子的內容將這段文字排列順序。

Observational Learning in Octopuses

____ Demonstrators were trained through a series of trials in which two balls, one red and one white, were presented to the animal. When the animal attacked the correct ball, it was rewarded with a piece of fish, and when it attacked the incorrect ball, it was punished by an electric shock.

____ Videotape analysis showed that observer octopuses increased their attention during each of the four trials.

____ Statistics on the observers' performance were analyzed and compared with those on the learning of the demonstrators.

____ Experiments to investigate the ability of *Octopus vulgaris* to learn by observation were conducted in three phases: training of demonstrators, observation of the task by untrained octopuses, and testing of observers.

____ In the testing phase, observer octopuses were tested with a session of five trials with both white and red balls randomly positioned. No reward or punishment was given for any choice made.

____ In the observational phase, an untrained octopus observed four trials during which a demonstrator in an adjacent tank attacked the ball it had been taught to attack.

15.2　實驗程序的描述

　　由於「方法」章節所描述的研究方法或實驗程序都屬作者過去開展的研究活動，所以通常要用過去式。有時，「方節」章節中的句子也會用到現在式。當然這些句子描述的不是作者在過去進行過的研究工作，而是敘述一般的普遍事實或實驗標準程序，也可能是指涉論文本身的內容，就像「論文導向」裏面的句子一樣。（關於動詞時態之進一步討論，請參考本書第三章。）

　　下文摘錄自一篇典型的方法章節，請注意文中的時態用法。

The Effect of Indentation on
Program Comprehension

Method

The experiment *was conducted* at a large university in the Midwest, and the subjects *were* 72 students from a junior-level Fortran and Pascal computer science course. Typical enrollees in this course *include* computer science and engineering students. The experiment *was administered* during a regular session of the class. At the time of the experiment the students *had* already *been exposed* to Pascal for four weeks, and each student *had written* at least two programs in Pascal.

　　The experimental design *was* of the "posttest only different treatment" variety. In this type of procedure, subjects *are* randomly *assigned* to one of several groups (in our case, three). Subjects in all groups *perform* the same tasks, with the only difference being the experimental treatment (in our case, the indentation of the programs). Performance measures (comprehension scores) *were collected* for each subject to see if the different treatments led to different levels of performance.

　　During the instruction session before the experiment, the subjects *heard* a prepared speech describing the experiment. Then the 72 subjects *were* randomly *divided* into three groups by stacking the three instruments in an alternating order to achieve an equal number of subjects in each group. The treatment *was* a Pascal implementation of the hangman game written in one of three styles of indentation. The data gathered *were* the student scores on a test of 10 comprehension questions. The tests for the control and "excessive" indentation groups *are shown* in Figure — ; the test for the moderate indentation group *is shown* in Figure —....

當作者描述實驗步驟時，應使用過去式：

> The experiment *was conducted* at a large university in the Midwest.
> The 72 subjects *were* randomly *divided* into three groups.

描述不受時間限制的普遍事實時，要用現在式：

> Typical enrollees in this course *include* computer science and engineering students.

至於學者常採用的標準程序，由於是普遍事實，所以要用現在式：

In this type of procedure, subjects *are* randomly *assigned* to one of several groups.

Subjects in all groups *perform* the same tasks.

當指涉研究報告的其它部份時，也要用現在式：

The tests for the control and "excessive"2 indentation groups *are shown* in Figure 3.

由於「方法」章節的內容大都為實驗程序（即作者過去的行為），所以句子多使用過去式，只有少數使用現在式。另外，如上例所示，「方法」章節還可能會用到過去完成式。關於過去完成式的用法，我們會在下一節進一步解釋。

最後要補充一點以結束本節的討論。有些學科的論文會用第二個章節來介紹作者開發的模型或技術；由於這類章節實際上是在作數學分析，所以大多使用現在式(請參閱本書第四章)。這類論文在「分析」章節之後通常會緊接著一章節，用來描述作者對該技術或模型所作的測試。由於這些測試不屬於數學分析，而是作者過去的活動，因此跟一般「方法」章節描述實驗程序一樣，要使用過去式。

練習 15-2 時態

請在下面文章中填上適當的動詞形式（提示：其中一些動詞可能是被動語態）。

Viewing Distances in VDU Work

The subjects _____ (*have*) two video display unit (VDU) work periods of 30 minutes each. The screen viewing distance _____ (*be*) 50 cm in one period and 70 cm in the other. The document viewing distance _____ (*be*) 50 cm in both periods. Between the two work periods, the subjects _____ (*rest*) for 45 minutes, during which time they _____ (*leave*) the experimental room. After a further rest of 10 minutes, subjects _____ (*perform*) the VDU task for 15 minutes. During this work period the screen viewing distance _____ (*adjust*) to the most comfortable position as indicated by each subject.

The VDU task _____ (*design*) so that frequent gaze shifts between the screen and document _____ (*be*) necessary. The screen and the document _____ (*contain*) a list of 20 names, each _____ (*follow*) by a four-digit number. The names on the screen and document _____ (*be*) identical, but

some of the numbers corresponding to the names _____ (*be*) different. The

subjects _____ (*have*) to compare the numbers for each name and press one

of two keys on the keyboard to indicate whether the numbers _____ (*be*)

identical or not....

如何使用被動語態與主動語態

前面講到，「方法」章節用於描述實驗步驟以及實驗材料。既然實驗步驟及實驗材料才是「方法」章節的重點，同時讀者亦明白是作者自己應用材料進行了實驗，所以在撰寫「方法」章節時一般都會使用被動語態。

有些作者偶爾還會使用 "we" 當作主詞，不過這通常是為了強調作者在實驗中的角色 — 例如，當作者提出假設或建議，或解釋行為目的時候，便會使用 "we" 當作主詞。此外，還有少數作者喜歡較口語化的表達，因此也會採用 "we"。然而，大部分學科（尤其在物理、化學等純科學領域）的研究報告都比較習慣採用被動語態，而不用 "we"。因此，讀者應該參閱一些刊登於著名學術期刊的文章，以確定所屬研究領域的學者是否有使用 "we" 的習慣。

請參看下列例句。大多數作者會捨句一而取句二，儘管句一也是正確的語法：

We immersed the samples in an ultrasonic bath for 3 minutes in acetone followed by 10 minutes in distilled water.

The samples were immersed in an ultrasonic bath for 3 minutes in acetone followed by 10 minutes in distilled water.

同樣，多數作者會選擇下面第二個句子：

To evaluate the influence of nitrogen and carbon monoxide on SiO_2 sputtering, *we performed two experiments* in which these gases were introduced through the leak valve during sputtering.

To evaluate the influence of nitrogen and carbon monoxide on SiO_2 sputtering, *two experiments were performed* in which these gases were introduced through the leak valve during sputtering.

請再看看下列例句。第一句表達了作者的信念，但卻因為使用了被動語態，讀起來很彆扭、很生硬。相比之下，第二和第三句都較可取。

For the second trial, the apparatus was covered by a sheet of plastic. *It was believed* that this modification would reduce the amount of scattering.

For the second trial, the apparatus was covered by a sheet of plastic. *We believed* this modification would reduce the amount of scattering.

For the second trial, the apparatus was covered by a sheet of plastic to reduce the amount of scattering.

15.3 對材料或設備的描述

撰寫科技論文時，作者有時候要花一整段甚至幾段來專門描述研究所採用的材料。這些材料可能包括實驗設備、機器、儀器、研究對象（如人、動物或材料）、化學品或其它材料、問卷或測驗、電腦軟件或數學模型等等。

當作者需要詳細描述實驗材料時，通常會先對材料做一概述，然後再詳細描寫材料的結構、主要成分或主要特性。若是描述儀器設備的話，則通常還會解釋這些設備的功能與運作方式。請參考下例：

A Twin-lens Reflex Camera

A twin-lens reflex camera is actually a combination of two separate camera boxes (see Figure 1). On top is the viewing box, which contains a fixed mirror (1) and ground glass (2). The viewing box is used only for viewing and focusing. The photograph is made on the film plane (6) in the lower box. Two lenses of equal focal length are mounted on a common plate (3) that is moved forward and backward to focus the camera. The viewing lens (4) is used for viewing and focusing; the taking lens (5) is used for taking the photograph. When the shutter release is pressed, the shutter in the taking lens opens, allowing light to pass through and form an image on the film plane.

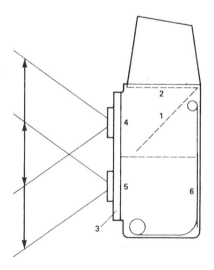

Figure 1. A twin-lens reflex camera.

如上例所示，對於材料或設備的主要組成之描述常常出現依空間順序的組織形式。（材料或設備的主要部份，通常是順著空間次序來描述的。）作者從上到下、從前到後或從左到右地描述某些設備的每個部分。這是最常見的組織形式，而且在描述許多不同零件所組成的設備時，此組織形式也特別適當。（這種描述方式很常見；尤其是當設備由許多不同零件組成時，這樣描述也就更合適。）

除此之外，我們還可據各部份的功能來依次描述。也就是說，作者按照設備運作的先後次序來描述各部份。若運作次序是固定不變的，那麼我們也可以說這是按時序的組織方式。例如，若按功能的次序來將上例重寫：

> On a twin-lens reflex camera (see Figure 1), light passes through the viewing lens (4) and is reflected by a fixed mirror (1) onto a ground glass (2). The photographer views the image on the ground glass and focuses the camera by moving a common plate (3) on which both the viewing lens and the taking lens (5) are mounted. When the shutter release is pressed, the shutter in the taking lens opens, allowing light to pass through and form an image on the film plane (6).

雖然材料描述有時候會跟「方法」章節的其餘部分分隔開來，然而卻常常與實驗步驟的描述合併在一起。如此一來，作者就可以在同一句中描述實驗程序及材料。請看下例：

Sample Preparation

All samples were prepared in <u>a V-80 molecular beam epitaxy system (Vacuum Generators)</u> that had a base pressure of 5×10^{-11} Torr. The substrates were <u>FZ Si(100) wafers</u> with a doping density on the order of 10^{15} cm^{-3}. Before they were introduced into <u>the vacuum system</u>, the substrates were cleaned by a wet chemical oxide etch regrowth procedure. In addition, the final removal of the surface oxide was carried out *in situ* by direct current heating of the sample to 900° C for 5 min. The substrate temperature was measured with <u>an infrared pyrometer</u> and maintained at 800° C during growth. The Si MBE layers were grown to a thickness of 2 mm at a growth rate of 0.8 mm h^{-1}, and were homogeneously doped with <u>Sb or In</u> by low-energy accelerated ion beam doping. <u>The dopant ion beams</u> were provided by <u>single grid broad-beam ion sources</u>; an ion energy of 200 eV was used. The ion flux was measured by <u>a Faraday cup</u> that was placed at the substrate position....

這個段落中有不少句子既描述了作者的行為，又描述了所採用的材料或設備（畫線的部分）。此種組織形式在科技研究報告中很常見，尤其在物理、化學以及生物學等領域。

描述實驗程序與材料時，為了採用最合適的組織形式，應該多參考所屬研究領域其他學者的文章。不同領域的學者可能有不同的習慣。例如，物理學家習慣的寫法可能會跟社會學家的有很大的差別。

時態

描述研究對象或材料之句子，可能會使用過去式或現在式。若句子的內容為不受時間限制的普遍事實，則應使用現在式；若句子的內容為特定、過去的行為或事件，則應使用過去式。例如，作者通常要用現在式來描述一般學者通常使用的標準設備。由於標準設備可為所有人使用，描述這類普遍事實的句子也就要用現在式。上面引述照相機的一段文字就是一例：因為文中的標準相機乃是任何人都可以購得、使用，而不是作者特別為了實驗而設計的，所以整個描述都應採用現在式。

> A twin-lens reflex camera *is* actually a combination of two separate camera boxes.

> The viewing box *is used* only for viewing and focusing.

下面一段文字為另一典型例子。段落首句交代作者過去的行為，因此使用過去式。第二和第三句則描述現在仍然可以為其他學者使用的某檯機器。因為這兩句描述的是不受時間影響之事實，所以都採用現在式。

> The work *was carried out* on the Imperial College gas atomizer, which has been described in detail elsewhere [4, 5]. The plant *operates* vertically upwards and *uses* a return gas flow to obtain a clear view of the atomizing jet. Under controlled conditions, oxygen *is fed* into the return gas at a level of 1% by volume to passivate the powder by forming a layer of oxide.

相反，在描述作者特別為了研究計劃而設計、製造或改裝之特殊設備，通常需要使用過去式。這是因為這些設備是過去為了特定用途而設計，而不是一般學者都可以使用的。

> The probes *consisted* of pieces of narrow plastic tubing inserted through wider pieces of plastic tubing, so that the smaller tubing *extended* 2 cm beyond each outer piece on one end and 8 cm beyond on the other end.

> Privacy was measured by summing the responses to a five-item questionnaire modified from one used by Sundstrom (1980). The scale *contained* five yes/no questions that *asked* whether the participant's workspace was enclosed by a partition or wall.... Questions used to assess the subjective evaluation of the workspace *asked* for ratings on seven-point scales....

注意，若採用不同的時態，句子的意義也會隨之改變。下面的例句由於使用了過去式的緣故，所以讀者能夠清楚知道作者描述的設備是為了實驗而特別設計並製造的：

> The sample holders *were* specially *designed* to prevent slippage during measurement. The samples *were held* by large aluminum clamps covered with sandpaper.

如果把句子的動詞改為現在式，句意就會改變：讀者會誤以為作者描述的設備或產品是任何人都可以購得並應用的。

> The sample holders *are* specially *designed* to prevent slippage during measurement. The samples *are held* by large aluminum clamps covered with sandpaper.

在描述樣本和抽樣（研究對象）時，時態的應用規則跟上述原則相若。對樣本（種群）的描述一般是不受時間限制的普遍事實，因此句子要使用現在式。同時這類句子常常會用到如 generally, typically 或 usually 等副詞。請看下列例句：

Students in these programs typically *have* three hours of instruction per day in French.

Enrollment in the course generally *consists* mainly of computer science and engineering students.

Most employees at this level *are* young and comparatively inexperienced.

　　相反，描述特定的抽樣或研究對象時則要採用過去式。這是因為這些研究對象是過去為研究計劃特別選取的。請參看下列例句：

The sample *consisted* of 350 grade 7 students from four school districts in a large Western city.

The average age of the first group of subjects *was* 22, and the average age of the second group *was* 40.

All of the salesmen in the sample *had* at least two years of experience in their current job.

之所以必須用過去式，是因為多數有關抽樣的事實，只在研究計劃中才有效。研究計劃一旦結束，這些事實可能就會馬上改變。例如，上面第一句所描述的抽樣個體，只要研究計劃一結束便會隨之解散；而第二句的研究個體，其年齡在研究計劃結束後都會增長；至於第三句，研究計劃完成後，那些業務員可能會轉換工作。因此，這些句子都要用過去式來描述。

　　此外，描述研究對象時偶爾還會用到過去完成式。當要敘述過去特定時間前已完成的行為或事件，便要用到過去完成式。以下面的句子為例，首句之所以用過去完成式來描述學生對電腦程式語言的學習，是因為這是實驗進行前已經發生的。而第二句則表示，在作者進行測試時，橋樑已經使用了五年。

At the time of the experiment, the students *had* already *been exposed* to Pascal for four weeks, and each student *had written* at least two programs in Pascal.

At the time of testing, the first bridge *had been* in use for five years.

練習 15-3 對材料和樣本的描述

　　請指出下列句子的描述對象：標準設備或材料、作者特別設計或改裝的材料、一般樣本、特定的抽樣研究。

1. The tests consisted of dialogues in which blanks were substituted for missing verbs.

2. Despite the fluency immersion students achieve in their second language, there are still major gaps in their acquisition and control of many aspects of grammar.

3. The calibrated bellows pump delivers known quantities of air through disposable gas sampling tubes.

4. The subjects were 60 college freshmen and sophomores enrolled in an introductory psychology course.

5. The VDU had a 14-inch screen with a background luminance of 6 cd/m^2.

6. The Minnesota Satisfaction Questionnaire uses a five-point Likert-type scale ranging from very satisfied (a value of 5) to very dissatisfied (a value of 1).

語態

在「方法」章節中，作者通常會使用被動語態來描述自己的行動，如實驗程序：

The subjects *were* randomly *divided* into three groups.

The samples *were immersed* in an ultrasonic bath for 3 minutes in acetone.

相反，若作者描述的不是自己的行動，而是實驗設備或材料的運作或反應時，則一般會使用主動語態。

The apparatus *measured* both instantaneous elastic deformation and subsequent stress relaxation.

The lasers *transmitted* upstream signals on preassigned optical wavelengths.

A dense wavelength-division multiplexing device at the remote node *separates* the signals and *routes* them onto dedicated distribution fibers.

要注意，上面例句所描述的設備可以自行運作，而不是作者來操作這些設備。

作者有時亦會使用被動語態來描述實驗設備的運作。如果用到被動語態，那就要用 by 開頭的片語來指出是甚麼設備導致了句子所描述的運作。

The white noise *was recorded by* a tape recorder.

Power *was supplied by* a portable generator.

The ion flux *was measured by* a Faraday cup.

請留意，只有及物動詞才可以有被動形式。及物動詞之後可以跟直接受詞，不及物動詞則不可以。因此，不及物動詞也就根本沒有被動語態。有關這問題的詳細討論，請參考本書第四章4.7節。

練習 15-4 方法章節

下面是一篇研究報告的導論，但「方法」章節卻尚未完成，只有大綱而已。請根據大綱加上適當的動詞、冠詞、介系詞及其它字詞造句，並組織句子完成「方法」章節。撰寫時要留心本章介紹過的時態及語態的使用原則。

The Influence of Tempo, Loudness, and Gender on Responses to Music

Music and marketing cross paths in several places where psychology can provide valuable insight. For example, music is a common background feature in advertising and is frequently present as an atmospheric feature in retail environments. Music is also an important product itself. In the United States alone, recorded music constitutes a $5.6 billion industry (Lieberman, 1988).

Consumers typically receive exposure to many hours of music each day, in homes, cars, the workplace, stores, restaurants, and other locations. Much of this exposure is involuntary and controlled by marketers. Given the pervasiveness of music in our lives and its potential importance to marketers, it is not surprising to see a resurgence of interest in the topic among consumer researchers....

It has been common practice in marketing studies to treat music as a unidimensional stimulus. For example, studies have examined the effects of music's presence or absence (Park and Young, 1986) and the effects of appealing versus adversive music (Gorn, 1982). The treatment of music as a unidimensional stimulus has led to inconsistent and conflicting findings. For example, studies have found the presence of music to enhance (Galizio and Hendrick, 1982; Hoyer et al., 1984), inhibit (Haley et al., 1984; Macklin, 1988), and have no effect (McEwen and Leavitt, 1976; Ogilvy, 1982) on responses to persuasive communication. . . . Moreover, the few studies that have attempted to isolate the effects of objective structural characteristics of music have tended to ignore the possibility of nonlinear or interactive effects of musical components (Kellaris and Kent, 1991)....

The present study extends previous research by exploring the influence of two objective stimulus properties of music—tempo and loudness—and gender on two types of hedonic responses to music: listeners' judgments of the music's emotional character and behavioral intentions toward the music.

Method

Overview

Experiment:

- subjects randomly assigned to treatment groups
- exposed to music from a loudspeaker
- asked to fill out a questionnaire

Stimuli:

- two levels of tempo (slow and fast)
- two levels of loudness (soft and loud)
- third factor: gender (male or female)

Subjects

- fifty-two volunteers (26 males and 26 females)
- recruited from an introductory class at a large urban university
- ages: from 19 to 34; median age of 21
- most subjects: some previous musical training
- no musical experts

Stimuli

- different versions of an original classical-style musical composition
  - two versions created in a digital sound studio: fast version (120 BPM) and slow version (60 BPM)
- loudness: manipulated by presetting volume controls on amplifiers that powered loudspeakers in listening rooms
  - average sound level of 60 dB (soft conditions) and 90 dB (loud conditions)

Procedure

- subjects taken to small soundproof listening room equipped with table and chairs
- subjects instructed:
  - not to talk
  - to leave the questionnaire face down on the table until after the music stopped
  - to complete the questionnaire immediately after the music finished

Measures

- subjects' judgments of the music's affective character measured by using 16-item adjective checklist
  - subjects circled adjectives that best described music
- behavioral intent toward the music measured by asking subjects whether they would want to listen to the music again

第十六章
結果章節

　　研究報告的「結果」章節，顧名思義，是用來介紹研究的結果，並對該結果加以評論或作總結。「結果」的文字部分會指出重要的結果並加以說明，或在此基礎上進一步展開推論。除了文字部分以外，「結果」章節通常還會包括圖表或表格，以及用數字詳細列出的完整研究結果。

16.1 基本內容及組織

　　「結果」章節的內容通常可分為三大類：

　　一、研究結果的介紹。通常是用一句話告訴讀者可以在哪個圖表中看到完整的研究結果。

　　二、對最重要的結果予以描述或概述。

　　三、對於研究結果的評論，或根據這些結果得出的推論。

　　這三類內容在同一章節中可能會重複多次；甚至有時候在每個段落均會出現。如果用這三類內容組成一個段落的話，第一類內容可作為段落的首句，第二類則是段落的主要部份，而第三類則是段落最後一兩句。請參考下例：

Incidence of Back Pain in Helicopter Pilots

Results

[1]Table 1 presents the data on the prevalence of back pain directly associated with flight. [2]Particularly high back pain prevalences were reported after flights of more than 2 hours duration or after a period of intensive flying. [3]Moreover, civilian pilots, with their greater accumulated flight time, reported a greater prevalence of back pain after flights of all durations. [4]It appears that both the flight duration and total accumulated flight time affect the incidence of back pain.

	Army Pilots ($n = 87$)		Civilian Pilots ($n = 39$)	
	%	(abs)	%	(abs)
After or during each flight	11	(9)	14	(5)
A flight < 2 h	11	(9)	33	(11)
A flight > 2 h	35	(28)	72	(26)
A flight with a high level of concentration	30	(24)	53	(18)
Period > 20 h/week	48	(38)	74	(26)

Table 1. Prevalence of back pain directly associated with flight.

在這個例子中，首句介紹了作者將要討論的數據，並告訴讀者可以在哪個表格中看到這些數據。第二和第三句則敘述了最重要的結果。第四句是對這些結果的評論──這個評論是根據表格一的數據得出的。

我們可以留意到，在描述表格的資料時，作者並沒有將所有數據羅列出來，而僅僅指出兩個最重要的事實。撰寫研究論文時，作者應避免把文章的內容跟圖表寫得一模一樣；換句話說，千萬不要在文章中把圖表的所有信息複述一遍。詳細的研究結果要用圖表列出，而資料之重要特性或趨勢則應該用文字來交代。例如，若要介紹下面圖表二的資料，下列句子便顯得不適當：

In 1986, enrollment was 20, in 1987, it was 30, in 1988, it was 40...

較為恰當的寫法應是這樣：

Enrollment increased dramatically between 1986 and 1991, reaching a peak of 60 students in 1990.

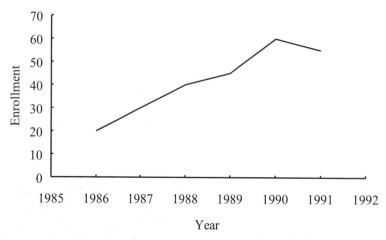

Figure 2. Enrollment in Chinese classes, 1986–1991.

　　如上例所示，介紹研究結果時，作者應將結果的涵義說明得清楚明白。不要光在圖表中把一大堆數據列出來，讓讀者自行解讀。作者最好直接告訴讀者這些數據呈現了怎樣的發展趨勢、蘊含了甚麼意義。另外，還要清楚交代基於圖表可以得出甚麼結論，而資料又是如何支持作者的推論等。如果報告還包括獨立的「討論」章節的話，那麼應留到「討論」章節再詳細討論研究結果。儘管如此，「結果」章節還是應該對研究結果做一些基本解釋，以便讓讀者容易了解此項研究究竟得到了甚麼樣的結果。此外，如有必要，也可以在這個章節說明數據分析的方法。

　　陳述研究結果時，作者討論的數據應「足以」支持自己對研究結果的解釋及推論。「足以」就是不要「過多」，不要列出過多的數據，讓讀者無法消化，或不能輕易看出數據如何能支持作者的解釋或推論。至於詳細的數據，則應用表格列出。

　　最後，要提供充足的圖表資料，充足到就算沒有文字的參照也能大致了解圖表的內容。大家會發現，如果圖表的標題與圖例標注清晰會很有用：例如在做會議簡報時，作者可以把這些圖標直接拿來當作投影片，這樣一來就算觀眾還未看到報告，也可以大致了解圖表的內容。

16.2 介紹研究結果

　　在「結果」章節之首，以及許多新段落的開首，常常會有句子介紹研究結果，這類句子通常會指出研究結果在哪個圖表或表格中列出。

> The variation in the temperature of the samples over time is shown in Figure 2.

> Figure 2 shows the variation in the temperature of the samples over time.

由於圖表所列出的研究結果不受時間限制，所以這類句子都使用簡單的現在式。除了主要動詞 *show* 之外，常用的動詞還包括 *present, display, summarize*（僅適用於作總結的圖表），*depict* 以及 *illustrate*（這兩個動詞只適用於圖形）。

如上例所示，在介紹研究結果時，可以將研究結果當作主詞，並採用被動語態表達；同時，也可以把圖表當作主詞，採用主動語態。那麼該如何決定使用哪種語態呢？在決定採用何種語態時，作者應考慮兩點：句子論述的重點以及作為主詞之名詞片語的長度。由於「結果」章節的重點是結果本身，所以在介紹研究結果時，將指稱結果之名詞片語當作主詞會比較好。不過一旦這個名詞片語太長，把它作為主詞便會令句子結構不平衡，看起來也不自然。要知道，一般人閱讀句子時，會期望儘快看完句子的主詞及動詞；若主詞太長的話，讀者可能要看很久才知道那是主詞。因此，若指涉研究結果的名詞片語太長，則不妨把該片語當作受詞，而把指涉圖表的片語當作主詞。有關這問題的進一步討論，請本書第九章9.4節。

此外，我們也可以採用其它形式來介紹研究結果。比如說開篇便單刀直入，指出結果，並用一個片語或括號告訴讀者可以參照哪個圖表。以下是常用的句型：

The temperature increased rapidly, as shown in Figure 2.

The temperature increased rapidly, as Figure 2 shows.

As shown in Figure 2, the temperature increased rapidly.

As Figure 2 shows, the temperature increased rapidly.

The temperature increased rapidly (see Figure 2).

16.3 敘述研究結果

在敘述或總結研究結果時，既然內容已成過去，因此通常會使用過去式。

After flights of less than two hours, 11% of the army pilots and 33% of the civilian pilots *reported* back pain.

The animals in the red group *chose* the red ball significantly more often than they *did* the white ball.

Enrollment in the course *increased* steadily from 1986 to 1990.

某些研究領域的作者或許會使用現在式敘述研究結果。然而，若採用現在式，那麼句子的涵義就會跟過去式的句子有所不同。就研究結果的有效範圍而言，兩種句子有重大的區別。使用過去式便意味著：「這是本研究的發現，僅在特定情況下有效。這個句子只是針對本研究的內容。」如使用現在式，其意思則是：「這是本研究所揭示的普遍事實。」也就是說，這個發現不單對研究樣本有效，而是對所有情況都有效。

Female listeners *found* loud music more irritating than male listeners *did*.
句子含義是，樣本中的女性比男性更討厭吵鬧的音樂。

Female listeners *find* loud music more irritating than male listeners *do*. 句子含義是，任何女性都比男性討厭吵鬧的音樂。

The level of indentation *had* a clear effect on comprehension scores. 縮進排印的程度明顯影響了樣本中的人的閱讀理解能力。

The level of indentation *has* a clear effect on comprehension scores. 縮進排印的程度會明顯影響到所有人的閱讀理解能力。

一般而言，在某些領域（如經濟學、社會學、心理學），作者常常以現在式陳述結果；然而，在其它領域（如物理學及化學），這種做法卻很罕見。

此外，描述由理論模型得出的結果應使用現在式，而敘述實驗結果則應使用過去式。這是因為由理論模型得出的結果乃是經過數學演算推出的，屬不受時間影響的事實，所以應該使用現在式。關於這點，請參看本書第十五章。

撰寫研究報告時，作者介紹研究結果通常會涉及下列三類內容：一、參數或變數在某段時期的變動；二、不同樣本、方法或研究對象之間的比較；以及三、不同參數或變數之間的關係。下文會介紹敘述這三類內容的常用句型。（請注意：下列句型的主要動詞都用過去式。）

一、參數或變數在某段時期的變動。用來描述參數變化的句子，一般會有表示變化（如增加或減少）的動詞或片語；參數會作主詞，至於表示時間、時期的片語則通常置於句末。

參數	過去式動詞	時間
Enrollment in medical schools	increased decreased rose	from 1985 to 1990.
The temperature	fell dropped declined went up went down remained constant remained unchanged	after oxygen was introduced. when more water was added.
Enrollment in medical schools	peaked reached a maximum reached a minimum	in 1989.
The temperature		after 30 minutes.

二、不同樣本、方法或研究對象之間的比較。交代這類內容的句子通常會用到比較級或最高級形容詞。

第一個項目	比較（過去式）	第二個項目
The new method	was faster than was slower than	the old method.
Older workers	scored higher than scored lower than	younger workers.

最高級形容詞

The *fastest* algorithm was the genetic algorithm.

Group 1 had the *highest* average score.

The third algorithm was the *most accurate*.

三、不同參數或變數之間的關係。常用的句型有兩類：第一類句子的主要動詞會用到如 *correlated* 或 *related* 等字眼；第二類則是複句，用附屬子句來描述其中一個參數的變動。

第一個參數	關係（過去式）	第二個參數
Grades	were correlated with were negatively correlated with were dependent on were independent of were determined by	study time.

第一個參數	過去式動詞	附屬連接詞	第二個參數	過去式動詞
Test scores	increased decreased rose fell	as when	study time	increased. decreased. rose. fell.

其它常用的句型還包括：

Test scores increased with an increase in study time.

Test scores increased with study time.

An increase in study time led to an increase in test scores.

16.4 對研究結果的評論或說明

評論研究結果時，可以用兩種形式來組織。第一種組織形式為先介紹某個項目的結果，繼而加以評論，然後再介紹另一個項目的結果並再加以評論。我們可以將這種組織形式稱為「個別評論」。當要介紹的結果有多項，並需要逐一評論時，採用這種方式就很恰當。下面的例子便採用了這種方式，作者敘述了三項主要結果，並在敘述每個結果後緊接著就作了簡短的評論。

Learning Styles and Computer-assisted Instruction

Results

The analysis of variance in the posttest scores is presented in Table 2. As can be seen from the table, the F for learning styles was 0.15478, which is not statistically significant, indicating no appreciable difference in post-test performance among the four learning style groups. The F for interaction was 0.72931 and was not statistically significant, indicating no appreciable relationship between learning style and instructional design.

The F of 0.93812 for instructional design was statistically significant at the $P < 0.01$ level, resulting from differences in the performance of the linear and branching groups....

Source	Sum of squares	d.f.	Mean square	P(F)	F
Learning styles	649.8785	3	216.6262	1.77	0.15478
Instructional design	0.7418082	1	0.7418082	0.01	0.93812
Instructional design × learning style	159.3705	3	53.12349	0.43	0.72931
Error	23532.68	192	122.5660		
Total	24342.66	199			

Table 2. Analysis of variance in CAI posttest scores.

第二種常用的組織形式為先介紹幾個不同項目的結果，然後針對這些結果做一綜合的評論或說明。我們可以稱這種組織形式為「綜合評論」。當要介紹一系列的結果，並對之做綜合評論時，就不妨以這種方式來論述。下面的例子便採用了這種方式，作者先陳述所有重要結果，然後根據這些結果給出了精簡概括的總結。

Observational Learning in Octopuses

Results

The octopuses (n = 30) that observed demonstrators attacking the red ball chose the red ball significantly more often than they did the white ball (129 red, 13 white in 150 trials), as shown in Figure 3 (A). Animals (n = 14) that observed demonstrators of the white group chose the white ball more often (7 red, 49 white in 70 trials), as shown in Figure 3 (B).

During the testing phase, the red observers made errors in 14% of the trials and the white observers made errors in 30%. However, if only the number of attacks to the wrong ball are considered, for both groups of observers the error rate was about 9%. Failure to attack did not correlate with choices in preceding trials. The randomness of the failure to attack does not favor the lack of discrimination between objects or the failure of learning, but may be related to a lack of reward after each trial.

These results suggest that untrained octopuses can learn a task by observing, for a short period of time (four trials), the behavior of another octopus....

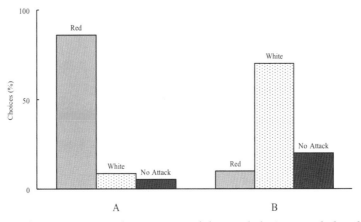

Figure 3. Choices expressed as percent of the total choices made by observers during testing: (A) red group observers, (B) white group observers.

評論的內容

評論研究結果通常包括下列內容：

（一）根據研究結果做推論。

（二）解釋研究結果，或說明導致該結果的原因。

（三）比較本次研究結果與過往研究的發現；例如，指出結果跟其它研究是否一致。

（四）若是工學研究報告，作者可能會對自己及其他學者所開發的方法或技術做比較。

（五）指出自己的理論模型跟實驗數據是否符合。

練習 16-1 評論內容

請根據上述五種評論方法來指出下面各句子的內容屬於何種評論，即：推論、說明、結果比較、技術比較、以及符合程度。

1. These data strongly support Stackman's (1985) suggestion that loudness has an important effect on subjects' affective judgments toward music.

   評論內容 _____

2. It appears that both the flight duration and total accumulated flight time affect the incidence of back pain.

   評論內容 _____

3. These findings are understandable because the initial annealing temperature determines the state of conformational structures.

   評論內容 _____

4. The difference between the average scores of the two groups suggests that the formatting style has an effect on comprehension.

   評論內容 _____

5. This gap is a result of the differences between the performance of the linear and branching groups.

   評論內容 _____

6. The recognition rate of our system is significantly higher than that reported for Chen's system.

   評論內容 _____

7. The results of this series of trials were all highly consistent with the predictions of the theoretical model.

   評論內容 _____

8. These results suggest that untrained octopuses can learn a task more quickly by observing the behavior of another octopus than by reward-and-punishment methods.

   評論內容 _____

時態

　　評論研究結果時，句子該用哪種動詞時態是依評論內容而定的。以下我們會討論各種評論的動詞時態。

　　（一）當評論的內容為根據研究結果而得出的推論時，句子的主要動詞通常要使用現在式。此種評論的動詞常常為表示臆測的意思，如 *appear, suggest* 或 *seem*，以及語態助動詞 *may*。

> It *appears* that because of their greater accumulated flying time, civilian pilots are subject to a higher incidence of back pain.

> The level of indentation *may have* an effect on students' test scores.

> These findings *suggest* that women strongly prefer slower music.

　　（二）當評論的內容為對於研究結果可能的解釋時，句子的主要動詞前常常會加上語態助動詞 *may* 或 *can* 之現在式動詞（此動詞有時候為被動語態。）

> The higher incidence of back pain in civilian pilots *may be* due to their greater accumulated flying time.

> These results *can be explained* by the differences between the learning styles of the two groups of subjects.

> One reason for this group's higher scores *may be* that the group was already accustomed to working with Pascal.

下面的句型也很常見：

> A possible explanation for this *is* that all of the oxygen was used up in the early stages of the reaction.

> This *may have occurred* because the reaction used up all the oxygen.

此外，在給出可能的說明時，作者還會常常使用現在式之臆測動詞，例如：

主詞	臆測動詞（現在式）	說明
It	seems appears is likely is possible	that the drug reduces the frequency and intensity of allergic reactions.
These data These results	indicate suggest imply	

　　說明研究結果的句子，通常會將說明的內容置於以 *that* 開頭的名詞子句，或以 *because* 開頭的附屬子句中。在不同的情形下，此種子句中的動詞可能會使用現在式、現在式加上助動詞 *may* 或過去式。若使用現在式則是表示作者的說明是普遍有效的事實；也就是說，他們認為說明的內容可能為不受時間影響的普遍事實。若使用助

動詞 *may*，其意思類近，但作者比較不確定此說明是否普遍有效。若使用過去式則表示說明僅對報告所討論的特定情形才有效。這時，作者只是猜測在本次特定情形下所發生的事情而已，並沒有主張這項說明對其它情況也有效。

> It seems that the drug *reduces* the frequency and intensity of allergic reactions. 作者認為此說明可能在一般情形下都有效。

> It seems that the drug *may reduce* the frequency and intensity of allergic reactions. 作者認為此說明可能在一般情形下都有效，不過沒有上面句子那麼確定。

> It seems that the drug *reduced* the frequency and intensity of allergic reactions. 作者只表示此說明在這次特定情形下有效，並沒有表示在一般情形下是否有效。

以虛主詞 *it* 開頭的句子，假如主動詞是 *seems* 或 *appears*，則可以省略虛主詞 *it* 而把名詞子句中的主詞當作整句的主詞。這樣的句子通常會比較簡潔。至於該運用哪一種時態，其原則與上述相同：若在一般情況下為真，則應用現在式；若只在特定情況下為真，則要用過去式。

> 原句：　　*It seems that the drug reduces* the frequency and intensity of allergic reactions.

> 修改句：　*The drug seems to reduce* the frequency and intensity of allergic reactions. 在一般情形下都為真。

> 修改句：　*The drug seemed to reduce* the frequency and intensity of allergic reactions. 只在這次特定情形下為真。

> 原句：　　*It appears that the drug reduces* the frequency and intensity of allergic reactions.

> 修改句：　*The drug appears to reduce* the frequency and intensity of allergic reactions. 在一般情形下都為真。

> 修改句：　*The drug appeared to reduce* the frequency and intensity of allergic reactions. 只在這次特定情形下為真。

（三）當評論的內容為作者與其他學者的結果比較時，應使用現在式，因為兩者無論是一致也好，矛盾也好，此等關係既然為邏輯上的事實，那麼便不受任何時間限制。這類句子如果有以 *that* 開頭的名詞子句，那麼該子句的動詞通常也會使用現在式。

> These results *agree* well with the findings of Smith, et al.

> These data *are* consistent with earlier findings showing that mice *avoid* bitter foods.

（四）當作者比較自己跟其他學者提出的技術性能時，評論該用哪種時態，則要視乎內容而定。如果作者根據論文的資料而做出的推論是普遍有效的，則應使用現在式，以暗示句子的內容為普遍的事實。如果作者想表示的評論內容僅在特定情況有效，則應使用過去式。

The values predicted by our model *have* a smaller degree of error than the values generated by Rickert's model *do*. 作者認為句子內容為普遍的事實。

These data show that the proposed method *is* faster and more accurate than the conventional method. 作者認為句子內容為普遍的事實，也就是說，無論任何情形，自己的方法都會比傳統方法快捷準確。

Our algorithm *required* consistently less processing time than Chen's algorithm. 作者只指出，在這實驗中，自己的演算法所用的時間比陳氏的演算法少，並沒有表示是否在任何情形下都會得出相同的結果。

（五）在比較根據自己的理論模型所得出的推測和實驗數據之間的吻合程度時，通常使用現在式，因為不論模型和數據一致與否，均不受時間限制。若句子包括以 *that* 開頭的子句的話，那麼子句的動詞通常也使用現在式。

The theoretical model *fits* the experimental data well.

The theoretical model *agrees well* with the experimental data.

There *is* a high level of agreement between the theoretical predictions and the experimental data.

The data *conform* closely to the predictions of the model.

The data *indicate* that the model *is* reliable and accurate.

The experimental measurements *are* very close to the predicted values.

然而，少數作者會將這種句子寫成過去式。這時，作者是把推測和數據之間的比較當作了過去的事件。

The theoretical model *agreed well* with the experimental data.

There *was* a high level of agreement between the theoretical predictions and the experimental data.）

練習 16-2 時態

下列段落都是摘錄自研究報告的「結果」章節。請在各段落中填上適當的動詞形式，並注意語態。

Quenching and Aging in PVC Films

The results _____ (*show*) in Figure —. The two tests of quenching from 153° C _____ (*have*) identical creep curves, confirming the thermoreversibility of quenching and aging as well as the reliability of the apparatus. The quench from 153° to 0° C _____ (*produce*) the least dense structure and the highest creep, whereas the quench from 96° to 0° C _____ (*yield*) the most dense structure, leading to the slowest creep behavior. These results _____ (*be*) understandable because the initial annealing temperature (T_0) _____ (*determine*) the state of conformational structures, from which the quenching takes place. For a higher T_0, greater excess free volume or molecular mobility _____ (*be*) likely to be frozen into the glassy matrix if quenching _____ (*perform*) properly. Thus molecular mobility _____ (*determine*) by the initial annealing temperature.

The Effect of Indentation on Program Comprehension

Table — _____ (*summarize*) the statistical analysis. The means of the ranks _____ (*show*) that Group 1 (no indentation) _____ (*exhibit*) the poorest performance, while Group 3 (moderate indentation) _____ (*perform*) the best. This _____ (*seem*) to suggest that indentation _____ (*have*) some effect on comprehension. On the other hand, the analysis of variance _____ (*indicate*) that we cannot reject the null hypothesis at the 0.05 level of significance.

The Effect of Semantic Complexity on the Comprehension of Program Modules

The proportion of elements correctly recalled for each problem at each level of difficulty _____ (*show*) in Table —. From the table it _____ (*be*) apparent that the complexity level _____ (*have*) no effect on immediate recall. This conclusion _____ (*support*) by an analysis of variance done on the data using problem pairings (six levels) and subjects (two per cell) as factors. There _____ (*be*) no significant difference in the number of elements recalled between the two difficulty levels, $F(1, 6) = 0.391$, $P > 0.05$. Similarly, there _____ (*be*) no difference among the problem pairs, $F(5, 6) = 0.718$.

Although complexity level _____ (*have*) no effect on immediate recall, it _____ (*do*) affect delayed recall. As Table — _____ (*show*), the subjects _____ (*recall*) less of the complex program segments than they _____ (*do*) of the simpler segments when tested 48 hours after their initial exposure.

The absence of an effect of difficulty level on immediate recall _____ (*be*) not surprising. Students often _____ (*develop*) good strategies for memorizing as a study skill and _____ (*can*) use these skills when they are needed. In this experiment, the short amount of time allowed for them to study the program segments _____ (*be*) probably not long enough for them truly to comprehend the modules. The reason for the effect of level of difficulty on delayed recall _____ (*be*) probably that the subjects _____ (*be*) able to process and integrate proportionately more of the simpler procedures than the complex procedures.

An Analysis of Broad-band Fiber Loop Architectures

Figure — _____ (*show*) fiber cross-sections averaged over the ten central offices (COs) included in the model. The results _____ (*indicate*) that the active double-star (ADS) cross-section _____ (*be*) sensitive to offered load, while the cross-section in the three passive architectures _____ (*be*) not. This _____ (*be*) because the feeder in the ADS _____ (*design*) on the basis of subscriber usage, while each of the passive architectures _____ (*give*) 16 subscribers at each remote node transparent 155 Mb/s video channels all the way from the CO.

練習 16-3 結果章節

根據本章介紹的標準寫法，請分別為下列兩幅圖表撰寫「結果」章節；每個段落要包括「結果」章節的三個基本項目，即：研究結果的介紹、主要結果的描述、以及對結果的評論。

1.

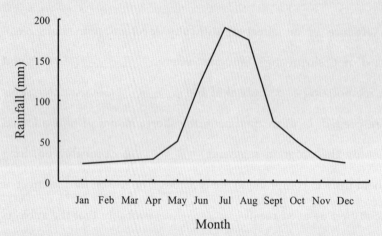

Figure 4. Monthly rainfall in Nabonia in 1992.

2.

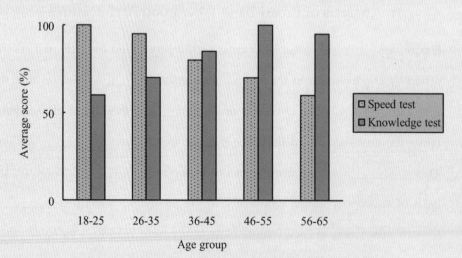

Figure 5. Average scores of workers in each age group
on speed and knowledge tests.

第十七章
討論章節

　　研究論文的「討論」章節旨在探討研究結果的各種蘊涵。作者在此章節中會說明該結果跟其他學者的研究結果之間的關聯。例如，這些結果是否能支持或反駁重要的理論或假設；或是否能豐富所屬領域的知識，並進而指出新的研究問題。一般來講，讀者（以及學術期刊的審稿人）所期待見到的學術成果、研究貢獻多出於這一章，因此「討論」章節可謂研究報告的點睛之筆。為了突出研究論文重點，作者在此章節要回答部分或所有下列問題：

- 作者所得到的研究結果是否符合自己原來的期望？如果沒有的話，為何沒有？
- 根據這些結果，我們可以做什麼推論？又可以得出什麼結論？
- 作者得到的結果是否跟其他學者的一致？如果不是，能否說明不一致的原因？
- 可以進行什麼實驗去確定、反駁或進一步擴充此項研究結果？
- 這些結果能否支持或反駁現有的理論？
- 能不能根據這些結果，建議如何修正現有的理論？
- 研究結果是否有實用價值？

　　由於「討論」章節的重點在於作者對研究結果的詮釋，所以作者在討論結果時千萬不要過於含蓄，而應該直接了當地告訴讀者自己對研究結果的想法與解釋。這點非常重要：根據一位科技寫作專家的說法，不少研究報告的結果其實相當有意思，但因為「討論」章節寫得太婉轉晦澀而被退稿。要寫出一篇成功的研究報告，僅僅得出有意思的研究成果是不夠的，作者還要清楚地說明這個成果如何重要，並要解釋為甚麼這個成果值得其他學者關注。

在進一步探討「討論」章節前，還要提醒大家，「討論」章節的英文為 "Discussion"，複數 "Discussions" 是錯誤的。

一般而言，「討論」章節常常是研究報告的最後一章。然而有些研究領域的報告，在「討論」章節後還有「結論」(Conclusion) 章節；而有時候「討論」章節並不稱作 "Discussion" 而稱作 "Conclusion"。此外，有些研究報告會把「結果」和「討論」章節合併，稱作 "Results and Discussion"；而該章節之後還有一個獨立的「結論」(Conclusion) 章節。至於該採用哪一種格式比較適合，作者可以參考一下所屬領域幾本著名期刊再做決定。

17.1 基本內容及組織

在「討論」章節之首，作者通常會再次回顧自己的研究並討論具體的研究結果，然後就開始針對結果討論比較廣泛的蘊涵以及這些結果對研究領域的貢獻。因此我們可以說，「討論」章節的焦點是由小到大、由窄到廣的。

「討論」章節大多包括下列內容：

一、研究目的：作者回顧研究的主要目的或假設。

二、結果概述：作者概述最重要的結果，並指出這些結果能否支持原來的假設，以及是否跟其他學者的結果一致。有時候，作者還會再次點出個別重要結果。

三、對於結果的說明：作者對自己的結果提出說明、解釋或猜測。

四、推論或結論：作者指出根據研究結果可進一步做哪些推論或結論。

五、研究方法或結果的限制：作者指出研究的限制條件以及其對研究結果的影響。

六、對進一步研究提出建議或解釋成果的實際用途：作者可以建議下一步的研究題目或方向，也可以指出如何將研究成果投入實際應用。

大多數研究報告會根據這六項內容來組織「討論」章節，但也有不少學者並不按上述次序來撰寫。他們可能會把一兩個項目省略掉，又或將第二、三、四項重複多次或穿插敘述。

我們可以參考以下「討論」章節。這段文字正是運用了上述的基本組織結構。

An Experimental Study on Integrating Formal and Functional Approaches to Language Teaching

Discussion

研究目的　This experimental study was designed to examine the effectiveness of one approach to integrating grammar into a French immersion curriculum. The findings indicate that classes which experienced

結果概述　an approach that integrated formal, analytic and functional, communicative activities in teaching the conditional made significantly higher gains in their ability to use this form in writing than did classes that did not experience this approach. Statistically significant gains were not revealed in speaking. However, an examination of the individual class data revealed greater and more consistent growth in speaking for the experimental than for the control classes, suggesting that they benefited somewhat from the experimental treatment in this area as well.

對於結果
的說明

The relatively smaller gains made by students in speaking than in writing may be attributed to several factors. Among these are the commonly observed lag between assimilation of a new rule and its automatization in speaking (James, 1980), as well as the competition provided by previously automatized rules in the learner's grammar. Detailed error analyses of the speaking data revealed the presence of interlanguage forms....

結論或推論

Overall, the findings of this study suggest that improvement of immersion students' oral and written grammatical skills can be achieved through curricular intervention that integrates formal, analytic and functional, communicative approaches to language teaching. Especially because of the consistency of the results for the experimental classes, we think that this integrated approach holds much promise for the improvement of language teaching in immersion programs.... The speaking results, however, suggest that more time and effort may be needed to allow students to assimilate fully their new grammatical learning....

研究的限制

This study could not separate the benefits that may have accrued from the increased opportunities for comprehension provided by the materials from those that may have accrued from the increased opportunities for production. Therefore, it cannot help resolve the theoretical debate on the importance of production in second-language learning (see Krashen, 1981 and Swain, 1985). Nor could the study isolate the effects of the various instructional features of the experimental materials. This information is important and would contribute to our understanding of both theoretical and practical issues in second-language learning, but one should not preclude the possibility that the key to improvement of second-language performance in the classroom may lie in the totality of the individual instruction features rather than in their isolation....

建議其他
研究題目

This research makes a step toward developing an effective approach for integrating grammar into French immersion. More research is called for concerning the effectiveness of the techniques used in this approach, if possible in teaching other aspects of grammar. In addition, there is a critical need for observational research in immersion classrooms so that effective strategies currently being used by immersion teachers to promote grammatical proficiency can be identified.

練習 17-1 「討論」章節的組織

下列句子摘錄自一篇研究報告的「討論」章節，但次序卻被打亂了。請根據上文介紹的基本組織形式，將下列句子重新排列。同時，亦請指出每句所屬的內容類別：研究目的、結果概述、對於結果的說明、研究的限制或關於未來研究的建議。

Loudspeaker Frequency Response and Perceived Sound Quality

____ This higher energy makes the speakers sound duller and also produces more upward spread of masking, which has a negative effect on clarity and fidelity.

內容類別 _____

____ Thus it would be preferable to use a continuous recording, both of the acoustical characteristics and of the listener's judgments, in order to obtain a more detailed understanding of the psychophysical relations.

內容類別 _____

____ The frequency response proved to be extremely important in determining perceived sound quality.

內容類別 _____

____ The data reveal that differences between loudspeakers mainly occur at lower frequencies, such as below 1000 Hz. The poorer loudspeakers usually have a pronounced energy boost somewhere in this low-frequency region.

內容類別 _____

____ The purpose of this work was to study the relations between the perceptual properties of loudspeakers and their frequency response.

內容類別 _____

____ The changing acoustical characteristics could be studied by some type of sonogram technique.

內容類別 _____

____ In a study of this type, the physical properties of the music program and the reproduction are continuously changing, and so is the listener's impression of the sound in its various dimensions.

內容類別 _____

____ It seems to influence all perceptual dimensions.

內容類別 _____

17.2 常用句型與時態

本節討論作者敘述上述基本內容時常用的句型以及時態的用法。

回顧研究目的

本書第三章曾指出，導論可以採用兩種不同的導向來介紹研究目的：若採用「論文導向」，敘述研究目的時便會以論文本身為焦點；而採用「研究導向」則會將研究活動做為句子的焦點。那麼當作者在「討論」章節回顧研究目的時，該採用哪種時態通常依導論所採用的導向而定。若導論採用了「研究導向」，「討論」章節便要用過去式來重述研究目的。請參看下列例句：

This research *investigated* the effects of two different learning methods.

This study *attempted* to isolate the roles of tempo and loudness in affecting subjects' reactions to music.

The aim of this research *was* to determine whether octopuses could learn new behavior by observing the behavior of a conspecific.

導論若採用了「論文導向」，則「討論」章節通常會使用現在完成式重述研究目的：

This study *has proposed* a new method for treating effluent from semiconductor plants.

This paper *has presented* a new algorithm for allocating bandwidth in networks.

In this paper, we *have proposed* a new technique for solving a well-known class of problems.

上述例句都用了主動語態，以 *this study, the aim of this study* 以及 *we* 等字詞為主詞。另外，有時候作者也可以使用被動語態的句子重述研究目的。請注意：只有及物動詞才有被動形式。

In this study, the effects of two different learning methods *were investigated*.
In this paper, a new technique *has been proposed* for solving a well-known class of problems.

採用主動語態的句子讀起來會較有力，而且作者可以把很長的名詞片語放在動詞之後。至於採用被動語態的好處是可以把研究主題當作主詞。（關於兩種語態的優缺點，請參考本書第十六章16.2節以及第九章9.3, 9.4節）。

若作者需要重述研究計劃原來的假設，則通常會使用過去式，而且描述假設內容的名詞子句也常常會使用助動詞 *would, could* 或 *might*。

The hypothesis tested in this research *was* that privacy *affects* job satisfaction.

We originally *assumed* that workers who enjoyed a greater degree of privacy *would be* more satisfied with their jobs.

We originally *hypothesized* that successful salesmen *would be* more adept at organizing client evaluation cues.

We *anticipated* that tempo *would have* a clear effect on subjects' attitudes toward the music.

The theory *suggested* that gender *might be* correlated with subjects' attitudes toward different types of music.

This evidence *led* us to infer that yield *could be improved* by subsurface irrigation.

結果概述

　　作者應該遵循第六章所介紹的基本原則來概述研究結果：換句話說，若作者認為結果只對本次研究有效，則要用過去式來概述；反之，若認為研究結果是普遍有效的，則要使用現在式。一般而言，在一些學科如心理學與經濟學等，現在式較為常見；而在其它學科如物理學和化學則較為少見。

All perceptual dimensions *seemed* to be influenced by the frequency response.

Females *reacted* adversely to louder music, whereas males *did* not.

The programmers *were* able to recall and execute more of the semantically simple procedures than the semantically complex procedures.

　　當討論研究結果能否支持原來的假設，或是否跟其他學者的結果或結論一致時，由於這類邏輯關係乃是不受時間限制的事實，作者通常會使用現在式來表達。

These test results *support* the original hypothesis that older workers would experience a decline in skills.

These results *are* consistent with the original hypothesis.

These results *provide* substantial evidence for the original hypothesis.

These results *contradict* the original hypothesis.

These results *appear* to refute the original hypothesis.

Our findings *are* in substantial agreement with those of Smith (1985).

The present results *are* consistent with those reported in our earlier work.

These yields *are* higher than would be expected according to the theory.

The experimental and theoretical values for the yields *agree* well.

The experimental values *are* all lower than the theoretical predictions.

　　然而，也有些作者會採用過去式來驗證研究結果是否跟推測相一致。這樣做是為了強調句子描述的事情是過去發生了的。若句子有指涉過去時間的片語，那麼更要使用過去式。

The weight losses observed in our study *were* greater than those reported by Wesson (1988).

In the first series of trials, the experimental values *were* all lower than the theoretical predictions.

對結果的說明

在說明研究結果的句子中，如果是為了表達這只是其中一種合理解釋，其主要動詞通常是表示可能性的現在式動詞。句子的主要動詞之後常會有以 *that* 開頭的名詞子句，子句的動詞則通常是過去式或現在式。如本書其它章節所示，若採用過去式，則表示作者的說明僅對本次研究的現象有效；若使用現在式，則表示此說明是普遍有效的。

說明只適用於本次研究結果：

主要子句（現在式）	That	說明（過去式）
It is possible It may be It is likely It is unlikely One explanation could be One reason for this could be These results can be explained 　　by assuming This inconsistency indicates	that	adding water *caused* the reaction rate to increase. an erroneous value *was attributed* to one of the quantities in Equation (3).

說明為普遍有效：

主要子句（現在式）	That	說明（現在式）
It is possible It may be It is likely It is unlikely One explanation could be One reason for this could be These results can be explained 　　by assuming This finding seems to show	that	adding water *causes* the reaction rate to increase. females *have* more sensitive hearing in the higher frequency range.

上面句子以 *that* 開頭的名詞子句可以改寫成獨立完整的句子。若要改寫，則要在主要動詞前加上語態助動詞，如 *may* 或 *could*。若說明只適用於本次研究結果，則應該使用現在完成式；反之，若此說明普遍有效，則應使用現在式。

說明只適用于本次研究結果：

Adding water *may have increased* the reaction rate.

An erroneous value *may have been attributed* to one of the quantities in Equation (3).

說明為普遍有效：

Adding water *may increase* the reaction rate.

Females *may have* more sensitive hearing in the higher frequency range.

　　作者若對自己的說明有十足的把握，那麼甚至可以連時語態助動詞也省略掉，直接使用簡單過去式或現在式。不過只有當作者非常確定自己的說明為正確無誤時，才能這樣寫。

說明只適用於本次研究結果有效：

Adding water *increased* the reaction rate.

An erroneous value *was attributed* to one of the quantities in Equation (3).

說明為普遍有效：

Adding water *increases* the reaction rate.

Females *have* more sensitive hearing in the higher frequency range.

　　說明研究結果常用表達方式還包括：*may be due to, can be attributed to, may be caused by* 以及 *may be because of*。使用這些詞句時，作者把要解釋的現象當作主詞，並用動詞後的介系詞片語說明導致該現象的理由。

This inconsistency *may be due to* an error in Equation (4).

This problem *may have occurred because of* a programming error.

This *may be because* the masking makes the speakers sound less clear.

Increases in absorption at high-doping levels *can be attributed to* dopant-induced stress.

The rapid decrease in the secondary electron yield *may be caused by* adsorbate sputtering followed by oxygen depletion.

推論或結論

　　在討論研究可能蘊涵的意義時，作者常使用現在式，而且常會使用如 *appear, suggest* 或 *seem* 之類的臆測動詞。之所以要用現在式，是因為作者已經不再討論研究結果，而是跟據這些結果來推論出普遍有效的結論。此外，研究結果及推論之間的邏輯關係不會改變。既然是不為時間限制的事實，那當然要用現在式。

　　其中一種常常用來作為結論的句子，是把研究結果當作主詞，或採用虛主詞，並用以 *that* 開頭的名詞子句來表達結論或推論。如果作者對結論或推論非常有把握，那麼名詞子句會使用現在式動詞；反之，若對自己的結論或推論的有效性不太確定，那麼名詞子句的動詞前會加上 *may*。無論如何，句子的主要動詞都要使用現在式。

主要子句（現在式）	That	推論或結論（現在式）
Our results indicate The data reported here suggest These findings confirm It appears Our conclusion is These results imply These data show These findings support the hypothesis Our data provide evidence	that	the mechanism *is* operative in both regions. 現在式：作者對此結論的有效性非常確定。 the reaction rate *may be* determined by the amount of oxygen available. 助動詞 *may*：作者比較不確定此結論是否有效。

此外，跟提出說明的句子一樣，作者也可以將上面以 *that* 開頭的名詞子句改為完整的句子，並在主要動詞前加上助動詞 *may* 或使用臆測動詞。這類句子要使用現在式。

The reaction rate *may be determined* by the amount of oxygen available.

The mechanism *appears* to be operative in both regions.

作者若對自己的推論或結論十分有把握，那麼有時連語態助動詞也可以省略掉，直接使用簡單過去式或現在式。不過只有當作者非常確定自己的說明為正確無誤時，才能這樣寫。

The reaction rate *is determined* by the amount of oxygen available.

The mechanism *is* operative in both regions.

研究方法或結果的限制

大多數研究工作都是在一定的限制條件下進行的，所採用的方法和得出的結果都會有一定的限制條件。指出研究限制的句子要採用甚麼時態，則要視乎句子內容而定。若敘述的事實是關於已完成的研究，則要使用過去式。

The number of people surveyed *was* quite small.

Only two sets of conditions *were tested*.

不過，若要指出研究方法、模型或分析之限制，則應該使用現在式。

The proposed model *neglects* several potentially important parameters.

Our analysis *is based* on two simplifying assumptions.

The method presented here *is* accurate, but *cannot be implemented* in real-time applications.

而作者若要猜測同一研究結果在其它情況下可能產生的改變，這時動詞便要使用現在式，並在前面加上助動詞 *may* 或 *might*。

Tests with other age groups *might yield* different results.

Our findings *may be* valid only for females.

An experiment using different initial conditions *might produce* different results.

另外，也有些作者會使用主詞 *we* 以及如 *admit* 或 *recognize* 等動詞，直接承認研究方法之限制。

We recognize that the degree of privacy is difficult to quantify.

We readily *admit* that a single short test may not fully reflect the subjects' level of competence.

新的研究題目或實際用途

當建議新的研究題目或進一步的研究方向時，作者常常會使用現在式動詞，並在動詞前加上語態助動詞 *would, could* 或 *should* （*should* 語氣較強，表示比較強烈的建議）。

It *would be* interesting to learn why oxygen is depleted during this type of sputtering.

Another interesting topic *would be* to examine how learning outcomes are related to concept attainment.

A more sophisticated system *could be used* to test a program with several branching levels.

Future research *could explore* the possible moderating role of gender on listeners' responses to other properties of music.

The generality of the gender moderated effect *could be assessed* in studies using other types of music and different exposure durations.

Experiments similar to those reported here *should be conducted* using different age groups.

提出建議的句子，通常會以 *we* 作主詞，主要動詞則用 *suggest* 或 *recommend*，並使用現在式。要留意，若用 *suggest* 或 *recommend* 當作主要動詞，動詞之後會有一個以 *that* 開頭的名詞子句，用來陳述建議。依據文法規則，子句的動詞必須用假設語氣。詳細說明請參考本書第三章3.3節。

We *suggest* that similar studies be conducted with other languages, such as Fortran.

We *recommend* that these experiments be repeated using a wider range of initial conditions.

有些作者習慣在「討論」章節或「結論」中提及自己正在進行或擬進行的相關研究。在這種情況下，可以使用現在進行式或未來式，而且最好以 *we* 當作主詞，以確定讀者瞭解作者是指自己的行動，而不是在建議其他人採取相關行動。請參看下列例句，首三句都清楚地告訴讀者是作者自己打算或正在進行研究，但最後一句卻採用了被動語態，這樣一來讀者便無法得知是誰進行了該項實驗：

> In the future, we *will investigate* the effect of using an oxygen ambient.

> We *are* now *conducting* experiments on low-temperature deposition.

> The present authors *are* currently *conducting* experiments on low-temperature deposition.

> Experiments on low-temperature deposition *are* now *being conducted*.

在指出研究之實際用途時，作者應使用現在式並加上助動詞 *may, might* 或 *should*（*should* 語氣較強，表示作者對自己研究的應用價值非常確定）。

> The results of this study *may lead to* the development of effective methods for teaching grammar to language immersion students.

> Our findings *may be useful* to educators and others involved in curriculum development.

> The results of this research *might help* consumers to make more informed food-purchasing decisions.

> The technique presented in this paper *should be useful* in reducing the amount of sludge emitted in wastewater from semiconductor plants.

練習 17-2 討論章節常用句子

下列句子都是「討論」章節的常見句子。可是這些句子並不完整，請根據句子的內容及括弧內的提示完成下列句子。

1. the sputtering yield of a monoatomic target / proportional to the energy deposited in nuclear collisions at the surface [作者原來的假設]

2. to investigate whether there are differences in the evaluation cues that successful and unsuccessful salespeople use for classifying sales leads [研究目的]

3. the losses of residue measured in our study / greater than those reported in previous research [結果概述]

4. program modules equated on surface complexity and on function / vary significantly in their semantic complexity [推論]

5. the energy deposited by the ions / rearrange the atomic structure of the damaged SiO_2 surface in the presence of oxygen [推論或說明]

6. the discrepancy / an increase in the value of the absorption coefficient / affect the induced carrier density significantly [說明]

7. Snow cover / to insulate the residues from extremes of cold and drying out / help account for the slow loss rates during the first winter at site A [說明]

8. it is difficult to measure comprehension / our method insufficiently precise [限制]

9. our student sample / not representative of the adult population [限制]

10. to study the chunking process as it operates in programming tasks [建議進一步之研究方向]

11. further study with large groups of professional programmers with varying degrees of experience [建議]

12. there are differences in the properties of salespeople's cues / no differences in the quantity of knowledge they have available [結論]

13. instructional design affects the outcome of education [結論]

14. structural differences in the starting material also strongly influence the sputtering yields [推論]

第十八章
結論章節

　　緊接在「討論」章節或「結果與討論」章節之後，有些研究報告還會有一個「結論」章節。本章會簡略討論這類章節的內容。

　　撰寫研究報告結論時，作者要把研究的主要發現清楚簡潔地總結出來。在這一章裡，不應出現任何前文中沒有論及的事實，也不應再將實驗程序或研究動機詳細複述一遍。

　　還有一點作者要緊記，那就是：「結論」章節旨在做總結，而非概述或重複論文的內容。要知道，「結論」章節不是摘要 (abstract)，因此要避免在「結論」章節再為整篇論文做摘要。此外，「結論」章節亦不是由論文出現過的句子拼湊而成，所以千萬不要直接複述論文其它章節的句子。

　　除了結論外，「結論」章節還可以建議下一步的研究方向或具體的研究題目，還可以指出本次研究的實際用途或效益，然而這些內容都並不是一定要寫。若該研究只有一兩種確定的用途或方向，則不要為了令結論看起來豐富充實，而勉強將一些無關緊要的題目寫進去。

　　其實，並不是所有研究報告都有「結論」章節。不少研究領域的學者都習慣在「討論」章節便給出結論，而不再另設「結論」章節。如果「討論」章節寫得如本書第七章建議般詳細，那麼大概也就毋須另設一章再做結論了。在決定研究報告要不要寫「結論」章節之前，作者還是應先翻閱一下意欲投稿的期刊，看看所屬研究領域有沒有獨立一章做結論的慣例。

　　若論文同時有「討論」及「結論」兩個章節，那麼「結論」章節便要寫得相當簡短精煉，只將研究的兩三個重要結論簡單地交代清楚即可。切記千萬不要再重複文章的任何內容讓讀者重讀一遍！

　　「結論」章節的拼法通常是單數 "Conclusion"，但有些研究領域的學者亦會將之寫成複數 "Conclusions"。如果結論只有一兩個主要重點，則使用單數形 "Conclusion" 會比較合適。如果結論有好幾個重點，那麼複數形 "Conclusions" 或許會比較適當；這時作者還可以考慮將幾個結論一一列出，並分別加上序號。然而，究竟採用單數型還是複數型，還是要視所屬研究領域的常規習慣而定。

18.1　基本內容及組織

　　「結論」章節通常會有下列幾項內容：

一、概述主要的研究活動（此項可有可無）。

二、陳述研究的主要結論。這部分可能會包括：

- 簡略複述最重要的結果。
- 指出結果的重要蘊涵。
- 對結果提出可能的說明。

三、建議其它研究題目或研究結果可能的用途（此項可有可無）。

　　下面一段文字摘錄自一篇研究報告的結論，我們可以看到上述內容都將在這段文字中出現：

The Effects of Indentation
on Program Comprehension

Conclusion

研究活動	This study investigated the effects of different methods of indentation on students' comprehension of a program written in Pascal.
主要結果及結論	Although subjects given a program with moderate indentation had higher average comprehension scores than subjects given programs with no indentation or excessive indentation, the difference was not large enough for us to conclude that one indentation standard should be preferred over another.
進一步的研究題目	However, the slightly higher comprehension scores associated with moderate indentation suggest further research with large groups of professional programmers and other languages, such as Fortran and Cobol.

18.2　時態

　　下面將簡單說明該用什麼動詞時態來撰寫上述內容。由於所使用的句型及時態跟「討論」章節相應的內容相同，所以下文只提一些基本原則，詳細的例子請參閱第十七章。

概述研究活動

　　「結論」章節的首句常常用來概述主要研究活動或目的（然而，也有不少作者省略此概述而直接敘述主要的結論）。當文章使用「論文導向」時（參考第十三章），通常會用現在完成式來概述研究活動；而當文章使用「研究導向」時，則應使用過去式。

論文導向

This paper *has presented* a new model for simulating the effect of elastic scattering on angular and depth distributions of excited photo and Auger electrons.

研究導向

Silicon substrates and MBE-grown silicon films doped with either Sb or In at various concentrations *were studied* by a time-resolved transient grating technique.

敘述主要結論

　　如果作者在結論中需要強調一些重要的研究結果，則通常會使用過去式。

Subjects given a program with moderate indentation *had* higher average comprehension scores than subjects given programs with no indentation or excessive indentation.

　　跟前兩章論及的原則相同（參考16.3與17.2節），如果結果是一般情形都為真的普遍事實（如數學命題），則應該使用現在式。

　　敘述研究的主要結論時，作者通常會使用現在式以及臆測動詞（如 *appears, seems* 等）或語態助動詞（如 *may, could* 等）。之所以要用現在式，是因為作者認為該結論並不是僅僅適用于本次研究結果，而是在指出一條普遍有效的結論。

On the basis of these results, we *cannot conclude* that one indentation standard should be preferred over another.

The results *indicate* that elastic scattering in the gold targets *has* a great influence on the angular and depth distributions of photo and Auger electrons.

The carrier recombination *appears* to be mainly of the SRH type in In-doped samples.

　　反之，如果對研究結果的解釋和結論只適用於本次研究，則要採用過去式。

The elastic collisions in the specimen *caused* the photoelectrons to originate at shallower layers.

　　如果作者以為其解釋大概是普遍有效的，但卻因為證據不足的緣故而不大肯定，則可採用語態助動詞（如 *may, could* 等）或臆測動詞（如 appears, seems 等）用來表示結論只是屬於臆測。由於結論的內容通常旨在指出具有普遍有效性的觀點，所以作者一般也都會採用現在式、語態助動詞或臆測動詞，而不用過去式。請參看下列例句，第一句採用了現在式，表示作者十分確定此解釋是普遍有效的。但第二、三句則不然，作者表示這個結論只是一種臆測而已。

> The elastic collisions in the specimen *cause* the photoelectrons to originate at shallower layers.

> The elastic collisions in the specimen *seem to cause* the photoelectrons to originate at shallower layers.

> The elastic collisions in the specimen *may cause* the photoelectrons to originate at shallower layers.

進一步研究或用途之建議

在建議新的研究題目或指出研究結果有哪些實際用途時，作者應使用現在式，也可以採用如 *may, should* 等語態助動詞。

> Experiments similar to those reported here *should be conducted* using a wider variety of materials.

> We *recommend* that these experiments be repeated using a wider range of initial conditions.

> The technique presented in this paper *may be useful* in reducing the amount of paper wasted.

> The results of this research *might help* consumers to make more informed food-purchasing decisions.

第十九章
摘要

研究論文一開篇就是摘要 (abstract)，用來概述整篇論文的內容。一篇寫得好的摘要能令讀者迅速瞭解論文的目的、方法、主要成果及結論。讀者可以根據摘要來決定是否有必要詳細閱讀整篇文章。若讀者認為有必要閱讀文章全文，摘要還可以讓讀者對接下來的文章正文的具體內容做好心理準備。

一般來講，摘要的篇幅並沒有一定的準則。有些期刊會有字數限制，所以作者要先查看欲投稿的期刊有沒有相關的規定。就算沒有字數限制，作者亦應翻看一下欲投稿的期刊，以便瞭解期刊中大多數摘要一般的長度。摘要內容要完整，但篇幅不宜過長，以免讀者嫌太長讀不下去。

由於摘要必須用簡短的篇幅交代豐富的內容，所以作者要記住，摘要的句子功能跟論文正文的略有不同。換句話說，正文的句子往往並不適用於摘要。因此，撰寫摘要時千萬不要把正文的句子原文照搬到摘要裡去。順帶一提，有些初學者在撰寫論文時，往往在摘要、導論、結論都重複一模一樣的句子。要提醒各位的是，文章中的各個章節都有不同的功能，所以適用於一個章節的句子，很可能並不適用於其它章節，這是大家要多加留意的要點。

最後，如果作者在完成整篇文章的具體內容之前打算將摘要寫好，這是十分困難的。這也是我們將摘要章節放到這本書的最後部分來介紹的原因。作者應該先努力將正文寫好（至少待初稿完成後），才動筆寫摘要。

19.1 基本內容及組織

摘要是研究報告的梗概和精華，因此其結構也跟研究報告相同。摘要應包括下列各項信息：

一、簡略描述研究背景。這項內容並不是一定要寫，有時候可以省略，尤其當摘要篇幅可能會過長的時候。

二、敘述研究目的或描述主要的研究活動。

三、描述研究方法。第二項與第三項內容可以合併為一句。

四、概述最重要的結果。

五、簡略地敘述主要的結論或建議（這項內容可有可無）。如果無法簡明扼要又具體地將結論陳述出來，則可以採用如 "The implications of the data are discussed in detail"、"The results are discussed in comparison with earlier findings" 或 "A mechanism is proposed to explain the results" 等句子來簡單交代。

練習 19-1 摘要內容

下面是一篇摘要，請據上文提過的五項基本信息將句子分類。

Preferred Viewing Distances to
Screen and Document in VDU Workplaces

Abstract

[1]Previous research has shown that during work at visual display units (VDUs) most subjects prefer viewing distances greater than 50 cm. [2]This study investigated whether this is also true in VDU tasks that require subjects to shift their gaze frequently between the VDU screen and a paper document. [3]Two conditions were compared: one in which both screen and document were located at the same viewing distance of 50 cm and another in which the distance to the document was 50 cm and the distance to the screen was 70 cm. [4]Gaze shifts between screen and document were made every 2 s. [5]The visual strain of 20 subjects aged 19–51 years was estimated with a questionnaire. [6]Contrary to expectation, visual strain was not greater when the viewing distances to screen and document differed. [7]When subjects were free to shift the screen to the most comfortable position, they preferred screen distances of 50–81 cm (mean 65 cm) despite gaze shifts to the document at 50 cm every 2 s. [8]These results are evidence against the widespread ergonomic concept that viewing distances to both screen and document should generally be

about 50 cm. [9]We suggest that VDU users should be allowed to select viewing distances of 50 cm or more that they find comfortable.

背景　　　　＿＿＿＿＿＿

研究目的　　＿＿＿＿＿＿

方法　　　　＿＿＿＿＿＿

結果　　　　＿＿＿＿＿＿

結論或建議　＿＿＿＿＿＿

19.2 時態

撰寫摘要時應使用什麼動詞時態，其規則其實跟論文其它章節相同。在這裡就簡單提一下，不再詳細贅述了。

一、介紹背景資料的句子，如果內容為不受時間限制的普遍事實，則應使用現在式。

An important variable affecting the comprehension of programs *is* their psychological complexity.

Carbonic acid often *has* a strong affect on streamwater chemistry.

如果句子為對研究趨勢的概述，則應該使用現在完成式。

Previous research *has shown* that during work at visual display units (VDUs) most subjects prefer viewing distances greater than 50 cm.

Much research *has been devoted* to investigating the quenching and aging of polymers.

二、若論文採用「研究導向」敘述研究目的或主要的研究活動，則應該使用過去式；反之，若採用「論文導向」，則要使用現在式。（少數作者採用「研究導向」時會使用現在完成式；不過，還是使用過去式比較恰當。）

研究導向

This study *investigated* the distances at which subjects prefer to work in VDU tasks that require frequent gaze-shifting between the VDU screen and a paper document.

Samples of neat solid ozone and ozone trapped in excess ice *were subjected* to laser photolysis at 308 nm.

論文導向

A numeric method *is proposed* for solving the symmetric matrix eigenvalue problem.

This paper *presents* a social planning model for analyzing the transition to nondepletable fuels.

三、至於實驗報告，則通常會使用過去式來描述實驗程序或方法。

> The visual strain of 20 subjects aged 19–51 years *was estimated* by means of a questionnaire.

> Modules *were presented* to student programmers to memorize.

如果論文旨在介紹模型、演算法、分析方法或技術，那麼作者應使用現在式來描述研究方法。

> A Monte Carlo model *is used* to calculate the photoelectron intensity.

> A numeric method for the symmetric matrix eigenvalue problem *is developed* by reducing the problem to a number of matrix-matrix multiplications.

有時候，作者可以用一句話來概括研究目的及研究方法。要撰寫這類句子，我們可以把句子的主要子句來敘述研究目的，而研究方法則用片語交代。請參考下面例句，用斜體字標示的片語正指出了研究方法。

> A numeric method for the symmetric matrix eigenvalue problem is developed *by reducing the problem to a number of matrix-matrix multiplications.*

除此以外，我們還可以用位於句首或句尾的片語來描述研究目的，而研究方法則用主要子句來描述。請參看下面的例句，以斜體字表示的片語交代了研究目的。

> *To study the effect of indentation on program comprehension,* programs with three levels of indentation were presented to different groups of subjects.

至於這類混合句子的主要動詞應該採用什麼時態，則仍須遵照上述規則；也就是說，當文章採用「研究導向」或是在描述實驗方法時，應該使用過去式，而當文章採用「論文導向」或是在介紹模型或數學分析時，則應該使用現在式。

四、概述主要結果的句子，通常要使用過去式。

> The scores of subjects who received a program written with moderate indentation *were* higher than the scores of the other two groups.

> On plots seeded with a no-till crop, residue losses *ranged* from 81% to 88% by harvest time.

然而，如果作者認為其研究結果不僅僅限於此次研究的特定情況，而是普遍有效的，則可能會使用現在式。

> Workers with more privacy *report* a greater degree of satisfaction with their jobs.

五、敘述結論或建議時，作者可能會使用現在式、臆測動詞或如 *may, should* 或 *could* 等助動詞。

> The experimental results *indicate* that in the presence of mullions wind-induced suctions *increase* dramatically at the wall edge area for almost all geometrical and exposure configurations.

> The strong seasonal fluctuations of CO_2 *may explain* variations in stream-water alkalinity and base-cation concentrations.

The pace of capacity expansion in the nondepletable sector *has* a strong influence on socially optimal energy prices and production rates.

有時候作者並沒有具體給出結論，而只採用如 "The implications of the data are discussed" 之類的句子來做簡單交代。由於這種句子描述論文本身的內容（如採用論文導向以敘述研究目的情形一樣），所以主要動詞應使用現在式。

練習 19-2 時態

下面是兩篇摘要。請填上適當的動詞形式（提示：部分動詞應該是被動語態）。

Wheat Residue Loss from Fields under No-till Management

Abstract

To successfully implement no-till crop management systems for winter wheat, knowledge _____ (*need*) of how rapidly large residue fragments _____ (*be*) lost. In this research, losses of surface-managed winter wheat residues _____ (*measure*) at five sites. Sites _____ (*sample*) periodically by using grab samples to determine weight loss per unit area. Thirty weeks after harvest, residue weight losses _____ (*range*) from 35% to 42%. Snow cover _____ (*provide*) insulation for residues, allowing decomposition to continue during winter when sufficient moisture _____ (*be*) present. On chemical fallow plots, there _____ (*be*) a 50 to 80% loss after a year. On plots seeded with a no-till spring crop, residue losses _____ (*range*) from 81 to 88% by harvest time. Contributions of various sources of residue mass loss _____ (*discuss*).

A Comparison of Successful
and Unsuccessful Salespeople

Abstract

Most salespeople _____ (*attempt*) to identify likely purchasers of a product by using evaluation clues stored in memory to classify potential customers. This study _____ (*investigate*) how these cues differ for successful and unsuccessful salespeople. The findings _____ (*suggest*) that successful and unsuccessful salespeople _____ (*have*; 普遍有效) the same number of cues in memory and that the two types of representatives _____ (*distribute*; 普遍有效) importance weights about the same across evaluation cues. Successful and unsuccessful salespeople _____ (*weight*; 普遍有效) many of the same cues differently, however. The standards they _____ (*use*; 普遍有效) to describe class members also _____ (*differ*; 普遍有效) for several cues, with successful salespeople generally using more stringent criteria. The authors _____ (*discuss*) the implications of the findings and _____ (*offer*) suggestions for future research.

練習 19-3 摘要

　　下面是一篇摘要的大綱，請根據大綱將摘要完成。請注意，撰寫摘要不需要副標題，下面大綱中出現的副標題要在撰寫摘要時將之刪掉。另外，要特別注意採用正確的動詞形式。

Semantic Complexity and the Comprehension of Program Modules

Abstract

Background

- an important variable affecting the comprehension of programs: their psychological complexity

- some previous work on surface or low-level semantic features that affect complexity

- little work done on the effects of higher-level semantic features

Purpose of article

- describe an experiment using pairs of program modules

- program modules had equivalent surface complexity and functions but included semantic constructs with varying complexity

Method

- modules presented to student programmers to memorize

- students tested on immediate recall, hand execution, and recall after a delay of 48 hours

Results

- students given semantically complex modules: significantly worse scores on hand execution and delayed recall

第二十章
會議簡報

科學與工程領域的研究人員常常需要在學術研討會當中發表自己新近的研究成果。此外，各領域的專業研究人員（如工業界的工程師與經理）也常常需要在會議中發表研發計劃、技術報告、市場分析報告或介紹新產品資料等。本章將討論如何準備研討會演講的內容以及一些實用的演講技巧。

20.1 準備

在準備會議簡報時，應隨時記得：簡報的目的並不僅僅在於「發表」某些訊息，而在於把這些訊息「傳達」(communicate) 給觀眾。報告人需要儘量確保觀眾能清楚瞭解所發表的訊息。因此在準備簡報時，應將主要目的著眼在組織簡報的內容（包括視覺教具），用來儘量確保觀眾能夠清楚領會主要重點。要做到這些並不難，那就是要事先妥善準備簡報內容。此外，只要報告人知道自己準備得充分，那麼在發表時也會顯得比較自信從容，因此也就能把簡報內容更有效地傳達給觀眾。

在準備講稿時，報告人應按照下面十個步驟來準備。

一、先瞭解觀眾，再決定適切的講義內容

在準備任何簡報或發言時，第一步就是要先瞭解自己的觀眾。誰會來聽我的發表？他們的知識背景如何？了解之後再根據觀眾的性質來決定簡報的內容。觀眾對會議題目究竟有多熟悉？他們能接受多少新訊息？他們希望聽到非常詳細、專業的發表，還是只需要報告人簡略地說明自己研究的主要重點？一般來講，以專業研究人員為對象的發表和以一般社會大眾為對象的發表，兩者會有很大的差別；而且來自不同專業領域的研究人員，也會有不同的興趣及需求。報告人必須努力確保能為觀眾提供一些他們渴求的新訊息，但同時又不能過多，以免造成觀眾在短時間內無法接受、消化的問題。

換句話說，你需要先瞭解觀眾，然後再明確簡報目的。在我們決定自己的簡報目的或開始組織簡報內容之前，我們必須先瞭解觀眾的性質，並考慮採用何種發表方式與內容比較適合。

二、決定想要表達的主要重點

在瞭解了觀眾的性質之後，我們便要決定在發表中所需要介紹的有哪些主要重點。有沒有什麼新訊息想和觀眾分享？是否需要給出論證過程？有沒有什麼希望能說服觀眾的新觀點？還是打算教他們如何做某件事？在考慮了這些問題之後，應該圍繞幾個主要重點展開，這也是整個簡報的基礎。

此外，我們還需要開始考慮發表的長度。是不是只需要做十幾分鐘的發言？如果是的話，那麼我們最好只選擇一兩個主要重點來討論。如果要做一個小時的簡報，那我們就有較多的時間來表達更多的信息。然而，即便是準備做很長的簡報時，我們都要牢記一件事：當一次簡報試圖覆蓋太多訊息時，總是會讓人無所適從，很少有觀眾聽完後能記得住那麼多訊息。因此，就算是做一個小時的簡報，我們最好還是把自己討論的主要重點限制在四項到五項重點。

其實在簡報結束之後，觀眾最多只會記得幾個比較突顯的內容。所以，千萬不要花費心思提供過多不必要的細節，而應細心選擇幾個有意思的主要重點，並儘量把這些重點表達清楚。

如果會議簡報是用來介紹自己的科技研究工作，那麼至少有四點一定要表達清楚：

- 為什麼要做這個研究（研究目的或動機）？
- 如何進行這個研究（研究方法）？
- 研究結果如何？
- 研究結果有什麼意義？

這四點和一般研究報告的組織結構（即導論、方法、結果、討論等章節）是相互對應的。然而，發表的內容並不應與書面報告一樣詳細。例如，在研究論文中，方法章節的目的在於詳細描述作者的實驗方法，以便讓其他學者能重複作者的實驗以確定其研究結果是否有效。相較之下，在發表中由於時間有限，我們並不能詳細

解釋實驗方法的所有細節，而且觀眾對這些細節可能也不會有太大的興趣。在簡短的簡報中，觀眾必須暫時假定我們的實驗方法沒有重大缺陷，所以我們只要簡略地描述即可。當描述研究結果時，也需要應用相同的原則：我們不需要詳細列出所有的數據，只要提供充分的資料來支持自己的結論即可。千萬不要提供太多複雜繁瑣的龐大數據模型或一大堆抽象的表格，以免觀眾無法瞭解或消化；如果他們根本看不出什麼才是主要結果，那麼這個簡報就無法達到「傳達」的目的，就算不上是成功的簡報。此外，應該儘可能地利用一目了然的圖表，避免插入複雜的表格。

三、支持主要重點的資料要準備充分

步驟二中所選擇的每項重點，在簡報中都必須提供相關的資料、論證或例子來支持自己的說法。然而，在選擇這些相關資料時，我們也必須視簡報的長度以及觀眾接受新訊息的能力來決定。由於受時間及觀眾接受能力的限制，我們大概最多只能選擇兩三項相關的資料來支持每項重點。千萬不要提供過多的詳細資料，以免跑題讓觀眾無法將注意力集中在演講的主要重點。必須記住：簡報的目的並不是要如數家珍地講述研究過程中的所有細節，而是要清楚地「傳達」幾個重要的觀點，這樣才能確保在發表結束後，這些觀點給觀眾當中留下深刻印象。

四、適當組織演講內容

準備好簡報的內容以後，下個步驟就是選擇適當的組織形式把這些內容加以整理，突出重點。例如，如果需要介紹實驗研究計劃的結果，那麼我們大概可以遵循傳統的組織形式，即先解釋研究背景及目的，然後描述實驗方法並列出研究結果，最後對結果的含義進行討論。如果需要描述如何做某件事情或製造某種東西，那我們可以按照步驟的先後順序來組織簡報的內容。如果需要比較兩種不同的方法或技術，則可以採用比較與對照的組織形式。在組織簡報內容時，應該採用和撰寫文章時類似的原則與形式，尤其是撰寫段落的原則和組織形式對安排演講的內容亦頗適用（請參閱本書第八章）。採用的組織形式必須適合簡報的內容，而且應該全篇一致地遵循這個組織形式。例如，在介紹實驗結果時，千萬不要突然開始進一步描述自己的研究目的。研究目的就應在「研究目的」那一板塊完成，若已經把研究目的的敘述清楚，那麼其它板塊就不應該再次出現前面的內容。

當簡報內容已有了初步的結構之後，應細心考慮這些內容是不是都屬必要，還是可有可無？缺乏經驗的報告人常犯的錯誤之一，就是在簡報中提供過多的資料。應該記住：簡報的目標是以最有效的方式將極少數具體的重點傳達給觀眾，而不是要證明自己很聰明或在一次發表中告訴觀眾自己所知道的一切事情。因此，凡是次要重點、不能直接支持或論證主要重點或不能使內容更聯貫的資料，都應省略。

五、準備講稿的大綱

第五個步驟是撰寫一篇講稿的大綱，作為練習簡報的依據。大綱應該相當簡略，只包括主要重點以及支持這些重點的資料。如果打算在發表時能參考大綱的內容，則應該把大綱寫在大資料卡片上（尺寸大約 A4 紙的一半）並使用三倍的行距。如此一來，如果在發表中需要參考資料卡的話，就能迅速又容易地找到卡片上的內容。此外，每張資料卡右上角應該加上序號，以便隨時確定卡片的順序是否正確。

　　在某些會議中，研究人員可以直接向觀眾朗誦自己已經寫好的研究報告。如果可以朗誦，那麼報告人就需要先把完整的報告內容寫出來，並事先演練一番。然而，很少有研討會鼓勵這樣直接朗誦研究報告的做法。在絕大多數研論會中，大家都期望報告人能對著觀眾說話，而不僅僅是向觀眾朗誦一篇報告（觀眾自己也認識字吧！）。而且在一般的情況下，報告人根本沒有足夠的時間把一整篇研究報告唸完（大多數會議的報告時間限制在二十分鐘以內）。所以，報告人應該準備好講稿或根據投影片的內容來發表，而不要直接朗誦研究報告。此外，報告人也不要嘗試把講稿逐字逐句地背下來。萬一花了幾個星期的時間好不容易背下講稿內容，結果在發表時觀眾中間問問題或有事情擾亂我們的注意力，　都很有可能導致我們無法正確回憶究竟在甚麼地方被中斷或突然想不起如何接下去……冷場，這不是很可怕的事情嗎？

　　所以，有經驗的報告人都不會逐字把簡報內容全部背起來，而會先以大綱的方式把主要重點寫下來，然後確保對這些重點以及支持重點的資料非常非常熟悉，最後再多多練習，以自然、口語化的方式表達這些內容並在不同重點之間自然過渡（至於應如何練習簡報技巧的問題，我們在下面將進一步討論。）只要我們細心準備並多多練習，我們就可以以自然、有效的方式來發表簡報，而不需要呆板地向觀眾朗誦報告。

　　在撰寫大綱時，應該記得：大綱是準備簡報時的重要工具，但它並不屬於簡報內容的一部分，而且我們也不會把它拿給觀眾看。所以，大綱的寫法應依個人的需求而定，並沒有一定的寫法。常常發表而且英文會話能力很強的人可能只需要很簡略的大綱，而其他人則可能喜歡手裏有個較完整的大綱。然而，無論發表的水平如何，大綱內容都應該儘量清楚、精簡。

　　簡報大綱通常至少要包含下列資料：

- 敘述報告主題。
- 陳述主要重點。在閱讀書面的研究報告時，讀者可以先閱讀摘要來大致瞭解整篇報告的主要重點或結果，而且在讀報告的主要部分時，只要讀者發現自己忽略了某個重點，他們可以隨時回過頭再重讀一遍。然而，簡報卻沒有「摘要」，而且觀眾也沒有「重讀」的機會。因此，報告人在解釋了研究主題及動機之後，應該馬上清楚、簡略地概述自己研究的主要重點或結果，以便讓觀眾對下面的內容有個心理準備。
- 提供資料以支持自己的重點，例如，描述實驗程序、材料以及主要結果。
- 指出結論或做總結。

六、準備有效的視聽輔助工具

　　適切的視聽輔助工具（如 Powerpoint、幻燈片、視頻錄像等等）是會議簡報成功不可或缺的要素。視聽輔助工具有幾種重要的功能：

- 如果報告人細心準備了含有視聽輔助工具內容的發表，那他就可以將這些工具當作簡報內容的提示，幫助自己回憶所要表達的重點。視聽輔助工具甚至可以完全取代演講人書面的大綱或筆記。

- 視聽輔助工具能使觀眾的注意力集中在報告人所表達的訊息上。當報告人想要強調某個重點時，最好能利用視聽輔助工具來支持該重點。如此一來，觀眾便會更加注意並更容易記住該重點。

- 視聽輔助工具能幫助我們清楚、有效地將很複雜的訊息傳達給觀眾。有些訊息難以用語言表達，而且就算能用語言表達也常會令觀眾覺得難以理解，不過假如以視聽輔助工具來表達，便可以很容易被觀眾所領會。例如，假設我們在科技會議中需要描述某種電子線路。對我們而言，利用圖形來解釋線路的結構一定比直接用口頭描述要容易得多，而且對觀眾而言，這樣也比較容易能瞭解線路的結構。

七、選用能提供具體訊息的標題

　　準備簡報時，應細心選擇適當的標題。好的標題能清楚地反映出簡報的內容。在這裏介紹一種很簡單的方法可以用來檢驗自己的標題是否適當：先把標題拿給一些朋友或同事看，然後請他們猜測簡報的內容。如果他們都猜不準，那就應該換新的標題才是。

八、準備清楚、切題的導論

　　簡報一開頭應冠以清楚、能提供具體訊息的導論。成功的簡報要求報告人在導論中提供充分的背景資料，以便觀眾瞭解簡報內容並認可簡報價值。簡報的導論必須將簡報主體部分的脈絡介紹給觀眾：簡單扼要地說明將要討論的是哪些題目或問題、它們的重要性以及整個簡報的重點。在做會議簡報時，不要讓觀眾對簡報的主要論點有任何猜疑。如果打算批評某個錯誤的理論或觀點，則應該在導論中直接告訴大家。如果打算介紹比現有技術還要更先進或更準確的技術，則應在導論中直接了當地說明。請記住：聽簡報不同於閱讀研究論文。觀眾在聽簡報時，不可能回頭「重溫」第一次沒聽清楚或沒聽懂的內容。因此，報告人有必要在一開始做簡報時就清楚表達自己的主要論點，以便讓觀眾知道究竟要提出哪些主張或訊息，而且也能對接下來報告人所提供的具體資料有個心理準備。

　　此外，在較長的簡報中，每次過渡到新的部分或次標題時，都應該再附上一個簡短的「迷你導論」，用來重述該部分的主要重點。正如研究論文中新段落的主題句一樣，此種「迷你導論」能幫助觀眾快速領會組織結構並對下面將介紹的詳細訊息有個心理準備。（請參閱本書第七章。）

　　一般來說，在簡報開始之前，會議主持人通常會先向觀眾介紹報告人。只有當主持人沒有介紹報告人時，報告人才有必要做自我介紹，否則只要說一句 "Good morning" 或 "Good afternoon" 就可以直接開始簡報。如果主持人只介紹了報告人的名字，而忘了提到他的學校（單位）或職位，那麼報告人可以補充這些信息。而且，如果報告人打算利用投影片以作為視聽輔助工具，那麼應該在第一張投影片上列出簡報的標題以及自己的姓名、學校（或單位）及職位。無論採用何種方式來介紹報告人，重要的是要迅速、順利地過渡到簡報的實質內容。

　　若有必要，報告人可以採用下面其中一種句型來做自我介紹（注意：說話越慢、越清楚越好）：

> Good afternoon/morning. My name is _____, and today I will be describing the results of research on _____ conducted at National Taiwan University, in Taiwan.
>
> Good afternoon/morning 或 Thank you. It's an honor / a pleasure to be here.
>
> Today I would like to report on _____.
> Today I will be reporting on _____.
> This afternoon I will report some of our findings concerning _____.
> In my report today, I'd like to present a new method for _____.
> My topic today is _____.
> Today I will be discussing _____.

　　有很多觀眾由於研討會剛開始，心裡還沒有靜下來而不會注意聽報告人的第一句話。因此，簡報的第一句話應該是 "Good afternoon" 或再次敘述簡報題目，而先不要急於表達重要的內容。

九、準備言簡意賅、有效的總結

　　一般來講，觀眾通常都會特別注意簡報最後的幾句話，所以報告人在簡報結束前，應以非常精簡的話語重述自己的主要重點——也就是最重要的結論或建議——以及支持這些重點的主要理由。這時，若能有效地強調自己的主要論點，則會給觀眾留下特別深刻的印象。

　　如果適當的話，在敘述了自己的結論之後，報告人還可以利用下列句子來鼓勵觀眾提出問題：

> If there are any questions, I'd be happy to take them now.
> If there are any questions, I'd be happy to answer them.

　　如果沒有時間給觀眾問問題，那麼報告人在做了總結之後，就可以以 "Thank you" 或 "This concludes my report. Thank you." 結束。

十、準備可以省略的內容

詳細回顧所準備的簡報內容，將三分之一左右的內容標出，作為必要時可以省略的內容。一般人在開始練習簡報之後，很快就會發現發表的時間過長。一般人（包括經驗豐富的人）剛一開始都會準備過多的內容。所以，當我們已經初步準備好了簡報的內容之後，應再次檢查所有的內容，並標明必要時可以省略的部分。

成功的簡報最重要的原則之一是：說話的速度應儘量放慢，很慢才行。對以英文為母語的人而言，適當的速度少於每分鐘一百個英文字。對非以英文為母語的人而言，適當的速度可能還要更慢。因此，如果自己準備做十五分鐘的簡報的話，則簡報的內容就絕不能超過一千五百個英文字。

20.2 練習

當我們把簡報內容都準備好了之後，就需要練習發表技巧了。勤於練習發表技巧，實為簡報成功的不二法門。唯有多練習，才能自然、流暢地把簡報各個部分連接起來。此外，唯有多練習才能確定所准備的簡報內容需要多長時間才能進行完畢，進而才能決定是否有必要增減一些內容。最重要的是：多練習發表技巧可以提高自信心，因此也可以讓我們在發言時能以最有效、最具說服力的話語來表達簡報的內容。只有細心練習，到了發表的時候，我們才不會手足無措。

練習簡報的方法很多。最簡單的方法是在家裡照鏡子練習，最好還可以錄音，如此一來，在練習完畢以後就可以試聽自己的簡報內容，並找出需要改進的地方。如果自己擁有或可以借到攝像機，可以把自己在練習發表時的情形拍下來，然後再觀看錄影帶。不論是聽錄音帶或看錄影帶，都應該注意自己是否有些地方暫停了太久，或在簡報不同部分時，過度得不太通順。另外，應該特別注意是否常常發出一些如「嗯」、「啊」等無意義的聲音或是常常重複如 "OK"、"good" 等口頭語。如果是的話，則應該設法改掉這些壞習慣。最後，也應該注意自己是否常常重複有些下意識的抽搐或手勢，或表現出其它影響觀眾的注意力的壞習慣。

此外，練習發表技巧最有效的方法是先向朋友、同事或同學做發表，並請他們記下對報告人表現的反映或建議可改進之處。在簡報結束了之後，請他們對簡報內容與表達方式做出評價並指出改進辦法。

在練習演講時，應該注意下列幾點：

銜接

多練習各個板塊或次題目之間的銜接過渡。過渡到新的次題目時，用以表示銜接的言辭無需特別複雜或刻意給人留下深刻的印象。事實上，最好的銜接方式就是自然地介紹新題目，這樣一般不太會引起觀眾的注意。不同次題目間的過渡必須清楚、自然、通順並合理。

在做銜接時，報告人可以多用如 "Now let me describe..." 以及 "Next, let's look at..." 等詞句來和觀眾建立一種融洽的感覺。然而，採用此種詞句卻並非必要。

例如，在介紹實驗結果時，假如直接把投影片打到螢幕上說 "Here are the results of the first test"，也無可厚非。

重點

　　準備幾種不同的表達方式來描述自己的主要重點。在簡報過程中，報告人通常需要多次重複主要論點。也就是說，在導論中應敘述一次，在提供證據以支持該論點之前或之後應再敘述一次，而且最後作總結時一定還要再敘述一次。如果每次重述同一個論點時都使用一模一樣的句子，那麼觀眾就難免會覺得簡報內容非常單調、枯燥乏味。因此，對於簡報的主要論點應該多準備幾種不同的表達方式。

設備操作

　　若在簡報中需要採用特別的設備，那麼報告人應先確定自己能夠熟練操作。在簡報開始前應該確定需要應用的設備可以正常運行，而且知道如何熟練操作它。如果在簡報過程中必須做某種表演或需要用到動態的模型，那麼還應確定自己的表演已很熟練，而且演示模型時也不會發生問題。

演講技巧

　　多練習發表技巧。訓練自己用清楚、專業的發表方式進行發表。在發表時，應該抬頭挺胸，不要駝背，聲音不要由喉嚨或胸部上方發出，而應該放鬆喉嚨與胸部，改用丹田周圍的肌肉發出既深又有力的聲音（不論男女都是如此）。在講話時，可以多利用自然的手勢，而且最好有些肢體動作。需要記住一點：觀眾是來聽人發表，而不是來聽蠟像發表！應該注意並改掉任何會擾亂觀眾注意力的壞習慣，如一直重複同樣一些口頭語、玩弄鉛筆或不斷地重複一模一樣的動作。最重要的就是要表現得自然！報告人需要讓觀眾看到：他和大家一樣都是有血有肉的人，而且他只希望介紹一些大家都會感興趣的研究。

　　如果需要用英文做特別重要的簡報，那就應該看看能不能找一位以英文為母語者或曾經參加過很多國際學術會議的教授，請他們試聽自己的簡報，並對發表技巧與內容提供一些改進意見。

　　在簡報中，應該儘量選用簡單的字詞與表達方式，而且發音應該做到又慢又清楚。千萬不要以為自己一定要用很複雜高深的言辭才能博得觀眾的尊敬，進而才能讓他們承認自己的研究價值。只要我們的簡報很清楚、組織有條理而且研究內容本身有一定的專業水準，那麼觀眾自然會尊敬我們，而並不會去注意我們使用的英文句子是否稍嫌簡單。

　　此外，在任何簡報中都應該避免生硬、不自然的句子。如果在文章中聽起來稍微生硬的句子，放在簡報中就會聽起來更加不自然。例如，在介紹某個圖表中的資料時，應避免如 "It is shown in this figure that…" 或 "It can be seen from this figure that…" 之類拙劣的被動句子，而應該簡單地說 "This figure shows that…" 或 "From this figure, we can see that…"。（請參考本書第四、六章。）

　　前文講到的關於英文寫作許多重要的修辭原則，對口頭上的溝通尤其適用。若報告人能熟練運用如「先提到舊訊息，然後才提到新訊息」以及「短的片語應該放在長的片語前」等修辭原則，則可以使觀眾更容易領會簡報內容。關於這些原則的詳細討論，請參閱本書第九章。

準備回答觀眾的問題

　　在發表簡報前應先針對觀眾可能提出的一些問題準備好答案。在簡報開始前，報告人可以先猜測觀眾可能會提出哪些問題，並針對這些問題準備好精簡的答案。為了節省時間，而且並不是所有的觀眾對每個問題都一樣有興趣，答案的內容應該儘量簡潔（想要詳細討論問題的觀眾，在簡報結束後還可以找報告人談一談）。如果可能的話，還可以請幾個朋友或同事提出一些自己沒想到的問題。只要報告人對自己的題目很熟悉，那麼在回答觀眾疑問時就應該不會有什麼困難，但是最好還是先準備充分，以確保到時候不會緊張出錯。

　　如果觀眾問了我們無法回答的問題，不要擔心，應該直接表示自己不知道或不確定應如何回答。沒有人知道所有問題的答案吧！我們可以坦白地對觀眾說："We don't have the answer to that yet"、"We aren't sure about that yet" 或 "We're still working on that question"。然而，我們需要記住：身為專業的研究人員，當我們表示 "I don't know" 時，這樣的答覆表示了我們有責任進一步研究這個問題，而且應在以後找機會為提出問題的人做進一步的解釋。

20.3 發表

　　對一般人而言，簡報最困難的一個部分就是如何克服怯場。想想要在幾十個甚至幾百個研究人員面前解釋自己的研究，而且若是國際科技討論會的話，則還要用英語發表！這怎麼會不令人緊張呢！

　　然而，事實上只要自己細心準備，就沒有什麼好著急費神的。感到緊張的唯一合理的理由就是因為自己沒有準備好。如果已經把簡報內容都準備妥當，而且已經把簡報練得很熟悉，那麼我們就根本就沒有理由感到緊張。

　　報告人如果是第一次做簡報而覺得很緊張，則應該提醒自己下列幾點：

　　一、自己已經細心準備了簡報內容並練得很熟練，現在只要再次重複自己已熟練的內容而已，這並不是那麼困難的事。

　　二、每個人都曾經有怯場的經驗，只要觀眾能看出報告人雖然有一點緊張但確實已準備了很好的簡報內容，那麼他們就會報以同情且會很有耐心。我們需要記得：觀眾本來就是和我們一樣的人，而不是一群食人妖怪。

　　三、怯場的感覺和經驗之間呈反比關係，當報告人經驗比較豐富時，怯場的感覺自然會逐漸消失。

　　需要做簡報時，為了進一步減少緊張的感覺，我們還可以注意下列原則：

在發表的前一天晚上保證睡眠充足。如果我們很疲倦地出場，當然不會有很好的發表。

穿得體的服裝、注意自己的姿勢

衣著必須如專業學者一般，才能讓觀眾信服自己就是專業研究人員。此外，由於穿著比較正式的衣服，所以到了發表的時候，自己也就會更加有自信。

應該抬頭挺胸並目視觀眾，而且手不應該塞到口袋裡。如果不必做任何手勢而且不知道雙手要做什麼，則可以在手上拿著筆記（無論需不需要筆記都是如此）。

不用擔心自己的英語

不要太擔心自己的英語是否正確。如果需要用英語做簡報，則應該儘量細心準備，而且應該多練習英語發表技巧。然而，到了發表的時候，不要擔心自己的語言能力不夠好。只要我們已經準備了清楚、有意思、內容充實的簡報，那麼雖然在英語表達方面有些小瑕疵，但我們還是可以獲得觀眾的肯定。

不要害怕觀眾

應把觀眾視為自己的朋友。在發表時，應該提醒自己：觀眾並不是一群飢餓、兇猛的怪獸，就算自己犯了錯，他們也不會馬上就來吞噬我們。觀眾都只是和我們一樣的人，他們來參加會議的理由，是因為他們對我們要發表的訊息很有興趣。他們是我們的朋友。

儘量找機會和觀眾認識。如果可能的話，則應在簡報開始前找機會和部分的觀眾見面聊天。如此一來，我們就更能放鬆自己，並把發表簡報視為和觀眾交談一樣（而事實上，發表簡報本來就如同和觀眾談話一樣）。

集中精神

把精力集中在所要表達的內容上。我們已經細心準備好了，因此在發表時只要專心按照自己原來的計劃來發表簡報內容即可。

盡情享受

放輕鬆、順其自然。要讓觀眾看出自己對簡報題目充滿濃厚的興趣，而且很熱心地想和觀眾分享自己的研究結果。

把發表視為很愉悅的過程。提醒自己最重要的一點：事實上，會議簡報能讓我們有機會做一些自己喜歡做的事情。對自己的研究做簡報本來就應該是一件很愉快的事——我們有機會與一大群和我們有相同興趣與教育背景的人討論一些大家都很感興趣的研究，豈不樂哉？

在閱讀了上述原則之後，相信我們一定能輕易地克服緊張的感覺，對不對？（如果讀者不信，那麼請再讀一兩遍！）。現在讓我們注意下面更加重要的發表技巧。

說話要慢

說話的速度要儘量放慢。在一開始發表時，自然會有一點激動，所以說話的速度一定會比在練習的時候還要快得多。因此，必須時刻提醒自己要減速、吐字要很清楚、發音很清晰，以便讓觀眾聽出每個字詞。這點極為重要，所以我要重複三次：說話要慢！說話要慢！說話要慢！

聲音洪亮

說話聲音要很洪亮。應該確定會議廳內的每個人都能聽得清楚。通常在發表中，我們說話的聲音會自然而然逐漸變小，所以應常常提醒自己：說話還要更大聲！（例如，在每次換投影片或資料卡時，可以再提醒自己一次。）

注意聽自己的聲音。由於頭骨震動的關係，在日常生活中，我們常常很自然地會以為自己的聲音聽起來已經很洪亮了，然而事實上對別人而言或許我們的聲音聽起來仍很微弱。因此，在發表時我們必須注意聽自己的聲音，並儘量用很深沉、很洪亮的聲音說話。

自然的動作

在發表中應展現一些自然的動作。應該時不時走來走去，並利用適當的手勢來強調簡報內容。不要在同一個地方站著不動，也不要一直躲在講台後面。

在發表中應常常目視觀眾。不要只讀筆記或投影片而不理睬觀眾。應該多看著觀眾，並嘗試令每個觀眾都以為我們是對著他/她一個人說話。

注意觀眾的反應

注意觀察觀眾對簡報內容的反應。要十分留意觀眾對簡報內容的感受。如果觀眾似乎不瞭解一些內容，那麼我們應該重複或換一種說法再次解釋。如果觀眾似乎很疲倦或對某些內容沒有興趣，則可以考慮省略其中一些細節，甚至直接跳到下個重點。

演講中需要變化

冗長的簡報應包括一些變化。一般人很難保持久坐不動，通常過了三四十分鐘就會開始感到疲勞而無法集中精力。如果需要做很長的簡報，那麼每三四十分鐘就該有些變化，如講笑話、讓觀眾有機會問問題或暫時切換題目。如此一來，觀眾就可以有機會換姿勢或放鬆一下，然後再重新開始注意簡報內容。

常常小結並請觀眾問問題。在簡報的每一部分結束時，應對該部分的重點及時做總結。如果簡報很長的話，還可以借這一機會給觀眾有機會問問題。（不過給觀眾發問的時間應控制得當，不能過長，以免影響到整個簡報的進行。若某個問題需要很長、很詳細的解釋，則應表示暫時保留此問題而在發表完畢時再回頭來討論。當然，不要忘記自己的諾言，在發表結束前一定要再提及此問題。）

20.4 中國人做英文簡報時的注意事項

如果你不是以英文為母語者，在做英文簡報時，當然會遇到一些特殊的問題。在本節中，我們將建議一些方法以幫助華人順利地發表英文簡報。

多利用以短小、簡單的字詞所組成之短小、簡單的句子。在簡報中不要使用如 "Following the addition of oxygen, the hardness of the samples was observed to increase significantly" 之類冗長、生硬的句子，說起來和聽起來都很彆扭。而應該說："Adding oxygen made the samples much harder"。

在發表時，說話要洪亮，發音要清晰。

在發表中說話要慢。應常常提醒自己：慢、慢、再慢！

不要把英文字詞的母音都吞掉了。華人說英語時，在發音方面最明顯的缺陷之一，是常常把英語母音都「切斷」了，尤其是短音的發音更是如此。在說英語時，需要把喉嚨放鬆，並把母音的聲音都拉長。請記得：喉嚨要放鬆，英語發音才會自然。需要放鬆！

應確定每個英文字詞的最後一個音節都發音清楚。尤其是當字尾是子音時，更需特別注意這點。華人說英語時常犯的另一個錯誤是英語字詞的最後一個音節或字母根本沒有發音。如果希望觀眾能瞭解我們的意思，那麼就必須把完整的字詞都發出來，不能任意省略其中任何一個音節！

應隨時使用完整的句子說話。每個句子必須為具有主詞、動詞之完整的獨立子句。所說的句子可以很簡短，但是應確保都是完整的句子。（請參考本書第四章 4.1 節。）

應該學習所屬專業領域中常用英文字詞的正確發音。尤其是當不知道字詞的哪個音節為重音時，應該查辭典確定。若可能的話，還可以請以英語為母語的朋友、同事或英語教師試聽自己的發表，並指出任何發音不正確的字詞並予以糾正。

不要以為英語專業術語正確的發音就是華人同學或同事常用的那種發音，有不少英語專業術語已經被納入中文而成為一種「科技中文」。然而，大家所用的發音和以英語為母語者的發音並不同。例如，在臺灣幾乎所有的人都把 *modem* 唸成 "mo*dem*"（第二個音節為重音），但以英語為母語者都說 "*mo*dem"（第一個音節為重音）。另外，大家通常都把 *DOS* 的發音當作和 *dose* 相同（發 "o" 的長音），然而在美國大家都把它唸成和 *doss* 相同的發音（發 "o" 的短音）。

要加強或改善自己的英語發音，最適宜的時刻就是「現在」，也就是說，我們不要等到需要做簡報的最後一個星期，才開始注意自己英文發音的問題。對於發音比較困難或複雜的英文字詞或凡是在書上看到的生字，都應該養成常常翻閱辭典的習慣，以查出正確的發音與重音。

把自己簡報中的所有關鍵詞都放到投影片中。如此一來，萬一自己對某個重要字詞的發音不清楚，觀眾還有機會在書面文字上看到這個字詞，明白你的意思。

在做英文簡報時，不要太擔心自己的英語是否有些小小的文法錯誤。重要的是：自己的姿勢、服裝都有專業水準，而且發音也很清晰。只要簡報的主要重點都能表達清楚（因為我們已經細心地準備了簡報內容，所以一定能表達清楚！），那麼觀眾一定可以原諒一些文法上的小瑕疵。其實，觀眾都能瞭解英語不是我們的母語，而且事實上他們也並不特別關心我們的英語是否很完美。他們所關心的是：我們是否能以很清楚的方式對於大家感興趣的題目提供一些有用的訊息。

　　有些讀者可能會懷疑，本章為何沒有列出很多在英文簡報中常用的句型以供讀者參考。然而，我們並不需要特別列出專門在簡報中用的句子，因為事實上，絕大多數在本書其它章節中所列出來的句型以及所討論的文法規則，對與簡報的內容而言都一樣適用。無論是書面的研究報告或口頭上的簡報，最重要的是能應用本書前後一貫所強調的三個基本原則：表達方式要正確、清楚及簡潔。

附錄

附錄一
標題頁

在本附錄中，我們將討論關於科技研究報告標題頁的一些注意事項。

標題頁的內容通常包括文章的標題以及作者的姓名、職位與地址。此外，有時候標題頁還包括一些答謝詞。標題通常在頁面正中、離上面邊界約整個頁高三分之一的距離。標題頁應列有作者的學校或研究機構的名稱以及完整的地址，以便讓期刊編輯能容易聯絡作者，而且最好也應提供傳真機或電話號碼以及電子郵件的地址。

標題頁通常應該為獨立於文章其餘部分的一張紙，除了標題與上述資料以外，沒有其他內容。有些學術期刊會指定標題頁一定要獨立於文章其他部分，而且作者的姓名只能放在標題頁上，在文章主要部分不要出現。如此一來，期刊編輯便能夠很方便地把文章送審：只要把標題頁拿掉、在文章主要部分蓋上編號並把文章轉交給審稿人即可。

如果作者喜歡的話，也可以在報告的第一頁上面重複文章的標題。

有些作者習慣把標題頁與摘要合併成一頁，然而，有不少學術期刊建議應該把標題頁與摘要分為兩頁。

有些期刊會要求作者在標題頁或摘要頁底列上關鍵詞 (key words)。

如果作者習慣用英文名字而且使用英文字母以表示中文的名字，則英文名字應該擺在表示中文名字的字母之前，而不要把英文名字放在這些字母和姓氏中間。例如，如果張三的英文名字是 Samuel，則他應該寫 "Samuel S. Chang" 或 "Samuel Chang"，而不要寫 "S. Samuel Chang" 或 "San Samuel Chang"。如果林寶玉的英文名字是 Paula，則她應該寫 "Paula P. Lin" 或 "Paula Lin"，而不要寫 "P. Paula Lin" 或 "Pao-yu Paula Lin"。

　　當研究報告不只有一個作者時，通常其中一個作者會負責和期刊編輯或其他學者通信。如果這作者的地址出現在標題頁上的話，則通常在作者的姓名後會有一個註解符號，而且在頁底會有個註解表示 "Responsible for correspondence"、"Addressee for correspondence" 或 "Corresponding author"（前兩者大概比較適用）。萬一此作者的通訊地址和標題頁上的地址不同，則在註解中可以表示 "Correspondence:"、"Address correspondence to:" 或 "Send correspondence to:"，並在後面提供通訊地址。

　　研究報告的作者在標題頁底常常會加上一個註解以表示謝辭。通常這註解的標題為 "Acknowledgements"（複數），然而如果內容只有感謝一個人或一個機構而已，則有些人會寫 "Acknowledgement"（單數）。下面為在 acknowledgements 中一些典型的常用句子。

> The authors are grateful for financial support from the China Technology Foundation.

> The authors wish to thank the China Technology Foundation for financial support of this research under grant 123-456-7890.

> This research was conducted with financial support from the China Technology Foundation.

> This work was supported by a grant from the China Technology Foundation.

> This research was funded by a grant from the China Technology Foundation.

> The authors gratefully acknowledge financial support from the China Technology Foundation.

> The author wishes to thank John Chen for offering many useful suggestions concerning the research in this paper and Mary Li for assisting with the data analysis.

> The authors are grateful to two anonymous referees whose valuable comments helped to improve the content of this paper.

> The authors wish to thank two anonymous reviewers for their comments regarding an earlier version of this paper.

附錄二
投稿信函

在投稿到專業學術期刊時，作者應該附上投稿信函，以表示自己的用意。投稿信函的內容可以既簡短又簡單，然而，由於禮貌的關係，此信函很重要而且不應該省略。在英文中，投稿信函稱作 "cover letter"。

以前，投稿信函需要採用大學研究所或研究機構正式的信紙，而且在信紙上面表示作者的通訊地址及聯絡資料。關於投稿信函的排版格式，商業書信的任何標準格式都適用。在信函上面列有期刊編輯的姓名、期刊的名稱以及期刊的地址。

當今投稿時，平時不必寄打印的硬拷貝 (hardcopy) 投稿信函或論文，而只寄電郵 (email) 的投稿信函並以電郵附件寄論文。然而，電郵的內容和以前的投稿信函大同小異。

一般學術期刊都會指定一位負責投稿事宜的編輯，投稿信函的抬頭應該是這位編輯的姓名。請注意：在一般歐洲語言的人名中，名字都擺在姓氏前，所以如果編輯的姓名是 James Smith 的話，則在信函的抬頭需要寫 Professor Smith，而不能寫 Professor James，後者就不禮貌。

下面列有兩封典型的投稿電郵。第一封為作者在初次投稿時可能會採用之信函，第二封則可以在投修正稿時採用。

在撰寫投稿電郵時，應注意：正式的英文書信應採用儘量清楚、簡潔的寫作方式，而且應該使用很自然的當代英文。投稿信函千萬不要以如 "Enclosed please find..." 之類生硬的詞句開頭，而只要簡單地寫 "Attached is..." 即可。不要對編輯表示 "I humbly submit the attached paper for your kind consideration"，而只要寫 "Please consider this paper for publication" 或 "I write to submit this paper for publication" 即可。電郵應該以一句簡單的 "Thank you" 結束。

投稿電郵例一

To: jamessmith@IJWT.tech.edu

From: jchen@ncuwidgets.edu

Subject: Manuscript submission to *International Journal of Widget Technology*

Dr. James Smith, Editor
International Journal of Widget Technology

Professor Smith:

Attached is a manuscript entitled "A New Design for Submersible Widgets."
Please consider this paper for publication in the *International Journal of Widget Technology*.

Thank you.

Sincerely,

John Chen

_____

John Chen
Professor
Department of Widget Science
National China University
100 Main Street
Central City, China 012345
Phone: 999-2345-6789
Fax: 999-1234-5678
Email: jchen@ncuwidgets.edu
Web: www.NCUwidgets.edu

投稿電郵例二

To: jamessmith@IJWT.tech.edu

From: jchen@ncuwidgets.edu

Subject: Manuscript resubmission

Professor Smith:

Attached is a revised version of our article "A New Design for Submersible Widgets" (manuscript no. 123-45-678).

We have revised the paper according to your directions and the suggestions of the referees and are resubmitting it for publication in the *International Journal of Widget Technology.*

Thank you.

Sincerely,

John Chen

———————

John Chen
Professor
Department of Widget Science
National China University
100 Main Street
Central City, China 012345
Phone: 999-2345-6789
Fax: 999-1234-5678
Email: jchen@ncuwidgets.edu

附錄三
參考資料目錄

　　科技研究報告的最後一部分通常為參考資料目錄。在本附錄中，我們將簡略地討論參考資料目錄的標準格式以及相關問題。

　　不同學術期刊或專業學會對參考資料目錄的格式有不同的標準，如所採用的標點符號、縮寫字詞以及訊息的順序可能都各有不同。例如，有些期刊在文章的名稱前後都加上引號，然而有些期刊則省略引號。有些期刊依字母順序排列參考文獻而不加上序號。然而，有些期刊則在每篇文獻前加上序號，並在文章中只使用序號以引述參考資料。在一般參考資料目錄的格式中，若參考文獻為期刊上的文章，則參考資料最後一項訊息是文章的頁數，然而，也有些期刊把出版年代當作最後一項訊息。在某些參考資料目錄中，在頁數前都加上縮寫 "pp."（即 "pages"）或 "p."（即 "page"），但不少常用的格式則省略這些字詞。在某些參考資料目錄中，所有期刊的名稱都縮寫，然而也有很多參考資料格式會把期刊的名稱全部寫出來。因此，在投稿之前，作者應先參考打算投稿的期刊曾刊登的幾篇文章，以確定該期刊所採用的參考資料目錄格式為何。

　　在查詢某個期刊所使用的參考資料目錄格式時，應該順便查詢文章中參考資料引述的格式，並確定自己引述參考文獻的方式符合擬投稿的期刊之標準格式。

　　在下面我們將簡略地介紹三種常用的參考資料目錄格式。第一種常用格式為許多科技專業期刊所採用之「序號格式」。第二種為不少科學及社會科學的專業期刊所使用之「APA 格式」，這格式原是美國心理學學會 (American Psychological Association) 所推行的。第三種則是人文學及部分的社會科學期刊所用之「MLA 格式」，這格式為美國現代語言學會 (Modern Language Association) 所推行的。（兩個學會推行的格式都會定期更新，所以最新的格式和本章介紹的可能會有出入，可參考各學會的網站。）然而，請注意：因為不少期刊所採用的參考資料目錄格式為這三種格式的變形格式，所以我們在下面僅提供此三種格式的基本描述。關於更詳細的描述，讀者應參閱個別專業期刊所印行的格式說明。

序號格式

當作者採用序號格式時，在文章中應使用阿拉伯數字來引述參考資料，阿拉伯數字前後應該用括號或方括號，或是把數字當作上標。請參考下例：

Submersible widgets are a relatively new development (4).

Submersible widgets are a relatively new development [4].

Submersible widgets are a relatively new development.[4]

在參考資料目錄中，參考文獻通常根據作者姓氏的第一個字母依字母順序排列（若有兩個以上作者，則依第一個作者的姓氏排列），而且在每一個參考文獻前加上序號：第一個參考文獻為 1、第二個文獻為 2 等等。然而，在某些期刊中，參考文獻的排列順序不是依字母的順序，而是依文獻在文章中出現的順序，亦即在文章中所提到的第一個參考文獻就為 1，在文章中所提到的第二個文獻為 2 等等。

下面就是以序號格式為基礎之典型的參考資料目錄：

1. A. J. Castelle and J. N. Galloway, Carbon Dioxide Dynamics in Acid Forest Soils, *Soil Sci. Am. J.* **54** (1990), 252–257.

2. A. Sedlacek and C. Wight, Photochemistry of Solid Ozone, *J. Phys. Chem.* **93** (1989), 509–511.

3. J. Smith, *Widgets in the Twentieth Century*, New York: Research Press, 1990.

4. D. E. Stott, H. F. Stroo, L. F. Elliott, R. I. Papendick, and P. W. Unger, Wheat Residue Loss from Fields Under No-till Management, *Soil Sci. Am. J.* **54** (1990), 92–98.

在此格式中，在序號後面第一項訊息是作者的姓名，而且作者的名字只用字母來縮寫。緊接在作者的姓名後是文章或書的名稱。如果是書名則應以斜體字表示，而且在書名後應表示出版城市、出版社以及出版年代。請參閱上面第三項參考文獻，尤其是應注意逗號及冒號等標點符號的用法。

如果參考文獻為期刊上的文章，則在文章的名稱前後就沒有引號。期刊的名稱應使用斜體字，而且通常都縮寫。在期刊的名稱後應表示卷號以及出版年代（出版年代通常放在括號裡），有時候卷號使用斜體字或粗體字。最後是文章的頁數，而在頁數前不需要寫 "pp."。

上面只不過是序號格式其中一個典型的例子而已。不同期刊所採用的格式可能和上面的格式有所差別。例如，有些期刊把作者的姓氏放在縮寫的名字前面，有些期刊把出版年代放在最後（緊接在頁數後面），有些期刊在文章名稱前後加引號，而有些期刊則甚至省略所有文章的名稱。因此，在投稿之前應先細心查詢擬投稿期刊之參考資料目錄格式究竟為何。

APA 格式

在 APA 格式中，在文章中應使用作者的姓氏及出版年代以引述參考資料。這些訊息通常應放在括號裡（有些期刊用方括號），如下：

Submersible widgets are a relatively new development (Smith, 1990).

如果在句子中提到作者的姓氏，則在括號中只需要寫出版年代。

According to Smith (1990), submersible widgets are a relatively new development.

如果句子直接引述作者的話，則在括號中還要包括引文的頁數。

According to Smith, submersible widgets are "a relatively new development" (1990, pp. 52–53).

在參考資料的目錄中，所有的參考文獻都根據作者的姓氏依字母順序排列。如果在目錄中列出同一個作者之兩篇以上著作，則這些著作應依年代順序排列（由最早期到最近期）。（如果同一個作者的兩個以上著作之出版年代都相同，則應依字母順序排列，並在出版年代後加小寫的字母，如 1990a, 1990b 等等）。

下面是此種格式的例子：

Castelle, A. J. & Galloway, J. N. (1990). Carbon dioxide dynamics in acid forest soils, *Journal of Soil Science, 54,* 252–257.

Sedlacek, A. & Wight, C. (1989). Photochemistry of solid ozone, *Journal of Physical Chemistry, 93,* 509–511.

Smith, J. (1990). *Widgets in the twentieth century.* New York: Research Press.

Stott, D. E., Stroo, H. F., Elliott, L. F., Papendick, R. I., & Unger, P. W. (1990). Wheat residue loss from fields under no-till management, *Journal of Soil Science, 54,* 92–98.

所有作者的姓氏都放在名字前（若文獻有兩個以上作者，則每個作者的姓名亦如此），而且名字都以字母縮寫。如果文獻有兩個以上作者，則在最後一個作者的姓氏前應該使用 "&" 符號以表示 "and" 的意思。然而，在文章中引述參考文獻時，則應該使用 "and" 而不用 "&" 符號。在參考資料目錄中，應該列出每篇參考文獻所有作者的姓名，但是在文章中引述個別的參考文獻時，如果某一篇文獻有六個以上作者，則只應寫第一個作者的姓氏並加上 et al. 兩個字詞（不需要用斜體字或逗號），如 "Smith et al."。如果某一篇參考文獻有兩個到五個作者的話，則在文章中第一次引述時，應該列出所有作者的姓氏，但是在第二、三次引述時則只需要寫第一個作者的姓氏並加上 et al.。

在上面的例子中，請注意：

- 出版年代都應該放在括號中。
- 在每個書名或文章的標題中，只有第一個字詞才需要大寫，其他字詞全部都是小寫。書名應該用斜體字來表示，但是文章的標題前後都不應該用引號。

- 和書名不同，在期刊的名稱中每個字詞都應該大寫。期刊的名稱應該使用斜體字，而且卷號應該使用斜體字或粗體字。
- 此外，如果某項參考文獻的出版資料超過一行字的話，則第二、三行必須縮進排印（縮進的距離大約五格）。

　　關於 APA 格式的進一步說明，請參考 *Publication Manual of the American Psychological Association*。

　　如同序號格式的情形一樣，不同的學術期刊可能會採用 APA 格式的不同變形格式。所以，個別期刊的格式可能和上述例子大致相同但有少許差別。

MLA 格式

　　在 MLA 格式中，在文章中的參考資料引述通常只包括作者的姓氏以及參考資料的頁數。這些訊息應該放在括號裡，但不應該有其他標點符號，也不需要寫 "p."，如：

> Submersible widgets are a recent development (Smith 110).

　　如果在文章中提到作者的姓氏，則在參考引述中只需要寫頁數而已，如下：

> Smith describes submersible widgets as a recent development (110).

　　在參考資料的目錄中，參考文獻根據作者姓氏依字母順序排列。作者的姓氏應擺在名字前（然而，假如文獻有兩個以上作者，則只應把第一個作者的姓氏擺在名字前，其他作者的姓氏擺在名字後）。在作者姓名後，應列出書名、出版城市、出版社以及出版年代。書名應該用斜體字表示。下面是 MLA 格式典型的例子。在這些例子中，請注意標點符號的用法。

> Smith, John. *Widgets in the Twentieth Century*. New York: Research Press, 1990.

> Smith, John, Charles H. White, and Roger Martin. *A History of Widgets*. New York: Gadget Press, 1991.

請注意：作者的名字不應該縮寫，而且在書名中應使用大小寫字母。

　　如果參考文獻有四個以上作者，則在參考資料目錄中只需要寫第一個作者的姓名並在姓名後加上 et al.。如果一項參考文獻的出版資料超過一行字的話，則第二、三行必須縮進排印（縮進的距離大約五格）。

　　上面例子的內容都是書名，而下面則是 MLA 格式列出文章之出版資料的方式。在這個例子中，請特別注意標點符號的用法。

> Smith, John H. "A Classroom Study of Computer-aided Learning in High Schools." *Journal of Computer Education* 33 (1991): 259–70.

　　關於多種其他參考資料的引述方式，MLA 都有詳細的規則。讀者可以參閱 *The MLA Handbook for Writers of Research Papers*。此外，如同另外兩個常用格式一樣，不同的大學或刊物可能會使用基本的 MLA 格式之不同的變形格式。

網上的參考資料

近年來，研究人員越來越需要頻繁地引述來自互聯網上的資料。至今為止，尚未形成任何成文的標準來規定如何引述網上發表的資料。儘管如此，作者們應採用一個統一的格式來註明每一個資料的出處，並保證為讀者提供足夠的信息以方便他們在網上查找來源。

一些網絡期刊或網站提供了如何在這些網站上引述出版物的指導。具體細節請留意一個關於「如何引述這份出版物」的解釋選項或者查看該網站版權聲明的附件。

下面給出一份關於引述網站出版物的基本格式供參考。如果你欲投稿的期刊沒有在這方面給出具體的要求，那麼你就可以按照這個基本格式來準備。

1. 作者姓名（姓在前）。如果沒有作者，則給出網站或出版物編輯的姓名。
2. 所引述文章的題目或網站的名字，用引號標註。
3. 網站的名字，也就是網站主頁所顯示的名字。
4. 編輯或翻譯人的名字，前面註明*編 (ed.)*、*譯 (tr.)*。
5. 如有，註明第幾版或第幾卷。
6. 出版日期。
7. 共有多少頁、段、或部分。
8. 支持網站運行的機構，如大學、研究所、出版社等。
9. 你訪問該網站出版物的日期。
10. 出版物的URL網址，用尖括號 ＜ ... ＞ 註明。

例：

> Fraser, Chris. "Mohism." *Stanford Encyclopedia of Philosophy*. Edward Zalta, ed. 2002. Twelve sections. Stanford University. 2 July 2004. <http://plato.stanford.edu/entries/mohism.html>.

> National Bureau of Statistics of China. Statistical Communiqué of the People's Republic of China on the 2005 National Economic and Social Development. 28 February 2006. 9 April 2009. <http://www.stats.gov.cn/tjgb/ndtjgb/qgndtjgb/t20060227_402307796.htm>.

> Sørensen, Knut. "Environmental Accounts in Norway." 20 September 2000. International Association for Research in Income and Wealth, 23 June 2010. <http://www.iariw.org/papers/2000/sorensen.pdf>.

其他注意事項

參考資料目錄的英文標題應該是複數 "References"，而不是單數。萬一正好只有一篇參考文獻，則有些作者習慣寫單數 "Reference"。另一個常用的標題是 "Works Cited"。

在投稿之前，應先查對自己參考資料目錄中的資料是否正確，例如，是否有一些作者的姓名拼錯了（我們也不希望別人把我們的名字拼錯，不是嗎？）。此外，應該細心檢查參考資料目錄中的標點符號是否符合預備投稿的期刊之標準格式。在參考資料目錄的初稿中，常常會出現標點符號上的錯誤，因此應特別注意在自己的報告中是否有錯誤。

請注意：不論是在文章中或在參考資料目錄中，在左邊的括號前都應該有一個空格，而且，除非右邊的括號後緊接著句號、逗號、分號或冒號等標點符號，否則在右邊的括號後也應該有一個空格。另外，在左邊的括號後及右邊的括號前不應該加空格。請參閱《科技論文英語寫作上冊》第五章 5.9節。

如果自己曾發表和此次研究報告相關的著作，則應該在參考資料目錄中列出。然而，我們不要讓參考資料目錄看起來像個人的履歷表。若自己過去的著作和此次研究沒有密切關聯，則應該省略之。

因為縮寫字詞 "et al."（即「和其他人」）原是拉丁文的外來語，所以在傳統上這些字詞得使用斜體字印刷（在英文中，外國語言的字詞都應該使用斜體字印刷）。然而，今日絕大多數辭典已把 "et al." 視為一般英文字詞而不是外語，因此現在一般期刊編輯會認為這些字詞已不需要用斜體字印刷。

在上面所討論的三種常用參考資料目錄格式中，在引述期刊上的文章時都省略卷、期以及頁等之縮寫字詞（即 Vol.、No.、pp. 或 p. 等）。然而，有些期刊在參考資料目錄中還包含這些縮寫字詞。例如，下例也是一種常見的格式。

Thomson, S. "New Developments in Signal Processing," *Journal of Signal Processing*, Vol. 22, No. 3, 1989, pp. 22–36.

最後，請注意：在列出文章的頁數時，不應使用 "～" 符號以表示「從幾頁到幾頁」之意（英文沒有這標點符號，而在數學與邏輯中，它的意思不是「到」而是「非」）。在英文中，應該使用 en-dash (–) 以表示「從…到…」之意。當代的電腦文書處理軟體都提供 en-dash 符號，然而，萬一在電腦上找不到此符號，則可以使用連字號 (-)。

習題答案

練習 2-1

device	可數	file	可數
hydrogen	不可數	hydrochloric acid	不可數
substrate	可數	deposition	不可數
telecommunications	不可數	system	可數
equipment	不可數	liter of acid	可數
research	不可數	concept	可數
software	不可數	term	可數
evidence	不可數	terminology	不可數
project	可數	gold	不可數
information	不可數	rain	不可數
biology	不可數	kilogram	可數
mass	不可數/兩用	efficiency	不可數

練習 2-2

1. 不可數，不可數，不可數，可數，可數，可數。
2. 不可數。
3. 可數，可數。
4. ·可數，不可數，可數。
5. 不可數，不可數，不可數，可數，可數，不可數，不可數，可數，不可數，可數，可數。
6. 不可數，可數，不可數。
7. 不可數，可數，可數，可數。
8. 不可數，可數。

練習 2-3

一般而言，一個名詞應使用定冠詞還是不定冠詞都有明確的答案；但有時候，答案要視乎作者意思而定。以下的答案都是文章本來的寫法。所以讀者也許會發現部分答案和自己的不同，但又覺得自己的答案也同樣合理。有這種情況的話，最好是請教母語為英語的老師，看你的用法是否也可接受。

1. In the late 1970s, the laser printer had just arrived on the market. It used a complex and expensive optical system to scan a diode laser beam in straight lines across a photoconductive drum. This optical system consisted of a rotary polygonal-mirror scanner and special focusing lenses. The laser beam is simultaneously modulated and deflected by the rotating mirror so that it repeatedly scans straight lines, forming an electrically charged image on the photoconductive drum. This image is then transformed into a visible image on paper by an electrophotoconductive process of the kind used by photocopiers.

   Vital to the optical system of the early laser printer was a high-precision, mirror-scanner motor needed to minimize fluctuations in the placement and straightness of the scanning lines. In laser printers, about 10 scanning lines are generated per rotation. Each line must scan exactly the same position on the photoconductive drum. If the shaft of the motor rotating the scanner wobbles, the scanning line also will deflect. The permissible runout angle for motor shafts of mirror scanners is about 5 seconds, depending on the system. In a typical scanner, the placement error should be less than 25 micrometers, which usually corresponds to a deflection angle change of less than 10 arc seconds. The line produced by laser printers may curve no more than ±0.1 millimeter over the entire scanning range of about 260 mm. To correct placement errors due to mirror wobble, cylindrical lenses often are used.

2. Thermonuclear fusion is the process through which light nuclei—such as hydrogen and its isotopes, deuterium and tritium—fuse at extremely high temperatures to produce heavier elements. It is the fundamental source of energy in the universe, providing the power for the sun and all other stars. Ultimately, all forms of energy used on Earth—including fossil fuels, hydroelectric power, and solar power—derive from fusion energy. Even the energy stored in uranium was originally a product of fusion reactions in a nearby supernova.

   Since nuclei are all positively charged, very high temperatures—over 100 million Kelvin—are required to give them sufficient energy to overcome coulomb electrical repulsion and to react. The basic problem of controlled fusion reactions is, therefore, to produce these high temperatures and simultaneously to confine the resulting plasma long enough and at sufficient density for the release of economically significant energy.

   There are two main approaches to the use of fusion for power generation: inertial confinement and magnetic confinement. Of these two, magnetic confinement has yielded the best results so far. Magnetic confinement makes use of the fact that the charged ions and electrons that make up the thermonuclear plasma tend to spiral around magnetic lines of force rather than move across them. With good design, therefore, magnetic "bottles" can be devised to contain <u>the</u> plasma even at very high temperatures, while <u>a</u> combination of magnetic field compression and other methods can be used for heating.

3. Early computers required <u>a</u> special environment, with raised floors to carry <u>the</u> interconnecting cables and large air-conditioning units to remove <u>the</u> dissipated heat; <u>the</u> maintenance man had to be summoned frequently. At <u>a</u> cost of over <u>a</u> dollar for either <u>a</u> discrete transistor or <u>a</u> bit of memory, <u>the</u> price of early computer systems generally came to <u>a</u> few million dollars. <u>The</u> high cost forced compromises on computer designers, such as <u>the</u> use of <u>a</u> single accumulator register as <u>the</u> source of one argument in every operation of computer logic or arithmetic. This simplified <u>the</u> control structure but generally necessitated time-consuming transfers of data that were extraneous to <u>the</u> intended calculation.

Since that time, <u>the</u> speed, cost, reliability, and size of computer circuitry have changed beyond recognition. <u>The</u> cost of <u>a</u> single transistor or bit of memory is less than <u>a</u> hundredth of <u>a</u> cent, circuits operate for thousands of hours without failing, and <u>a</u> computing unit that far exceeds <u>the</u> capabilities of <u>the</u> ENIAC measures about <u>a</u> centimeter on <u>a</u> side, consumes <u>a</u> fraction of <u>a</u> watt, and can be bought for only <u>a</u> few dollars. This has been brought about, on <u>the</u> supply side, by <u>a</u> remarkably diverse body of new technology and, on <u>the</u> demand side, by <u>the</u> emergence of new, massive, and diverse applications of computational resources, which for <u>the</u> most part bear little resemblance to those for which <u>the</u> general-purpose computer was originally intended.

4. Radio astronomy—<u>the</u> measurement of radio frequencies emitted by interstellar molecules—is <u>the</u> chief method for observing how stars form from interstellar clouds of gas and dust, or die and release such clouds. We live about 30,000 light years from <u>the</u> center of our galaxy, but interstellar dust blocks most of <u>the</u> distance from view by optical telescopes. However, radio waves travel through <u>the</u> dust and can be recorded by special receivers, since <u>the</u> wavelengths are much longer than <u>the</u> size of <u>the</u> dust grains.

Radio telescopes are somewhat similar to optical telescopes. Radio waves from interstellar space are reflected off <u>the</u> antenna—a bowl-shaped mirror—onto <u>a</u> secondary mirror. <u>The</u> waves are reflected down to <u>the</u> center of <u>the</u> bowl, where they enter <u>a</u> radio receiver, or radiometer. <u>The</u> signal is then amplified, filtered, and processed by <u>a</u> detector with <u>a</u> short integration time—about 0.1 ms, or <u>the</u> response time suitable for <u>a</u> loudspeaker.

In making <u>an</u> observation, <u>the</u> astronomer typically steers <u>the</u> antenna toward <u>a</u> radio source, such as <u>a</u> nebula. <u>The</u> signals from various species of molecules—at least 40 have been identified so far—are measured by tuning <u>the</u> receiver to <u>the</u> wavelength characteristic of each species. <u>The</u> observed peak output power of many regions of <u>an</u> interstellar cloud can be plotted as <u>a</u> map with isophotes.

5. Computers would seem much friendlier if it were possible to verbally ask them for information or command them to carry out <u>a</u> task, and if they could respond by talking in natural, conversational English. However, <u>the</u> prospects for automatic recognition of fluent, continuous speech in <u>the</u> near future are not encouraging, in part because of <u>the</u> complexity of <u>the</u> task and in part because of inadequate research support.

A fundamental question in automatic speech recognition by computers is how much information is contained in the acoustic wave patterns that make up the words and sentences used in communicating by voice. In other words, can the machine decipher a voice command and act on it simply by decoding the wave pattern, or does it need to know certain additional information? In all cases, the answer seems to be that extra knowledge must be programmed into the computer.

Speech recognition by a computer comprises two operations. The first is the decomposition of acoustic wave patterns into the basic sounds or elements of speech, called phonemes. Existing speech recognition machines do this job with no more than 65 percent accuracy, in part because the wave patterns corresponding to neighboring phonemes tend to overlap. The second operation is to arrange the phonemes into words and the words into sentences, taking into account that a substantial fraction of the phonemes may be misidentified, and it is here that the need for linguistic and contextual knowledge arises.

6. The molecules of most fuels have far too many atoms for combustion to proceed as a concerted event. Imagine the tangle that would arise if the eight carbon atoms and the 18 hydrogen atoms of an octane molecule (C_8H_{18}) were to disengage from one another and combine all at once with the surrounding molecules of diatomic oxygen (O_2), forming the new chemical bonds of carbon dioxide (CO_2) and water (H_2O). No fuel burns that way. Instead the breakdown of fuel molecules and the formation of combustion products proceed in long sequences of steps; each step involves only a small rearrangement of chemical bonds.

A step of this type is termed an elementary reaction; the various molecules created along the way are called reactive intermediates, and the set of all elementary reactions that together account for the net chemical transformation is the reaction mechanism. The equation describing the overall chemical reaction that takes place in a flame gives no hint of what the individual molecular changes are; the equations describing elementary reactions, however, do represent real chemical events at the molecular level. Only when all the important elementary reactions are known can the path from fuel to combustion products be accurately described in terms of the rearrangements of atoms in molecules.

7. As far as chemists and biologists are concerned, the basic building blocks of matter are atoms and molecules, combinations of atoms that are bound together electrically. An atom consists of a nucleus, which has a positive electric charge, surrounded by one or more electrons that are negatively charged. The electrons are over a thousand times less massive than the nucleus, but they usually occupy a volume with a diameter more than ten thousand times that of the nucleus. Thus, to all intents and purposes, the size of an atom is determined by its electrons.

Since oppositely charged particles attract one another, electrons in an atom tend to stay as close to the nucleus as possible. If one of the electrons is given additional energy, however, the force binding that electron to the nucleus is partially or totally overcome. When the compensation is partial, we speak of a process of excitation; when total, of ionization.

The more the attractive force within the atom is counterbalanced, the greater the separation of the excited electron and the nucleus. If one electron in an atom is at a much greater distance from the nucleus than all the others, the atom is called a Rydberg atom, the highly excited electron a Rydberg electron, and the rest of the atom (the nucleus plus the less distant electrons) the core of the Rydberg atom.

8. More complex circuits are generally more specialized in their functions and thus are less in demand. The efforts of integrated circuit designers have focused on developing commercially viable products using integrated circuits in the face of this and other constraints.

   Undoubtedly the most successful such product has been the memory circuit, which makes large data bases practical; the second most successful class of devices has been the microprocessor and its successor the microcomputer, which is, literally, a computer on a chip. The programming of microcomputers often involves a program written permanently into a special read-only memory (ROM) on the chip during the manufacturing process, which makes it possible to use this class of circuits in a wide variety of ways.

9. The expansion of the universe was discovered when it was found that cosmic objects move away from us with speeds that are higher the farther away the object is located. The speed at which objects move away from us increases by about 15 km/sec for every 10^6 light years distance from us. The expansion must be imagined not as the penetration of a limited amount of matter into empty space surrounding it, but as an increasing dilution of matter everywhere in the universe. Each point can be considered the center of this dilution. Indeed, regardless of his location in the universe, an observer would see exactly the same thing with respect to the objects around him; that is, objects would recede from him at the rate of 15 km/sec/10^6 light years. The expansion of the universe does not distinguish any point and is the same all over space.

   This expansion leads to a remarkable conclusion when we try to extrapolate it toward the past: one can easily calculate that about 18 billion years ago the density of matter must have been infinite. Thus we can indeed calculate approximately the date of the Primal Bang.

   It is important to keep in mind that the Primal Bang is not a local phenomenon. The descriptions of it in the popular literature are often grossly misleading; it is wrong to imagine that the Primal Bang occurred at a given point in space, matter being expelled in all directions. Actually, the Primal Bang was the beginning of a decompression of an infinite universe. This means that the whole universe, the infinite space, was filled with an infinite density of matter at time zero. Immediately afterward the density became finite though still very high. With the passage of time the density decreased further until it reached the present value.

10. The function of a bus is to transfer information in the form of electric signals between the different parts of an electronic system. The generic term for system components connected by a bus is devices. A group of devices is connected to a bus segment.

    Only one device, the bus master, is allowed to control the bus and initiate data transfers at any one time. Several masters may be present on a bus, so contention between them must be resolved using arbitration rules.

A bus master either oversees the transfer of data between devices or, more often, exchanges information with one or more slaves. The bus master selects slaves by placing address information on the bus; each slave compares this information with its own address. If the addresses match, the master and slave establish a connection and the slave becomes a responder. Addresses that identify more than one slave are called broadcast addresses. A particular device may act as both master and slave, but not at the same time.

Once the slaves are connected, the bus master exchanges data with them over the bus. The master breaks the connection with its responders after all the data have been transferred. This sequence of actions—making a connection, transferring data, breaking the connection—is called a transaction. The master may either relinquish bus mastership after a transaction or continue with other transactions.

練習 3-1

在大多數情況下，句子應使用甚麼動詞時態，一目瞭然；但有些情況中，卻必須看作者意思而定。下面的答案都是原文的寫法。所以讀者或許會發現自己的答案與這裏所提供的不同，但自覺已依據書中的原則作答。如果是這樣的話，不妨請教英語系國家的老師，看自己的答案是否真的站得住腳。

1. In February of 1899 the British ship *Southern Cross* put 10 men ashore at Cape Adare in Antarctica, thus beginning the first expedition to endure a year on the world's southernmost continent. Today many zoologists credit the expedition, which ushered in the "heroic" era of Antarctic exploration, with a discovery that has intrigued them for almost a century: the coldest marine habitat in the world is actually alive with fishes. The team's zoologist, Nicholai Hanson, did not survive the year on the icy land, but before his death he collected examples of previously unknown fish species.

   Almost a century later investigators are still trying to understand the adaptations that enable fish to survive in a region once thought to be virtually uninhabitable. Of particular interest are the evolutionary adaptations of the suborder Notothenioidei, a group of teleosts, or advanced bony fishes, that are related to the perchlike fishes common in virtually all marine habitats. This suborder of between 90 and 100 species is primarily confined to the Antarctic region; there it dominates, accounting for an estimated two thirds of the fish species and 90 percent of the individual fish in the area.

2. Figure 2 shows the current-voltage (I-V) characteristics of aluminum contacts on boron-doped polycrystalline diamond films deposited from gas mixtures with different concentrations of boron. The I-V characteristics were determined by applying a voltage to the Al contact on the diamond film surface while grounding the rear of the Si substrate. Poor rectifying characteristics were obtained as a result of excess reverse leakage current. When the boron concentration increased, the forward current decreased. This decrease in the forward current may be attributed to impurity scattering on the diamond film. For a

given temperature, the mobility decreased with increasing impurity concentration because of enhanced impurity scattering. The smaller forward current was due mainly to the smaller hole and electron mobility.

The I-V characteristics of diamond films deposited with various boron concentrations and annealed at a constant temperature in helium ambient at 900° C for 30 min. are shown in Figure 3. After the annealing treatment, there was no deterioration in the I-V characteristics of the undoped films. In the boron-doped films, the leakage current for the 10V forward voltage doubled and deterioration in the rectifying characteristics was observed.

3. The amplification of ultrashort pulses in erbium-doped fiber amplifiers (EDFAs) has been intensively studied both theoretically and experimentally. Several theoretical models have been proposed that use different gain descriptions for the pumped erbium ions [2-6]. Numerical studies have shown that an accurate analysis requires the use of the Maxwell-Bloch equations with all the higher-order dispersive and nonlinear terms [7]. However, previous studies have all been concerned with the amplification in an EDFA of a single ultrashort pulse with negligible gain saturation. For this case, our previous work has shown that solving the Bloch equations for the pumped erbium ions is equivalent to using a complex Lorentzian gain profile [9]. Here we extend our previous results to include the important phenomenon of gain saturation, which occurs in the amplification of the pulse train in the amplifier.

This paper presents a model that fully characterizes the amplification of an ultrashort soliton pulse train in an EDFA. This model employs the general formalism of a two-level system to treat the coupled set of Maxwell-Bloch equations. The model provides a general expression for the propagation of the pulse train in the amplifier. The population relaxation time in the Bloch equation is modified to include the pumping rate, and the pump absorption is taken into account by solving the pump intensity evolution equation. This approach allows us to estimate the range of pulse widths where the simpler rate-equation approximation [8] is valid. The paper also discusses the problem of the nonlinear nonreciprocity of soliton transmission in EDFAs with different pumping configurations.

4. For three and a half centuries after their discovery, the Galilean satellites of Jupiter were studied through telescopes. Then, on 20 August 1977, the first of two Voyager spacecraft was launched from Kennedy Space Center. A year and a half later, the two spacecraft passed through the Jupiter system, and in a few days the Galilean satellites were transformed from small points of light into four separate worlds that could be mapped and studied in great detail. Hundreds of high quality images of the two largest moons, Ganymede and Callisto, were obtained. These objects are of great interest not only because of their great size—Ganymede is larger than the planet Mercury, Callisto only slightly smaller—but also because of their composition. All the planets and moons studied in detail prior to Voyager are composed of rock and, in some cases, metal. Ganymede and Callisto, however, have densities so low—1.9 and 1.9 g/cm^3—that roughly half their mass must be ice. There are many other icy bodies in the solar system, including the planet Pluto and most of the moons of Saturn, Uranus, and Neptune. Ganymede and Callisto have provided the first look at this previously unexplored class of planetary objects.

5. For many years now, kinship <u>has been recognized</u> as an important factor in human social behavior, and recent studies <u>have demonstrated</u> that kinship <u>influences</u> the social behavior of many other species as well. The widespread occurrence of nepotism, or favoritism shown to genetic relatives, and the rarity of close inbreeding among free-living animals <u>imply</u> that most animals <u>possess</u> mechanisms for distinguishing relatives from nonrelatives and close from distant kin.

However, until the last few years little attention <u>was paid</u> to mechanisms of kin identification. In this paper, we <u>consider</u> some of the theoretical and empirical issues relevant to animal kin recognition, <u>describe</u> recent work on this topic, and <u>outline</u> several mechanisms by which kin might be identified. Finally, we <u>summarize</u> the results of our four-year laboratory and field investigation of kin recognition using ground squirrels.

6. The origin of stars <u>represents</u> one of the most fundamental unsolved problems of contemporary astrophysics. Stars <u>are</u> the basic objects of the universe. Indeed, the discovery of the nature of most stars as hydrogen-burning thermonuclear reactors and the subsequent development of the theory of stellar evolution <u>rank</u> among the greatest triumphs of twentieth-century science. Deciphering stellar genesis, on the other hand, <u>has proven</u> to be a formidable challenge for astronomers. Until a quarter of a century ago, only a rudimentary understanding of the subject <u>existed</u>. This state of comparative ignorance <u>prevailed</u> because no substantive body of empirical data <u>existed</u> that could be used to critically test even the most basic hypotheses concerning stellar origins.

In our galaxy, stars <u>form</u> within the dust-enshrouded dense cores of molecular clouds. The obscuration provided by the solid grains that permeate the clouds <u>renders</u> newly forming stars (protostars) completely invisible at optical and shorter wavelengths. Moreover, the molecular gas that gives birth to young stars <u>is</u> itself extremely cold (10 to 20 K) and, with a few exceptions, <u>can</u> only <u>be observed</u> in emission in the submillimeter and millimeter regime, a spectral window opened by radio astronomers only in the 1970s.

During the last two decades, impressive advances in technology <u>have provided</u> astronomers with the ability to observe star-forming regions in considerable detail at infrared, millimeter, and submillimeter wavelengths. With this new instrumental capability, a direct assault on the star-formation problem <u>became</u> possible. Indeed, over the last few years, observations with filled-aperture telescopes and interferometric arrays <u>have produced</u> a series of remarkable, exciting, and unexpected discoveries that <u>have begun</u> to remove the veil of mystery that surrounds the star-formation process in our galaxy. As a result of these discoveries, we <u>are beginning</u> to understand the processes of star formation and early stellar evolution and <u>are developing</u> the foundation for a coherent theory of star formation.

7. The experimental apparatus used <u>is shown</u> in Fig. 3. The reactant gas pressure <u>was set</u> at 3.3 kPa (25 Torr). An optical pyrometer <u>was used</u> to monitor the substrate temperature, which <u>was maintained</u> at about 820° C by keeping the microwave power at 450 W. CH_4-CO_2 gas mixtures without additional H_2 gas <u>were used</u>. The flow rate of CO_2 <u>was fixed</u> at 30 sccm and the flow rate of CH_4

was varied from 19.2 to 20 sccm. Then the silicon substrates <u>were prepared</u> for diamond deposition by carrying out the following steps.

8. As Figure 1 <u>shows</u>, Africanized honeybees <u>are</u> nearly indistinguishable in appearance from the bees familiar in North America and Europe, and sting for sting they <u>are</u> no worse than our own honeybees. What <u>has earned</u> the Africanized bees the undeserved notoriety as killer bees <u>is</u> their extreme aggressiveness. Numerous studies <u>have documented</u> the fierce defensive behavior of this bee (Michener 1972; Collins et al. 1982; Rinderer 1986; Boreham and Roubik 1987). Many <u>have reported</u> that a particularly dangerous attribute of the bees <u>is</u> their aggressiveness after slight jarring or vibration of the hive. Africanized bees <u>can react</u> to an intruder three times faster than do European bees, <u>can inflict</u> ten times as many stings, and <u>will pursue</u> their aggressors over much longer distances, up to a kilometer. However, some evidence <u>suggests</u> that climate <u>has</u> more influence on aggressiveness than racial differences and that Africanized bees <u>are</u> more aggressive under warmer conditions (Brandenburgo et al. 1977).

9. In recent years an extraordinary increase <u>has occurred</u> in the attention, both popular and scientific, that <u>has been paid</u> to mutation and its consequences. The sources of this interest <u>are</u> the recognition that components of our environment <u>pose</u> a largely unevaluated threat to the conservation of genetic material and the realization that mutations frequently <u>have</u> serious consequences for human health that encompass, at the least, birth defects and cancer. The resulting research effort <u>has improved</u> our understanding of the fundamental genetic substance, DNA, and of the intricacies of its metabolism and organization into genes.

Modern investigations into the mutation process <u>involve</u> the structure of DNA and all the processes that <u>affect</u> it. Inherent in the now-classical description of DNA structure by Watson and Crick in 1953, and immediately recognized by them, <u>was</u> the notion that variations in the electronic structures of the DNA bases <u>could cause</u> incorrect base pairings, and hence mutations. In the early models, however, DNA <u>was viewed</u> as structurally static when not undergoing replication. More recently, the identification of numerous families of alternative structures <u>has led</u> to an expanded view of DNA as far more variable in form. Some of these structures <u>provide</u> explanations for mutational events that <u>were</u> previously mysterious, and others <u>offer</u> intriguing hints for future exploration.

10. Maps <u>are</u> one of the oldest forms of written communication. Land boundary maps on clay tablets <u>were being used</u> in Babylonia as early as 2200 B.C. Through the centuries various materials <u>have been used</u> for maps. The ancient Egyptians <u>used</u> sheets of papyrus, the Chinese <u>used</u> pieces of silk, Eskimos <u>made</u> maps on seal skins, and Polynesians <u>used</u> a network of bamboo canes, with each crossing point indicating an island. Today printed maps <u>pervade</u> our lives, ranging from sketch or location maps in newspapers and advertisements, to parcel maps showing property boundaries, to small-scale maps in atlases.

The techniques used to produce maps <u>have changed</u> dramatically over the past fifty years, in a transition from field workers and mule trains to jet aircraft, satellites, and computers. Before World War II, the predominant method for creating maps <u>was</u> field surveying. After World War II, map-making methods

<u>began</u> to include manual photogrammetry (measurement from photographs). Although manual photogrammetry <u>is</u> still used today, it <u>is being supplanted</u> by digital cartography, and computers <u>are becoming</u> the hub of the mapping process.

Soon after their introduction in the 1950s, digital computers <u>were used</u> for various phases of the mapping process, especially for trigonometric calculations of survey data and for orientation of aerial photographs on map manuscripts. In addition, computer-controlled plotters <u>were used</u> to draw simple outline maps. The process of collecting data for the plotters <u>was</u> slow and expensive, and the drawings <u>were</u> not as precise as those produced by the best manual cartography. Only in the last ten to fifteen years <u>has</u> it <u>become</u> technologically feasible and cost-effective to assemble and use the data required to automate the mapping process.

練習 3-2

1. Physics <u>is</u> a subject that has fascinated him since high school.

2. Smith's approach as well as Turner's <u>has</u> several serious shortcomings, which <u>render</u> it unsuitable for practical applications.

3. The on-chip RAM and two I/O ports <u>are</u> an important part of the chip.

4. Each of the samples <u>was</u> annealed for 20 minutes.

5. The number of passengers using the airport <u>has</u> increased each year since 1984.

6. After the members of the examination committee and the department chairman <u>approve</u> the plan, it should be submitted to the Dean's Office.

7. After the members of the examination committee or the department chairman <u>approves</u> the plan, it should be submitted to the Dean's Office.

   After the department chairman or the members of the examination committee <u>approve</u> the plan, it should be submitted to the Dean's Office.

8. The increase in the number of free hydrogen atoms along with the higher temperature <u>causes</u> the reaction rate to increase.

9. Be careful how your research team <u>interprets</u> those figures. Statistics <u>are</u> sometimes highly misleading.

10. An attribute name or a class name <u>is</u> entered in this dialog box.

11. Also of interest <u>is</u> why samples immersed in solution A exhibited a higher growth rate.

12. The automatic power-saving function <u>is</u> just one of the many features that <u>make</u> the Droog 2000 the most cost-effective system on the market today.

13. All of the authors <u>have</u> sent in their papers and every paper <u>has</u> been received.

14. A number of samples <u>were</u> collected from a different geographical region to see whether the phenomenon occurred there as well.

15. Included in the search <u>are</u> all child nodes on the right-hand side of the node of interest.

16. A major problem with this type of system <u>is</u> the many errors that occur in the acceleration stage.

練習 4-1

1. Given an input rate r, we can obtain the solution using equation (3). If r is unknown but T is known, we can apply equation (5).

2. The amount of fluorine incorporated into the film on the substrate surface can be controlled by reducing the amount of water added to the immersing solution. When there is less water, more fluorine atoms are released, as shown in the reaction equation above. Because of the increase in free fluorine atoms in the solution, a greater amount of fluorine is incorporated into the film.

3. While there are at least a dozen major different designs for devices that use magnetic fields to control thermonuclear fusion, the best results to date have been achieved with the tokamak, which was developed in the 1960s by Soviet scientists seeking to overcome the inherent instability of earlier magnetic confinement schemes. After the announcement in 1969 of results showing much longer confinement of the plasma under fusion conditions, the United States redirected its fusion program to emphasize tokamak research, and today major tokamak projects are being conducted by the U.S., the European Economic community, Japan, and China.

4. Although physics has made monumental strides in the last hundred years, theoretical descriptions of complex phenomena such as turbulent flow in fluids have remained outstanding unsolved problems. The difficulty lies in the nonlinear character of the mathematical equations which model the physical systems: the Navier-Stokes equations for fluid flows and Newton's equations for three or more interacting particles. Since these equations do not generally admit closed-form analytical solutions, it has proved extremely difficult to construct useful theories that would predict, for example, the drag on the wing of an airplane or the range of validity of statistical mechanics. However, in the last ten years, considerable progress has been made, using a unique synthesis of numerical simulation and analytical approximation.

   The key to recent progress has been the use of high-speed digital computers. In particular, high-resolution computer graphics have enabled the "experimental mathematician to identify and explore ordered patterns which would otherwise be buried in reams of computer output. In many cases the persistence of order in irregular behavior was totally unexpected; the discovery of these regularities has led to the development of new analytical methods and approximations which have improved our understanding of complex nonlinear phenomena.

練習 4-2

1. A communication network can be modeled as a graph, and a network under attack or with other sources of failure can be modeled as a random graph. A graph, in the sense used here, consists of vertices (or points) and edges. Each vertex corresponds to a command center or other node in a communication network. Each edge represents a two-way communication link between two

command centers. In a random graph, an edge may fail, leaving intact the vertices connected by the edge, or a vertex may fail, destroying all the edges connected to the vertex.

2. Slime molds reproduce by means of spores, each of which is an independent, one-celled organism. However, the cells originating from spores divide repeatedly, and eventually the offspring swarm together in a heap to form a common amoeboid mass. The original cell boundaries sometimes disappear, and the once-independent cells take on specialized functions, somewhat like organs in a larger animal. The creeping mass of protoplasm, in some cases as large as 30 cm in diameter, is difficult to classify as plant or animal or, indeed, as either a collection of individuals or a larger, single organism. At any rate, it is one of the most curious examples of self-organization in all biology.

練習 4-3

1. Let X be the Cartesian product of these sets, and let A be their union.

   Let X be the Cartesian product of these sets and A be their union.

2. Consider the circuit shown in Figure 2. We can draw its Norton-equivalent circuit as shown in Figure 3.

   Consider the circuit shown in Figure 2; its Norton-equivalent circuit can be drawn as shown in Figure 3.

3. Assume the input power of port 1 is P1 and the output power of port 2 is P2. Then we have the following equation.

   Assume the input power of port 1 is P1 and the output power of port 2 is P2; then we have the following equation.

4. Suppose C can be factored into a product of D and a cube q. Then we replace C in the above expression by q.

   Suppose C can be factored into a product of D and a cube q; then we replace C in the above expression by q.

5. The samples were fabricated by a standard chemical vapor deposition process. N-type Si (100) substrates were scratched using diamond powder to enhance the nucleation density of the deposits.

   The samples were fabricated by a standard chemical vapor deposition process, and N-type Si (100) substrates were scratched using diamond powder to enhance the nucleation density of the deposits.

6. Rearranging the above equation, we obtain the solution.

   By rearranging the above equation, we can obtain the solution.

   If we rearrange the above equation, we can obtain the solution.

練習 4-4

A centralized compression service <u>is</u> economical, but it hampers creativity when developers want to experiment with applications and data. Accordingly, digital video interactive (DVI) technology <u>offers</u> another kind of compression:

edit-level video, done on the developer's DVI system in real time. Edit-level video is lower in quality than the presentation-level video made by centralized compression but is adequate for software development.

The user employs edit-level video to develop and test new software. When the user has made his choices and polished the program, he sends the final analog video through the centralized compression service. When the presentation-level compressed video comes back, the user substitutes it for the edit-level files. The newly developed software runs just as it did in testing, but now with higher-quality video.

The heart of the DVI video display processor is two chips: one for processing images stored in memory, the other for displaying the processed images. Each chip is a CMOS chip containing about 132,500 transistors. The set can connect to almost any computer, as long as it has the requisite computing speed and data transfer bandwidth–usually this means a 16-bit or 32-bit processor that operates at a clock speed of 6 megahertz or higher.

練習 4-5

1. When researchers a few years ago uncovered a strong link between the sunspot cycle and weather patterns on Earth, many atmospheric scientists were intrigued. Indeed, the correlation seemed so convincing that a few meteorologists even began to plug solar activity into official long-range forecasts. But the whole notion has taken a battering recently, and it may have a tough time recovering.

   Many skeptics, in fact, have always said that the postulated correlation was not as firm as it seemed. For starters, they pointed out that it could only be traced back about 40 years, which struck them as too short a record to be convincing. On top of that, solar activity seemed to affect weather patterns one way when winds in the stratosphere above the equator were blowing in a westerly direction and another way when they were easterly; statistically speaking, that effectively cut in half an already short record. And most disturbing was the absence of any physical mechanism to explain such behavior. But the skeptics nevertheless had a hard time disproving the link, which had withstood every statistical test—until the winter of 1989.

2. Chain-propagating steps alone are insufficient to account for flames. It was recognized in the 1930s that chain-initiating, chain-terminating, and chain-branching steps are also necessary. The 1956 Nobel prize in chemistry was awarded jointly to Cyril N. Hinshelwood of the University of Oxford and Nikolai N. Semenov of the Institute of Chemical Physics in Moscow for their leading roles in showing how the main features of oxidation reactions could be explained in terms of branched-chain reaction mechanisms. (At the time of their research chemists had only provisional ideas about what the actual elementary reactions might be and almost no information at all about the values of the rate coefficients.)

3. While scientists and engineers agree that fusion can work, there is no general agreement on what will be the most economical and desirable type of fusion reactor. To date, the best results have been achieved with the tokamak, a

doughnut-shaped machine with powerful magnetic coils, and the optimism that a viable reactor <u>can be built</u> <u>has been</u> primarily <u>based</u> on the tokamak's performance. Although it now <u>appears</u> probable that tokamak reactors <u>will</u> one day produce energy at a cost around that of petroleum and below the cost of solar energy, many scientists <u>think</u> that alternative magnetic fusion devices <u>could produce</u> energy even more cheaply.

4. The sun <u>produces</u> the heating and confinement needed for atomic fusion through its immense gravitational fields. On earth, large-scale fusion reactions <u>have been achieved</u> for 30 years in thermonuclear weapons, where the temperature <u>is provided</u> by a plutonium bomb explosion and the confinement <u>is</u> simply by inertia—that is, the reaction <u>goes</u> so fast that the fusion fuel, lithium deutride, <u>does</u> not <u>have</u> time to disperse. Inertial confinement <u>is</u> one of the two principal approaches to the use of fusion for power generation. Inertial fusion reactors <u>would use</u> lasers, electron beams, or ion beams to compress and heat pellets of fuel, allowing them to explode in chambers and thereby drive energy generation equipment.

練習 4-6

1. The aim of this paper is to propose a new simulation method that dramatically reduces the time needed to carry out the simulations.

2. Increasing the annealing temperature above 900° C causes the samples to become brittle.

3. Adding more oxygen makes the deposition rate increase significantly.

   Adding more oxygen increases the deposition rate significantly.

4. Let N represent the number of customers and t represent the time.

5. Assume that half of the customers exit the system at the same time.

6. Let there be 10 processors in the network.

7. The author should consider proving theorems I and II instead of only stating the theorems.

8. We suggest solving the problem by using a Fourier transform.

   We suggest that the author solve the problem by using a Fourier transform.

   We suggest that a Fourier transform be used to solve the problem.

9. The referee recommends accepting the paper for publication.

   The referee recommends that the paper be accepted for publication.

10. The success of this method depends on solving equation (5) quickly.

11. Let X be the desired recognition accuracy and S be the desired recognition speed.

12. We discussed treating practical applications of the new technique in the paper, but we decided doing so would make the paper too long.

練習 4-7

1. These figures show that the classification accuracy increases as the size of i and j increases.

   From these figures it can be seen that the classification accuracy increases as the size of i and j increases.

2. We believe that the annealing treatment improved the electrical characteristics of the films.

   The annealing treatment appears to have improved the electrical characteristics of the films.

   It appears that the annealing treatment improved the electrical characteristics of the films.

3. The difference between the two curves can be attributed to the different values of b used in the two cases.

4. Now that we have modified the method, we can use it to analyze the oscillator.

   Now that the method has been modified, it can be used to analyze the oscillator.

5. Consider the following example.

6. It would be desirable for the country's economy to improve quickly.

   The country needs to improve its economy quickly.

   We hope the country's economy will improve quickly.

7. From these data it can be seen that the self-phase modulation and the self-frequency shift are enhanced by forward pumping.

   These data show that forward pumping enhances the self-phase modulation and the self-frequency shift.

8. Coding of coefficients is difficult to accomplish in real time.

   It is difficult to code the coefficients in real time.

9. The appearance of C-H bonds can be attributed to the large number of non-equilibrium hydrogen atoms in the plasma.

   C-H bonds appear because of the large number of non-equilibrium hydrogen atoms in the plasma.

10. These values can now be substituted into the equations of motion to obtain the solution.

    We can now substitute these values into the equations of motion to obtain the solution.

11. Assume that the arrival rate can be modeled as a Poisson process.

    In this example, we assume that the arrival rate can be modeled as a Poisson process.

In this example, it is assumed that the arrival rate can be modeled as a Poisson process.

12. Figure 6 indicates that the theoretical model predicts the experimental values accurately.

The theoretical model predicts the experimental values accurately, as Figure 6 shows.

練習 4-8

1. When it was tested, the system provided excellent performance.

When the system was tested, it performed well.

When tested, the system performed well.

When we tested the system, it performed well.

2. If users plan to carry out complex calculations, they should purchase a high-performance workstation.

For complex calculations, a high-performance workstation is recommended.

3. This type of network is insensitive to differences in scale, translation, and rotation, but it requires an unusually large number of processing elements and connections.

4. If we attempt to solve the equation in this form, we encounter several difficulties.

If we attempt to solve the equation in this form, several difficulties arise.

Attempting to solve the equation in this form leads to several difficulties.

5. This algorithm provides accurate results but requires a great deal of processing time.

6. The sensors detect errors quickly and feed information about them to the controller.

Errors are quickly detected by the sensors and information about the errors is fed to the controller.

練習 4-9

1. After the mapping of A_i from L_1 to L_p is determined, the next array dimension can be processed in the same way.

After determining the mapping of A_i from L_1 to L_p, we can process the next array dimension in the same way.

After we determine the mapping of A_i from L_1 to L_p, we can process the next array dimension in the same way.

2. When Smith's method was applied in our simulations, the modeled objects had an unrealistic shape.

When we applied Smith's method in our simulations, the modeled objects had an unrealistic shape.

3. By choosing an appropriate reference plant model and robustness filter, we can use the IMC structure to produce a controller of the desired order.

If an appropriate reference plant model and robustness filter are chosen, the IMC structure will produce a controller of the desired order.

4. When the input pulse width is decreased further, pulse splitting due to SFS is observed.

5. After performing the simulations, we obtained the following results.

The results of the simulations were the following.

6. To write effective software programs for banks, software engineers need training in both computer science and finance.

7. Verifying the prototype at this stage allows specification errors to be detected and corrected earlier.

By verifying the prototype at this stage, we can detect and correct specification errors earlier.

8. In an NPN bipolar junction transistor, for example, there are three parts: the collector, base, and emitter.

An NPN bipolar junction transistor has three parts: the collector, base, and emitter.

9. Unlike Chen's method, our method does not use external forces to join the panels in the model together.

10. If we apply the finite difference method, we can find the elastic force for an M × N grid of points in vector form as follows.

According to the finite difference method, the elastic force for an M × N grid of points in vector form is the following.

By the finite difference method, the elastic force for an M × N grid of points in vector form is as follows.

11. After the iterative procedure for producing the codebook is performed, each cluster contains a different number of spectral vectors.

12. To develop a high-performance bicycle, engineers must use lightweight materials.

A high-performance bicycle requires lightweight materials.

Lightweight materials are an important part of a high-performance bicycle.

In the design of high-performance bicycles, it is important to use lightweight materials.

13. Before discussing the design of the damper, we must identify the main design factors.

The design of the damper will be discussed below. First, however, the main design factors must be identified.

14. The results indicate that the proposed load compensation technique significantly improves system performance.

15. If this analysis is applied directly to the present case, two difficulties arise.

練習 4-10

1. In this case, it would be necessary to search for only the largest subset template.

2. The samples were wrapped in foil and placed in an oven.

3. From the two parameter studies, we can conclude that the appropriate parameters for the recognition system are $N = 12$, $M = 4$, and $T = 18$.

   The two parameter studies indicate that the appropriate parameters for the recognition system are $N = 12$, $M = 4$, and $T = 18$.

4. Without loss of generality, we can assume that the applied force is always in the +y direction.

   We can assume without loss of generality that the applied force is always in the +y direction.

5. The mathematical model presented above was used to develop a computer program to generate the complete tooth profile.

   On the basis of the mathematical model presented above, we developed a computer program to generate the complete tooth profile.

   Using the mathematical model presented above, we developed a computer program to generate the complete tooth profile.

6. The technique partitions a data set into only two subsets.

7. A general observer-based scheme for generating residuals is depicted in Figure 2.

8. The system can be divided into two basic parts.

9. This is a problem of great complexity in classical physics.

10. The parameters measured in the experiment were used to test the model.

練習 4-11

1. When a formal financing system does not exist, a pre-selling system is established to make the market more effective. This type of system can be found in a number of Asian countries.

2. A centralized compression service is economical, but it hampers creativity when developers want to experiment with applications and data. Accordingly, digital video interactive (DVI) technology offers another kind of compression: edit-level video, done on the developer's DVI system in real time. Edit-level video is lower in quality than the video made by centralized compression but is adequate for software development. Users employ edit-level video to devel-

op and test new software. When they have made their choices and polished the program, they send the final analog video through the centralized compression service. When the presentation-level compressed video comes back to them, they substitute it for the edit-level files. Their newly developed software runs just as it did in testing, but now with higher-quality video.

3. The solar water heater used in the experiment is shown in Figure 2. At the top left of the water heater is a cold-water inlet, where water flows into the apparatus. The main portion of the heater consists of many coils of plastic pipe connected together in an accordion fashion and covered with a sheet of heat-absorbing plastic. The water flows through the pipes, absorbing heat from the sun, and then exits the heating apparatus through the outlet at the lower right of the heater. From the outlet the water flows into an insulated storage tank in the basement of the house, from which hot water is drawn when needed.

4. While scientists and engineers agree that fusion can work, there is no general agreement on what will be the most economical and desirable type of fusion reactor. To date, the best results have been achieved with the tokamak, a doughnut-shaped machine with powerful magnetic coils, and the optimism that a viable reactor can be built is primarily based on the tokamak's performance. Although it now appears probable that tokamak reactors will one day produce energy at a cost around that of petroleum and below the cost of solar energy, many scientists and engineers think that alternative magnetic fusion devices could produce energy even more cheaply.

練習 4-12

1. In this paper we introduce a new method for selecting the location of actuators.

2. To achieve realistic modeling, we need to develop a method for avoiding penetration of objects.

3. We will now discuss issues concerning the implementation of this architecture.

4. Next, we will find the service time for cycle k using the random number stream R_i.

5. Section 3 presents our method for computing the feedback gain matrix.

6. Existing methods for assigning bandwidth in networks are not suitable for this case.

7. Mitchell [4] described an efficient technique for transferring files in a distributed operating system.

8. The government has enacted new legislation intended to stimulate investment in technology.

9. The company has developed a new program for training operators of machinery used to produce integrated circuits.

10. This document proposes a model for guiding the development of technology at research institutes operated by the government.

練習 4-13

1. The alignment problem is simpler in imperative languages than in the functional language Alpha.

2. The cost function and alignment algorithm are also similar to those in [11].

3. The cost of the filter is about half that of the approach in (Wason, 1990).

4. Compare the voltage drop between node 1 and node 2 with that between node 3 and node 2.

5. Lane developed an alternative approach with performance similar to that of the method in (Long, 1992).

6. The accuracy of the new robot arm is greater than that of the conventional one.

   The new robot arm is more accurate than the conventional one.

7. Machine recognition of handwritten Chinese characters is more difficult than machine recognition of handwritten English letters.

   Developing a machine to recognize handwritten Chinese characters is more difficult than developing one to recognize handwritten English letters.

8. This strategy yields a greater variance reduction than the strategy proposed in [3].

9. These results are consistent with those of Rogers et al. (1985).

10. Low-frequency noise is filtered out more effectively by the AGC than by the limiter.

    The AGC filters out low-frequency noise more effectively than the limiter does.

練習 4-14

1. Smith [15] gave a parametric solution for the eigenvalue assignment.

2. SPS is an extensible operating system for creating system services.

3. Lee's algorithm can be divided into two parts.

   Lee's algorithm has two main parts.

4. Many applications of fuzzy neural networks have been reported.

5. This problem was solved by adopting the following approach.

   The following approach was adopted to solve this problem.

6. Each character image is identified as belonging to a set of m candidate characters.

7. The main difference between Lee's approach and ours is that our method is much simpler to use.

   Our method is much simpler than Lee's approach.

8. The institute has been in operation for twenty years.

9. Software can be used to program some I/O devices so that they share interrupts with other devices.

   Some I/O devices can be programmed by software to share interrupts with other devices.

   Some I/O devices can be programmed to share interrupts with other devices.

10. Figure 4(a) illustrates the effect of the Rayleigh number on the wall temperature of the inner cylinder.

    The effect of the Rayleigh number on the wall temperature of the inner cylinder is illustrated in Figure 4(a).

練習 5-1

1. Consider the circuit shown in Figure 10-1, where R_1 is in port 1 and R_2 is in port 2.

2. As just mentioned, the input and output impedance of the attenuator should match those of the original circuit.

3. The personal computer, which became popular in the 1980s, has had a far-reaching impact on the way research in this field is conducted.

4. 句子的標點符號正確。子句 "who do not enjoy teaching" 是限定關係子句。

5. Professor Thompson, sitting in the second row, raised his hand to ask a question.

6. The difference between their method and ours is as follows.

7. 句子的標點符號正確。片語 "as shown in Figure 8" 作限定片語使用。但此片語也可合理地解釋為非限定片語，所以在 "source" 後加上逗點亦是正確的。

8. The market radius decreases as population density increases, as shown in Figure 5.

9. 句子的標點符號正確。片語 "sitting in the back" 作限定片語使用。

10. Sales revenue in the local computer industry has grown rapidly over the last three years, as shown in Figure 4.

11. 句子的標點符號正確。

12. Let a represent x and b represent y.

13. An object's radar cross section (RCS) may depend more on its shape than on its physical size. A small truck, with its sharp edges and abrupt flat surfaces, can reflect electromagnetic waves better than a smooth-edged jumbo jet. The RCS of a pickup truck (measured head-on at microwave frequencies) is about 200 square meters, while that of a jumbo jet airliner is only about 100.

14. The last twenty years have seen major developments in clinical transplantation, particularly of such vital organs as the heart, liver, and kidneys. However, despite these apparent breakthroughs, the success of tissue transplants remains dependent on first overwhelming and then chronically suppressing the pa-

tient's immune system with a variety of drugs. The drug therapy currently in use has many undesirable side effects (particularly in children), because it is based on nonselective cyclotoxic drugs, which indiscriminately kill all rapidly dividing cells. An encouraging development of the 1980s was the introduction of cyclosporin A, an immunosuppressant with more specific effects on the immune system that leave the patient with some resistance against infection. Nevertheless, even this immunosuppressive drug is not free from side effects, including damage to the kidneys.

練習 6-1

下面是一些修改建議。有些句子可能不只一種修改方式，因此除了下面的答案之外，可能還有其他答案。

1. In this paper, we propose an algorithm to handle noisy and uncertain data. The proposed algorithm easily handles false negative training instances.

   In this paper, we propose an algorithm for processing noisy and uncertain data that easily handles false negative training instances.

2. The values obtained in the first two trials are compared in Figure 3.

   The values obtained in the first two trials are plotted in Figure 3.

3. Many applications of fuzzy neural networks have been reported.

4. The procedure is described below.

5. The second method uses a more complex formulation.

   The second method is more complex.

6. For comparison, consider the performance of Chen's method.

   In comparison, consider the performance of Chen's method.

   By comparison, Chen's method... [直接描述陳氏的方法]

7. Section 6 summarizes the results. For simplicity, the results have been divided into two sets.

8. The reasons for this poor performance are the following.

   The reasons for this poor performance are that... [直接敘述理由]

9. This paper investigates the effects of three types of mutation on the performance of genetic algorithms.

   In this paper, we study the effects of three types of mutation on the performance of genetic algorithms.

10. Table 4 compares the speed of our algorithm with that of the other algorithms.

11. In this paper, we analyze the stability of clamping with passive friction forces.

    In this paper, we investigate the stability of clamping with passive friction forces.

12. The data have been simplified so that the problem can be treated more easily in the finite element analysis.

The data have been simplified to facilitate treatment of the problem using finite element analysis.

13. To meet this requirement, we must develop an optimization technique for implicit-form problems.

To meet this requirement, an optimization technique for implicit-form problems must be developed.

14. This allocation technique may lead to longer delays in time-insensitive applications and blocked connections in time-sensitive applications.

15. The shortcomings of the general cell mapping method can be eliminated by combining it with interpolated cell mapping.

16. To examine the variation in tensile strain along the free edge, we have plotted the relationship between tensile strain and element number in Fig. 5.

17. A larger scale of operations is needed not only to reduce manufacturing costs, but also to justify investment in R&D.

18. The major difference between Chang's method and ours is that our technique does not rely on external forces to ensure smooth, natural animated motion.

Unlike Chang's method, our technique does not rely on external forces to ensure smooth, natural animated motion.

19. The proposed algorithm is faster than Matsumoto's method and uses much less memory.

20. Because our design approach considers both the algorithm level and architecture level, it produces a programmable, low-cost filter design with an accumulation-free tap structure.

練習 6-2

1. The proposed method greatly improves the accuracy of the analysis.

2. In section 4 the performance of the proposed method is compared with that of several existing methods.

Section 4 compares the performance of the proposed method with that of several existing methods.

3. Section 2 briefly surveys existing blending techniques.

In section 2, we briefly survey existing blending techniques.

Section 2 presents a brief survey of existing blending techniques.

4. This policy may waste a considerable amount of bandwidth.

5. Section 6 concludes the paper.

Section 6 is the conclusion of the paper.

The conclusions of the paper are presented in section 6.

6. The triggers were activated sequentially.

7. The modal controllability can be expressed more compactly as follows.

8. The level sufficient for successful identification depends on several factors.

9. High-temperature processing reduces yield.

   When high-temperature processing is used, yield is reduced.

10. The stability of these solutions will be analyzed below.

11. Chen [5] defines the problem in a similar way.

    Chen [5] states the problem in a similar way.

12. To compare the performance of the two processors, we ran another series of tests.

13. This technique can be used to improve the performance of CAD systems.

14. The compiler is responsible for inserting communication instructions. Instructions will be inserted wherever the compiler judges they should be.

    The compiler inserts communication instructions wherever it judges they should be.

    The compiler inserts communication instructions in appropriate locations.

15. With this new method, the severity of the staircase effect can be substantially reduced.

    This new method substantially reduces the severity of the staircase effect.

16. The speed can be adjusted by the technique described in section 2.

練習 6-3

　　下面是一些修改建議。有些句子可能不只一種修改方式，因此除了下面的答案之外，可能還有其他答案。

1. The reaction occurred slowly.

   The reaction was slow.

2. Several researchers have observed that in solving this type of problem genetic algorithms tend to fall into local minima.

   Several researchers have observed that in solving this type of problem genetic algorithms tend to converge to local minima.

3. A valid schedule must have an iteration period greater than or equal to this bound.

   For a schedule to be valid, its iteration period must be greater than or equal to this bound.

   No valid schedule has an iteration period shorter than this bound.

4. We must provide more than one plot.

5. The experimental results show that the proposed algorithm outperforms the conventional method.

6. This study has compared the effects of computer-assisted instruction and traditional instruction techniques.

7. The analysis is invalid.

8. To reduce the hardware cost, we must develop a more efficient filter design.

   To reduce the hardware cost, a more efficient filter design must be developed.

9. Designing an on-line control system for this application is a complicated task.

10. The electrical properties of the films improved after the films were doped with boron.

    Boron doping was found to improve the electrical properties of the films.

    We found that boron doping improved the electrical properties of the films.

    Boron doping improved the electrical properties of the films.

11. The iterations continue until the convergence test is satisfied.

12. The simulation results show that the proposed control algorithm quickly and effectively adjusts the cutting system in response to different cutting conditions.

    As the simulation results show, the proposed control algorithm quickly and effectively adjusts the cutting system in response to different cutting conditions.

練習 6-4

1. Note that the analysis presented above is not applicable to nonlinear systems.

2. Many filter designs have been proposed in the literature.

3. Solving equation (5) directly would be time-consuming.

4. Many new applications of neural networks have been proposed in the last ten years.

5. An on-chip buffer is needed for raster-scan ordering of the pixels.

6. These results show that hypothesis H_1 is false.

   These results imply that hypothesis H_1 is false.

   From these results, we can conclude that hypothesis H_1 is false.

7. Three types of events are defined in the program.

8. Another advantage of this method is that we need only a shifter and an adder to complete the circuit.

   Another advantage of this method is that only a shifter and an adder are needed to complete the circuit.

9. The purpose of mission planning is to maximize instrument operating time subject to various constraints.

10. These figures clearly show that the classification accuracy increases as i and j increase.

練習 6-5

1. An interesting question is whether the relationship between these chromosomes is an original form or is itself a result of evolution.

2. Let us now consider how the circuit works.

3. We must now explain why the samples immersed in the HF solution showed increased selectivity during the second deposition phase.

4. Section 3 discusses the types of applications in which the proposed algorithm outperforms the conventional method.

5. In section 4 we evaluate the performance of the proposed method in comparison with that of the conventional method.

   In section 4 we compare the performance of the proposed method with that of the conventional method.

6. In the second experiment, we investigated whether the amount of fluorine incorporated into the film depends on the amount of water in the immersing solution.

練習 7-1

下面是一些修改建議。有些句子可能不只一種修改方式，因此除了下面的答案之外，可能還有其他答案。

1. Another type of network used in neural-network-based object recognition is the neocognitron, which is a hierarchical multilayered network based on the model of the human visual system. The initial stage is an input layer, and each succeeding stage has a layer of S-cells followed by a layer of C-cells. Thus layers of S-cells and C-cells are arranged alternately throughout the whole network. A detailed analysis of the training process used with this type of network can be found in Matsumoto [8].

   The neocognitron has two disadvantages. First, the training process is very slow, because the number of cells in the model increases almost linearly with the number of objects it is required to learn to distinguish. Second, the network must be completely retrained for each new set of patterns.

2. Housing is an extremely heterogeneous product, reflecting the uniqueness of each building site, the long life of the structure, and particularly the decentralized means of production. Decentralization shows up sharply in a comparison with the automobile, which for most people is second only to housing in size and cost. Only a few manufacturers produce automobiles. In housing, however, the 100 largest developers produce only about 15 percent of the annual new construction. The remainder is mostly built by companies of small or medium size or by individuals—all with their own idea of what constitutes a house. Moreover, the builder, unlike the automobile manufacturer, makes no systematic effort to control the quality of maintenance once the product has been sold.

Instead the owner must deal with an even more decentralized system of local repair and remodeling services—all with their own views of what should be done. Local building codes are one of the few sources of standardized construction and maintenance procedures, yet they are notorious for differing from one another and for being circumvented by owners in any event.

練習 7-2

下面是一些修改建議。有些句子可能不只一種修改方式，因此除了下面的答案之外，可能還有其他答案。

1. To the observer, a change in state is a sudden and dramatic event, one that renders a material essentially unrecognizable after it occurs. Certainly, at first glance, an ice cube seems to have more in common with a quartz crystal or a diamond than it does with the steam pouring from a kettle of boiling water. On a microscopic scale, however, all three forms of water contain the same two atoms of hydrogen to one of oxygen, and all are held together by the same electromagnetic force. Moreover, despite the apparent abruptness of a change in state, the sequence of events that precedes it is anything but sudden and dramatic; typically, it is a smooth and unremarkable continuum. Lower the temperature of a glass of water degree by degree and at some point the change from water to ice will take place. Experience tells us at what temperature the change will occur, but no simple theoretical formula predicts it.

2. In the 1920s, researchers realized that the brain was in ceaseless electrical activity, so the idea became popular that memories could take the form of recurrent electrical signals between cells. But memories can withstand all sorts of shocks to the head or brain—from concussion to electroconvulsive therapy—that totally disrupt this electrical activity. So memories cannot be stored in purely electrical form. On the other hand, such damage does tend to result in loss of very recent memory—for events minutes to hours before the shock—which is why people who have been in crashes often cannot remember the events that led up to the accident.

   Hence researchers came to believe that memory exists in at least two forms: memory for very recent events—called short-term memory—which is relatively labile and easily disruptable, and long-term memory, which is much more stable. Not everything that gets into short-term memory becomes fixed in the long-term store. A filtering mechanism selects things that might be important and discards the rest. If this were not the case—if we remembered everything that impinged upon us—we would soon become hopelessly overloaded.

練習 7-3

1. We are developing a new memory product with large capacity, low power requirements, and fast access speed.

2. My report discusses how to increase sales, improve quality, and develop new products.

3. The terms will be a sequence of either 1's or 0's.

4. In our latest work, we have prepared fiber with liquid crystal cladding, set up a measurement system, and derived theoretical formulas.

5. The selection criteria for government-funded R&D projects are the following:

    - Develops a major technology essential to economic growth

    - Requires substantial funding

    - Fills a gap in private firms' development plans

6. The new method is simpler, faster, and more accurate than the conventional method.

7. The indirect control method has two advantages: it eliminates the need to install flux sensors and it is easy to use at low speeds.

8. When the principal point lies on the right side of the graph, the angular velocity is negative and the direction of the friction force is counterclockwise. When the principal point lies on the left side of the graph, the angular velocity is positive and the direction of the friction force is clockwise.

練習 7-4

1. When designing practical controllers, one often encounters systems with uncertain parameters, which can be represented mathematically as follows.

    When designing practical controllers, one often encounters systems with uncertain parameters. These systems can be represented mathematically as follows.

2. This type of job dispatching, which is called dynamic load balancing, balances the workload of the processors.

    Because it balances the workload of the processors, this type of job dispatching is called dynamic load balancing.

3. The upper row displays eight icons, which users can assemble into query graphs.

4. Since the results of the first trial were surprising, we repeated the experiment using a new set of data.

    The results of the first trial were surprising, so we repeated the experiment using a new set of data.

5. Live-line workers approach their jobs with the care accorded lion training and skydiving. *Because a significant electrostatic field surrounds a live power line for several tens of meters and increases in strength the nearer to the line*, a lineman's body is energized well before he touches the conductor. Within a meter or so, the field may be 20-30 kV less than the conductor's voltage. Despite that difference, a human body has a relatively small mass, and *when the lineman contacts the line with his wand* a current of no more than a few microamperes is induced in his body. *Because of that difference in voltage*, however, an arc will leap between conductor and wand as the lineman approaches the conductor. (*Although not strong enough to be fatal*, such sparks can cause a brief loss of sensation in the hand.)

6. The lineman's wand and steel-mesh suit prevent the spark from touching his body: the arc jumps from line to wand rather than to a gloved hand or finger, and the suit equalizes the charge across its surface, *working on the principle of a Faraday cage. After the lineman is bonded,* contact is maintained through a short tie, *called a bonding lead,* from suit to conductor. The suit, *required at voltages above 150 kV,* also protects the lineman against the corona effect, the ionization of the air around a person's body *that results in a distinct buzzing sound and a prickly sensation on such protruding body parts as the ears.*

練習 8-1

1. (b) What ultimately limits divers' time under water is nitrogen gas.

2. (c) The two Voyager spacecraft revealed much about the dynamics of the atmospheres of the outer planets.

3. (b) The horse's great running ability coupled with its large size places unusual demands on its legs.

4. (a) The leech's simple body plan makes it an attractive animal to the experimental biologist.

5. (c) There are two basic types of cogeneration systems.

6. (c) Algorithmic computing and neurocomputing complement each other well.

練習 8-2

1. 比較與對照。

2. 歸納法。

3. 空間順序。

4. 定義。

5. 因果分析或定義。

6. 依時間順序。

7. 列舉法。

8. 因果分析。

9. 由概括到個別描述。

10. 邏輯論證。

11. 段落一：由概括到個別描述、由個別到概括描述及因果分析合用。

　　段落二：由概括到個別描述。

　　段落三：由概括到個別描述和由個別到概括描述合用。

　　段落四：空間順序。

　　段落五：分類法以及比較與對照。

　　段落六：比較與對照以及由概括到個別描述。

練習 9-1

1. In this paper, we propose a new service for digital mobile communication systems. This service allows two or more users to hold a secure electronic conference.

   In this paper, we propose a new service for digital mobile communication systems that allows two or more users to hold a secure electronic conference.

2. A block of four DIP switches is located on the bottom of the UT240. These DIP switches can be used to configure the unit for different types of systems. The correct DIP switch settings are shown in Table 2 below.

   On the bottom of the UT240 is a block of four DIP switches, which can be used to configure the unit for different types of systems. The correct DIP switch settings are shown in Table 2 below.

3. Much recent research on machine pattern recognition has focused on the use of neural networks. An important step in most existing neural-network-based methods is extracting the features of the patterns to be recognized. The quality of feature extraction largely determines the recognition rate achieved.

4. A distinctive feature of the MOS resistor is that its resistance value can be adjusted by varying the gate voltage. Thus the MOS resistor can be used to tune the gain of the wideband amplifier. However, the parasitic capacitance of the MOS device degrades the frequency response slightly.

5. If the CPU address does not match the tag, a cache miss occurs. When a cache read miss occurs, the controller will check whether the alter bit of the cache line involved is clean or dirty. If the alter bit is dirty, the controller will update the main memory with the data currently stored in the cache.

6. The solar water heater used in the experiment is shown in Figure 2. At the top left of the water heater is a cold-water inlet, where water flows into the apparatus. The main portion of the heater consists of many lengths of plastic pipe connected together in an accordion fashion and covered with a sheet of heat-absorbing plastic.

7. The atomic structure of ceramics gives them a chemical stability that makes them impervious to environmental degradation, such as dissolution in solvents. The strength of the bonds in ceramics results in characteristics such as a high melting point, hardness, and stiffness. Also, because many ceramics are composed of metal oxides, further oxidation is often impossible.

8. This paper investigates the financial investment and technological requirements involved in putting nitrogen-based techniques for fabricating widgets to use in commercial manufacturing. These techniques are an attractive investment, because their per-unit cost is lower than that of traditional methods of manufacturing widgets. However, before nitrogen-based techniques can be adopted, a number of technical problems must be overcome.

9. A bus master either oversees the transfer of data between devices or, more often, exchanges information with one or more slaves. The bus master selects slaves by placing address information on the bus; each slave compares this information with its own address. If the addresses match, the master and slave

establish a connection and the slave becomes a responder. Addresses that identify more than one slave are called broadcast addresses. A particular device may act as both master and slave, but not at the same time.

10. Perceptions of odors and colors operate according to different principles. Color perception involves a lexical system which is organized in memory in a relatively abstract and rigidly controlled way. By contrast, the characteristics of odor perception are flexibility and adaptability, and a relatively concrete but open-ended nonverbal coding system. This manner of organization in turn affects odor memory. What is stored about odors is not likely to involve semantic categories which can be used to retrieve odors. Rather, odor memory involves perceptually unitary episodes described in idiosyncratic terminology.

練習 9-2

1. This article also discusses the problem of the nonlinear nonreciprocity of soliton transmission in an EDFA with different pumping configurations.

2. In this paper an internal model control method is used to develop a fully digital servo control for an AC induction motor.

   In this paper we use an internal model control method to develop a fully digital servo control for an AC induction motor.

   In this paper a fully digital servo control for an AC induction motor is developed through the use of an internal model control method.

3. This paper investigates the molecular director configuration of a closed cylinder of liquid crystal with negative dielectric anisotropy in an external field.

4. A global calibration scheme is proposed to resolve the coordinate equivalence problem encountered when CAD systems are integrated with robot manipulators.

   We propose a global calibration scheme to resolve the coordinate equivalence problem encountered when CAD systems are integrated with robot manipulators.

5. In section 7, we describe experiments in which the proposed method is applied to control a standard industrial robot manipulator.

   In section 7, experiments are described in which the proposed method is applied to control a standard industrial robot manipulator.

   Section 7 describes experiments in which the proposed method is applied to control a standard industrial robot manipulator.

6. In this report, an efficient algorithm is developed that employs the concept of static equilibrium to determine the stability of clamping.

   In this report, we develop an efficient algorithm that employs the concept of static equilibrium to determine the stability of clamping.

練習 9-3

1. In strong light conditions, the solar cell may deliver a supply voltage that is so high that the LCD display segments cannot be switched off.

2. The techniques used to produce maps have changed dramatically over the past fifty years, progressing from field workers and manual surveying to satellites and computers. Before World War II, the predominant method for creating maps was field surveying. After World War II, map-making methods began to include manual photogrammetry. Although manual photogrammetry is still used today, it is being supplanted by digital cartography, and computers are becoming the hub of the mapping process.

3. In recent years an extraordinary increase has occurred in the attention, both popular and scientific, that has been paid to mutation and its consequences. The sources of this interest are the recognition that components of our environment pose a largely unevaluated threat to the conservation of genetic material and the realization that mutations frequently have serious consequences for human health. This interest has led to research that has improved our understanding of DNA and of its metabolism and organization into genes.

4. As Figure 1 shows, these insects are physically dissimilar from species common in North America, and they have a voracious appetite. Numerous studies have documented the unusually large amount of vegetation an individual of the species can consume in a single day (see, for example, James 1982, Halton 1987, Mayumi 1989, and Brandom 1992).

5. During the last two decades, impressive advances in technology have led to the development of sophisticated new instruments such as filled-aperture telescopes and interferometric arrays, which have provided astronomers with the ability to observe star-forming regions in considerable detail at infrared, millimeter, and submillimeter wavelengths. Over the last few years, observations with these and other instruments have produced a series of remarkable, exciting, and unexpected discoveries concerning the star-formation process in our galaxy. As a result of these discoveries, astronomers are beginning to understand the processes of star formation and early stellar evolution.

6. The test apparatus samples and records the rate of evaporation over a 4 × 5 meter area. The apparatus is based partly on the design described by Susky and Hopfeld [4], although it is easier to move and assemble than their device, requiring only two people for transportation and setup.

練習 9-4

1. The intensity and frequency of earthquakes can be measured using seismometers. A seismometer consists of a mass suspended by a spring or other elastic mechanism inside a metal frame that is anchored to the ground. A magnet is attached to the mass and an electric coil to the frame. Any vibration of the ground shakes the seismometer's frame, but inertia tends to hold the mass in its place. Thus the coil on the frame moves in relation to the magnet on the mass, and this movement generates an electrical signal that represents the intensity and frequency of the movement.

2. The amount of fluorine incorporated into the silicon film can be controlled by reducing the amount of water added to the immersing solution. When less water is added, more fluorine atoms are released, as shown in the reaction equa-

tion. Because the number of free fluorine atoms in the solution increases, a greater amount of fluorine is incorporated into the film.

3. Since each sensor receives information from only a limited range, information from many sensors must be combined.

4. As landfills are closed, many communities are passing recycling laws and constructing waste-to-energy plants. Although waste-to-energy plants face many of the same technical, regulatory, and political obstacles as conventional power plants, some issues are peculiar to them. Unlike most power plants, municipal waste incinerators burn many different types of materials, creating different types of toxic byproducts. Whereas fossil fuel plants may pollute the air, waste incinerators may pollute the earth. Since most ash is buried along with garbage in municipal landfills, environmentalists fear that contaminants may seep into groundwater.

練習 9-5

1. 這段文章主要有兩個問題：一、在第二個句子中，*this method* 究係何指，並不清楚。二、第三個句子的句首 *therefore* 暗示了一個事實上並不存在的邏輯關係：第二個句子所陳述的事實，既不會是作者作實驗的原因，而且在邏輯上也不會推演出「這些作者會去作實驗」。這段文章可修正如下：

> Roski [3] studied the characteristics of the built-up edge (BUE) and developed a chamfered main edge cutting tool. His cutting method involves tool geometries that produce a BUE that flows away continuously in the form of a separated secondary chip. In the research reported here, we studied the mechanism underlying secondary chip formation by conducting cutting experiments on carbon steel and pure aluminum.

2. 究竟甚麼「基於」("based on") 不同成本之間的取捨情形？這個句子的表面意思是：這篇論文以不同成本之間的取捨為基礎，但這根本就是一派胡言。作者的意思大概是：非線性程式化的問題係以不同成本之間的交易為基礎。可是，這問題究竟如何「以不同成本之間的交易為基礎」，則沒有交待清楚。有些作者如何濫用 *based on* 這模糊不清的字眼，從這句中可見一斑。這句可修改如下：

> This paper has presented a nonlinear programming problem that determines the optimal market size by finding the optimal trade-off between the operating cost and the travel cost.

3. 這段文章有幾個問題：一、在第二個句子中，作者說 "based on" 是甚麼意思？二、第三個句子的 *search algorithm* 究係何物？（作者在還沒介紹這個演算法之前，就已開始討論如何改善它。）此外，第三個句子也提到「其他屬性」，可是這些屬性究竟是甚麼事物的屬性，也不夠清楚。弄清這些邏輯的「跳躍」，這段文章的原作者就把文章修改如下：

> In this paper, we analyze the stability of clamping with passive friction forces. The concept of the instant center of rotation is employed to trans-

form the stability analysis into a search for a static equilibrium state. Other properties of clamping are also studied and applied to develop an efficient algorithm for determining the stability of clamping.

4. 這段文章主要的問題是第三和第四個句子間的關係不清：一、在第三個句子中，作者告訴我們：多種名稱都必須有 "the same semantics"。但作者卻沒有解釋 *semantics* 的意思。（它們都必須為名詞嗎？還是它們都必須指同一件事物？）二、在第四個句子中，作者舉了三個例子，但這些究竟是甚麼事物的例子並不清楚。由於第三個句子提過 "the same semantics"，所以讀者可能已假設第四個句子的例子是想幫助讀者瞭解 "the same semantics"。然而，事實上，這些例子又像是「多種名稱」的例子。三、在第四個句子中，形容詞 *good* 意思非常模糊，作者應用上較精確的形容詞。

   我們可省略第三個句子，並改寫第四個句子：

   A distinctive feature of the data model is how names are used. Users can specify multiple names for classes, attributes, methods, and reference relationships. For example, *person, people,* and *human* could all be used as names of a class which contains information about persons. When users want to retrieve information about persons, they can use any one of these names in their query.

5. 第二個句子所提到的問題究竟是甚麼？在第一個句子中，作者只指出一個事實，而沒提到任何「問題」。我們可省略 *problem* 這字詞，並把第二個句子修改得較具體一點：

   The reaction between n-butyl bromide and phenoxide ions exhibits a slow reaction rate because the two substances consist of different phases. Many investigators have attempted to increase the speed of this reaction by using various catalysts.

6. 在這段文章中，從第三個句子到第四個句子的轉接令人眼花撩亂，因為轉接過程中，作者已更換了主題，卻沒提醒讀者。第三個句子仍在討論 INY，可是第四個句子已經開始描述 INZ，並把 INZ 所應用的方法和 INY 所應用的作一對照。作者應在第三個句子之後加上一新句，以指出討論的主題已改變。下面是一種修改方式：

   Vendor selection is one of the most important parts of the purchasing process. Recently, the concept of dimensional analysis was used to propose a vendor performance measure and to obtain an index called INY. The performance criteria used in INY include quantitative and qualitative criteria. In this paper, a new vendor performance index called INZ is proposed as an alternative to INY. For qualitative criteria, a two-directional evaluation is employed instead of the one-directional approach used in INY. Then all scores for quantitative and qualitative criteria are combined into a sum of weighted averages. The use of INZ is compared with that of INY by means of several examples.

練習 12-1

步驟一: 句子 1, 2, 3

步驟二: 句子 4, 5, 6, 7, 8, 9 （前半部分）

步驟三: 句子 9 （後半部分）

步驟四: 句子 10

步驟五: 句子 11

練習 12-2

As the standard of living has improved in the last ten years, beer, a Western beverage, has become very popular in China. With an estimated annual production of 6 million cubic meters, China has become the fifth-largest beer-consuming nation in the world, after the United States, Germany, the United Kingdom, and Russia. Of the thousands of breweries in China, most are located in rural areas, use outdated technology, and, until recently, have been little concerned with pollution. For each cubic meter of beer produced, these plants in general generate 20-30 cubic meters of effluent, much more than that reported to be produced by modern plants in Western nations. As a result of this heavy output of effluent, the brewery industry has become one of the major polluters in China.

練習 12-3

Knowledge of the wind-induced local pressures expected to act on the building envelope during its lifetime is needed for the rational design of glass and cladding on buildings. This requirement has become more important in recent years because of the popularity of tall buildings with large areas of glass and lightweight cladding. Fluctuations in pressure on wall surfaces are caused by the turbulence in the wind flow approaching the building and by flow disturbances generated by the building and its surface elements, such as mullions or vertical ribs. Mullions and ribs are common because of cladding requirements or simply for decorative purposes.

Wind standards and building codes state guidelines for the design of building cladding. However, the applicability of these guidelines to buildings with mullions or ribs is doubtful. In addition, wind tunnel modeling commonly assumes that the surfaces of the buildings being simulated are smooth. It is unclear whether wind pressures measured on smooth building surfaces can also represent those acting on a model with mullions or ribs.

練習 12-4

下面是練習 12-4 的修改建議。除了下面的解答之外，可能還有其他寫法可以適用。

One of the most challenging problems in the field of computer vision is the analysis of visual motion from image sequences. Besides its relevance to the understanding of biological vision systems, motion analysis has many practical applications in areas such as robotics, vehicle navigation, traffic safety, intelligent vehicle and highway systems, aviation, and space exploration. One of the major areas of interest in motion analysis is passive ranging. In passive ranging, the 3-D environment of a moving camera is reconstructed by analyzing a sequence of images obtained by the camera.

練習 12-5

1. Many studies <u>have examined</u> the relationships between physical characteristics of the work environment, attitudes, and behavior.

2. Goodrich (1982) <u>found</u> that the use of a VDT focuses workers' attention. He <u>suggested</u> that use of a VDT would reduce workers' need for privacy.

3. Several different measures of these factors <u>have been employed</u> to study a variety of samples and settings.

4. The effects of devices such as VDTs <u>have been investigated</u> by several authors (Brown, 1982; Forman, 1986; McGee, 1988).

5. Roberts (1987) <u>showed</u> that interaction with a VDT tended to increase employees' levels of fatigue, muscular tension, and eyestrain.

6. Degree of openness <u>is</u> an important characteristic of the physical work environment (Smith, 1990).

7. Several researchers <u>have found</u> that muscle aches and joint pain can be reduced by the use of adjustable workstation furniture (Kleeman, 1988; Roberts, 1990; Paul, 1993).

8. Several authors <u>have suggested</u> that office technology affects the ways in which employees work (Kruk 1987; Smith 1989; Black, 1990).

9. Stellman et al. (1987) <u>found</u> that stress effects are greater for clerical employees than for managerial employees.

10. The negative effects of improper VDT use and poor work station design <u>are</u> [或 <u>can be</u>] costly (Kruk, 1989).

11. A number of researchers <u>have demonstrated</u> that physical characteristics of the work environment have an impact on outcome variables such as satisfaction, motivation, and performance (Becker, 1981; Sundstrom, 1982; Carlopio, 1991).

12. Kleeman (1988) <u>suggested</u> that VDT users are more prone to stress symptoms than are non-VDT users.

練習 12-6

1. 作者把研究結果當成普遍的事實。

2. 結果被限制為只在特定情形下有效。

3. 建議。

4. 結果被限制為只在特定情形下有效。

5. 結果被限制為只在特定情形下有效。

6. 作者把研究結果當成普遍的事實。

7. 結果被限制為只在特定情形下有效。

8. 假設。

9. 作者把研究結果當成普遍的事實。

10. 結果被限制為只在特定情形下有效。

練習 12-7

　　下面是練習 12-7 文獻回顧的修改建議。除了下面的解答之外，可能還有其他寫法可以適用。

Several researchers have found that workers prefer architecturally private offices to open offices and that the lack of privacy affects the level of job satisfaction (Sundstrom, 1982; Oldham, 1988). Oldham and Brass (1979) studied employees before and after they moved to an open-plan office and found that job satisfaction declined considerably after the move and remained low at the time of a follow-up survey. In a similar study of office workers, Hedge (1982) found that the open office caused too many disturbances and distractions. In a laboratory experiment, Block and Stokes (1989) found that subjects were more satisfied working in a private office than in one they had to share with three other individuals.

Several studies have reported a relationship between privacy and overall job satisfaction (Sundstrom, 1980; Burt et al., 1981), but only a few researchers have considered the relationship between privacy and individual aspects of job satisfaction. Altman (1975) suggested that privacy may function to reduce overload and the number of distractions by providing the worker the ability to regulate the number of outgoing and incoming interactions. Steele (1973) found that privacy increased an employee's sense of social status in the company. Justa and Golan (1977) hypothesized that privacy may give the worker a greater sense of freedom. Sundstrom (1986) suggested that privacy generally serves to improve working conditions.

練習 13-1

Depletion of atmospheric ozone is a major environmental problem, especially in the polar regions [1]. Several studies have examined the photodissociation of ozone and subsequent reaction of the fragments with O_3 [2-11], H_2O [12-23], and other small molecules [24-31]. However, the importance of ozone photochemistry in stratospheric ice crystals is largely unknown [32, 33], and to our knowledge little/no experimental research on this reaction in the solid state has been reported until now. In this paper, we describe cross sections for photodestruction of solid ozone….

...Studies performed on CO_2 levels within the soil profile have established that significant variations in soil CO_2 occur seasonally, between soils, and with depth (Richter and Jacobs, 1972; Miotke, 1974; Rightmire, 1978; Gunn and Trudgill, 1982; Buyanovsky and Wagner, 1983). Measurements of CO_2 concentrations for an entire annual cycle <u>are</u> rare, <u>however</u>, and most of these <u>have been</u> reported for just one depth. Moreover, <u>although</u> annual CO_2 cycles <u>have been</u> studied extensively under agricultural conditions (Buyanovsky and Wagner, 1983), to our knowledge there <u>have been</u> <u>no/few</u> intensive investigations into CO_2 dynamics and the possible effects on water quality in mountainous and forested regions....

練習 13-2

1. 論文導向

2. 論文導向

3. 研究導向

4. 論文導向

5. 研究導向

6. 研究導向

7. discusses / explores / investigates / considers / examines 等等（時態為現在式）

8. was

9. investigated / examined / explored / identified 等等（時態為過去式）

10. presents / provides / describes 等等（時態為現在式或未來式）

練習 13-3

下面是練習 13-3 建議的解答。有些句子可能不只有一種正確的寫法，因此除了下面的解答之外，可能還有其他答案可以適用。

...However, at high doping levels these conventional methods usually give erroneous t values because of the resistivity and short lifetime in such materials. In the research reported here, carrier recombination was investigated in MBE-grown silicon films highly doped with Sb or In. Unlike earlier work, the transient grating method was used under strong pumping conditions in an attempt to obtain more accurate values of t.

或

...However, at high doping levels these conventional methods usually give erroneous t values because of the resistivity and short lifetime in such materials. The purpose of this research was to investigate carrier recombination in MBE-grown silicon films highly doped with Sb or In. Unlike earlier work, we used the transient grating method under strong pumping conditions in an attempt to obtain more accurate values of t.

…Indeed, many immersion educators have called for curriculum-based research on how to improve immersion students' oral and written grammar skills.

The purpose of this research was to conduct an experimental study to determine whether middle-school immersion students' acquisition and use of a specific grammatical form could be improved and to develop curricular materials integrating formal and functional approaches in order to effect this improvement. The results of this research should be of interest to educators involved in designing language immersion programs and teaching materials.

或

…Many immersion educators have called for curriculum-based research on how to improve immersion students' oral and written grammar skills.

In this research, an experimental study was conducted to determine whether middle-school immersion students' acquisition and use of a specific grammatical form could be improved, and curricular materials integrating formal and functional approaches were developed in order to effect this improvement. The results of this research may be of interest to educators involved in designing language immersion programs and teaching materials.

練習 14-1

下面是練習 14-1 建議的解答。有些句子可能不只有一種正確的解答，因此下面列出兩個動詞形式。

1. Consider 或 will consider; are; is proposed 或 will be proposed; consists; is; be introduced.

2. Assume 或 will assume; increases 或 will increase; is; represents; is expected 或 can be expected; will place 或 places; will begin 或 begin; may impose、will impose 或 imposes.

練習 15-1

Experiments to investigate the ability of *Octopus vulgaris* to learn by observation were conducted in three phases: training of demonstrators, observation of the task by untrained octopuses, and testing of observers. Demonstrators were trained through a series of trials in which two balls, one red and one white, were presented to the animal. When the animal attacked the correct ball, it was rewarded with a piece of fish, and when it attacked the incorrect ball, it was punished by an electric shock.

In the observational phase, an untrained octopus observed four trials during which a demonstrator in an adjacent tank attacked the ball it had been taught to attack. Videotape analysis showed that observer octopuses increased their attention during each of the four trials.

In the testing phase, observer octopuses were tested with a session of five trials with both white and red balls randomly positioned. No reward or punishment was given for any choice made.

Statistics on the observers' performance were analyzed and compared with those on the learning of the demonstrators.

練習 15-2

The subjects had two video display unit (VDU) work periods of 30 minutes each. The screen viewing distance was 50 cm in one period and 70 cm in the other. The document viewing distance was 50 cm in both periods. Between the two work periods, the subjects rested for 45 minutes, during which time they left the experimental room. After a further rest of 10 minutes, subjects performed the VDU task for 15 minutes. During this work period the screen viewing distance was adjusted to the most comfortable position as indicated by each subject.

The VDU task was designed so that frequent gaze shifts between the screen and document were necessary. The screen and the document contained a list of 20 names, each followed by a four-digit number. The names on the screen and document were identical, but some of the numbers corresponding to the names were different. The subjects had to compare the numbers for each name and press one of two keys on the keyboard to indicate whether the numbers were identical or not....

練習 15-3

1. 特別設計的材料

2. 對一般母體的描述

3. 標準設備

4. 特定樣本

5. 特別設計的設備

6. 標準材料

練習 15-4

下面是練習 15-4 的建議解答。有些句子可能不只有一種正確的寫法，因此除了下面的解答之外，可能還有其他答案可以適用。

An experiment was conducted in which subjects were randomly assigned to treatment groups, exposed to music from a loudspeaker, and asked to fill out a questionnaire. The stimuli included two levels of tempo (slow and fast) and loudness (soft and loud). Gender (male or female) was the third factor.

Fifty-two volunteers (26 males and 26 females) were recruited from an introductory class at a large urban university. The ages of the subjects ranged from 19 to 34, with a median age of 21. Most of the subjects had some previous musical training, but none were musical experts.

The stimuli consisted of different versions of an original classical-style musical composition. Two versions of the music were created in a digital sound studio: a fast version (120 BPM) and a slow version (60 BPM). Loudness was manipulated by presetting the volume controls on the amplifiers that powered the loudspeakers in the listening rooms. An average sound level of 60 dB was produced under the soft conditions and 90 dB under the loud conditions.

Each group of subjects was taken to a small soundproof listening room equipped with a table and chairs. The subjects were instructed not to talk, to leave the questionnaire face down on the table until after the music stopped, and to complete the questionnaire immediately after the music finished.

The subjects' judgments of the music's affective character were measured by using a 16-item adjective checklist, on which the subjects circled the adjectives that they thought best described the music. Behavioral intent toward the music was measured by asking the subjects whether they would want to listen to the music again.

練習 16-1

1. 和其他學者的研究結果作比較。

2. 根據研究結果作推論。

3. 對研究結果提出說明。

4. 根據研究結果作推論。

5. 對研究結果提出說明。

6. 和其他學者的技術作比較。

7. 比較實驗數據和理論模型。

8. 根據研究結果作推論。

練習 16-2

下面解答是原作者的寫法。在解答中，我們用方括號表示其他可能的選擇。

1. The results <u>are shown</u> in Figure —. The two tests of quenching from 153° C <u>have</u> identical creep curves, confirming the thermorever-sibility of quenching and aging as well as the reliability of the apparatus. The quench from 153° to

0° C produced [或 produces] the least dense structure and the highest creep, whereas the quench from 96° to 0° C yielded [或 yields] the most dense structure, leading to the slowest creep behavior. These results are understandable because the initial annealing temperature (T_0) determines the state of conformational structures, from which the quenching takes place. For a higher T_0, greater excess free volume or molecular mobility is most likely to be frozen into the glassy matrix if quenching is performed properly. Thus molecular mobility is determined by the initial annealing temperature.

2. Table — summarizes the statistical analysis. The means of the ranks show that Group 1 (no indentation) exhibited the poorest performance, while Group 3 (moderate indentation) performed the best. This seems to suggest that indentation has [或 had] some effect on comprehension. On the other hand, the analysis of variance indicates that we cannot reject the null hypothesis at the 0.05 level of significance.

3. The proportion of elements correctly recalled for each problem at each level of difficulty is shown in Table —. From the table it is apparent that the complexity level had [或 has] no effect on immediate recall. This conclusion is supported by an analysis of variance done on the data using problem pairings (six levels) and subjects (two per cell) as factors. There was no significant difference in the number of elements recalled between the two difficulty levels, $F(1, 6) = 0.391$, $P > 0.05$. Similarly, there was no difference among the problem pairs, $F(5, 6) = 0.718$.

   Although complexity level had [或 has] no effect on immediate recall, it did [或 does] affect delayed recall. As Table — shows, the subjects recalled [或 recall] less of the complex program segments than they did [或 do] of the simpler segments when tested 48 hours after their initial exposure.

   The absence of an effect of difficulty level on immediate recall is not surprising. Students often develop good strategies for memorizing as a study skill and can use these skills when they are needed. In this experiment, the short amount of time allowed for them to study the program segments was probably not long enough for them truly to comprehend the modules. The reason for the effect of level of difficulty on delayed recall was [或 is] probably that the subjects were [或 are] able to process and integrate proportionately more of the simpler procedures than the complex procedures.

4. Figure — shows fiber cross-sections averaged over the ten central offices (COs) included in the model. The results indicate that the active double-star (ADS) cross-section is sensitive to offered load, while the cross-section in the three passive architectures is not. This is because the feeder in the ADS is designed on the basis of subscriber usage, while each of the passive architectures gives 16 subscribers at each remote node transparent 155 Mb/s video channels all the way from the CO.

練習 16-3

　　下面是練習 16-3 建議的解答。有些句子可能不只有一種正確的寫法，因此除了下面的解答之外，可能還有其他答案可以適用。

1. The monthly rainfall in Nabonia in 1992 is shown in Figure 3. The monthly rainfall was about 25 mm from January to April, after which it increased dramatically, peaking at about 200 mm in July. Between July and November, the amount of rain gradually returned to about 25 mm per month. It appears that there is a distinct rainy season in Nabonia that lasts from June to September.

2. Figure 4 shows the average scores of the workers in each age group on the speed and knowledge tests. Younger workers scored higher than older workers on the speed test, but lower than older workers on the knowledge test. The results suggest that younger workers may be more adept at jobs that require great speed, whereas older workers may be more capable of doing jobs that require more knowledge.

練習 17-1

1. The purpose of this work was to study the relations between the perceptual properties of loudspeakers and their frequency response. [研究目的]

2. The frequency response proved to be extremely important in determining perceived sound quality. [結果概述]

3. It seems to influence all perceptual dimensions. [結果概述]

4. The data reveal that differences between loudspeakers mainly occur at lower frequencies, such as below 1000 Hz. The poorer loudspeakers usually have a pronounced energy boost somewhere in this low-frequency region. [結果概述]

5. This higher energy makes the speakers sound duller and also produces more upward spread of masking, which has a negative effect on clarity and fidelity. [說明]

6. In a study of this type, the physical properties of the music program and the reproduction are continuously changing, and so is the listener's impression of the sound in its various dimensions. [限制]

7. Thus it would be preferable to use a continuous recording, both of the acoustical characteristics and of the listener's judgments, in order to obtain a more detailed understanding of the psychophysical relations. [建議]

8. The changing acoustical characteristics could be studied by some type of sonogram technique. [建議]

練習 17-2

下面是練習 17-2 建議的解答。有些句子可能不只有一種正確的寫法，因此我們在每一題下列有兩三個不同的建議。

1. We originally assumed that the sputtering yield of a monoatomic target would be proportional to the energy deposited in nuclear collisions at the surface.

   It was originally assumed that the sputtering yield of a monoatomic target would be proportional to the energy deposited in nuclear collisions at the surface.

Existing theories suggested that the sputtering yield of a monoatomic target would be proportional to the energy deposited in nuclear collisions at the surface.

2. The purpose of this study was to investigate whether there are differences in the evaluation cues that successful and unsuccessful salespeople use for classifying sales leads.

3. In general, the losses of residue measured in our study were greater than those reported in previous research.

4. The results show that program modules equated on surface complexity and on function may vary significantly in their semantic complexity.

   Our findings indicate that program modules equated on surface complexity and on function may vary significantly in their semantic complexity.

   Program modules equated on surface complexity and on function may vary significantly in their semantic complexity.

5. It seems that the energy deposited by the ions rearranges the atomic structure of the damaged SiO_2 surface in the presence of oxygen.

   The energy deposited by the ions may rearrange the atomic structure of the damaged SiO_2 surface in the presence of oxygen.

   It is possible that the energy deposited by the ions may rearrange the atomic structure of the damaged SiO_2 surface in the presence of oxygen.

   The energy deposited by the ions appears to rearrange the atomic structure of the damaged SiO_2 surface in the presence of oxygen.

6. The most likely cause of the discrepancy was an increase in the value of the absorption coefficient, which could affect the induced carrier density significantly.

   The discrepancy was likely due to an increase in the value of the absorption coefficient, which could affect the induced carrier density significantly.

   The discrepancy may be due to an increase in the value of the absorption coefficient, which might affect the induced carrier density significantly.

   It is likely that the discrepancy was caused by an increase in the value of the absorption coefficient. This may have affected the induced carrier density significantly.

7. Snow cover appeared to insulate the residues from extremes of cold and drying out, which would help account for the slow loss rates during the first winter at site A.

   Snow cover appeared to insulate the residues from extremes of cold and drying out, which might help account for the slow loss rates during the first winter at site A.

   Snow cover may have insulated the residues from extremes of cold and drying out. This could help account for the slow loss rates during the first winter at site A.

Snow cover could have insulated the residues from extremes of cold and drying out, which might explain the slow loss rates during the first winter at site A.

8. We recognize that it is difficult to measure comprehension, and our method may have been insufficiently precise.

It is difficult to measure comprehension, and our method may have been insufficiently precise.

It is difficult to measure comprehension, and our method may be insufficiently precise.

9. We cannot claim that our student sample is representative of the adult population.

Our student sample may not be representative of the adult population.

We recognize that our student sample may not be representative of the adult population.

10. An important direction for further work might be to study the chunking process as it operates in programming tasks.

An important topic for future research would be to study the chunking process as it operates in programming tasks.

Future research could examine the chunking process as it operates in programming tasks.

An interesting topic would be to study the chunking process as it operates in programming tasks.

11. These findings suggest further study with large groups of professional programmers with varying degrees of experience.

We suggest further study with large groups of professional programmers with varying degrees of experience.

Further studies should be conducted with large groups of professional programmers with varying degrees of experience.

12. In summary, we find differences in the properties of salespeople's cues, but no differences in the quantity of knowledge they have available.

These findings provide evidence that there are differences in the properties of salespeople's cues, but no differences in the quantity of knowledge they have available.

The results indicate that there are differences in the properties of salespeople's cues, but no differences in the quantity of knowledge they have available.

There appear to be differences in the properties of salespeople's cues, but no differences in the quantity of knowledge they have available.

13. The results of this study suggest that instructional design affects the outcome of education.

Our findings indicate that instructional design affects the outcome of education.

These results imply that instructional design may affect the outcome of education.

Instructional design appears to affect the outcome of education.

14. The results indicate that structural differences in the starting material also strongly influence the sputtering yields.

These data suggest that structural differences in the starting material also strongly influence the sputtering yields.

Structural differences in the starting material also appear to strongly influence the sputtering yields.

Structural differences in the starting material also appear to have a strong influence on the sputtering yields.

練習 19-1

背景：句子 1

研究目的：句子 2

方法：句子 3, 4, 5

結果：句子 6, 7

結論或建議：句子 8, 9

練習 19-2

To successfully implement no-till crop management systems for winter wheat, knowledge is needed of how rapidly large residue fragments are lost. In this research, losses of surface-managed winter wheat residues were measured at five sites. Sites were sampled periodically by using grab samples to determine weight loss per unit area. Thirty weeks after harvest, residue weight losses ranged from 35% to 42%. Snow cover provided insulation for residues, allowing decomposition to continue during winter when sufficient moisture was present. On chemical fallow plots, there was a 50 to 80% loss after a year. On plots seeded with a no-till spring crop, residue losses ranged from 81 to 88% by harvest time. Contributions of various sources of residue mass loss are discussed.

Most salespeople attempt to identify likely purchasers of a product by using evaluation clues stored in memory to classify potential customers. This study investigated how these cues differ for successful and unsuccessful salespeople. The findings suggest that successful and unsuccessful salespeople have the same number of cues in memory and that the two types of representatives distribute importance weights about the same across evaluation cues. Successful and unsuccessful salespeople weight many of the same cues differently, however. The standards they use to describe class members also differ for several cues, with successful salespeople generally using more stringent criteria. The authors discuss the implications of the findings and offer suggestions for future research.

練習 19-3

　　下面是練習 19-3 建議的解答。除了下面的解答之外，可能還有其他答案可以適用。

An important variable affecting the comprehension of programs is their psychological complexity. Although some previous work has been done on surface or low-level semantic features that affect complexity, little work has been done on the effects of higher-level semantic features. This article describes an experiment using pairs of program modules that had equivalent surface complexity and functions but included semantic constructs with varying complexity. The modules were presented to student programmers to memorize. The students were tested on immediate recall, hand execution, and recall after a delay of 48 hours. Students given the semantically complex modules scored significantly worse [或 had significantly worse scores] on hand execution and delayed recall.

註釋

第二章註釋

1. Adapted from Takefumi Inagaki, "Better Laser Printers for Less," *IEEE Spectrum,* March 1989, p. 42.

2. Adapted from Eric J. Lerner, "Magnetic Fusion Power," *IEEE Spectrum,* December 1980, p. 44.

3. Adapted from Glenn W. Preston, "The Very Large Scale Integrated Circuit," *American Scientist,* Vol. 71, September-October 1983, p. 466.

4. Adapted from IEEE Spectrum staff, "Sharper 'Eyes' for Star Gazers," *IEEE Spectrum,* August 1980, p. 26.

5. Adapted from Arthur L. Robinson, "Communicating with Computers by Voice," *Science,* Vol. 203, No. 23, February 23, 1979, p. 734.

6. Adapted from William C. Gardiner, Jr., "The Chemistry of Flames," *Scientific American,* Vol. 246, No. 2, February 1982, pp. 88–89.

7. Adapted from James E. Bayfield, "Rydberg Atoms," *American Scientist,* Vol. 71, July-August 1983, p. 375.

8. Adapted from Glenn W. Preston, "The Very Large Scale Integrated Circuit," *American Scientist,* Vol. 71, September-October 1983, p. 471.

9. Adapted from Victor F. Weisskopf, "The Origin of the Universe," *American Scientist,* Vol. 71, September-October 1983, pp. 475–76.

10. Adapted from W. Kenneth Dawson and Robert W. Dobinson, "What a Bus Is and How It Works: A Primer," *IEEE Spectrum,* October 1986, pp. 52–53.

第三章註釋

1. Adapted from Joseph T. Eastman and Arthur L. DeVries, "Antarctic Fishes," *Scientific American*, Vol. 255, No. 5, November 1986, p. 96.

2. Adapted from work by Chia-fu Chen and associates, National Chiao Tung University, Hsinchu, Taiwan.

3. Adapted from Sien Chi, C. W. Chang, and S. Wen, "Ultrashort Soliton Pulse Train Propagation in Erbium-Doped Fiber Amplifiers."

4. Adapted from Steven W. Squyres, "Ganymede and Callisto," *American Scientist*, Vol. 71, January-February 1983, p. 56.

5. Adapted from Warren G. Holmes and Paul W. Sherman, "Kin Recognition in Animals," *American Scientist*, Vol. 71, January-February 1983, p. 46.

6. Adapted from Charles J. Lada and Frank H. Shu, "The Formation of Sunlike Stars," *Science*, Vol. 248, May 4, 1990, p. 564.

7. Adapted from work by Chia-fu Chen and associates, National Chiao Tung University, Hsinchu, Taiwan.

8. Adapted from Scott Camazine and Roger A. Morse, "The Africanized Honey-bee," *American Scientist*, Vol. 76, September-October 1988, p. 465.

9. Adapted from John W. Drake, Barry W. Glickman, and Lynn S. Ripley, "Updating the Theory of Mutation," *American Scientist*, Vol. 71, November-December 1983, p. 621.

10. Adapted from Steven C. Guptill and Lowell E. Starr, "Making Maps with Computers," *American Scientist*, Vol. 76, March-April 1988, pp. 136–137.

第四章註釋

1. Adapted from Eric J. Lerner, "Magnetic Fusion Power," *IEEE Spectrum*, December 1980, p. 45.

2. Adapted from Roderick V. Jensen, "Classical Chaos," *American Scientist*, Vol. 75, March-April 1987, p. 168.

3. Adapted from Joel E. Cohen, "The Counterintuitive in Conflict and Cooperation," *American Scientist*, Vol. 76, November-December 1988, p. 578.

4. Adapted from Barry F. Madore and Wendy L. Freedman, "Self-Organizing Systems," *American Scientist*, Vol. 75, May-June 1987, p. 256.

5. Adapted from Arch C. Luther, "You Are There…and in Control," *IEEE Spectrum*, September 1988, pp. 46–47.

6. Adapted from Richard A. Kerr, "Sunspot-Weather Link Is Down But Not Out," *Science*, Vol. 248, May 11, 1990, p. 684.

7. Adapted from   William C. Gardiner, Jr., "The Chemistry of Flames," *Scientific American*, Vol. 246, No. 2, February 1982, p. 89.

8. Adapted from Eric J. Lerner, "Magnetic Fusion Power," *IEEE Spectrum*, December 1980, p. 44.

9. Adapted from Eric J. Lerner, "Magnetic Fusion Power," *IEEE Spectrum*, December 1980, p. 44.

10. Adapted from Arch C. Luther, "You Are There…and in Control," *IEEE Spectrum*, September 1988, pp. 46–47.

11. Adapted from Eric J. Lerner, "Magnetic Fusion Power," *IEEE Spectrum,* December 1980, p. 44.

第五章註釋

1. Adapted from John A. Adam, "How to Design an 'Invisible' Aircraft," *IEEE Spectrum*, April 1988, p. 28.

2. Adapted from John C. Rodger and Belinda L. Drake, "The Enigma of the Fetal Graft," *American Scientist*, Vol. 75, January-February 1987, p. 51.

第六章註釋

1. Adapted from Trudy E. Bell, "Earthquake Prediction: Keeping an Ear to the Ground," *IEEE Spectrum*, May 1988, p. 47.

第七章註釋

1. Adapted from Philippe Brou, Thomas R. Sciascia, Lynette Linden, and Jerome Y. Lettvin, "The Colors of Things," *Scientific American*, Vol. 255, No. 3, September 1986, p. 80.
2. Adapted from William C. Baer, "The Shadow Market in Housing," *Scientific American*, Vol. 255, No. 5, November 1986, p. 29.
3. Adapted from Judith Goldhaber, "The Quest for Quark Soup," *New Scientist*, November 13, 1986, p. 40.
4. Adapted from Steven Rose, "Memories and Molecules," *New Scientist*, November 27, 1986, p. 40.
5. Exercises 5 and 6 adapted from Gary Stix, "Working Hot: Life at 765 kV," *IEEE Spectrum*, September 1988, p. 56.

第八章註釋

1. Adapted from Glenn Zorpette, "An Underwater Visit to Aquarius," *IEEE Spectrum*, March 1988, p. 25.
2. Adapted from Andrew P. Ingersoll, "Atmospheric Dynamics of the Outer Planets," *Science*, Vol. 248, April 20, 1990, p. 308.
3. Adapted from Milton Hildebrand, "The Mechanics of Horse Legs," *American Scientist*, Vol. 75, November-December 1987, p. 594.
4. Adapted from Gunther S. Stent and David A. Weisblat, "The Development of a Simple Nervous System," *Scientific American*, Vol. 246, No. 1, January 1982, p. 100.
5. Adapted from Joel Fagenbaum, "Cogeneration: An Energy Saver," *IEEE Spectrum*, August 1980, p. 30.
6. Adapted from Robert Hecht-Nielsen, "Neurocomputing: Picking the Human Brain," *IEEE Spectrum*, March 1988, p. 36.
7. Adapted from Ted Simons, Steve K. Sherrod, Michael W. Collopy, and M. Alan Jenkins, "Restoring the Bald Eagle," *American Scientist*, Vol. 76, May-June 1988. p. 254.
8. Adapted from Glenn Zorpette, "An Underwater Visit to Aquarius," *IEEE Spectrum*, March 1988, p. 24.
9. Adapted from H. Kent Brown, "Advanced Ceramics," *Scientific American*, Vol. 255, No. 4, October 1986, pp. 148–149.
10. Adapted from Stuart Ross Taylor, "The Origin of the Moon," *American Scientist*, Vol. 75, September-October 1987, p. 474.
11. Adapted from Milton Hildebrand, "The Mechanics of Horse Legs," *American Scientist*, Vol. 75, November-December 1987, p. 596.
12. Adapted from P. David Fisher, "Shortcomings of Radar Speed Measurement," *IEEE Spectrum*, December 1980, p. 28.
13. Adapted from Stuart Ross Taylor, "The Origin of the Moon," *American Scientist*, Vol. 75, September-October 1987, p. 469.
14. Adapted from Trygg Engen, "Remembering Odors and Their Names," *American Scientist*, Vol. 75, September-October 1987, p. 499.
15. Adapted from Aldo V. LaRocca, "Laser Applications in Manufacturing," *Scientific American*, Vol. 246, No. 3, March 1982, p. 80.
16. Adapted from H. Kent Brown, "Advanced Ceramics," *Scientific American*, Vol. 255, No. 4,

October 1986, p. 147.

17. Adapted from Trygg Engen, "Remembering Odors and Their Names," *American Scientist*, Vol. 75, September-October 1987, p. 501.

18. Adapted from Andrew P. Ingersoll, "Atmospheric Dynamics of the Outer Planets," *Science*, Vol. 248, April 20, 1990, p. 314.

19. Adapted from R.N. Bracewell, "Numerical Transforms," *Science*, Vol. 248, May 11, 1990, p. 697.

20. Adapted from Trudy E. Bell, "Earthquake Prediction: Keeping an Ear to the Ground," *IEEE Spectrum*, May 1988, p. 47.

21. Adapted from work by Chia-fu Chen and associates, National Chiao Tung University, Hsinchu, Taiwan.

22. Adapted from David Schwartzman and Lee J. Rickard, "Being Optimistic about the Search for Extraterrestrial Intelligence," *American Scientist*, Vol. 76, July-August 1988, p. 364.

23. Adapted from work by Ching-fa Yeh and Chun-lin Chen, National Chiao Tung University, Hsinchu, Taiwan.

24. Adapted from Patricia D. Moehlman, "Social Organization in Jackals," *American Scientist*, Vol. 75, July-August 1987, p. 366.

25. Adapted from David Schwartzman and Lee J. Rickard, "Being Optimistic about the Search for Extraterrestrial Intelligence," *American Scientist*, Vol. 76, July-August 1988, pp. 365–366.

第九章註釋

1. Adapted from H. Kent Brown, "Advanced Ceramics," *Scientific American*, Vol. 255, No. 4, October 1986, pp. 148–149.

2. Adapted from W. Kenneth Dawson and Robert W. Dobinson, "What a Bus Is and How It Works: A Primer," *IEEE Spectrum*, October 1986, pp. 52–53.

3. Adapted from Trygg Engen, "Remembering Odors and Their Names," *American Scientist*, Vol. 75, September-October 1987, p. 501.

4. Adapted from Steven C. Guptill and Lowell E. Starr, "Making Maps with Computers," *American Scientist*, Vol. 76, March-April 1988, pp. 136–137.

5. Adapted from John W. Drake, Barry W. Glickman, and Lynn S. Ripley, "Updating the Theory of Mutation," *American Scientist*, Vol. 71, November-December 1983, p. 621.

6. Adapted from Charles J. Lada and Frank H. Shu, "The Formation of Sunlike Stars," *Science*, Vol. 248, May 4, 1990, p. 564.

7. Adapted from Trudy E. Bell, "Earthquake Prediction: Keeping an Ear to the Ground," *IEEE Spectrum*, May 1988, p. 47.

8. Adapted from Katherine Wollard, "Garbage in, Power out," *IEEE Spectrum*, June 1988, p. 42.

第十二章參考資料

Thomas E. Kesler, Randy B. Uram, Ferial Magareh-Abed, Ann Fritzsche, Carl Amport, and H. E. Dunsmore, "The Effect of Indentation on Program Comprehension," *International Journal of Man-Machine Studies*, Vol. 21, 1984, pp. 415–428.

G. Holmen and Harald Jacobsson, "The Influence of Oxygen on SiO_2 Sputtering," *Journal of Applied Physics*, Vol. 68, No. 6, September 15, 1990, pp. 2962–2965.

Barbee T. Mynatt, "The Effect of Semantic Complexity on the Comprehension of Program Modules," *International Journal of Man-Machine Studies*, Vol. 21, 1984, pp. 91–103.

Herbert H. P. Fang, Liu Guohua, Zhu Jinfu, Cai Bute, and Gu Guowei, "Treatment of Brewery Effluent by UASB Process," *Journal of Environmental Engineering,* Vol. 116, No. 3, May/June 1990, pp. 454–460.

Theodore Stathopoulos and Xiwu Zhu, "Wind Pressures on Buildings with Mullions," *Journal of Structural Engineering,* Vol. 116, No. 8, August 1990, pp. 2272–2291.

Chandra Shekhar and Rama Chellappa, "Passive Ranging Using a Moving Camera," *Journal of Robotic Systems,* Vol. 9, No. 6, 1992, pp. 729–752.

D. E. Stott, H. F. Stroo, L. F. Elliott, R. I. Papendick, and P. W. Unger, "Wheat Residue Loss from Fields Under No-till Management," *Soil Sci. Am. J.,* Vol. 54, 1990, pp. 92–98.

P. M. Bongers, C. T. J. Hulshof, L. Dukstra, and H. C. Boshuizen, "Back Pain and Exposure to Whole Body Vibration in Helicopter Pilots," *Ergonomics,* Vol. 33, No. 8, 1990, pp. 1007–1026.

James R. Carlopio and Dianne Gardner, "Direct and Interactive Effects of the Physical Work Environment on Attitudes," *Environment and Behavior,* Vol. 24, No. 5, September 1992, pp. 579–601.

Kimberly DuVall-Early and James O. Benedict, "The Relationships Between Privacy and Different Components of Job Satisfaction," *Environment and Behavior,* Vol. 24, No. 5, September 1992, pp. 670–679.

第十三章參考資料

D. E. Stott, H. F. Stroo, L. F. Elliott, R. I. Papendick, and P. W. Unger, "Wheat Residue Loss from Fields Under No-till Management," *Soil Sci. Am. J.,* Vol, 54, 1990, pp. 92–98.

Arthur J. Sedlacek and Charles A. Wight, "Photochemistry of Solid Ozone," *Journal of Physical Chemistry,* Vol. 93, 1989, pp. 509–511.

A. J. Castelle and J. N. Galloway, "Carbon Dioxide Dynamics in Acid Forest Soils in Shenandoah National Park, Virginia," *Soil Sci. Am. J.,* Vol. 54, 1990, pp. 252–257.

Stephen G. Powell and Shmuel S. Oren, "The Transition to Nondepletable Energy: Social Planning and Market Models of Capacity Extension," *Operations Research,* Vol. 37, No. 3, May-June 1989, pp. 373–383.

Ricardo Carelli, Rafael Kelly, and Romeo Ortega, "Adaptive Force Control of Robot Manipulators," *International Journal of Control,* 1990, Vol. 52, No. 1, pp. 37–54.

V. Grivitskas, M. Willander, D. Noreika, M. Petrauskas, J. Knall, and W. X. Ni, "Carrier Lifetime in MBE Grown Si:Sb and Si:In Layers Measured by the Transient Grating Method," *Semiconductor Science and Technology,* Vol. 3, 1988, pp. 1116–1121.

Elaine M. Day and Stan M. Shapson, "Integrating Formal and Functional Approaches to Language Teaching in French Immersion: An Experimental Study," *Language Learning,* Vol. 41, No. 1, March 1991, pp. 25–58.

第十四章參考資料

Shing-tung Yau and Ya Yan Lu, "Reducing the Symmetric Matrix Eigenvalue Problem to Matrix Multiplications," *SIAM Journal of Scientific Computing,* Vol. 14, No. 1, January 1993, pp. 121–136.

Stephen G. Powell and Shmuel S. Oren, "The Transition to Nondepletable Energy: Social Planning and Market Models of Capacity Extension," *Operations Research,* Vol. 37, No. 3, May-June 1989, pp. 373–383.

Ricardo Carelli, Rafael Kelly, and Romeo Ortega, "Adaptive Force Control of Robot Manipulators," *International Journal of Control,* Vol. 52, No. 1, 1990, pp. 37–54.

H. J. Salane and J. W. Baldwin Jr., "Identification of Modal Properties of Bridges," *Journal of Structural Engineering,* Vol. 116, No. 7, July 1990, pp. 2008–2021.

第十五章參考資料

Elaine M. Day and Stan M. Shapson, "Integrating Formal and Functional Approaches to Language Teaching in French Immersion: An Experimental Study," *Language Learning,* Vol. 41, No. 1, March 1991, pp. 25–58.

Thomas E. Kesler, Randy B. Uram, Ferial Magareh-Abed, Ann Fritzsche, Carl Amport, and H. E. Dunsmore, "The Effect of Indentation on Program Comprehension," *International Journal of Man-Machine Studies,* Vol. 21, 1984, pp. 415–428.

Graziano Fiorito and Pietro Scotto, "Observational Learning in *Octopus vulgaris,*" *Science,* Vol. 256, April 24, 1992, pp. 545–546.

V. Grivitskas, M. Willander, D. Noreika, M. Petrauskas, J. Knall, and W. X. Ni, "Carrier Lifetime in MBE Grown Si:Sb and Si:In Layers Measured by the Transient Grating Method," *Semiconductor Science and Technology,* Vol. 3, 1988, pp. 1116–1121.

Ali Unal, "Gas Atomization of Fine Zinc Powders," *International Journal of Powder Metallurgy,* Vol. 26, No. 1, 1990, pp. 11–21.

Kimberly DuVall-Early and James O. Benedict, "The Relationships Between Privacy and Different Components of Job Satisfaction," *Environment and Behavior,* Vol. 24, No. 5, September 1992, pp. 670–679.

Kevin W. Lu, Martin I. Eiger, and Howard L. Lemberg, "System and Cost Analyses of Broad-Band Fiber Loop Architectures," *IEEE Journal on Selected Areas in Communications,* Vol. 8, No. 6, August 1990, pp. 1058–1067.

James J. Kellaris and Ronald C. Rice, "The Influence of Tempo, Loudness, and Gender of Listener on Responses to Music," *Psychology and Marketing,* Vol. 10, No. 1, January/February 1993, pp. 15–29.

第十六章參考資料

P. M. Bongers, C. T. J. Hulshof, L. Dukstra, and H. C. Boshuizen, "Back Pain and Exposure to Whole Body Vibration in Helicopter Pilots," *Ergonomics,* Vol. 33, No. 8, 1990, pp. 1007–1026.

Graziano Fiorito and Pietro Scotto, "Observational Learning in *Octopus vulgaris,*" *Science,* Vol. 256, April 24, 1992, pp. 545–546.

Barbara J. Cordell, "A Study of Learning Styles and Computer-assisted Instruction," *Computers Educ.,* Vol. 16, No. 2, 1991, pp. 175–183.

H. H. D. Lee and F. J. McGarry, "A Creep Apparatus to Explore the Quenching and Aging Phenomena of PVC Films," *Journal of Materials Science,* Vol. 26, 1991, pp. 1–5.

Thomas E. Kesler, Randy B. Uram, Ferial Magareh-Abed, Ann Fritzsche, Carl Amport, and H. E. Dunsmore, "The Effect of Indentation on Program Comprehension," *International Journal of Man-Machine Studies,* Vol. 21, 1984, pp. 415–428.

Barbee T. Mynatt, "The Effect of Semantic Complexity on the Comprehension of Program Modules," *International Journal of Man-Machine Studies,* Vol. 21, 1984, pp. 91–103.

Kevin W. Lu, Martin I. Eiger, and Howard L. Lemberg, "System and Cost Analyses of Broad-Band Fiber Loop Architectures," *IEEE Journal on Selected Areas in Communications,* Vol. 8, No. 6, August 1990, pp. 1058–1067.

第十七章參考資料

Elaine M. Day and Stan M. Shapson, "Integrating Formal and Functional Approaches to Language Teaching in French Immersion: An Experimental Study," *Language Learning,* Vol. 41, No. 1, March 1991, pp. 25–58.

Alf Gabrielsson, Bjorn Lindstrom, and Ove Till, "Loudspeaker Frequency Response and Perceived Sound Quality," *Journal of the Acoustics Society of America,* Vol. 90, No. 2, Pt. 1, August 1991, pp. 707–719.

Barbee T. Mynatt, "The Effect of Semantic Complexity on the Comprehension of Program Modules," *International Journal of Man-Machine Studies,* Vol. 21, 1984, pp. 91–103.

James J. Kellaris and Ronald C. Rice, "The Influence of Tempo, Loudness, and Gender of Listener on Responses to Music," *Psychology and Marketing,* Vol. 10, No. 1, January/February 1993, pp. 15–29.

G. Holmen and Harald Jacobssen, "The Influence of Oxygen on SiO_2 Sputtering," *Journal of Applied Physics,* Vol. 68, No. 6, September 15, 1990, pp. 2962–2965.

V. Grivitskas, M. Willander, D. Noreika, M. Petrauskas, J. Knall, and W. X. Ni, "Carrier Lifetime in MBE Grown Si:Sb and Si:In Layers Measured by the Transient Grating Method," *Semiconductor Science and Technology,* Vol. 3, 1988, pp. 1116–1121.

Barbara J. Cordell, "A Study of Learning Styles and Computer-assisted Instruction," *Computers Educ.* Vol. 16, No. 2, 1991, pp. 175–183.

David M. Szymanski and Gilbert A. Churchill, Jr., "Client Evaluation Cues: A Comparison of Successful and Unsuccessful Salespeople," *Journal of Marketing Research,* Vol. XXVII, May 1990, pp. 163–174.

D. E. Stott, H. F. Stroo, L. F. Elliott, R. I. Papendick, and P. W. Unger, "Wheat Residue Loss from Fields Under No-till Management," *Soil Sci. Am. J.,* Vol. 54, 1990, pp. 92–98.

第十八章參考資料

Thomas E. Kesler, Randy B. Uram, Ferial Magareh-Abed, Ann Fritzsche, Carl Amport, and H. E. Dunsmore, "The Effect of Indentation on Program Comprehension," *International Journal of Man-Machine Studies,* Vol. 21, 1984, pp. 415–428.

V. Grivitskas, M. Willander, D. Noreika, M. Petrauskas, J. Knall, and W. X. Ni, "Carrier Lifetime in MBE Grown Si:Sb and Si:In Layers Measured by the Transient Grating Method," *Semiconductor Science and Technology,* Vol. 3, 1988, pp. 1116–1121.

Koichi Takeuchi and Kenji Murata, "Monte Carlo Simulation of Photoelectron Emission from a Gold Specimen," *Journal of Applied Physics,* Vol. 68, No. 6, September 15, 1990, pp. 2955–2961.

第十九章參考資料

Wolfgang Jaschinski-Kruza, "On the Preferred Viewing Distances to Screen and Document at VDU Workplaces," *Ergonomics,* Vol. 33, No. 8, 1990, pp. 1055–1063.

Barbee T. Mynatt, "The Effect of Semantic Complexity on the Comprehension of Program Modules," *International Journal of Man-Machine Studies,* Vol. 21, 1984, pp. 91–103.

Arthur J. Sedlacek and Charles A. Wight, "Photochemistry of Solid Ozone," *Journal of Physical Chemistry,* Vol. 93, 1989, pp. 509–511.

D. E. Stott, H. F. Stroo, L. F. Elliott, R. I. Papendick, and P. W. Unger, "Wheat Residue Loss from Fields Under No-till Management," *Soil Sci. Am. J.,* Vol. 54, 1990, pp. 92–98.

Theodore Stathopoulos and Xiwu Zhu, "Wind Pressures on Buildings with Mullions," *Journal of Structural Engineering,* Vol. 116, No. 8, August 1990, pp. 2272–2291.

A. J. Castelle and J. N. Galloway, "Carbon Dioxide Dynamics in Acid Forest Soils in Shenandoah National Park, Virginia," *Soil. Soc. Am. J.,* Vol. 54, 1990, pp. 252–257.

Stephen G. Powell and Shmuel S. Oren, "The Transition to Nondepletable Energy: Social Planning and Market Models of Capacity Extension," *Operations Research,* Vol. 37, No. 3, May-June 1989, pp. 373–383.

David M. Szymanski and Gilbert A. Churchill, Jr., "Client Evaluation Cues: A Comparison of Successful and Unsuccessful Salespeople," *Journal of Marketing Research*, Vol. XXVII, May 1990, pp. 163–174.

Koichi Takeuchi and Kenji Murata, "Monte Carlo Simulation of Photoelectron Emission from a Gold Specimen," *Journal of Applied Physics*, Vol. 68, No. 6, September 15, 1990, pp. 2955–2961.

參考書目

Vernon Booth, *Communicating in Science*, 2nd ed. (Cambridge University Press, 1993).

Colburn A. Carelli, "Can We Talk? The Art of Giving Effective, Interesting Technical Presentations," Society for Technical Communication, R.O.C. Chapter, 1995.

Richard M. Davis, "Publication in Professional Journals: A Survey of Editors," *IEEE Transactions on Professional Communication* PC-28 (2), June 1985, pp. 34–42.

Robert A. Day, *How to Write and Publish a Scientific Paper* (ISI Press, 1979).

Joan Detz, *How to Write & Give a Speech* (St. Martin's Press, 1984).

George Gopen and Judith Swan, "The Science of Scientific Writing," *American Scientist*, Vol. 78, No. 6, pp. 550–558.

James G. Gray, Jr., *Strategies and Skills of Technical Presentations* (Greenwood Press, 1986).

Mark H. Henry and Harold K. Lonsdale, "The Researcher's Writing Guide," in Bruce O. Boston, ed., *Stet! Tricks of the Trade for Writers and Editors,* (Editorial Experts, 1986), pp. 108–12.

Thomas Huckin and Leslie Olsen, *Technical Writing and Professional Communication for Nonnative Speakers of English* (McGraw-Hill, 1991).

B. Luey, *Handbook for Academic Authors* (Cambridge University Press, 1987).

J. H. Mitchell, *Writing for Professional and Technical Journals* (John Wiley, 1968).

Peter L. Petrakis, "How to Abstract a Scientific Paper," in Bruce O. Boston, ed., *Stet! Tricks of the Trade for Writers and Editors* (Editorial Experts, 1986), pp. 134–36.

John Swales, *Aspects of Article Introductions*, Aston ESP Research Report No. 1 (University of Aston, 1981).

Robert Weissberg and Suzanne Buker, *Writing Up Research* (Prentice Hall, 1990).

國家圖書館出版品預行編目 (CIP) 資料

科技論文英語寫作 / 方克濤著 . -- 初版 . -- 新北
市 : 全華圖書 , 2015.01
　　面；　公分
ISBN 978-957-21-9727-1(平裝)

1. 英語 2. 論文寫作法

805.175　　　　　　　　　　103026115

科技論文英語寫作 (2023新版)

作　　者 / 方克濤

發 行 人 / 陳本源

執行編輯 / 黃艾家

封面設計 / 林彥彣

出 版 者 / 全華圖書股份有限公司

郵政帳號 / 0100836-1號

印 刷 者 / 宏懋打字印刷股份有限公司

圖書編號 / 09128

初版三刷 / 2023年1月

定　　價 / 650元

Ｉ Ｓ Ｂ Ｎ / 978-957-21-9727-1

全華圖書 / www.chwa.com.tw

全華網路書局 Open Tech / www.opentech.com.tw

若您對本書有任何問題，歡迎來信指導book@chwa.com.tw

臺北總公司（北區營業處）
地址：23671新北市土城區忠義路21號
電話：(02) 2262-5666
傳眞：(02) 6637-3695、6637-3696

中區營業處
地址：40256臺中市南區樹義一巷26號
電話：(04) 2261-8485
傳眞：(04) 3600-9806（高中職）
　　　(04) 3601-8600（大專）

南區營業處
地址：80769高雄市三民區應安街12號
電話：(07) 381-1377
傳眞：(07) 862-5562